Gateways to Forever

Liverpool Science Fiction Texts and Studies

Editor David Seed, *University of Liverpool*

1. Robert Crossley *Olaf Stapledon: Speaking for the Future*
2. David Seed (ed.) *Anticipations: Essays on Early Science Fiction and its Precursors*
3. Jane L. Donawerth and Carol A. Kolmerten (eds) *Utopian and Science Fiction by Women: Worlds of Difference*
4. Brian W. Aldiss *The Detached Retina: Aspects of SF and Fantasy*
5. Carol Farley Kessler *Charlotte Perkins Gilman: Her Progress Toward Utopia, with Selected Writings*
6. Patrick Parrinder *Shadows of the Future: H. G. Wells, Science Fiction and Prophecy*
7. I. F. Clarke (ed.) *The Tale of the Next Great War, 1871–1914: Fictions of Future Warfare and of Battles Still-to-come*
8. Joseph Conrad and Ford Madox Ford *The Inheritors*
9. Qingyun Wu *Female Rule in Chinese and English Literary Utopias*
10. John Clute *Look at the Evidence: Essays and Reviews*
11. Roger Luckhurst *'The Angle Between Two Walls': The Fiction of J. G. Ballard*
12. I. F. Clarke (ed.) *The Great War with Germany, 1980–1914: Fiction and Fantasies of the War-to-come*
13. Franz Rottensteiner (ed.) *View from Another Shore: European Science Fiction*
14. Val Gough and Jill Rudd (eds) *A Very Different Story: Studies in the Fiction of Charlotte Perkins Gilman*
15. Gary Westfahl *The Mechanics of Wonder: The Creation of the Idea of Science Fiction*
16. Gwyneth Jones *Deconstructing the Starships: Science, Fiction and Reality*
17. Patrick Parrinder (ed.) *Learning from Other Worlds: Estrangement, Cognition and the Politics of Science Fiction and Utopia*
18. Jeanne Cortiel *Demand My Writing: Joanna Russ/Feminism/Science Fiction*
19. Chris Ferns *Narrating Utopia: Ideology, Gender, Form in Utopian Literature*
20. E. J. Smith (ed.) *Jules Verne: New Directions*
21. Andy Sawyer and David Seed (eds) *Speaking Science Fiction: Dialogues and Interpretations*
22. Inez van der Spek *Alien Plots: Female Subjectivity and the Divine*
23. S. T. Joshi *Ramsey Campbell and Modern Horror Fiction*
24. Mike Ashley *The Time Machines: The Story of the Science-Fiction Pulp Magazines from the Beginning to 1950*
25. Warren G. Rochelle *Communities of the Heart: The Rhetoric of Myth in the Fiction of Ursula K. Le Guin*
26. S. T. Joshi *A Dreamer and a Visionary: H. P. Lovecraft in his Time*
27. Christopher Palmer *Philip K. Dick: Exhilaration and Terror of the Postmodern*
28. Charles E. Gannon *Rumors of War and Infernal Machines: Technomilitary Agenda-Setting in American and British Speculative Fiction*
29. Peter Wright *Attending Daedalus: Gene Wolfe, Artifice and the Reader*
30. Mike Ashley *Transformations: The Story of the Science-Fiction Magazine from 1950–1970*
31. Joanna Russ *The Country You Have Never Seen: Essays and Reviews*
32. Robert Philmus *Visions and Revisions: (Re)constructing Science Fiction*
33. Gene Wolfe (edited and introduced by Peter Wright) *Shadows of the New Sun: Wolfe on Writing/Writers on Wolfe*
34. Mike Ashley *Gateways to Forever: The Story of the Science-Fiction Magazine from 1970–1980*

Gateways to Forever

The Story of the Science-Fiction Magazines from 1970 to 1980

The History of the
Science-Fiction Magazine
Volume III

MIKE ASHLEY

LIVERPOOL UNIVERSITY PRESS

First published 2007 by
Liverpool University Press
4 Cambridge Street
Liverpool L69 7ZU

Copyright © 2007 Liverpool University Press

The right of Mike Ashley to be identified as the author of this work has been asserted by him in accordance with the Copyright, Designs and Patents Act, 1988

British Library Cataloguing-in-Publication data
A British Library CIP record is available

ISBN 978 1 84631 002 7 hardback
ISBN 978 1 84631 003 4 paperback

Typeset by Koinonia, Manchester
Printed and bound by CPI Group (UK) Ltd, Croydon, CR0 4YY

Contents

Preface

When I began this volume it was intended to complete my trilogy of the history of the science-fiction magazines, and cover the years from 1970 to the present, or at least to the year 2000. The first volume, *The Time Machines*, had covered 25 years, from 1926 to 1950, from the first all-sf magazine, *Amazing Stories*, through the domination of its chief rival, *Astounding Stories* (now *Analog*), to the post-war years and the beginning of the end for the pulp magazines. The second volume, *Transformations*, covered 20 years, from 1950 to 1970, charting the death of the pulps, the domination of the digest magazines led by *Galaxy* and *F&SF*, and the emergence of the New Wave revolution in *New Worlds*. The early fifties saw the Golden Age of the science-fiction magazines with probably the greatest concentration of talent and quality fiction that the field had seen.

With all that charted, it was left for me to explore the remaining 30 years and bring everything up to date. But always in the back of my mind was the niggling question, 'What do I do about the seventies?' To many readers, the science-fiction magazines ceased to be important in the seventies, with the popularity of the paperback novel, and the last 30 years is simply a catalogue of decline. But that isn't the case, especially in the seventies. The seventies was certainly a turning point, but it wasn't simply one that saw the magazine pass the baton on to the paperback and bid it good luck. In fact, despite certain problems and hardships, the magazines generally flourished in the seventies, facing all the challenges that were thrown at them. And there were plenty.

The start of the decade saw the death of John W. Campbell, the editor of *Analog*, who had dominated the field for over thirty years and who is credited with the maturing of science fiction in the late thirties and early forties by dragging it out of the pulps and into the modern world. There were many who held Campbell in god-like awe and wondered how the field could survive his passing. In fact his passing had quite an impact on the field, which I explore here through several threads.

Also at the start of the decade emerged the phenomenon of the 'original anthology series', that is a regular anthology that ran all new short fiction. These included Damon Knight's *Orbit*, Robert Silverberg's *New Dimensions* and Terry Carr's *Universe* which, along with several others, took the magazines on at their own game and often beat them in winning awards for their short fiction. Many predicted that the anthologies would supersede the magazines, yet the magazines survived. How they did this and whether Roger Elwood had a part to play is another major thread I explore.

You can always be sure that if the magazines do not provide what readers want, then they will find an alternative. The seventies saw the emergence of several alternatives to the professional sf magazine, in addition to the original anthologies. There was a rise in small-press and semi-professional magazines, some, such as *Galileo*, proving so successful that they burst through into the professional ranks. Others remained specialist but also served a vital role, such as *Unearth* which became a forum for new writers, *Pandora* which served the feminist movement, and *Shayol* which demonstrated how you could produce a top-quality, beautifully illustrated slick magazine even on a limited budget. The seventies also saw the flowering of the role-playing game (RPG), the best-known being *Dungeons and Dragons*, and with these came their own magazines, many, such as *The Space Gamer*, *The Dragon* and *Ares*, running fiction. Was this a healthy expansion of the field or a dangerous division which would weaken the traditional sf magazine? And there were other rivals. The growth of underground and adult comics and graphic novels, perhaps best symbolized by the popularity of *Heavy Metal* magazine. And the growth in popular-science magazines, of which *Omni* was the success story of the decade.

In 1977 came the blockbuster film *Star Wars*, followed by *Close Encounters of the Third Kind* and *Alien*, which set new standards in science-fiction films and brought with them a rise in sf media magazines, such as *Starlog* and *Starburst*, which began to supersede the traditional fiction magazines in the public's eyes as the new sf magazines. They gave rise to a new form of media fandom, alongside which ran *Star Trek* fandom with its own fanzines and conventions.

Was all this competition and rivalry healthy for the science-fiction field, and how did it affect the old-style sf magazine? I needed to untangle these complicated webs and follow through the individual threads to see what effect they had on both the traditional magazines and the development of science fiction.

What was especially noticeable about the seventies was the emergence of another major wave of new writers, the greatest blossoming of talent since the early fifties and the first new generation to flourish since the passing of Campbell. Amongst them were Michael Bishop, Octavia Butler, Orson Scott Card, William Gibson, Joe Haldeman, Vonda McIntyre, George R. R. Martin, Jerry Pournelle, Kim Stanley Robinson, Bruce Sterling, John Varley, Joan Vinge, Howard Waldrop, Connie Willis and Chelsea Quinn Yarbro. It was important to see who discovered and supported these writers and how in turn they influenced the field. Much of this was down to the new editors who controlled the field during the seventies – in both magazines and anthologies – including Ben Bova, James Baen, Ted White, Damon Knight, Terry Carr and Robert Silverberg – but it was helped by another phenomenon that took hold at the start of the decade, the writers' workshop. The best known and most successful was the Clarion Writers Workshop, organized by Robin Scott Wilson. Its success rate has been remarkable, but just how did it affect the shape of science fiction and influence the magazines and anthologies?

Noticeable amongst those new writers was the number of women, heralding the arrival of the feminist movement. Just what factors contributed to the rise of feminism in sf in the seventies and what roles the magazines and anthologies played was yet another question.

And wrapped around all of this was the greater scrutiny to which the field was being subjected: both from without, with the growth of academic publications devoted to the study of science fiction (*Extrapolation, Science-Fiction Studies, Foundation*), and from within, with the development of fan magazines into critical reviews (*Riverside Quarterly, Algol, Thrust*). How was this perceived and what effect did this have? Linked to this was the attitude of the literary establishment to science fiction, brought into focus by the views of Polish writer Stanislaw Lem who became one of the best-selling writers of science fiction during the seventies but who openly despised genre sf.

These were the storms that buffeted the science-fiction magazines during the seventies, yet at the end of the decade we see *Isaac Asimov's Science Fiction Magazine* becoming the best-selling new sf magazine in years, outselling *Analog* from the start. Yet, despite the success of *Asimov's*, it was perceived by many as appealing to a juvenile market, one attracted by the success of *Star Wars*. Was it necessary for science fiction to 'dumb down' in order to survive?

By the time I had explored all of these issues, I knew I would not have space to consider the eighties and nineties as well. Not when I needed to plot the emergence of the internet with its webzines and fan groups, the arrival of cyberpunk, slipstream and steampunk and many other corridors of the new sf, plus the revival of interest in high-tech hard sf. So I have saved all of that for a fourth volume.

This volume, then, explores the years 1970 to 1980. There is some overlap at the start with *Transformations* in order to pick up where certain threads began, and at the end I run on into the early eighties for a few items in order to follow a few threads to their conclusion, or to a logical place to pause. The book is divided into five chapters. The first three follow a time arc from 1970 to 1977 into which many of the activities mentioned conveniently fit. The first chapter looks at the traditional sf magazines *Analog*, *Galaxy*, *F&SF* and *Amazing* during these years, including how *Analog* coped with the passing of Campbell. Chapter 2 considers the role of the original anthology series, including the impact of the writers' workshops, of feminism and of Roger Elwood. Chapter 3 explores the growth of the semi-professional magazine, including the overlap with the allied fields of fantasy and weird fiction, plus the emergence of critical and academic sf magazines, the RPG magazines and adult comics. Chapter 4 picks up all these threads from 1977 onwards and charts the rise of new magazines including *Galileo*, *Asimov's* and *Destinies* and the emergence of the media magazine in the wake of *Star Wars* and the popular science magazine with *Omni* and *Future Life*. Chapter 5 looks back over the seventies and assesses and evaluates what had happened and where sf was going.

As with the previous volumes there is a set of appendices. The first looks at the international scene with the growth of sf magazines around the world, while the others provide a quick checklist to all of the sf magazines of the seventies, together with their editors and cover artists. I've added a further appendix for this volume which is a schedule of magazine sales figures. I've also included a chronology. Whereas in past volumes my discussion was linear and could be followed through in date order, in this volume I have had to split my discussion, and I thought a chronology would help establish a backbone to what was happening.

The volume stands on its own as a study of the sf magazine scene and the events that impinged upon it in the seventies, but it helps establish the context if you have also followed the story through the two earlier books. To provide continuity, however, I have given relevant backgrounds to all the people and magazines as I introduce them.

I hope you'll agree with me that the seventies was far from a period of decline for the magazines but one that showed how robust and adaptable they were during the decade when science fiction at last emerged from being a minor genre into one of both academic and literary importance as well as a major money-spinner. Science fiction was at last coming of age.

Mike Ashley
Chatham, October 2006

Note

Throughout this volume I use the abbreviation sf for science fiction and not that dreadful neologism 'sci fi'. Other frequently used abbreviations, usually spelled out in full the first time, are prozine for professional magazine, semi-pro or semi-prozine for semi-professional magazine, fanzine for fan magazine, and Worldcon for World Science Fiction Convention. Whenever I cite a story title, I provide its original magazine or anthology source in brackets, e.g. (*Analog*, January 1971). If the story is serialized over more than one issue, I note the first and last issues joined by a dash, e.g. January–February 1971. If a magazine, usually a bi-monthly, has a double cover date, I refer to both dates joined by a slash, e.g. January/February 1971. All short story titles and serials are given in quotes but all magazine and book titles are given in italics.

Acknowledgements

I hardly know where to begin in thanking the scores of people who have helped me with this volume, helped not only in providing information but in giving feedback and support in a wide variety of ways. First and foremost my thanks has to go to my amazingly stoic wife, Sue, who puts up both with my frequent isolation and with several tons of books and magazines moving in and out of the house, cluttering up every nook and cranny. She is remarkable.

It is impossible, otherwise, to rank my thanks, for all help has been vital and important. If anyone deserves to be high on this list, though, it is John Boston, who read through all the first draft of the book and commented, often in fine detail, on virtually everything, often bringing me up short by making me rethink what I was trying to say. This book would be considerably weaker without his essential contribution.

There were many who provided feedback and commentary on specific sections. Robert Silverberg not only gave me crucial feedback on those sections that dealt with his role but also helped put much of that in perspective. Ben Bova was likewise generous in providing thoughts and memories on his time at *Analog* and, along with Frank Kendig and Dick Teresi, of their days at *Omni*. Ted White was similarly helpful with his comments on the days at *Amazing* and *Heavy Metal*. Amanda Bankier deftly kept me on the straight and narrow by helping me through the section on feminism, and I am also grateful to Jeanne Gomoll for her help and advice.

Many writers and editors provided specific background data on their work and I list them here in alphabetical order, though all were equally vital: Neville Angove, Sam Bellotto, Jr., Ruth Berman, Michael Bishop, Pat Cadigan, Orson Scott Card, Samuel R. Delany, Terry Dowling, Gardner

Dozois, Scott Edelstein, Arnold Fenner, Edward L. Ferman, David Galef, David Gerrold, Norman Goldfind, Joe Haldeman, Harry Harrison, David Hartwell, Van Ikin, Steve Jones, Duncan Lunan, Vincent McCaffrey, Shawna McCarthy, Elinor Mavor, Michael Moorcock, Kevin O'Donnell, Jr., Gerald W. Page, Andrew Porter, Jerry Pournelle, Charles C. Ryan, Pamela Sargent, Stuart David Schiff, Darrell Schweitzer, George Scithers, Keith Seddon, David A. Sutton, Gordon Van Gelder, John Varley, Lois Wickstrom and Connie Willis. There were also many, alas no longer with us, who over the years responded to my early requests for information, including Jim Baen, Terry Carr, William Crawford, Robert Hoskins, Ejler Jakobsson, Damon Knight, Sam Moskowitz and Roger Zelazny. There were many who helped provide data for the coverage on international magazines and I have thanked those individually in Appendix 1.

Finally there are those ever-reliable individuals at the other end of an e-mail who patiently respond to my seeming interminable requests to provide obscure information or to double-check facts. I am especially grateful to Ned Brooks who provided me with endless scans from his remarkable collection of amateur magazines, which helped plug gaps in my collection. My thanks to William G. Contento, who produced a variety of data from his formidable book and magazine database enabling me to produce several of the charts, and to Bud Webster for sharing his data on authors' first sales. My thanks, as always, to Victor Berch, Richard Bleiler, Stephen Holland, Dennis Lien, Steve Miller, Andy Sawyer and Phil Stephensen-Payne for checking long-buried facts or tracking down obscure references for me, and to Dave Cail, Jetse de Vries, Pierre-Paul Durastanti, Bruce Gillespie, Attila Nemeth, Mark Owings and Doug Sulipa for filling in gaps when I had almost given up hope.

To all of these, and any I have inadvertently omitted, my sincere thanks.

Tables

Chronology

The following timeline lists the first and last issues of magazines during the period 1970 to 1980, together with any significant editorial or other changes. It also lists debuts of major authors. Unless specifically noted, all dates relate to the cover date of the magazine, which, in most cases, is the off-sale date, meaning that the issue would have appeared a month or two earlier.

1970

January	First volume of *Infinity* with first story by George Zebrowski. Edward Bryant debuts in *Adam* and *New Worlds*.
February	First volume of *Nova*. Vonda McIntyre debuts in *Venture*.
March	Jack Dann debuts in *If*.
April	Gordon Eklund debuts in *Fantastic*.
July	Alan Dean Foster debuts in *The Arkham Collector*.
September	First issue of *Bizarre Fantasy Tales*. Pamela Sargent debuts in *F&SF*.
October	First issues of *Forgotten Fantasy* and *Cinefantastique*. Michael Bishop debuts in *Galaxy*.
November	First volume of *QUARK/*.
December	Connie Willis debuts in *Worlds of Fantasy*.

1971

January	First issue of *Witchcraft & Sorcery*.
February	George R. R. Martin debuts in *Galaxy*.
March	Final issues of *Science Fiction Greats*, *Startling Mystery Stories*, *Bizarre Fantasy Tales*, *Worlds of Fantasy*, *Worlds of Tomorrow* and *New Worlds*. Also final issue of first series of *Science Fiction Review*. F. Paul Wilson debuts in *Startling Mystery Stories*.

April	Final issue of *Magazine of Horror*.
May	Jerry Pournelle debuts in *Analog*.
June	Last issue of *Forgotten Fantasy*. First volume of *Clarion* with first story by Octavia Butler. *New Worlds* reappears as anthology *New Worlds Quarterly*.
July	Death of John W. Campbell, Jr. (11 July).
August	Final volume of *QUARK/*.
September	First volume of *Universe*. George Alec Effinger debuts in *Fantastic*.
December	First volume of *New Dimensions*. Rachel Pollack debuts in *New Worlds*.

1972

January	Ben Bova becomes editor of *Analog*. First *Star Trek* convention held in New York.
February	Publication of *Again, Dangerous Visions*.
March	First issue of *Foundation*.
April	First Roger Elwood original anthology, *Signs and Wonders*.
May	Howard Waldrop debuts in *Analog*.
June	Lisa Tuttle debuts in *Clarion II*.
July	First issue of *Eternity*.
November	*Algol* becomes semi-professional.

1973

January	Appearance of *The Alien Critic*. Marta Randall debuts in *New Worlds*.
February	First issue of *Thrust*. Spider Robinson debuts in *Analog*.
March	First issue of *Science-Fiction Studies*.
April	First issue of *Vertex*.
June	First issues of *Dark Fantasy* and *The Haunt of Horror*. *Weird Tales* revived.
July	First issue of *Whispers*.
August	Final issue of *The Haunt of Horror*.
October	John Shirley debuts in *Clarion III*.

1974

January	*Dungeons & Dragons* role-playing game launched.
February	First issue of *Science Fiction Monthly*.
March	James Baen becomes editor of *Worlds of If*.
April	Joan Vinge debuts in *Orbit*. Cherry Wilder debuts in *New Writings in SF*.

June	First issue of *The Diversifier*. Final issue of revived *Weird Tales*. James Baen becomes editor of *Galaxy*.
July	Charles R. Saunders debuts in *Dark Fantasy*.
August	John Varley debuts in *F&SF* and *Vertex*.
September	First volume of *Stellar*. Last issue of *Witchcraft & Sorcery*.
October	First issue of *Midnight Sun*. Pat Murphy debuts in *Galaxy*.
November	Last issues of *Worlds of If* and *Science Fiction Adventures*.
December	Last volume of *Nova*.

1975

January	World's first home-computer kit offered.
February	Final issue of *Eternity*.
March	First issues of *REH: Lone Star Fictioneer*, *The Space Gamer* and *The Strategic Review*. David Bischoff debuts in *Perry Rhodan*.
April	James Patrick Kelly debuted in *Galaxy*.
June	*Vertex* switches to tabloid format.
July	Final issue of *Thrilling Science Fiction*.
August	First issues of *Stardust* and *Void*. Final issue of *Vertex*.
September	First issue of *Nickelodeon*.
October	First volume of *Weird Heroes*. Terry Dowling debuts in *Enigma*.
November	First issue of *Other Times*.

1976

February	Final issue of *Other Times*.
March	First issue of *Odyssey*. David Langford debuts in *New Writings in SF*.
April	Appearance of *Analog Annual*.
May	First volume of *Andromeda*. Last issue of *Science Fiction Monthly*.
June	*The Strategic Review* relaunched as *The Dragon*. Only issue of *S.F. Digest*. Last issues of *Odyssey* and *Macabre*. Kim Stanley Robinson debuts in *Orbit*.
August	First issue of *Starlog*. Last volume of *New Worlds* anthology with debut story by Geoff Ryman.
September	First issues of *Galileo*, *Ariel* and *Phantasy Digest*.
November	Bruce Sterling debuts in *Lone Star Universe*.
December	First issue of *Chacal*. Cynthia Felice debuts in *Galileo*.

1977

January	First issues of *Isaac Asimov's SF Magazine*, *Vortex* and *Unearth*, the last with debut story by Paul Di Filippo. James Tiptree, Jr.'s identity revealed in *Locus*.

February   Final magazine issue of *Void*.
March   Last issue of *Luna Monthly*. *Thrust* revived as semi-prozine. Pat Cadigan debuts in *Chacal*.
April   First issue of *Heavy Metal*. Charles Sheffield debuts in *Galaxy*.
May   First issue of *Cosmos*. Last issue of *Vortex*. *Star Wars* released (25 May).
June   First issue of *Fantasy Tales*. William F. Wu debuts in *Andromeda*.
July   James Blaylock, William Gibson and Somtow Sucharitkul all debut in *Unearth*.
August   First volume of *Chrysalis*. Robert Lynn Asprin and Orson Scott Card debut in *Analog*; John Crowley debuts in *Whispers* (anthology).
September   Final volume of *New Writings in SF*.
October   First volume of *New Voices in Science Fiction*.
November   First issues of *Shayol* and *Skyworlds*. Last issues of *Cosmos* and *Weird Heroes*. John J. Pierce becomes editor of *Galaxy*. *Close Encounters of the Third Kind* released (16 November).

1978
January   First issues of *Questar* and *Starburst*. Last pocketbook edition of *Perry Rhodan*.
April   First issue of *Future*. Reappearance of *New Worlds* as semi-prozine. Craig Shaw Gardner debuts in *Unearth*.
May   John Kessel debuts in *Galileo*.
June   First issues of *Asimov's SF Adventure Magazine* (29 June) and *Fantasy Newsletter*.
July   Diana Paxson debuts in *Asimov's*, Rudy Rucker in *Unearth* and David J. Schow in *Galileo*. John J. Pierce resigns as editor of *Galaxy* (31 July).
August   Final issue of *Skyworlds*.
September   Final volume of *Andromeda*. Sol Cohen sells *Amazing* and *Fantastic* to Arthur Bernhard (15 September).
October   First issues of *Omni* and *Pandora*. Last volume of *Ariel*.
November   First volumes of *Destinies* and *Shadows*. Barry Longyear debuts in *Asimov's*.
December   First issue of *Sorcerer's Apprentice*. Stanley Schmidt becomes editor of *Analog*.

1979
January   Final issue of *Unearth*. Rick Kennett debuts in *Enigma*.

February	Final issue of *The Diversifier*. Jo Clayton debuts in *Asimov's*.
March	*Algol* becomes *Starship*.
April	Elinor Mavor now editor of *Fantastic* and *Amazing Stories*. *Eternity* revived. *Alien* premiered (25 April).
June	Hank Stine becomes editor of *Galaxy*.
July	Final issues of *Asimov's SF Adventure* and *Midnight Sun*.
August	Michael Kube-McDowell debuts in *Amazing*.
September	*Science Fiction Chronicle* launched as separate magazine. Final semi-pro issue of *New Worlds*. Timothy Zahn debuts in *Analog*.
October	First issue of *Ad Astra*.
November	Wayne Wightman debuts in *Amazing*.
December	*The Cygnus Chronicler* relaunched as semi-prozine.

1980

January	Final issue of *Galileo*. Ted White becomes editor of *Heavy Metal*. Robert Sheckley becomes fiction editor of *Omni*.
February	Davis Publications buys *Analog* (20 February).
March	First issues of *Ares* and *Something Else*. Final issue of *Stardust*.
July	Final issue of *Galaxy*. Michael Swanwick debuts in *New Dimensions*. Harry Turtledove debuts in *Universe*.
September	Susan Shwartz debuts in *Analog*.
October	Final issue of *Fantastic* and final volume of *Orbit*.
November	Final issue of *Dark Fantasy*.

I

Goodbye to all That:
The Old Gateways

One Step ... Forwards?

On 20 July 1969 man first left his footprint on the Moon. One of science fiction's great dreams had been achieved. At the time, it seemed it must herald a new dawn in space exploration. Further lunar landings were planned, and there was no reason to doubt that there would be a working colony on the Moon by the end of the century. The pictures transmitted, especially that of the Earth seen from the Moon, looking alone and fragile in space, gave impetus to the ecological movement. The manned moon missions were one of those significant moments in history that affects the beliefs, perceptions, hopes and desires of millions.

Science-fiction fans were jubilant. More drama was to follow with the near-tragedy of the *Apollo 13* mission when for four days the fate of three astronauts hung in the balance as they struggled to return safely to earth. John W. Campbell, Jr., the editor of *Analog* magazine and generally acknowledged as the father of modern science fiction, called it 'the greatest cliff-hanger in history'.[1] But Campbell was also one of the first to recognize that the writing was on the wall for the Apollo programme. Just a few months after the *Apollo 13* mission he wrote:

> there is a type of barrier that makes it impossible for our human culture to reach the stars. There are already signs of that barrier developing – and, as Shakespeare said, 'The fault, dear Brutus, is not in our stars, but in ourselves, that we are underlings.'[2]

Those words announced a story by Stanley Schmidt, 'The Unreachable Stars', which appeared in the April 1971 issue. The story is set on Earth

1 *Analog* 85:6 (August 1970), p. 4.
2 *Analog* 87:1 (March 1971), p. 157.

millennia hence, where nuclear power provides all the fuel requirements but where technology has otherwise receded and there is little understanding of the nature of space and the stars. The belief that man had once travelled to the Moon is dismissed as legend. Benign aliens try to revive Earth's climb back to the stars. One of the aliens explains the short-sightedness of mankind since the twentieth century. Public pressure had forced governments to look inwards at domestic problems such as pollution, population and poverty. The development of nuclear power solved the energy and pollution problems in the short term and, satisfied that they had achieved their goals, humanity ceased further innovations. Society stagnated.

Campbell and Schmidt had read the signs. The Apollo lunar missions ended with Apollo 17. Eugene Cernan was the last man to stand on the Moon, on 14 December 1972. Unfortunately, Campbell, whose work in reshaping and developing science fiction in the pages of *Astounding* (the original name for *Analog*) had done much to stimulate interest in space exploration, did not live to see the end. He had died of an abdominal aortic aneurysm on 11 July 1971 at the age of only 61.

It was a time of endings and of changes. With the last of the manned lunar missions, America did indeed look inwards. The Vietnam War, civil unrest, student riots, energy crises, rampant inflation – all this and more made any further Apollo missions seem misguided[3] and the light that had shone briefly flickered and went out.

Well, almost. It continued to glow in the pages of the science-fiction magazines, but they too had their storms to weather. The economic, political and social unrest that buffeted the American nation during the 1970s also battered the sf magazines. Not all survived and none was left unaffected. Yet at the same time as the sf magazines tried to cope, the fans and writers responded. Just as 20 years earlier the dawn of the 1950s had seen a flowering of new talent, so did the start of the 1970s. The period was second only to the early 1950s in seeing the emergence of many important new writers who would regenerate the magazines and give them a new lease of life. It also saw a burgeoning of new ideas and a diversity of expression both in how science fiction was written (such as the growth in the feminist movement and in a greater freedom of expression) and in the way it was packaged (with traditional sf magazines under threat from original anthology series, gaming magazines, media magazines, under-

3 An opinion poll taken just a few months after the Apollo 11 moon landing in 1969 showed that 50 per cent of Americans thought the country should 'do less' in space, and only 20 per cent thought they should 'do more'. This compared to 58 per cent who were in support of the lunar programme in 1965. See James R. Hansen, *Spaceflight Revolution* (Washington: NASA, 1995).

ground comics, graphic novels and much more), all regulated by reader and market demands.

In this first chapter, which covers the years up to 1977, I will explore how these storms affected the traditional sf magazines, alongside the contributions by both new and established writers. It was a frenetic period when they faced a variety of challenges.

The Gathering at the Gate

At the dawn of the 1970s, it was a diverse and seemingly ill-prepared group of magazines that faced the oncoming decade. In addition to *Analog*, there were five other major sf and fantasy magazines published in the United States, plus a number of lesser magazines and various reprint titles. The oldest was *Amazing Stories*, which had been the first all-sf magazine when it appeared in April 1926. In the subsequent 44 years it had seen good times and bad and was only now starting to emerge from a particularly lean period during which it had subsisted primarily on reprints from its archives, a blight which had also affected its companion title, *Fantastic*. Ted White had taken over as editor of both magazines from the May and June 1969 issues respectively.

Amazing had several all-reprint companion titles, which were handled directly by the publisher, Sol Cohen. These included *Thrilling Science Fiction*, *Science Fiction Greats*, *Space Adventures* and *Science Fiction Adventures*, all produced at minimal cost. The magazines' previous publisher, Ziff-Davis, had bought all serial rights to the stories, allowing Cohen to reprint the stories without further payment to the authors. Although he was legally correct, this practice was frowned on by the newly formed Science Fiction Writers of America, which placed an embargo on the magazines. This led to considerable acrimony and blighted the reputation of all of Cohen's magazines. Yet the reprint magazines sold almost as well as *Amazing* and *Fantastic* and, because they were cheap to produce, they effectively subsidized the older magazines.[4] It was regarded as an unethical but necessary evil.

The Magazine of Fantasy and Science Fiction (or *F&SF* for convenience) was the most stable and consistent of the magazines. Since 1965, it had been edited by Edward L. Ferman, son of the magazine's publisher (and one of its founders), Joseph Ferman. *F&SF* had evolved with the times and, though it retained a remarkable consistency in format and appearance

---

4 See comment by Ted White in *Amazing Science Fiction Stories* 44:4 (November 1970), p. 135.

over those 21 years, it had moved on from being a reflective magazine of 'slick' fantasy to publishing the widest spectrum of creative and imaginative fiction. *F&SF* was arguably the most popular magazine among hardcore genre enthusiasts, although its circulation was half that of *Analog*'s. It had won the Hugo Award in 1969 and 1970 (and would win again in 1971 and 1972).

F&SF had a companion magazine called *Venture*. This had first appeared in 1957 but had run for only ten issues. It had been revived in May 1969 in anticipation of a growing interest in science fiction as a result of the Apollo missions. In both incarnations *Venture* concentrated on longer stories with a strong action element, but its second life was even shorter than its first, and it folded after six issues in August 1970. Sales apparently never exceeded 20,000 copies.[5]

Galaxy, which in the 1950s had generated most of the influx of talent to the field, had seen, along with its companion *If*, a change of editor and publisher in 1969. This would have a dramatic effect on the direction and the fate of both magazines. Under its previous editor, Frederik Pohl, *If* had been aimed primarily at new readers and those who enjoyed adventure-orientated sf, a policy that had won it three Hugo Awards in succession (1966–68). Under the new editor, Ejler Jakobsson, *If* retained much of that appeal, but *Galaxy*, which had published more mature, sociological science fiction, became more experimental at a time when readers were still divided over the value of the New Wave revolution.

Like *Venture*, other magazines were revived. In a moment of flushed optimism, Universal, the publisher of *Galaxy* and *If*, revived their companion titles *Worlds of Tomorrow* and *Worlds of Fantasy* in the summer and autumn of 1970, but both lasted only three issues. The indefatigable William L. Crawford, who had more or less created the small-press semi-professional magazine in 1934 with *Marvel Tales*, revived his fifties magazine, *Spaceway*, in 1969, but was never able to achieve sufficient financial backing or distribution, and that magazine folded after four issues in June 1970. He did not throw in the towel, however. Instead he bought the subscription list to the weird-fiction magazine *Coven 13*, which folded in March 1970, and revived it as *Witchcraft & Sorcery*, one of the new breed of small-press magazines, of which much more later.

The popular editor Robert A. W. Lowndes, who had, during the forties and fifties, edited the magazines *Future Science Fiction* and *Science Fiction* amongst others, forever struggling with a minimal budget and production values, was editing a clutch of reprint titles including *Magazine of Horror* and *Startling Mystery Stories*. A change in the parent company and

---

5 See news report in *Luna Monthly* #18 (November 1970), p. 2.

a tightening of belts saw his magazines dropped after April 1971. One other reprint title, the beautifully produced *Forgotten Fantasy*, from Nectar Press in Hollywood, was also short-lived, lasting for only five issues from October 1970 to June 1971. Its failure had more to do with distribution than content, but the passing of all these titles gave the impression that there was no longer a market for old material.

Britain still had two sf magazines at the start of 1970 but none to speak of by the end of the year. The Australian-financed but British-edited-and-published magazine, *Vision of Tomorrow*, arguably the first true sf slick magazine, had appeared in August 1969 but poor distribution killed it after 12 issues. *New Worlds*, Britain's oldest sf magazine and the one which, in the hands of Michael Moorcock, had whipped up the New Wave into a tsunami during the latter part of the sixties, had now also run out of energy and had folded, as a magazine, in May 1970, but would return the next year as a paperback anthology.

The inability of the new and smaller magazines to survive showed that the magazine field had lost its previous domination of the newsstands and had become a difficult domain to enter. During the 1950s and especially since the 1960s, science fiction had prospered in paperback. This benefited novels in particular, but short-story collections (by a single author) and anthologies (by multiple authors with an overall editor) also sold well. In Britain, John Carnell, the founding editor of *New Worlds*, had seen the coming trend and had wound up Nova Publications and sold *New Worlds* in 1964. He began a regular anthology of new science fiction called *New Writings in SF*. The concept had originated with Frederik Pohl and *Star Science Fiction*, published from 1953 to 1959. By the early seventies the concept had reblossomed, and a number of original anthology series appeared, including *Orbit, Infinity, Nova, New Dimensions* and *Universe*. *Infinity*, edited by Robert Hoskins and published by Lancer Books, was of special interest because it came from the same publisher as the original magazine *Infinity*, which ran from 1955 to 1958 and saw itself as a 'lineal descendant' of that magazine. The original anthology would seriously rival the digest magazines in the quality and originality of its fiction during the 1970s.

One other development, that would have more far-reaching effects as the decade progressed, was just knocking on the door when the 1970s began. In *Transformations* I discussed how the Comics Code introduced in 1954 had effectively prohibited graphic horror and weird-science art in comics. Since 1954 the major comics publishers had avoided horror and weird sf, concentrating on the clean-cut heroics of the superheroes. However, in December 1964, James Warren circumvented the code by publishing *Creepy*, a quarterly of black-and-white illustrations, in magazine rather than comics format. Magazines were not covered by the Comics Code, allowing Warren to recreate the original horror and terror images of the previous decade. The success of *Creepy* led to *Eerie* in 1966 and then, more relevant to sf, *Vampirella* in September 1969, created by long-time sf fan Forrest J Ackerman.

This, then, was the somewhat disorganized army that assembled at the gates in 1970, ready to explore the future. It is time to consider them in more detail.

The King is Dead ...

The biggest shock to hit science fiction at the start of the decade, arguably since the start of the sf magazines in 1926, was the death of John W. Campbell. He had been in poor health for some years but his death was nevertheless sudden and unexpected. He died of heart failure quickly and quietly at home while watching television on 11 July 1971.[6] Campbell had been employed by Street and Smith in September 1937 as sub-editor to F. Orlin Tremaine on *Astounding Science Fiction*, starting from the December 1937 issue. Although Tremaine retained overall editorial control, Campbell had a fairly free hand, and gained complete control after Tremaine left in May 1938. At the time of Campbell's death, there was sufficient material in hand for his assistant Kay Tarrant and art director Herbert Stoltz to assemble issues until December 1971. Campbell can therefore claim editorship of 409 consecutive issues over 34 years, a record that no one else has yet equalled for any sf magazine.[7]

Campbell's importance had been to direct authors to produce a more sophisticated form of science fiction than had been prevalent in most of the sf magazines during the 1930s. He was not the first to try this. David Lasser, editor of Hugo Gernsback's *Wonder Stories*, had tried to do much the same in 1932/33, but he lacked the financial support and wherewithal of Campbell's publisher, Street and Smith and, unfortunately, Gernsback fired Lasser just at the time that his editorial drive was starting to have an effect. As a consequence, many of the writers that he was developing transferred to *Astounding Stories*, then edited by F. Orlin Tremaine. Some of those same authors continued to write for Campbell, but Campbell was a strict regimentarian when it came to the type of stories he wanted, and

6 See obituary by Isaac Asimov in *Luna Monthly* #27S (August 1971).
7 Stanley Schmidt has edited 339 issues of *Analog* as at the end of 2006. Edward L. Ferman edited 320 issues of *F&SF* from 1964 to 1991.

not all could cope with the discipline that he imposed. Those who did –
most notably Robert A. Heinlein, Isaac Asimov, Theodore Sturgeon, Fritz
Leiber, A. E. van Vogt, C. L. Moore and Eric Frank Russell – went on to
create most of the original and thought-provoking science fiction stories
of the 1940s, many of which are still considered classics of the field.

But it would also be true to say that Campbell's most significant period
of influence was over by the end of the 1940s. Thereafter an expanding
market, with editors, writers and readers only too aware of the 'atomic
age', allowed science fiction to develop and, taking Campbell's lead, the
field grew and matured. Horace L. Gold at *Galaxy* and Anthony Boucher at
F&SF were as important to the growth of sf in the 1950s as Campbell had
been in the 1940s. Likewise in the 1960s, Frederik Pohl (Gold's successor
at *Galaxy* and *If*), Cele Goldsmith at *Amazing Stories* and Michael Moorcock
at *New Worlds* allowed the field greater scope. A new generation of editors
working in the pocketbook field, in particular Damon Knight and Terry
Carr, were also developing the field.

During the fifties and sixties Campbell had come to be seen, in some
people's eyes, as eccentric. He had promoted dianetics (the predecessor
to scientology), experimented with the Hieronymous machine and the
Dean device, and actively encouraged any form of alternative science.
Although stories based on traditional science continued to appear in
Astounding, renamed *Analog* from 1960, a large percentage drew upon
psi powers, blurring the borders between science fiction and fantasy.
Campbell's readers were nothing if not loyal, and clearly enjoyed a good
argument. One of the main features of *Analog*, often eclipsing the fiction
in the reaction they drew from readers, was Campbell's editorials. He went
out of his way to be provocative, always challenging the status quo, to the
extent that if too many people agreed with him, he would change the
argument again. What Campbell enjoyed was a strong debate and lateral
thinking, and his editorials always stimulated readers and writers alike,
though not always positively. Isaac Asimov, arguably Campbell's most
devoted disciple, later confessed, 'I could hardly ever read a Campbell
editorial and keep my temper.'[8] In his later years, Campbell's editorials
became more provocative than ever. He would make alarming statements in order to force the reader into thinking through or countering
his argument. Campbell did not always agree with these statements, and
if anyone followed his argument they would see why he made them, but
not everyone could get into Campbell's mindset and, as a consequence,
he frequently angered readers. Of course, that was what he wanted to

8 Isaac Asimov, 'Introduction', in Harry Harrison (ed.) *Astounding, John W. Campbell
Memorial Anthology* (New York: Random House, 1973) Sphere edition, p. 12.

do. He loved it. Consider some of these statements from various editorials over the two years prior to Campbell's death.

> On peace in Vietnam: 'All the misery of South Vietnam could also be stopped, even more quickly, by a thorough, saturation, overlapping hydrogen bombing of the area. That would leave no one alive to complain.'[9]

> On banning cigarette adverts: 'tobacco is not habit-forming, and discontinuation causes no withdrawal symptoms whatever'.[10]

> On pollution and the population explosion: 'We can solve the whole sticky problem by getting rid of about eighty percent of the human population of the planet.'[11]

> On the anti-Vietnam-War protestors and others of the 'now' generation: 'stop trying to tell us how to run the world: you're saying "I don't know how to do these hard things – you do 'em!" You're still a child howling for "Daddy!" to solve the problems you want handled. And kicking Daddy in the shins because he doesn't do it fast enough to suit you brats.'[12]

> On over-zealous ecologists: 'All across the country, Concerned Ecologists have been fighting and winning their battles to prevent the use or construction of nuclear power planets. Already completed and ready-to-go power plants have been stopped by legal injunctions thanks to the wise Caring Ecologists. Who don't have the foggiest notion what the hell they're talking about, of course.'[13]

Most of these comments brought protests from readers and allowed Campbell to extend his argument and score points. Sometimes, the responses went beyond *Analog*. It was unusual for fellow editors to attack one another but that is what happened following Campbell's editorial 'A Difference of Intelligence' in the October 1969 issue. Drawing on research published in the *Harvard Education Review* and elsewhere, Campbell drew the conclusion that 'Black children had lower IQs, and learned more slowly, than White children did' (p. 4). Campbell was using this editorial to explore the nature of intelligence and see how this might differ between racial or ethnic groups. He concluded, 'The Blacks appear to have a subtly different *type* of intelligence' (p. 177).

There were many who believed that Campbell was racist. He easily

9 Campbell, 'Face Against Peace', *Analog* 83:3 (May 1969), pp. 6–7.
10 Campbell, 'The Lynch-Mob Philosophy', *Analog* 83:5 (July 1969), p. 176.
11 Campbell, 'Red Tide', *Analog* 85:4 (June 1970), p. 178.
12 Campbell, 'The "Now" Generation', *Analog* 86: 3 (November 1970), p. 176.
13 Campbell, 'Ecological Notes', *Analog* 88:1 (September 1971), p. 175.

gave that impression because of his anglocentric views, his domination of any argument and his intransigence, but strictly he was not racist.[14] Racism is bigotry based on non-rationalized emotion. Campbell based all his conclusions on empirical evidence.

Ejler Jakobsson, the new editor at *Galaxy* and *If* took exception to Campbell's attitude. He devoted his editorials in the November 1969 *Galaxy* and December 1969 *If* to lambasting Campbell for his selective evidence, and wondering what planet he inhabited, concluding, 'Mr. Campbell is made of strong stuff. On his planet I would rapidly become paranoid.'[15]

Jakobsson's editorials brought more response in the pages of *If* and *Galaxy* than Campbell's original comments did in *Analog*. While some supported Jakobsson's reaction, others sided with Campbell. One correspondent raised a matter relevant to all of Campbell's editorials when, after admonishing Jakobsson for missing Campbell's point, he suggested, 'So fish your October issue of *Analog* out of the trash can and read what Mr Campbell says instead of what you think he is going to say.'[16] It was evident, once the dust settled, that most respondents could see the argument that Campbell was developing, though they may not have agreed with it. Jakobsson's reaction demonstrates that those not sufficiently acquainted with Campbell would draw too rapid a conclusion on superficial issues and miss the deeper analysis. Longer-term readers of *Analog*, and evidently other sf magazines, accepted Campbell for what he was. A hard-headed rationalist who wanted readers to take those extra mental steps to see through the emotional reaction to the hardcore pragmatism beneath. Only by doing that could you develop the logic necessary to extrapolate to the next and further levels, a requirement, in Campbell's eyes, for realistic and rational science fiction. Gordon R. Dickson once remarked, 'What John [Campbell] really loved wasn't science fiction but idea fiction'[17] and it was that wrangling with ideas to extrapolate a logical conclusion that so fascinated Campbell and which he projected to his authors.

14 Evidence in Campbell's own words will be found in his letter to Isaac Asimov on 18 November 1958, reprinted in Perry A. Chapdelaine Sr. (ed.), *The John W. Campbell Letters Volume II* (Franklin, TN, AC Projects, 1993) pp. 477–87. He states, amongst much else, 'I don't care who runs the world – provided only he's the best man. I don't give a damn whether he's black, white, yellow or purple with chartreuse polka-dots. If the Blacks can take the world away from us, *by their superior achievements* ... it's theirs until somebody out-achieves them.' Frederik Pohl also did not believe that Campbell was racist. See F. Pohl, *The Way the Future Was* (New York: Del Rey, 1978), pp. 83–4, paperback edition.

15 Ejler Jakobsson, 'Editor's Page', *If* 19:10 (December 1969), p. 3.

16 James C. Fairfield, letter, 'Hue and Cry', *If* 20:3 (March 1970), p. 157.

17 Gordon R. Dickson in an interview by Sandra Miesel in *Algol* #31 (Spring 1978), p. 33.

Stanley Schmidt recalled:

> People assumed he believed everything he wrote and while I may
> be mistaken, I have the strong impression that this was not the case.
> Rather, Campbell believed that the surest way to get people to really
> think about something – especially something they have long consid-
> ered settled – is to show them a radically contrasting viewpoint [...]
> different enough and convincingly enough presented that they feel
> infuriated into trying to refute it.[18]

The main thrust of his latter-day editorials was on military issues, inevitably arising out of Vietnam, and ecological problems. A technocrat, he
was of the view that military superiority and technological progress were
both necessary for the advancement of civilization and that no matter
what consequent problems arose, science would find the answer.

Many of his leading contributors held similar ideas, including Poul
Anderson, Gordon R. Dickson and Harry Harrison. One new author who
emerged in Campbell's final days and was amongst his last 'discoveries'
was Jerry Pournelle, whose work came to epitomize the Campbellian
viewpoint. Pournelle was 37 when he made his first sale to Campbell and
had an impressive curriculum vitae behind him. He had Ph.D.s in both
psychology and political science, had worked in the aerospace industry,
was a professor of political science at Pepperdine University, and had
been an adviser to the Mayor of Los Angeles. He had also recently had
published (with Stefan T. Possony) a book on technology and the military,
The Strategy of Technology (1970). He had tried to break into *Astounding*
during the 1950s without success, while in the 1960s Campbell had
tried to prise articles from him about the space programme, with which
Pournelle had been deeply involved. Pournelle had sold a couple of espionage novels under the alias Wade Curtis[19] before he sold his first story to
Campbell, 'Peace with Honor' (May 1971). Though set in a future alliance
between the United States and the Soviet Union, it otherwise reads as a
very contemporary story, since it concentrates on internal corruption to
manipulate both a peaceful presidential succession and withdrawal from
the alliance. Its scenario would become all the more potent when the
Watergate scandal broke a year later.

Pournelle's stories echo many of Campbell's philosophies. 'A Spaceship
for the King' (December 1971–January 1972) explores the belief that
advanced technology is necessary for political progress and that polit-

---

18 Stanley Schmidt, 'Changing the Guard', *Analog* 99:1 (January 1979), p. 8.
19 *Red Heroin* (1969) and *Red Dragon* (1971). The first carried an endorsement from
Robert A. Heinlein, a friend of Pournelle's and whose work Pournelle's early stories most
resemble.

ical short-sightedness usually thwarts such plans. A colony world seeks to regain its independence, but can only do so if it rediscovers starship technology. 'Ecology Now' (December 1971) was the first of three stories run under the Wade Curtis alias and featuring Bill Adams, a troubleshooter for the nuclear industry. Adams has to combat protestors at a nuclear power plant. One of the protagonists voices an opinion recently expressed in a Campbell editorial: 'Without the best technology we can develop … we won't live in danger. We just won't live at all.'[20] In fact, it was so recent (September 1971) that Campbell may well have borrowed the sentiment from Pournelle, showing how much in tune their thinking was.

Pournelle told me:

> I was selling non-fiction about nuclear power to the regular magazine trade, and I had come to many of the same conclusions that Campbell did. I had been reading Campbell editorials since high school, and I was pretty well in agreement with most of them, so it's not astonishing that much of that came through in my stories.[21]

Perhaps Pournelle's most controversial story was 'The Mercenary' (July 1972). Pournelle was in the process of editing the story to Campbell's demands at the time Campbell died, and Ben Bova subsequently bought the story as originally written. It introduced Pournelle's best-known character, John Falkenberg, the commander of a small army of merce-naries, who finds employment resolving problems throughout the loosely organized galactic CoDominium. Falkenberg's philosophy is that 'war is the normal state of affairs'. In this story he is brought in to sort out polit-ical rebels in a backward mining colony. His solution is to lure the rebels into the capital's stadium and slaughter them. Campbell had discussed a similar tactic in his provocative May 1969 editorial.

Pournelle's work was so much part of the Campbell heritage that when the John W. Campbell Award for the best new writer of each year was instigated in 1973 by Condé Nast in tribute to Campbell, it was no surprise that Pournelle was the first recipient.

Campbell's strong presence was a key feature of *Analog* and held together a loyal readership, many of whom had grown up with the magazine. While *Analog* was still regarded as one of the 'big three' (alongside *Galaxy* and *F&SF*), its fiction lacked the scope and originality that had revitalized the field in the 1940s. If anything the fiction had become predictable, though that in itself had its benefits. Readers knew what to expect. At a time when the New Wave was battering at the ramparts of sf, Campbell

20 'Ecology Now', *Analog* 88:4 (December 1971), p. 96.
21 Personal e-mail, Pournelle/Ashley, 9 May 2006.

held firm and did not swerve from the course he had maintained for three decades. Indeed, it was as much against the traditional Campbell outlook as anything else in sf that the rebels were fighting. Far from being in the vanguard of science fiction, *Analog* was part of the 'old school'. The magazine had not won the Hugo Award since 1965, and neither had many stories. Its last major work was probably Frank Herbert's 'The Prophet of Dune', serialized at the start of 1965 and which in the book version as *Dune* (1966) won both the Hugo and Nebula awards. Other notable winners included two of Anne McCaffrey's Pern stories, 'Weyr Search' (October 1967), which tied for the Hugo, and 'Dragonrider' (December 1967–January 1968), which won a Nebula. The last story purchased by Campbell to win an award, though he did not live long enough to know it, was 'The Missing Man' by Katherine MacLean (March 1971), a typical Campbellian story about a man whose psychic talent is sufficiently advanced that he can pick up on people's emotional distress from remote locations and aid their rescue.

Tales of psi powers had dominated *Analog* since the late forties. One of the most regular contributors to Campbell's final issues was James H. Schmitz, whose engaging stories about telepath Telzey Amberdon, who can read both human and alien minds, read as much like fantasy as sf. While there was some humour in *Analog*, particularly in the works of Harry Harrison and Jack Wodhams, and still some hard science, most notably Hal Clement's recent return to the high-gravity world of Mesklin for the serial 'Star Light' (June–September 1970), the bulk of *Analog's* fiction during Campbell's last years depicted military action, usually as part of Earth's means of controlling former planetary colonies or repressive alien cultures. In this respect, Pournelle's Falkenberg series was simply part of a long line of Campbellian militarist sf, of which other recent examples included the works of Mack Reynolds, Christopher Anvil's Interstellar Patrol series, Gordon R. Dickson's Dorsai series, Keith Laumer's Bolo stories and Lloyd Biggle's serial 'The World Menders' (February–April 1971). The latter should be compulsory reading for all prospective military do-gooders, as it portrays the consequences of trying to liberate a slave society without the liberators understanding the nature of the culture.

Another author whose work challenged existing military principles was the Campbell near-discovery, F. Paul Wilson. I say 'near', because Wilson first appeared in print in the final issue of Robert Lowndes's *Startling Mystery Stories* (March 1971) with the sf-horror story 'The Cleaning Machine'. Wilson had been submitting stories to Campbell for over a year and made his breakthrough with another sf-horror story, 'Ratman' (August 1971).

That story, about an interstellar rat exterminator who works as an undercover agent, was held over in order to fit into a sequence of stories, the LaNague series, that Wilson was developing with Campbell. It began in *Analog* with the complex story 'Wheels within Wheels' (September 1971). Wilson has long espoused the role of the individual over the state[22] and, in a precursor to the LaNague sequence 'The Man With the Anteater' (July 1971), showed the basic weakness in a government that tries to get the best out of people without considering what motivates them. He took this further in 'Wheels within Wheels', portraying a native society, symbolic of any aboriginal race, who have become dominated by Terran settlers and have lost all individualism, consigning themselves to fate. One Earthman (the son of the man with the anteater) shows the natives how to fight back, though he pays for it with his life. It was a story finely tuned to the state of society in the late 1960s during the turbulence of the civil-rights movement following the assassination of Martin Luther King, and with the move toward greater self-determination for the Native Americans encapsulated in Nixon's 'Special Message on Indian Affairs' in 1970. When Wilson reworked and expanded the story into the book version, *Wheels Within Wheels* (Doubleday, 1979), it became the first recipient of the Prometheus Award for libertarian sf.

Wilson's story gave a positive message at a time when a general pall of despondency was settling over the content of science fiction, reflecting the grim, violent world from which most readers were trying to escape. It was something that, as we progress through the seventies, we shall see got worse before it got better. Although it also seeped into *Analog*, mostly via Campbell's increasingly oppressive editorials, *Analog* remained the most positive of the sf magazines. Readers had come to expect this from Campbell. His philosophy for 30 years had been that mankind could solve any problem, given time and opportunity, and the sf he had published explored those opportunities. In addition to F. Paul Wilson's stories, we find Ted Thomas creating a viral cure that solves all drug addiction in 'The Swan Song of Dame Horse' (June 1971), while Colin Kapp turns the abilities of a saboteur to advantage in 'Letter from an Unknown Genius' (August 1971).

Yet even in *Analog* one could feel a hint of defeatism. Despite Wilson's optimism, we find in 'The Man with the Anteater' that the hero's sister and brother-in-law had fled to a remote colony 'unable to cope with Earth any more' (p. 58). Gordon R. Dickson's serial 'The Outposter' (May–July 1971), the last Campbell would see through into print, also feels disap-

---

22 See Gary Lovisi's interview with Wilson in *Paperback Parade* #40 (October 1994) in which Wilson refers to himself as a 'rational anarchist' and 'radical capitalist' (p. 63).

pointingly defeatist in portraying the dregs of society being deported from Earth to control pollution and overpopulation, rather than positive action being taken to solve the problem.

It is possible that the cracks were showing in Campbell's positivism, perhaps owing to his failing health and the depressing state of society. One wonders what more Campbell would have achieved at *Analog* had he lived longer, but it is unlikely to have been much. Although he had continued to develop new writers in his final years – Lee Killough, Alan Dean Foster[23] and Andrew Stephenson, in addition to F. Paul Wilson and Jerry Pournelle – these might as easily have debuted under a successor editor. Campbell's strength, after his first few years, was not in the development of new writers – indeed, his forceful letters may have been off-putting to many young aspirants – but in his ability to make seasoned writers continue to think laterally and develop new ideas out of the old. Few stories in Campbell's *Analog* are likely to be revered as great literature, but they were never intended to be. However, they can and should be revered as highlighting the abilities of human creativity, the triumph of brainpower over adversity and therefore the unstoppable progress of mankind. It is impossible to read any of Campbell's 409 issues without feeling amazed at the potential of human ingenuity over human fallibility. Campbell's form of science fiction worked because it always gave hope.

There were the inevitable outpourings of praise and respect for Campbell after his death. Most echoed the sentiments of Frederik Pohl when he wrote that 'he was the greatest editor that science fiction ever had.'[24] Theodore Sturgeon said, 'You were – you are – the very best in the world at what you do.',[25] while Kelly Freas went so far as to say, 'To me, John W. Campbell stood just a few steps down the stairs from God.'[26] The one that I thought captured the man's outlook best came from a reader, Maydene Crosby, who wrote, 'No fading away for John W. Campbell, Jr. – Thank God! – no mental deterioration, no senile fuzziness, no blurring of that compassionate desire to see not only both sides of the coin but the edge as well.'[27] Others remembered the man. Both Lester del Rey and Eric Frank Russell recalled his 'pixie'-like nature, Russell saying, 'People who did not know him personally could be misled by his liking for ruthless argument

---

23 Foster's first sale had been to August Derleth (who died just a week before Campbell) and appeared in *The Arkham Collector*, Summer 1971, but it was his appearance in *Analog* with 'With Friends Like These ...' (June 1971) that first established his name.

24 *Locus* #90 (12 July 1971), p. 8. This was a view still held seven years later: see interview in *Galileo* #9 (July 1978), p. 9.

25 *Locus* #91 (22 July 1971), p. 7.

26 *Locus* #90 (12 July 1971), p. 9.

27 *Analog* 88:3 (November 1971), p. 172.

and his sly needling of opponents, all of which arose from his love of discussion and his pixieish sense of humor.'[28] And there was no denying the sense of deep personal loss. Harry Harrison wrote, 'he was a warm and wonderful human being. A friend. A man who was really without malice, who believed in people and in mankind.'[29] However, Vincent Di Fate probably best summed up Campbell's contribution:

> A man who believed in things *that* strongly, who was that uncompromising and whose overwhelming manner and vast intellectual resources were such that he could make you believe almost anything, had to become a legend. But the legend in no way exceeds what he was as a man, for in the midst of all that strength was a compassion which gave him the will to encourage the growth of others – and that, in a world where *self* has inordinate meaning, is truly an accomplishment.[30]

Even in the 30 years since Campbell's death the legend has not dimmed. Although his career may now be seen in perspective, his editorial achievements are generally still held in high regard. When revising *Billion Year Spree* in 1986, Brian W. Aldiss wrote, 'John Campbell was a bit of a philistine and a bit of a chauvinist. But first and foremost he was a bit of a miracle.'[31] More recently Roger Luckhurst has remarked that Campbell's 'intolerant right-wing editorials … teetered on self-parody'.[32] There is some truth in that if anyone holds a strong unfaltering position for long enough he will come to appear antiquated, inflexible and difficult; 'cranky' is the word I have most often seen applied to Campbell. Campbell's model of sf had perhaps become too rigid over the years and allowed little room for expansion.

There are more hostile views. R. A. Lafferty believed that Campbell was 'the worst disaster ever to hit science fiction',[33] arguing that Campbell did not develop his stable of new writers but simply removed their brains and replaced them with a preprogrammed roll. Campbell's greatest critic of recent years is Gary Westfahl. In two blistering articles,[34] Westfahl belittles much for which Campbell is credited and seeks to place him in a less

---

28 *Analog* 88:3 (November 1971), p. 169. See also *Locus* #90, p. 2.

29 *Locus* #90, p. 9.

30 *Locus* #91, p. 8.

31 Brian W. Aldiss and David Wingrove, *Trillion Year Spree* (London: Victor Gollancz, 1986), p. 227.

32 Roger Luckhurst, *Science Fiction* (Cambridge: Polity Press, 2005) p. 160.

33 R. A. Lafferty, 'The Case of the Math-eaten Magician', in Martin H. Greenberg (ed.), *Fantastic Lives* (Carbondale, IL: Southern Illinois University Press, 1981), p. 68.

34 Gary Westfahl, 'A Convenient Analog System', *Foundation* #54 (Spring 1992) and '"Dictatorial, Authoritarian, Unco-operative": The Case against John W. Campbell', *Foundation* #56 (Autumn 1992).

emotive perspective, coming to the conclusion that Campbell was more of a critic than an editor and not 'a particularly talented editor'. Rather, Campbell liked to operate from a position of power and used that as a hammer with which to bludgeon his writers into following his lead. The evidence Westfahl produces does show, as I have explored in these three books, that Campbell's ability to influence writers waned during the 1950s and 1960s, and it also shows that Campbell was not good at the nuts-and-bolts of editing. Campbell always read every story submitted and had no filtering process. Such a saturation of manuscripts has rapidly numbed lesser men and could not be sustained for 30 years without something going by the board. Campbell had clearly honed his skills at recognizing a story's qualities so that he did not have to waste valuable time or clog his mind with poor material. But he left all the other editorial tasks to his assistant, Kay Tarrant, so that he could develop ideas and authors. What this means is that Campbell was not so much an editor as a mentor, and a mentor with vision. This may have given him a seeming God-given power over mortal scribes, but that was what most mortal scribes wanted. This was clearly stated by Greg Bear who, at the time of Campbell's death, had sold only one minor story and that was to Robert Lowndes at *Famous Science Fiction* in 1967. When he learned of Campbell's death he wrote a final personal letter to him, saying:

> I'm not quite twenty years old, and I have no real idea what I'm going to be. I have hopes of being a writer, hopes which I've tried to foist on you since the age of fourteen by submitting manuscripts, not a one of which you accepted. But there were letters ... But whatever I become, there'll be a small part of you in me. You may not agree with all the ideas I'll try to deliver in my life, but like it or not, you'll be there.[35]

Those are not the words of an author cowed into submission by an over-authoritarian editor. They are the words of a neophyte to a master. Campbell doubtless enjoyed such adoration. It is a form of immortality.

Campbell was a man who not only shaped modern science fiction and established a model that many copied, but who left a legacy, in the shape of *Analog*, that continues to this day. No one else has had such a significant influence on the field. It may have stayed too narrow as the field of science fiction broadened in the late sixties, but Campbell had established a firm base from which writers could explore and experiment, knowing they were safely tethered. The problem was that Campbell never cut the leash, but by the sixties the new generation of writers were anxious to explore further.

35 *Analog* 88:3 (November 1971), p. 171.

At the start of this volume, therefore, we can say farewell to Campbell and see where his legacy takes us. Science fiction was once again on the move.

... Long Live the King

The task of selecting a successor to Campbell was not an easy one. Ben Bova told me:

> When Campbell suddenly died, the management realized that they knew nothing about the magazine. It made a modest profit every month and it was very inexpensive to produce. Also, it was Number One in its field and the management felt some pride about that. So they asked Kay [Tarrant] to submit a list of people she thought could handle the job. Kay, in turn, asked a half-dozen of the magazine's steadiest contributors to put together lists of possible people for the job.[36]

It took them three months to come to a decision. During that period rumours abounded. Frederik Pohl, Lester del Rey and Clifford D. Simak were all mentioned, though Simak professed he was never approached. According to Harry Harrison, Campbell had asked both him and Poul Anderson to take over. Harrison turned it down because he believed *Analog* was Campbell's magazine and it should end with him. He also did not want to live in New York.[37] It was much the same with Poul Anderson, who did not want the hassle of moving or commuting from California. Anderson suggested Pournelle but Pournelle, who also lived in California, didn't want the hassle either for the remuneration offered.

There was one name that was on most, possibly all, of the lists, and that was Bova's. Bova was invited for an interview along with several others. It was not until Bova had been editor for a year that he asked Condé Nast's president (who had been vice-president and had made the final decision) why he was chosen:

> He told me that nobody in management knew much about the magazine, but its cover page said 'science fiction and science fact'. So he made a point to read some of the fiction and nonfiction that each candidate had written for the magazine. 'And Ben,' he told me, 'yours were the only ones I could understand!'[38]

Bova was 38 when he took over *Analog*. Like Pournelle, he had a firm

36 Personal e-mail, Bova/Ashley, 1 April 2006.
37 *Vertex* 3:2 (July 1975), p. 20.
38 Personal e-mail, Bova/Ashley, 1 April 2006.

grounding in the aerospace industry. He had been a technical writer and marketing manager for Avco-Everett Research Laboratory since 1960. He had sold a juvenile sf novel (*The Star Conquerors*) to Winston Publishing in 1959 and began selling both fiction and non-fiction regularly to the sf magazines the following year. He had first appeared in *Analog* in 1962 and most recently in collaboration with Harlan Ellison with 'Brillo' (August 1970), about the first robot policeman.

Bova had his work cut out for him. Over a hundred manuscripts a week poured into *Analog*'s office and none had been read since Campbell died. Bova worked through around two thousand of them in his first few weeks. Although his name was listed as editor from the January 1972 issue, he did not feel a full ownership until the March 1972 issue. But his presence soon became evident, primarily through just two stories.

The March 1972 issue ran Frederik Pohl's 'The Gold at the Starbow's End'. Pohl had appeared only once before in *Analog* in a posthumous collaboration with Cyril Kornbluth, 'The Quaker Cannon' (August 1961).[39] Throughout the fifties and sixties Pohl had been too occupied either writing for or editing *Galaxy* and *If* to worry too much about selling to Campbell, though the fact that he didn't clearly irked him. He recalled in his autobiography, 'In all of John's thirty-four years I never sold him a story that was all my own. Fair mortified my feelings, he did.'[40]

But Pohl and Campbell had very different ideologies. They were at the extremes of the political scale. Campbell was an ardent capitalist. Pohl had once, briefly, been a communist. His science fiction often satirized capitalism and frequently showed the negative side of American society, so it would never have passed first base with Campbell, no matter how good it was. Curiously, 'The Gold at the Starbow's End'[41] is close to being a Campbell story because the humans triumph over great odds. A group of astronauts are sent on what proves to be a false mission but they use the time to improve their intelligence and ultimately transcend humanity. Pohl regarded the story as one of his best. It was nominated for both the Hugo and Nebula awards and topped the poll by readers of *Locus* as the best novella of the year.

Three issues later Bova published 'Hero' by Joe Haldeman, the first in his Forever War sequence which was later reworked into the award-winning novel *The Forever War* (1974). This is arguably one of the most important stories published during Bova's editorship and of great signifi-

39 When Pohl was a literary agent he revised two stories by Milton Rothman that appeared in the August and October 1939 issues of *Astounding* under the alias Lee Gregor, but these do not count amongst Pohl's output.

40 Pohl, *The Way the Future Was*, p. 81.

41 Expanded to novel length as *Starburst* (1982).

cance in Bova's first year as it allowed him to stamp his individuality on the magazine. The story begins only 25 years in the future and so is able to depict an America relatively close to home in people's minds, though certain key technological advances have been made. Of major import is the discovery of near-instantaneous travel (subjectively) through black holes in space, though Haldeman refers specifically to collapsars rather than wormholes, which has since become the preferred terminology. This allows cheap space travel but it also brings mankind into conflict, albeit unwittingly, with a race of aliens, the Taurans. Thus starts the Forever War which, though it is within the lifetime of the soldiers, distances them in time from the Earth. Each time they return to Earth for R and R, life has moved on by a century or two, and the two main protagonists witness changes alien to them in a relentless breakdown of society. In effect they have found that they can exist only in the society of the military itself.

'Hero' and its immediate sequels[42] are powerful stories with strong characterization and a realism that could only have come from direct experience. Haldeman had served for over a year in Vietnam, effectively as a support engineer, but had still witnessed direct combat. His first published novel *War Year* (1972) had been about his experiences. Some years later he realized that he was one of the few writers of science fiction who had actually served in combat and used that as a basis for sf. Reflecting on this he wrote:

> I don't have to put too much imagining effort into writing about a Vietnam ambush, and I could probably do a fair job describing an ambush in the twenty-fifth century, or the twelfth; a better job than I could synthesize from completely second-hand sources. In that sense, there's no substitute for having been there, at least so long as you do come back to write about it.[43]

Haldeman had returned from Vietnam to be perturbed by the changes in American society in the short time he had been away. It was this alienization that was the seed for the Forever War. Combined with the verisimilitude of the narrative, they gave 'Hero' both a raw power and an emotional impact.

'Hero' would never have been bought by Campbell. He supported the involvement in Vietnam and he would not have liked the evolution of American society projected in so negative a manner. Haldeman had submitted the story to Campbell, who rejected it with a customary three-

42 'We Are Very Happy Here' (November 1973), 'The Best of All Possible Worlds' (November 1974) and 'End Game' (January 1975).

43 Joe Haldeman, 'Science Fiction and War', *Isaac Asimov's Science Fiction Magazine* 10:4 (April 1986), p. 32.

page letter arguing on such points as that men and women would never fight in combat together, that it was anti-war and that there was far too frequent use of four-letter words, which would lose many subscribers.[44] Once Bova took over, though, he asked to see the story and ran it complete, regardless of any potential adverse reaction.

The subsequent success of *The Forever War* ('Hero' was nominated for a Hugo, and *The Forever War* won both a Hugo and a Nebula), and its now venerated classic status,[45] vindicates Bova's wisdom in publishing it. But at the time it did generate much retaliation from indignant readers. The most notorious letter came from a reader in San Bernardino, California, saying:

> 'Foundlings Father' was an overlookable crudity, but you really gave us all the finger with 'Hero'. All it was, was a rewrite of 'Starship Troopers', *without* the political philosophy that gave Heinlein's story its distinction, but *with* large doses of genital recreation, which gave it no distinction at all. [...] A sex story *could* be also a story of ideas about science and society, but it usually isn't; a sex flavor is likely to drown out the rest.[46]

Bova's response made it clear where he stood. 'If all you got out of "Hero" was sex, you have a problem!'

'Hero' was clearly a story of its time and a good example of how radically society and attitudes were changing in the early 1970s. It is disappointing that some of those who seemed resistant to change were the very individuals you would expect to embrace it, namely the science-fiction fans and in particular the readers of the sf magazines. The stories run by Bova in his first year, in particular 'Hero', 'The Gold at Starbow's End' and Pournelle's 'The Mercenary', brought considerable adverse comments, primarily over the graphic description of sex and violence and the use of bad language. Ironically these objections had started even earlier with a reaction to Kelly Freas's illustration to Jack Wodhams's 'Foundlings Father', the story referred to in the above letter. This had appeared in the December 1971 issue and Freas had drawn a naked man seen from the back holding up one finger in an obscene gesture. Just this one picture drew a host of rabid comments including:

> You people in New York City seem not to realize that out here in the provinces we aren't nearly so blasé. This is an outrageous thing and for what it's worth, I'm telling you so.

44 See Haldeman's guest of honour speech at the 48th World SF Convention in The Netherlands in August 1990 printed in *Quantum* #40, Fall 1991, p. 7.

45 The novel was voted 12th on *Locus*'s all-time poll for pre-1990 novels in 1998 and has been reprinted in the Gollancz SF Masterworks series.

46 *Analog* 90:4 (December 1972), p. 175.

I'm sorry if I appear too thin-skinned or overly prudish, but it would seem that with the death of Mr. Campbell the snickering little boys have taken over.[47]

Bova seemed delighted to be able to point out that both Wodhams's story and the artwork had been acquired by Campbell,[48] but, perhaps still feeling a little uncertain, Bova also asked readers what their feelings were about sex in sf. There was a significant response – indeed, it was a subject that filled the letter columns of the other magazines (*Galaxy* even conducted a survey, as we shall see) – and though there were the inevitable disgruntled readers, others were more realistic. The May 1973 issue contained several letters of support, commending Bova's editorial work and defending the relevance of sex and war in sf. These readers also noticed how sensitive some of *Analog*'s correspondents had become. It is likely that the change of editorship gave an opportunity for some of the old-guard readers to react, but it is also likely that as Bova began to imprint his preferred stories into the magazine, some of the more intractable old-guard gave up. There were several who threatened to cancel their subscriptions, and may well have done so, but overall *Analog*'s subscriptions rose by over 8 per cent during Bova's first two years, with total paid circulation up by nearly 7 per cent, reaching an all-time high of over 116,500 during 1973.

Bova was clearly doing something right, and he was reaching a new and expanding readership. He was able to sustain that difficult juggling trick of keeping enough of the old regular contributors and much that was traditional in *Analog* – at least at the outset – alongside new material that was following the new expansion of sf since the revolution of the late sixties.

Bova's record of new writers is impressive. Those whose fiction first appeared during his editorship include Howard Waldrop[49] ('Lunchbox', May 1972), Gary Alan Ruse ('Nanda', August 1972), Spider Robinson ('The Guy With the Eyes', February 1973), William Tuning ('Survivability', May 1973), Kevin O'Donnell ('The Hand *Is* Quicker', October 1973), P. J. Plauger ('Epicycle', November 1973), Brenda Pearce ('Hot Spot', April 1974), Eric Vinicoff with Marcia Martin ('Swiss Movement', June 1975), John M. Ford ('This, Too, We Reconcile', May 1976), Bud Sparhawk ('The Tompkins Battery Case', August 1976), Jayge Carr ('Alienation', October

---

47 Both quotations come from *Analog* 89:1 (March 1972), p. 175.

48 This wasn't the first time pictures of naked men had appeared in *Analog* or *Astounding*. One had even featured on the cover of the July 1954 issue, drawn by Alejandro. However none had been depicted in quite such a defiant pose.

49 His story was one of the last to be acquired by Campbell. It is surprisingly un-Campbellian and not especially Waldropian, though in its portrayal of an unusual Martian life-form's reaction to the first human landing it contains seeds of the anarchic Waldrop to come.

1976) and Orson Scott Card ('Ender's Game', August 1977). It's a list of which to be proud. It is evident that not only was Bova encouraging new writers, he was also developing a diverse and creative stable of talent. Several of these writers went on to win major awards. Robinson, Plauger and Card each won the John W. Campbell Award for Best New Writer, and Brenda Pearce was nominated.

Plauger had several stories in *Analog*, most notably 'Child of All Ages' (March 1975), a touching story of a girl who is immortal and has to keep reinventing herself every generation so as to blend in to society. However the demands of Plauger's business career curtailed his writing and after a sequel to this story, 'The Con Artist' (December 1976), he did not appear again in *Analog* for 15 years.

Spider Robinson, on the other hand, rapidly established his name. His first few stories were all light-hearted bar yarns set at Callahan's Place – a series that has since become self-perpetuating. There was a sudden change with his novella 'By Any Other Name' (November 1976) which portrayed a turbulent future North America where civilization has crashed following the release of an artificial virus that heightens people's awareness of pollution. The story won a Hugo award and was the basis for Robinson's first novel *Telempath* (1976). Hot on its heels came another novella, 'Stardance' (March 1977), created with his wife Jeanne Robinson, a professional dancer. She had developed the concept of a zero-gee dance and in the story this allows a disabled dancer not only to express herself but to communicate with an angelic alien race. This beautiful story ran away with all the top awards, leading to the fuller story in 'Stardance II' (September–November 1978) and the subsequent trilogy of books. In 1980 Jeanne Robinson was invited by NASA to perform her zero-gee dance in space, an opportunity lost when the *Challenger* disaster curtailed the Civilians-in-Space programme.

Bova also developed new writers who had debuted elsewhere. This was the case with Joe Haldeman, who had sold his first story to Ejler Jakobsson, but won his spurs under Bova. The same was true of George R. R. Martin, who had also debuted in *Galaxy*. Martin's first appearance in *Analog* was with an article. A computer devotee and chess fan, Martin wrote about the increased ability of computers to play and win at chess in 'The Computer was a Fish' (August 1972). Thereafter, although Martin sold to other magazines and anthologies, his major stories nominated for awards all appeared in *Analog*, and he was also nominated for the Campbell Best New Writer Award primarily on the strength of his *Analog* appearances. 'The Second Kind of Loneliness' (December 1972), is an emotional story of a man isolated on the edge of the solar system, monitoring a space portal and reflecting upon his deeds. 'With Morning Comes Mistfall' (May 1973) is another atmospheric piece set on a remote world where rumour has exaggerated gossip and created the belief that the world has murderous mist-wraiths. 'A Song for Lya' (June 1974), the best of these early stories and his first to win a Hugo Award, is a study of the effect of an alien religion on colonists and goes to the heart of what constitutes faith.

Martin also collaborated with new writer Lisa Tuttle on 'The Storms of Windhaven' (May 1975). Somewhat in the same vein as Anne McCaffrey's Pern series, it proved very popular, especially amongst feminist circles because it is about a girl's fight for independence. It generated a couple of later sequels.

Martin's work appeared regularly in *Analog* in the seventies. Other important titles included 'And Seven Times Never Kill a Man' (July 1975) and his first novel, 'After the Festival' (April–July 1977), better known in book form as *Dying of the Light* (1977).

Bova was fortunate in being able to acquire 'Of Mist, and Grass, and Sand' (October 1973) by Vonda McIntyre. This beautiful tale of a female healer and her attempts to save the life of a young boy on a post-apocalyptic Earth won McIntyre her first Nebula award and it was also runner-up in that year's Locus poll for best short story.[50] The story had considerable impact at the time and helped generate greater recognition for the many women writers working in the field and the growth in feminist sf, something I shall return to in more detail later.

Both McIntyre's and Martin's stories are lyrical and, generally, non-technical, creating vivid alien worlds populated by thinking and caring individuals. Like Haldeman's stories, they are driven by character and emotion and are not afraid to explore human failings. In Bova's hands, *Analog's* fiction was becoming softer, more human and more approachable but without losing that hard edge of realism and excitement.

Bova also attracted to *Analog* major writers who had not previously appeared there. We have already seen Frederik Pohl's solo debut. Larry Niven really ought to have been an *Analog* author but never sold a story to Campbell because he was put off by the three-month turn-round for rejections.[51] That changed when Bova took control, and Niven became a regular. Amongst his contributions was the award-winning 'The Hole Man' (January 1974) where a Martian expedition discovers that aeons ago advanced alien visitors had controlled a quantum black hole. A meddling

---

50 When expanded into the novel *Dreamsnake* (1978), it won the Hugo, Nebula and Locus awards and remains one of the landmark works of the 1970s.
51 See Darrell Schweitzer's interview with Niven in *Thrust* #21 (Fall 1984), p. 13.

Earthman releases it, setting in train the ultimate fate of the solar system. Campbell would have loved the idea but would probably have regarded the denouement as the start of the story. Bova, on the other hand, let the implications hang in the reader's mind.

Like Niven, Greg Benford could also have been an *Analog* author had he not been unsettled by Campbell's racist views. Benford was one of the masters of technological sf in the vein of Hal Clement and Poul Anderson. Once Bova attracted him to *Analog*, the result was a surprise. 'Doing Lennon' (April 1975) was not a hard-sf story but a clever extended joke about a billionaire who arranges to be cryogenically frozen and when revived claims he is John Lennon. The story has remained perennially popular. Benford's next *Analog* story, 'Beyond Grayworld' (September 1975), was more typically hard sf, though even this story of a man's assignment to terraform an inhospitable world holds some surprises.

In contrast to Niven and Benford, Barry Malzberg was not a typical *Analog* author, but Bova brought him into the fold. Ironically, 'Closing the Deal' (March 1974), a spoof on the whole matter of psi powers, had sufficient gall to have amused Campbell and might well have appeared under him. Harlan Ellison, whose only sale to Campbell had been a collaboration with Bova, 'Brillo' (August 1970), put in his first solo *Analog* appearance with his anti-war story 'Sleeping Dogs' (October 1974), which has such an awesome conclusion of alien retaliation that it is hard to believe that Campbell would have left it alone. Gene Wolfe put in just one appearance with his irreverent but strangely poignant 'How I Lost the Second World War and Helped Turn Back the German Invasion' (May 1973), a story which I suspect would barely have hit Campbell's desk.

David A. Drake was a writer somewhat in the Pournelle mould, though he also enjoyed Lovecraftian horror and the wide realms of fantasy. His first appearance in *Analog* was with a military story, 'Contact!' (October 1974), but of more interest was 'Nation Without Walls' (July 1977), the first of his stories about future cop Jed Lacey, depicting a future when computers and security surveillance had banished privacy. It was an idea in many people's minds as the real 1984 approached, and it was one that CCTV, the internet and telecommunications would soon obligingly deliver.

Gardner Dozois had been steadily building a reputation in the original anthologies but had scarcely appeared in the magazines, even though he had debuted in *If* in 1966. 'The Visible Man' (December 1975) was only his third story in the professional magazines and his only appearance in *Analog*. It deals with a high-security criminal who is treated so that he can see no one, even though they can all see him. It is the ultimate in alienation or ostracization, and the criminal has to fathom out a way of surviving. It was, on the surface, an ideal *Analog* puzzle story, but the underlying story was quite different as Dozois portrays a corrupt and unfair society. Dozois later reflected that he was sure that Bova knew this, 'but he was tolerant enough to allow it to go through'.[52]

One of the major captures for *Analog*, because of his popularity, was Roger Zelazny, an author of both vision and creativity but one leaning to the fantastic rather than the technical and thus not one you would expect in the magazine. Yet Bova secured from him two superb stories which seemed ideally suited to the magazine he was shaping and to the psychoses of the mid-seventies. Both 'The Engine at Heartspring's Center' (July 1974) and 'Home is the Hangman' (November 1975) are insightful studies of what constitutes soul and nobility. By contrast, Zelazny's one serial in *Analog*, 'Doorways in the Sand' (June–August 1975), reads like a throwback to the Kuttneresque serials in *Startling Stories* in the late forties.

Bova maintains that 'as the editor of *ASF* I didn't have to go out and seek contributors. Writers like Zelazny sent their stories to me because they thought of *ASF* as the top of the field. Perhaps they had been rejected earlier by Campbell, but they *wanted* to be seen in *Analog*.'[53] That may be so, but I think that Bova understates his own role as a broadminded editor determined to present the best possible magazine. It became a partnership, albeit informal, between editor and contributor to produce a magazine that not only entertained but provided an inspiring but provocative vision.

Besides his own discoveries and those established writers whom he welcomed into the fold, Bova continued to develop some of Campbell's more recent discoveries and other new writers. In addition to Jerry Pournelle and F. Paul Wilson, there was Stephen Robinett (writing initially as 'Tak Hallus') who produced a mixture of satirical and dramatic fiction, including the serial 'Stargate' (June–August 1974), the climax of a short series about the invention of a matter-transmitter and the corporate development of instantaneous space travel. Stanley Schmidt, the future editor of *Analog*, went one huge step further in 'The Sins of the Fathers' (November 1973–January 1974) and a series of sequels, and moved the Earth physically to another galaxy in order to save it from an inevitable doom. Although this is sf on a cosmic scale, the super-science, provided by a group of benevolent but guilt-ridden aliens, takes place mostly off-stage and the story focuses on the lives of a few individuals trying to cope with and manage this cataclysmic event. In outline the story sounds like

52 See Michael Swanwick, *Being Gardner Dozois* (Old Earth Books, 2001), p. 92.
53 Personal e-mail, Bova/Ashley, 15 May 2006.

some of the cosmic sf of the thirties, but the changes in sf are evident in this story being character-driven, with the emphasis on people, rather than science-driven, with the emphasis on catastrophe.

The February 1976 issue welcomed Greg Bear to *Analog*. I quoted Bear earlier in his eulogy to Campbell, and at last he was an *Analog* writer. He had sold his very first story when only 15 to Robert Lowndes for *Famous Science Fiction*, but he regarded that as a 'fluke' and it was eight years before his next story, 'The Venging', appeared in the June 1975 *Galaxy* and then 'A Martian Ricorso' in *Analog*. This tale of a dying Mars that might just have been shows some signs of the extreme-sf Bear would soon be writing, and there was even more indication in 'The Wind from a Burning Woman' (October 1978), a tense story of the Earth threatened by an asteroid, but it was not until the early eighties that Bear's name really came to the fore.

These examples show that Bova was letting writers take their own lead and not dictating in the Campbell manner. That's not to say that Bova did not interact with writers, but he preferred to give them space. The result was very evident in *Analog*, which felt more liberated and expansive and had greater depth. At times Bova ran fiction of considerable dystopian gloom, the type Campbell shunned. Perhaps the most extreme was 'Pigeon City' (November 1972) by Jesse Miller, depicting future inner-city squalor. But Bova could also see a joke and 'Not Polluted Enough' (April 1973), George Scithers's ecological spoof, was just the kind of story Campbell would have enjoyed.

The period 1972/74 felt transitional as new writers appeared while many of the old regulars faded away. 'The Symbiotes' (September 1972) was James H. Schmitz's last appearance. Although he had sold to other magazines, Schmitz was uniquely Campbellian, thriving on the interplay of ideas. Apart from two more stories in *If*, Schmitz wrote no more. Clifford Simak, now approaching 70, continued to produce novels, including some less-than-successful fantasies, but his appearances in *Analog* were limited, with only the serial 'Cemetery World' (November 1972–January 1973) of any import. Isaac Asimov had long since ceased to be a major contributor to *Analog* and his few stories there during the 1970s are of little consequence, although 'Mirror Image' (May 1972) was a pleasing return to Lije Baley and R. Daneel Olivaw. One surprise contributor was Alfred Bester, who had written little sf for well over a decade but returned with a flurry of items in the mid-seventies, including the serial 'The Indian Giver' (November 1974–January 1975).[54] This rather convoluted novel

54 Published in a revised edition in book form as *The Computer Connection* (1975) in the USA and *Extro* (1975) in the UK.

about how a supercomputer seeks to save the human race against the machinations of a group of immortals has only a hint of the Bester of former years, but was nevertheless welcome.

Another loss was Harry Harrison. Apart from the alternate-world romp, 'A Transatlantic Tunnel, Hurrah!' (April–June 1972), already in hand when Campbell died, Harrison appeared only once more, with another serial 'Lifeboat' (February–April 1975). That was in collaboration with Gordon R. Dickson and was of special historical import because a creative session had been filmed by James Gunn in which Dickson, Harrison and Campbell developed the story-line and plot.[55] Even the work of Poul Anderson was sparse in *Analog* during Bova's tenure. This was perhaps inevitable, as Anderson had produced a number of top-quality hard sf stories during the 1960s, many of them for *Analog*, and in the seventies he shifted more towards fantasy. Only 'The People of the Wind' (February–April 1973), a clever study of an alien culture, stands out amongst Anderson's few items in *Analog* at this time.

Anderson's erstwhile collaborator and another *Analog* regular was Gordon R. Dickson, a tireless perfectionist, ever hard at work on a variety of projects. His contributions to *Analog* in the seventies were mostly serials, though he also began a new series with 'Enter a Pilgrim' (August 1974), depicting the Earth enshackled by a powerful alien race. It was some while before Dickson developed the series, which eventually resulted in the book *The Way of the Pilgrim* (1987), but en route he created one of the most sinister and hateful of alien masters in a series that causes one to consider the nature of all imperialists and freedom fighters. Of Dickson's serials, Sandra Miesel described 'The Far Call' (August–October 1973) as 'the finest realistic novel about the space program yet written'.[56] The story plots the many problems and political machinations that plague the first manned expedition to Mars. It is arguably Dickson's best work, yet it is surprisingly overlooked. Dickson worked on it for years – some evidence of his research at Cape Kennedy surfaced in *Analog* in the article 'A Matter of Perspective' (December 1971). He remained unsatisfied with the *Analog* version and rewrote it at least three more times before the book version appeared in 1978.

One of the most popular of *Analog*'s old-guard contributors was Frank Herbert whose 'Children of Dune' (January–April 1976) brought to a conclusion the initial sequence of Dune novels. Dune was closely associ-

55 The film, 'Lunch With John Campbell', is included on the DVD *John W. Campbell's Golden Age of Science Fiction* compiled by Eric Solstein (DMZ, 2002) along with other author interviews.

56 Sandra Miesel on Dickson, in Noelle Watson and Paul E. Schellinger (eds), *Twentieth-Century Science-Fiction Writers* (St James's Press, 1991), p. 212.

ated with the Campbell days, even though the previous novel in the sequence, 'Dune Messiah', had been serialized in *Galaxy*. Herbert did not entirely abandon *Analog*, though his two remaining stories there were a collaboration and a shared-world story. So 'Children of Dune' may be seen as a suitable demarcation delineating the final closure of any lingering influence on *Analog* which Campbell may have had, and leaving the world open for Bova.

There were other changes and losses. One would be less obvious to readers. Kay Tarrant, who had served as Campbell's assistant almost since day one, and who had stayed on to support Bova at the outset, retired in 1973 with effect from the October issue. She was replaced by Diana King. Her professionalism and reliability in handling the day-to-day affairs of the magazine had allowed Campbell and Bova to concentrate on the authors and stories. In Bova's words she was 'a dedicated, selfless, tireless assistant'.[57] Campbell used to claim that Miss Tarrant forbade any sexual content in the fiction, but this was Campbell's excuse for discouraging it himself. Miss Tarrant retired to her home in Hoboken, New Jersey, and died in March 1980, aged 74.

A more obvious passing was the death of P. Schuyler Miller in October 1974 at the age of just 62. Miller had provided 'The Reference Library' review column since October 1951. He never regarded himself as a critic but his knowledge of the field was significant so that his opinions were frequently regarded as authoritative. Many readers commented that his column was the first feature in *Analog* they would turn to. His place was taken for the rest of the seventies by Lester del Rey with occasional inter-jections by Algis Budrys, Spider Robinson and others, but the spark that had been Miller's passion for science fiction had gone.

One contributor who did remain a regular throughout the Campbell/ Bova changeover was Kelly Freas, and his role should not be underes-timated. His presence with both the cover art and interior illustrations meant that visually *Analog* looked unchanged, providing a continuity that allowed Bova to work his magic but still present a familiar and enduring image. Freas was an all-rounder capable of producing highly technical space art as well as deeply human images. He could capture a scene from a story and give it added depth, often with a hint of humour – his aliens invariably had some human characteristic that caught the eye and brought them alive. Another Campbell regular who continued through Bova's years was John Schoenherr. His art was less humanistic but he was superb at creating alien landscapes and beings. Between them Freas and Schoenherr provided 43 per cent of the covers for Bova's issues. The

57 Personal letter, Bova/Ashley, 16 September 1977.

others were spread over a dozen artists, including Jack Gaughan, but the two major new names to emerge were Rick Sternbach and Vincent Di Fate. Both could depict extremely technical art ideally suited to *Analog*.

One element that distinguished Bova's *Analog* from Campbell's was the number of women contributors. Campbell had certainly published work by women – Judith Merril, Katherine MacLean, Pauline Ashwell, Anne McCaffrey, Leigh Richmond and (unknowingly) Alice Sheldon – but they appeared only occasionally and were seldom high-profile. Years could pass between such contributions. This was to some degree a reflection of the times. There were not that many women sf writers about and those there were tended to gravitate towards the more liberal magazines such as *F&SF*. By the early seventies that was changing and women writers were making their presence felt. *Analog* was, to some degree, something of a last bastion to storm. Bova was more than happy to consider work by women writers, but it took a while for their work to find its way into *Analog*.

One of the first, rather delightfully, was the octogenarian Miriam Allen deFord, who had been writing for over fifty years and had frequently appeared in *F&SF* and *Galaxy* but never in *Astounding/Analog*. Her story 'PRD and the Antareans' (December 1972) is a light-hearted account of how aliens are repulsed from Earth by a secret formula that creates a near-instant sex change amongst males. Anne McCaffrey, Vonda McIntyre and Sonya Dorman followed, along with Cynthia Bunn and Brenda Pearce. However, it was not until 1977 that the presence of women became most noticeable and then chiefly because Bova put together a 'Special Women's issue' for June 1977. Bova discovered he had sufficient material on hand to put together a near-complete issue, though he commissioned an extra story from Joan Vinge. The only male author in the issue was George R. R. Martin with a serial episode. The editorial, science article and book review column were all by women. Unfortunately, apart from Janet Aulisio, all the illustrations and covers were by men. There were five complete stories, two of which would go on to win the Hugo and Nebula awards respectively. These were 'Eyes of Fire' by Joan D. Vinge and 'The Screwfly Solution' by Raccoona Sheldon.

Joan Vinge was at that time the wife of writer Vernor Vinge and she had first appeared in print in the anthology *Orbit 14* in 1974. Her debut in the magazines had been in *Analog* in collaboration with her husband with 'The Peddlar's Apprentice' (August 1975) but she was soon going solo. 'The Media Man' (October 1976), later revised as 'Legacy', formed part of her Heaven's Belt setting put to good use in her serial 'The Outcasts of Heaven's Belt' (February–April 1978). These two works depict a well-thought-through society, benefiting from Vinge's anthropological background as well as her husband's scientific input. It was populated by individuals struggling to survive after a civil war has robbed them of their primary means of support. In many ways it is a grand old space opera in the tradition of Andre Norton and Leigh Brackett but updated with a modern perspective. 'Eyes of Amber' has a similar rationalized planetary romance background – it's set on a habitable Titan – but its pleasure comes from the way Vinge infuses the tropes of the fairy tale into an alien setting, in this case an American Indian legend about a man and a wolf.[58] Vinge admitted that the background to these stories was suggested by her husband, who encouraged her early writing. She was, for a period in the late seventies, seen as the token *Analog* woman hard-science writer.

Raccoona Sheldon was another alias for Alice Sheldon, alias James Tiptree, Jr. She had debuted in *Analog* with 'Birth of a Salesman' in 1968. She made one other appearance in *Analog*, as Tiptree, with 'Your Haploid Heart' (September 1969), an ingenious story of a society desperate to join the 'human'-oriented Galactic Federation but hampered, so it believes, by the strange nature of their sexual reproduction, which alternates each generation. Curiously, neither of these stories caused much of a wave, and her ground-breaking work appeared elsewhere – mostly in original anthologies and *F&SF*. By the time 'The Screwfly Solution' appeared in *Analog*, Tiptree was a much-lauded author, but her true identity had only just leaked out and was still not widely known.[59] Few readers would therefore have linked Raccoona Sheldon to Tiptree. 'The Screwfly Solution' is one of her most audacious stories, following the effects on a husband and wife of the growing power of a cult, the Sons of Adam, whose wish to eradicate all women spreads like a virus.

The concept of a special women's issue was frowned on by some readers who saw it as something of a gimmick and wondered why the stories had not been spread through various issues. Bova's immediate response was because he had sufficient stories to hand and, as he implied in announcing the issue in the previous 'In Times to Come' feature, it was an opportunity to showcase the growing number of women writers. He confirmed this to me:

> At the time, I thought the Women's Issue would call attention to the fact that many more women were writing – and reading – science fiction than in previous years. I hoped that by emphasizing this in one issue we might gain women readers.[60]

58 See interview with Joan Vinge by Robert Frazier in *Thrust* #16 (Fall 1980), p. 7.
59 It had been revealed in the January 1977 issue of *Locus* but was not revealed in *Analog* until May 1978.
60 Personal e-mail, Bova/Ashley, 1 April 2006.

When a reader survey was conducted in 1981, it showed that women represented 24.9 per cent of the respondents, which was double that when the survey was previously undertaken in 1958.[61] Just when that number increased during those two decades is not known, but it is more likely to have been during the post-Campbell years. I will return to the matter of the growth of feminism in sf in a later chapter.

The need to widen *Analog's* market was obviously one that Bova was keen to explore. The seventies was a time of considerable change within the sf market and it was necessary to experiment and keep ahead of developments. The early seventies had seen a huge surge in the number of original anthologies. Bova recognized that new readers were probably turning to paperbacks first rather than magazines, and there was a need to promote *Analog* within the paperback market. As far back as 1952 Campbell had compiled *The Astounding Science Fiction Anthology* in hardcover which had appeared in two abridged parts in paperback in 1956/57. From 1963 he compiled an annual anthology of the best stories from *Analog*, entitled simply *Analog 1*, *Analog 2*, and so on, issued in hardcover by Doubleday, but only the first three of these appeared in paperback in the United States. Bova had similarly compiled *Analog 9* in 1973, but this again did not make it into paperback. *Analog* was not penetrating the pocketbook market.

Following a suggestion by Sam Moskowitz, Bova issued an *Analog Annual*, released in April 1976 in standard pocketbook form by Pyramid Books. It was priced at $1.50, half as much again as an issue of *Analog*, but it also contained more wordage, running to 256 pages. It featured a complete novel by P. J. Plauger, 'Fighting Madness', acquired specifically for the *Annual*, and not since published separately in book form in English, plus three stories and an article. It also contained several illustrations, so was in one sense a repeat of the magazine content, though it had no other columns besides an editorial.

The book's back cover promised that *Analog Annual* would be published each year, but it wasn't. Instead Condé Nast reviewed their own marketing and explored other areas. First, in January 1977, they launched Analog Records with a dramatized recording of Asimov's story 'Nightfall' issued on a standard long-playing vinyl disc. A year later they began Analog Books. This was a joint venture between *Analog*, Baronet Books and Ace Books. Bova provided the editorial direction, and the books were published in trade paperback by Baronet and mass-market paperback by Ace.

The first two titles, issued in March 1978, were a retrospective, *The Best of Astounding*, edited by Anthony Lewis, and the all-new *Analog Yearbook*, compiled by Bova. The yearbook, especially in the trade paperback edition,

61 See *Astounding* May 1958, pp. 135–6 and *Analog* 27 April 1981, pp. 7–14.

felt far more like a magazine than the annual, and a decent one at that. It ran to 300 pages, priced at $1.95 (in the mass-market edition) and included six stories, two articles, Bova's introduction and a guest editorial by Greg Benford. Each story was illustrated and there was even a book review column by Barry Malzberg and a film column by Jeff Rovin. Bova's introduction openly promoted the magazine though, rather curiously, did not include a subscription address. *Analog Yearbook* was effectively a thirteenth issue and looked a positive way ahead. Both the annual and yearbook sold fairly well, but Bova told me, 'I don't think they increased the sales of the magazine as I had hoped.'[62] In fact, this was the start of the period of the slow but increasing fall in *Analog*'s circulation. It was three years before the next yearbook appeared, and much had changed in that time, as we shall see later.

Bova's two final major discoveries, Robert Asprin and Orson Scott Card, debuted in the same issue, August 1977, both with military-based fiction, still a major feature in *Analog*. Asprin's story, 'Cold Cash War', was written as a satire of military fiction and portrayed a future where corporate multinationals had effectively superseded governments and fought against each other with mercenary armies in what was effectively a computerized wargame. Wargaming was starting to be a big industry by 1977 and would have an impact on the sf magazines, as I shall explore later. The story was a promising start but most of Asprin's later work was in the fantasy field and he sold nothing else to the sf magazines.

Orson Scott Card, though, was another matter. 'Ender's Game' also features war games – virtual-reality games in zero-gee involving genetically enhanced children who eventually fight a real battle against alien invaders. The story was controversial from the start, not simply because it depicted children at war, but because it blurred the distinction between game-playing and real conflict, yet it was a sign of a maturing attitude amongst *Analog*'s readers that they were generally supportive of the story.

Card had originally conceived of the idea of zero-gee wargames as a play for his local repertory theatre in 1970, but reworked it as a story after Bova rejected Card's earlier submission, 'Tinker'. Bova also initially returned 'Ender's Game' with suggestions for cuts. Reluctant to edit it, Card sent it to James Baen at *Galaxy* who rejected it. Card edited some of the battle scenes and Bova bought it in June 1976, though it took a year to get into print. By that time Card and Bova had developed a good working relationship and, with Bova's help, Card's writing skills were honed.[63] As

62 Personal e-mail, Ashley/Bova, 2 June 2006.
63 See Cliff Moser's interview with Card in *Science Fiction Review* #32 (August 1979), p. 34 and Card's essay 'Mountains Out of Molehills', *Foundation* #45 (Spring 1989), pp. 63–72.

a consequence, a number of stories followed in quick succession after 'Ender's Game', including the beautiful 'Mikal's Songbird' (May 1978) about the training of a young boy to become an emperor's songbird. Card had discovered within himself a fascination for the rite of passage from child to adult, a theme which recurs in many of his best works.

It's a theme that has its parallels in science fiction. The genre had taken a long time to mature and more than once had been a rebellious teenager and young adult, but the seventies saw it entering a more sedate middle age and ready to produce offspring. A new generation of writers was emerging, in *Analog* and elsewhere, who were able to look at science fiction afresh and learn from its mistakes but also benefit from its achievements. The science-fiction editors were the guardians of this process, helping to train the new Songbirds.

Bova's ability to take over from Campbell was a major achievement. One thing that Bova did not do, and should never be accused of doing, was to take on Campbell's mantle. He was his own man from the start. Nor did he seem to be overawed by Campbell's legacy. Bova told me, 'I never felt his "shadow over my shoulder",' adding, 'I did feel that I agreed with his basic editorial outlook and tried to satisfy *ASF*'s readers with the kinds of stories they wanted – *except* that I tried to stretch their outlook (just as Campbell had done, more than once) by including stories with new ideas, from writers both new and well-known.'[64]

Intriguingly, *Analog* serialized Robert Silverberg's last major serial completed before his retirement from sf, 'Shadrach in the Furnace' (August–October 1976). This had, as its central theme, the secret plans of an old tyrant to have his persona transferred to the body of a young man, who has hitherto been his doctor and keeper. The tyrant, Genghis Mao Khan, is the epitome of evil, whereas his doctor, Mordecai Shadrach, is beneficent and idealistic. But it would be wrong to suggest that Silverberg had Campbell and Bova in mind in this story, with characters taken to extremes. Shadrach's solution to the problem is to link their two lives so that if Shadrach dies so does the Khan. Shadrach rules with the Khan as figurehead. Bova, on the other hand, had succeeded in laying Campbell completely to rest. In the space of a few short years it was definitely Bova's *Analog*.

Bova had restored an excitement and authority to *Analog* that had been lacking for many years. His achievements did not go unrecognized. He won the Hugo Award for best professional editor five years in succession from 1973 to 1977. What may have felt equally if not more rewarding

64 Personal e-mail, Bova/Ashley, 1 April 2006.

was the response from readers. After the howls of protest in the early months, and doubtless a number of cancelled subscriptions, the reactions had become more modulated. One Canadian reader, writing in the March 1975 issue, said:

> The main thing which distinguishes *Analog* from all other SF magazines on the market is honesty and integrity. Your magazine, Mr. Bova, is not only a company trying to stay in business, it is a magazine trying to help the healthy evolution of science fiction as well.[65]

Bova had certainly done that. He had allowed science fiction to move ahead, once again, in the pages of *Analog*, primarily through encouraging new writers and removing barriers, while keeping a level head for science fiction in the aftermath of the New Wave revolution. By 1978, Bova was ready to move on, wishing to return to writing. Before considering that transition, we need to see what was happening amongst *Analog*'s rivals during Bova's editorship.

The Forgotten Editor

The second of the 'big three' magazines was *Galaxy*. If Campbell's *Astounding* dominated the forties, then Horace Gold's *Galaxy* dominated the fifties, or at least the first half of that decade. It returned to dominate much of the sixties in the capable hands of Frederik Pohl. But at the end of the sixties Pohl had returned from a science-fiction festival in Brazil to discover that the magazine's proprietor, Robert M. Guinn, had sold *Galaxy* (and its companion titles *If*, *Worlds of Tomorrow* and *Worlds of Fantasy*) to the Universal Publishing and Distributing Corporation (UPD). The change was effective from the July 1969 *Galaxy*.

The head of UPD was Arnold E. Abramson. He had founded the company in 1945. It established itself with the DIY magazine *Family Handyman* (from 1951) and similar hobby and sports periodicals. The company's reputation went downhill when Abramson established a series of sleazy pocketbook imprints in the early fifties such as Uni-Books, Royal Books and most notoriously Beacon Books. These are all now highly collectable for their cover art and books by such authors as Charles Willeford and Orri Hitt. They had published some science fiction, often under suggestive titles, such as Fritz Leiber's *The Sinful Ones* (1953), a reprint of his novella 'You're All Alone' (*Fantastic Adventures*, July 1950), with soft-core porn passages added by the publisher. When Guinn sold the *Galaxy Science-Fiction Novels*

---

65 Letter from John S. Barker, *Analog* 95:3 (March 1975), p. 177.

series to Abramson in 1959, it was promptly adapted to fit in with Beacon Books' image, managing to place an innuendo even into Olaf Stapledon's superman novel *Odd John* (1959). Amongst the reprints of respectable but now retitled classics, were a few original novels that genuinely pushed boundaries and received more prestigious publication later, such as Brian Aldiss's satirical *The Male Response* and Philip José Farmer's *Flesh*, but mixed with less distinguished items such as *Pagan Passions* by Randall Garrett and Larry M. Harris and *The Sex War* by Sam Merwin, Jr.

This experience did not bode well for the sale of the magazines to Abramson. Pohl chose not to continue as editor, though his young assistant, Judy-Lynn Benjamin, remained, elevated to the role of managing editor. Overall editorial control passed to Ejler Jakobsson (his first name was pronounced Eye-ler, but he was usually called Jake). Jakobsson is one of the forgotten editors of science fiction. Born in Finland in 1911 he had come to the United States in 1926, already well-steeped in the adventure fiction of Jules Verne. He entered the Columbia University School of Journalism where he was nearly thrown out because of his interest in science fiction. In the end he left voluntarily to become a reporter and then a story editor on radio dramatizations until he, and his wife Edith, began to write for the pulps, mostly the shudder pulps *Horror Stories, Terror Tales* and similar, in the late 1930s. Jakobsson was also soon editing pulps for Popular Publications.

Curiously, Jakobsson had succeeded Pohl nearly thirty years before on the pulp *Super Science Stories*. Jakobsson stayed with Popular throughout the 1940s, becoming a departmental head with responsibility for such magazines as *Famous Fantastic Mysteries* and *Detective Tales*. He edited the revived *Super Science Stories* from 1949 to 1951, and the once-prestigious pulp *Adventure* from January 1951 to March 1953. Thereafter he worked as a book editor and briefly as a TV story editor before entering Abramson's publishing enterprise in 1960.

Jakobsson was thus no newcomer to either editing or science fiction. The team he established around him was also strong. Judy-Lynn Benjamin was just 26. She had graduated from Hunter College, New York, with a degree in English in 1965. Her speciality had been James Joyce and she edited a volume of essays on his works, *The Celtic Bull*.[66] Within a few weeks she had applied for a job as assistant to Frederik Pohl at *Galaxy* and *If*. Pohl was in a dilemma. 'She was just what I needed in almost every way', he later wrote, but Judy-Lynn was an achondroplastic dwarf, meaning that although her torso was of normal size, her arms and legs were about half the usual length, so that she stood a little under four feet

66 University of Tulsa, 1966.

tall. Pohl was concerned about her abilities to cope in an office environment, but he need not have worried. She was a remarkable bundle of energy whose heart seemed bigger than her body. Pohl recalled:

> She turned out to be one of the best assistants I ever had. She learned everything that had to be learned the first time around. Although she had never knowingly read a science fiction story before she came to work at *Galaxy*, within two months she was able to predict, from reading the proofs, which stories the readers would like best.[67]

Benjamin had an instinctive understanding of what constituted a good story. Now elevated to managing editor under Jakobsson, Benjamin virtually ran the magazine. The result was a useful blending of minds. Jakobsson enjoyed science fiction because of its endless possibilities. He was of the view that 'sf was not only a form of literature but a vitally important one that had more to say about the human present and future than any other form of speculative writing'.[68] Benjamin's love of Joyce was proof of her own delight in experimental fiction, but both editors also liked work firmly rooted in story. Her later record as publisher of Del Rey Books demonstrated how keen her senses were in predicting the public taste in escapist fiction. This came through in *Galaxy* and *If* where she and Jakobsson could experiment with both forms.

The third member of the team was Jack Gaughan as associate (later full) art director. Gaughan had been a regular contributor to *Galaxy* throughout the sixties and had won the Hugo Award for best professional artist in three consecutive years from 1967 to 1969, as much for his work in *Galaxy* and *If* as for his paperback covers, mostly for Ace Books. He also won the fan artist Hugo in 1967. Gaughan was immensely popular, both for his work and because he was a genial human being. He worked hard and could produce stunningly detailed artwork or quick sketches and caricatures as required. It was Jack's responsibility to create an image for the magazine. With the United States still in the final days of 'flower power' and the hippie movement, Gaughan created an avant-garde image with flowing covers, often lacking in detail but suggestive of freedom and movement and often depicted in bright, day-glow colours. You knew instantly that both *Galaxy* and *If* were about other-worldly escapism, reflecting the stories that Benjamin and Jakobsson were acquiring.

There was arguably a fourth member of the team, though he went uncredited, and that was Gardner Dozois. He would become renowned

67 Frederik Pohl, *Locus* #303 (April 1986), p. 21.
68 Personal letter Jakobsson/Ashley, 4 February 1974.

for his supreme editorship at *Asimov's Science Fiction Magazine* in the 1980s and 1990s, but it all started here at *Galaxy* and *If*:

> I was originally brought in to break the then-infamous '*Galaxy* backlog', the slush that had piled up unread for a number of months between Fred Pohl leaving as editor and Jake taking over, which I did, in a marathon session that took about a week and a half; I then continued reading the slush regularly until sometime in mid 1971, when I moved to Philadelphia.[69]

Galaxy's reputation in 1969 was still strong. Its policy had never been as prescriptive as *Analog*'s and neither Gold nor Pohl had looked specifically for high-tech sf – rather the opposite. Gold had liked to explore how humans would cope with the pressures of society in the future, and Pohl enjoyed teasing those societies. *Galaxy* often ran humorous, light stories, but it did not fight shy of exploring the unusual. The sixties saw it publishing the exotic science fantasies of Jack Vance and Cordwainer Smith, the hard science of Larry Niven and the experimental psychological fiction of Robert Silverberg. Although Pohl was not himself a major advocate of the New Wave, he gave his writers considerable freedom of expression, not least Harlan Ellison, whose award-winning work in both *Galaxy* and *If* was helping regenerate science fiction from the stagnation of the early sixties.

Pohl had always treated *Galaxy* as the senior magazine. While *If* carried the less sophisticated fiction, it also ran some of the more experimental and daring work. It was aimed at a readership more recently attracted to sf, so its fiction was usually easier to assimilate, but amongst its more formulaic contributors, such as C. C. MacApp, A. Bertram Chandler (whose Rim stories featuring Lieutenant John Grimes were ideally suited to readers attracted to the sf magazines after the success of the TV series *Star Trek*) and Fred Saberhagen, it occasionally had more challenging material, such as stories by Harlan Ellison and Gene Wolfe, early work by James Tiptree, Jr., and serials by Robert A. Heinlein. Pohl had also instigated a policy of featuring a story by a new writer each issue and Larry Niven, Alexei Panshin, Bruce McAllister, Gardner Dozois and George Scithers amongst others could all claim to have been an '*If* first'.

Jakobsson and Benjamin maintained the distinction between the magazines. Most of the contents of their early issues were either stories acquired by Pohl or parts of continuing series initiated by Pohl. There was material by James Blish, Poul Anderson, Frank Herbert (the serial 'Dune Messiah'), Larry Niven, Clifford Simak (a powerful story equating robots

---

69 Personal e-mail, Dozois/Ashley, 13 August 2006.

with the civil rights movement, 'I Am Crying All Inside', August 1969),
Fritz Leiber, Hayden Howard, A. Bertram Chandler and A. E. van Vogt.

Pohl was listed as editor emeritus for the first year and wrote the
occasional editorial or article, even the occasional story, notably the excru-
ciatingly titled 'The Merchants of Venus' (*If*, July/August 1972), which
turned out to be a prelude to his Heechee series. This continuity was
helpful in smoothing the transition and a worried readership. One reader
later wrote: 'I had my doubts when your magazines changed ownership
and editors in '69, but now I confess you've made the *Galaxy/If* combo a
treat to receive each month.'[70]

One sad loss, though, was that of Willy Ley. He had been *Galaxy*'s science
columnist since the first issue and was also one of the prime supporters
of the Apollo programme. Cruelly, Ley died on 24 June 1969, less than a
month before the first manned moon landing. There was a handful of 'For
Your Information' columns remaining, which ran until the November
1969 *Galaxy*, and Ley had almost finished another series, 'The Story of
Our Earth', which appeared in *If* (September 1969–January 1970). His
place as science editor was taken by Donald H. Menzel, who was even
older than Ley and had been involved with Hugo Gernsback in the days
of *Science and Invention*. Menzel never made his presence felt and only
contributed a couple of rather facile articles, though his name remained
on the masthead for three years. He did, though, with the support of
Judy-Lynn Benjamin, succeed in influencing an international commission in naming one of the craters on the moon after Willy Ley. You can't
see it from Earth, as it is on the far side of the Moon, forever looking out
towards the stars.[71]

Jakobsson was determined to make his mark, and evidently to appeal
to the younger, hippier market. For a man approaching sixty, his attempt
at hip lingo in his forecast of stories in the September 1969 issue – 'I dig
the music – now let's have the libretto' (p. 81) – was embarrassing then,
let alone now.

Working with Jack Gaughan, he arranged for certain stories to be
decorated with elaborate graphics, properly integrated with the story. The
first to receive the treatment was 'The Last Night of the Festival' by Detroit
fan Dannie Plachta, in the February 1970 issue. Plachta had written
several short, sharp stories for *Galaxy* and *If*, often with clever, surprise
endings. This tale, though, was longer and more intense, recounting, in
extravagant language, the final days of an oppressed part of mankind
whose only remaining pleasure can be found in the Festival. Gaughan

70 Letter by Roy J. Schenck in *If* 21:7 (September/October 1972), p. 4.
71 It's situated at 43°N, 154°E. See 'Editorial', *Galaxy* 31:1 (December 1970), p. 2.

provided a set of illustrations and rococo illuminations to match the florid text. The style was similar to several baroque tales of the day, especially the work of Roger Zelazny and Michael Moorcock.

The second to be treated this way was even more dramatic. Harlan Ellison's 'The Region Between' (March 1970) was one of five stories by various writers written to develop a scenario created by Keith Laumer of an individual's after-life following euthanasia. Ellison used this as an opportunity for a soul's odyssey as it seeks to be reunited with a cosmic almighty but is ensnared by an evil succubus. Rather than simply illustrate the story, Gaughan used integrated graphics and visual tricks to create pace, atmosphere and depth, a true marriage of art and language.

There was a mixed reaction to the experiment, but readers seemed generally supportive. However, the real test came with a short comic-strip serial by Vaughn Bodé. Bodé was a young artist already becoming influential in the underground comic scene. He had provided several cover and interior illustrations for both *Galaxy* and *If* during Pohl's tenure, but, when Pohl left, Bodé's commissions dried up, purportedly because there was a clash of personalities between him and Judy-Lynn Benjamin. In 1969 Bodé won the Hugo Award as best fan artist, and Jakobsson, keen to tap into this wider market, commissioned Bodé to provide a comic strip.[72] The result was 'Sunpot', featuring the space adventures of the pneumatically endowed Belinda Bump, which began in the February 1970 issue. Bodé's wonderfully exaggerated imagery and sharp humour had won him much acclaim in the adult comic field, especially with the Cheech Wizard,[73] but there was a more mixed reaction from *Galaxy*'s readers. Bodé soon experienced problems with the 'dusty editors',[74] who tried to censor his work. Bodé came to the view that the strip was too avant-garde for the majority of *Galaxy*'s still rather conservative readers. Whatever the case, it might have been useful had the experiment continued for longer, but Bodé grew frustrated with the paranoia of the editors and submitted a final strip where he killed off all the characters. This was never run, and the strip last appeared in the May 1970 issue. Jakobsson never explained its disappearance but generally the comic-strip and flamboyant artwork was perceived as an experiment that had failed.

72 The story as told by Ted White is that White had commissioned Bodé to draw a comic strip for *Fantastic*, and when Judy-Lynn Benjamin learned of this she made Bodé an increased offer to work for *Galaxy*. See *Fantastic* 20:2 (December 1970), p. 135.

73 The Cheech Wizard featured in the 'Deadbone' strip that had originally been drawn for the weird-fiction fanzine *Anubis* in 1968 and subsequently ran in *Cavalier* from May 1969 to March 1970.

74 See Bodé's note in George W. Beahm, *Vaughn Bodé Index* (privately printed, 1976), p. 51.

There were further experiments. Believing the market was expanding, Abramson decided to revive both *Worlds of Tomorrow* and *World of Fantasy*. *Worlds of Tomorrow* had been started in 1963 as a sop to Pohl when Guinn would not agree to publish *Galaxy* monthly. The magazine ran some interesting material, not least Philip José Farmer's first Riverworld serial. Pohl saw it as somewhere he could run rather more extreme material not best suited for *Galaxy* or *If*. When it was revived in June 1970 (undated), Jakobsson chose to emphasise the extreme. Most of the stories in the issue have sex as their central theme, the most extreme being Piers Anthony's 'The Bridge', where a beautiful female manikin is created in order to harvest sperm for a dying world. George H. Smith, noted for his many sex-and-sleaze novels, led the issue with 'In the Land of Love', set in a grossly overpopulated and hippified future where one individual rebels against the constant love-ins. One of the few stories of any merit in the first issue was 'The State vs. Susan Quod', the last story by occasional sf (and mostly westerns) writer, Noel Loomis. The story considers the extent to which androids should be treated as humans. Of some interest in the other two issues which appeared in December 1970 (dated Winter) and March 1971 (dated Spring) were the short novel 'The Dream Machine' by Keith Laumer,[75] which considers the nature of reality, and Gary K. Wolfe's first story, 'Love Story'. Dean R. Koontz was also present with his little-known 'Unseen Warriors', set after a nuclear war where couples are fearful of producing mutant children.

Worlds of Fantasy had seen only one experimental issue in September 1968, tapping in to the upsurge in interest in fantasy fiction following the success in paperback of Tolkien's *The Lord of the Rings* and Robert E. Howard's Conan books. Sales were sufficiently gratifying that the magazine would probably have seen further issues had Guinn not gone through with the sale of the various Galaxy titles. When Abramson did revive it, in September 1970, Jakobsson did not feel he was sufficiently well versed in fantasy fiction to edit it. The role passed to Lester del Rey, who had also compiled the first issue, and had remained with *Galaxy* and *If* in an assistant capacity, as features editor. Del Rey probably welcomed the diversion. His wife, Evelyn, had died in a car accident in January 1970. Judy-Lynn Benjamin provided emotional and moral support and the two soon drew close together. They were married on 21 March 1971.

Del Rey had more editorial acumen than Jakobsson and secured some major names and interesting material for the magazine. The policy was to run one long story per issue. For the three issues that appeared these were 'Long Live Lord Kor!' by Andre Norton, in which time manipula-

75 Issued in book form as *Night of Delusions* (1972).

tors try to rework the early history of a planet destroyed by a nuclear war, 'The Tombs of Atuan', the second Earthsea novel by Ursula Le Guin, and 'Reality Doll',[76] Clifford Simak's intriguing quest story which explores dreams and perceptions on an alien world of legend. These novels alone were worth the price of admission but there was an interesting selection of short fiction, especially in the third issue. This not only had the first appearance by Connie Willis, 'Santa Titicaca', but the wonderfully anarchic 'The Man Doors Said Hello To', by James Tiptree, Jr., and the historical fantasy 'Death of a Peculiar Boar' by Naomi Mitchison, the only appearance in a science-fiction magazine by this distinguished author of historical fiction and fantasy.

Although del Rey edited the second issue, Jakobsson had a greater hand in the third and fourth issues, much to del Rey's frustration, as Jakobsson insisted in including some science fiction. Del Rey took more and more of a back seat, finding himself having to juggle contents and often edit stories severely to fit in with Jakobsson's last-minute changes. Even so, *Worlds of Fantasy* was far superior to *Worlds of Tomorrow*, but that served it no better when the distribution of both magazines was so poor that they failed to attract much attention and sales were dismal.

In addition to the strong sexual content of *Worlds of Tomorrow*, Jakobsson felt bold enough to include four-letter words in the sacred pages of *Galaxy*. The author was Robert Silverberg. In 'The Throwbacks', the first of his Urban Monad series that became *The World Outside*, Silverberg has his twenty-fourth-century historian reflecting on the twentieth century's obsession with obscene language. The words 'fuck' and 'cunt' are so old-fashioned and meaningless to him that he repeats them over and over to himself. 'They sound merely antiquated. Harmless, certainly,' he concludes.[77] Harmless or not, Silverberg's audacity caused an outcry amongst readers. *Galaxy* only ran an occasional letter column and none of the protests appeared there or in *If*, but Silverberg knew of them: 'These explorations of the innately innocuous nature of sexual slang touched off so many irate letters from the readership that the publisher became aware of the situation and asked Jakobsson to reinstate the old magazine taboos.'[78]

When Robert A. Heinlein's novel 'I Will Fear No Evil' was serialized soon after, one reader queried why the 'f' word had been censored at the end of the novel simply into 'f—'. Jakobsson responded that it was not

76 Published in book form as *Destiny Doll* (1971).
77 See *Galaxy* 30:4 (July 1970), p. 44.
78 Robert Silverberg, memoir to 'Going Down Smooth', in Frederik Pohl, Martin H. Greenberg and Joseph D. Olander (eds), *Galaxy: 30 Years of Innovative Science Fiction* (New York: Playboy Press, 1981) vol. 2, p. 36.

down to him or Heinlein, adding: 'The real story may never be told; but remember, there are distributors, retailers and local ordinances to deal with.'[79]

It is a pity that Jakobsson did not say more in order that readers understood exactly what had happened, but there must have been a sharp reaction to Silverberg's use of the words. It is likely that Abramson was concerned that he might lose the second-class mailing privilege accorded to magazines by the postal authority, which would have been a big financial blow. In addition, the postal authority might have fined them for sending obscene material through the mail. This was a major factor that caused reluctance amongst many magazine publishers to be too sexually free, whereas it was not a factor affecting books. Jakobsson evidently had to move cautiously.

Nevertheless, management felt a need to take stock and get a better understanding of who their readers were and what they thought. Associate publisher Bernard Williams devised a survey form, incorporated in the December 1970 *Galaxy*, asking a range of questions on demographics and preferences, including the use of swear words. Selected results were published in the May/June 1971 *Galaxy*, as follows:

1. More than two-thirds of readers are aged between 18 and 39.
2. 74.4 per cent of that age group had received a college-level or better education.
3. 64 per cent liked occasional fantasy published alongside sf.
4. Nearly 80 per cent 'gave four-letter-and-cussword freedom of expression to *Galaxy*'.
5. 91 per cent voted for real-life sex in a story if it was important to the story.[80]

Jakobsson did not say how many readers returned the survey form so we do not know how representative it was. It may be that the responses were from a preponderance of the younger age group, though Jakobsson does say that the oldest respondent was 73. The respondents clearly had no problem with sex or bad language. Unfortunately, no question was asked specifically about Bodé's comic strip or Gaughan's ornate artwork. A diluted question was asked about whether readers liked the illustrations in that specific issue (December 1970), but Jakobsson did not report on that.

Reader reaction to Heinlein's novel, which concluded in that same

79 Pohl, Greenberg and Olander, *Galaxy*, p. 2.
80 Details are summarised from Jakobsson's editorial in *Galaxy* 31:6 (May/June 1971), pp. 2, 165.

December 1970 issue, was mixed, with the inevitable number who found it 'offensive' and 'pornographic'. The sf premise is that of an aged and terminally ill man whose brain is transplanted into the body of a young, healthy woman. Thereafter the story explores the interplay between the two 'minds' within the body and the male half's reaction to living a sexually free lifestyle. Though the novel is generally regarded as one of Heinlein's poorest – it is frequently self-indulgent in what is clearly a wish-fulfilment story – it proved popular amongst the growing libertarian movement.

One interesting point is that at the outset it is made clear that the body receiving the old man's brain must be of the same rare blood group. Heinlein was also of a rare blood group and Jakobsson discussed the matter of blood-donation in his editorial in the August/September 1970 *Galaxy*. He subsequently revealed that, according to the National Rare Blood Group, there was an 'unusually impressive response from your ranks'.[81]

'I Will Fear No Evil' was Heinlein's last novel to be serialized in the sf magazines, though there would be a few extracts from later works. Indeed, he had only one more story in any sf magazine so, although no one realized it at the time, it was another sign of the passing of the old guard, as was also becoming evident in *Analog*.

There was one old-guard writer, though, who continued to push barriers and provoke readers for good or ill, and that was Theodore Sturgeon. *Galaxy* was his main magazine market in the early seventies. In the midst of all the discussion about sex in sf, Sturgeon wrote a guest editorial 'After Sex – What?' (April 1971). Sturgeon had been one of the prime movers in liberating sex in sf in material published 20 years earlier. His message was that that battle had now been won and that writers risked spoiling the liberation if sex was overused. It was time to move on. Instead, he advocated that we look closer at the whole human being and its relationship with its environment. He also urged writers to be more subtle and readers to be more perceptive.

Did he practise what he preached? Almost certainly. Sturgeon's stories in *Galaxy* had been consistent in their outlook over the previous 20 years. All the more remarkable then that it was not until this time that Sturgeon won his first Hugo and Nebula awards with 'Slow Sculpture' (February 1970). The story's strength lies not in its science-fiction premise, which involves a cure for cancer, but in the relationship between healer and patient, revealing the symbiotic power of human bonds – the 'whole being' as Sturgeon asked us to comprehend. The half-dozen other stories that Sturgeon had in *Galaxy* and *If* at this time explore, in subtle ways, the

81 See *Galaxy* 31:5 (April 1971), p. 139.

human approach to manipulating or controlling major developments so as to minimize the consequences. This may be as a result of medical discoveries, such as perfect birth control in 'Necessary and Sufficient' (April 1971), or the effect of wealth as in 'Occam's Scalpel' (*If*, August 1971), or the relationship with aliens as in 'Case and the Dreamer' (January 1973). Sturgeon always led by example.

It is interesting that the writers prepared to push the barriers were not the new generation but the older ones. Unabashed by the uproar that he had caused in his recent stories, Robert Silverberg continued to submit one excellent novel after another. He had been on a roll for three years, producing a rapid series of quality stories and novels. This continued into Jakobsson's *Galaxy* for three more years. In all of these works, just as with Sturgeon, Silverberg studied the human condition and our relationship with the world. 'Downward to the Earth' (November 1969–March 1970) considers what is human and what is alien as a man seeks to fuse with an alien culture. 'The Tower of Glass' (April–June 1970) considers the relationship between man and his gods in a biblical allegory where one man is worshipped as a god by his androids but in turn looks to the heavens for his own salvation. 'A Time of Changes' (March–May 1971) has another man on a mission but this time in a distant colony where all individualism has been suppressed. The protagonist determines to liberate that society but first he has to discover his true self. These novels are all about self-discovery, culminating in Silverberg's single greatest work, 'Dying Inside' (July–September 1972). This highly charged introspective novel is all about self as a telepath struggles with the consequences of losing his powers. Amazingly, although all these novels were nominated for awards, only 'A Time of Changes' won a Nebula. Yet the characterization in 'Dying Inside' is as potent as you will find in any great work of literature and the gradual draining of the protagonist's talent, rather like dementia in a normal human, is tangible.

'Dying Inside' may have lost a Hugo because Silverberg was competing against himself, with *The Book of Skulls*, and both books lost out to Isaac Asimov's 'The Gods Themselves'. That novel had started and ended in *Galaxy* (March–May 1972) with the middle instalment in *If* (March/April 1972), a ploy necessary to complete the serial before book publication. In fact, the middle instalment, set entirely in another dimension, a totally alien environment from which mankind is drawing energy to overcome the energy crisis, is amongst the most original of Asimov's works of fiction, but the novel as a whole is fairly traditional. It is evident that both the fans (for the Hugo) and the SFWA committee (for the Nebula) were going for the populist rather than the literary vote.

Silverberg and Sturgeon topped the pile of *Galaxy*'s senior contributors in the early seventies. There were also works by James Gunn, James Blish, Robert Sheckley, Philip Jose Farmer (his second Riverworld serial 'The Fabulous Riverboat', *If*, June–August 1971), Keith Laumer, Frank Herbert, even Jack Williamson, with a serial 'The Moon Children' (July/August–November/December 1971). Jakobsson could not rest on his laurels, however, relying on the old regulars. It was important to encourage a new generation of writers.

The September 1969 *Galaxy* saw the first appearance of Joe Haldeman. 'Out of Phase', about the alien infiltration of Earth, had been returned by Pohl with suggestions for revision. Haldeman made the changes and returned the story just after Pohl had left. He wondered whether his letter, saying he had made the suggested changes, gave the story the green light, by-passing the slush pile. Thereafter he mischievously recommended this as a way for all new writers to get into print. Haldeman wrote a sequel to this story, 'Power Complex' (*Galaxy*, September 1972), where the aliens infiltrate as far as the US President. He also contributed two stories about undercover agent Otto McGavin's interplanetary exploits, 'To Fit the Crime' (*Galaxy*, April 1971) and 'The Only War We've Got' (*Galaxy*, January 1974), which later formed part of *All My Sins Remembered* (1977). These are all relatively minor stories, though, compared to 'Time Piece' (*If*, July/August 1970), which proved to be Haldeman's trial run for 'Hero'. Both feature soldiers in combat across the universe, with instantaneous travel through 'holes' which removes them from any contact with the Earth they know. The one stable place is a planetary hospital and retreat called Heaven, but they only get there when they are severely wounded. Haldeman wrote this immediately upon his return from Vietnam and it is fired with the same angst that inspired 'Hero'. Interestingly, Haldeman told me, 'I don't think I consciously thought of it as presaging a novel, and I'm pretty sure I didn't write *The Forever War* with that story in mind.'[82]

At the same time as Haldeman's debut in *Galaxy*, the September 1969 *If* carried the first story by Chelsea Quinn Yarbro, 'The Posture of Prophecy'. It was another that had been bought by Pohl, making her one of the last of his *If* firsts. Yarbro later called it 'trivial', but although it's more of an outline than a story, there's enough material for a novel crammed into vignette form. It considers an alien viewpoint of Earth and the fate of the first baby conceived in space. Yarbro also sold Jakobsson 'Frog Pond' (*Galaxy*, March 1971), a fairy-tale of mutation in which the stranger a girl meets turns out to have batrachian blood.

David Gerrold had already sold the well-known episode 'The Trouble

---

82 Personal e-mail, Haldeman/Ashley, 18 May 2006.

with Tribbles' to *Star Trek* and scripts to other TV series before he turned to writing short stories, the first of which appeared in the December 1969 *Galaxy*. This was 'Oracle for a White Rabbit', which introduced his Human Analogue Computer, Harlie. Acting rather like a spoiled teenager Harlie soon grows up and finds it difficult to understand how humans could have created him. The stories were collected as *When Harlie Was One* (1972).

Like Gerrold, William Rotsler was also into fantasy films, though of a more erotic nature. Since 1966 he had directed films with such titles as *Suburban Pagans* and *Overexposed*, with storylines that seemed straight out of Abramson's Beacon Books. Rotsler did much more besides, though. A science-fiction fan of over twenty years' renown, he was famed for his cartoons and won the fan artist Hugo Award four times, starting in 1975. He turned his hands to various art forms over the years, including sculpture, and his first published story, 'Ship Me Tomorrow' (*Galaxy*, June 1970) brought together many of these endeavours in a slight piece about the ideal dream woman. His fiction, though, would soon go from strength to strength.

Jakobsson was the first to get Jack Dann into print with 'Traps' (*If*, March 1970), one of his early collaborations with George Zebrowski. Dann had already sold a story to Damon Knight for *Orbit*, but that would take nearly two years to make it into print. Meanwhile Jakobsson published another Dann/Zebrowski collaboration, 'Dark, Dark, the Dead Star' (*If*, July 1970). Dann later felt that these early collaborations were 'not really serious',[83] and though both show signs of apprentice work, they are strong studies of transformation and alienation that typify much of Dann's later writings.

'Piñon Falls' in the combined October/November 1970 *Galaxy* marked the debut of Michael Bishop. This tale, which reads like a combination of Jorge Luis Borges, Clifford Simak and Ray Bradbury, tells of the consequences of the discovery of a strange winged man. It has an atmosphere of fantasy rather than sf, along with a lyrical beauty that attracted Jakobsson. Bishop had tried to sell the story to *F&SF*, where it had been rejected, though *F&SF* would become Bishop's major magazine market over the next few years. Jakobsson acquired two more stories from Bishop including his major break-out piece, 'Death and Designation Among the Asadi' (*If*, February 1973), a truly haunting story of a human struggling to understand an alien society.[84]

In fairness, the person who really 'discovered' Bishop (and, for that matter, Haldeman and Connie Willis), by finding his story amongst the slush pile of submissions was Gardner Dozois, working as Jakobsson's

---

83 See Gregory Feeley's interview with Dann, *Thrust* #21 (Fall 1984), p. 9.
84 This story was subsequently expanded as *Transfigurations* (1979).

first reader.[85] He also found Jakobsson's last major discovery of this early period, George R. R. Martin, though his tale 'The Hero' (*Galaxy*, February 1971), dealing with how war heroes are created, reads light years away from the lyrical, pastoral works Martin would soon be producing.

Jakobsson continued to develop writers who had only recently started selling sf, some of whom had been discovered by Pohl. One, who shone only briefly in the sf firmament but who nevertheless burned into the mind, was T. J. Bass, the pseudonym used by physician Thomas J. Bassler, another *If* first. 'Half Past Human' (*Galaxy*, December 1969) was the first in a series that looked at how society and humanity had changed 400 years hence under pressure from overpopulation. In a rather Wellsian image, a new race of humans, the Nebishes, exist in vast hives beneath the Earth's surface controlled by a supercomputer, while a few original humans try and survive on the surface, which is given over to crops. Bass had a vivid imagination and a wonderful command of English. The series continued until 'Rorqual Maru' (*Galaxy*, January 1972) and was reworked into book form as *Half Past Human* (1971) and *The Godwhale* (1974), both novels receiving Nebula nominations. Pressure of work and family commitments forced Bassler to stop writing just at the point that his name was becoming established, and sf lost a potent talent.

Stephen Tall was the alias adopted by professor of biology, Compton Crook. Tall had been writing short fiction under other aliases for over forty years, but had only turned briefly to science fiction in 1955 when he sold 'The Lights on Precipice Peak' to *Galaxy*. It was over ten years before he returned to the field with 'Seventy Light Years from Sol' in *Worlds of Tomorrow* (November 1966), the first of his series about the explorations of the crew of the starship *Stardust*. It looked like he might be about to start a different series with 'Allison, Carmichael and Tattersall' in the April 1970 *Galaxy* about further space explorers set closer to home, venturing to the Jovian moon Callisto. But he later returned to the *Stardust* characters, mostly in *Galaxy* and *If*. These stories have a period feel and would not have been out of place in the pulps for their stereotyped characters and adventurous settings, but Tall was writing with 1970s vision and the ecological issues he raised were highly topical: ideal, in fact, for the new motto Jakobsson had created for *Galaxy* as featuring 'the best in Pertinent Science Fiction'. Tall's most powerful ecological message, though, appeared in a non-series story, 'This is My Country' (February 1971). Man has destroyed all life on Earth, including his own, and only robots continue to function, striving to imitate man through his books, such as *Gone With the Wind*.

---

85 See Tim Sullivan's interview with Dozois, *Fantasy Review* #85 (November 1985), p. 7.

Gerald Jonas, writer for *The New Yorker* and sf book critic for the *New York Times*, was an infrequent contributor to the magazines, and then usually to *F&SF*. 'The Shaker Revival' marked his sole appearance in *Galaxy* (February 1970). Written in an investigative style, it looks at the rise of the New Shakers and presages the growth of extreme religious cults in the seventies and eighties.

Howard Waldrop had made his first sale to *Analog*, but it was a whole year before his next story appeared and that was in *Galaxy*. 'A Voice and Bitter Weeping' (July 1973), written with Jake 'Buddy' Saunders has Texas secede from the United States and the dispossessed Israeli army brought in to force them back. It's a violent story with some chill humour, not unlike Haldeman's work, and formed the basis for the novel *The Texas–Israeli War: 1999* (Ballantine, 1974). Waldrop's work was just too oddball for the magazines at that time.

Greg Benford had been producing competent work since his first sales in 1965/66, mostly for *F&SF* and *Amazing*, but one of his first major stories was 'In the Ocean of Night', the novella out of which his 1977 novel grew and which appeared in the May/June 1972 *If*. This told of the discovery of an alien starship hidden within a comet and its impact on human society. Algis Budrys used the novel as a launchpad to herald a new generation of writers who were taking sf forward.[86] He linked Benford with Joe Haldeman and George R. R. Martin – both of whom were *Galaxy* discoveries – and John Varley (who would soon be a *Galaxy* star).

Budry's discussion was not in his review column in *Galaxy* but in *F&SF*. Budrys had dropped something of a bombshell and resigned 'on air' so to speak at the end of his column in the November 1971 *Galaxy*. He was tired of reviewing, but also felt that the majority of the books he was reading had little to offer – 'the most popular writers are semi-literate' is how he began. The column passed to Theodore Sturgeon who, like Budrys, provided insightful essays rather than reviews. Budrys evidently got a second wind because three years later he was reviewing books again on a fairly regular basis for *F&SF*, and kept that going for 18 years. His departure from *Galaxy* raised the question of the state of science fiction in book form, while his subsequent comment in *F&SF* was indicative of the fact that the salvation of science fiction was emerging from the new writers in the magazines.

Another name Budrys linked with that group was James Tiptree, Jr., the alias that for ten years fooled the entire sf world and hid the identity of Alice Sheldon. I shall discuss her work in more detail later but it is worth remembering that most of her early work had appeared in *If* and *Galaxy*,

---

86 See his book review column in *F & SF* 55:1 (July 1978), pp. 54–8.

starting with 'The Mother Ship' (*If*, June 1968) and including 'Parimu-tuel Planet' (*Galaxy*, January 1969) and 'Happiness in a Warm Spaceship' (*If*, November 1969) – the only one of her early *Star-Trek*-inspired stories to see print. These acceptances were all down to Frederik Pohl, but one later story made it in to Jakobsson's *Galaxy* – 'Mother in the Sky with Diamonds' (March 1971), a story that brought humanity to the space-ways. Tiptree brought a rebellious freshness to science fiction, twisting the field into shapes that hadn't been seen before, and you can see that development starting in these early stories. Sheldon later wrote, '*If* gave a home to the worst turkey I ever launched, which let me see why it was no good – and to the best I early achieved.' The magazine was, as she termed it, 'a friend to experiments'.[87]

One of the great experimenters was R. A. Lafferty. He did much to raise smiles and occasional eyebrows, and was particularly at home in *Galaxy* and *If* and had been so since he first appeared there in 1960. He continued to contribute with only slightly decreasing regularity during the first half of the seventies. If his stories had any recurrent theme, it was one of bewildered humanity who would be paranoid if they only knew what was going on. 'The All-at-Once Man' (*Galaxy*, July 1970) suggests there are a small group of immortals on Earth who know everything. Their omniscience turns to faking history in 'Rivers of Damascus' (*Galaxy*, February 1974). 'About a Secret Crocodile' (*Galaxy*, August 1970), one of his most amusing stories, considers how a diversity of small, secret organizations interact to control each other and the world. The same idea surfaces in a rather more sinister way in 'All But the Words' (*Galaxy*, July 1971) which suggests that one reason why no aliens have contacted us is because we're so boring, a concept reworked in 'Parthen' (*Galaxy*, May 1973) when alien conquerors threaten to enslave one half of Earth and destroy the other, only to find that no one's much bothered either way. Lafferty's work is rife with wonderful off-the-wall phrases, some highly applicable to his work. In 'The All-At-Once Man' he advises, 'Try being a little lopsided sometimes, men. You'll live longer by it.' (p.87) All of Lafferty's work was 'a little lopsided', and it may well live longer than many of its contemporaries. I will be quoting Lafferty again.

There was a group of writers who brought much humour to the magazines. Almost as anarchic as Lafferty and at times equally humorous was Larry Eisenberg. He had developed a series for *F&SF* about a scientist called Duckworth whose bright ideas seem great at first but always end

---

87 James Tiptree, Jr., introduction to 'The Night-Blooming Saurian', in Frederik Pohl, Martin H. Greenberg and Joseph D. Olander (eds), *Worlds of If: a Retrospective Anthology* (New York: Bluejay, 1986).

in disaster. The series shifted to *If* in 1970 and later to *Galaxy*, providing much-needed escapist humour. Harry Harrison revived his series about interplanetary conman Slippery Jim DiGriz in 'The Stainless Steel Rat Saves the World' (*If*, October 1971), the first of three new novellas. Although Ron Goulart contributed primarily to *F&SF*, he appeared occasionally in *If*, holding up to ridicule a world slightly out of kilter. He was often at his best when looking at how increased automation thwarted and frustrated humankind, such as in 'What's Become of Screwloose?' (July 1970) and 'Dingbat' (November/December 1973).

Both *Galaxy* and *If* became homes to several British sf writers bereft of a magazine market in Britain. Many were also dispossessed by the domination of the New Wave, with only John Carnell's *New Writings in SF* as an occasional market. Their work often added a dimension of wonder and awe that was frequently missing from their soul-searching American counterparts, and this contrast is especially evident in *Galaxy* and *If*.

Michael Coney was a British writer recently uprooted to the West Indies and soon to move on to Canada. He had sold his first two stories to the Anglo-Australian magazine *Vision of Tomorrow* but for the next few years *Galaxy* and *If* became his major market. Coney used short stories to experiment with ideas that he might later rework into novels. His first appearance in *Galaxy*, 'Discover a Latent Moses' (April 1970), and its sequel 'Snow Princess' (January 1971), formed the basis for his novel *Winter's Children* (1974). Earth has been overcome by a new ice age or 'nuclear winter' and the survivors scratch an existence in caves. Although a green land still exists, the survivors cannot envisage a life there as the world has lost its dreamers. Coney later turned the idea on its head, depicting a future colony, the Peninsular, ruled by dreamers, artists and the idle rich, supported by spare-part-organ-donor bonded servants. This series began in *Galaxy* with 'The Girl With a Symphony in Her Fingers'[88] (January 1974). It showed that dreamers alone would be no better at furthering society than the hunter-gatherers of the Ice Age. Coney had followed a similar theme in 'The Sharks on Pentreath' (February 1971) where people can visit anywhere they like via virtual links with miniature robots. Both depicted societies withdrawing into themselves. That concept was also behind Coney's most intriguing idea, which was born in *If*. 'The Never Girl' (January/February 1973) and 'A Woman and Her Friend' (March/April 1973) posit a future form of immortality where individuals over the age of 40 can have their brains transplanted into new-born children.

---

88 This title was used for the British edition of the book arising from the series but the US edition was called *The Jaws that Bite, the Claws that Catch* (1975), reflecting the nonsensical pointlessness of many of the characters' lives.

So popular does this become that the shortage of children means that brains are stored in tanks, and later in androids. When reworked into book form it took the title *Friends Come in Boxes* (1973). Although Coney never became a major writer, he was a fecund store of ideas which always made his work fascinating.

Scottish scientist Duncan Lunan made his professional debut with 'The Moon of Thin Reality' (June 1970),[89] for which Gaughan provided one of his more detailed space covers. It was the first in Lunan's Interface series, where mankind gains access to alien matter transmitters, and has elements not unlike Frederik Pohl's Heechee series.

Like Lunan, Colin Kapp's work was rooted in solid technology, and he was equally at home in *Analog*, but for *If* he provided two serials of cosmic proportions. 'Patterns of Chaos' (January/February–May/June 1972) is a van-Vogtian tale of a machine capable of projecting outcomes from chaos that proves vital in deciding a future interstellar war. This novel had all the flair of the thirties pulp sf extravaganzas and delighted readers. Despite the title, his other serial, 'The Wizard of Anharrite' (November/December 1972–March/April 1973), is solid sf, reading rather like a merger of the works of Leigh Brackett and Poul Anderson. It explores the conflict between an earth-based mercantile council and a slave-based colony emerging out of its feudalism under a super-scientist who masquerades as a wizard.

While Kapp was thrilling the minds of *If* readers, James White was doing the same at *Galaxy*, but with more moderated science. 'Dark Inferno' (January–March 1972) has a major accident occur on an Earth–Ganymede passenger ship and the doctor finds himself having to bring everyone through safely. 'The Dream Millenium' (October–December 1973) has the first interstellar colonization ship on a knife-edge as they find themselves running out of possibilities. Whereas Kapp went for the technological fireworks, White produced two tense thrillers focused on human actions.

Fellow Irish writer Bob Shaw had found a satisfactory American market in the pages of Ted White's *Amazing* and *Fantastic*, where he continued to explore his slow-glass concept. He appeared in *Galaxy* with 'Orbitsville' (June–August 1974), a novel which neatly combines the super-science of Kapp with the tension of White. Humans discover a vast Dyson Sphere surrounding a distant star. A man, whose family is held hostage elsewhere on the Sphere, crashes millions of miles away and has to find a

---

89 Lunan had made an earlier sale to Joseph Wrzos at *Amazing Stories* in 1967 but that story, 'Derelict', languished in the files for seven years until appearing in the April 1974 issue.

way back to rescue his family. A similar study of a Dyson Sphere had just appeared in 'The Org's Egg' (*Galaxy*, April–June 1974) by Frederik Pohl and Jack Williamson – indeed the final episode appeared in the same issue as the first episode of 'Orbitsville'. Unlike Shaw's novel, though, Pohl and Williamson's is built on a cosmic scale with a cast of thousands (indeed each individual may be replicated many times as a consequence of a new means of instantaneous travel).

Like Shaw, John Brunner's main magazine market in the United States was with Ted White and he had just one appearance in *Galaxy*, with the serial 'Web of Everywhere' (March–April 1974). As with Lunan's series, Brunner looks at the impact of the discovery of instantaneous travel but rather than across galaxies, he studies the consequences on Earth, showing how such an invention would ultimately bring the total collapse of civilization. The novel was written during one of Brunner's most creative periods and shows his skill at building one idea on top of another.

Galaxy had published a couple of vignettes by Arthur C. Clarke and was fortunate to gain advance publication of his novel 'A Rendezvous with Rama' (September–October 1973), the now classic account of a mysterious asteroid-size alien craft that enters our solar system, is explored and then continues on its way. Like Shaw's 'Orbitsville', Clarke's 'Rama' was a fascinating study in world-building, but arguably one of the most distinctive and imaginative worlds created in science fiction appeared in Christopher Priest's 'Inverted World' (*Galaxy*, December 1973–March 1974). In this novel, which grew out of Priest's fascination with calculus, we are introduced to Earth City, a completely enclosed society that is hauled along on tracks heading towards some unknown Optimum. Behind the city time speeds up, while ahead it seems to slow down. People who venture too far from the city become distorted in shape and disjointed in time. The world along which Earth City travels is not spherical but hyperbolic. This bizarre world took some explaining, especially as Priest had not fully thought it through himself. He had been thinking about the concept for some years and he eventually wrote it at white-hot pace during the summer of 1973,[90] with no idea as to how it would end until he got there, but that creative speed carries you through the story. The reader can make any number of allegorical parallels or simply enjoy the story at its bewildering face value – such is the depth of good story-telling.

The British and Irish writers brought an extra dimension to the variety of fiction appearing in *Galaxy* and *If*. There is no denying that during Jakobsson's years the two magazines published much that was enjoyable and helped bring new writers on board. Both magazines continued

90 See interview with Priest in *Science Fiction Monthly* 1:12 (January 1975), p. 26.

to some degree in the form originally conceived by Gold and developed by Pohl. Certainly *If* remained the more experimental and original – Jakobsson dubbed it 'the magazine of alternatives', and it fitted that epithet well. Perhaps *Galaxy* lacked some of the drive and creativity that it had previously had. Jakobsson worked hard at the outset to inject a new personality but within a year that had flagged and *Galaxy* lacked any clear direction. It survived more on its reputation, operating on autopilot rather than through any new initiative. This suggests that once Pohl's backlog had been worked through and Gardner Dozois had gone, Jakobsson was left without any fuel in the burner. It may also be that both Arnold Abramson and Judy-Lynn Benjamin convinced Jakobsson not to experiment too much, causing him to lose that verve that made his first year so interesting. Readers had noticed the change, as the following extracts show from two letters three years apart. Firstly, in the March– April 1971 *If*, one reader said:

> Congratulations on your fine editorial work in *Galaxy* and its sister publications. I've been reading them for over a decade and though there have been some lousy stories, I can say on the whole I've enjoyed them tremendously. And perhaps look forward with more anxiety to each new issue since you took over, than before. I think this is only to see what's going to happen next. In fact I think most magazines are pretty exciting these days.[91]

But a couple of years later this became:

> although I've still found *Galaxy* and *If* the best mags around, they have had a dead quality which leaves the reader with the idea that nobody cares. I like editorials, I like letter columns and it is great to see an editor–reader relationship. It means we are being listened to. That editors do care.[92]

Although each letter is by a different correspondent, they echo sentiments that turn up progressively through the issues. In his first year Jakobsson had tried to generate a responsive relationship with readers but that faded. While *If* retained a regular letter column, *Galaxy* had only an occasional one, until July 1972 when Jakobsson announced that he would introduce a regular forum and pay $10 for the most interesting letter and $5 for any others he ran. While this sparked a series of discussions, Jakobsson again stood back and he never felt part of the process. His editorials, when he bothered to write any, were anodyne and shallow.[93]

---

91 Letter by John A. Beck in *If* 20:10 (March/April 1971), p. 191.
92 Letter by Nicholas Grimshawe in *If* 22:5 (May/June 1974), p. 170
93 Jakobsson also had the embarrassment of publishing a plagiarism. The September/

This was due in part to sheer overwork. UPD was a relatively small company producing a large number of books and magazines. While Jakobsson had primary responsibility for *Galaxy* and *If*, he had not relinquished his role in the book department and continued to be involved in the paperback imprint of Award Books, which he had helped to launch in 1964. Award Books became the main science-fiction imprint of UPD, publishing two or three books a month, including anthologies that Jakobsson compiled anonymously from material in the magazines.

Not only were Jakobsson's energies spread thinly but so were those of art director Jack Gaughan. Gaughan later explained:

> The original notion was that I would send out stories and pick the artists to illustrate them. What happened is that the magazine was put together on Thursday and the art had to be done by Monday. That's why it was only me – I didn't have time to send out any stories.[94]

Sometimes Jakobsson would read extracts from stories over the phone which Gaughan would record and use for his illustrations. On two occasions, his artwork was lost in the mail and Gaughan had to redo all of the artwork from memory in one day. Gaughan regarded it as 'artistic suicide'. Dan Steffan, who knew Gaughan well, told me:

> My understanding is that those years were not happy ones for Jack, who by this time was cynical and frustrated by the sf industry's refusal to move out of the mentality of the old pulp magazines. He went into several years of decline after his time with those magazines.[95]

The inevitable result was that Gaughan's illustrations looked hurried, even scribbled, adding to the feeling that 'nobody cared'. Gaughan stepped down as art director after the May 1972 *Galaxy*, having illustrated almost the entirety of 22 successive issues of *Galaxy* and twenty of *If*. For the next 18 months most covers were supplied by the London-based art studio of Brian Boyle who worked for the UK imprint of UPD, Tandem Books. Though technically competent, Boyle's art looked clinical and lacked the soul that made Gaughan's work live when at its best.

Gaughan's tired covers and Jakobsson's lack of presence did not help sales. When UPD took over *Galaxy* and *If*, circulation had been falling. From an average paid circulation per issue of 75,300 for *Galaxy* and 67,400

October 1971 *If* carried 'To Kill a Venusian' by Irwin Ross which was a direct copy of the well-known 'Nine-Finger Jack' by Anthony Boucher, originally published in *Esquire* in 1951. No one can be expected to know every story and identify such copies, but readers spotted it instantly, adding to the belief that Jakobsson was not concentrating.

94 See discussion with Jack Gaughan by Ginger Kaderabek in *Isaac Asimov's Science Fiction Magazine*, 3:4 (April 1979), p. 47.

95 Personal e-mail, Steffan/Ashley, 20 May 2006.

for *If* during the year ended October 1968, sales dropped to 51,479 and 44,548 respectively during 1968/69 – a fall of over 30 per cent. Sales continued to drop and did not recover until 1972 when a subscription drive boosted sales, though it did not necessarily boost income. Subscription houses that handle mass mailings on behalf of publishers will take a premium for their service and the returns only increase income if the subscribers renew for a second year.

At the same time, UPD had a problem with distribution. Readers regularly complained that they could not find the magazines in their area. Though news-stand sales improved, distribution remained a problem and, most importantly, income had been cut during the crucial two years after the purchase of the magazines.

Abramson had used various tactics to cut costs and maximize income. His first act had been to reduce the number of pages in *Galaxy* from 196 to 160. Besides the obvious savings, it meant that both *If* and *Galaxy* had the same number of pages, which streamlined the printing and binding processes. Next, as an experiment, he extended the on-sale time of what would have been the January 1970 issue of *Galaxy*, which was redated February as a consequence. The cover date of the magazine is the date when the magazine goes *off* sale and copies are returned to the warehouse. The longer a copy remains on sale the more likelihood there is that a few extra copies will be sold. Jakobsson did not report back on this and the continued slide in sales does not suggest that it had much effect, but nevertheless Abramson took the next logical step.

Abramson needed to spread his overheads and so revived *Worlds of Tomorrow* in June 1970 and *Worlds of Fantasy* in September. To compensate, *If* went bi-monthly from its May 1970 issue and *Galaxy* followed suit with its August issue. *If* remained bi-monthly thereafter and though *Galaxy* returned to a monthly schedule in December it reverted to being bi-monthly in July 1971 and did not become monthly again until September 1973.

At the same time that *Galaxy* went bi-monthly it increased its page count by 20 per cent to 192, with a corresponding price rise of 25 per cent from 60 cents to 75 cents. The same happened at *If*. This was only a temporary compensation, as the page count dropped to 176 from May 1971. At that same time, *Worlds of Fantasy* and *Worlds of Tomorrow* were dropped. The bi-monthly printing and distribution of *Galaxy* and *If* were done concurrently, rather than alternate months.

The overall effect of all of this, in very crude terms, was to increase income to the order of about 25 per cent, while holding the extra printing and distribution costs to about 10 per cent. Abramson also tapped further into the British market. UPD owned the British publisher Tandem Books. Starting in May 1972, Tandem printed their own British edition of both *Galaxy* and *If*. To all intents these were identical in content to the American edition, but the covers – which were now printed on a thicker, better-quality, glossy card – carried a British cover price (25p) and was renumbered as 'UK No. 1' and so on.[96] It is possible that the UK sales were not included in the circulation figures that Universal were required to publish each year by law. The data were provided to support advertising rates and this was only relevant to the North American continent. Nevertheless, the appearance of the UK edition coincided with the sudden increase in news-stand sales for *Galaxy* and *If*, both up by around 6,000 copies, a proportion of which might have been UK sales.

At the same time, though, Abramson entered into some less-than-successful deals. Firstly, in May 1972 he agreed a sale of two of his more lucrative titles, *Golf* and *Ski*, to the Times Mirror Company for an undisclosed sum. These two titles had a circulation ten times that of *Galaxy* and *If* and their sales continued to improve after the change in management. A year earlier Abramson had been an investor in a new magazine called *On the Sound*, aimed at the social elite on Long Island Sound. Unfortunately, they did not support the magazine, though Abramson, believing it had potential, bought the title in October 1972. The magazine continued to struggle and eventually folded in May 1974. In the short space of 18 months, Abramson had sold off two of his major magazines and acquired one that was floundering.

This was the start of Abramson's financial problems in relation to *Galaxy* and *If*, a situation not helped by the start of the oil crisis in October 1973, which pushed the United States into the worst recession for 40 years.

It would not have helped the already overworked Jakobsson when in May 1973 Judy-Lynn del Rey left to take up an editorial post at Ballantine Books. Within days she had secured a six-book deal with Arthur C. Clarke, starting with *A Rendezvous with Rama*, which she had been working on preparing for serialization in *Galaxy*. She did not abandon the magazines completely. One of her first projects at Ballantine was to contact Leigh Brackett to urge her out of retirement. In fact, Brackett had been considering the same thing and was working on a new planetary adventure, *The Ginger Star*. Not only was this signed up for Ballantine

96 One of the odd changes as a result of the British edition was that the redesign caused the title of *If* to be shown on the masthead as *Worlds of If*. When *If* was first published the full title had been *If Worlds of Science Fiction*, but over the years the cover design had given the impression that the title was *Worlds of If Science Fiction*, a name further embedded in the mind with the companion *Worlds of Tomorrow*. The title always remained officially *If*, but from May 1972 it was more likely that readers would refer to it as *Worlds of If*.

Books but the advanced serialization of it appeared in *If*, starting in the January/February 1974 issue.

Judy-Lynn made her mark instantly and in March 1977 was elevated to editor-in-chief of the newly created imprint Del Rey Books, which was so successful that it subsidized much of Ballantine's other operations for a few years. She became vice president of Ballantine Books in 1978 and formally the publisher of Del Rey Books in 1982.

She was replaced at *Galaxy* and *If* by Albert Dytch. Dytch's stay at the magazines was brief, a little over three months. It was during his tenure that some writers noticed significant changes in their published stories. One of these was Christopher Priest, whose serial 'The Inverted World' was tampered with. Priest commented:

> please believe that throughout the serial there are a multitude of petty re-wording, with the copy-editor indulging himself in an orgy of rewriting towards the end. These aren't abridgements, incidentally, although the story has been cut slightly: I'm talking about seemingly pointless tamperings with dialogue, narrative, structure of sentences and paragraphs. To my eye, the book now reads very badly indeed.[97]

Another who suffered was Duncan Lunan. His Interface series had been delayed for several reasons, not least a postal strike in Britain, and the sixth story did not appear till the November/December 1973 issue of *If*. Lunan relates:

> When it came to the sixth story, 'How to Blow up an Asteroid', they changed it so much that the seventh and eighth stories could no longer be published in sequence. They also introduced some bizarre male chauvinism, for which I had to apologise when taken to task by Vera Johnson and Anne McCaffrey. It put paid to the series, which had two more stories to go and a second series of eight to follow, as well as three related novels.[98]

Lunan was told that the changes had been made by Judy-Lynn del Rey, but that seems unlikely. She always worked closely with her authors and prided herself on not meddling with manuscripts. It is possible that Jakobsson himself made the changes. Harlan Ellison tells of such an experience. When he sold Jakobsson 'Cold Friend' for the twenty-third special anniversary issue, he did so on the condition that it was kept exactly as written. This took place after Judy-Lynn del Rey had left. Ellison discovered when the October 1973 issue was announced that his story had

97 See letter by Christopher Priest in *The Alien Critic* #9 (May 1974), p. 25.

98 Personal e-mail, Lunan/Ashley, 18 May 2006. Vera Johnson was a British fan and writer.

been retitled 'Know Your Local Mailman' and, following a phone call to Jakobsson, learned of other changes.[99] Jakobsson had to recall the proofs and revise everything (though some still slipped through). Jakobsson was evidently the transgressor here. Barry Malzberg is of a similar opinion. He told me, 'Jake's meddling with manuscripts was notorious. He was not only an interfering editor of the worst sort but a *terrible* writer who screwed up work. A Pamela Sargent story was destroyed by him.'[100]

Pamela Sargent's story was 'If Ever I Should Leave You', published in the January/February 1974 *If.* When reflecting on this some years later, Sargent wrote:

> I glanced at the story after it was published and it was horrifying – all these dumb lines I hadn't written. The story was told in the first person by a nameless protagonist, but apparently some dufus at *If* – not the editor as far as I could tell – decided my narrator should have a name. The name he decided on was Nanette. And the other changes were worse – clumsy bits of exposition that were wrong, details that made no sense.[101]

Sargent had to struggle to get any redress from the publisher and it was not until James Baen took over that a letter from Sargent, together with an apology, was published in *Galaxy*.[102] Sargent was evidently of the view that Jakobsson had not done the revisions. The fact that Dytch left after only three months may say it all.

He was replaced by James Baen. Baen was just a few months younger than Judy-Lynn del Rey. He had joined Ace Books in 1971 and had worked his way up via the accounts and complaints departments to become the assistant editor on the gothic romances, where he remained for six months. With his move to UPD, he was appointed as managing editor in August 1973 with effect from the November 1973 *Galaxy* and January 1974 *If.* But things moved fast. With the next issue, dated March 1974 but on sale from 1 January, Baen was made full editor of *If.* Six weeks later Jakobsson resigned, with effect from 15 February. 'Reasons: overwork and health and a complicated amalgam of factors I won't bore you with,' he told me, adding, 'The last four years at the helm of *Galaxy* have easily been the most rewarding of my working life.'[103] The last issue

99 Harlan Ellison, memoir to 'Cold Friend', in Pohl, Greenberg and Olander, *Galaxy*, vol. 2, pp. 103–4.

100 Personal e-mail, Malzberg/Ashley, 19 May 2006.

101 See Jill Engel, 'Letters from Upstate New York: a Correspondence with Pamela Sargent', *Nova Express* 3:3 (Winter 1991), p. 5.

102 See *Galaxy* 36:1 (January 1975), p. 157.

103 Personal letter, Jakobsson/Ashley, 4 February 1974.

he compiled was that for April 1974, though his name was still recorded as editor on the May 1974 issue.

Jakobsson was only 62, but he had clearly had enough. Although he had lent little of his personality to either *Galaxy* or *If* after his first few issues, he did strive to make the magazines diverse and challenging, running much top-flight material. He was, of course, ably supported by Judy-Lynn del Rey and with her departure the pressure fell back on Jakobsson. He must have seen capable hands in James Baen, although he did recommend to Abramson that Frederik Pohl be re-engaged as editor. There was, albeit briefly, some interest from Pohl, but he declined. With Jakobsson's departure James Baen was firmly enthroned as the editor of both *Galaxy* and *If*. Jakobsson retired to his home in Pleasantville, near Westchester, New York (where Abramson also lived), where he died in October 1984 aged 72, the forgotten editor of sf.

How the Mighty Fall

Baen regards the May/June issue of *If* and the June 1974 *Galaxy* as the first over which he had direct control. The change in presentation was immediate. The table of contents spread over two pages to allow a brief outline of each story or feature. In *Galaxy* there was a new forum where each month a different author would discuss different aspects of science fiction. Contributors in the first year included Alexei and Cory Panshin, Isaac Asimov, Poul Anderson, Dick Hoagland and Frederik Pohl. Theodore Sturgeon continued the book column, though this was taken over by Spider Robinson from June 1975.

From the April 1974 *Galaxy*, Baen instigated a new science column, 'A Step Further Out', by Jerry Pournelle. The feature became extremely popular. Pournelle had a broad knowledge of all matters scientific. A. E. van Vogt remarked, 'Of all the people I have met in my life, Jerry is one of the most colossally educated in science.' He also said of him, 'Jerry has Isaac Asimov's memory in a younger body.'[104] Pournelle also had strong views. It was not long before he was whipping up support on issues of ecological concern ranging from overpopulation to whaling to the effect of tuna fishing nets on dolphins.

Baen also reintroduced a regular letter column in *Galaxy* and encouraged interplay between correspondent and contributor – usually Pournelle. Baen often used to add his own comments so that, although he seldom wrote a specific editorial, you felt his presence.

104 See *Galaxy* 35:7 (July 1974), p. 171.

Baen created or boosted similar features in *If* with one significant addition. He brought in Richard Geis to contribute a regular column, 'The Alien Viewpoint'. The column was ostensibly to review fan magazines, or fanzines, but Geis was given a wide remit to talk about matters of interest to the sf world. Those who did not know Geis were in for a treat. He was a long-time fan who had published, off and on, a fanzine variously called *Psychotic*, *The Alien Critic* and *Science Fiction Review*. Both the magazine and he won a slew of awards. Geis was renowned for his ego-bursting jibes, his anti-establishment viewpoint and his remarkable ability to assess a situation in a few perceptive and often funny sentences. One gimmick he used was to talk with his own alter ego, called Alter. Alter was chained up somewhere deep in his mind and was frequently trying to escape or come up with some scheme that annoyed Geis. Geis introduced Alter to readers of *If*, cautiously at first but Alter soon had his way. Right from the start Geis's column was a hit.

Within a couple of issues Baen had transformed both magazines, giving them a vibrancy and character which they had long been lacking. He also further brightened the covers, bringing in such relatively new artists as Rick Sternbach, Wendy Pini and Stephen Fabian. Though Sternbach's humans always looked a bit mechanical, his space and technical artwork was second to none. Pini's covers were colourful with a fantasy edge. With a style resembling Virgil Finlay's, Fabian could produce both exotic and erotic pictures within fantastic settings.

Baen also strove to secure a good line-up of fiction, though here he was fighting against severe odds. Cash flow at UPD had become tight, partly because of Abramson's earlier financial deals, but also because of the spiralling economic climate. In October 1973, six of the major oil-exporting countries, represented by OPEC, had placed an oil embargo on the West. The dramatic rise in oil prices had a consequent impact on other costs. Uncertainty in the stock exchange led to a dramatic fall in share values, and during 1974 inflation rose by over 12 per cent.[105] UPD was in dire financial straits. Baen told me:

> When I got there, the editorial budget was $4,500 per issue and payments were generally made shortly after acceptance; about three months into my tenure the corporate crunch came. The per-issue allowance was dropped to $2,750 and started slowing down to the point where payments were generally being made six months after publication – or worse.[106]

105 From November 1973 to December 1974 the Dow Jones Industrial Average fell from a high of 956.58 to 616.08, and at one point was as low as 570. The Consumer Price Index rose from 46.3 in December 1973 to 51.9 in December 1974.
106 Personal letter, Baen/Ashley, 20 December 1977.

Baen, while doing his best, had to take short cuts where he could. For *If*, he bought a new robot story from Isaac Asimov, 'Strangers in Paradise', even though it had been rejected by Judy-Lynn del Rey two years before. He acquired two stories from Robert Silverberg, both of which had seen prior publication in British magazines over twelve years before.[107] There was also bottom-drawer material from Mack Reynolds, James H. Schmitz and James Blish. On the plus side, though, Baen had some popular serials to offer. In *If* was Fred Saberhagen's 'Berserker's War' (May/June–July/August 1974) and Poul Anderson's Dominic Flandry adventure 'A Knight of Ghosts and Shadows' (September/October–November/December 1974), while in *Galaxy* was Edgar Pangborn's welcome 'The Company of Glory' (August–October 1974), set in the same world as his much-acclaimed post-apocalypse novel *Davy*.

Amongst the short fiction, Joe Haldeman contributed another sardonic war story to *Galaxy*, 'The Private War of Pvt. Jacob' (June 1974), which looked at the grisly way soldiers could keep renewing themselves. Ursula Le Guin appeared with a prequel to her novel *The Dispossessed*, 'The Day Before the Revolution' (August 1974), which went on to win the Nebula, Jupiter and Locus awards. There was a chilling chess fantasy by Fritz Leiber, 'Midnight by the Morphy Watch' (*If*, August 1974), while Frederik Pohl completed another story from an idea by Cyril Kornbluth, 'The Gift of Garigolli' (*Galaxy*, August 1974).

Baen was also bringing several new authors on line, of whom more in a moment. He was certainly doing his best to put vitality back into *Galaxy* and *If*, even though the magazines were hanging on by a thread. The letter column in the November/December 1974 *If* was full of praise for his efforts, many remarking how quickly he had turned them from being 'bland' and 'lifeless' to 'a real treat', and subscriptions flooded in. In fact, in that year he not only preserved the subscriptions boosted by the previous year's subscription drive, but increased them. For the first time ever, in 1974, *If*'s total paid circulation was greater than *Galaxy*'s – 50,355 compared to 47,789.

And that was when the thread unravelled.

One of the consequences of the oil embargo and rising inflation was that it caught up with a general malaise in the paper industry. No one had been planning for the increased demand in paper. Paper consumption had risen by over 35 per cent in the decade prior to 1973 but, with the recession, paper companies had cut back on their budgets for upgrading

---

107 'House Divided' in the May/June 1974 *If* had appeared in the December 1958 *Nebula*. 'The Man Who Came Back' in the December 1974 *Galaxy* had appeared in the February 1961 *New Worlds*.

equipment and expanding plants. The sudden ecological awareness had imposed further restrictions on paper companies to clean up their systems and stop discharging toxins into rivers, and many old paper mills had closed down. The price of paper had risen steeply and supplies were dangerously low, leading to a rapid rise in costs.

UPD were already in financial straits and the paper supply had to be rationed. Baen explained the situation bluntly in the final issue of *If*: 'We ran out of paper – the kind of paper we can afford to buy, that is. We still have access to quantities sufficient for one magazine, but not two.'[108]

From the January issue *If* was combined with *Galaxy*. The page-count was reduced to 160 and soon after (in April) the price rose to $1. You might think that, as *If* now had the greater circulation, the merger would be the other way round, but *Galaxy* was the senior title (by two years) and had always had more gravitas. *If* had always felt like the junior partner, literally, because it often had more fun without having to take too much of the blame. In its 22 years *If* had passed through three publishers and no fewer than eight editors. It had won three Hugo awards and published works that had won four Hugos and a Nebula. At its most popular, in the mid-sixties, it had helped attract to the sf magazines younger readers who might graduate to *Galaxy* and others. It had also been a lure for new writers and the number of '*If* firsts' who had gone on to greater things is significant.

At the time there was a slight hint that maybe the merger was temporary and perhaps, in the hands of a more financially sound publisher, that might have been possible. But no one seriously believed that. *If* would not be the only victim of the paper shortage, but it was certainly the greatest loss.

Yet the entrepreneurial Jim Baen used it to his advantage. He genuinely saw the merger as a benefit, because he could bring all the benefits of *If* to *Galaxy* and focus the sparse resources on one magazine. Baen may have sighed at having to say farewell to *If*, but the grieving was brief. There was a job to do, and he knew how to do it.

Baen's positive attitude was evident in the magazine, not least in his editorial in the March 1975 issue. Entitled 'If This Goes On (and On and On)...', it recognized that the world had problems but Baen could see no benefit in sitting around moaning and giving in to it. Science already had the answers to most of these problems. He told contributors to submit not stories of doom and gloom but stories that gave hope, courage and solutions.

108 James Baen, 'Editorial', *If* 22:8 (November/December 1974), p. 6. Baen explained further, in *The Alien Critic* #11 (November 1974) p. 5, that *If*'s increased circulation was still not enough to compensate for the heavy increases in the cost of paper.

Baen had already published one story that stood as a good example. 'Allegiances' (February 1975) by Michael Bishop was, on the face of it, a fairly pessimistic story. The United States had become a continent of domed cities, the urban nuclei, and the world outside had been left to revert to nature. America had cut itself off from the rest of the world and was unaware of developments elsewhere. And therein lies Bishop's solution: America needed to embrace the rest of the world, not isolate itself.

Baen received several uplifting stories, many of them humorous. Hayford Peirce's 'High Yield Bondage' (August 1975) has a group of aliens stranded on Earth who manipulate the financial markets as a way of escaping and, at the same time, solve most of Earth's problems. Similar is Kevin O'Donnell's satirical 'Shattered Hopes, Broken Dreams' (January 1976). Earth has great hopes of joining a galactic partnership but the plans are thwarted when two of the alien contacts visit an American football match and discover how violent Earth people are. The number of stories appearing at this time wherein aliens visit Earth and try to solve our problems was clearly a cry for help.

There were also some powerful high-tech space stories, none better than 'Tinker' (July 1975) by Jerry Pournelle. Inspired by a query from Jim Baen for one of Pournelle's science columns, the story covers in detail the rescue of a space-liner in the asteroid belt in the midst of much political scheming. There were similar strong science-based adventures by A. Bertram Chandler (another of his Rimworld stories) and Larry Niven.

There were also powerful military stories, not as frequent or as high-profile as in *Analog*, but no less potent. Chief amongst them were the stories by David A. Drake featuring Colonel Hammer and his troop of mercenaries known as Hammer's Slammers, which began with 'Under the Hammer' (October 1974). Like Haldeman, Drake had served in Vietnam, much of the time as an interrogator with the 11th Armored Cavalry Regiment. The series has been compared to Jerry Pournelle's Falkenberg stories, but any similarity is superficial; Pournelle considers military engagements against political machinations, while Drake concentrates on military tactics in alien environments.

Amongst other military sf that Baen ran were several stories by Fred Saberhagen, including his Berserker series of alien war machines bent on destroying anything that crosses their path, and Stephen Robinett's 'Helbent 4' (October 1975) about a Terran war-machine that returns from space to an alternate Earth of limited technology. Spider Robinson had the nerve to write a humorous story set in Vietnam, though 'Overdose' (September 1975) is really about how a soldier foils an alien invasion by sharing his drugs with it.

Baen wanted to capture that feel-good factor and allow readers a means of escape from the daily frustrations of life, while still recognizing and exploring those problems. It became an extremely eclectic magazine. Now that *If* was incorporated with *Galaxy* – and enshrined in the title (which for the next three years remained officially as *Galaxy incorporating Worlds of If*) – Baen had far more elbow room. *If* had not been averse to a little fantasy fiction, and the first combined issue led with Roger Zelazny's new Amber serial 'Sign of the Unicorn' (January–March 1975). Zelazny's first two novels in this series, *Nine Princes in Amber* and *The Guns of Avalon*, had appeared in book form only, with no prior magazine serialization. They had proved very popular with a rapidly growing fan base. The third novel was eagerly anticipated, as it had been three years since the previous book, so it was a significant coup for Baen. The novels are science fantasy at their most entertaining, full of quests, puzzles and mysteries. Amber is the perfect world of which earth is but one shadow, but Amber is under threat. In the first two books, Prince Corwin had been ejected from Amber and had to find his way back and investigate the nature of the threat. Inevitably, not all is as it seems, especially as the ruling family of Amber, of which Corwin is one of the brothers, is about as dysfunctional a family as you'll ever find. As a consequence, it was easy for Zelazny to leave threads open to explore in further novels. *Galaxy* was fortunate to secure publication of the next two, 'The Hand of Oberon' (May–September 1976) and 'The Courts of Chaos' (November 1977–February 1978).

The Swedish writer Sam Lundwall, who had been making a name for himself as a student of science fiction from an international perspective, also came through with a story of shadows of alternate worlds, 'Nobody Here But Us Shadows' (August 1975), though this story, of a woman displaced from her alternate Earth and unable to return, was on a more scientific basis.

Galaxy also ran the wonderful satire by Larry Niven and Jerry Pournelle, 'Inferno' (August–October 1975), where the narrator, a science-fiction writer who dies as a result of a silly stunt at a convention, finds himself being escorted down through the various pits of Hell, just as happened in Dante's original masterpiece. Niven had been bursting to update *Inferno* for years and both writers took every opportunity to use the novel to satirize every aspect of modern society.

The scientific features and the desire to explore positive outcomes brought *Galaxy* into line with *Analog*'s publishing philosophy, while the incorporation of such fantasies as 'Inferno' and the Amber series reminded one of *Unknown*, the former companion to *Analog* in the days when it was *Astounding*. Did this make Baen's *Galaxy* a merger of the best of *Analog* and

Unknown? Not really, though the potential was there. The new *Galaxy* was really two magazines struggling to succeed but held back by the economic problems of UPD. In later years we shall see how, with *Destinies* and its successors, Baen was able to get closer to the *Analog* model, but he was currently far too constrained. Moreover, the two aspects of *Galaxy* were as likely to cancel each other out, as the more like *Analog* that *Galaxy* became, the less readers would want the fantasy element, and vice versa. Baen needed to keep a fine balance, which he handled well, but to do that he needed a large and reliable stable of writers. He had done well to secure Pournelle and Zelazny, but the financial position, which delayed payments to authors, was a major hurdle. Nevertheless, Baen's growing track record in showing what he had achieved at *Galaxy*, plus his tenacity, would bear fruit. By 1976, Baen was attracting some strong names, but until then he had to rely heavily on new writers.

Fortunately Baen's track record in discovering new talent was good and had started from the day he stepped through UPD's doors. Early discoveries were William John Watkins ('The People's Choice', *If*, May/June 1974), Thomas Wylde ('Target of Opportunity', *Galaxy*, September 1974) and James Patrick Kelly ('Dea Ex Machina', *Galaxy*, April 1975), writing simply as James Kelly. Baen published the first solo stories by James Blish's wife (soon, alas, to be his widow), Judith Ann Lawrence ('Opening Problem', *Galaxy*, July 1974). He also published a couple of early stories by Greg Bear starting with 'The Venging' (*Galaxy*, June 1975), which was labelled a '*Galaxy* first' although Bear had had one prior story published.[109] This fascinating tale of humans confronting an alien religion contains some high-tech physics and shows that Bear started how he meant to continue.

Baen printed the first professional sales by American Indian Craig Strete. Strete had previously published these stories in his radical fanzine *Red Planet Earth*, which set out to show that even in the gregarious and purportedly open world of science fiction there was still bias and prejudice. Strete's 'Time Deer' (*If*, November/December 1974), which was nominated for a Nebula, jarringly contrasts beautiful Native-American imagery alongside prejudice and violence.

Strete's story was published as an '*If* first' – the last one. So too was 'Angel Fix' by Raccoona Sheldon (*If*, July/August 1974). No one yet knew that Raccoona Sheldon was also James Tiptree, Jr., and that both masked the identity of Alice Sheldon. In hindsight, one can see considerable similarities of style and, more significantly, rebellious humour, between 'Angel Fix' and other contemporary Tiptree work, but no one was looking

109 A brief tale, 'Destroyers' in *Famous Science Fiction*, Winter 1967.

for it at the time, although Tiptree and Sheldon were known to know each other! The story fitted ideally into Baen's publishing philosophy as it dealt with an alien who comes to Earth with an invention – a kind of dimensional portal – that only works for good guys. It was typical of the stories *Galaxy* was publishing in the early fifties – Sheckley could have written it – but just as suited to the early seventies.

Baen published first or early stories by several women writers in *Galaxy*, including Lisa Tuttle ('Changelings', March 1975), Pat Murphy ('No Mother Near', October 1975) and Nancy Kress ('The Earth Dwellers', December 1976) – all three of which dealt with child–parent relationships. *Galaxy* was a good market for feminist writers and ran several stories by Joanna Russ whose primary sf market was the liberal *F&SF*. Baen was brave enough to publish Russ's novel 'We Who Are About To...' (January–February 1976), a bleak and uncompromising story that split the sf field along gender lines. The plot concerns a passenger spaceship that is forced off course and crashes on an inhospitable world. The one female, who is also the narrator, is the only person who understands that any attempts to salvage an existence and develop a colony is doomed and that it is best that they all die. She refuses to be forced into bearing the next generation. Most men who reviewed the book at the time despised it, whereas it was hailed by women as a major work for the women's liberation movement. Although treated as a feminist work, the novel has much wider implications and is a stark reminder of the pressures of society to conform to stereotypes.

Baen's most prolific discovery, at least for the next four years before he moved on to become a management consultant, was Arsen Darnay. Darnay worked for the Environmental Protection Agency at the time, so it is not surprising that several of his stories deal with ecological issues, including his first. 'The Splendid Freedom' (*Galaxy*, September 1974) tells of a man from a distant colony who returns to Earth as part of a coming-of-age odyssey but is not aware, because of implanted images, that the Earth is no longer habitable. Darnay was born and raised in Hungary and did not settle in the United States until 1953. The experiences of wartime Europe and the subsequent Soviet command over Hungary would have had a profound influence on Darnay, which is reflected in his fiction. He later wrote, 'I am intrigued about the future because I am sure that it will be radically different from the present – but not from our past.'[110] Thus we find in 'The Eastcoast Confinement' (*Galaxy*, October 1974) a future American dictatorship where dissidents are herded into vast walled camps. The same setting provides the background for his one

110 Arsen Darnay, 'The Future is the Past', *SFWA Bulletin*, 13:4 (Fall 1978), p. 12.

serial in *Galaxy*, 'Helium' (April–July 1975),[111] which depicts a North America divided between high-tech urban societies and nomadic tribal hinterlands. Darnay's future visions were bleak but he demonstrated that societies had the answers to their problems if only they were prepared to communicate and compromise, the two requirements that few societies in conflict practise. Perhaps his most memorable story was 'Plutonium' (*Galaxy*, March 1976),[112] which uses a scientific rationale for reincarnation as a basis for exploring the karmic evolution through history of an SS concentration camp guard and two of his Jewish victims. Darnay's stay in the sf field was brief but, like a paper cut, it was noticeable.

Despite the cuts biting deeper and *Galaxy* missing issues for the last two months of 1975, Baen remained determined to put together the best that he could, and this paid off. 1976 and 1977 were remarkable years, considering. In addition to Joanna Russ's serial, Zelazny's fourth Amber novel and Darnay's 'Plutonium', Baen published three further high-profile serials – 'Children of the State' by Larry Niven (September–November 1976), 'Gateway' by Frederik Pohl (November 1976–March 1977), the first of his Heechee novels, and 'The Dosadi Experiment' by Frank Herbert – plus four excellent stories by John Varley. Varley had rapidly made a name for himself with just a handful of stories, mostly in *F&SF*, and was at the peak of his early form with his contributions to *Galaxy*. He was still developing his connected future history known as the Eight Worlds and these stories are spread over different periods, but they have several things in common. Varley was one of the few male writers capable of producing convincing stories told through the female viewpoint, as happens in both 'The Phantom of Kansas' (February 1976) and 'Bagatelle' (October 1976) – the latter introducing his popular police detective Anna-Louise Bach. Varley also created some wonderful future forms of art, such as sculpturing with the weather in 'The Phantom of Kansas' and an alien dance in 'Gotta Sing, Gotta Dance' (July 1976). He is also able to bring tension into all these stories – a hunt for a murderer in 'The Phantom of Kansas' and for a human bomb in 'Bagatelle', and a fight against time to restore a man's personality to his body in 'Overdrawn at the Memory Bank' (May 1976). High-tech future visions, strange art forms, suspense and a female viewpoint meant that Varley's stories had something for everyone, and it was no surprise when all four of these stories featured high in the *Locus* award poll and other awards for that year.

Baen continued to discover and develop new writers and relied on them heavily to fill the magazine – Thomas Wylde, Christopher Irwin,

111 Published in book-form as *A Hostage for Hinterland* (1976).
112 Expanded in book-form as *The Karma Affair* (1978).

Dennis Schmidt, Greg Bear, Lisa Tuttle, Steven Utley. The last major new name he discovered was Charles Sheffield, who had a rash of stories in *Galaxy* through 1977 starting with 'What Song the Sirens Sang' (April 1977), where a politician seeks to project the future. Several of these early stories were humorous, involving the invention of and consequences of matter transmission, but particularly touching was 'The Long Chance' (November 1977).[113] A man has his wife frozen, hoping that she can be revived when a treatment for her incurable disease has been found, and he likewise has his body frozen so he can rejoin her at some future date. Sheffield's own wife had died in June 1977 of cancer and he had turned to writing as a way of dealing with the deep grief he felt. The poignancy at the end of this story is almost too much to bear.

Baen's efforts reaped rewards. *Galaxy's* circulation, boosted to some degree by some crossovers from *If*, rose considerably from 47,789 at the time Baen took over to 81,035 by the time he left. Baen told me:

> *Galaxy*, to the best of my knowledge, has been earning its keep since I got there – and doing considerably more than paying its way. The trouble is that the corporation that owns the magazine has been in severe financial distress so that there has been no relationship between income deriving from the magazine and expenditures made to maintain it. It got very depressing towards the end of my tenure, and indeed was the main reason I left.[114]

Abramson confirmed the status of *Galaxy*.

> We see no immediate likelihood that *If* will be revived but we're protecting the title by carrying it on the cover of *Galaxy*. No one knows what the future holds but there's no near-term possibility that *Galaxy* will be chopped. Not after what we've invested in it to turn it profitable.[115]

Despite Abramson's support, *Galaxy* missed occasional months, and the price, which had been dropped to an experimental 95 cents in September 1975, continued to rise, back through $1 in May 1976 to $1.25 in June 1977. Readers were increasingly complaining that they could not find the magazine and that the subscription service was unreliable. Against this, Baen was struggling to provide top-quality work but was unable to make prompt payment to authors. Some had to wait as long as a year after publication before payment came through. There was only so much one

113 Also known as 'At the Eschaton', this story was expanded into the novel *Tomorrow and Tomorrow* (1997).

114 Personal letter, Baen/Ashley, 20 December 1977.

115 Personal letter, Abramson/Ashley, 1 February 1978.

could take. In August 1977 Baen accepted an offer from Tom Doherty to become a senior editor at the newly revamped Ace Books. His last official issue of *Galaxy* was for October 1977, though his inventory of stories continued to appear for a while.

At the same time that Baen left, Abramson felt that they were getting on top of the problem. He advised *Locus* of the position: 'At the end of our fiscal year, March 31, 1975, we owed sf writers and artists in excess of $40,000. As of now [November 1977], and including all material in the November issue, our indebtedness is less than $8,000.'[116]

To pay these debts Universal had needed to sell the family silver. Their only other major magazine, *Family Handyman*, was sold at the end of 1976. They closed down their New York offices and relocated to Abramson's home at Westchester.

Baen had really been *Galaxy*'s last hope. His departure left the magazine in amateur hands and though it would struggle on for another two years (though only another 12 issues), it looked throughout like a wounded animal waiting to die. I shall return to its fate later.

Sex and Drugs and Rock 'n' Roll

The oldest surviving sf magazine was *Amazing Stories*. It had appeared on the stands during March 1926 (cover date April), almost four years before *Astounding Stories of Super Science* – the magazine later to become *Analog* – embraced sf into the pulp field. In its first few years, *Astounding* had debased the field, but it then rapidly recovered and, under editor John W. Campbell, had created the world of 'modern' sf of the forties and fifties. *Amazing* had gone the other way, sinking into a morass of juvenile space antics and the Shaver Mystery under Raymond Palmer in the forties and churning out masses of formulaic fodder in the fifties. There was a brief period around 1953–54 when *Amazing* turned its back on the pulps, but it was not until the early sixties, under the guiding hand of Cele Goldsmith Lalli, that *Amazing* at last became respectable. During a nova-like flash of wonder, Lalli discovered and developed writers Roger Zelazny, Ursula K. Le Guin, Thomas M. Disch, Piers Anthony and others.

But that recovery was short-lived. *Amazing*, and its companion *Fantastic*, were sold in 1965 to the Ultimate Publishing Company run by Sol Cohen. Cohen used Ziff-Davis's vast archive, and the fact that the company had acquired second serial rights from authors, to reprint fiction without further payment. This practice saved him around $8000 a year on fees.

---

116 Letter, Arnold E. Abramson, *Locus* #207, December 1977, p. 12.

Cohen's first editor, Joseph Wrzos (who used the name Joe Ross), insisted that both *Amazing* and *Fantastic* run some new fiction, but this was usually limited to one story or serial episode per issue. Wrzos carefully selected some of the best of the older fiction from *Amazing*'s early days, and all might have been satisfactory had Cohen not compounded the problem by starting several new magazines consisting entirely of reprints. Two of these, *Great Science Fiction* and *The Most Thrilling Science Fiction Ever Told*, reprinted more recent stories, and this annoyed currently active writers who felt they should have received at least a token payment. Cohen was quite within his rights, because it had been standard practice amongst all publishers to acquire second serial rights – in fact sometimes all rights. Prior to the 1950s, little science fiction from the pulps was reprinted, so authors did not expect any subsidiary payments. They sold a story, and that was that. But from the fifties on, there was a greater likelihood of book or anthology rights being taken up in the booming pocketbook field and so writers paid more attention to what rights they sold.

Cohen fell foul of the newly formed Science Fiction Writers of America (SFWA), who demanded that Cohen make payments for reprints. Cohen refused and the SFWA boycotted the magazines. The SFWA advised its members not to submit work to the magazines and discounted any sales there as counting towards membership of the SFWA amongst new writers. This controversy left a cloud over the magazines that never really lifted, and negotiations dragged on until 1973. Eventually Cohen agreed to make flat-fee token payments, but these were always minor. The SFWA did not want to push Cohen too far for fear of losing another market, no matter how small. Cohen's argument was that the reprint titles were selling well and therefore subsidizing *Amazing* and *Fantastic*. It was an unsatisfactory resolution, but it held.

It made it difficult to work for Cohen. There was a rapid change-over of editors: Wrzos passed the baton to Harry Harrison, who soon passed it to Barry Malzberg, who even more rapidly passed it to Ted White. White took over in October 1968 but, because both magazines were bi-monthly and because Malzberg had acquired material some months ahead, the first issues to which White could put his name were the May 1969 *Amazing* and the June 1969 *Fantastic*. White had accepted on condition that he be allowed to phase out the reprints. There was a short-term compromise whereby he reduced them to one per issue and it was not until the March 1972 issue that he was able to drop them completely. In the meantime, Cohen syphoned the reprints into a rash of reprint magazines. In addition to *Great SF* (which became *Science Fiction Greats*) and *The Most Thrilling SF Ever Told* (which became *Thrilling SF Adventures*), there were *Science Fiction*

Classics, Space Adventures, Strange Fantasy, Science Fantasy, Weird Mystery and others which flourished during 1969 to 1972. These weren't all bad. There was some good material in the archives – though there was a lot that was awful, and Cohen was not discriminating. And these magazines sold almost as well as the two parent magazines, and on a negligible budget. So *Amazing* and *Fantastic* survived, despite steadily dwindling sales, because of the reprints.

White had nothing to do with the reprint titles. These were assembled solely by Cohen, initially with the help of local fans Herb Lehrman and Arnie Katz who selected suitable fiction, but later Cohen did this all himself. White concentrated on the two leading magazines and did all that he could to change their image and make them into the most exciting magazines his limited budget could afford. He had one key attribute that his predecessors lacked. White was at heart a science-fiction fan – an active one, meaning one who is involved in fan activities, namely writing for fanzines, producing fanzines and attending conventions. You would have to go back 30 years to Raymond Palmer to find the last editor of *Amazing* who was (or had been) an active fan. None of White's fellow editors – Bova, Jakobsson, Ferman – were or had been active fans either, though they would attend conventions in a professional capacity.

White had been born in February 1938, a few months before Palmer took over at *Amazing*, and had been raised on a diet of Palmer's magazines, especially his later title *Other Worlds*. White liked Palmer's personal style. He projected himself from his magazines, which reflected his showman personality. Palmer had included 'The Club House' in his magazines, a column run by Rog Phillips, which reviewed fanzines and fan organizations. It was through this that White became involved in fandom, starting his own fanzine *Zip* in 1953 and soon after running the Washington Science Fiction Association. He later merged forces with Greg Benford who, since 1954, had been producing his own fanzine called *Void* with his twin brother Jim. White was co-editor of this from 1958 to 1962.[117] White's main involvement in fandom, apart from being good at organizing people, was as an artist rather than a writer and he became noted for the layout of his fanzines. He did not start writing seriously until 1959 when he became a contributing editor of the jazz magazine *Metronome*.[118] He sold his first short stories (both in collaboration) to *Amazing* and *If* on the same day in 1962, and they both appeared in print on the same day in January

117 A further issue which had been half started was finished and released in 1969.
118 White is as passionate about jazz and rock music as he is about science fiction and fantasy. He was involved in helping to produce the early issues of the rock magazine *Crawdaddy* in 1966.

1963 – 'Phoenix' with Marion Zimmer Bradley (*Amazing*, February 1963) and 'I, Executioner' with Terry Carr (*If*, March 1963). His first book (also with Terry Carr), *Invasion from 2500*, appeared in 1964. He was assistant (later associate) editor of *F&SF* from the November 1963 issue to May 1968. He also served a term as associate editor at Lancer Books, under Larry Shaw. In 1967 he had tried to launch his own magazine, *Stellar*, and got as far as acquiring stories and putting a dummy issue together, but the financial burden proved too heavy. Some of the stories he selected later surfaced in *Amazing* and *Fantastic*. He continued his fan activities and was co-chairman of the 1967 World Science Fiction Convention in New York. At the 1968 World Convention he won the Hugo Award for Best Fan Writer.

Being an active fan is both a help and a deterrent in editing a professional magazine. One benefit is that you have a network of contacts who may be only too willing to help. You also know what fans like and what they look for in a magazine – and with some twenty years of reading and experience behind him White knew exactly what he wanted. One problem, though, is not to pander too closely to fans. There is a danger of making the magazine look like an exclusive club with its own jargon and close-knit concerns. But if you don't appeal to the fans, both in the choice of fiction and in the overall character of the magazine, you will probably fail to appeal to the wider world.

This matter of White's approach to the magazine was important. At the time that White took over, *Amazing*'s circulation was around 38,500, that of *Fantastic* around 37,000. Most of that was news-stand sales. Only 4 per cent of *Amazing*'s circulation was by subscription, compared to nearly 10 per cent at *Galaxy* and around 35 per cent at *Analog* and *F&SF*. If White could develop his subscription base and encourage fans to promote the magazines, it would make a considerable difference to sales. However, according to White, Sol Cohen regarded subscription-fulfilment as a burden, since his wife handled it out of their garage in Queens, and never sought subscribers.[119]

White addressed this problem in one of his early editorials:

> The magazines – *all* sf magazines – have been going through a slow but inexorable decline in sales. There was a time when *Amazing Stories* sold around 150,000 copies of an issue. The day is apparently gone when we can sell *one third* as many copies.
>
> A lot of reasons have been advanced to explain this decline in sales. The most obvious – but also most superficial – is that the day of the sf magazine is done, that today's sf magazines are anachronisms which

---

119 Personal e-mail, White/Ashley, 27 August 2006.

have outlived their usefulness. I'm not convinced of that. It may be true, but I don't believe it yet. I will believe it if, when I have put out the best possible magazine I can put out, the sales show no change. Then I will concede defeat. But not yet. Not now.[120]

He exhorted his readers to continue buying the magazine, to check newsstands to make sure that the magazine was properly displayed and, if it was not there, to ask why, and to provide feedback to the publisher. White was using the fan base to support and promote the magazine.[121] He ran all of the features one expects in a good magazine over and above the fiction. He brought back a lively letter column, plus the return of the fan column, 'The Club House', run initially by John Berry and later by Susan Wood. There was a wide range of perceptive book reviews. White's editorials were always informative, if at times self-indulgent, and there were always interesting articles on subjects relevant to sf, such as Gregory Benford's series 'The Science in Science Fiction'.

White also had a wide interest in comic fandom, something that, as an organized force, was still in its infancy in the sixties. But White was aware of the new generation of comic-book artists whose talents were generally ignored by the sf magazine field. He wanted to attract many of these artists – Vaughn Bodé, Jeff Jones, Steve Hickman – and perhaps in the process develop a cross-over market with the comic-book field. However, as with the fiction, at the outset White was saddled with having to use cover paintings purchased cheaply from European magazines. He made the best of the situation by commissioning authors to write stories based on the cover – his first being Gregory Benford with 'Sons of Man' (*Amazing*, November 1969), a story linking the fabled Bigfoot with the discovery of a wrecked spacecraft on the Moon.

Eventually Cohen relented and White was able to use original covers. White was the first to publish work by New-Zealand-born artist, Mike Hinge, whose bold, exaggerated style, often in vibrant colours, had not been to everyone's taste. White had hoped that Mike would become art director but at the last minute plans fell through. In the end White remained his own art director, usually under the alias J. Edwards, spending many hours not only commissioning and selecting the artwork but also pasting up the magazine's covers. He ran covers by many of the comic-book artists, including Jeff Jones, Dan Adkins and John Pederson, and the first professional work by Mike Kaluta.

---

120 Ted White, 'Editorial', *Amazing Stories*, 43:4 (November 1969), pp. 142–3.
121 White estimated that active sf fandom probably represented around one-thirtieth of *Amazing*'s circulation, which would be around 1,250 people: see *Amazing Stories*, 43:4 (November 1969), p. 126.

Right from the start White insisted upon making a visual impact with a new layout and new typography (though he had to make several changes before he was satisfied). The use of a smaller typeface allowed the magazine to contain at least seventy thousand words of new material – the equivalent of any other sf magazine – in addition to the reprints. To help pay for this the cover price was raised to 60 cents. Both *Galaxy* and *Analog* were already 60 cents but they had more pages. However, once *F&SF*, which had only 128 pages, raised its price in July 1969, it was easier to do the same at *Amazing* and *Fantastic*, which had 144 pages. Unfortunately, as White later reported, the price increase had a detrimental effect on both magazines, but especially *Fantastic*, where sales of the December 1969 issue (the first at 60 cents) fell by 10,000. It wiped out any benefit from the increased price.[122] The 60-cent cover price remained for over four years, but after a year the page count dropped from 144 to 128.

From the September 1970 *Amazing*, White also revamped the magazine logo on the cover to give it a more modern look, presenting all the lettering in lower case, and he also revised the magazine's name to *Amazing Science Fiction Stories*, trying to separate it, albeit slightly, from its past connotations. It became *Amazing Science Fiction* from March 1972. White would probably have preferred to change the title even more radically. He had wanted to change the name of *Fantastic*, considering reverting to *Fantastic Adventures*. Readers advised against that, suggesting *Fantastic Stories* or *Fantastic Visions*. White settled on *Fantastic Stories*, which was how the name was already presented on the cover and masthead, even though the official title remained *Fantastic*. From the August 1971 issue, *Amazing* was given a thicker, card-like cover, rather than paper. Together with the vivid day-glow colours of Mike Hinge's artwork, the magazine looked far more modern and sophisticated.[123] Hinge's work was at last appreciated. In 1973 he was nominated for the Hugo as Best Artist, losing out to Kelly Freas.

White was no fan of the experimental New Wave but he was all for more daring fiction exploring adult themes and saw no reason why these stories could not co-exist alongside more traditional stories. By running both forms in *Amazing*, he hoped he could make the old and the new influence each other. This had been evident in White's own fiction. His early novels, such as *Phoenix Prime* (1966) and *The Sorceress of Qar* (1966), showed the pulp influences of Edgar Rice Burroughs and Leigh Brackett, and his Captain America novel *The Great Gold Steal* (1968), showed his

122 See 'Editorial', *Fantastic* 20:1 (October 1970), p. 5.
123 Ironically, Hinge's style had not been adapted for the 1970s. He had submitted one of these covers to *Amazing* in the early 1960s but it had been rejected.

fascination for the comic field. But some of his later fiction in *Amazing*, especially stories like 'Growing up Fast in the City' (May 1971), with its bleak view of urban society and the growing drug culture, used techniques also used by the New Wave writers. White's tastes, therefore, were not restricted to any one school of fiction, allowing *Amazing* and *Fantastic* to appeal to a wide spectrum of readers.

This was evident in his early issues. The May 1969 *Amazing* featured the latest Star Kings novelette by Edmond Hamilton, 'The Horror from the Magellanic'. This series, where the twentieth-century John Gordon swaps bodies with a man from two hundred millennia in the future, had started with 'The Star Kings' in *Amazing* back in September 1947. While Hamilton was now writing better than ever, the story and characterization were unadulterated pulp adventure. In the next issue, White began the serialization of Robert Silverberg's new novel 'Up the Line' (July–September 1969), a complex time-travel adventure with elements of new-age libertarianism, sexual freedom and even transtemporal incest.

Although the Swinging Sixties were at an end and flower power was fading fast, the influence of psychedelia had left its mark on White, and infiltrated his magazines. Jakobsson had tried a similar approach at *Galaxy*, but there it looked out of place. With White it seemed more natural. Of some significance was Philip K. Dick's serial, 'A. Lincoln, Simulacrum' (*Amazing*, November 1969–January 1970), better known by its book title *We Can Build You* (1972). Though it is not usually ranked amongst Dick's most notable works, it is important in understanding his fears about the nature of reality. It includes a memorable discussion between an android reconstruct of Abraham Lincoln and a greedy entrepreneur on what it is to be human. Throughout the novel it becomes apparent that the android has a greater awareness of reality than the humans. In fact, the humans seek to escape reality by experiencing fugues created via hallucinogenic drugs. The novel had been written in 1962 and Dick had hoped it would help him break out of science fiction into the mainstream, but it was rejected. It was not until 1969 that the novel appeared in *Amazing* with a new final, explanatory chapter added by White (which is deleted from the book version). Here, then, is a novel written for a wider audience but dealing with the very things that fascinated the counter-culture of the late sixties: sex, drugs and the nature of reality. At that time, Dick was developing a following amongst the counter-culture, members of which had been attracted by his enigmatic classic, *The Three Stigmata of Palmer Eldritch* (1965).

Though White was not going out of his way to pander to the drug culture, he could relate to it. This was evident from an article, 'Science

Fiction and Drugs', that White wrote pseudonymously in the June 1970 *Fantastic*. He believed we were entering the 'psychedelic seventies' in which alcohol would be out and drugs would be in. White didn't overtly promote the free use of drugs, but he evidently favoured drugs over alcohol and suggested that science fiction needed to consider how the possible legalization of some drugs might affect the future. White was open to a greater liberalization of science fiction, in line with what was happening to youth nationwide. He saw science fiction as a vehicle to push back the barriers of the 'establishment', with no suppression of soft drugs, 'healthy sex', or free expression. Both *Amazing* and *Fantastic* were becoming 'hippie' sf magazines.

In this respect, Philip K. Dick was the ideal writer for *Amazing*. As Pournelle was to *Analog* and Sturgeon to *Galaxy*, so Dick should have been to *Amazing*. Alas, Dick contributed no more to either *Amazing* or *Fantastic*. In fact, he had nothing else of any substance in any sf magazine, but *Amazing* became the closest to a Phildickian magazine that there was. Some of this may be seen in the work of Ursula K. Le Guin. Her straightforward drug-image story, 'The Good Trip', appeared in *Fantastic* (August 1970), and *Amazing* serialized her novel of dream worlds, 'The Lathe of Heaven' (March–May 1971). This story, about a patient whose dreams can alter reality, reads like a tribute to Dick. Robert Silverberg's 'The Second Trip' (July–September 1971) is also in the vein of Philip K. Dick, raising the question of the nature of identity. In the future, criminals have their personalities erased and replaced by new ones, but in the case of one criminal, a former artist, his old personality fights back.

Le Guin's 'The Lathe of Heaven' had the following effect on one writer: 'But after first plowing into the first pulpy pages of the 1971 *Amazing* in which *Lathe* came out, my toe-nails began to curl under and my spine hair stood up.'[124] That was James Tiptree, Jr., who owed her first sale to *Fantastic*,[125] when it was edited by Harry Harrison. Tiptree was another writer in the Dick/Le Guin vein, though with a renegade mischievousness. White was able to acquire four stories from Tiptree, the first two of which had been rejected by other markets. 'I'm Too Big But I Love to Play' (*Amazing*, March 1970) is almost a parody of Dick, featuring a high-energy alien struggling to create a human persona. 'The Peacefulness of Vivyan' (*Amazing*, July 1971) could almost be her homage to Le Guin, as it shares some similar images to the start of 'The Lathe of Heaven'. The two

124 James Tiptree, Jr., in *Universe SF Review*, September/October 1975, reprinted in *Meet Me at Infinity* (2000), p. 290.
125 'Fault', *Fantastic*, August 1968. According to Julie Phillips in *James Tiptree, Jr. The Double Life of Alice Sheldon* (2006), letters of acceptance for 'Fault' and 'Birth of a Salesman' (from *Analog*) arrived on the same day in October 1967 (p. 215).

best contributions, 'The Man Who Walked Home' (*Amazing*, May 1972) and 'Forever to a Hudson Bay Blanket' (*Fantastic*, August 1972), were also first submissions to Ted White, or so he believed. Both are concerned with time travel but while the latter is humorous, the former is a sombre, haunting tale of the consequences of experimentation. It ranks alongside her very best stories.

While White did what he could to attract good fiction and new writers, *Amazing* had been in a wilderness for the previous five years. Most of the major writers were deterred from contributing because of the SFWA boycott, but also because the payment rates were so low. White was only able to pay one cent a word – the same rate the pulps had paid in the thirties – whereas *Galaxy* and *F&SF* were paying three cents and *Analog* was paying five cents. This meant that, unless he was proactive, White would only ever see the rejects from the other magazines. However, he knew he might have a chance at some of the best experimental fiction, which had no ready market elsewhere, and thereby attract writers who did not otherwise click with the establishment. One such was Piers Anthony.

Anthony had yet to write his best-selling Xanth series or to develop his present image as a writer of formulaic juvenile entertainment. At the end of the sixties he was regarded as one of the more original and challenging writers in the field, based on such novels as *Chthon* and *Macroscope*. At this early stage in his career he was having problems finding a regular market. Typical was the plight of his novel 'Hasan', a fantasy modelled on an episode in *The Arabian Nights*, which had received a dozen rejections from publishers. Anthony sent the manuscript to Richard Delap, who reviewed it in *Science Fiction Review*. Ted White saw the review, asked to see the novel and within three weeks had bought it for *Fantastic*, where it was serialized from the December 1969 issue. This was one example where White's links to the fan press and his proactivity reaped dividends. Piers Anthony was also pleased with the outcome. Anthony, who seldom has a good word to say about editors, remarked, 'Though I have my differences with Ted White, I regard him as a better writer than credited, and an excellent editor.'[126]

White also published Anthony's next novel, *Orn*. This was the sequel to *Omnivore* and ought to have been taken up by the same publisher, Ballantine Books, but Anthony was having contractual problems with them and the novel languished. White ran it in *Amazing* (July–September 1970). The novel (which originally had a different title) was subsequently published by Avon Books. Interestingly, both Ted White and George Ernsberger of Avon had suggested revisions to the novel but Ernsberger agreed to wait

126 Piers Anthony, *Bio of an Ogre* (New York: Ace Books, 1988), p. 195.

and see the changes that Anthony made in response to White's requests, in case he chose to publish that version. It was clear that White's editorial acumen was respected and it was White's version, using White's title, that Ernsberger used. These sales helped Anthony through a difficult period.

Other writers who refused to be categorized and who seemed at home in Ted White's world began to appear in the magazine. These included David R. Bunch, Avram Davidson, Philip José Farmer, R. A. Lafferty, Richard A. Lupoff, Barry N. Malzberg, Alexei Panshin and Christopher Priest. Farmer sent White a story, 'The Oogenesis of Bird City' (*Amazing*, September 1970), which had been a self-contained section in the original version of Farmer's 'Riders of the Purple Wage' but which was deleted prior to its appearance in *Dangerous Visions*. Richard Lupoff had also contributed one of the landmark stories to Ellison's *Again, Dangerous Visions*, 'With the Bentfin Boomer Boys on Little Old New Alabama', and White would eventually publish the sequel to that story, 'The Bentfin Boomer Girl Comes Thru' (*Amazing*, March 1977). These, and other connections, make White's *Amazing* something of a spiritual kin to *Dangerous Visions*.

Perhaps the most notorious amongst the renegades was its former editor Barry Malzberg. Malzberg's short fiction was unique in the sf magazines, often little more than streams of consciousness, or momentary reflections, or simply episodes. Malzberg wrote as much, if not more, for the mood and atmosphere as for the telling of a story. If Malzberg could make readers think differently, he was content. Such was his eulogy, 'A Soul Song to the Sad, Silly, Soaring Sixties' (*Fantastic*, February 1971).

No other editor gave writers this kind of opportunity on such a scale. The closest was Ejler Jakobsson at *Galaxy* and *If*, and because of the greater prominence of those titles they are usually regarded as the more experimental magazines of the period. But, as we have seen, Jakobsson's experiments were short-lived during 1970 and he was soon brought back into line by his publisher. Despite what one might say about Sol Cohen, he was accommodating of White's radicalism, provided it delivered the goods.

White tried various experiments, not just with the fiction. He had originally negotiated with Vaughn Bodé for a comic strip, but Bodé, against his better judgment, entered into an agreement with *Galaxy*. White was still keen to have a comic strip and commissioned the young artist Jay Kinney to produce what became '2000 AD Man', a four-page satirical strip of a man from the year 2000 reflecting over past events, such as the assassination of President Nixon and the presidency of Spiro Agnew. After some delays, it appeared in the December 1970 *Fantastic*. White had intended that 'Fantastic Illustrated' become a regular feature, and had a second strip lined up by Art Spiegelman, but no more appeared. There was friction between the readers of sf magazines and those of the comics, and the sf field had yet to embrace the underground comics field. Also, Cohen was of the view that comics and fiction did not mix and instructed White to drop it. Soon after, White's flexibility was reduced when *Fantastic*'s page count was reduced. White was ahead of his time and would eventually be able to indulge his interests when he became editor of *Heavy Metal*.

While White was publishing experimental work from more challenging writers, he was also nurturing new talent and welcoming back into the fold some of the older writers. One of the first newcomers was Gordon Eklund. He appeared with 'Dear Aunt Annie' in the April 1970 *Fantastic*, which was nominated for a Nebula Award as one of that year's best novelettes. Eklund became one of the more creative new writers of the seventies, presenting a fresh face on old themes. After his first year Eklund wanted to write full-time but was wary of the financial risk. White made a special deal with him:

> I told him that I would guarantee to buy, sight-unseen, *any* story he couldn't sell to a higher market – provided he himself honestly thought it was a good story. I would be his guarantor that he wasn't wasting his time writing stories that might not sell. It was, as far as I know, a unique deal, and it enabled Gordon to write full-time and to sell widely. I was his safety net.[127]

White was able to publish some of Eklund's more thought-provoking works, including 'Beyond the Resurrection' (*Fantastic*, April–June 1972), 'The Ascending Aye' (*Amazing*, January 1973), 'Moby, Too' (*Amazing*, December 1973) and 'Locust Descending' (*Fantastic*, February 1976).

White also published the second story by British writer Ian McEwan, 'Solid Geometry' (*Fantastic*, February 1975), a macabre tale of a young man who becomes fascinated by shapes and singular dimensions. Apart from the erotic element, it is actually a fairly old-fashioned story, but it has since been filmed and McEwan has become a respected writer in British literary circles. He won the Somerset Maugham Award in 1976 for his first story collection, *First Love, Last Rites*, which included 'Solid Geometry'.

Other new writers whom White encouraged include Gerard F. Conway ('Through the Dark Glass', *Amazing*, November 1970), George Alec Effinger ('The Eight-Thirty to Nine Slot', *Fantastic*, April 1971), Grant Carrington ('Night-Eyed Prayer', *Amazing*, May 1971), F. M. Busby (who sold his first story in 1957 and waited 15 years before selling his second,

---

127 Personal e-mail White/Ashley, 27 May 2006.

'Of Mice and Otis', *Amazing*, March 1972), Thomas Monteleone ('Agony in the Garden', *Amazing*, March 1973), John Shirley ('Silent Crickets', *Fantastic*, April 1975) and Keith Taylor, whose 'Fugitives in Winter' (*Fantastic*, October 1975, under the alias Denis More) was the first in his historical fantasy series about the Celtic bard Felimid. All of their work was challenging, often daring, seldom traditional and often bleak. They echo the angst of those years when traditional hopes and values had been called seriously into question.

White published two stories by long-time sf fan Roger Ebert who had already established himself as a major film critic. He had also written the screenplay for Russ Meyer's *Beyond the Valley of the Dolls* (1970). Both are rather macabre tales, 'After the Last Mass' (*Fantastic*, February 1972) and 'In Dying Venice' (*Amazing*, May 1972), the latter reflecting changes in the film industry.

White gave over the December 1971 *Fantastic* to stories arising from the Guilford Writers' Conference, held in Baltimore by Joe Haldeman's brother Jack (usually called Jay) and Jack's wife Alice. The stories are good examples of the blend of traditional and New Wave fiction that White was publishing. They ranged from White's own violent and bleak view of future society, 'Things Are Tough All Over', Effinger's spoof on the superhero character 'The Awesome Menace of the Polarizer', Jack Dann's sharp vignette 'Cartoon', Gardner Dozois's war paranoia tale 'Wires', and Jack Haldeman's tale of revolution 'Garden of Eden'.

White did not ignore the older generation of writers. He published new work by Raymond Z. Gallun, Ross Rocklynne and Frank Belknap Long, as well as by others who had not written much sf recently, such as Wilmar Shiras, Noel Loomis and Gardner F. Fox. Alongside these he used some of the best work by leading writers, including Bob Shaw, John Brunner, Brian Aldiss, Fritz Leiber, L. Sprague de Camp, Poul Anderson, Robert Silverberg, William F. Nolan and Jack Vance. These latter writers were represented strongly amongst the serials, and one of the strengths of *Amazing* and *Fantastic* was their powerful novels. However, because both magazines were bi-monthly, White usually ran serials in two episodes, rather than three, and that meant that the serial often filled over half the magazine. As a consequence, he was limited in his use of novellas or novelettes, which is why the novels were complemented by a number of often very short stories. This could sometimes lead to a lack of balance in an issue, so increasingly – and certainly once the magazines' frequency began to slip – White switched to using longer works complete in one issue.

Although readers would look to *Analog* and *Galaxy* for the more mature, reasoned and traditional sf tales, and to *F&SF* for more literary tastes, one could not deny an excitement about *Amazing* and *Fantastic*, where the experimental fiction and sheer audacity of some stories made you feel you were at the cutting edge of new fiction. Far more than the other magazines, *Amazing* was the link between the New Wave of the sixties and the cyberpunk revolution of the eighties.

Fantastic was at the forefront of the growth of interest in fantasy fiction, and though it never seemed to reap the benefits in terms of increased sales, it was important as a vehicle for developing the field. It published, for instance, a rare sword-and-sorcery novella by Dean R. Koontz, 'The Crimson Witch' (October 1970), it ran a new Elric story by Michael Moorcock, 'The Sleeping Sorceress' (February 1972) and one of the finest, yet overlooked, fantasy novels of the seventies, 'The Son of Black Morca' by Alexei and Cory Panshin (April–September 1973).[128] It ran stories about the witch Arcana by Janet Fox, starting with 'A Witch in Time' (September 1973), as well as one of the last historical fantasies by Thomas Burnett Swann, 'Will-o-the-Wisp' (September–November 1974). *Fantastic* also ran a series of relentless parodies of various forms of fantasy fiction written by Richard Lupoff under the alias Ova Hamlet. These included such revelations as 'War of the Doom Zombies' (June 1971) and 'The Horror South of Red Hook' (February 1972), lampooning in turn Robert E. Howard and H. P. Lovecraft.

The presence of L. Sprague de Camp was both noticeable and important in *Fantastic*. He had a wonderfully nostalgic fantasy in the *Unknown* tradition, 'The Fallible Fiend' (December 1972–February 1973). He also contributed a series of articles about pioneers of classic fantasy, 'Literary Swordsmen and Sorcerers' (began June 1971), including Robert E. Howard, L. Ron Hubbard, H. P. Lovecraft, Lord Dunsany, E. R. Eddison, J. R. R. Tolkien and William Morris. But most important of all were the new Conan stories contributed by de Camp with Lin Carter. The first, 'The Witch in the Mists', ran in the August 1972 issue, and White later reported that sales of that issue exceeded not only all the other issues of *Fantastic* that year, but all the issues of *Amazing* as well.[129] White could rely on any Conan issue selling an extra 10,000 copies. After this success *Fantastic* ran far more sword-and-sorcery stories, including Lin Carter's Thongor stories and Fritz Leiber's Grey Mouser tales. The subtitle of *Fantastic* was amended to read 'sword & sorcery and fantasy' from April 1975 and Sol Cohen issued one further one-off reprint title, *Sword & Sorcery Annual*, in the spring of 1975.

128 Published in book form as *Earth Magic* (New York: Ace Books, 1978).
129 See White's editorial in *Fantastic* 22:5 (July 1973), p. 116, with additional data provided by personal e-mail, White/Ashley, 26 May 2006.

Although *Amazing* ran the whole range of science fiction, it was most typified by its stories dealing with the social or psychological stresses of the future. In Bob Shaw's 'One Million Tomorrows' (November 1970–January 1971), humans have become immortal but also sterile. In 'The Stone That Never Came Down' (October–December 1973), John Brunner explores the implications of a drug that enhances human empathy in a world on the brink of breakdown. In 'To Walk With Thunder' (August 1973) – a complete short novel that came to White because it was too long for *Analog* – Dean McLaughlin considers how pollution control might itself be used as a weapon against a wayward population.

There were many stories emphasizing future sex in all its forms, far more than in any of the other sf magazines. White led the way with his own 'Growing Up Fast in the City' (*Amazing*, May 1971), which had been written for Ellison's *Dangerous Visions*. It considers the lives of students in the near future, with doses of casual sex. The story brought a hostile response from some readers who regarded it as pornographic. It was nothing compared to what lay ahead. Some of Barry Malzberg's stories seemed to have no motive other than to shock. 'On Ice' (*Amazing*, January 1973) involves a drug-induced frenzy leading to a climax of buggery and possession. 'Upping the Planet' (*Amazing*, April 1974) concerns a man having to masturbate every hour for 24 hours in order to save the planet from an alien invasion.

Probably the two most controversial stories, though, were 'The Kozmic Kid' (*Fantastic*, July 1974) by Richard Snead and 'Two of a Kind' (*Amazing*, March 1977) by Rich Brown. Snead's novella, set against the background of seventies drug culture, uses the pinball machine as a metaphor for exploring reality. Some read the story as an extended drug trip but most appreciated its originality (despite some similarity to the rock opera *Tommy*) and its daring concept. This was Snead's first and only known story.

Rich Brown's story, though, was by far the most controversial and still starts arguments today. It was inspired by White's story 'Things Are Tough All Over' from the special Guilford Conference issue, but Brown took the story to extremes. Set in an anarchic future where government agents hunt blacks for meat and sport, the greater part of the story is taken up by the graphic rape of a black woman and the slaughter of her rapists. Apart from the futuristic setting and some minor sf trappings such as laser guns, the story could as easily have been set in the present day and reads as little more than an excuse for sex and violence.

So far as White knew, none of these controversial stories affected sales one way or the other. There were as many letters supportive of 'Two of a Kind' as those objecting to it. Clearly readers had come to expect that there would be nothing bland in White's magazines and that each issue would contain something memorable.

Controversy aside, White published much respectable science fiction and fantasy. This included 'Junction' by Jack Dann (*Fantastic*, November 1973), about a small Midwestern town separated from causality and surrounded by chaos. Dann was for a long time unsatisfied with various drafts of this story and continued to work at it for some years. A later expansion, 'Islands of Time', appeared in the September 1977 *Fantastic* and the two parts were later united with other text as the final book-length version, published in 1981. White also serialized, as two novellas, Dann's novel 'Starhiker' (*Amazing*, June–September 1976), a mind-expanding voyage of discovery into a completely alien civilization. Dann's erstwhile collaborator, George Zebrowski, had only one appearance in White's *Amazing*, 'The Cliometricon' (May 1975), a fascinating study of a machine that observes alternate histories. He would return to *Amazing* in later years with two sequels to the story. Zebrowski's partner, Pamela Sargent, also had only one sale to White, but that was 'Father' (*Amazing*, February 1974), which was later reworked as the opening for her novel *Cloned Lives* (1976). It follows the emotions and anguish that a scientist suffers when he agrees to be cloned, and watches what are effectively his alternate lives.

Other powerful stories included 'His Hour Upon the Stage' (*Amazing*, March 1976), a telling story by Grant Carrington about the last live actors, and 'Tin Woodman' (*Amazing*, December 1976), a delightful first-contact story by Dennis Bailey and Dave Bischoff. Both stories were finalists for the Nebula Award. Parke Godwin sold White two beautiful Celtic fanta-sies, 'The Lady of Finnegan's Hearth' (*Fantastic*, September 1977) and 'The Last Rainbow' (*Fantastic*, July 1978). Starting with 'The Incredible Umbrella' (*Fantastic*, February 1976), Godwin's occasional collaborator, Marvin Kaye, delighted readers with a series of humorous fantasies in the *Unknown* style, about a professor whose umbrella transports him to various worlds of fiction.

Despite the unforgiving conditions under which White had to work, he produced two remarkable magazines. His achievements were not ignored by the fans. *Amazing* was nominated three times for the Hugo Award (1970, 1971 and 1972), each time coming in third behind *F&SF* and *Analog*. When that category was superseded by Best Professional Editor, White was nominated every year from 1973 to 1977, though he never finished higher than third.

Yet this recognition was not reflected in sales. Despite all he did to make

Amazing and *Fantastic* amongst the most exciting and arguably the most challenging magazines of the early seventies, circulation continued to fall. *Amazing*'s sales had been around 38,500 when White took over in October 1968. By October 1975 they were down to under 23,000, a fall of over 40 per cent. The equivalent figures for *Fantastic* were similar, from 36,900 down to 22,500. White had made some progress in raising the number of subscribers, particularly to *Fantastic*, but it was far from enough.

At this time rumours abounded that Cohen was looking to sell the magazines. Several potential buyers showed signs of interest, though no serious negotiations ensued. One interested party was Roger Elwood, who had thought of running the magazine as *Roger Elwood's Amazing Stories*, but that came to naught. I shall discuss Elwood in far more detail in the next chapter. Edward Ferman also spoke once to Cohen about the possibility of buying the magazines and combining them as a companion to *F&SF*, but nothing came of it. There were other rumours, most extremely vague,[130] but in the end Cohen decided to keep the titles.

White knew nothing of this at the time, and it probably would not have helped his confidence if he had. The lack of progress was soul-destroying, especially as the work on the magazines consumed so much of White's time and creative energy that he had little left for writing. Payment for his services – and he was not just the editor but also the art director, which included cutting and pasting each issue – was minimal (a 'pittance' he called it), and certainly not a living wage, so he needed to write to earn a living. He had some assistance in reading the slush-pile submissions and the proofs, mostly unpaid, from a number of friends, variously Arnie Katz, Alan Shaw, Grant Carrington and Moshe Feder. In October 1974 White introduced a controversial scheme whereby unsolicited submissions from writers with no previous sales had to be accompanied by a 25-cent reading fee, which would be refunded if the story were accepted. This fee went to the first readers, Grant Carrington and Rick Snead, who should have been paid by the publisher. It was an unpopular move since it hit the very writers White was seeking to encourage. It was a sign of desperation.

Because of his workload, White occasionally made mistakes and was often apologizing in the magazines. Add to this frequent problems with the printers, and papers being lost in the post,[131] and what ought to have been a pleasure was becoming an ordeal. White occasionally vented

130 See 'Rumor Department', *Locus* #151 (1 December 1973), p. 1. Ferman confirmed in a personal e-mail to me that he had approached Cohen, and White himself confirmed the Elwood rumour.

131 White did all his editorial tasks at his home in Falls Church, Virginia, while Cohen's offices were in Flushing, New York.

his views in his editorials, and in so doing sometimes clashed with his publisher. Although Sol Cohen was the active partner in the Ultimate Publishing Company, a 50 per cent share was owned by Arthur Bernhard, who did not always like the political views expressed by White.

But it was Cohen who vetoed White's editorial for the March 1975 *Amazing*. White later admitted this was not surprising because the editorial was an attack on Cohen's own publishing policy. White yearned to be able to edit a magazine that had some financial backing by a publisher with a vision. He wanted to produce a full-size slick magazine and put forward his proposals. Cohen rejected them and this time it was the last straw. White resigned. He explained his reasons in an article in *Science Fiction Review*:

> I am tired of editing two magazines which limp from month to month on the inadequate budget and over-extended energies of a very few people. I have edited *Amazing* and *Fantastic* for more than six years ... and my energies are depleted. I am paid a literal pittance to get these magazines out, I am perennially late with deadlines, and to a great extent they have become a minimally subsidized hobby.
>
> When I began with the magazines I brought to them a lot of energy and enthusiasm and a great many ideas for their improvement ... Well, I have put into effect nearly every idea which I was allowed to follow through on ... and I have spent most of my energy and enthusiasm.[132]

In an editorial six years before he had said that he did not yet believe that the day of the sf magazine was over: 'if, when I have put out the best possible magazine I can put out, the sales show no change. Then I will concede defeat.' This felt like the time.

However, after a long phone call, Cohen convinced White to stay on another year. A few changes were instigated. Cohen ceased publication of the remaining reprint magazines, *Science Fiction Adventures* (with the November 1974 issue) and *Thrilling Science Fiction* (with the July 1975 issue). The cover price was raised again to $1 from the October 1975 *Fantastic* (November 1975 *Amazing*). This led to another drop in sales and from the start of 1976 both magazines were placed on a quarterly schedule.

White found himself editing both magazines not for another year but for another three years. To his credit, despite the drain on his energies and the continued slide in sales – though there was a brief recovery in 1977 – the contents showed no deterioration. The covers became more dramatic, especially with the exotic work of Stephen Fabian and quality

132 Ted White, 'Uffish Thots', *Science Fiction Review* #12 (February 1975), p. 38.

work by Tom Barber and Douglas Beekman. White saw *Amazing* through its fiftieth anniversary issue, which should have been dated April 1976 but because of the schedules was dated June 1976 (but did appear on the correct anniversary in March). He also saw *Fantastic* through its twenty-fifth anniversary in June 1977. He managed to acquire a good range of material from the rising generation of authors – George R. R. Martin, Charles Sheffield, Brian Lumley, Darrell Schweitzer, Craig Shaw Gardner and others. Some of these later issues looked and read amongst the best.

But it was all becoming financially burdensome. Cohen reported that the magazines had lost $15,000 in 1977, and that was the year when sales improved, albeit briefly. Cohen tried to find a new publisher but eventually, in September 1978, he sold his half-share in Ultimate Publishing to his partner Arthur Bernhard. White could see the writing on the wall and resigned in late October. He returned all the manuscripts in his possession to their authors.

Once again *Amazing* and *Fantastic* were to see a new editor and further changes, all of which I shall discuss later. White heaved a huge sigh of relief as he handed in his resignation. At last he could get back to writing. No longer did he have to feel like a slave on a never-ending treadmill. No longer did he have to act as go-between for Cohen and the SFWA.

White had achieved wonders with these magazines. He succeeded in publishing daring and challenging fiction, some of it over-the-top and self-indulgent, but much of it worthy and important, as much to their authors as to the readers. White gave support to a cluster of authors who would not have found it easy to sell their material elsewhere and who, thanks to White, managed to develop their craft and move on to greater things. It is difficult to imagine what other editor would have been as long-suffering as White or as dedicated. *Amazing* and *Fantastic* might never have survived to their half- and quarter-centuries had it not been for him. He had much to be proud of and little to regret in looking back over those issues.

Within a year he would be back as editor of *Heavy Metal*, of which more later. It is time to consider the last of the surviving magazines from the fifties and sixties, *The Magazine of Fantasy and Science Fiction*.

The Anchor Mag

While its rivals went through all manner of changes and conflicts, *F&SF* sailed a straight and true course throughout the decade. It had the same economic vicissitudes to overcome but it took them in its stride. By the end of the decade its circulation had risen by 23 per cent from 50,300 to 62,000 while at the same time *Analog*'s circulation had peaked and dropped again by 5 per cent (110,330 to 104,600). Whereas *Amazing* lost readers every time it raised its cover price, *F&SF*'s readers remained loyal, even though it had doubled its price from 60 cents at the start of the decade to $1.25 at the end. There had been a slight increase in page count from 128 to 160, but that was not really important. What was important was that *F&SF* delivered the goods month after month. We can show this in purely statistical terms by looking at the number of awards (Hugo, Nebula, Locus) which stories in *F&SF* either won or were nominated for, together with the number of stories selected for the various annual anthologies of the year's best science fiction. The results for the five main sf magazines are shown in Table 1.1. I have simply allocated one point each time a story was nominated for an award or reprinted in a 'year's best' anthology. I have not allocated extra points for stories which won awards. I have not included points for nominations or winners of Best Magazine or Best Editor.

Table 1.1 *Magazines with most story nominations, awards or 'Year's Best' selections*

Year	F&SF	Analog	Galaxy	If	Amazing
1970	10	2	13	5	2
1971	16	6	9	8	–
1972	28	23	7	5	3
1973	17	18	10	9	1
1974	30	29	12	5	3
1975	41	34	12	–	5
1976	23	10	10	–	6
1977	22	30	–	–	1
1978	27	23	–	–	–
1979	23	17	–	–	–
1980	30	14	–	–	1
TOTAL	267	206	73	32	22
Av/Yr	24.3	18.7	10.4	6.4	2.0

Although Ben Bova received the Hugo for Best Professional Editor six times in the years 1973 to 1979 (missing only 1978), more stories from *F&SF* received some kind of recognition than from any of the other leading magazines.

The reason for *F&SF*'s success was consistency, in all its forms: a regular monthly schedule, the same editor throughout, the same instantly recognizable format, and a proven reliability for the quality and diversity of its stories. If those are the reasons, how was it achieved, and why were other magazines not following the formula?

The differences between *F&SF* and the other magazines was one of background. Most of the sf magazines, including *Analog* and *Amazing Stories*, had developed through the pulp magazines. They were dedicated to a particular group of readers – those who enjoyed a good action or adventure yarn – and to a particular style of writing. Campbell pulled *Astounding/Analog* out of that pit to a degree, but its roots remained there. Much the same applied to *Galaxy*, for although that had never been a pulp magazine – and indeed Gold's original purpose was to distant itself from the pulps – it still bore some of that stigma and was soon surrounded by a host of pulps turned digests.

Although *F&SF* was also a digest, it had a literary heritage. The literary world and genre fiction have traditionally been poles apart and have always had an uneasy relationship. You can, without too much difficulty, trace its roots back to H. L. Mencken and *The Smart Set*. Mencken and George Nathan had edited *The Smart Set* – the leading literary magazine of the post-World-War-One decade – but, with its sale to Hearst's empire in 1923, the two set up *The American Mercury* with A.A. Knopf. The *Mercury* soon became the literary review of the twenties, the little magazine with the big circulation. Mencken stepped down as editor in 1933 and a year later the magazine was sold. By 1939 it had been acquired by its former business manager Laurence Spivak, who established Mercury Press. This published *American Mercury* and started *Ellery Queen's Mystery Magazine* (*EQMM*) in 1941 and *The Magazine of Fantasy and Science Fiction* in 1949. Spivak's vice-president and general manager was Joseph Ferman, who had been the circulation manager at Knopf when they published the *Mercury*. Ferman acquired Mercury Press from Spivak in 1955. Although the *American Mercury* had been sold in 1950, its name continued in the company and that continuity, particularly through Joseph Ferman, was a key factor in establishing both *F&SF* and its former partner *EQMM* as sophisticated magazines with literary blood flowing through their pages.

So, at its basic level *F&SF* was part not of the science-fiction world but of the literary establishment, a fact that has never been lost on its editors. When Anthony Boucher and J. Francis McComas developed the magazine, it was always intended to appeal more to the book world than the magazine world. It rarely carried internal illustrations, apart from occasional cartoons, and initially the magazine had a single column of print per page, not two columns as in most magazines. This had changed by the sixties, but the lack of interior artwork always gave it a more literary feel and, of course, allowed for more wordage. Robert P. Mills and Avram Davidson continued that sophisticated, literary image. The magazine received commendations from Clifton Fadiman, Basil Davenport, Orville Prescott, Bennet Cerf and others whose opinions were highly regarded amongst the literary world.

By the late fifties, with the departure of Boucher, the magazine allied itself more closely with the sf field and ran material by many of the same writers, but it never fully lost that image of a literary journal that was on the outside looking in, whereas the sf magazines were firmly on the inside looking out.

Edward Ferman worked briefly as an editorial assistant on the magazine when he was fresh out of college but, wanting a wider experience, he worked as an assistant editor at Prentice-Hall, in 1959, moving on to the financial institution of Dunn and Bradstreet, where he produced financial papers. The dual literary and financial background was useful for his future handling of F&SF. He returned to F&SF in 1962 as the managing editor, which meant that he compiled the issues in the New York office from manuscripts selected by Avram Davidson, who by then lived in Mexico. Davidson stepped down as editor at the end of 1964 and Joseph Ferman was looking for a replacement. Isaac Asimov believes that it was he who suggested Edward, then aged 27, and makes it clear that he soon slipped into the role.[133] Joseph Ferman remained the editor of record for a year, and the titled passed formally to Edward from the January 1966 issue. From November 1970 he also took over as publisher.

So, in addition to having a literary background and being more acceptable to the literary mainstream, F&SF had a consistency in its editorial and publishing vision. As Ferman wrote later, celebrating the magazine's twenty-fifth anniversary, 'F&SF has … under five editors … strayed not at all from the goal announced in Volume 1, Number 1, of "offering the best in imaginative fiction".'[134]

And that was the third key element in the magazine's success. It had the broadest policy of them all. It had no restrictions on the depth or intensity of the scientific content of stories, no problems over whether their message was positive or otherwise and no real arguments over the sexual, religious or racial content of a story, provided it broke no laws. Frequently

---

133 See Isaac Asimov, *In Joy Still Felt* (New York: Doubleday, 1980), pp. 345–6. Asimov states that Edward became editor from the December 1964 issue. In the October 1974 editorial for F&SF, Ferman states that his first issue was for November 1964.
134 Edward Ferman, 'Editorial', F&SF 47:4 (October 1974), p. 6.

F&SF had published stories rejected by other magazines because of some stereotypical taboo, but rarely did Boucher or Davidson flinch. Ferman's criteria were that the stories should be well-written and that he should enjoy them. That's all that mattered.

There are other factors that caused *F&SF* to stand apart, especially during the seventies and eighties. Ferman had not started out as a science-fiction reader. He had much broader tastes but clearly knew what he liked, and liked things that were out of the ordinary. But he would not argue the point over some small matter, like Campbell, or go for the cutting edge, like White or the anthologists we shall explore shortly, or try and create a stable of writers who wrote to order. In one sense he was an innocent in a world all too easily tarnished. Ferman kept away from ideologies, waves, trends or revolutions and just kept compiling the best magazine he could from the four hundred or so manuscripts he received every month.

And the final factor, if there is a line to draw, is that to Ferman – both father and son – this was very much a family business. Unlike Bova, Jakobsson and White, Ed Ferman had no senior publisher to answer to. From 1970 on, he was his own boss. He moved his editorial and publishing offices to his large Victorian house in Cornwall, Connecticut, where he was assisted by his wife Audrey, who handled subscription details and became the business manager. Until 1974 Andrew Porter, the publisher of *Algol*, served as assistant editor and first reader. Several others served in that role until Anne Jordan, the founder of the Children's Literature Association, took over in 1980. Ferman treated running Mercury Press as a nine-to-five job, recognizing it more as a 'cottage industry' than big business.

This disciplined, but relaxed approach permeated the magazine. It was always friendly and welcoming, like being part of a family, and the consistency of design and presentation meant that you felt you were coming home whenever you opened an issue. It was an atmosphere created from the start by Boucher and sustained over the years by the Fermans.

Another cornerstone in the magazine's consistency was the regularity of its non-fiction columns. Isaac Asimov had contributed his informal science column to every issue since November 1958, and would continue to do so until February 1992 – 399 in total. Gahan Wilson contributed a macabre cartoon to most issues from 1965 to 1981. There was a regular book review column which had been run by Judith Merril in the late sixties, then James Blish till 1975 and then Algis Budrys, with occasional other contributors, while Baird Searles contributed a film review column from 1970 to 1984. *F&SF* did not usually run a letter column, although Ferman did experiment with one in the late seventies. Though Ferman clearly needed feedback, he did not feel that readers wanted to read it and preferred to encourage reader involvement through occasional literary competitions.

So, you knew what to expect from *F&SF*, and you also knew you would find the widest range of science fiction and fantasy in any magazine. It was a very rare issue that did not include something of value. In 1972, for instance, nine of the twelve issues each contained one or two stories that were nominated for (and in two cases won) awards. In 1975 that applied to eleven out of the twelve issues. Such was the reliability that has made *F&SF* the most consistently enjoyable magazine of the last 50 years.

Part of the magazine's charm is its diversity. As the title says, most issues contained a range of science fiction (hard science or experimental or any point in between) and fantasy (which might include ghost stories or heroic fantasy – the latter a definite change under Ferman, as Boucher did not like it). It occasionally ran reprints from sources of which readers might not be aware. The January 1970 issue, for instance, reprinted the ghost story 'Ride the Thunder' from a 1967 issue of the truck-driver's magazine *Overdrive* and could thus claim to introduce Jack Cady to his most appreciative audience, though it would be a few more years before the wider weird-fiction market existed for his work.

There were a few writers generally regarded as *F&SF* writers, for even though they might occasionally sell to other magazines, their work seemed ideally suited to *F&SF*. These stories were sometimes eccentric, sometimes satirical. A good example at the start of this period was the work of Sterling Lanier. Although he had first appeared in *Analog*, and occasionally appeared in *If*, Lanier is best remembered for his series featuring the tall tales of Brigadier Ffellowes whose exploits, in the vein of Lord Dunsany's Joseph Jorkens, take him into the world of the fantastic and supernatural. But *F&SF* was also known for its softer, more lyrical stories that scarcely featured enough science to be science fiction, but could not have been anything else. A good example were the stories by Zenna Henderson. Her stories about the 'People', which had been running in *F&SF* since 1952 and continued up to 1980, were not only fine science-fiction stories but also perfect parables of refugees across the world. The People are humanoid extraterrestrials, distinguished by their psychic powers, who came to Earth many decades ago and struggle to blend in and survive. The sf element is minimal but is the device that allows the stories to serve as allegories of their time. Others often regarded as typical *F&SF* authors, even though they sold elsewhere, include Reginald Bretnor, Leonard Tushnet, Kit Reed, Ward Moore, Harvey Jacobs and Raylyn Moore, to name but a few from the late sixties and early seventies. If there is any common denominator amongst these writers, it is that they produced material that was off-beat, atypical and ill-definable, which, rather than defining a typical *F&SF* story, serves to emphasise that *F&SF* was open to a wide variety of approaches and attitudes. The work of these writers, which might seem out of place elsewhere, felt entirely at home in *F&SF*, where it served like dressing and spice to add flavour to the issue and acted as a contrast to the more conventional fare.

There were, of course, other writers whose work added spice to any issue, and often more than that. The most notable of these was Harlan Ellison and, though Ellison may be considered *sui generis*, his work always seemed more at home in *F&SF* than anywhere else. Ellison contributed twelve stories to *F&SF* during the seventies and these included some of his most challenging work. 'Corpse' (January 1972) sets the mood for a wave of stories dealing with the modern-day gods we worship but in no way prepares the reader for what are Ellison's two most emotionally intense stories, 'Basilisk' (August 1972) and 'The Deathbird' (March 1973). Despite the inevitable comparisons, 'Basilisk' is not specifically about Vietnam, but considers how the gods of war manipulate our baser instincts to achieve their ends. 'The Deathbird' twists religion on its head, and, in revealing how the Earth reached its chaotic state, also shows the healing power of death. It is impossible to read these stories without being both emotionally and physically drained. They are epitaphs to mankind's inhumanity.

Ellison noted at the time that 'Adrift Just off the Islets of Langerhans: Latitude 38° 54' N, Longitude 77° 0' 13" W' (October 1974) was 'one of the most difficult I've ever attempted'. It uses characters and imagery from the cinema as symbols in man's quest to reclaim his soul. 'Croatoan' (May 1975) rose out of a writer's workshop where Ellison set the task of exploring the theme of the place where all lost things go. Once again Ellison brought the razor close to our conscience, our collective irresponsibility, and reveals the children of the sewers where aborted foetuses are flushed.

Ellison was honoured by *F&SF* with one of its occasional special author issues (July 1977). This concept, the brainchild of Joseph Ferman, began with a Theodore Sturgeon issue in September 1962. Other authors so honoured in the seventies were Poul Anderson (April 1971), James Blish (April 1972), Frederik Pohl (September 1973), Robert Silverberg (April 1974) and Damon Knight (November 1976). Ellison wrote three stories for his issue, each a different ember in the fire of his mind and, although all three are powerful evocations of life, it was 'Jeffty is Five', about the loss of innocence and the wonder of childhood, that caught readers' imaginations. It not only won virtually all the major awards at the time, but 22 years later when *Locus* ran an all-time poll, it came out top as everyone's favourite short story. If there is a single author whose work represents the best of *F&SF* in the seventies – not just in the quality of the fiction but in its intensity, its rebelliousness and its impact – it is Harlan Ellison.

The authors honoured by the special issues usually delivered something unusual, but there are some interesting parallels between some of the stories. Poul Anderson had been an occasional but regular contributor since the early fifties. Although closely associated with sf, *F&SF* also gave Anderson an opportunity to experiment with fantasy. For his special issue, Anderson managed to combine elements of sf, fantasy and mystery. In 'The Queen of Air and Darkness' a private investigator called Sherrinford (the name Conan Doyle had once considered for Sherlock Holmes) is looking for a lost boy on a remote world that has never been fully explored and where some believe there may be an alien intelligence. Anderson weaves a conclusion that is a masterwork of creativity in what is in many ways a quintessential *F&SF* story. Anderson had only six further stories in *F&SF* in the seventies, including a late addition to his Time Patrol series of the fifties, 'Gibraltar Falls' (October 1975). 'Goat Song' (February 1972), like 'The Queen of Air and Darkness', won both the Hugo and Nebula, though they are two very different stories. In 'Goat Song', a supercomputer has taken on a godlike sentience and controls the human race through drugs and false promises. Yet both stories share the idea that humanity prefers to live with illusions rather than reality. Indeed, it shares with Ellison's 'The Deathbird', the message that unchallenged beliefs are the true enemy of the soul.

James Blish was, alas, nearing the end of his writing career and 'Midsummer Century', the short novel in his special issue (April 1972), was one of his last works. Of Wellsian, even Stapledonian vision, the story takes us along with the mind of a young astronomer which is propelled over twenty thousand years into the future to become linked to a super-computer. From this he learns that civilization has risen and fallen repeatedly and that currently a degenerated humanity is in conflict with a race of evolved birds for mastery of the planet. Blish regarded the story as an old-fashioned adventure tale, but, like 'Goat Song', it is a study of mankind's resilience and its ability to see beyond its beliefs to a greater goal.

Frederik Pohl takes this baton from Blish in his special story, 'In the Problem Pit' (September 1973). Here, in the relatively near future, government has established a number of think tanks that meet in underground caves and try to solve the nation's and their own problems. The think tanks become a means in themselves as a 'big brother' way of monitoring people and their thoughts, and the individuals pass through the pits and become cleansed, ready to start again. Pohl sees an Orwellian future, but a more benign one.

The fact that stories such as these were appearing in the aftermath of Vietnam and a turbulent time in American history was no coincidence. Science fiction and fantasy were the best media for writers to put such turmoil in context and speculate on cause, effect and solution. To some writers, certainly Ellison, and perhaps to some readers, this fiction was cathartic. But whereas science fiction of the thirties, forties and fifties saw man looking outward at what we could achieve, by the seventies man was looking inward at what we had failed to achieve. Within these special stories, though, even Ellison's, there was usually a glimmer of hope. Mankind unceasingly traps itself in cages and has to redesign the cage in order to escape. The hardest cage from which to escape is that created by our own fears and prejudices. It was by working through these neuroses that science fiction, which, like the society of the time, had become tormented and distraught, could be reborn. Blish might have been reflecting on this. There is a line in 'Midsummer Century' where the scientist, trapped in the future and learning of mankind's fate, believes that 'His only option was to try to figure out some way of changing an age, and then hope that the age would find some way to rescue him.'[135]

The one special story that does not fit into this argument is Robert Silverberg's 'Born with the Dead' (April 1974). Coming towards the end of a remarkably creative period, this story was the product of a writer who was becoming dejected and depressed with the world around him and saw no positive outcome. In 'Born with the Dead' a process has been created which allows the recently dead to be revived, but this causes isolation rather than rejoicing. The reborn do not want to mix with their former loved ones, resulting in a divided society. This story was a highly personal one for Silverberg, written during a difficult period of his life when hard decisions had to be made, and the story reflects that inner turmoil.

By contrast, in the last special issue of the seventies, Damon Knight's 'I See You' (November 1976) is essentially positive. It foresees a future where all privacy has been lost – in Knight's case as a result of a form of time-viewer, though much of this is happening now through the growth in the internet and telecommunications – and where society adjusts so that the benefits outweigh the problems. If these special issues are in any way a guide to changing moods through the seventies, it seems that the problems raised in the early stories might be finding their own solutions in the second half of the decade.

135 James Blish, 'Midsummer Century', F&SF 42:4 (April 1972), p. 21.

The special issues were obviously tributes to writers of repute whose careers were long-established. *F&SF* was also good at encouraging new writers. Ferman might not always buy an author's first story – *F&SF*'s demands for quality writing might limit that – but he certainly supported writers as they began to master the craft. The list of new writers who either debuted in the seventies or sold the majority of their early work to *F&SF* is a long one and I shall only cover some of the writers here, but it includes Pamela Sargent, William Walling, Phyllis Eisenstein, John Morressy, David S. Garnett, Lisa Tuttle, John Varley, Tom Reamy, Michael Reaves, Jane Yolen, James P. Kelly and Alan Ryan.

'Landed Minority' (September 1970) was Pamela Sargent's first sale, though she almost never submitted it. It was her partner, George Zebrowski, who pulled the story out of the bin and suggested she submit it to *F&SF*.[136] Two months later back came a cheque and a contract. It's a competent enough story set in a post-holocaust university, an unusual but, as it turns out, appropriate setting to explore a world torn between disaster and hope. Her next appearance in *F&SF*, though, showed a significant advance in her writing skills. In 'Gather Blue Roses' (February 1972), a Jewish mother, who had survived a Nazi death camp, discovers that her daughter, like her, is telempathic. The mother had to experience not just her own agonies in the concentration camp but those of all the others, yet she believes that the suffering will be even harder for her daughter in the future. It was this story that placed Sargent's name on the map and she confirmed her abilities with 'Bond and Free' (June 1974), where she steadily reveals the true nature of a girl held in a remote hospital. All of Sargent's early work, including that built into her first novel, *Cloned Lives*, has this deep sense of apartness.

Michael Bishop had submitted his stories to *F&SF* from the start but his early stories were rejected and first appeared in *Galaxy* and *If*. However, Bishop soon made the grade with Ferman with a potent fantasy, 'Darktree, Darktide' (April 1971), which reveals the secret of an old woman's immortality. Bishop contributed a couple more short stories and then discovered his métier at the novella length. 'The White Otters of Childhood' (July 1973), set in the sixth millennium and strangely reminiscent of Walter Miller's *A Canticle for Leibowitz*, contrasts two human cultures, one of which has achieved transcendence and the other of which castigates itself for failing to do so. As in 'Death and Designation Amongst the Asadi', which appeared in *If* a few months earlier, Bishop is able to create

---

136 See Jeffrey Eliot's interview with Sargent, *Fantasy Newsletter* #52 (October 1982), p. 19.

an alien environment which is both puzzling and yet strangely familiar.[137] Although on the surface 'Cathadonian Odyssey' (September 1974) is a tribute to Stanley Weinbaum's 'A Martian Odyssey', this post-Vietnam version is harsh and unyielding. Humans succeed in all but obliterating the native *squiddles* despite the self-sacrifice of the natives in helping a woman stranded on their planet. 'Men are hardly creatures,' Bishop observes, 'Men are the ultimate vermin.' By the time *F&SF* published 'The Samurai and the Willows' (February 1976), Ferman was writing, 'Bishop is perhaps not the most prolific of the best new writers of sf ... but it would be hard to think of another who has produced high quality work so consistently.' Bishop's fiction has the ability to take the reader into an alien world and to witness its strangeness while conveying an empathy for its inhabitants.

Bishop told me, 'My reading of *F&SF*, of anthologies compiled from the contents of past issues of *F&SF,* and my fondness for certain writers who often appeared in the magazine's pages – Ray Bradbury, Damon Knight, Harlan Ellison, Zenna Henderson, etc. – did indeed strongly influence my own early fiction.'[138]

From the exotic estrangement of Bishop there are several degrees of arc to the cybertech vividness of John Varley, though both were comfortably at home in *F&SF*. Varley hit the science-fiction scene with the force of an atom bomb in the mid-seventies and was, according to John Clute in the *Encyclopedia of Science Fiction*, 'soon thought to be the most significant writer of the 1970s'. Brian Aldiss was more reserved, saying that Varley's work had 'a richness, but no wholeness'.[139] What Varley delivered was a passion and conviction that made him the most exciting new writer since Roger Zelazny, ten years earlier.

Varley had only started writing because he needed money and it seemed a good idea at the time. He was inspired by Robert Heinlein's James Forrestal Memorial Lecture delivered at the US Naval Academy at Annapolis (Heinlein's alma mater) in April 1973 and which Varley read when it was printed as the guest editorial in the January 1974 *Analog*. Heinlein set down five rules for success in writing.[140] Varley, then a devoted fan of Heinlein, followed them to the letter, and it worked instantly. He made two near-simultaneous sales, to *F&SF* and *Vertex*, both appearing in

137 Bishop told me that Ejler Jakobsson rejected 'White Otters of Childhood' on the grounds that it was too melodramatic (personal e-mail, Bishop/Ashley, 31 May 2006).

138 Personal e-mail, Bishop/Ashley, 31 May 2006.

139 Aldiss, *Trillion Year Spree*, p. 362.

140 The rules are: First: you must *write*. Second: You must *finish* what you write. Third: You must refrain from rewriting except to editorial order. Fourth: You must place it on the market. Fifth: You must *keep* it on the market until sold.

print within weeks of each other. *F&SF* ran 'Picnic on Nearside' (August 1974), the first in what would prove to be his Eight Worlds Future History. The big-hitters, though, came the following year: 'Retrograde Summer' (February 1975), 'The Black Hole Passes' (June 1975) and 'In the Bowl' (December 1975). These contained all the fixtures and fittings of solid high-tech science fiction, but with the new hardware and cultural software of the coming millennium. Varley was able to weave all the new sciences and tropes into his fiction – cloning, cybernetics, black holes, ecology and a feminist viewpoint – and he did it with such panache that he made his worlds believable, maybe even inevitable. While some critics, such as Aldiss and Thomas Disch, felt that Varley was playing with gimmicks and pandering to the fans,[141] others saw the underlying effects of his work. Varley was able to create a tense and very real story with genuine characters in a world that many of us sensed was not far away. His use of computers and nanotechnology presaged the world of cyberpunk. His work was part of the continuum that threaded through the seventies and formed a melding of the old hard-tech school with the resurgent New Wave experimentalists (soon to become the cyberpunks) and the feminists. Varley's work of the seventies was a milestone in the evolution of science fiction.

Varley burned like a nova and his first wave of creativity began to dim by the early eighties. But that was not before he had produced some of the most memorable science fiction of the decade. *F&SF* carried much of the best of this – though James Baen at *Galaxy* and George Scithers at the new *Isaac Asimov's SF Magazine* also caught some, Baen even believing he had discovered Varley.[142] His later works in *F&SF* included one of his occasional planetary adventures, 'In the Hall of the Martian Kings' (February 1977), and 'The Persistence of Vision' (March 1978), arguably his best story of the decade, which won both the Hugo and Nebula awards and topped the *Locus* poll. This story has Varley moving towards the transcendence of Bishop's work in his depiction of a remote deaf-blind community that has achieved a higher level of understanding than the rest of humanity and succeeds in escaping from the world.

A new writer who seemed highly suited to *F&SF*, and yet who appeared sparsely, was James Tiptree, Jr., though it is noticeable that the work *F&SF* did publish was amongst her best. 'Painwise' (February 1972) was a story that Ferman had rejected but it haunted him and he asked to see it again. On the surface, this might seem a minor story about a man rewired by

---

141 See Thomas M. Disch, 'Books', *F&SF* 60:2 (February 1981), p. 42, reprinted in Disch, *On SF* (Ann Arbor: University of Michigan Press, 2005), p. 99.
142 Personal e-mail, Varley/Ashley, 31 May 2006.

aliens so that he suffers no physical pain but is tormented by psychological anguish, but the underlying allegory relates the lack of humanity's pain to the anguish of the Earth. It is, in fact, a hymn to the ecological movement. 'And I Awoke and Found Me Here on the Cold Hill's Side' (March 1972) deals with a man's physical and sexual attraction to various aliens on board a giant space station. As with all of Tiptree's work, the story conveys a deeper message and a complex one dealing with the extent to which men become slaves to their physical urges, even when it drives them into forbidden areas. The story has a companion piece in what is probably Tiptree's best-known story, 'The Women Men Don't See' (December 1973). It is a more straightforward story of a small group of men and women stranded after a plane crash and their encounter with aliens. The women choose to leave with the aliens in preference to the world of men. In both stories the aliens form a catalyst for slavery on the one hand and freedom on the other. Tiptree's stories were dealing with how humanity had become trapped by its own cultural and moral chains.

While the stories discussed in the last few pages tended to catch the headlines in *F&SF*, they were only part of a wide variety which the magazine published and which reflected its broad personality. As its title suggests, it was originally a magazine of fantasy – the very first issue was called simply that, but science fiction was added because of its commercial importance. During the late fifties the magazine was one of the few markets for fantasy and weird fiction, though *Fantastic*, under Cele Goldsmith, and the British *Science Fantasy* provided worthy material in the early sixties. By the late sixties fantasy was back in vogue after the success of *Lord of the Rings* and the Lancer editions of Robert E. Howard's Conan stories, yet surprisingly few magazines benefited from this popularity. *F&SF* preferred more literary fantasy over sword and sorcery, but it had bowed to the latter in the late sixties with Jack Vance's Dying Earth stories featuring Cugel the Clever. These stories were more exotic, ingenious and better-written than the basic heroic fantasy. Alas, Vance contributed only one more Cugel tale, 'The Seventeen Virgins' (October 1974). Roger Zelazny contributed the serial 'Jack of Shadows' (July–August 1971), set on a parallel Earth with a permanent dark side, but disappointingly Zelazny appeared no more in *F&SF*, the magazine that had seen many of his major early works. Fritz Leiber contributed a few of his Grey Mouser stories, though these were now turning up in a variety of markets. With 'Inn of the Black Swan' (November 1972), Phyllis Eisenstein began a series featuring Alaric the Minstrel, abandoned at birth and seeking an understanding of his life. Thomas Burnett Swann contributed several new historical fanta-sies. Even Larry Niven ventured into the fantastic, though, as you might expect, his fantasy has a scientific rationale. In Niven's ancient world, magic was derived from *mana* which was in everything, but it was being used up and when all *mana* had gone magic would cease to exist. It was a form of ecological fantasy. The concept had been introduced in 'Not Long Before the End' (April 1969) and reappeared in several stories including the excellent 'What Good is a Glass Dagger?' (September 1972).

Other fantasies included the eccentric Dr Esterhazy stories by Avram Davidson, set in a kind of Ruritanian alternate Europe, and which began in 'Polly Charms the Sleeping Woman' (February 1975). Towards the close of the seventies both Stephen Donaldson and Stephen King contributed to *F&SF*: King with the start of his Dark Tower series in 'The Gunslinger' (October 1978) and Donaldson with a couple of fairy-tale-style fantasies, 'The Lady in White' (February 1978) and 'Mythological Beast' (January 1979). The true mistress of the fairy-tale, Jane Yolen, also became a regular contributor, starting with 'The Lady and the Merman' (September 1976).

There were four stories by Tom Reamy, at least three of which stand out as amongst the finest fantasies in *F&SF* during the seventies. Reamy was seldom satisfied with his own fiction and it was years before he submitted any for publication. His stories in *F&SF* are Bradburyesque in their study of evil in small-town America. They all revolve around the mythical town of Hawley, Kansas, which is touched with the strange. These were 'Twilla' (September 1974), 'San Diego Lightfoot Sue' (August 1975) which won the Nebula Award, 'The Detweiler Boy' (April 1977) and 'Insects in Amber' (January 1978). Reamy won the Campbell Award for Best New Writer in 1976. Alas he died the following year of a heart attack, aged only 42. Reamy was a potent force in the small-press movement and I shall return to him later.

Darker tales of fantasy and the supernatural were also present. From amongst the Grand Masters were stories by Manly Wade Wellman and L. Sprague de Camp, the latter with a series about the mild-mannered Willy Newbury who has become ensorcelled and is drawn into supernatural adventures which begin in 'The Lamp' (March 1975). In addition to the multi-award winning 'Catch That Zeppelin!' (March 1975), an unsettling story of shifting between alternate realities, Fritz Leiber contributed his last novel and one of his best works of the supernatural, 'The Pale, Brown Thing' (January–February 1977), better known in book form as *Our Lady of Darkness* (1978). It's an autobiographical novel of an ageing writer trying to understand his paranoia about visions he has of strange creatures. It justly won the World Fantasy Award. Karl Edward Wagner made his magazine debut in *F&SF* with 'In the Pines' (August 1973) but

surprisingly sold no more to Ferman. Ferman had also published the first
story by Charles L. Grant in 1968 and ran several of his dark tales in *F&SF*
during the seventies.

Although superficially science fiction, Robert Silverberg's 'The Stochastic
Man' (April–June 1975) is more in the vein of a dark horror novel where
a statistician discovers that the future is immutable and nothing he can
do can stop it. It was one of his last novels before his brief departure from
sf and, like 'Born with the Dead', is permeated with despair. Silverberg
soon bounced back after a period of rejuvenation, and *F&SF* presented
his triumphant return with the magisterial 'Lord Valentine's Castle'
(November 1979–February 1980), the first of his Majipoor Chronicles and
the start of a whole new generation of Silverberg works.

Ferman promoted the material of British writer Robert Aickman,
reprinting some stories from collections and running several new items
of which the vampire story 'Pages From a Young Girl's Diary' (February
1973) won the first World Fantasy Award for short fiction. Ferman also
published the Lovecraftian tales of another British writer, Brian Lumley,
starting with 'Haggopian' (June 1973) and including 'Born of the Winds'
(December 1975), which was nominated for a World Fantasy Award.

Ferman published the works of many British writers. He even created
a special All-British issue in April 1978 with work by Brian Aldiss, John
Brunner, Kenneth Bulmer – his last professional magazine appearance –
Richard Cowper, Christopher Priest, Keith Roberts and Ian Watson. Most
of these writers were or would become *F&SF* regulars – in fact it was the
only magazine to which Cowper sold, with just one exception. Cowper
– the alias used by John Middleton Murry, Jr. for his sf and fantasy – had
been writing books since the early fifties but had only turned to science
fiction in the late sixties, and only to short fiction in the mid-seventies.
His work was quintessentially British, similar to that of Keith Roberts and
John Wyndham, most of it with that charming blend of the pastoral with
the unusual. He first appeared with 'The Custodians' (October 1975),
about a remote monastery built at a nexus of time which is able to witness
events into the future. However, the real hit came with his next story,
'Piper at the Gates of Dawn' (March 1976). Set in a flooded post-apocalyptic Britain, where only the highlands remain as islands, society has
reverted to a medieval state, but there is hope of a new Messiah. The story
proved so popular that Cowper developed it into a trilogy, the White Bird
of Kinship.

Christopher Priest's contribution, 'The Watched', is one of his Dream
Archipelago series and develops an idea similar to that used in Damon
Knight's 'I See You', a world where all privacy has gone, this time because

mini-cams are so common. Everyone is aware of this and, with time, free will ceases to exist. Priest's only other story in *F&SF* was 'Palely Loitering' (January 1979), a story of a man who can move through time yet finds that those he seeks prove all too elusive. These stories were part of Priest's transition from genre to mainstream fiction, emphasising the literary significance of *F&SF*.

Despite the emphasis on fantasy, *F&SF* always welcomed high-tech science fiction if it could be written with more people than wires. It is perhaps surprising to find that Gregory Benford, who would seem to be the ideal *Analog* author, appeared more regularly in *F&SF*. His first sale had been to the magazine as a result of a story competition, and his later contributions included such fine stories as 'Deeper Than the Darkness' (April 1969), 'Icarus Descending' (April 1973), 'The Anvil of Jove' (July 1976) and 'A Snark in the Night' (August 1977). 'Icarus Descending' was one of a wave of stories, popular at the time, of Earth threatened by near-Earth objects. It was a collaboration with Gordon Eklund, who had started to sell to *F&SF* soon after his debut in Ted White's magazines. 'Seeker for Still Life' (January 1971), 'Grasshopper Time' (March 1972), 'Treasure in the Treasure House' (August 1974) and 'Beneath the Waves' (March 1974) are all tender stories of human–alien relationships, the last-named dealing with merpeople. One of Eklund's best stories for the magazine was 'Sandsnake Hunter' (March 1975), a credible creation of an alien world.

There were other good planetary adventures by Stephen Tall (several of his *Stardust* stories, including the very popular 'The Bear With the Knot in His Tail', May 1971), Joseph Green, Gerald Pearce, Keith Laumer and George R. R. Martin. Frederik Pohl contributed the serial 'Man Plus' (April–June 1976) which, like his earlier *Analog* story 'The Gold at the Starbow's End', tells of a mission doomed to failure – this time a cyborg mission to Mars – that produces remarkable results. Ben Bova and Jerry Pournelle also put in appearances, Bova with a story on earthquake predictions, 'A Slight Miscalculation' (August 1971). Asimov appeared with the robot story 'Thou That Art Mindful of Him –' (May 1974), written for the anthology *Final Stage* which Ferman compiled with Barry Malzberg, but most of Asimov's stories for the magazine formed part of his Black Widowers series of club puzzles he was already writing for *Ellery Queen's Mystery Magazine*.

There was a confidence about *F&SF* in the seventies (which continued into the eighties) which was not so evident in the other magazines, not even *Analog*. Such confidence allows the editor to take risks at times or become self-indulgent, and there were a few moments in the seventies when *F&SF* was clearly having fun for its own sake. Philip José Farmer had been on a roll in the late sixties and early seventies, producing a series of metafictional biographies which wove fictional characters into real life. These had included the lives of Tarzan and Doc Savage. He also adopted the persona of Kurt Vonnegut's fictional author Kilgore Trout and, with Vonnegut's permission, wrote one of the books attributed to Trout in *God Bless You, Mr Rosewater* (1965). This was 'Venus on a Half-Shell' serialized, in an abridged form, in the December 1974 and January 1975 issues, complete with a mock photograph of Farmer in a long beard and cap as Trout. The story was an outright pastiche of space opera, but written through Trout's perspective as perceived by Farmer from Vonnegut's novels. In agreeing that Farmer could write the book, Vonnegut had stipulated that he be in no way associated with it. However, Farmer had done such a good job that many reviewers and academics were convinced that it was by Vonnegut. Also an offhand and erroneous remark by Leslie Fiedler that Farmer would have written the book even without Vonnegut's permission added to Vonnegut's dissatisfaction with the whole affair. Farmer had to admit his authorship and publish various disclaimers, and Vonnegut refused Farmer permission to write any more books as by Trout. By now Farmer had been writing so many books in the guise of others that he found it difficult to write as himself and had a writer's block.[143] For a while, he produced a series of stories as written by various fictional authors including Jonathan Swift Somers III, Harry Manders, Paul Chapin and Rod Keen, all of which appeared in *F&SF* over the next few years.

The Kilgore Trout novel was not the only metafiction that *F&SF* published but it was by far the most notorious. John Sladek wrote a series of clever parodies of authors' works which included 'Engineer to the Gods' by R*b*rt H**nl**n (August 1972), 'Broot Force' by *s**c *s*m*v (September 1972) and 'Solar Shoe Salesman' by Ph*l*p K. D*ck (March 1973). In addition, Barry Malzberg and Harry Harrison battled each other in their collaborative 'The Whatever-I-Type-is-True Machine' (November 1974).

There was plenty of humour in addition. Running throughout the decade were the crazy misadventures of missionary Crispin Mobey in various remote or not-so-remote places as chronicled by Gary Jennings, starting with 'Sooner or Later or Never Never' (May 1972). There was Ray Russell's 'The Fortunes of Popowcer' (February 1971), where a character refuses to exist, Gene Wolfe's spoof, 'Tarzan of the Grapes' (June 1972), M. John Harrison's affectionate parody of the space opera 'The Centauri

---

143 See interview with Farmer in *Science Fiction Review* #14 (August 1975), p. 20.

Device' (January 1974), plus stories – though never enough – from Ron Goulart and R. A. Lafferty.

Throughout the seventies *F&SF* seemed at peace with itself. Unlike its rivals it underwent no editorial changes, no drastic drop in circulation (quite the reverse) and felt no need to champion any cause or pursue individual campaigns. It was reliable, trusted and distinctive; it allowed contributors and promised readers the greatest diversity of fiction with an assured editorial quality. With all the changes battering the field in the seventies, *F&SF* felt like the one secure place around which all else was turbulent.

New Blood, New Clothes

The number of new professional sf magazines during the early seventies was minimal and, with one major exception, of little import. That one exception was *Vertex*. It could so easily have been the most important and most influential magazine in the field if it had been in the right place at the right time. It so nearly was.

Vertex was born at the World Science Fiction Convention held in Los Angeles from 1–4 September 1972. Donald J. Pfeil was the editor of two men's magazines, *Knight* and *Adam*, which were published in Los Angeles by imprints of the Mankind Publishing Company. Mankind was the senior company, its name based on the studies of peoples and history that it published both in books and in its magazine of popular history, *Mankind*, which had been issued since May 1967. Pfeil had been a science-fiction fan since the early fifties and often ran stories in *Adam* by sf writers, including Harlan Ellison, Norman Spinrad and Edward Bryant, whose first story to see print, 'They Come Only in Dreams', was in the January 1970 *Adam*.

Inspired by the convention, Pfeil suggested to his publisher, Bentley Morris, that it would be good to publish a top-quality slick sf magazine, like nothing else around. Much to his surprise, a week later Morris agreed, but gave him a deadline of just 33 days to get the material ready to fit into the publishing schedule. The original title for the magazine was *Vector*, but it was changed at the last minute to *Vertex*, a more significant name since it meant the apex or summit of achievement. Payment rates were good, between $125 and $600 per story, depending on length and author reputation, and between $100 and $300 for artwork.[144]

Pfeil revealed his 33-day deadline in his first editorial, along with the general state of panic in which the issue was produced. That may not

144 See news item in *Locus* #123, 22 September 1972.

have been wise, since it suggested an issue compiled without too much care. In appearance the magazine was striking. A true slick, saddle-stapled in quarto-sized flat format, running to 96 glossy pages, heavily illustrated throughout, though not yet with sufficient advertising to support the cost. It was priced at $1.50, when all other magazines were still 60 cents, but it instantly looked good value for money.

Pfeil was assisted at the outset by William Rotsler and Forrest Ackerman. Rotsler tracked down artists and artwork and made contact with writers. Forrest Ackerman provided an interview with Ray Bradbury, a feature by Charles Neutzell on the art of his father, Albert Neutzell, and a transcription of Robert A. Heinlein's 1941 World SF Convention speech, 'The Discovery of the Future'. Ackerman had not consulted Heinlein over this printing, which incurred Heinlein's wrath and led to *Vertex* reaching a separate agreement with him.

More important, though, was the quality of the content, and here the magazine was a little disappointing. Of the eight items of fiction, three were reprints, all from the original anthology market. William Rotsler's 'Patron of the Arts' had been revised since its appearance in *Universe 2*. Robert Silverberg's 'Caught in the Organ Draft' came from Roger Elwood's *And Now Walk Gently Through the Fire...*, and Terry Carr's fine 'The Dance of the Changer and Three', an unusual study of alien life, came from Joseph Elder's *The Farthest Reaches*. One other item was a reprint, Larry Niven's intriguing article, 'The Theory and Practice of Time Travel', from his recent collection, *All the Myriad Ways*.

The most striking story in the issue, labelled 'the most controversial story ever written by Harlan Ellison', was 'Bleeding Stones'. Pollution in New York reaches such levels that the gargoyles around St Patrick's Cathedral come alive and begin a mass slaughter of humanity. Pollution was also the theme of Harry Harrison's less graphic 'We Ate the Whole Thing'.

What made *Vertex* stand out was the slick magazine format. Unlike the digest magazines, *Vertex* ran plenty of photographs and the size allowed for a variety of fillers, news items, reviews, book covers and sufficient space so that the stories and artwork did not feel cramped. The first few issues ran several art portfolios, with work by Tim Kirk (June 1973), Josh Kirby (August 1973) and George Barr (December 1973). It was a feature it should have maintained, as it was well suited to the format, but Bill Rotsler, who organized this feature, had difficulty obtaining sufficient quality material.[145]

Vertex's covers were often stylized and depicted none of the usual sf

---

145 See letter from Rotsler, *The Alien Critic* #10, August 1974, p. 27.

images or stereotypes and though it clearly stated 'The Magazine of Science Fiction' on the cover, it would not have been perceived as one by some and so attracted a wider readership than usual. With a strong emphasis on scientific articles and news. Gregory Benford and Jerry Pournelle both contributed scientific articles at first, and there were frequent articles about the space programme. *Vertex* was an early attempt at what *Omni* would achieve four years later.

The author interviews were amongst the most historically important items. Besides allowing readers an opportunity to see photographs of the authors, which was not common at that time, the interviews were long and perceptive. A full list is Ray Bradbury (April 1973), Robert Silverberg (June 1973), Poul Anderson (August 1973), Frank Herbert (October 1973), Philip K. Dick (February 1974), Harlan Ellison (April 1974), Ursula K. Le Guin (December 1974) – fans would no doubt have been intrigued to see her brandishing a pipe during the interview – Judy-Lynn del Rey (April 1975), Harry Harrison (June 1975), Terry Carr (July 1975) and Norman Spinrad (August 1975). There were also interviews with Erich von Daniken (August 1974) and Leonard Nimoy (June 1975).

Perhaps the most contentious item which *Vertex* published was an essay by Joanna Russ, 'The Image of Women in SF' (February 1974), which I shall consider in more detail in the next section. Russ was concerned over how women were portrayed in science fiction and drew attention to the inadequacy of much work in depicting how personal and family relationships may change over time. It brought a surprisingly naïve response from Poul Anderson and a more thoughtful and revealing one from Philip K. Dick. The exchange revealed how at last writers were becoming or being made more aware of the shortcomings of sf in the past and of the need for considerable change. It was part of a continual learning process that had been kicked off by the New Wave revolution of the late sixties but was only now bearing fruit.

The fiction in *Vertex* was, unfortunately, most often the weakest part. It ran some good fiction, but not enough. Larry Niven explored various consequences of matter transmission in 'The Alibi Machine' (June 1973) and 'All the Bridges Rusting' (August 1973). There was the last previously unpublished short story by Robert A. Heinlein to appear in an sf magazine, although 'No Bands Playing' (December 1973), which was actually written in 1947, was not sf but a fictionalized account of the immunization programme that Heinlein and others went through in the thirties.

'In the House of Double Minds' (June 1974) was the last short story that Robert Silverberg completed before his retirement (though he had two novels to finish). It deals with children who are raised specifically to be oracles, following the separation of the two halves of their brain. In the same issue, John Brunner delivered a wonderfully British story of a professor who stumbles upon the next step in evolution in 'Bloodstream'. Most memorable amongst Edward Bryant's several contributions was 'Sharking Down' (February 1975) where the fate of the final city of Cinnabar is decided by a battle between a robot shark and a genetically recreated megalodon.

Only one story from *Vertex* made it to a Nebula final ballot – William Carlson's 'Sunrise West', a novella run in two episodes (October–December 1974). It's set in the future following America's economic collapse and a return to barbarism in a country that includes animals with scientifically enhanced intelligence. It's a well-written adventure, typical of many at the time that considered a post-catastrophe United States.

Vertex discovered several new writers. Although John Varley's first sale was to *F&SF*, it was only by a matter of days and *Vertex* managed to get 'Scoreboard' into print earlier (August 1974).[146] It's a wargame story where Varley looks at the consequences of a conflict on the asteroid Ceres. Joseph Patrouch, Jr.'s first sale, 'One Little Room an Everywhere' (February 1974), is a humorous story of advanced aliens who are amazed that humans have advanced technology but have not progressed beyond carnal sex. Greg Bear had been writing columns for the fan magazines but had not made a professional sale for seven years before *Vertex* bought his article on planetaria, 'The Space Theater' (April 1974). Thomas Easton had sold an erotic novel in 1971, and a sale to *Adam* brought him to *Vertex* with 'End and Beginning' (December 1974), an account from the future looking back on the final days of an Arab–Israeli conflict. Stephen Goldin's wife, Kathleen Sky, made her debut with 'Door to Malequar' (July 1975), where the real secret of an artist's colony is revealed. More often than not, it was the new writers who gave *Vertex* its freshness and character as a magazine which was prepared to experiment. Over the years that freshness has turned slightly stale so that *Vertex* is now something of a period piece, but an interesting one.

Vertex had several regular contributors – William Rotsler, Neil Shapiro, Herman Wrede, Mildred Downey Broxon, F. M. Busby – but no one classifiable as a *Vertex* author. Besides its newness and slickness, *Vertex* was not around long enough to develop a personality. In fact, its slickness defines it. There was too much material of average quality that just slid

146 'Scoreboard' and 'Picnic on Nearside' appeared in the August 1974 issues of *Vertex* and *F&SF* respectively, but as *Vertex* was bi-monthly, its issue came out in early June, almost a month before the *F&SF* issue appeared.

through the mind. It looked good, with its artwork and format, but was otherwise too shallow. Pfeil delighted in running a 'Potpourri' of very short stories, most of which were little more than extended jokes. Forrest Ackerman attempted to write 'the shortest ever story ever told', 'Cosmic Report Card' (June 1973), which in theory was one letter, but in practice relied on a set of notes to make sense. Pfeil stated in his first editorial that his purpose was to 'please and entertain', and that he did, but lightly, with too little to challenge.

The print run for the first issue of *Vertex* had been 100,000 copies with the intention of increasing this to 500,000 by the year-end. That was clearly overambitious, although after the first four issues an exuberant Don Pfeil was remarking, '*Vertex* is enjoying outstanding sales, and it appears that our upcoming ABC audit will show it to be outselling any other sf magazine on the market.'[147] That probably related to news-stand sales only, as *Analog*'s total sales at that time were 114,000, beyond *Vertex*'s print run. But its news-stand sales were 65,000, which *Vertex* might well have exceeded. With a cover price twice that of *Analog*'s, that would have made *Vertex* profitable, despite the extra production costs. *Vertex* had attempted to encourage subscriptions, but even its charter rate was twice that of *Analog*'s and, by its second year, it still had only 4,300, a tenth of *Analog*'s. By then news-stand sales had fallen to under 50,000.

The paper shortage of the early seventies was also having its impact. The paper used had changed from glossy to matt from June 1974, but the drastic change came with the June 1975 issue. *Vertex* shifted to tabloid format and used all newsprint paper, looking more like *Rolling Stone* than a science-fiction magazine. At the same time, it shifted to a monthly schedule and reduced its price to $1. It was a valiant effort to keep the magazine going, and Pfeil believed it might improve distribution, but instead it bombed. *Vertex*'s main attraction had been its up-market slickness and polish, but this was now lost and, despite attempts to sustain the variety of content, it now looked cheap and ugly. The idea to start a new Flash Gordon comic-strip serial in the August 1975 issue was also misguided. These final three issues, which ran some reasonably good fiction by Harlan Ellison, John Varley, F. M. Busby, Scott Edelstein and Ed Bryant (another Cinnabar story), are amongst the hardest to find.

The publisher tried to find a buyer for the magazine, but the paper restrictions made it less viable. Such paper as Mankind was able to secure was allocated to the more lucrative titles, and *Vertex* had to go.[148] Had it

---

147 Don Pfeil, letter in *The Alien Critic* #7, November 1973, p. 15.
148 See news stories in *Luna* #59 (November 1975), p. 9 and *Locus* #174 (3 June 1975), p. 1.

not been for the economic climate, and had *Vertex* been edited with a more qualitative eye, it could have become a significant force. It remains readable but disappointing, and is now a museum piece of what might have been.

Another experiment in format and presentation was happening at the same time in Britain. The publisher New English Library (NEL) had a good art department and was proud of its bright and vibrant paperback covers. They received many requests for copies of the covers and NEL decided to publish a poster magazine which became *Science Fiction Monthly*. During the development stage it was agreed to extend this to running stories and features, though the emphasis remained on the art.

This was at a time when the science-fiction world was rediscovering its roots and several books appeared which were superficially surveys of science fiction but were really excuses to reprint plenty of lurid covers from old pulps and books. The way had been led by Jacques Sadoul's *Hier, l'an 2000* (Denoël, 1973), with English-language editions as *2000 AD*, from Souvenir Press in the UK and Henry Regnery in the US in 1975. At the same time, Anthony Frewin compiled *100 Years of Science Fiction Illustration* (1974), and more would follow. James Gunn wrote *Alternate Worlds, the Illustrated History of Science Fiction* (1975), Hilary and Dik Evans went back to the earliest sources for *Beyond the Gaslight* (1976) and New English Library, encouraged by the success of *Science Fiction Monthly*, commissioned Brian Aldiss to compile a poster-size book, *Science Fiction Art* (1975). Harry Harrison would later bring together an illustrated history of sex in science fiction, *Great Balls of Fire* (1977).

The first issue of *Science Fiction Monthly* appeared on the last Wednesday of January 1974.[149] It was in large tabloid format (40 cm x 28 cm) with 28 unstapled pages, selling for 25p. The cover was a partial reproduction of Bruce Pennington's dustjacket painting for Arthur C. Clarke's *2001*, and the full cover was reproduced inside as a double-page spread. This was the main selling point of the magazine. Five of the pages opened up into poster-size paintings, and there were another four single-page reproductions.

The artwork reproduction was excellent. The magazine ran work by Tim White, Bruce Pennington, Josh Kirby, E. M. Clifton-Day, Gareth Colman, David Hardy, David Pelham, Roger Dean, Jim Burns and many more, at last giving some identity to the all-too-often-anonymous cover artist. The overall editorial director was Patricia Hornsey, but Michael Osborn

---

149 All issues were undated, carrying only an issue and volume number, but technically the first issue was for February 1974 and it continued on a monthly schedule.

was art editor and responsible for the magazine's appearance and format, along with art director Cecil Smith and designer Jeremy Dixon. At the outset, Aune Butt and Penny Grant had responsibility for acquiring the textual material, but this passed to Julie Davis from the eighth issue.

Alongside the posters, everything else seemed incidental, although the editorial team did a good job in assembling a full package. At the time, it was Britain's only regular monthly market for short sf and it was flooded with manuscripts at the rate of 400–500 a month. Since it usually published only two or three fiction items each issue, and it liked to include at least one major name, and sometimes used reprints, the scope for new authors was limited and it's surprising that any managed to break through. Yet both Terry Greenhough and Chris Morgan owe their first sales to *Science Fiction Monthly*. David S. Garnett's first British appearance was in the December 1974 issue and Garry Kilworth's magazine debut was in April 1976.

The magazine launched a short-story competition, but it was some months before the results were decided. The winner was David Coles who had previously sold a story to John Carnell's *New Writings*, and his story, 'Horizontal Spy', about psionic espionage, appeared in the January 1975 issue. Other winners included the best Commonwealth entry, 'Time and Again', by David James, which uses what is now called the 'groundhog-day' principle of being trapped in a time loop, and the best 'Foreign' entry by Christine Stinchcombe, 'Return to Earth', a New Age look at Earth's former inhabitants. Unfortunately, none of these authors established a reputation in the field.

Amongst British authors there were several contributions by reliables Brian Stableford, Ian Watson and Robert Holdstock, and occasional appearances by Brian Aldiss, Christopher Priest, Josephine Saxton, Bob Shaw and Robert Wells. The American stories were mostly reprints but the occasional new story appeared, including 'Shatterday' by Harlan Ellison (September 1975) and 'The Highest Dive' by Jack Williamson (February 1976).

The format only allowed for relatively short fiction, and it is a credit to its contributors that the stories were usually of a high quality and attracted reader attention rather than serving as filling between the art. There were many mood stories or sharp tales written around clever ideas. Some of the more unusual stories include Greenhough's debut, 'The Tree in the Forest' (March 1974), about the fate of explorers on an alien world; 'Dark Icarus' by Bob Shaw (May 1974) on the perils of future flying; 'Song of the Dead Gulls' by Chris Penn (November 1974), a chilling portrayal of the fate of an irradiated village; 'Our Loves so Truly Meridional' (February

1975), Ian Watson's clever twist on racial equality, and 'The Antique Restorer' by Bruce Crowther (October 1975) where a time scoop allows a computer to resynthesize people from the past. Janet Sacks, in NEL's book department, gave a more permanent home to a representative selection of the magazine's fiction by compiling a *Best of Science Fiction Monthly* after the first year.

The magazine's features included a series of profiles of sf artists. Walter Gillings contributed an incisive overview of various classic authors' works, with each profile accompanied by a classic reprint, and he also ran 'The Query Box', responding to readers' questions. It was in *Science Fiction Monthly* that the original series of my 'History of the Science Fiction Magazine' appeared (April–July 1974). There were other articles by John Brosnan on sf cinema, and Peter Weston on the various themes of sf. There were author interviews, which occasionally developed into a special feature. The April 1975 issue, for instance, ran a new story by Edmund Cooper, 'Jupiter Laughs', along with a profile and interview by James Goddard. There were features on Harlan Ellison (September 1975), J. G. Ballard (November 1975), Keith Roberts (January 1976) and Robert Silverberg (April 1976). Other interviews included Christopher Priest (January 1975), Samuel Delany (April 1975), Bob Shaw (October 1975), Harry Harrison (December 1975) and D. G. Compton (May 1976). There was a special Australian issue in August 1975 to tie in with the World Convention in Melbourne and which ran new fiction by Lee Harding and Cherry Wilder.

The magazine ran a regular news column, which included information of fan conventions and publications and, as a consequence, *Science Fiction Monthly* worked well at promoting and stimulating fandom.

The magazine sold well at the outset with a reported circulation of 150,000 by the third issue.[150] However, the poster novelty eventually ran its course and, although *Science Fiction Monthly* worked hard at boosting its other features, outside factors soon had their effect. Britain suffered even more than America from the economic bleakness of the seventies. The magazine's cover price rose rapidly through 30p in October 1974 to 35p (May 1975), 40p (January 1976) and 50p (April 1976). Circulation plummeted to below twenty thousand, which was insufficient to sustain the magazine's high production costs. In what proved to be its last number (May 1976) the editor rather cruelly ran a long, vehement letter from a reader in Stoke-on-Trent saying how much the magazine was an 'utter waste of money' and that he was convinced it would be dead before the end of the year.

150 See *Locus* #159, 11 May 1974, p. 7.

NEL replaced it with *S.F. Digest*, from the same editorial and production team. It was intended to be a quarterly with the first issue out in mid-May 1976. It was half the size of *SF Monthly*, in quarto format, but still only 48 pages for 50p. It ran some interior art, but no more double-spread posters. The emphasis was on fiction, with four new stories by Brian Aldiss, John Brosnan, Rachel Pollack and Michael G. Coney, plus a reprint of Silverberg's 'In the House of Double Minds'. There was an interview with Dr Christopher Evans and a new column by Maxim Jakubowski.

This magazine had more potential than *SF Monthly*, but alas its fate was decided even before the print was dry on the first issue. New English Library was undergoing a merger with Hodder and Stoughton and the decision was made to axe NEL's magazine department. With it went once again Britain's hope of a regular sf magazine.

Science Fiction Monthly is remembered today mostly for its artwork and seldom for its fiction, but it ran some worthy material, gave British writers at least the chance of a home sale and encouraged new writers.

There were a couple of other items of passing interest that NEL published as companions to *SF Monthly*. NEL (under its Four Square imprint) had long been the British publisher of the works of Edgar Rice Burroughs, and in September 1975, on the centenary of Burrough's birth, they issued a one-off edition called simply *Edgar Rice Burroughs*,[151] compiled by Penny Grant. It was in the same large tabloid format as *SF Monthly*, but with only 28 pages. It included an article by Walter Gillings on Burroughs's life and work. There were many cover paintings and photographs and features on all aspects of Burroughs's writings, plus an interview with Michael Moorcock about his interest in Burroughs's work and his involvement in the filming of *The Land That Time Forgot*. This has now become a fascinating collector's item.

Of far less interest was *Ghoul*, a horror-oriented quarto-size companion to *S.F. Digest*, also issued in June 1976. This was also edited by Penny Grant and written almost entirely by R. Chetwynd-Hayes under a variety of silly pen-names, bowing to his penchant for ghoulish humour. *Ghoul* was no loss when NEL's magazine department closed, but *S.F. Digest* was.

Science Fiction Monthly had presented mostly traditional British sf, but the long shadow of *New Worlds* continued to darken publishers' doors. *New Worlds* itself was appearing as a paperback anthology, which I shall discuss in the next section. In 1975 the London printer and publisher PPLayouts, run by Andrew Ellsmore, put out a magazine called *Other Times*. This was

151 The promotion called it the *Edgar Rice Burroughs Centenary Magazine* but the last two words are missing from the actual issue.

in the same large-flat slick format as the final issues of *New Worlds* and had much the same publishing philosophy, calling itself 'an international speculative quarterly'. It acknowledged the support and help of Michael Moorcock, Hilary Bailey and Christopher Priest. It ran indefinable stories, similar to those in *New Worlds*, by John Sladek and Barry Malzberg in the first issue (dated November 1975/January 1976) and Gregory FitzGerald and Edward Bryant in the second issue (February 1976), along with brief mood pieces, articles and pictorials. Priced at 60p for its 48 pages, it was even more expensive that *Science Fiction Monthly* and offered far less. Under-capitalized and over-ambitious, it passed away after two issues.

Soon after the demise of *S.F. Digest*, *Vortex* came along. This was a very attractive magazine with full colour interior and cover artwork printed on glossy paper in quarto format. Its 48 pages sold for 45p and it called itself, rather oddly, 'The Science Fiction Fantasy'. It came from the firm of Cerberus Publishing in Bushey Heath in Hertfordshire.

Editor Keith Seddon was only 19. He had secured the editorship because his father knew the publisher, Edward Shacklady, who in the normal course of events published aviation magazines. Seddon believed he could secure Michael Moorcock's new novel and the project was born. Seddon's interest was broader than the New Wave, with a fascination for speculative fiction in the widest sense. In his first editorial he complained about the lack of such a market in Britain, which he regarded as 'the richest in possibilities'.[152]

The stories in the first issue did not reflect this richness. 'First Entry' by Steve Axtell is a stream of consciousness rediscovery of life and birth. 'The Englishman's Lady' by Ravan Christchild is mock Moorcock, the first of a quasi-steampunk series of time travel in an alternate Edwardian age. There was some of the real thing with the serialization of Moorcock's 'The End of All Songs', already available in book form in the United States but not yet published in Britain. There was also a reprint of Robert Holdstock's 'The Touch of a Vanished Hand', a moving story of the loneliness of space, which had previously appeared only in a small circulation fanzine.[153]

Moorcock's serial and Christchild's series dominated the next few issues which otherwise contained only minor stories by unknown authors, some pseudonymously. There were, though, interviews with artists and authors: James Cawthorn (January 1977), Rodney Matthews (February 1977), Michael Moorcock (April 1977) and Eddie Jones (May 1977). The fifth issue showed signs of development, with a new story by Terry Greenhough, 'A Gift of Time', and the start of Colin Kapp's serial, 'The Chaos

152 See 'Editorial', *Vortex* 1:1 (January 1977), p. 1.
153 *Zimri* #7 (January 1975).

Weapon'. Unfortunately this was the last issue, leaving Kapp's serial unfinished until published complete by Ballantine Books in the United States later that year.

The magazine was proving more expensive than originally planned, mostly because of the publisher's insistence on full-colour artwork throughout. There were 50,000 copies printed of the first issue, reducing to 35,000 for the fifth, and sales of those first few issues were between 15,000 and 20,000 copies. The magazine might have survived had it not been for the cost of paper and colour printing, and the absence of any substantial advertising revenue. Also, Seddon had been working excessive hours in putting the magazine together, with no editorial assistance. The publisher, whose view of science fiction was planets and rockets, was dissatisfied with the direction Seddon had been taking the magazine, and fired him after he had assembled the sixth issue (dated June/July but never distributed). He sought the services of Peter Weston, who showed interest but was dubious of the publisher's abilities.[154] In the end, further conflict arose between Shacklady and Seddon's father over the way his son had been fired and all plans fell through, another lost market. It would be five more years before Britain finally got a regular and reliable magazine.

The only other professional magazines to appear before 1977 were *The Haunt of Horror* and a revival of *Weird Tales*. Neither of these was a sf magazine *per se*, and they form part of a separate evolution which was generating a growth in magazines of weird and supernatural fiction and which would soon, thanks to the popularity of Stephen King and Dean R. Koontz, bring the fields closer together. I shall save discussion about that for Chapter 3.

There was another, much bigger challenge facing the sf magazines during the early seventies. The start of the decade brought a gathering flood of anthologies bearing original short fiction, promising high wordage rates and greater freedom for writers on a wide range of subjects. These anthologies were seen not only as rivals to the magazines, but also as their successors.

154 See Peter Weston, *With Stars in My Eyes* (Framingham, MA: NESFA Press, 2004), pp. 244–7.

2

All This and Elwood Too:
The Rival Gateways

The Threat from Within

When the first science-fiction magazines emerged, they did not have much competition for their readership. Those who enjoyed science fiction would find some amongst the other pulps, and occasionally in book form – usually in comparatively expensive hardcovers – but in terms of reading matter there was not much about. They could turn to the cinema, and by the 1930s the talkies were of sufficient quality for sf films to be of interest – especially once such classics as *Frankenstein* and *King Kong* hit the screens. But this did not really dent the readership for the magazines – if anything it enhanced it.

But over the years more and more has emerged to capture the attention of readers and to divert them away from the magazines. Indeed, most of the history of the sf magazine has been a war of attrition against these other temptations. If we leave aside the cinema, radio and television for the moment and concentrate on the printed page, the first major rivals were the sf comic books, especially the superhero comics which seriously rivalled the lower-level hero pulps and eventually defeated them.

The main enemy of the sf magazine, however, was the growth of the pocketbook from the late forties onwards and particularly by the early sixties. By then there was sufficient top-quality science fiction appearing in cheap paperbacks – especially novels – that readers did not need to turn to a science-fiction magazine at all. There were more than enough books to absorb their time. The growth of the short-story anthology – both those that selected from old magazines and those that chose the best from each year – must have superseded the magazine in the hearts and minds of many readers. Even so, there was at least a symbiosis between these publications, the magazine providing the raw material and the anthology reprinting the best.

Then came the threat of the original anthology. That is, the anthology that ran all new fiction, rather than any selected from earlier sources. This was riding right into the heart of magazine territory and threatening to lure away not only their readers but their writers too. The phenomenon of the original anthology mushroomed in the seventies to such an extent that many believed that it would supersede the magazine and that the days of the magazine were numbered. This section will look at the rise and fall of the original anthology and chart its impact on the magazine world.

The first regular original anthology sf series had been *Star Science Fiction* edited by Frederik Pohl and published in the United States by Ballantine Books. It ran for six volumes between 1953 and 1959, with an additional *Star Short Novels* in 1954. As discussed in *Transformations*, in 1957 Pohl believed the series might work better as a digest magazine, and one issue appeared in magazine format in January 1958 but sold poorly because of dealer resistance at that time to new magazines. Ian Ballantine had never been wholly behind the magazine experiment and *Star* was converted back to pocketbook format for three final volumes. The series as a whole was successful and set a standard that many would later try and emulate. It also helped to establish the criteria that distinguished between the original anthology and the magazine.

The chief benefit of the book was that it would stay on the bookstall for longer than a monthly or even bi-monthly magazine. If it sold well it could be reprinted. There was also the possibility of hardcover and paperback editions, British editions and translations. In simple terms the book had a longer lifetime than a magazine issue, allowing greater exposure and a higher profile of the book and, of course, its contents. The natural extension of this is that the contributors could well earn more for their work. Although the initial advance might be at a similar wordage rate, the opportunity for reprints and other sales meant that the book might go into profit and, if the authors had a contract allowing them to share in that profit, then they would receive further royalties.

These are two big advantages to the publisher, editor and contributor. So what are the drawbacks? Why, if it is so advantageous, did Frederik Pohl want to return to the magazine format? Pohl had said that he had felt constrained by the pocketbook format. This takes several forms. Firstly, there is the obvious physical limit of the book itself. In the fifties, the wordage in a pocketbook was about the same as in a magazine, around fifty thousand. If the book appeared only once or twice a year, the editor could buy only that much material, whereas a monthly magazine could clearly buy six to twelve times as much. The editor is thus limited in the amount of fiction he can buy, and that is a frustration for both him and the contributor. The contributor therefore stands a better chance of selling a story to a magazine than to an anthology, unless that anthology is itself monthly, and there is little benefit in that as it promptly negates one of the main advantages, that of prolonged sale time.

The other restriction goes to the heart of what distinguishes a magazine from an anthology. A magazine, by its very name, is a miscellany. It doesn't run only fiction, but has other features, including book reviews, letter columns and topical articles, all of which give the magazine a distinct personality and continuity. The editor of an anthology is denied most of these features because the material will rapidly be out of date and seem pointless if the book is reprinted.

So the big advantages of the magazine are its frequency, its topicality and its diversity. This was certainly enough to fight back against the anthology's two main weapons of higher payments and greater profile. This was what was learned from publishing *Star Science Fiction*, and it showed that with the advantages on both sides the original anthology and the magazine could co-exist.

That assumed, of course, that all else remained equal. However, by the end of the fifties magazine distribution was in turmoil. Pocketbooks were gaining the ascendance and with it a chance for the original anthology to try and encroach further into the magazine's domain. The next step, though, did not happen in the United States but in Britain, which gives us a chance to explore the British scene at the start of the seventies.

The British Dimension

The individual who had seen the writing on the wall for the fiction-magazine market was John Carnell. He had been the founding editor of *New Worlds* in 1946 and had also edited *Science Fantasy* and the British edition of *Science Fiction Adventures*. He had been involved in the founding of the British Science Fiction Book Club and later became the first British literary agent to specialize in science fiction. Because of Carnell, many British sf writers had a prosperous home market in the fifties, which helped them develop.

But by the early sixties magazine readership in Britain was in decline. Magazines such as *New Worlds* were already an anomaly. Most of the major popular fiction magazines had faded away during the Second World War and never recovered afterwards. *The Strand* had died in 1950 – technically merged with *Men Only*, which was a fate worse than death. It had been revived briefly in 1961 as *The New Strand*, with the emphasis on crime fiction, but it lasted only 15 issues. *Lilliput*, the other major survivor from the war, had ceased in July 1960. The weekly *John Bull* had folded in February 1960. The only fiction-carrying magazines to survive in Britain, apart from science fiction, were crime-fiction titles and women's magazines.

At the start of 1964 Carnell conducted a survey amongst his readers. In addition to finding that the average age of the respondents was 26.1 (down from 30.8 in 1958 when he had last conducted the survey), he discovered that 20 per cent of readers read no sf magazine other than *New Worlds*, while the remaining 80 per cent read on average three other magazines. By comparison those same readers acquired an average of four paperbacks per month, some as many as twenty. Carnell had conducted a survey in 1953 as well, so he had three sets of data on which to base the following conclusions.

> The obvious assumption here ... is that the older reader is no longer buying sf magazines (the average has halved in ten years) and the majority of sf readers are buying more and more paperbacks in this medium. ... I would even go as far as to assume that the majority of older readers have given up the magazines entirely and now only buy paperback sf. This is evident from the number of paperbacks published or distributed here each month (an average of 8) with circulations around 30,000 copies each (except the imported editions which are around 10,000) against an average of 3 per month and half the foregoing circulation four years ago – when sf magazine sales were twice what they are today.[1]

The decision to cease publication of *New Worlds* and *Science Fantasy* had already been made in December 1963 when Carnell entered into an agreement with Transworld Publishing to produce a regular original anthology, *New Writings in SF*, to be issued in pocketbook format by Corgi Books and in hardcover by Dennis Dobson. As it happened, *New Worlds* was reprieved, and I shall return to that shortly, but Carnell was already moving on. The first *New Writings* appeared in August 1964 and for the next two years sustained a regular quarterly schedule, but by 1967 it had started to waver, primarily because the hardcover sales were slipping and Dobson's wanted the books on sale for longer. At least two volumes per year appeared thereafter, usually in the spring and autumn, and there were occasions when the Corgi paperback edition appeared before the hardcover.

1   E. J. Carnell, 'Survey Report 1963', *New Worlds* 47:141 (April 1964), p. 3.

New Writings is an undervalued series. It would run in total for longer and with more volumes than any similar American series: 14 years and 30 volumes. Carnell edited it for 21 volumes, until his death in March 1972, and Kenneth Bulmer sustained it for 9 more. Under Bulmer the hardcover edition came from Sidgwick & Jackson, but Transworld remained loyal throughout and all 30 volumes appeared in a consistent format.

Carnell filled *New Writings* with the type of science fiction that he enjoyed, and it remained the last bastion of traditional Britishness against the onslaught of the New Wave. It was to all intents a continuation of the *New Worlds* of the fifties, with many of the same writers who had not been able to adjust to the sf revolution or did not feel at home in the American market. Philip E. High, Edward Mackin, John Kippax, Donald Malcolm, Dan Morgan and others had all previously appeared in *New Writings* since Volume 1. There was also work by writers whose fiction was appreciated in America – James White, Colin Kapp, Keith Roberts, Brian Aldiss – and Carnell also provided an outlet for Australian and Canadian writers – Damien Broderick, Vincent King, Lee Harding, H. A. Hargreaves and more. Even Americans occasionally found their way into its pages – Frederik Pohl, James H. Schmitz, Donald A. Wollheim – but no one who would substantially rock the boat. *New Writings* was never groundbreaking. It was comfortable, enjoyable and occasionally old-fashioned – the kind of book that helped you relax rather than made you feel you were on a crusade.

Carnell tended to stick to his stable of clients but Bulmer widened the scope. Harry Harrison who, perhaps surprisingly, had not appeared in any of Carnell's volumes, led Bulmer's first volume with 'An Honest Day's Work' which contrasted the human element with computer warfare. Brian Aldiss returned and appeared in several volumes with groupings of his strangely reflective enigmas.

Bulmer gave a few writers their first professional outings. Charles Partington, who had been one half of the team who had produced the semi-prozine *Alien Worlds* in 1966 and who had sold a weird tale to August Derleth for the anthology *Dark Things* in 1971, made his British professional debut with a study of prejudice, 'Sporting On Apteryx' (#23, 1973). Noted fan writer David Langford debuted in the professional world with a typically madcap 'Heatwave' (#27, 1975). Fellow fan Leroy Kettle, who went on to write various pseudonymous horror novels with John Brosnan and who later still became an honoured policy adviser to the British government on disability rights, made his first sale with 'The Great Plan' (#28, 1976).

Bulmer's major discovery, though, was the New Zealand writer (though

Australian resident), Cherry Wilder. Remarkably Wilder was the first woman writer to be published by *New Writings* with 'The Ark of James Carlyle' in Volume 24 (April 1974). Wilder had sold various men's adventure stories and literary stories to Australian magazines since the mid-fifties but only turned to science fiction in 1973. Bertram Chandler suggested she send her story to *New Writings* but, believing there was sexism amongst male editors, she submitted the story under a male pseudonym. Once it was accepted she revealed her true identity. According to Wilder, 'Ken Bulmer was delighted ... the story "made him sweat", when I was a chap, but when I was a woman he found it "evocative".'[2]

The story deals with space explorers trying to understand the nature of a strange life-form, the quogs, whose ability to communicate initially confuses the explorers. Just what section made Bulmer sweat I do not know, but there is an episode when a group of quogs remove the clothes from another. As they are of indeterminate sex, the observer is puzzled by it. If that is the scene, then Bulmer's view that a woman writing it is more evocative than a man suggests he believed that women brought a greater freedom and sensuality to the field. The story is clearly by a seasoned writer and Wilder – the name Cherry Grimm adopted for her sf – was soon selling widely to other anthologies and magazines, and had two more stories in the *New Writings* series. There were other women who contributed to *New Writings* after her, but none who reached her stature.

Bulmer succeeded in moving *New Writings* with the times without ever becoming too experimental. 'The emphasis of the series is changing very slightly,' he wrote in 1975, 'but I like to put in one or two of the "old-fashioned" stories when they are well done.'[3] In fact, under Bulmer, even the more traditional writers sharpened their skills, producing more penetrating, contemporary work. Donald Malcolm's 'The Enemy Within' (#25, 1975), for instance, shows how drugs help resolve a menace introduced by the return of mankind's first starship. Bulmer also provided a market to the new generation of writers – Christopher Priest, David S. Garnett, Michael G. Coney and Robert Holdstock all made occasional sales. Perhaps no story feels more contemporary by twenty-first century standards than Ian Watson's 'To the Pump Room With Jane' (#26, 1975), which considered a global drought.

New Writings continued to appear on a twice-yearly basis through the first half of the seventies, though sales diminished. Volume 30, though

2 Interview with Wilder by Miriam Hurst in September 1999, on the internet at http://nzsfw.sf.org.nz/articles/article05.htm

3 Letter by Kenneth Bulmer in *Science Fiction Review* #15 (November 1975), p. 50.

copyrighted 1977, was never issued in hardcover and did not appear until the paperback edition in September 1978. Without Sidgwick & Jackson's support, Transworld suspended the series, although Bulmer had the next two volumes compiled. Despite its increased irregularity, the loss of any market was a blow to British writers, especially when the British scene looked so bleak. Both Carnell and Bulmer had succeeded in sustaining a market for the storyteller, which was increasingly rare in Britain.

New Worlds could not have been further removed from *New Writings*. Michael Moorcock had taken it in a completely different direction, following a course already emerging in British sf in the works of J. G. Ballard and, to some extent, Brian Aldiss, and in the wider literary avant-garde by such authors as William Burroughs. Soon christened the New Wave, it brought an outcry from traditionalists but a growing coterie of new writers – Charles Platt, Langdon Jones, Graham Charnock, David I. Masson, Michael Butterworth – saw the potential and pushed the boundaries of science fiction (some now called it speculative fiction) way beyond anything seen hitherto. Significantly, there were several American writers – Thomas M. Disch, Norman Spinrad, John Sladek, James Sallis, Roger Zelazny amongst them – who found that *New Worlds* gave them a greater freedom of expression than any American market. A revolution was starting.

Moorcock's original plan to have a large-format magazine had been dashed by his publisher, David Warburton, who felt sales would be better if *New Worlds* were in pocketbook format. It did indeed sustain sales for a while, allowing the magazine better display in the bookracks. Sales of the early issues were around twenty thousand, greater than the final Carnell issues.

But, as related in *Transformations*, in 1967 the publisher Roberts & Vinter suffered financial setbacks and *New Worlds* almost folded again until rescued by an Arts Council grant. Now Moorcock had his glossy large format, but the experimentalism of the magazine and charges of obscenity brought against it eventually lost it major distribution in Britain through W. H. Smith. The magazine succumbed at the start of 1971, at which point Moorcock took the same route as Carnell, seven years earlier, and entered an agreement for a paperback version of *New Worlds*. The first volume was published in Britain by Sphere Books in September 1971, with a simultaneous American edition from Berkley Books.

Almost as a pilot to that transformation, Langdon Jones, erstwhile associate editor of *New Worlds*, had compiled an anthology *The New SF*, published by Hutchinson in hardcover in 1969 and issued under their

Arrow paperback imprint the following year.[4] It was labelled 'an original anthology of modern speculative fiction', its cover blurb saying, 'From the world of Science Fiction writing there has come a totally new literature, a Space Age fiction created by writers to whom new material demanded new techniques. Now they use the new techniques to explore territory way beyond the original Science Fiction bases.'

That was the publishing hype, but in fact the contributors, who included Giles Gordon, James Sallis, Brian Aldiss, Michael Butterworth, John Sladek and Thomas M. Disch, used less-experimental techniques than in the large-format *New Worlds*. It was not the techniques that were important – they were a superficial effect to shift reader's perceptions; what was important was the substance of the story. J. G. Ballard, whose radio interview by George MacBeth was printed in the anthology, contrasted the traditional and new forms of science fiction:

> Modern American science fiction [is] an extrovert, optimistic literature of technology, whereas I think the new science fiction, that other people apart from myself are now beginning to write, is introverted, possibly pessimistic rather than optimistic, much less certain of its own territory.[5]

This reflected a mood of the time, which grabbed American science fiction a few years later. The contributors to *New Worlds* perceived a world running down. Entropy was a key word in the image of the magazine, becoming a synonym for the decline of civilization. It was used by various authors in various ways but was perhaps best exemplified in Pamela Zoline's story 'The Heat Death of the Universe' from the July 1967 issue, which used the physical and mental decline of a housewife trapped by her routine as a metaphor for the collapse of society.

From the bright-eyed optimism of early science fiction, glorying in the mastery of science and the conquest of outer space, there was a shift in awareness to the state of the planet (socially, politically, ecologically) and the state of humanity itself. In contrast to outer space, this became termed 'inner space'. It was a phrase coined by J. B. Priestley as far back as 1954 but was reintroduced by J. G. Ballard in 1962, and it was his usage that stuck.[6]

---

4 Hutchinson had originally asked Moorcock to compile this anthology, but he passed it over to Jones. Moorcock provided the introduction and commissioned some of the contributions.

5 Ballard interviewed by George MacBeth, 'The New Science Fiction, 2: Prospective Narrative', BBC Radio, The Third Programme, London, 29 March 1967.

6 In 'They Came from Inner Space' (*The New Statesman and Nation*, 16 (1953), p. 712) Priestley argued that science fiction had sought to explore outer space rather than 'the hidden life of the psyche'. His definition of 'inner space', regarding mankind's fears and

The fiction published in *The New SF* and *New Worlds* was not science fiction in the usual sense, and indeed Charles Platt frequently argued that *New Worlds* was not a science fiction publication. It was, though, a close ally. Most of the anxieties and problems mankind was facing in the late twentieth century were ones brought on by technology. It was a subject addressed by Alvin Toffler in his book *Future Shock*, published in May 1970. The book was labelled 'a study of mass bewilderment in the face of accelerating change' and looked at mankind's inability to cope with the rapid pace of change that had hit society in the last few decades – and would continue to do so. It was no mere coincidence that science fiction was undergoing a revolution at this same time. The New Wavers, under Ballard's 'inner space' banner, had moved from looking at the wonders of science to the effects of those wonders, psychologically and sociologically. One could imagine that while science fiction was the prophet and, to some degree, the conscience of science, the New Wave had become the prophet and conscience of science fiction. The New Wavers were monitoring the symptoms of Toffler's 'future shock'.

The book version of *New Worlds* saw some compromise towards a traditional readership without totally sacrificing its principles – though it did label itself 'the Science Fiction Quarterly' on the cover of the first volume. In his editorial, Moorcock remarked:

> Although identified with a so-called 'new wave', we have always preferred to publish as wide a spectrum of speculative and imaginative fiction as possible. We have encouraged experiment, certainly, but we have not published unconventional material to the exclusion of all else. It would have been stupid to do so since we ourselves and, we assume, our readers enjoy all kinds of fiction.[7]

He was even more critical in the second volume:

> Just as one tires of reading too many space adventure stories or engineering problem stories, so it's possible to become quickly bored with the more recent kinds of sf – the wistful and inconsequential mood piece, the typographical trickery used to hide a sparsity of content or, perhaps worst of all, the baroque 'myth' story produced by too many of today's once-promising young writers. The bulk of so-called New Wave

---

anxieties, is close to Ballard's in 'Which Way to Inner Space?' (*New Worlds* #118, May 1962). However, throughout the fifties and sixties the phrase was used loosely by the media to mean either that part of outer space which encircled the Earth and the Moon, or the remote places of the Earth's surface, or the world beneath our feet or the ocean's depths. It also came to mean that part of our psyche where our subconscious lurks or where we go on a drug trip. The phrase was never fully understood and has generally dropped out of usage.

7 Michael Moorcock, 'Introduction', *New Worlds 1* (1971), p. 10.

science fiction has no more claim to be worthy of serious attention than the bulk of so-called Old Wave sf. Most of the stuff is barely entertaining, much is irritatingly whimsical or portentous.[8]

Was this a sign that Moorcock was turning his back on the New Wave? Not at all. As he went on to explain in this second editorial, any form of fiction, especially if constrained by genre definitions, soon finds itself at the limit of expression and needs to break out of that genre. What Moorcock wanted to do with *New Worlds* – what he had always wanted to do – was to release science fiction and all other forms of speculative fiction from the bonds of genre identification and let it find its level within the mainstream. The labelling of these anthologies as 'science fiction' did not help his case, but it was a marketing decision made by Sphere simply because a science-fiction anthology generally sold more copies than a mainstream anthology. Moorcock, therefore, had to aim his comments primarily at a science-fiction readership, in the hope that it might broaden their thinking, and also that at least some of the broader mainstream readership – who, in Britain, had been supportive of *New Worlds* – would take his message on board.

The first volume of the anthology *New Worlds*, which included a few reprints from earlier magazine issues that had been banned from full distribution and thus not readily available, ran a selection of material from the conventional to the experimental, much of it unremittingly bleak. The opening story, 'Angouleme' by Thomas M. Disch, formed a suitable continuity from the previous *New Worlds*, with its grim vision of street gangs of murderous children in the near future. Keith Robert's 'The God House',[9] though a post-catastrophe story, is more akin, in mood and setting, to his alternate-world Pavane series. Nevertheless, in its vision of a new generation bringing violence back to the world, it has a kinship with Disch's tale. Almost all hope is dashed in Barrington Bayley's 'Exit from City 5', which sees the end of the universe and an uncertainty about the fate of those who managed to escape beyond, 'into non-being'. 'The Lamia and Lord Cromis', one of M. John Harrison's Viriconium stories, is a bleak and decadent literary fantasy highlighting a move in the field of 'heroic' fantasy much like that being taken by Moorcock in his Dancers at the End of Time series. There is some light relief in two amusing tales by John Sladek, of which 'Pemberly's Star-Afresh Calliope' is a wonderful pastiche of the scientific romance and a progenitor of the steampunk movement.

The next few volumes of *New Worlds* were all in a similar vein – inven-

8 Michael Moorcock, 'Introduction', *New Worlds 2* (1971), p. 9.
9 This, along with 'Monkey and Pru and Sal' in the second volume, formed part of his episodic novel, *The Chalk Giants* (1974).

tive and original fiction, often depressingly grim, but most written in a more conventional style without resorting to linguistic or typographic games. Unlike Carnell's *New Writings*, which had been modelled on early Campbellian sf, there was little that was uplifting. The stories seldom gave solutions to the problems and in this sense the stories are more realistic than most science fiction. There was an inevitability and immutability about life and events that portrayed man's involvement as futile. George Zebrowski's 'The History Machine' in Volume 3 (1972) concentrates not simply on the past, but on the individual watching the past. He cannot influence it, but the past continues to influence him.

Moorcock rescued several stories originally lined up for Kenneth Bulmer's magazine *Sword & Sorcery*, an intended companion to *Vision of Tomorrow* which had folded even before its first issue when *Vision* collapsed. Despite that magazine's title, these were not conventional sword-and-sorcery stories but more akin to 'dark fantasy'. They included Christopher Priest's 'The Head and the Hand' (#3, 1972), which is neither sf nor fantasy but a macabre story about performance art and the ultimate in self-mutilation. Moorcock and Sladek also encouraged Emma Tennant to return to fiction and she published her first new work in ten years, 'The Crack'[10] (#5, 1973), in which she uses the concept of a London divided by an earthquake to explore cracks in society.

US writers continued to find *New Worlds* a home for their more grim stories, which were out of place in the United States. In addition to Sladek, Disch and Zebrowski, there was work by Jack Dann, Pamela Sargent and Norman Spinrad. Spinrad's 'No Direction Home' (#2, 1971), is perhaps more positive than most. Set in a future San Francisco where everyone is dependent on drugs, a young lad discovers the wonders of abstinence.

Moorcock was keen to develop new writers, stating in Volume 2 that it would be *New Worlds'* policy in future to publish the work of at least one new writer each issue. That volume marked the first sales of Rachel Pollack (as Richard A. Pollack) and William Woodrow. Woodrow sold one more story to *New Worlds* but Pollack went on to become one of the exciting fantasists of the 1980s. Her first story, the rather Pythonesque 'Pandora's Bust', blends sexual and religious images and is a clear indication of the direction her work would take. Moorcock's other discoveries include Marta Randall (writing as Marta Bergstrasser) in Volume 5, and Robert Meadley, Eleanor Arnason and Ronald Anthony Cross (all in Volume 6).

Most of the stories were illustrated. Richard Glyn Jones served as art editor, securing the work of Jim Cawthorn, Mal Dean and Keith Roberts. Dean's work had been highly representative of *New Worlds* in

10 Expanded in book form as *The Time of the Crack* (1973).

his flamboyant and often sensational imagery. He died at the age of only 32 of pneumonia brought on by treatment he was receiving for cancer in February 1974. Moorcock wrote a tribute to him in *New Worlds 8*.

In addition to the fiction there were assorted features. Charles Platt interviewed Alfred Bester in the fourth volume, and there was a review column by M. John Harrison in each issue, worked into the guise of an article to sustain some topicality.

The early volumes of *New Worlds* sold well – around twenty-five thousand copies in Britain, plus the US edition. The editorial director at Sphere, Anthony Cheetham, was supportive, but when Cheetham left in 1972 to establish his own Futura Publications, ownership of the series grew rather tenuous. Moorcock's energies were also directed elsewhere so that after the long delayed fifth volume appeared, early in 1973, he passed the editorial reins to Charles Platt. Platt had been resident in the United States since 1970 and, since 1972, had been a consulting editor for Avon Books, establishing their 'rediscovery' line of classic sf. When Berkley decided to drop the US edition of *New Worlds*, Platt took it on at Avon. By then the fifth volume had been missed so, rather confusingly the British *New Worlds 6* appeared in the United States as *New Worlds 5*. Likewise the British *New Worlds 7* was published in the United States as *New Worlds 6*, and in this case Platt provided his own editorial and added an extra story, Rachel Pollack's 'Black Rose and White Rose', which was not in the British edition. By the time Avon issued that volume, Platt had resigned over a dispute in publishing a Philip K. Dick title. Avon already had production problems with Sphere Books who provided the typesetting, and so the US edition was discontinued. Platt had worked with Hilary Bailey (Moorcock's wife at the time) on the British Volume 7, but thereafter Bailey edited them with some assistance by Diane Lambert. *New Worlds* eventually transferred from Sphere to Corgi with Volume 9 in 1975, which made *New Worlds* and *New Writings* stable mates again.

Freed of the burden of editing *New Worlds* – Moorcock later admitted that he had lost his editorial touch and could no longer read sf[11] – Moorcock returned as a contributor, with several long stories in his wonderfully decadent Dancers at the End of Time series, starting with 'Pale Roses' (#7, 1974). Bailey attracted further new and up and coming writers, including A. A. Attanasio, Bruce Boston, Nigel Francis, and the first fiction by Geoff Ryman, 'The Diary of the Translator' (#10, 1976). Brian Aldiss, Barry Bayley, Keith Roberts and M. John Harrison remained regular contributors throughout and there was the occasional appearance

11 See Moorcock's introduction to M. Moorcock (ed.), *New Worlds, An Anthology* (London: Flamingo, 1983), p. 25.

by Harvey Jacobs, Ian Watson and even Joanna Russ. John Clute took over the review spot.

Bailey's issues were in much the same vein as Moorcock's, maintaining a good degree of experimentalism and ingenuity restrained by good story-telling. Bruce Gillespie, who had read all of the original anthologies for various articles and reviews in *S.F. Commentary*, claimed, 'New Worlds has been the most consistently interesting series of original fiction anthologies.'[12]

The freedom of expression allowed by *New Worlds* was refreshing, if at times overused. In an era before political correctness, *New Worlds* had no problem in publishing stories about invalids and thalidomide children. There was a feeling that the authors enjoyed their liberty even though, by the mid-seventies, the revolution had subsided. Battles had been won and lost and much that was good about the New Wave had been absorbed into the more liberal sf in the United states – though it was a while before its longer-term benefits would be evident in Britain.

At the time neither Moorcock nor Platt seemed especially satisfied with their achievements. Moorcock wrote, 'To this day I don't know if *New Worlds* achieved anything which would not have happened anyway,' adding, 'we had lost the spark which had made the monthly magazine what it was'.[13] Platt reflected, 'We didn't think that we were going to take over the world, but we did think we could push science fiction in our direction a bit. And to some extent we were right; although I never imagined this slow slide back into conventionality would occur.'[14] Moorcock's and Platt's reservations about their achievements should not be overemphasised. The many-headed hydra that was science fiction might look in many directions at once and take a long time to decide which route to follow, but it advanced steadily nonetheless. Although *New Worlds* had alienated the traditionalists, this was outweighed by the encouragement it gave to new writers who saw that science fiction had far greater potential than most had imagined. The overexperimental work was a fad, but the underlying changes – placing sf within a wider perspective of language and vision, liberating fiction from the bondage of sf tropes and celebrating unconventionality – were far more deep-seated and sustained a movement that survived the seventies and became re-energized in the eighties.

12 Bruce Gillespie, 'The Original Fiction Anthologies, 1973–1975', *SF Commentary* #48/49/50 (October–December 1976), p. 136.

13 Michael Moorcock, 'Introduction', *New Worlds, An Anthology*.

14 Charles Platt in his 'Profile' by Douglas E. Winter, *Science Fiction Review* #47 (Summer 1983), p. 27, reprinted in Charles Platt, *Dream Makers, Volume II* (New York: Berkley Books, 1983), p. 296.

New Worlds remained with Corgi Books for only two volumes but, following disagreement over their editorial interference, Moorcock and Bailey decided to stop the series after Volume 10, which appeared in August 1976. Moorcock no longer had the energy to negotiate with a third publisher. After more or less continuous publication for 30 years, *New Worlds* looked like it would be laid to rest. But it refused to die and would soon return in a most surprising form in a semi-professional capacity, which I shall return to later.

Although Moorcock led the advance guard in the revolution, he was not entirely alone and there was another revolution happening in the United States, which also saw the growth of original anthologies.

Experiments in Orbit

Two years after John Carnell started *New Writings in SF* in Britain, Damon Knight launched *Orbit* in the United States. That is the only connection you can make between them. Knight used as his model Frederik Pohl's *Star Science Fiction*, but only inasmuch as both were anthologies of all-new fiction. *Star* published some of the best sf of the fifties but Pohl drew upon what was happening in the field at the time, especially at *Galaxy* and *F&SF*. Knight, however, wanted writers to strive for greater originality. In that sense Knight's *Orbit* was closer in intent to Moorcock's *New Worlds* and perhaps Harlan Ellison's *Dangerous Visions*. Knight later declared, '*Orbit* has never had anything to do with the stylistic experimentation of the *New Worlds*/New Wave scene.'[15]

Yet, despite Knight's disclaimer, the innovative US writers of sf were reacting to the same world and the same literary trends as Moorcock and the *New Worlds* brigade, and allowing them space often led to similar results. Thus it is not surprising that P. Schuyler Miller remarked, 'As editor of this series of anthologies of original "speculative fiction" ... Damon Knight seems to have appointed himself the American guru of the so-called 'New Wave'.'[16] Though in content *Orbit* was probably closer to *F&SF* than to *New Worlds*, it was peppered with more experimentalism than Ferman's magazine.

Knight defined his purpose for *Orbit* as follows:

> Each volume ought to redefine the field in such a way as to draw in
> more good stories, so that more and more good stuff gets written. In

---

15 Knight in interview with Paul Walker in *Luna Monthly* #34, March 1972, p. 3.
16 P. Schuyler Miller, 'The Reference Library' *Analog* 91:5 (July 1973), p. 167–8.

order to do this, you've got to let go of your rigid conceptions of what science fiction is, and let it grow in whatever direction it can.[17]

Knight believed that if you loosened editorial restrictions, the field could move forward and that there should be a rise in quality. It was limited, inevitably, by his own judgement and perceptions, but he endeavoured to expand those perceptions to keep, in his words, 'the boundaries fluid'.

As the only original sf anthology appearing in the US market at that time, sales were high, allowing Knight to pay good rates, between four and five cents a word, the equivalent of *Analog*, and he never paid less than $200 for a story. In addition to the US hardcover from Putnam and the paperback from Berkley, there was (from 1967) a British paperback edition from Panther Books and (from 1968) a British hardcover from Rapp & Whiting. There was also a Science Fiction Book Club edition and occasional translations. So, at the outset, *Orbit* was profitable and an ideal market.

Besides his liberal tastes, Knight also had the advantage of time. At the start *Orbit* was scheduled to appear once a year so, unlike a magazine editor having to acquire material to fill a monthly or bi-monthly issue, Knight declared that for the first volume he had eight months in which to select his material. By the fourth volume, in 1968, it was appearing biannually, but that still allowed Knight substantial time.

Knight had the time not only to be selective but also to work with authors to develop the type of story he wanted. The writers responded. The first few volumes of *Orbit* were highly regarded, with stories nominated for, and sometimes winning, awards. In the first volume the short story Nebula (awarded by the SFWA) went to Richard McKenna's 'The Secret Place'; in the third volume Nebulas went to both Richard Wilson's 'Mother to the World' and Kate Wilhelm's 'The Planners', while from the fourth volume, Robert Silverberg's 'Passengers' won the Nebula in 1970.

Perhaps Knight became the victim of his own success. Some have suggested that there was a clique amongst SFWA members consisting of those from the Milford Writers Conference (of which more shortly), many of whom were appearing in *Orbit*, and who were working together to concentrate the vote for *Orbit* stories.[18] Whatever the circumstances, the final ballot for the 1971 Nebula contained six stories from *Orbit 6* and *Orbit 7*, and only one other (from *If*). There was allegedly a reaction to this amongst other SFWA members who voted for the 'no award' option

17 Knight, in interview with Paul Walker in *Luna Monthly* #34, March 1972, p. 2.
18 See Knight in interview with Paul Walker, pp. 4–5.

and, as a consequence, none of the stories won.[19] Thereafter, no further stories from *Orbit* won any award, even though they continued to be nominated.

The success and initial popularity of the *Orbit* series at the same time as a comparative malaise in the magazines led to a rapid increase in all-new anthologies, both one-off titles and regular series. From 1970, Knight no longer had the field to himself.

Despite the opposition, Knight remained true to his vision, a vision that saw the series through 21 volumes over 14 years. Gene Wolfe believed, 'Knight is probably as good as editors ever get.'[20]

The author whose work is perhaps most representative of *Orbit* is Gene Wolfe. He had stories (sometimes more than one) in 14 of the 21 volumes. Damon Knight did not discover Wolfe – he had sold a ghost story to *Sir* in 1965, after nine years of writing, and Frederik Pohl bought his first sf story for *If* in 1966 – but it was through *Orbit* that Wolfe established his name. It was thanks to Knight's liberal policy that Wolfe was able to write unrestrained, because few of Wolfe's stories fit comfortably into any one genre. His first notable story was 'How the Whip Came Back' in *Orbit 6* (1970), where a future world government decides to treat all prisoners as slaves on a lease system. It was his next *Orbit* story, 'The Island of Dr. Death and Other Stories' (#7, 1970), that put his name on the map, and the one most believe should have won the Nebula Award. It concerns a child, ignored by his drug-addicted mother, who becomes so absorbed in a story that the characters become more real (and visible to his parents) than the child. The story is all the more remarkable for being related in the second person, present tense, taking you into a projection of the child's psyche. The story is key to an understanding of many of Wolfe's early works, which deal with the blur between reality, imagination, dreams and memories. The theme featured again in 'The Toy Theater' (#9, 1971), one of Wolfe's own favourites, this time blurring manikins with the puppeteer, and in 'The Fifth Head of Cerberus' (#10, 1972), which compares a society of clones against one of shape-shifters. 'Alien Stones' (#11, 1972) concerns the exploration of an abandoned space ship which, once again, is not what it seems. Of his other contributions, 'Seven American Nights' (#20, 1978) stands out as a topical vision of a Moslem's perceptions as he tours a post-apocalyptic United States.

19 The story with the highest number of votes was Gene Wolfe's 'The Island of Doctor Death and Other Stories'. When reading the final vote, Isaac Asimov mistakenly announced that story as the winner. The official story was that members mistakenly voted for the 'no award' option believing it to mean they were abstaining. Wolfe eventually got his revenge when 'The Death of Doctor Island', from *Universe 3*, won the Nebula in 1974.

20 See Melissa Mia Hall's interview with Wolfe in *Amazing Science Fiction Stories*, September 1981, p. 126.

Wolfe's fiction represents one of the best facets of *Orbit*, which is to make the reader look beyond the basic story and not accept the first interpretation. *Orbit*'s contents were like Chinese boxes, constantly opening on to something new.

The other main contributor to *Orbit* was Knight's wife, Kate Wilhelm, with stories in all but three volumes. According to Knight, she was probably the most important influence upon the series, primarily because she refused to be bound by genre definitions.[21] Her work in *Orbit* was never formulaic and even though she used many of the basic trappings of science and sf, they were simply a means by which to explore individuals in extreme circumstances. All of the stories are worth considering, but three stand out from the seventies. 'The Infinity Box' (#9, 1971), a chilling study of a corruptive psi power, caused Theodore Sturgeon to remark that Wilhelm 'never needs to prove, after this, that she is a strong and capable writer who knows exactly what she is doing'.[22] 'Where Late the Sweet Birds Sing' (#15, 1974), the basis for her 1976 award-winning book, shows further corruption, this time of an isolated group trying to survive after a nuclear war. 'Ladies and Gentlemen, This is Your Crisis' (#18, 1976) is a remarkable prediction of reality television, showing that Wilhelm can be as speculative as the best of them, as well as creative and imaginative. The cumulative effect of these stories, and such other gems as 'The Encounter' (#8, 1970), 'The Scream' (#13, 1974) and 'Moongate' (#20, 1978), not only unsettle the reader but continue to haunt them long afterwards. It is this disquiet that typifies much of the content of *Orbit*, leaving the reader disturbed rather than comforted.

Another writer whose work was representative of *Orbit*'s unboundaried freedom was R. A. Lafferty. He was in 16 of the volumes, each story marked by his usual obliqueness. The best was 'Continued on Next Rock' (#7, 1970) which tells of a group of misfit archaeologists who uncover, but don't fully comprehend, a record in stone of an eternal love story. Lafferty deliberately leaves the story ambiguous, reflecting the continuous cycle of time. It was not always easy to know when Lafferty was being serious and when he was just having fun with words, but his stories constantly forced the reader to look at life from a new angle. At the conclusion of 'When All the Lands Pour Out Again' (#9, 1971), a mischievous satire on life and death built upon a sudden change in continental drift, Lafferty writes that three wise men were 'walking in a direction that had not yet been renamed', and that was often how it felt reading *Orbit*.

One aspect of *Orbit* was the number of contributions by female writers,

21 See Knight in interview with Paul Walker.
22 Theodore Sturgeon, 'Galaxy Bookshelf', *Galaxy* 32:5 (March/April 1972), p. 87.

besides Kate Wilhelm. Joanna Russ had been a regular contributor since the first volume, but she only put in two appearances in the seventies. 'Gleepsite' (#9, 1970) and 'Reasonable People' (#14, 1974), both relatively minor stories that prompt us to be more aware of ourselves and our surroundings. Carol Emshwiller, Carol Carr, Grania Davis, Sonya Dorman, Raylyn Moore, Doris Piserchia, Kit Reed, Joan Vinge and Josephine Saxton all put in occasional appearances. Ursula K. Le Guin's two contributions, 'Direction of the Road' (#12, 1973) and 'The Stars Below' (#14, 1974) are both introspective fables looking at the world through different perspectives. Of Vonda McIntyre's two contributions, 'The Genius Freaks' (#12, 1973) raises issues about the ethics of selective breeding.

There was much else of import in *Orbit*. Harlan Ellison had two stories: 'Shattered Like a Glass Goblin' (#4, 1968) and 'One Life, Furnished in Early Poverty' (#8, 1970). The latter, one of Ellison's emotional visitations to childhood, is a reminder of how little we can change things. Michael Bishop's 'The Window in Dante's Hell' (#12, 1973), one of his stories set in a future domed Atlanta, is a similar tale of dashed wish-fulfilment. Joe Haldeman's 'Counterpoint' (#11, 1972) is not really sf at all, for all that it stretches into the future, but is a sombre story of the lives of two individuals from disparate backgrounds whose fortunes pivot around their experiences in Vietnam. Tom Reamy's 'Under the Hollywood Sign' (#17, 1975) is a disturbing but compelling story of a policeman haunted by angel-like aliens whom he sees at any violent death. This was one of two stories that Reamy sold simultaneously at the start of his career, though it took nearly two years to get into print.

Amongst the other writers whose careers Knight helped to launch, two were especially significant. Joan D. Vinge had not had a chance to become as cynical or pessimistic as many of *Orbit*'s contributors, and though her debut story, 'Tin Soldier' (#14, 1974), has a deep sadness in its study of a quasi-cyborg who ages slower than those he once knew, it has a positive ending. Similarly, 'Mother and Child' (#16, 1975) is a touching but rewarding story of how an alien comes to understand humans through observing a mother and her child. Kim Stanley Robinson debuted with two stories in *Orbit 18* (1976), 'In Pierson's Orchestra' and 'Coming Back to Dixieland', both overlooked at the time but now relevant in tracing the author's development and the influence of music in his work.

Despite these and many other stories of substantial merit, there was much in *Orbit* that readers did not understand or appreciate. Although Knight claimed that he did not associate *Orbit* with New Wave fiction, he nevertheless published much that was experimental, including some by *New Worlds* authors Charles Platt, James Sallis and Graham Charnock.

He published many stories that were plotless and inconsequential or just plain silly. The work of Steve Chapman and Felix Gotschalk in particular came in for much criticism either because of the weakness of their ideas or as a result of their factual errors (or sometimes both). Some of these inconsequential stories were nevertheless powerfully written, one of the best being Edward Bryant's 'Dune's Edge' (#11, 1972), where five people try to conquer a huge dune, though as an allegory of the shifting fragmentation of society it seemed lost on some. But other stories were little more than jokes. Ed Wellen was especially adept at these, including two in Volume 15 (1974): 'If Eve Had Failed to Conceive' which was simply a full stop/period, and 'Why Booth Did Not Shoot Lincoln', which was a complete blank. Knight may have found them fun, but few readers did. They might have been acceptable as fillers in a monthly magazine, but one expected far more from an anthology.

These story games, which increased during the seventies, turned people against *Orbit*. Whereas many readers felt that *Orbit* had had a promising start, by the seventies it had become too obscure and offered little reward for the effort needed.

Knight's desire to keep the boundaries 'fluid' and to counter his own natural bias meant that he had to keep adjusting the limits of acceptability. As the volumes developed, so the material became increasingly esoteric. By the second half of *Orbit*'s life we find critics, all highly respectful of Knight as an editor, becoming dissatisfied. While they always found something of merit in each volume, these were countered by stories described variously as 'workshop stories' (Doug Fratz), 'half-written stories or sketches' (John Foyster) or 'finger exercises' (Algis Budrys). P. Schuyler Miller catalogued them as 'Pictures. Visions. Hallucinations. Nightmares.'[23] Theodore Sturgeon reacted to the experimentalism as early as Volume 9, believing that *Orbit* was already in danger of 'evoking many more experimentally subjective attempts than anyone needs – to the ultimate dead-end'.[24] Darrell Schweitzer, reviewing *Orbit 17* in 1975, wondered whether 'the series ha[d] moved beyond maturity into advanced senility'.[25]

The problem was that many people – especially those within sf circles – had high expectations of Damon Knight. He was a renowned critic, a respected instructor, an experienced editor, a highly regarded author, and an afficionado of the field. When Damon Knight produced something, all heads turned, and if the product was not 100 per cent top drawer

23 P. Schuyler Miller, 'The Reference Library' *Analog* 91:5 (July 1973), p. 169.

24 Sturgeon, 'Galaxy Bookshelf'.

25 See respective reviews in *Thrust* #10 (Spring 1978), pp. 41–2; *Foundation* #11/12 (March 1977), p. 165; *F&SF* 52:3 (March 1977), p. 32; and *Science Fiction Review* #18 (August 1976), p. 37.

then expectations were dashed. In short, while most editors would be judged by their best work, Knight was judged by the worst. Algis Budrys summed it up in his review of *Orbit 18* from which I briefly quoted above. His review was more of an essay on the techniques of editing an original anthology. He said, in part:

> I think … that Knight makes many of the right moves; he conserves what is best of the established; aids the transition of apprentices into full establishment, and introduces not only new individuals but new approaches. … And yet, I think *Orbit* looks a little better in its description than it does in actuality.

He concludes his assessment by saying:

> Knight is … a major creative technician; a splendid analyst of story functions, a skilled handler of writers, an individual with a clear-cut personality – in short a top-flight editor – and he puts out a good product. But not as good as it ought to be.[26]

Knight was, arguably, a victim of his own superiority. But, by that very token, when Knight got it right, he got it very right. If he had not, then *Orbit* would not have been the success and influence that it was, and many writers would not have been so proud to appear in it. But when he got it wrong, he got it very wrong. Despite his efforts to maintain a high standard, the overall effectiveness of *Orbit* slipped away until it became almost a parody of itself. Knight found this hard to accept at the time – he was extremely defensive about any bad reviews – but in time he came to recognize the series' shortcomings. Reflecting on his belief that he intended to acquire the best work by the best writers, no matter what kind it was, he said:

> When I came to edit *Orbit* I tried to live up to this ideal and found that I couldn't. I bought five or six stories in a row from Gardner Dozois and Gene Wolfe and other writers and then rejected other stories which they must have had every reason to think I would buy. So it goes.[27]

Michael Bishop, who found working with Knight humbling, recorded that not only did Knight reject his 'The House of Compassionate Sharers' (which went to David Hartwell's new magazine *Cosmos*) but also Gardner Dozois's 'A Special Kind of Morning' (which went to Silverberg's *New Dimensions*), Gene Wolfe's Nebula-winning 'The Island of Doctor Death and Other Stories' (to Terry Carr's *Universe*) and Larry Niven's Hugo-

---

26 Both quotes are from Budry's review in *F&SF* (March 1977), pp. 30–34.
27 Damon Knight, 'Knight Piece' in Brian W. Aldiss and Harry Harrison (eds), *Hell's Cartographers* (1975), p. 134.

winning 'Inconstant Moon' (which went into Niven's collection *All the Myriad Ways* with no prior publication).[28]

After good sales in the first five or six years, they began to slump. Putnam dropped the series in 1973, the thirteenth volume appearing in March 1974 after a long delay. Harper & Row picked it up, but it lost its paperback edition from Berkley and its British editions. Knight responded to some criticism that the series had lacked personality and introduced several new features, including illustrations and a competition, so much so that Algis Budrys remarked, 'Of all the books there are, this is the most magazine-like.'[29]

Harper valiantly supported it for eight volumes, but the schedule slipped and in 1977 they announced they were dropping the series, citing poor sales and the lack of a paperback edition.[30] They honoured their contract and saw it through to Volume 21, which did not appear until 1980. Knight tried to find a new publisher but none was forthcoming. The original anthology field had been swamped by this time and sales of all such books had dropped dramatically.

There was much that Knight could be proud of with *Orbit*. He had, to all intents, regenerated the original-anthology field in America and published many noteworthy stories. He gave writers considerable freedom – perhaps too great for their and his own good, but it nevertheless gave them space to experiment and there can be no doubt that many of them – especially Gene Wolfe and Kate Wilhelm – became better writers because of it. It raised awareness amongst the magazines that things needed to change and contributed to the overall improved standards in the sf magazines during the seventies. Soon after the *Orbit* contract was cancelled, Knight told me:

> I think the idea is viable, but I can't prove it. Several of the other series have already gone under, and one or two more are shaky, but one keeps hearing of new ones popping up. The series, in fact, are a lot like science-fiction magazines. When I began *Orbit* there was some significant differences in content – you could say certain things in hardcover and paperback that you couldn't in a newsstand magazine. Those differences have all but disappeared, and the only distinction there is left, except for the format itself, is one of quality.[31]

28 See Michael Bishop, 'Light Years and Dark', *Isaac Asimov's SF Magazine* 8:4 (April 1984) included in Bishop's collection, *A Reverie for Mister Ray* (Hornsea: PS Publishing, 2005), pp. 95–6.

29 See Budry's review in *F&SF*, March 1977.

30 See news report in 'Orbit Decays', *Locus* #201 (May 1977), p. 3.

31 Personal letter, Knight/Ashley, 17 October 1977.

That it failed was partly because of market forces beyond Knight's control – which we shall consider as the Elwood factor – but partly because Knight became blinded by his own ideology. You don't redefine the field without helping people to understand it. Unfortunately, too many readers were not prepared to put in the intellectual effort required to gain an appreciation of many of the stories. Other editors learned from this and thus what became *Orbit's* downfall helped others succeed.

The Depths of Infinity

The initial success of *Orbit* and the remarkable critical success of Harlan Ellison's *Dangerous Visions*,[32] published by Doubleday in 1967, awakened American publishers to the potential of the original anthology. From just one volume in 1966 and two in 1967, their numbers would rise to nine in 1970, twelve in 1971 and peak at twenty-nine in 1973. In 1973, there were half as many original anthologies as there were individual monthly issues of the professional sf magazines (29 compared to 62). And that counts only American adult original sf anthologies and excludes reprints of UK volumes, juvenile anthologies and fantasy/supernatural volumes. If you include all of those, the figures increase by more than half.

Three new series emerged in 1970. These were *Infinity* from Lancer, edited by Robert Hoskins; *Nova* from Delacorte Press, edited by Harry Harrison; and *QUARK/* from Paperback Library, edited by Samuel Delany and Marilyn Hacker. There was still room for these to be different from each other and sufficiently diverse from *Orbit*, *New Worlds* and *New Writings*.

Infinity was the first to appear in January 1970. This was a direct descendant of the magazine *Infinity*, which ran from 1955 to 1958. That had been edited by Larry Shaw and published by Irwin Stein. Stein subsequently established Lancer Books in June 1961 and Larry Shaw returned as their editor in 1963. It was Shaw who helped negotiate the paperback editions of the Robert E. Howard Conan books, which first appeared in 1966. Shaw moved on at the end of 1968 and was replaced by Robert Hoskins. Hoskins, then aged 35, was a childcare worker by profession, but had changed to working for a literary agency in 1966 before becoming Lancer's editor.

Hoskins was keen to revive the original *Infinity* magazine, but costings revealed that it would have to sell at least fifty thousand copies from the first issue to be viable. Stein did not think that possible as a magazine, but

---

32 See *Transformations*, pp. 256–7 for a discussion of *Dangerous Visions*.

thought that it could be as a paperback anthology. Once Stein had made up his mind, Hoskins had just two months in which to assemble the first volume.[33] That he managed to compile such a star-studded issue at such short notice was a testimony to his abilities. He was not able to pay the full top rates, but 2 to 4 cents a word.

Infinity One was published in January 1970 in standard pocketbook format with a striking black cover by Jim Steranko. It ran to 253 pages and was priced at 75 cents. The title page declared it as 'a magazine of speculative fiction in book form', even though it ran none of the traditional magazine features. The statement shows that Stein was trying to appeal to both markets which at the start of the seventies were still relatively closely linked. The term 'speculative fiction' also shows that the New-Wave argument had reached Hoskins and he wanted the series to attract the new generation of readers and writers as much as the old. He was able to appeal to the older generation in the first volume with a special introduction by Isaac Asimov[34] and by reprinting Arthur C. Clarke's story 'The Star' from the first issue of the original *Infinity* to cement the connection. There were new stories throughout the series by a sufficient number of established writers to attract even the most die-hard traditionalist, including Poul Anderson, Gordon R. Dickson, James E. Gunn, Katherine Maclean, Robert Silverberg, Clifford Simak and Ron Goulart.

Across the five volumes, Hoskins encouraged a number of new writers, including Alan Brennert, Edward Bryant, Scott Edelstein and Dean R. Koontz. Koontz, who was still building up his reputation, had stories in four of the five volumes, including some of his best work of the period. 'Nightmare Gang', in #1, presaged the dark fantasy for which he would become renowned. It deals with a violent gang raised from the dead by their charismatic leader and made immortal. Koontz turned the idea round for 'Altarboy' in *Infinity Three* (1972), in which an executioner who traps the souls of his victims has to face their wrath when he is defeated by an even more vicious killer. In 'Ollie's Hands' (#4, 1972) an individual is isolated by his power to bond psychically with others. The fifth volume contained his novella, 'Grayworld',[35] a Kafkaesque odyssey through a series of increasingly nightmarish dreamworlds.

Hoskins bought the first story by George Zebrowski, 'The Water Sculptor of Station 233' (in #1), a sensitive tale of a scientist who is trying to repair the Earth's biosphere, and his relationship with an artist. Zebrowski

33 These and other background details come from correspondence between Robert Hoskins and the author in October 1977.

34 Asimov's introduction was actually an essay reprinted from *Lithopinion*, the in-house magazine of the Amalgamated Lithographers of America.

35 Later expanded into the novel *The Long Sleep* (1975) as by 'John Hill'.

contributed to three other volumes in the series, including his impressive collaboration with Grant Carrington, 'Fountains of Force' (#4), one of the first stories to explore the possibilities of wormholes in space (though here they're called rat holes).

Hoskins had several other regulars amongst his writers. Robert Silverberg was in all five volumes. He was writing at the peak of his form at this time, producing stories of creative energy and imaginative scope. 'The Pleasure of Our Company' (in #1) includes the intriguing idea of computer-generated personality cubes which recreate historical characters from the past with whom you can hold conversations. 'In Entropy's Jaws' (#2, 1971) is a clever experimental story of a telepath disjointed in time, mostly in the far future. It seems dated now, but at the time was topically psychedelic. In 'Caliban' (#3, 1972), a man from 1967 is catapulted into the vain twenty-second century. It also reads like an acid trip and both stories were included in Silverberg's 1972 collection called, not surprisingly, *The Reality Trip*. Unlike the previous three stories, 'What We Learned from This Morning's Newspaper' (#4, 1972), reads like a throwback to Silverberg's early work and deals with the old idea of what we would do if we suddenly had next week's newspaper. In the fifth volume, though, we are back in Silverberg's present-day psyche with 'The Science Fiction Hall of Fame', a highly evocative piece about a man so obsessed by science fiction that he gradually shifts out of reality. There is a subtext to the story, though, that the world of pulp sf adventure may not be the way he wants to go. This presaged Silverberg's retirement from the sf field in 1975.

Barry Malzberg was also in all five volumes, sometimes as K. M. O'Donnell. Like most of his short tales at the time, these were dark, manic outbursts, shaking a fist at the universe. 'Inter Alia' (#3) is an especially potent story of conspiracies and who is really running the asylum. It was one of several stories by a new generation of writers with a deep anger about the state of the world but who felt powerless to do anything about it other than through fiction. *Infinity* served as a suitable soapbox for their spleen. Other such works include Anthon Warden's 'Timesprawl' (#2), where the protagonist seeks to escape the regimentation of the twenty-second century by rediscovering his past identity,[36] and 'Legion' (#2) by Russell Bates, which follows attempts to rebuild an injured man from the parts of others, all of whom had died violently, and whose pain and anger he inherits. Bates was a full-blooded Kiowa Indian and the story may be read as a parable on the fate of the American Indians in current society.

---

36 I know nothing about Anthon Warden but, reading between the lines of Hoskins's notes on the author, I suspect it was one of Hoskins's own pen names.

In 'Beyond the Sand River Range' (#3), Ed Bryant took the American Indian viewpoint of their subjugation by the Europeans and laughs at the likely prospect for the white man following the arrival of advanced aliens. Arthur C. Clarke had a similar outlook in 'Reunion' (#2), one of his rare short-story outings of the period, when our ancient ancestors return to Earth with a message of hope that any remaining white people can be cured. There was a deeper concentration of rebellious stories in *Infinity* than in most of the other anthologies at the time.

Not all stories in *Infinity* were experimental or angry, though they all reflected the political and social angst of the time. In Poul Anderson's 'The Communicators' (#1) a message had been received from space 200 years before at a time when the Earth was imperilled by a global war. Only now can efforts be made to translate it but it may be too late to do anything about the consequences and the fate of organic life. A similar apocalyptic mood prevails in 'A Time of the Fourth Horseman' by Chelsea Quinn Yarbro (#3), which later formed a key sequence in her first novel, and in Edward Bryant's 'The Road to Cinnabar' (#2), the first of his Cinnabar stories which explore the final city at the end of time where energy has all but been spent.

Despite the general downbeat tone of many of the stories, they were impressively written, developing strong and original ideas. As one of the first anthologists of an original series, Hoskins was tapping into the wellspring of talent and new voices that were emerging in the early seventies. *Infinity* was a good series, capturing the fears and concerns of the day, and deserved to succeed. Unfortunately by the end of 1972 Lancer Books were in administrative and financial chaos. They underwent a complete reorganization as a consequence of which, in November, both Irwin Stein and Robert Hoskins resigned.

The sales of *Infinity* were sufficient for Lancer to agree to continue it, though Volume 5, which had already been completed, was delayed and not published until June 1973. *Infinity Six* was subsequently completed and scheduled for release in December 1973. However, Lancer's problems had not gone away. They suspended publication of all their books in September 1973 and filed for bankruptcy that November. Learning of Lancer's impending fate, Hoskins managed to retrieve all of the manuscripts and returned them to their authors. Some of the stories were subsequently repurchased for a new anthology series called *Gamma* that Hoskins developed for Curtis Books, planned as a quarterly. Unfortunately, even before Hoskins had delivered the final copy, the Curtis imprint was discontinued in February 1974. The book passed to Curtis's sister company, Paperback Library, but tragically the whole manuscript was lost in the mail between

Hoskins's agent and the publisher. Hoskins did not know of this for a year and then tried to rebuild the whole anthology. He eventually delivered it in 1976 but thereafter it entered publishing limbo and was never seen again.[37]

Hoskins firmly believed that the future of the short story was in the anthology market rather than magazines. In his editorial for *Infinity Four* he wrote: 'The magazine field will continue in its trend toward specialization, and it may be that the fiction magazine will finally go the way of the dodo. But if it does, the paperback anthology is there to take up the slack.'

He repeated that belief to me in a letter in October 1977 saying, in part, 'The paperback today is the magazine of yesterday.' We shall continue to explore whether that is, indeed, the case.

Hoskins compiled several other reprint anthologies but had no further opportunities to work on an original series. Instead he returned to full-time writing. He died in June 1993 aged 60.

From Nova to Quark

Harry Harrison was no stranger to editing. He had stepped in many times to take over from others at various magazines: *Science Fiction Adventures* and *Rocket Stories* in 1953, *Impulse* in 1966 and *Amazing Stories* and *Fantastic* in 1967. He had also edited plenty of reprint anthologies, including (jointly with Brian W. Aldiss) an annual selection of the year's best science fiction, starting in 1967. Harrison had also compiled the first original themed anthology, *The Year 2000*, which came out from Doubleday in February 1970 but had been contracted for as far back as 1966. It had arisen from a discussion that Harrison had had in 1965 with Kingsley Amis, who believed that a book advance might allow better payment rates for authors than from a British magazine. Harrison saw the wisdom in this and was keen to develop it, but his move from Britain to the United States and various travels and other commitments prevented him from developing the idea until 1969, after he had stepped down from editing *Amazing* and *Fantastic*.

It was then that he also worked up the idea for a series of original anthologies, which he called *Nova*. At that time *Infinity* had not appeared and Harrison did not agree with how Knight was developing *Orbit*. 'I

---

37 Popular Library went into hiatus in 1977 when its parent company, CBS, acquired Fawcett Publications. Popular Library was sold to Warner Publishing in 1981 after four years of legal discussions.

thought he was missing great areas of SF in his series', Harrison told me.[38] In his introduction to *Nova One*, which was published by Delacorte Press in February 1970, Harrison remarked that while the sf magazines might no longer have taboos, they did have 'editorial distinctness', which might influence a writer subconsciously, while he believed that the stories submitted to him had a liberating effect on the authors. He also remarked, as had Knight, that the more 'leisurely pace' of the book editor had allowed him to read more and be more discerning.

His remarks could be interpreted as implying that *Nova* had no 'editorial distinctness' but of course it did, as do all anthologies. Harrison was known for his humour, and consequently several of the stories were light-hearted – certainly far brighter than any in *Orbit*. Harrison also liked a distinctive story and while he was open to experimental material, he clearly favoured a solid narrative.

Harrison also used friends and connections, as any editor will rather than leaving the anthology entirely open. There is a small coterie of contributors in every volume – the series ran to four. There was no surprise in finding Brian Aldiss in all four. He brought a mordant touch in 'Swastika!' (#1, 1970) in which it is revealed that Hitler was alive and living in Ostend and that in fact this was not that much of a secret. 'The Ergot Show' (#2, 1972) is a colourful exploration of a future society which feels like a taster for his novel *The Malacia Tapestry* (1976). 'The Expensive Delicate Ship' (#3, 1973) is one of Aldiss's most profound stories, despite its brevity, and uses a variety of juxtaposed images and events to present a parable on life and death. Despite the pulpish title, 'The Monsters of Ingratitude IV' (#4, 1974) is another of his melancholic studies of how artists cope with the future. These four stories capture both the humour and the deftness of observation in Aldiss's work.

A much less obvious regular but an extremely welcome one was Naomi Mitchison. She was a member of the famous Haldane family and a great achiever in her own right. Her interests were diverse and *Nova* captured just a small part of them, especially her concern over ecological and ethnological issues. In the first volume Harrison reprinted 'Mary and Joe', an episode from *Memoirs of a Spacewoman* (1962), one of the few reprints he used. Like 'Miss Omega Raven' in Volume 2, it was concerned with how one copes with mutation. 'The Factory' (#3) considered pollution. All her concerns were brought together in one ecological plea in 'Out of the Water' (#4).

If Mitchison was caring for our environment and Aldiss for our artistic values, Barry Malzberg was, in his usual blunt way, serving the collective

38 Personal letter, Harrison/Ashley, 12 July 1977.

conscience. He managed to get eight stories into the four volumes, all of them short but all of them like thistles beneath the saddle. They express a rage over humanity's hopelessness in caring for the Earth and the likelihood of spreading this to other worlds. In Malzberg's world you meet violence with violence, but does it achieve its ends?

Thankfully these cautionary tales were leavened with some humour. Robin Scott Wilson opened the first volume with 'The Big Connection', almost a period piece now, where two high hippies try and cope with a close encounter. Robert Sheckley mercilessly parodied the space opera in 'Zirn left Unguarded...' (#2) and the alien invasion story in 'Welcome to the Standard Nightmare' (#3) and produced one of the best of all time-paradox tales in 'Slaves of Time' (#4) in which the unhappy protagonist struggles to stop himself from inventing a time machine. Other parodies were provided by Philip José Farmer, who lampooned the medical profession in 'The Sumerian Oath' (#2), and John Sladek who, in 'The Steam-Driven Boy' (#3), discovers what happens if you try and change time by kidnapping a president at birth and replacing him with a less than adequate robot.

Harrison was good at recognizing new talent. He had, after all, bought James Tiptree's first sf story for *Fantastic*. In *Nova 2* he ran her 'And I Have Come Upon This Place by Lost Ways', another parable, this time on the importance of science in the destiny of man. Harrison ran two stories by new-timers in *Nova 3* and six in *Nova 4*. Most of the authors did not progress further. The major discovery was Tom Reamy with 'Beyond the Cleft' in *Nova 4*. Reamy had sold this story to Harrison on the same day that he sold 'Under the Hollywood Sign' to Damon Knight, but Knight could not get that story in print earlier than *Orbit 17*, in October 1975, so to Harrison goes the honour of bringing Reamy into the professional fold in December 1974. 'Beyond the Cleft', with its horrific study of children's decline into cannibalism, was the penultimate story in *Nova 4* and needed something to restore the balance. Harrison concluded with 'Our Lady of the Endless Sky' by another newcomer, Jeff Duntemann. This is a beautifully uplifting tale of how prayer may yet be the answer to Earth's woes.

Nova was a rewarding series. Harrison knew how to file off the rough edges. It lacked the experimental extremes of *Orbit* and *New Worlds*, and provided more meaningful hard-sf than *New Writings*. Yet the series was overlooked by the readers. Only one of its stories, 'Jean Duprès' by Gordon R. Dickson (#1), was short-listed for a Hugo Award, perhaps because it was the most traditional item – about the encounter between humans and aliens. Two other stories figured on the *Locus* poll for their years: 'Now + n ... Now – n' (#2), where Robert Silverberg brings his skills to bear on exploring an individual's telepathic contact with himself through time, and Philip José Farmer's 'Sketches Among the Ruins of My Mind' (#3), a poignant tale of frustration and memory loss. Yet so much else, including work by Gene Wolfe, David Gerrold, Frank M. Robinson ('East Wind, West Wind' (#2), a catastrophe story of smog), Norman Spinrad and all those I have discussed above, seems to have been overlooked.

It may not have been helped by the difficulty in finding *Nova*. Delacorte Press dropped the hardcover edition after the first volume, though continued it in paperback, selling the hardcover rights to Walker. That, and other commitments, delayed the second volume, which did not appear until May 1972. Walker editions had low print runs, were seldom promoted and were notoriously difficult to find. The paperback editions came out two years later – too late for award considerations. *Nova 3* appeared so late from Dell that it was retitled *The Outdated Man*. The hardcover of the final volume did not come out until late in 1974, with the paperback edition from Manor Books. Both had only scattered distribution.

By then Harrison was tiring of editing and wanted to return to full-time writing, so he dropped the series. It has become one of the forgotten ones of science fiction, and yet contained material every bit as good as that of its companions. It is ironic that it should have suffered from the same complaint that plagues most sf magazines – that of distribution.

QUARK/ (the editors always referred to it in full capitals and with the final slash, though the publisher liked to print it all in lower case) was a literary quarterly of speculative fiction. Had it not been for that latter phrase and the fact that one of the co-editors, Samuel Delany, had earned a reputation as one of the major new names in science fiction, it might have been easier not to treat *QUARK/* as part of the sf scene at all, because its connections are tenuous.

In 1970 Hy Steirman, publisher of Paperback Library, approached Samuel Delany and his then-wife, Marilyn Hacker, to put together a quality quarterly both to raise the publisher's image and profile and to attract new and serious writers. A significant budget was assigned, purportedly $5000 for the editorial, plus additional production costs so that the book could be printed by offset lithography rather than the traditional letterpress, allowing for a better-quality product and a greater use of graphics. Delany had been chosen not only because of his reputation as a fiction writer but also on the strength of the literary criticism he had been writing since 1967. Both he and Hacker had credentials amongst the literary establishment and genre fiction – Delany had already won four

Nebula Awards from the SFWA and a Hugo by this time, and he was still only 28.

Delany and Hacker used as their models such anthology series as *New World Writings* which had run from 1962 to 1964, edited by Vance Bourjaily, and had published stories by Saul Bellow, Thomas Pynchon and Norman Mailer. Similar was Bellow's own *the noble savage* (1960–62) and currently the *New American Review* which New American Library had started in 1967, edited by Theodore Solotaroff, and which had published Philip Roth, Donald Barthelme, John Barth and other literary alumni. In fact *New American Review* was published in both hardcover (Simon & Schuster) and paperback, but Steirman did not go that far. *QUARK/*, like *New Worlds*, would appear only in paperback, but priced at $1.25 (when most paperbacks were still around 75 cents or 95 cents at most) to emphasise its prestige. The first volume came out in November 1970 and appeared on a quarterly schedule in February, May and August 1971.

The name 'quark' must have been significant, yet the editors made nothing of it. At the time it was one of the new scientific buzz words, a name for one of the fundamental though hypothetical units of matter. The word itself came from James Joyce's *Finnegan's Wake*, where it was used in an almost pejorative way to mean the sound of the squawking made by crows. Joyce was saying that King Mark (of the Tristan and Isolde legend) had no voice of his own so the crows must talk for him. The word not only had scientific and literary connotations, therefore, it also implied something both new and exciting, fundamental, and a voice on behalf of the elite.

The editors chose not to explain the title but concentrated instead on the phrase 'speculative fiction' or 's-f', denouncing its originator, Robert Heinlein, and instead claiming that in 'the search for quality, *QUARK/* hopes to add new resonance to those initials'.[39] In other words, they wanted to push the boundaries of speculative fiction as far from the original 'sf/science fiction' base as possible. *QUARK/* was stating the same objective as *New Worlds*, but this time financially supported by a publisher keen to improve literary standards.

How could *QUARK/* fail? The fact that it ran for only four volumes, with Steirman pulling the plug in May 1971, might suggest that it did fail, but Delany told me that the project had been conceived as a non-profit venture and that sales figures were pleasantly surprising.[40] *QUARK/* was evidently not a commercial failure. Indeed, the decision to stop the series had been made before sales figures for the first volume had been received.

---

39 Delany and Hacker, 'Editorial', *QUARK/* #1 (November 1970), p. 7.
40 Paraphrased from a personal letter, Delany/Ashley, 3 October 1977.

Delany told me that Steirman reacted to the hostile reviews that the series received. These reviews (which I have not been able to find) were critical of the publisher and implied hostility toward the editors where none existed. Paperback Library was being accused of the exact opposite of what they were trying to achieve. Much of this attack must have come from outside the science-fiction field, because most of the sf magazines and fan press ignored *QUARK/*. Amongst the sf professional magazines, only *Amazing Stories* reviewed the first volume. Ted White criticised not Paperback Library but Delany and Hacker, claiming that they had 'delivered the dud of the year' and called *QUARK/* 'easily the most self-indulgent collection of its kind since *New Worlds* folded shop as a British magazine.'[41]

Not all reviews were hostile. Jonathan Post, writing in *Luna Monthly*, was prepared to 'hold off judgment until a few more numbers have been published', while recognizing that the first issue included 'both new and old-time sf people doing new/old/good/bad/interesting/silly things'. By the fourth volume Samuel Mines, the old-time editor who had allowed exciting things to happen at *Startling Stories* and *Thrilling Wonder Stories* in the early fifties, rather enjoyed the volume, regarding it as 'pretty good fun overall'.[42] The chief lambasting came from Darrell Schweitzer. He severely criticized *QUARK/ 3*, not only for the weakness of the content, which he called 'lumps of style, totally devoid of any plot, theme, characterisation, settings, emotional depth, or meaning in any way',but for claiming the contents were speculative fiction, arguing that only four of the eighteen items came anywhere close to that.[43]

The question is, then, whether *QUARK/* was relevant to science fiction or not. In the first volume, Delany offered an open view of 'SF', initials he preferred not to define but used as representative of a literature freed from the shackles of convention or prejudice. He likened the evolution of SF to that of poetry, suggesting that they are the only forms sufficiently free from conformity to be both creative and inventive. He did not want to define the material used – in whatever artistic form it took. The anthology's content should allow the reader a totally new perspective of the world. His SF, therefore, was subjective, not objective. It was of intent rather than content.

This is something different from Ballard and Moorcock's New Wave. That was addressing the malady of science and society with the hope of highlighting contemporary ills. Delany's SF is outside of that and could

---

41 Ted White, *Amazing Science Fiction Stories*, 45:3 (September 1971), p. 110.

42 See respective reviews in *Luna Monthly* #23, April 1971, p. 28 and #35/6, April/May 1972, p. 51.

43 See Darrell Schweitzer, *Luna Monthly* #41/2, October/November 1972, pp. 56–7.

use New-Wave techniques as just one of a number of methods to aid perspective. Delany's SF therefore was a tool to allow the observer to refocus on the world. *QUARK/*'s content was fundamentally ambiguous, presenting powerful images and dramatic scenes that are not clearly set in any familiar or identifiable context, whether mundane or one recognizable from the body of science fiction, and leaving it to the reader to interpret and assign significance.

It would have helped had *QUARK/* included more graphic features, because illustrations made it easier for readers to adjust. The primary graphic in the first volume was a series of illustrations by Russell FitzGerald related to the cover, which depicted two faceless men, one black, one white, coming together under the US flag. The cover was called Appomattox, after the conclusive battle of the American Civil War, and both the cover and the interior graphics were representative of a conjoining of the black and white races. But there is an added dimension. The cover shows the white man holding a hypodermic syringe while the black man holds what appears to be a sacrificial dagger or some form of totem, and this is where the speculative element arises. Is FitzGerald suggesting that the union of the two races has created a society that is ultimately self-destructive, or were the syringe and totem symbols of a transcendental relationship? It is certainly an image that causes the observer to ponder, and it allows a level of speculation that is far freer than the narrative word. There were similar provocative covers on the other three volumes.

QUARK/ needed the time to develop and mature so that both readers and writers could explore the potential of Delany's expanded SF. Inevitably, though, the first few volumes were filled by writers either already known for their New Wave work – Thomas M. Disch, James Sallis, Hilary Bailey, John Sladek, M. John Harrison, Charles Platt and Michael Moorcock – or were already *sui generis* and known to be radical or nonconformist – Philip José Farmer, Josephine Saxton, R. A. Lafferty, Avram Davidson, Joanna Russ and Christopher Priest. There were also several new writers already establishing strong reputations and prepared to push boundaries: Edward Bryant, Gordon Eklund, Vonda McIntyre, Gardner Dozois.

This is an impressive list of contributors and, if we do not restrain our perceptions as to whether these stories should fit into one category or another, but simply follow the stories wherever they take us, the results can be enjoyable, as Samuel Mines discovered. To my own thinking, the one author who captured the essence of *QUARK/* immediately was Ursula K. Le Guin. 'A Trip to the Head', in the first volume, is a disorientating story of a man struggling to discover his identity and place in the world. We all go through that, sometimes never get through it, and Le Guin deftly built a genuine story around this sense of dislocation. Le Guin was an ideal contributor for *QUARK/*. She later wrote in an essay in *Galaxy*, 'If science fiction has a major gift to offer literature, I think it is just this: the capacity to face an open universe. Physically open, psychically open. No doors shut.'[44]

Le Guin was for no barriers, no definitions, no limits. Other writers were less open, not always sure of the freedom, and their stories feel more constrained. Joanna Russ came close to Le Guin with her discovery of self in 'The View from This Window'. Joan Bernott's 'My Father's Guest' extends that self-discovery to a greater awareness of the immortality of memory. It is perhaps pertinent that the woman's perception of immortality (through memory and inheritance) is seen as positive, whereas in Greg Benford's 'Inalienable Rite', where it is achieved through transplants, it is seen as negative. In his story only the rich can be immortal and eventually the others take their revenge. Benford's is a straightforward sf story with minimal layered imagery and, as such, feels out of place in *QUARK/*, where the mood of the volume soon has you seeking new meanings and looking for transcendence. Some of the authors deliver that sense of discovery in quite a sly way. In 'Dogman of Islington' Hilary Bailey tells what, on the surface, appears an amusing but rather superficial story of a pet dog that suddenly starts to speak. However, she delivers a neat twist at the end when, after the dog is killed, the owners wonder whether a new set of puppies sired by that dog might have something else to offer. She does not say whether this is something they want and the reader can interpret it either way, thus ending the story on what might be a note of wonder or of fear.

That was the secret of *QUARK/*. To have multilayered stories that allowed for a range of interpretations and caused the reader to question the world about them with a view to a better understanding. All stories are capable of this, not just science fiction, and that was Delany's point. He was not trying to change science fiction, he was trying to encourage some science-fiction writers to contribute to a more perceptive, transcendent art form.

Only one story from *QUARK/* seemed to meet the approval of the sf fraternity: Larry Niven's 'The Fourth Profession' in Volume 4. It made it onto the *Locus* poll and was singled out in reviews. This is a Kuttneresque tale of humanity's association with an alien ambassador and the gradual awareness of our position in the universe. It was a good science-fiction story, and it was not a bad *QUARK/* story, but it still did not quite fit. It was too ordinary.

44 Ursula Le Guin 'Escape Routes', *Galaxy* 35:12 (December 1974) p. 44, reprinted in Ursula Le Guin, *The Language of the Night* (New York: Putnam, 1979).

Schweitzer's decrial of *QUARK/3* should have been a celebration that the editors were finding material that pushed the boundaries of both mundane fiction and sf. In fact *QUARK/3* contains some of the best stories in the series: 'Dog in a Fisherman's Net' by Delany himself, Lafferty's 'Encased in Ancient Rind', Bailey's 'Twenty-Four Letters from Underneath the Earth', Kate Wilhelm's 'Where Have You Been Billy Boy, Billy Boy', M. John Harrison's 'Ring of Pain' and Brian Vickers's novella 'The Coded Sun Game'. These are all stories that shake the readers into opening their minds and bear witness to the consequences of what we are doing to the world and ourselves.

The complete contents of *QUARK/* should not be read in one or two sessions because they are too potent – at least the best ones are – but they have to be read while the mind is unlocked. They are, at their best – and Le Guin, Lafferty and Bailey offered that – some of the best short fiction of their day. It is disappointing that *QUARK/* was not accepted so readily by the wider world – perhaps it was perceived as a gimmick, with science-fiction writers trying to muscle in on true art. By the same token, it was viewed cynically by some (not all) of the sf world, who failed to go those extra steps to understand it.

It was, like *New Worlds*, too advanced for the sf world of the early seventies. Its like would return in the nineties with a far different reception.

Universe and New Dimensions

QUARK/ and *New Worlds* were series trying to take science fiction where most readers were not ready to go. *New Writings* was the other extreme and perhaps too traditional. *Orbit* was the true field leader, but set itself too high a target and was suffering as a result. Both *Infinity* and *Nova* were nearer to the area that satisfied the sf readership, but neither had the chance to reach its potential and both became victims of the market. So, while the growing number of new original anthology series seemed to suggest a fertile market, nothing had yet established itself.

But all that was about to change. In the autumn of 1971 two new series began that would strike a chord with readers and survive the vagaries of publishing for several years. The first, in September, was Terry Carr's *Universe*, followed in November by Robert Silverberg's *New Dimensions*. *Universe* appeared in paperback only, from Ace Books, where Carr was in charge of the Ace Science Fiction Specials series. *New Dimensions* was issued in hardcover by Doubleday, so many readers may not have seen the first volume until it appeared in paperback from Avon Books in August 1973.

These two series would dominate the anthologies throughout the seventies and, for a while, dominate the awards. Virtually every year during the first half of the seventies a story from one or the other would win one of the major awards. These series have come to be regarded as special, even more so than *Orbit*, running some of the most respected sf of the decade. How did they do it when the other anthologies had such problems, and how did they beat the magazines at the same game?

Carr had conceived of editing such a series as far back as 1968, when he had started the line of Ace Specials. At that time he had suggested calling the series *Nova*, before Harrison adopted the title. Carr was inspired by both *Orbit* and, unusually, Carnell's *New Writings in SF*, a series he read regularly when selecting stories for the annual volume of the year's best science fiction that he compiled with Donald Wollheim.[45] These sources of inspiration could not be more of a contrast, the common ground being that Carr wanted to run traditional science fiction but with a modern treatment. He amplified this in his introduction to *Universe 1*:

> *Universe* is a science fiction series first and foremost; you'll find an occasional fantasy story here, but it will be one I bought because I liked it so much I couldn't bring myself to reject it – and there'll be no 'speculative fiction' at all.[46]

Carr remarked that he understood the urge to break boundaries and was impressed by some of the stories that emerged, but he also believed that the boundaries were there so that people knew what they were buying. Although this placed Carr firmly in the traditional camp – and his background in fandom and much of his prior editing work further emphasized this – the novels he had been acquiring for the Ace Specials since the series started in 1968 were always more literary and with a rebellious streak. These included *Rite of Passage* by Alexei Panshin, *Past Master* by R. A. Lafferty, *Picnic on Paradise* by Joanna Russ, *Mechasm* by John Sladek, *The Black Corridor* by Michael Moorcock and *The Left Hand of Darkness* by Ursula K. Le Guin. Readers knew Carr well by reputation. They knew that he liked a good solid story, which delivered on several levels, was reliable and never cut corners.

Silverberg's inspiration was slightly different:

> I decided to start *New Dimensions* because I felt the magazines were paying insufficient attention to craftsmanship and literary technique, partly because of deadline pressure and partly because of unconcern with such matters, whereas the original anthologies of the day seemed

---

45 Carr in interview with Paul Walker, *Luna Monthly*, #65 (Fall 1976), p. 6.
46 Terry Carr, 'Introduction', *Universe #1* (1971), p. 8.

overly concerned with experimentation at the expense of narrative values. My model for *New Dimensions* was Frederik Pohl's *Star Science Fiction* series, which still seems to me the most successful of all the original anthologies.[47]

In his introduction to the first *New Dimensions*, Silverberg remarked on the extremes of some of the other anthologies and vowed that he would try to negotiate a middle course. This was close to Carr's attitude, but Silverberg's fiction was known to be experimental and thus the middle ground to him was likely to be slightly further to the radical left than Carr's. One could expect, therefore, that *New Dimensions* would be more avant-garde than *Universe*.

Readers would anticipate this purely from the editors' reputations and their own comments. Ultimately, though, it was the books that mattered. In basic physical comparison, although both books ran to around the same number of pages (246/249), *New Dimensions* was in hardcover with smaller print and more words per page. In *Universe* Carr had a full-page drawing by Alicia Austin to illustrate each story, a nice touch but it reduced the available wordage. (In fact he dropped the illustrations with the change of publisher from Volume 3.) So *Universe* contained 12 stories totalling 68,000 words and *New Dimensions* had 14 stories and 88,000 words. Since in paperback both books cost 95 cents, the Silverberg might have looked better value for money.

Each volume shared three of the same authors, four if you count Silverberg, as he had a story in *Universe*. In fact it was one of the best: 'Good News from the Vatican', about the election of a new Pope, with the final selection going to a robot. The story won the Nebula Award. The other common authors were R. A. Lafferty, Edward Bryant and Barry Malzberg – not too surprising as all three were establishing a track record amongst the anthologies. They tended towards the experimental or unusual but there are differences between their stories. Lafferty's 'Nor Limestone Islands' in *Universe* is more of a satirical fable in the style of *Gulliver's Travels*, while 'Sky' in *New Dimensions* takes us into a sceptically stylized drug trip. The *Universe* story is the more accessible, though it lacks the impact of 'Sky'. Malzberg's two stories are also significantly different. 'Notes for a Novel About the First Ship Ever to Venus' in *Universe* is exactly that, a series of brief episodes that trace the fate of the first Venusian expedition. As ever, with Malzberg, the story is more about what goes wrong than what goes right and how we never learn. 'Conquest' in *New Dimensions*, however, is much more of a teaser. It's the type of story Malzberg does best, pitting

47 Personal letter, Silverberg/Ashley, 6 August 1977.

the wits of a human against those of an alien in a story that questions the very nature of checks and balances and is much more satisfying than the *Universe* story. Bryant had two stories in *Universe*. 'Jade Blue' is another of his atmospheric Cinnabar stories and a clever tale of manipulating time. 'The Human Side of the Village Monster' is far more visceral, set in a decaying future where butchers deal in babies and food takes on a whole new meaning. His story in *New Dimensions*, 'Love Song of Herself', is as different again, an exotic if intangible mood story of regeneration in a post-apocalyptic world.

These three shared authors show that Carr had tended to opt for the more direct story, but the added layers of mood and interpretation in the Silverberg volume make those stories more memorable. This is much the same for the rest of *New Dimensions*. In commissioning their fiction, Carr had circulated details only amongst already-published authors, whereas Silverberg was open for submissions from allcomers. Perhaps writers found it easier to respond to Silverberg's open approach, as he certainly had the wider selection of names with better-quality stories. Silverberg was also able to pay a higher rate, around five cents a word, while Carr could only pay between two and four cents a word. However, Carr did have a share arrangement for all future royalties arising, something not catered for in Silverberg's contract (or in Knight's for *Orbit*).[48]

'Vaster Than Empires and More Slow' ranks as one of Ursula Le Guin's best stories and is the centrepiece of *New Dimensions*. It works on several levels, a basic story of interplanetary exploration with an ecological message, but a far deeper, personal story about the nature of intelligence. It's the type of story Carr would also have loved, and in fact Carr reprinted it as one of two stories from *New Dimensions* for his 1972 round-up, *The Best Science Fiction of the Year*. It would not be until *Universe 5* that Carr would secure a new Le Guin story with 'Schrodinger's Cat'.

Carr also selected Philip José Farmer's 'The Sliced-Crosswise Only-on-Tuesday World' from *New Dimensions* for his year's-best volume, as did Lester de Rey – it was the only story from that volume to be chosen twice. Although beautifully written, this story of a world where population control means that individuals can only be conscious one day a week was not that original,[49] but it was topical.

Other notable stories in *New Dimensions* were 'A Special Kind of Morning' by Gardner Dozois, where he used new techniques in which to focus the wartime memories of an old soldier, and 'The Wicked Flee',

48 See interview with Carr in *Luna Monthly* #65, Fall 1976, p. 6.
49 A similar idea had been used by John Christopher in 'Summer's Lease', *Argosy*, July 1959.

by Harry Harrison, an ingenious chase through time of a heretic carried out by the Vatican. These were stories that would also have worked in *Universe*. Those that were special to Silverberg were the more experimental ones, such as Harlan Ellison's 'At the Mouse Circus', Thomas M. Disch's 'Emancipation' and Robert Malstrom's 'The Great A'.

Universe 1 did not have quite the match for these. There is the effective satire of George Alec Effinger's 'All the Last Wars at Once', where all human prejudices and aggression are brought out once and for all in a rapid series of gladiatorial-style contests. 'West Wind, Falling' by Gregory Benford and Gordon Eklund, is a hard-sf story of a cometary liaison but with a sardonic twist. Joanna Russ's 'Poor Man, Beggar Man' is a historical fantasy, set at the time of Alexander the Great, but is far more a study of Alexander's soul. 'Mount Charity' by Edgar Pangborn was set in the world of *Davy*.

By any standards the first volumes of both *Universe* and *New Dimensions* were high-quality, containing material which took stock of the current state of the field and helped nudge it forwards, especially in *New Dimensions*.

With the second volumes – and this time Carr had opened *Universe* to allcomers – Carr had the edge over Silverberg. *Universe 2* included another great Silverberg story, 'When We Went to see the End of the World', Harlan Ellison's 'On the Downhill Side' and William Rotsler's tale of a new art form 'Patron of the Arts'. All three were nominated for awards, although once again it was *New Dimensions* that published the Hugo winner, R.A. Lafferty's 'Eurema's Dam'. Lafferty had proved time and again in magazines and anthologies that he could always produce the off-the-wall story, the one that never fitted into any category, and often the one that everyone remembered afterwards even if they couldn't remember where they'd read it. 'Eurema's Dam' isn't necessarily his most creative story, but it is one of his most memorable – a wonderful twist on the idiot-inventor theme – and it was the only story to win him a Hugo, though even then he had to share it. Lafferty's quirky, irreverent, indefinable stories were often the sauce that added that final piquant flavour to any magazine issue or anthology and he was writing at his very best in the early seventies.

Universe and *New Dimensions* continued this dance throughout the seventies. The two volumes complemented each other perfectly, *Universe* running the more straightforward material and *New Dimensions* the more avant-garde, with much overlap in between. They would sometimes exchange material. Silverberg told me:

> Terry and I were close friends and we kept each other informed about what we were buying. On occasion, when one of us had closed an issue

and wouldn't be buying for the next one for eight or ten months, we would turn stories over to each other for possible purchase. I'm pretty sure he gave me a Tiptree that way and maybe a Vance, and I believe I passed things along to him.[50]

Both series suffered a change of publisher with the third volume. Carr had left Ace by then but secured a hardcover edition from Random House with a paperback from Popular Library. This gave him extra money and more room to play with and from Volume 3 he began to run longer stories. Silverberg lost his commercial hardcover edition (though Volume 3 had an advance edition from the Science Fiction Book Club) and had paperback only from Signet Books for Volume 4 until Harper & Row took over the series from Volume 5 – thus making it a stablemate of *Orbit*. Ironically Doubleday, which had dropped *New Dimensions*, took on *Universe* from Volume 6. This unsettling change of publishers disrupted the publishing schedules for the books. Two volumes of *Universe* appeared in 1974 (#4 and #5) and none in 1975. Even so, the two series usually appeared in print within a month or two of each other, with *Universe* most often the first. However, *New Dimensions* lost its paperback edition after Volume 5 (in 1975) and was not restored until Volume 11 (in 1980).

They both ran award winners in their third volumes, though Silverberg was not to be outdone. Whereas *Universe 3* ran the Nebula winner with Gene Wolfe's masterful 'The Death of Dr. Island and Other Stories', *New Dimensions III* ran two Hugo winners, 'The Ones Who Walk Away from Omelas' by Le Guin and 'The Girl Who Was Plugged In' by Tiptree – the latter regarded by some as a precursor to the cyberpunk movement. *Universe 4* evened the balance by running the following year's Nebula winner, 'If the Stars are Gods' by Eklund and Benford. *New Dimensions IV* had no major award winners, probably because it consisted of two long stories and a bunch of small ones. The longest story – almost half the book – was 'Strangers' by Gardner Dozois. This reworked the undine folktale in having a human forsake what makes him human in order to love a female alien, with the legendary sacrificial consequences. Although Dozois began it as a novelette for Silverberg, it grew and grew and he had to compress certain sequences to make it a manageable length – even then it came in at 40,000 words. It is to Silverberg's credit that he ran it complete. Dozois subsequently unzipped the compressed sections for the full-length novel published four years later.

Sales of both *Universe* and *New Dimensions* were never high. They were a critical success rather than a commercial one. They sustained their

50 Personal e-mail, Silverberg/Ashley, 13 June 2006.

Table 2.1 *Comparison of major anthologies and magazines with most story nominations, awards or 'Year's Best' selections, 1970–80*

Anthology/Magazine	Total story nominations or reprintings	Total issues/ volumes covered	Average score
Universe	64	10	6.40
New Dimensions	62	10	6.20
Orbit	61	16	3.81
Stellar	16	5	3.20
F & SF	267	132	2.02
Analog	206	132	1.56
Omni	36	27	1.33
*New Worlds**	13	10	1.30
If	32	32	1.00
Galaxy	73	82	0.89
Destinies	8	9	0.89
Asimov's	28	34	0.82

* Only the ten anthology 'issues' are included here, excluding the semi-pro issues. If those are included, *New Worlds*'s average drops to 0.75.

impact throughout the decade. One way in which that can be measured is to see how often stories from them were either selected for the year's best sf anthologies or nominated for major awards. Table 2.1 covers the major anthology series and magazines that ran through the decade and saw more than four volumes. I have allocated one point for each time a story was reprinted or nominated. I have not added anything extra if a story won. I've then divided that total by the number of magazine issues or volumes published during that period to give an overall average per issue/volume.

Clearly the major anthologies outscored the magazines by a significant margin. Some of this is clearly because the anthologies have the luxury of refining their selection for just one or two volumes a year, whereas the magazines had to produce a monthly issue regardless of whether top-quality material was always available. In this regard it is perhaps relevant that *Destinies*, which I shall discuss later, which tried to hit a bi-monthly schedule, scores the lowest out of the main anthologies. Nevertheless, *Universe*, *New Dimensions* and *Orbit* continued to score consistently through the decade.

Despite this, during most of this period the Hugo Award for best editor went to Ben Bova. Carr, Knight and Silverberg were always nominated but never won. So let me emphasize it here. Their three series contributed significantly to improving the quality and diversity of science fiction published during the 1970s. The writers responded to the openness of these editors and this raised readers' expectations. The magazines were forced to respond and with their editorial changes, science fiction matured significantly.

There was one other US original anthology series of the mid-seventies that deserves a mention and one British one.[51]

The American one was *Stellar*, which scores highly in the chart. Plans for it were started by Judy-Lynn del Rey almost as soon as she took up her editorial post at Ballantine Books in May 1973, and the first volume appeared in September 1974. Its name was suggested by its illustrious predecessor at Ballantine, *Star*. It was really a showcase anthology for Ballantine authors, so it was not as open or as purposeful as *New Dimensions* or *Orbit*. It reflected del Rey's view that science fiction should be fun, and it was her idea to restore some balance to science fiction after the experimental and message-driven sf of recent years. Some critics thus downplayed *Stellar* as comfort reading and of little consequence, but it's hard to agree with that interpretation when the first volume contained Vernor Vinge's 'The Whirligig of Time' and Robert Silverberg's 'Schwartz Between the Galaxies' – this last a companion piece to 'The Science Fiction Hall of Fame' and another castigation of the current state of popular sf – and the second volume ran Asimov's award-winning 'The Bicentennial Man' and the early Howard Waldrop story, 'Sic Transit....?', a collaboration with Steven Utley.

Stellar certainly was fun, immaculately packaged as one expected from Ballantine, but it wasn't lightweight. It ran several latter-day stories by Clifford Simak, a late Philip K. Dick story, and long stories by Stephen Donaldson, James P. Hogan, Charles Sheffield and James Tiptree, Jr. *Stellar* received many long stories, so much so that del Rey also published *Stellar Short Novels* in October 1976. The series ran to *Stellar* #7 in August 1981 when del Rey's other duties became too demanding for her to continue the series.

Britain also developed an original series at this time, *Andromeda*, edited by Peter Weston, published by Futura Books and named after Roger

51 There was nearly another. Noted Vietnam veteran Gus Hasford, author of the book filmed as *Full Metal Jacket*, started work in 1972 on a paperback magazine called *Grok*, aimed chiefly at college students, but it came to nothing.

Peyton's specialist sf bookshop in Birmingham, where Weston also hailed from. Weston was a leading British fan and the publisher of the magazine *Speculation*, Britain's premier fan magazine of serious sf study and analysis, which had run from 1963 (called *Zenith* at first) to 1973.[52] Weston had high standards for science fiction but no special axe to grind. He simply presented the best material he could find, though admitted that it did not come easily.[53] As a result *Andromeda* was on no regular schedule, but appeared only when Weston was satisfied that he had sufficient quality material. Most fiction was by British writers – the first volume included Brian Aldiss, Michael Coney, Robert Holdstock, Bob Shaw, Terry Greenhough, Naomi Mitchison and Christopher Priest (with 'An Infinite Summer') but US authors were not ignored, and both Harlan Ellison and George R. R. Martin were present with strong stories. Ian Watson, Tom Shippey (writing as Tom Allen), David Langford and Bob Rickard were added to the roster in the second volume, along with US writers Scott Edelstein and Richard Geis. This volume also published the first works by Mike Scott Rohan and William F. Wu. Many of the same authors were present in the third and final volume, along with Fritz Leiber and his now classic 'Black Glass', David Redd, Larry Niven and Darrell Schweitzer. All of the stories in *Andromeda* were solid science fiction, mostly hard-sf, rather like an advanced version of *New Writings in SF*. Unfortunately, sales did not support what was a first-class series and no more volumes appeared. Britain was desperate for new markets in the mid-seventies, especially after the demise of *Science Fiction Monthly* and *Vortex*. Weston showed what could be achieved, but it would be a few more years yet before Britain once more had a regular market on home soil.

Of course, anthologists did not need to create a regular series in order to deliver an original sf anthology. There were a considerable number of other titles that were having their impact on the field, for good or for ill.

The New Generations

The success of Harlan Ellison's *Dangerous Visions* had alerted publishers to the potential of the all-original anthology. Even while *Orbit* was establishing itself, and long before *Infinity*, *Nova*, *Quark* and all the rest, publishers began to issue the occasional volume of new fiction.

This wasn't in itself new but hitherto such anthologies had been the exception. The first post-war original sf anthology had been *The Girl*

52 Though the final issue, #33, was not actually distributed until August 1976.
53 Weston recalls his trials with submissions in *With Stars in My Eyes*, pp. 240–44.

With the Hungry Eyes compiled by Donald Wollheim with contents originally acquired for a new pulp magazine but, owing to the whims of his
publisher, Joseph Meyers, this was switched to pocketbook format and
issued as an original anthology from Avon Books in 1949. The first major
hardcover all-original anthology had been *New Tales of Space and Time*
edited by Raymond J. Healy and published by Henry Holt in 1951, but
this had started no trend. Healy had produced another volume, *Nine Tales
of Space and Time* in 1954, at the same time that August Derleth compiled
Time to Come, but whereas such original anthologies were more regular
in the field of supernatural fiction, they had yet to catch on in science
fiction, where the magazines held sway.

But by the end of the sixties the magazines were having an uncertain
time, and this despite the first manned lunar landing. There was more
optimism in the book-publishing field. The first to test the waters was the
publisher Trident Press in New York who approached literary agent Joseph
Elder to compile an anthology of space stories. The result was *The Farthest
Reaches*, published in August 1968. It had an impressive line-up, with
stories by Arthur C. Clarke, Jack Vance, J. G. Ballard, Robert Silverberg,
Brian Aldiss, Poul Anderson and John Brunner amongst others. Its title
suggested stories delving into the farthest reaches of space and time but it
was a wide remit. Some of its best stories included two wonderful studies
of alien life, Terry Carr's unpredictable 'The Dance of the Changer and
Three' and Brian Aldiss's evocative 'The Worm That Flies'. This volume
was well received. It went through two printings plus a British hardcover
edition and a US paperback edition.

The next to appear was *Three for Tomorrow*, published by Meredith Press in
October 1969. It was edited by Robert Silverberg but, because it contained
an introduction by Arthur C. Clarke, the subsequent British edition gave
the impression that Clarke had compiled it. This was the first of the new
generation of themed anthologies for which Silverberg went back to an
idea developed in the early fifties. In 1951 historian and fantasy writer
Fletcher Pratt had developed the idea of assembling a volume of three
long stories all of which were written around a common theme which
was set out in an introduction. The idea was sold to Twayne Publishers
in New York and the projected series took on the endearing name of the
'Twayne Triplets'. The first volume, *The Petrified Planet*, appeared in 1952,
compiled by Pratt but published anonymously. This was the only genuine
science-fiction volume produced. The second of them, before the series
was dropped, was *Witches Three*, a fantasy volume which reprinted two
stories and ran only one new novella, 'The Blue Planet' by Pratt. *The Petrified Planet*, though, was another matter. Pratt's friend, Dr John D. Clark,

provided an introduction that set up the conditions on an unusual planet. Then three authors – Fletcher Pratt, H. Beam Piper and Judith Merril – provided new stories set on that world. Both Pratt's and Piper's stories were promptly reprinted in magazines, of which there was an abundance in 1952, but Merril's 'Daughters of Earth' remained out of print for 15 years until resurrected in the British *New Worlds* in 1967.

The Twayne Triplets idea was a good one, and stories for at least two other volumes were commissioned, but Twayne encountered financial problems and the books were never completed. They were amongst the earliest of the 'shared-world' concept that would be revived in the eighties. Silverberg's development was less restrictive than Twayne's. The foreword he received from Arthur C. Clarke for *Three for Tomorrow* simply highlighted that technological growth had both positive and negative consequences and the authors were left to take it from there. Silverberg considered what might happen if a new drug which caused amnesia polluted the water supply in 'How We Were When the Past Went Away'. Roger Zelazny explored how to circumvent the regimentation of a computerized society in 'The Eve of RUMOKO', while James Blish highlighted the problem of society's own waste in 'We All Die Naked'.

What is pertinent about this anthology, and the many like it that followed, is that the stories were specially commissioned around a theme and thus were unlikely to have been written by the author under any other circumstances. The themed anthology was thus adding to the great ocean of sf literature, not detracting from it. There are those who have argued that when anthologies published new stories they were depleting the stock that might otherwise go to the magazines. That may well have been the case for stories submitted to the series anthologies, although some writers may have written material knowing it might be acceptable to Knight, Carr or Silverberg but not necessarily acceptable to any of the magazine editors. That was part of the liberation of science fiction in the seventies.

Following the success of *Three for Tomorrow*, Silverberg repeated the concept on a yearly basis. Subsequent volumes with guest forewords were *Four Futures* (1971), with an introduction by Isaac Asimov, and *The Day the Sun Stood Still* (1972), with an introduction by Lester del Rey. Thereafter Silverberg dispensed with the guest foreword and provided his own. The remaining 'triplets' were *Three Trips in Time and Space* (1973), *Chains of the Sea* (1973), *No Mind of Man* (1973), *Threads of Time* (1974), *The New Atlantis* (1975), *The Crystal Ship* (1976), *Triax* (1977) and *The Edge of Space* (1979). Terry Carr also experimented with the concept just once with *An Exaltation of Stars* (1973) where he commissioned works from Silverberg,

Zelazny and Edgar Pangborn on the theme of a transcendental experience.

These anthologies were generally popular and, because the story lengths allowed the contributors to develop plot, setting and character and they were not unduly restrained by Silverberg's themes, the stories were often nominated for and occasionally won awards. The shining example is Norman Spinrad's 'Riding the Torch' from *Threads of Time*. Although superficially the anthology needed three time-related stories, Spinrad's story has little to do with time, and everything to do with mankind's ability to live with itself. The story was nominated for the Hugo, came in third as the most popular novella of the year amongst *Locus* readers, and won the Jupiter Award.

The ultimate themed anthology – or so it was intended – was *Final Stage*, compiled by Edward L. Ferman and Barry Malzberg. It had a chequered history before it was eventually published by Charterhouse in June 1974. The idea was that contributors would produce the story-to-end-all-stories on a series of themes. The choice of authors was almost inevitable but appropriate because each delivered what was asked of them. Asimov tackled the ultimate robot story, Harlan Ellison the ultimate in future sex, Philip K. Dick had fun with time travel, Harry Harrison brilliantly lampooned the space-opera genre and in so doing produced the ultimate in pulp adventure, Brian Aldiss took us deep into inner space in what must have been the most difficult ultimate, but achieved nonetheless. The years have moved on and the stories no longer seem state-of-the-art as they once did, but it remains a statement of the times. It was nearly ruined. A meddling copy-editor at Charterhouse revised stories with no consultation, leading to the book being boycotted by its own editors and authors. Charterhouse went into liquidation and it was not until Penguin Books published their paperback edition in May 1975 that the full texts were restored.

What finally cemented the importance of the all-original anthology was Harlan Ellison's second blockbuster, *Again, Dangerous Visions*, even bigger and more startling than the first. It was published by Doubleday in February 1972. Half as big again as *Dangerous Visions*, it could no longer be the taboo-breaking leviathan of five years earlier, but it could still present some of the most thought-provoking fiction of the day. Ursula K. Le Guin won the Hugo award for her powerful study of an alien world, 'The Word for World is Forest' and Joanna Russ won a Nebula for her definitive feminist story, 'When it Changed', depicting a world where women have learned to live without men. The anthology received a special award later that year at the 1972 World SF Convention and it also topped the *Locus* poll for that year's best original anthology. Twenty-seven years later when *Locus* conducted its all-time-best-anthology survey, it came in fourth – and the original *Dangerous Visions* topped the poll.

No one could really compete with Ellison's giant anthologies. He succeeded in achieving for 'the New SF' far more in these two massive volumes than was achieved by the totality of *QUARK/* and *New Worlds* and possibly *Orbit* too, and that was because these volumes refused to be ignored. Readers might take or leave many of the original anthologies, but you could not ignore *Dangerous Visions* or *Again, Dangerous Visions*. Even if you did not read them, you heard about them or you encountered their consequences in the next fiction you read. They stand there at the dawn of the seventies like two vast monoliths signalling the change in science fiction as it moved from games-in-the-back-yard to literature-on-the-main-stage.

Publishers, ever keen to jump on the bandwagon without really thinking it through, saw the all-new sf anthology as the big seller of the future (or at least as far into the future as publishers are able to think, which seldom requires a new calendar). As a consequence, the period from 1972 to 1977 saw a huge upsurge in original anthologies. It also saw an upsurge in reprint anthologies. Publishers did not necessarily distinguish between them, and most of the reading public may not have done either. But writers and editors most certainly did. Eventually one editor emerged who would dominate the original anthology market to the point that he is accused of contributing to its demise. That was Roger Elwood, and I shall deal with his role shortly.

The other important aspect of the original anthology was that it provided a market for those who might not have automatically felt at home in, or able to break into, the magazine market. These were the new writers, fresh from school, so to speak, and women writers, many of whom had long felt ostracized by the science-fiction mainstream but now had an opportunity to create their own. It is those two aspects I want to deal with here.

One of the key roles of a science-fiction editor is to spot and develop new talent. Without the science-fiction magazines to help develop that talent, there would be considerably fewer good science-fiction writers around – because they would have had no route by which to learn their trade and break into the professional realms.[54]

54 Damon Knight produced a chart showing the connection between the number of magazines and the number of new writers which was published in Robin Scott Wilson (ed.), *Clarion* (New York: Signet, 1971).

That was certainly the case in the thirties and forties and, to a large degree, in the fifties and sixties. There was one supplementary development in 1956 when Damon Knight and Judith Merril (with long-distance help from James Blish) founded the Milford Science Fiction Writers Conference in Milford, Pennsylvania. This was a writers' workshop to foster mutual commentary and criticism on unpublished stories. Membership was, however, limited to writers who were already published. Beginners could attend, even if they had sold only one story, but they must have at least made that breakthrough. It was a very informal affair, lasting only a week, and was almost a summer holiday for writers, giving them an opportunity to receive and provide feedback within a constructive format. It continued on an annual basis until 1972 when the concept was exported to England by James Blish and his wife and continues to this day. While the original Milford helped new writers, that was not its primary purpose. It was a medium for all.

The big change came when Robin Scott Wilson established the Clarion Writers' Workshop at Clarion State College, Pennsylvania, in 1968.[55] Wilson had sold a few stories to the sf magazines since 1964, writing as Robin Scott. He visited the Milford Conference in 1967 to learn from the participants, and Damon Knight and Kate Wilhelm helped him establish the student workshop at Clarion. This was a far more intense gathering – six weeks instead of one. It was set within an academic framework and aimed primarily at new writers, including unpublished ones. The visiting lecturers varied from year to year, with Damon Knight, Kate Wilhelm and Harlan Ellison amongst the most regular. Others in the early years included Samuel R. Delany, Thomas Disch, Fritz Leiber, Judith Merril, Joanna Russ and James Sallis.

After the first workshop had finished, Wilson wrote, 'If publication of student work is a proper criterion of success, Clarion – with three stories sold before the end of the session, all by previously unpublished authors – must be accounted successful.'[56]

This was out of a total of 25 students, not all of whom were registered for the full six weeks. Wilson reported, 'The youngest of our participants was 18; the oldest 64. Both were unpublished; both sold stories during the workshop.'[57]

Harlan Ellison, who was the God-of-fiction's gift to the workshop,

55 It moved to Tulane University in 1971 and to Michigan State University in 1972 where it remains, but keeping the original name. Other Clarion Workshops have since been established in Seattle and in Australia.

56 Robin Scott Wilson, 'The Clarion Science Fiction Workshop', *Extrapolation* 10:1 (December 1968), p. 5.

57 Wilson, 'The Clarion Science Fiction Workshop', p. 7.

and whose sessions always seemed to be amongst the most memorable and effective at Clarion, noted in 1972, 'Out of a hundred students at Clarion/Tulane in the four years of its existence, more than half have sold, continue to sell, and seem on their way to making successful careers at *writing what they want to write.'*[58]

Although his example may not be typical, Edward Bryant's experience shows just how Clarion could work for some. He attended the very first workshop in 1968. He recalled:

> I was lazy at Clarion. Finally I got round to writing an original story for Fritz Leiber. It was Leiber's week and Fritz disliked the story intensely. Luckily the story had been done right at the end of the week; he'd had time to read it, but there hadn't been time to workshop it. So, it was held over for Harlan's week. Well, Harlan comes along and suddenly the tone of the workshop changes. Suddenly, everything is high energy and a terrific amount of work, a lot of badgering on the part of Harlan, telling us that we're all lazy, unambitious creeps and that we'd better shape up or we're not going to live through Friday. So I took this new story and did some additional work on it and Harlan bought it for *Again, Dangerous Visions* – he'd just opened the book and it was the first story he bought for it. Aside from having a profound effect on my ego, I now had a sudden ambition for professional writing.[59]

The following endorsement also came from Octavia Butler:

> My only preparation specifically for writing science fiction came in 1970 when I went to Clarion, Pennsylvania, for the Clarion Science Fiction Writer's Workshop. This was a six-week session of writing, criticizing and being criticized. The teachers, one for each week, were Joanna Russ, Samuel R. Delany, Harlan Ellison, Fritz Leiber, Kate Wilhelm and Damon Knight. [...] It's the best writing class experience I've ever had and I recommend it to anyone who is serious about writing science fiction.[60]

Not everyone was in favour of the Clarion approach. Harry Harrison, for example, remarked, 'It's like being in an army camp. But if you want fascist type methods, if you want to be browbeaten – fine.'[61]

But the results speak for themselves. Table 2.2 lists those Clarion alumni who attended the workshop during its first ten years, 1968–77,

---

58 Harlan Ellison, *Again, Dangerous Visions* (1972), introduction to story by Evelyn Lief. Cy Chauvin reported the precise figures as 93 participants, of whom 35 had actually sold stories: see *Amazing Stories*, December 1973, p. 120.

59 Edward Bryant interviewed by Melissa Mia Hall, *Fantasy Newsletter* #48 (June 1982), p. 31.

60 Octavia Butler interviewed by Jeffrey Elliot, *Thrust* #12 (Summer 1979), pp. 19–20.

61 Harry Harrison interviewed by John Brosnan, *Vertex* 3:2 (June 1975), p. 20.

Table 2.2 *Schedule of Clarion alumni who subsequently made professional sales, 1968–77*

Author	Workshop	First Professional sale and/or publication
C. Davis Belcher	1968	'The Price', *Orbit* #5, 1969
Edward Bryant	1968	'The 10:00 Report is Brought to You By...', *Again, Dangerous Visions*, 1972; first appearance 'They Come Only in Dreams', *Adam*, January 1970
Evelyn Lief	1968	'Bed Sheets are White', *Again, Dangerous Visions*, 1972; first appearance 'The Inspector', *Clarion*, 1971 (third sale)
Patrick Meadows	1968	Already sold 'Countercommandment', *Analog*, December 1965
Joseph Wehrle, Jr.	1968	'The Bandemar', *Clarion*, 1971; 'Connoisseur', *Void* #4, 1976
Russell L. Bates	1969	'Legion', *Infinity* #2, 1971
Joan Bernott	1969	'My Father's Guest', *Quark* #1, 1970
Grant Carrington	1969	'Night-Eyed Prayer', *Amazing*, May 1971
Glen Cook	1969	*The Swap Academy*, 1970; first sf sale 'Song from a Forgotten Hill' to *Worlds of Tomorrow*, 1970, but magazine folded before publication
Michael Fayette	1969	'The Man on the Hill', *Infinity* #1, 1970
Liz Hufford	1969	'Tablets of Stone', *Orbit* #8, 1970
Octavia Butler	1970	'Crossover', *Clarion*, 1971; sold 'Childfinder' to *The Last Dangerous Visions* (unpublished)
Gerard F. Conway	1970	'Through the Dark Glass', *Amazing*, November 1970
George Alec Effinger	1970	'The Eight-thirty-to-Nine Slot', *Fantastic*, April 1971; first sale 'Sand and Stones', *Clarion II*, 1972
Mel Gilden	1970	'What About us Grils', *Clarion*, 1971; 'What's the Matter with Herbie?', *Orbit* #12, 1973.
Steve Herbst	1970	'An Uneven Evening', *Clarion*, 1971; 'Old Soul', *Orbit* #11, 1972
Vonda N. McIntyre	1970	already 'Breaking Point', *Venture*, February 1970
Maggie R. Nadler	1970	'The Secret', *Clarion*, 1971; 'The Pill', *Fantastic*, April 1972

Author	Workshop	First Professional sale and/or publication
David J. Skal	1970	'Chains', *Clarion*, 1971; 'They Cope', *Orbit* #11, 1972
Robert Thurston	1970	3 stories in *Clarion*, 1971; 'Punchline', *Orbit* #9, 1971
Arthur Byron Cover	1971	First sale to Ellison's *The Last Dangerous Visions* (unpublished); 'Gee, Isn't He the Cutest Thing', *The Alien Condition*, ed. Stephen Goldin, 1973
Scott Edelstein	1971	'The Victim', *Vertex*, August 1973
Lisa Tuttle	1971	'Stranger in the House', *Clarion II*, 1972; 'Dollburger', *F&SF*, February 1973
David Wise	1971	2 stories in *Clarion III*, 1973; 'Achievements', *New Dimensions* #5, 1975
Robert Wissner	1971	2 stories in *Clarion II*, 1972; 'The PTA Meets Che Guevara', *Alternities*, ed. David Gerrold, 1974
Mildred Downey Broxon	1972	'Asclepius Has Paws', *Clarion III*, 1973; 'Grow in Wisdom', *Vertex*, October 1974
F. M. Busby	1972	Already 'A Gun for Grandfather', *Future*, Fall 1957 and 'Of Mice and Otis', *Amazing*, March 1972
William J. Earls	1972	Already sold 'Jump', *Analog*, October 1969
Susan C. Lette	1972	First sale to Ellison's *The Last Dangerous Visions* (unpublished); 'Timmy', *Weird Tales*, Summer 1974
J. Michael Reaves	1972	'The Breath of Dragons', *Clarion III*, 1973; 'Passion Play', *Universe* #5, 1974
John Shirley	1972	'The Word "Random", Deliberately Repeated', *Clarion III*, 1973; 'Silent Crickets', *Fantastic*, April 1975
Don Stern	1972	2 stories in *Clarion III*, 1973; 'Reunion', *F&SF*, September 1979
Alan Brennert	1973	'Nostalgia Tripping', *Infinity* #5, 1973
Robert Borski	1973	'In the Crowded Part of Heaven', *Science Fiction Emphasis*, ed. David Gerrold, 1974
Daniel P. Dern	1973	'Stormy Weather', *If*, November 1974
Seth McEvoy	1973	'Which in the Wood Decays', *Orbit* #17, 1975
Jeff Duntemann	1973	'Our Lady of the Endless Sky', *Nova* #4, 1974
George M. Ewing	1973	'Black Fly', *Analog*, September 1974

Author	Workshop	First Professional sale and/or publication
Carter Scholz	1973	'The Eve of the Last Apollo', *Orbit* #18, 1976
Darrell Schweitzer	1973	'The Story of Obbok', *Whispers*, December 1973 (though previously sold to an unpublished Lin Carter anthology)
Michael Conner	1974	'Extinction of Confidence, the Exercise of Honesty', *New Constellations*, ed. Thomas Disch and Charles Naylor, 1976
James P. Kelly	1974	'Dea ex Machina', *Galaxy*, April 1975
Bruce Sterling	1974	'Man-Made Self', *Lone Star Universe*, ed. George Proctor and Stephen Utley, 1976
Robert Crais	1975	'With Crooked Hands', *Clarion SF*, ed. Kate Wilhelm, 1977; 'The Dust of Evening', *2076: The American Tricentennial*, ed. Edward Bryant, 1977
Gregory Frost	1975	'In the Sunken Museum', *Twilight Zone*, May 1981
Bill Johnson	1975	'Stormfall', *Clarion SF*, ed. Kate Wilhelm, 1977; 'Meet Me at Apogee', *Analog*, May 1982
Lois Metzger	1975	'No Specific Time Mentioned', *Clarion SF*, ed. Kate Wilhelm, 1977; 'Mara', *Woman Space*, ed. Claudia Lamperti, 1981
Kim Stanley Robinson	1975	'Coming Back to Dixieland' and 'In Pierson's Orchestra', *Orbit* #18, 1976
Michael Ward	1975	'Delta D and She', *New Dimensions* #12, 1981
Marc Scott Zicree	1975	'The Leader of the Club', *Clarion SF*, ed. Kate Wilhelm, 1977; *Space Stars* TV series, 1981
Cynthia Felice	1976	'Longshanks', *Galileo* #2, December 1976
Eileen Gunn	1976	'What Are Friends For?', *Amazing*, November 1978
Paul Novitski	1976	Already sold 'The Wind She Does Fly Wild', *Amazing*, August 1973, as 'Alpajpuri'
Tony Sarowitz	1976	'The Prologue to Light', *Galaxy*, October 1977
Peter J. Andrews	1977	'The Collected Poems of Xirius Five', *Fantastic*, October 1978
Michael Orgill	1977	Already sold 'The Mind Angel', *The Mind Angel*, ed. Roger Elwood, 1974

and shows the first professional story sale. Where their first sale was to one of the Clarion anthologies, I have added their second sale. I have excluded those who only made one sale. They are listed in order of the year they attended.

The chart lists 56 authors. If we exclude those who had already made sales, that leaves 50. If we leave aside those first sales to a Clarion anthology we find that 29 (58 per cent) still made first sales to an anthology. Nine of those stories were bought by Damon Knight for *Orbit*, perhaps not too surprising as Knight was a key player at Clarion. Five were acquired by Harlan Ellison; three by Robert Hoskins for *Infinity*, and two by David Gerrold. Gerrold would buy several further stories by Clarion alumni, as we shall see shortly. We should include in this list Ted White, who bought eight first stories for *Amazing* or *Fantastic*.

Norman Spinrad was not sure that the number of sales was necessarily a good thing, 'I have the notion that what the students from Clarion are encouraged to do is to mistake quality for quantity. The students measure their worth by how much stuff they have in print.'[62] Harry Harrison made the additional point, when considering the influence of the lecturers, 'I am against the idea that theirs is the only kind of science fiction to write. Offhand, I would say that theirs is the only kind of science fiction *not* to tell young writers to write.'[63]

Harrison's point is borne out to some extent because almost a third of the alumni sold stories only to one or other of the lecturers and made few further sales. But by the same token over 50 per cent of these students have continued to write, establishing a significant career in sf. The Clarion conditioning, if that is what it was, worked for them. Of the remaining 20 per cent, many have gone on to work in related areas of journalism or editing, or continue to make occasional sales.

From 1970 to 1972, New American Library put forward a prize for the best stories from each workshop. The winner in 1970 was Robert Thurston, with second place going to Vonda McIntyre. In 1971, Ed Bryant and Robert Wissner were joint winners. In 1972, Vonda McIntyre won with her now-classic story, then entitled 'Mist, Grass and Sand', with F. M. Busby second. Their work, if not already sold elsewhere, plus other stories from the workshops, were printed alongside essays by some of the tutors in three annual anthologies, *Clarion*, *Clarion II* and *Clarion III*, all edited by Robin Scott Wilson.

There is an excitement about much of the fiction in the Clarion anthologies, and a lot of anger. It was the voice of a generation. Although

62 Norman Spinrad in interview with Arthur Cover, *Vertex* 3:4 (August 1975), p. 7.
63 Harry Harrison, interview in *Vertex* 3:2 (June 1975), p. 20.

some of the stories were clearly the work of new writers, sometimes self-conscious, a little overzealous, even pretentious, there is a chemistry that you only find with new work. That thrill when everything comes together and glows. That wonder, when a new butterfly first unfurls its wings. That passion when you are determined to succeed. These anthologies spark with that energy, and returning to them with the hindsight of knowing which of these authors went on to great things – Bryant, Butler, Effinger, McIntyre, Scholz, Shirley, Tuttle – only adds to their magic.

What is most noticeable about these stories is how mainstream they are. Very few of them are traditional science fiction. They may contain some nuts-and-bolts technology, and a number are set in the future or a variant world, but that is often incidental. The stories are about people, life, goals, desires, hopes, fears – all the matter of existence. They stand as good fiction regardless of genre. There is an essay by Joanna Russ in the first volume of *Clarion*, where she decried the desire to categorize fiction into genres. Genre fiction, she claimed, was both stale and constricted, and she argued that 'The genre must die before it can become real art.'[64] The new generation of writers were breaking down the barriers. They didn't need the New Wave – in danger of becoming a genre of its own. They didn't need any labels. They only needed imagination, and science fiction and fantasy made better use of that than anywhere else.

When Theodore Sturgeon reviewed the first *Clarion* anthology for the *New York Times*, he called it 'the most significant book about science fiction now available' because of its 'immediacy'. He spoke of the dedication of these students, noting, 'This new relevance, this new dedication, is exploding all over the landscape of science fiction – in the magazines, in the new paperback originals, in the anthologies of originals and in the hardbacks. The old hands will have to look lively.'[65] In Sturgeon's eyes science fiction was being reborn.

Clarion and Milford have encouraged many similar writers' workshops. I have already mentioned the Guilford Conference, run by Jay Haldeman. This later relocated to Philadelphia and became known as the Philford Conference. There is the Turkey City workshop which came together in the mid-seventies out of an informal group of Texan writers, and which is now held in Austin, Texas, and the Sycamore Hill workshop started in North Carolina in 1984. No longer did the determined would-be writer have to suffer alone amongst a growing pile of magazine rejection slips. The writers' workshops and the original anthologies were a major factor in developing new talent.

64 Joanna Russ, 'Genre', in Scott Wilson (ed.), *Clarion*, p. 185.
65 Theodore Sturgeon, 'If ...?', *New York Times*, 5 March 1972, p. 37.

One editor who provided a further showcase for this talent was David Gerrold. In 1969 he assembled an anthology of all-new stories by all-new writers including Vonda McIntyre, Gardner Dozois, James Tiptree, Chelsea Quinn Yarbro and Ed Bryant. Called *Generation*, it was scheduled to appear in 1970 but delays beyond the control of both Gerrold and his publisher Dell Books, meant that the book did not appear until July 1972. As Gerrold noted, 'some of these new talents were a little impatient and have gone on to become more than just "up-and-coming" writers.' Nevertheless, the premise remained so that even though it included work by Piers Anthony, Barry Malzberg, Gene Wolfe and David R. Bunch, they still represented a new generation of writers. Despite the time lapse, Gerrold published some authors' first sales, amongst them Dennis O'Neil (though he had already been writing for comic strips), Kathleen Sky and Joseph Pumilia. Most of the new stories in *Generation* resort to clichés more than those in *Clarion*, and there are a number of gimmick stories such as Roger Deeley's 'The Shortest Science-Fiction Story Ever Told', Stephen Goldin's 'Stubborn' and even Piers Anthony's 'Up Schist Crick', though the latter has more polish. Needless to say, James Tiptree's two contributions are superior, but the stories by Ed Bryant, Gardner Dozois and Vonda McIntyre all show the promise that these authors would deliver.

Gerrold, usually assisted by Stephen Goldin, compiled several more anthologies of new talent, *Protostars* (Ballantine, 1971), *Science Fiction Emphasis* (Ballantine, 1974), *Alternities* (Dell, 1974) and *Ascents of Wonder* (Popular Library, 1977). *Science Fiction Emphasis* was labelled #1; the title was supposed to mean an emphasis on talent and was intended as the start of a series presenting new stories by new writers, though no more appeared under that title. Not all writers were new or young talents – Wallace Macfarlane was in his fifties and had been selling sf since 1949 – but most had sold only a few stories and were writers of the seventies: Joseph Pumilia, Felix Gotschalk, Robert Borski and Michael Bishop amongst others. Bishop's contribution, 'On the Street of Serpents', filled almost a third of the book. It is an intense, dream-like vision, where the author finds himself projected 20 years into a future Spain where icons from the past have been kept alive. The story was nominated for a Nebula. It also caught the eye of Betty Ballantine who asked whether Bishop had a novel in preparation, and this led directly to the publication of his first book, *A Funeral for the Eyes of Fire*, the next year.

Alternities was the new title for what was originally *Generation 2*. It was not packaged as a showcase of new talent, although that's what it was. Gerrold's intention was to restore some fun into a genre that was becoming overly paranoid. Unfortunately, the results were too often pretentious and gimmicky. Science fiction can be fun but it needs to be well-crafted first and jokes such as Duane Ackerson's 'Sign at the End of the Universe' fail to impress. There are occasional good stories but unfortunately, despite the quality of such names as Vonda McIntyre, Edward Bryant, James Sallis, David R. Bunch, Barry Malzberg, Jack Haldeman and early work by Greg Bear, Arthur Byron Cover and Robert Wissner, this volume was far less successful than *Science Fiction Emphasis*. Steve Brown, who would later edit the magazine *Science Fiction Eye*, and who was also a Clarion alumni (workshop of 1974), besides calling *Alternities* 'an anthology of such unremitting awfulness', recalled that it 'was elevated to cult status at Clarion '74' as an example of bad writing. It demonstrates that new writers should not be left simply to enjoy themselves. The Clarion experience imposed a discipline and that needed to be sustained by future editors until the writer was sure of his craft.

Fortunately, the last of Gerrold's showcases, *Ascents of Wonder*,[66] was considerably better. The title was a pun on sf's ability to create 'a sense' of wonder, which Gerrold wanted to restore. This was ideal for new writers, who can approach science fiction with total freedom, unshackled by the past. It included many powerful stories. 'Love Among the Symbionts' is a touching exploration by J. Michael Reaves of a psychic encounter between a mute paraplegic and a blind woman, each compensating for the other's deficiencies. Lisa Tuttle and Steve Utley recreate a forgotten episode in the adventures of Tom Sawyer and Huck Finn in 'Tom Sawyer's Suborbital Escapade'. In 'The Exempt', George Alec Effinger reveals how a booth in New Orleans is the entropic alternative centre of the universe. Daniel P. Dern's 'White Hole' is an inventive twist on the black-hole obsession by having an alternative point of creation rather than destruction. Most of the authors in this anthology were Clarion students and they were now exercising that discipline over their writing while allowing their imagination to fly.

The Hugo committee had twice before issued a Hugo Award for Best New Writer. In 1953 it went to Philip José Farmer and in 1956 to Robert Silverberg. In 1959 there was no overall winner and the final vote was for 'No Award'. Brian Aldiss, who otherwise received the most votes, received a special plaque.

In 1973 the award was revived, though not as a Hugo. Condé Nast, the publishers of *Analog*, sponsored a John W. Campbell Award for Best New Writer. It is presented at the Hugo ceremony but is not in itself a Hugo Award. The winner in 1973 was Jerry Pournelle. In 1974 it was a tie between Lisa Tuttle and Spider Robinson. In 1975 it went to P. J.

66 This was the final version of *SF Emphasis* #2.

Plauger, in 1976 to Tom Reamy, in 1977 to C. J. Cherryh and in 1978 to Orson Scott Card. Several Clarion alumni were amongst the nominations: Alan Brennert, George Alec Effinger, Carter Scholz, Bruce Sterling, Robert Thurston, in addition to the victor Lisa Tuttle.

In 1977 George R. R. Martin assembled a showcase volume of Campbell Award winners, called *New Voices in Science Fiction*. This picked the winners and runners-up from the first three years of the award, plus Martin himself, and ran six all-new stories. The results were good examples of the position these authors had reached, all developing along their own lines in a more liberated genre where most barriers had long since fallen. There is a confidence in them which reflected the renewed confidence of the science-fiction field as a whole. New writers had never had such opportunities for learning their craft and publishing their material, and the field was being regenerated as a result.

Anthologies did not have it all their own way. Magazines had, of course, always been supportive, but it was less easy for a commercial magazine to concentrate solely on new writers. The best they could do was encourage and promote a new author spot each issue, as happened at *If* under Pohl (and continued under Jakobssen and Baen) and at *New Worlds*.

Then, in March 1976, three Boston-based fans, John M. Landsberg, Jonathan Ostrowsky-Lanz and Craig Shaw Gardner, who had met on a writing course run by Hal Clement, began to formulate the possibility of publishing a magazine devoted to new writers. The idea had been Landsberg's to produce in some dim-and-distant future, but Ostrowsky was keen to act instantly. Gardner was more reserved, but all three worked together, raised the finance, and the final result, cleverly called *Unearth*, 'the magazine of science fiction discoveries', appeared in November 1976, dated Winter 1977. It was in a saddle-stapled, digest-size format, running to 96 pages for $1 and with a black-and-white cover by Steven Gildea.

No sooner had *Unearth* been launched than Landsberg earned a place in medical school, leaving Ostrowsky to run the magazine on a daily basis. Nevertheless the two regularly liaised, Landsberg helping when he could, and both always agreeing on the final line-up.

Unearth was cleverly packaged. It was established solely as a magazine for writers who had yet to make their first sale. But recognizing that these names would have no drawing power, the editors added other features. They reprinted a well-known author's first sale together with a new introduction by them talking about how the sale came about. For the first issue Harlan Ellison provided the background on 'Glowworm'. It was fitting that Ellison should be the first choice as he had always been so actively supportive of new writers. Landsberg provided an advice column for new writers, which he subsequently handed over to Ellison. Hal Clement contributed a column on getting the science right in sf, while Gardner provided book and film reviews.

As for the new writers, the star of the issue and the first of several major writers *Unearth* would launch, was Paul Di Filippo. 'Falling Expectations', written in present-tense, mock-Malzberg style, had been penned for a fanzine and Di Filippo vowed in the contributors' column that this would be the last sf story he would ever write (a joke added by the editors). Some may have taken him at his word because it would be over eight years before he returned to the field to establish one of the most dynamic careers of recent years.

The first issue of *Unearth* received a merciless review from Lester del Rey in *Analog*. He not only declared the magazine a 'ripoff', because of the price in relation to the wordage, but opined that it was 'not at all recommended,' adding:

> The whole idea of a magazine by previously unpublished writers is wrong. The other magazines pay far better and offer more prestige. Any new writer with a good story is going to try the better market first, as a rule. What is left, since all magazines of science fiction welcome new writers, won't have much to offer.[67]

So much for the theory, but the practice may be vastly different. New authors may be intimidated by the idea of approaching the major magazines, or may try them at a time when the magazine is not acquiring new material or, more importantly, they may write stories which have a style and approach not suited to the traditional magazines but which are nonetheless meritorious. The latter had been proved by the number of new writers appearing in the more experimental anthologies, but as these appeared only once a year at best, selling to one of them was like winning the lottery. *Unearth*, with its encouraging new policy, provided a much better chance of taking the first step on to the ladder. Although *Unearth* did not pay top rates, it did at least pay something. Their standard rate was half a cent a word but with a minimum payment of $20, so a two-thousand-word story would earn a cent a word. That was what Ted White was paying at *Amazing*.

Bova supported del Rey's views,[68] but there were far more who supported *Unearth*. Algis Budrys gave it an encouraging review in the December 1977 *F&SF*, and sent in a letter of support which appeared in issue #2. He also gave permission to reprint his first sale, 'Walk to the

---

67 Lester del Rey, 'The Reference Library', *Analog* 97:4 (April 1977), p. 168.
68 See Bova's comment in response to a letter in the December 1977 *Analog*, p. 178.

World' which appeared, with his commentary, in the third issue. By then *Unearth* had full-colour covers and with the fourth issue it went perfect bound. That issue included a highly complimentary article by Theodore Sturgeon looking back over the first four issues. These issues had also run positive letters by James Tiptree and Robert Silverberg, who sent in their subscriptions. Others who also allowed their first stories to be reprinted and provided a commentary were Hal Clement, Norman Spinrad, Kate Wilhelm, Roger Zelazny, Damon Knight, Poul Anderson, Philip K. Dick, Michael Moorcock and Fritz Leiber. Harlan Ellison, always responsive with his time, provided the opening of a story, 'Unwinding', for new writers to complete as a competition. The winner was Rachel Susan Canon whose collaborative story appeared in the eighth issue, dated Winter 1979.

Alas, Canon did not make a career out of science fiction, but the number of writers who did following their appearance in *Unearth* is remarkable. Here is the list by issue:

#1, Paul Di Filippo
#2, Timothy R. Sullivan
#3, James P. Blaylock, William Gibson, Somtow Sucharitkul
#5, D. C. Poyer, Steve Vance
#6, Craig Shaw Gardner
#7, Rudy Rucker.

That's nine major new writers in eight issues. More than that: it was nine new talents, whose creativity would transform sf over the next decade, especially William Gibson. Theodore Sturgeon spotted his talent. In his round-up of the first four issues he highlighted Gibson as 'one to watch'. *Unearth* also serialized Rucker's first novel, 'Spacetime Donuts', or at least the first two-thirds of it before it folded. It also published some of the earliest artwork by Clyde Caldwell and Barclay Shaw.

Unearth had been welcomed by a core of readers. It was selling most of its print run of 6,000 by the end of the first year, with a good subscription base, and continued to grow. However, that growth needed added capital, and cash flow was becoming a problem. The shoestring budget on which they had operated for two years ran out at the end of 1978. A new sponsorship deal announced in the eighth issue, which had been delayed for three months to capitalize on the deal, failed to materialize. Efforts to find an investor or a buyer failed and the magazine ceased. But creatively it was a success and a sign of the potential of the semi-professional magazine.

The years between 1970 and 1977 had seen a significant turn-about in the field. From the generally depressed and uncertain days of 1969, science fiction had pulled itself up by its bootstraps, tapping into the energy of new writers, new editors and a new freedom.

The Female Perspective

One of the most noticeable and welcome changes in science fiction in the seventies was the increase in the number of women writers and the rise of feminism. There had long been a belief that very few women contributed to science fiction prior to the seventies, and even that women were not welcome in the magazines. It was one of those mantras that if chanted enough became self-fulfilling and by the late sixties and early seventies many people believed it.

In fact, women had contributed to the science-fiction magazines from the very start when Clare Winger Harris (listed initially as Mrs F. C. Harris, so there was no gender disguise) came third in a story competition run in the December 1926 *Amazing Stories*. Gernsback and his successors published several women writers: Amelia Reynolds Long, Lilith Lorraine, Catherine L. Moore and Leslie F. Stone, all amongst the first generation, all quite prolific. More joined their ranks during the forties and fifties, with Leigh Brackett one of the most popular contributors to the pulps.

Connie Willis recognised this and corrected the balance in her essay 'The Women SF Doesn't See'. She not only highlighted many of the women who wrote sf, she also made the following important observation:

> People are always asking me how *I* stormed the barricades, and my answer is always that I didn't know there *were* any barricades. It never occurred to me that SF was a man's field that had to be broken into. How could it be with all those women writers? How could it be when Judith Merril was the one editing all those *Year's Best SF*s? I thought all I had to do was write good stories and they'd let me in. And they did.[69]

Even those who accepted that women contributed to the pulps believed it was harder to breach the barrier of *Astounding/Analog* under John W. Campbell, maintaining that he was prejudiced against women. This was despite the fact that Campbell published many women, including Judith Merril, Katherine MacLean, Wilmar Shiras, Kate Wilhelm, Pauline Ashwell and Anne McCaffrey.[70] Campbell was supportive of these writers and encouraged their careers. Anne McCaffrey made it clear how helpful

---

69 Connie Willis, 'The Women SF Doesn't See', *Isaac Asimov's Science Fiction Magazine* 16:11 (October 1992), p. 8.

70 He was also the first to get James Tiptree, Jr. into print, with a strong feminist story, 'Your Haploid Heart'.

Campbell was when she was developing the world of Pern. 'He was pointing out the weak links,' she recalled, 'So he made me write 'Dragon-rider', the two-parter in *Analog*, and pushed me on.'[71]

Yet the perception of Campbell as a barrier continued. Ursula K. Le Guin believed that Campbell would reject her because she did not like what he stood for. When thinking about male editors generally, she wrote, 'I don't feel the men are agin me. Campbell would have been, because I was agin him.'[72] This cannot have been from direct experience. When the editor of *Playboy* ran her story 'Nine Lives' (November 1969), under the byline U. K. Le Guin, thus hiding her gender, Le Guin called it 'the first (and ... only) time I met with anything I understood as sexual prejudice ... from any editor or publisher'.[73]

There were views being expressed elsewhere that might cause Le Guin to form that opinion against Campbell. Joanna Russ remarked in 1971: 'within the memory of living adolescents, John W. Campbell, Jr. proposed that "nice girls" be sent on spaceships as prostitutes because married women would only clutter everything up with washing and babies'.[74] I have not found any place where Campbell said this and neither has Eric Leif Davin[75] who believes it was originally said by Robert S. Richardson in his article 'The Day After We Land on Mars', written for the *Saturday Review*. Richardson writes:

> Can we expect men to work efficiently on Mars for five years without women? Family life would be impossible under the conditions that prevail. Imagine the result of allowing a few wives to set up housekeeping in the colony! After a few weeks the place would be a shambles.[76]

He added, in an extended version written for *F&SF*, that it might be necessary to send 'nice girls' to Mars to relieve the sexual tension, something that he did not believe should be regarded as immoral. Russ would be right to take issue with Richardson, but it is unfortunate that her memory of the remark caused her to malign Campbell. The remark did not even appear in *Analog* but, remarkably, in that most liberal of the magazines, *F&SF*.

71 See interview with Anne McCaffrey by Chris Morgan, *Science Fiction Review* #44 (Fall 1982), p. 21.

72 Ursula K. Le Guin in *Khatru* #3/4 (November 1975), p. 77.

73 Ursula K. Le Guin, *The Wind's Twelve Quarters* (New York: Harper and Row, 1975), p. 105.

74 Joanna Russ, 'The Image of Women in Science Fiction', reprinted from *The Red Clay Reader* #7, 1970 reprinted in *Vertex* 1:6 (February 1974), p. 55.

75 Eric Leif Davin, *Partners in Wonder* (Lanham, MD, Lexington Books, 2006), p. 142.

76 Robert S. Richardson, 'The Day After We Land on Mars', *Saturday Review*, 28 May 1955, reprinted and expanded in *F&SF*, December 1955, p. 50.

Campbell clearly did have his limits. Kate Wilhelm recalled that when she sold her first story to him, he sent her a form to be notarized, swearing that she was indeed the author. Yet she knew of no male author who had had to do this.[77] When Anne McCaffrey submitted 'A Womanly Talent' (*Analog*, February 1969) she wished to portray the heroine as a truly liberated woman but Campbell argued that she must be shown in a more traditional role. McCaffrey produced a more subtle portrait which provided Campbell with his superficial image but which, deep down, revealed that women have greater abilities than most people recognize.[78]

Perhaps the most damning view of Campbell by a woman came not from a new writer but from a seasoned one. Leslie F. Stone had been a popular contributor to the early sf magazines. In March 1974 she gave a talk to the Baltimore Science Fiction Society called 'Day of the Pulps'. She recalled her early sales and remarked that although a friend of hers had warned her that a woman writer would prove unacceptable in the sf field, she found she was welcomed by Gernsback and his fellow editors. However, when she visited John W. Campbell, just after he had become editor in 1937, he rejected a story she had submitted to his predecessor, saying, 'I am returning your story, Miss Stone. I do not believe that women are capable of writing science-fiction – nor do I approve of it.'[79]

Perhaps that was Campbell's view in his first weeks in office, but it can't have lasted long, as he ran a story by Amelia Reynolds Long in his first issue (December 1937) and another in July 1939, plus Leigh Brackett from February 1940 and C. L. Moore from February 1942. He also welcomed women contributors to *Unknown*. Stone admitted that Campbell later reversed this policy, but she never submitted anything else to him.

In this same speech Stone recalled that Horace L. Gold was a 'male chauvinist', as he had written on one of his rejection slips, 'Why not face up to it. Women do not belong in science-fiction!' She also learned that when Groff Conklin reprinted one of her stories in his 1946 anthology, *The Best of Science Fiction*, he believed it was by a man and when he discovered her identity commented, 'I didn't believe women could write science fiction.' He must soon have changed his mind as he reprinted many stories by women in later anthologies.

From such distant memories grew the belief that women were not welcome in the sf magazines and, as a consequence, some writers masked their names in order to sell. As we have seen, Vonda McIntyre submitted

77 Kate Wilhelm, 'Women Writers', *The Witch and the Chameleon* 1:3 (April 1975), p. 22.

78 See Anne McCaffrey, 'Romance and Glamour in Science Fiction', *Science Fiction, Today and Tomorrow* (New York: Penguin, 1975) p. 282.

79 Leslie F. Stone, 'Day of the Pulps', speech printed in *Fantasy Commentator* 9:2, Fall 1997, p. 101.

her first story under her initials, V. N., Alice Sheldon created the male persona of James Tiptree, Jr., and Cherry Wilder submitted her first story under a male alias. They did this under a misapprehension that had become a firm fact to many.

What is true is that there were considerably fewer women writing sf than men and that sf, with its high-tech, macho adventures, had always seemed a more male-oriented form of literature, with women relegated to a subordinate role. The image of the brass-bra'd bimbo needing to be rescued from the bug-eyed monster became all too symbolic and difficult to forget – even though most of this had faded with the passing of the pulps in the early fifties. Kate Wilhelm, who started to sell sf in 1956, regarded much of what had appeared in the pulps as 'immature'[80] and there is a view that women writers are usually more mature in their outlook than men – especially men writing adventure fiction.

With the majority of writers being men and, more significantly, the majority of editors, no one had much incentive to take it the next step. There had been some women sf editors, but they were not in a position to effect change. Mary Gnaedinger's *Famous Fantastic Mysteries* was chiefly a reprint magazine. Though both Lila Shaffer at *Amazing Stories* and Bea Mahaffey at *Other Worlds* had general day-to-day control they were still answerable to Howard Browne and Ray Palmer respectively, and they had minimal influence over encouraging any science fiction that reflected a feminist outlook. The only female magazine editor who was able to make an impact was Cele Goldsmith at *Amazing Stories* and *Fantastic* from 1958 to 1965. In her capable hands, much of the formulaic imagery was discarded and the magazines became more mature. Amongst Goldsmith's discoveries were Phyllis Gotlieb and Ursula K. Le Guin.

Although women were not editing the magazines, they could edit anthologies. Merrill's annual selection of the *Year's Best S-F*, which ran from 1956 to 1968, was highly influential in changing attitudes towards science fiction and broadening perceptions through the diverse and less formula-driven material she reprinted. She did the same in her book-review column in *F&SF*, as did Joanna Russ, the two of them constantly challenging the status quo.

Moreover, the change in editorial personae at the main magazines at the start of the seventies – including one more woman, Judy-Lynn Benjamin – led to a wider understanding in what was becoming a more liberated genre. It is possible that, with the passing of Campbell, the barrier that women felt was there was lifted. Damon Knight claimed that he favoured stories by women writers because he knew they would not contain stereo-

80 See comments in *Khatru* #3/4 (November 1975), pp. 9–10.

typical characters. He stated that 30 per cent of the stories in the first ten volumes of *Orbit* were by women.[81]

Certainly by the early seventies, more women were selling to the magazines and more women were reading them.

The data on the latter is limited to specific magazines but one of the more reliable ones was *Astounding/Analog*. A reader survey conducted in 1958 showed that 11.9 per cent of respondents were female (the total number of respondents is not given). When that survey was repeated in 1981, the figure had risen to 24.9 per cent.[82] *Locus*, the only magazine to survey its readers each year, showed that during the 1970s the proportion of women who responded to the survey rose from 19 per cent in 1971 to 23 per cent in 1981, but Charles Brown believed that this figure was low and reflected that men were more likely to respond to surveys than women. He undertook an analysis of subscriptions and found that women represented 35 per cent of subscribers in 1978.[83] *F&SF*'s survey of its readers in 1982, with 3,000 responses, also showed a 35 per cent female readership, which rose to 40 per cent by 1994.[84] In 1975, Vonda McIntyre did some rough-and-ready calculations and discovered that the female membership of the SFWA was 17.6 per cent, that amongst the original anthologies 23.1 per cent of the stories were by women, and that 25 per cent of the nominees or winners of major awards were women.[85] There is some degree of consistency between these figures.

Although the magazine market was receptive to women writers, it was also still receptive to the old-guard male writers, so that while feminist issues were at last being recognized, too many of the old chauvinist plots and characters continued to appear. Things were changing, but slowly. Vonda McIntyre, writing in 1975, remarked:

> SF in general is not, as I had believed, maturing. I discovered that the vast majority of SF writers either ignore the feminist movement, hoping it will evaporate in the sunlight of anti-abortion groups or the dew of Chivalry; or they resist it actively, kicking, screaming and forcing the most offensive stereotypes possible into their fiction to prove their beliefs.[86]

The change needed was so fundamental that it was clearly not going to happen overnight, or even in one decade. Writers, both male and female,

---

81 Damon Knight, letter in *The Witch and the Chameleon* 1:3 (April 1975), p. 25.

82 See *Astounding*, May 1958, pp. 135–6 and *Analog*, April 1981, pp. 7–14. A survey by *Galileo* also showed a a similar figure (26 per cent), see *Galileo* #10, September 1978, p. 9.

83 See *Locus* #219 (February 1979), p. 10.

84 See *F&SF*, June 1982, p. 5 and February 1995, p. 6.

85 See *Khatru* #3/4 (November 1975), p. 88.

86 Vonda N. McIntyre, 'About Two Million, Six Hundred and Seventy-Five Thousand, Two Hundred and Fifty Words', *The Witch and the Chameleon* #3 (April 1975), p. 13.

needed to change their whole world-view and, with many old-guard writers, that might prove impossible. This was evident to some degree in an exchange of correspondence that arose following the publication of Joanna Russ's essay 'The Image of Women in SF' in *Vertex* (February 1974).[87] Russ argued that most women were portrayed as subservient and that family dynamics and the relationship of the wife/mother had scarcely changed, even in stories set in the far future. This brought a rebuff from Poul Anderson (June 1974) who argued that if women were largely ignored or portrayed poorly in science fiction it was not deliberate. Anderson was in turn rebuffed by Philip K. Dick (October 1974), who conceded that Russ was right. Dick remarked, 'I have long said, science fiction may touch the sky but it fails to touch the ground.'

Writers needed to look deep into their souls and explore future societies as they should be, and could well be, not simply as extensions of the present. Vonda McIntyre, after having read nearly three million words of science fiction during 1974, though frustrated over the lack of change, did draw some hope from the new generation of writers – not just emerging women authors but John Varley, P. J. Plauger, William Carlson, Joe Haldeman and even some of the old guard, notably Hal Clement:

> Many writers are genuinely trying to free themselves and their fiction from the assumptions we were all taught as divine truth. Whatever their flaws and failures, they are trying. [...] Speaking as someone who has been through the process, I have to say that changing takes hard work and thought and a refusal to allow the past to dictate your life. SF readers and writers must stop looking to the past: we must resist being expected to accept its crippling 'ideals' over and over again in the future. SF may change more slowly than our own reality, but it will change.[88]

The three books most often cited as having started the feminist sf revolution, or at least as early key texts, are *The Left Hand of Darkness* by Ursula K. Le Guin (Ace Books, 1969), *Walk to the End of the World* by Suzy McKee Charnas (Ballantine, 1974) and *The Female Man* by Joanna Russ (Bantam, 1975). None of these had any prior magazine publication. Russ's book, although not published until 1975 was written in 1970. Le Guin created a planetary society that was androgynous for most of the year, during which time they were sexually inactive, but with short intervals when their bodies shifted to either a male or female form. Le Guin wanted to explore what kind of society that would have created. Charnas's book is set in a post-apocalyptic society, dominated by men, where women are

---

87 This essay was revised from its original publication in *The Red Clay Reader* #7, 1970.
88 McIntyre, 'About Two Million'.

treated as slaves. In Russ's book, her protagonist forms a psychic bond with three women in very different societies, allowing Russ to explore the varying roles of women. All three books contrast male and female lives and perceptions, emphasizing how women are regarded as subordinate while demonstrating their true potential.

At the same time, Marion Zimmer Bradley was evolving her series of Darkover novels from the original planetary adventures in the style of Leigh Brackett to deeper studies of societies and the roles of men and women. The change first became noticeable in *The World Wreckers* (1971), but took off with *The Heritage of Hastur* (1975) where Bradley explored not only repressed homosexuality but also the question of how sexual relations work in a telepathic society. The next book, *The Shattered Chain* (1976), was the first where Bradley explored in detail a female society, the Free Amazons of Darkover, who live outside the structured society. Writing this book was a liberation for the author:

> I don't think I will ever again be able to write the kind of story where the woman is a passive nonentity, there for the hero to admire – but then I don't think, once I stopped imitating Leigh Brackett, that I ever did. Even as early as *Door Through Space* [1961], my women were independent and had their own ideas. But they *have* evolved and changed; and, even more, the climate of science fiction has changed, so that I can now write of them as I always knew them to be.[89]

The Darkover series developed an active feminist following and Bradley encouraged others to contribute to the series with various Darkover anthologies. As we shall see later with *Star Trek*, there is an appeal, especially to women writers, to develop cultures and individuals within already existing fictional societies. Bradley broadened the way that was already opening through her work and that of Le Guin, Russ and Charnas, encouraged by their book editors and publishers Frederik Pohl, Terry Carr and Donald Wollheim.

Though these books stand as landmarks within the world of feminist sf, they should not overshadow similar advances in the magazines and anthologies. A good starting place would be 'When I Was Miss Dow' by Sonya Dorman in *Galaxy* for June 1966. A protean life form is transformed into a female assistant to a scientist and the female/male interaction is perceived from an objective viewpoint. In 'For the Sake of Grace' (*F&SF*, May 1969), the first prose sale by Suzette Haden Elgin who, like Dorman, was already known as a poet, a young girl strives for an equal

---

89 Marion Zimmer Bradley, 'An Evolution of Consciousness', *Science Fiction Review* #22, August 1977, p. 45, reprinted from *The Diversifier* #18 (January 1977).

opportunity to advance herself in a strict, patriarchal society. It was later reworked into her Coyote Jones series, starting with *The Communipaths* (1970). Octavia Butler's first appearance, 'Crossover' (*Clarion*, 1971) is a dark story of a woman struggling to overcome the vicissitudes of life.

In these examples, the female protagonist is able to tell her story and express it in terms of her world. They are stories about how women come to terms with their existence and strive for something better. There were those writers who took it further, most notably Joanna Russ. Russ had written several stories featuring the female protagonist Alyx for Damon Knight's *Orbit* series, plus a novel *Picnic on Paradise* (1968). Alyx was a forceful character who undertook assignments throughout the timelines and served as a model for young women. Russ's short story 'When it Changed', in Ellison's *Again, Dangerous Visions* (1971), was set on the world of Whileaway, which also appeared in her novel *The Female Man*. Whileaway is a self-contained female society where a plague has wiped out all men and the women have existed in perfect isolation for six centuries. All is well until a spaceship arrives with four men who are viewed with distrust by the women, while the men believe they will be welcomed. Men are portrayed as threatening and disruptive, certain to bring an end to the harmony of Whileaway.

The writer who would come to symbolize the feminist movement, though chiefly in retrospect, was James Tiptree, Jr., the alias of Alice Sheldon. Until Tiptree's identity was revealed in 1977,[90] she was believed to be a man, and it actually upset some when they discovered her identity, because some women had hoped that for once there was a man who had an empathy with women. Not all of Tiptree's stories are feminist in outlook. Some of the early ones, notably 'Happiness is a Warm Spaceship' (*If*, November 1969), revealed her fascination with *Star Trek*. Her first sale, though, 'Fault' (*Fantastic*, August 1968) explored what it was like to be out of synch with the world. 'The Mother Ship' (*If*, June 1968) is an intriguing study of a woman who distrusts all men and is first drawn to three giant women aliens until she learns that their true objective is to enslave Earth, whereupon she allies herself with her male worker. Two of her stories, 'The Last Flight of Dr Ain' (*Galaxy*, March 1969) and 'Amberjack' (*Generation*, 1972) are masterful examples of her ability to work in the very short form, both stories being little more than two thousand words. Both explore, in entirely different ways, female control over men. She adapted the same thinking with alien life-forms in 'Love is the Plan, the Plan is Death' (*The Alien Condition*, 1973) where, despite (in fact, because of) every effort by the male to protect his mate during the long harsh

90 See news story in *Locus* #198, 30 January 1977, p. 1

winter, it is she who has the power to survive. 'The Girl Who Was Plugged In' (*New Dimensions 3*, 1973), argued by some as the earliest cyberpunk story, tells of how an ugly and ungainly young girl hides from the world but projects herself through an animated cyborg. Tiptree's masterpiece, all the more powerful for its simplicity, is 'The Women Men Don't See' (*F&SF*, December 1973) where the women in the story find it preferable to live with aliens than with men.

Throughout these stories, some more subtle than others, Tiptree portrays an unsettling picture for men of how women are the secret masters, regardless of male strength. Some of Tiptree's later stories are spoiled by overstating their message. 'Houston, Houston, Do You Read?' (*Aurora*, 1976), discussed further below, is similar to Russ's 'When it Changed' in envisioning a world devoid of men.

Tiptree's pseudonymity lasted for ten years, from 1968 to 1977. It is perhaps significant that for the first half of that career, 1968–72, when she was at her most productive, 21 stories appeared in magazines and only six in anthologies. In the second half, 1973–77, as her pace slowed down, five appeared in magazines but eight in anthologies. In fact from 1971 onwards, the majority of her stories appeared first in anthologies. This reflects the changes occurring in the short-story field at that time. The magazines were undergoing significant editorial changes, with only Ferman and White being receptive to her stories after 1970, while the editors of the blossoming anthology field were actively pursuing her work.

Moreover, there seemed a greater freedom of expression in the anthologies than in the magazines, although I am not convinced that this was fully put to the test. During the early-to-mid-seventies the anthologies became the smart place to appear and the magazines became – and often looked – old fashioned.

Besides the welcome provided by anthologists David Gerrold, Harlan Ellison and Robert Silverberg to Tiptree's work, there was more potential for anthologies to develop themes and thereby more flexibility to explore feminist issues, as well as more opportunity for women editors. Yet the road to producing a genuine feminist anthology was not a simple one.

The first attempt was a joint effort, and an interesting experiment. For *Two Views of Wonder*, Thomas N. Scortia and Chelsea Quinn Yarbro devised a process whereby a man and a woman would each write a story based on a common theme. They allowed the woman to select a theme first, from a list of 25, and then found a man also prepared to write around that theme. This went on through six pairings. Neither partner knew the identity of the other, to avoid collusion. The result was a rare opportunity to compare how men and women treated the same subject. As each author was individually creative, the pairing tried to omit extremes. Thus Miriam Allen deFord, known for her mystery fiction as well as her science fiction, was paired with crime writer Joe Gores, Pamela Sargent was paired with Michael Kurland, Sydney Van Scyoc with Reginald Bretnor, George Zebrowski with Tamsin Ashe, Yarbro was matched with Harlan Ellison and Scortia with Willo Davis Roberts.

One needs to know each writer's individual style well in order to avoid reading too much into the experiment. That aside, it is fascinating to see how different each story is within each pairing, at least in terms of plot and characters. The creative process, no matter how common the denominator, is distinctly individualistic. Yet when it comes to treatment, there is no indication that the women chose to write softer, more human stories or that the men wrote violent adventures. The experiment underscores primarily how individual all true talents are. If there was any distinction, it was that the men were inclined to bolder, brasher statements, more vivid images, and black humour. The women worked their imagery more, bringing out subtler shades, and their humour and observation tended towards the ironic. But I would not say that these comparisons are universal. In fact, if I were not aware of the bylines on most of the stories, I don't think I could have distinguished the author's sex – although Ellison's story stands out as uniquely his work. George Zebrowski's story struck me as far more subtle than Tamsin Ashe's and without knowing the author identities I might have switched those round. When Theodore Sturgeon read the anthology he concluded that, 'the experiment demonstrates that there is no significant difference between the males and females in approach or texture'.[91]

One might argue that some of the authors, knowing the nature of the experiment, might have tried to write as asexually as they could, though it's difficult to see evidence of that. It was an interesting experiment and one worth refining and repeating, but it did nothing to develop a feminist perspective. Yarbro did not seem wholly satisfied with the result, remarking, 'it did give me a very strong object lesson in the fact that the times aren't a-changing as much as we tell ourselves they are'.[92] This comment was aimed as much at the collaborative process with Scortia, where she often found herself relegated to the role of secretary, as it was over the book's content.

Pamela Sargent, who took part in the experiment, took the next step. She wanted to compile an anthology of stories by women that explored

91 Theodore Sturgeon, 'Bookshelf', *Galaxy* 34:7 (April 1974) p. 122.
92 Chelsea Quinn Yarbro in *Khatru* #3/4 (November 1975), p. 38.

female issues. Rather than commission new ones, Sargent sensibly selected reprints, demonstrating, in effect, what had already been achieved. It took her two years to find a publisher willing to take it on. One editor queried whether she would find enough stories, demonstrating their ignorance of the field, but it was a challenge nonetheless. The anthology, *Women of Wonder*, was eventually published by Vintage Press, a division of Random House, in January 1975. It contained 12 stories, presented in chronological order, from Merril's 'That Only a Mother' (1948) to Vonda McIntyre's 'Of Mist, and Grass, and Sand' (1973). The selection served several useful purposes. It not only made available a good cross-section of stories by women, and demonstrated that women had been writing feminist sf for at least 25 years, it also showed that the sf magazines and anthologies, even though mostly edited by men, were already publishing such stories. All of the stories reprinted in *Women of Wonder* and *More Women of Wonder* (1976) had originally been selected for publication by men, as had all but one of the stories in *The New Women of Wonder* (1978). Robert Silverberg, Damon Knight and Harlan Ellison stand out amongst these editors and it is none too surprising that these were amongst the most active editors in liberating science fiction. The late sixties and early seventies was a moment right for change and women, quite rightly, took full advantage of it.

The time was due for an anthology of all new feminist, or rather humanist, stories and *Aurora: Beyond Equality* eventually appeared in May 1976, though work began on it in 1974. The editors, Vonda McIntyre and Susan Janice Anderson, wanted to avoid all stereotypes and extremes. Their request to contributors stated that they were looking for stories 'which would explore the future of human potential after equality between the sexes had been achieved' – in other words, genuine humanist stories. They reveal in the anthology that many of the stories they received were unusable because authors went to extremes and that it took them a year to get the collection together. They eventually selected eight stories, plus an essay by Le Guin on how she came to write *The Left Hand of Darkness*. Three of the stories were by men – Dave Skal, P. J. Plauger and Craig Strete. At the time, James Tiptree's story would also have counted as being by a man, so the editors believed they had chosen an even balance with four women contributors: Mildred Downey Broxon, Joanna Russ, Marge Piercy and Tiptree again, but writing as Raccoona Sheldon. At the time the editors believed Tiptree and Sheldon were two separate writers.

Unfortunately, even these stories were not truly humanistic. They did not portray a society as it would exist after total equality. Most of the stories tended to show how hopeless men were and how superior women could be. Only Marge Piercy's 'Woman on the Edge of Time' portrayed a non-sexist future, where even the male and female pronouns have been replaced by 'per'. This was an extract from her forthcoming novel of that name, published by Knopf later in 1976, so was not written especially for the book. Both of Sheldon's stories depict (or in one case imagine) worlds without men. 'Houston, Houston, Do You Read?', as Tiptree, depicts a future where plague has eradicated men. An all-male space-ship crew enters this future via a time warp and the women, unsure that they could cope again with men, eradicate them, but save their sperm. The story went on to win the Hugo, Nebula and Jupiter Awards, though not everyone approved of it. Marion Zimmer Bradley, for one, called it 'one of the worst novelettes to appear at *any* time in the past fifty years', adding that had the genders been reversed in the story it would have been pilloried as 'vicious hate propaganda'.[93] Yet that is a very superficial interpretation. Most of Tiptree's stories have many layers of interpretation and the story projects such an extreme view in order to jolt stereotyped preconceptions.

The anthology was a brave attempt but perhaps a step too soon. Three years after it appeared, McIntyre stated:

> Susan and I would like to re-edit *Aurora* now … Writers today are caught up with the theme that we wanted to have stories written about. It would be nice to have a bunch of humanistic science fiction stories collected in one place … I'm not ashamed of *Aurora*, I think there was some really good fiction in it, though I don't think it was completely successful in terms of what we set out to do. We didn't *get* any stories that were more humanistic than the ones in the book.[94]

It demonstrates a problem with original themed anthologies, when writers are asked to work to a set of criteria. It restricts their natural creative freedom and, as so often happens to people when asked for something outright, their minds do not focus. Much better that writers produce material to their own criteria, for whatever market, and such stories can later be reprinted in themed anthologies.

Feminist issues could not be forced. They worked best when infiltrated, and they had been doing that within the sf magazines and serial antholo-gies, for many years, as Pamela Sargent's anthologies showed. As we have seen, all of the magazine editors during the seventies were publishing women writers and feminist fiction in the sf magazines without fanfare. We need only refer back to Ben Bova's work at *Analog*, publishing Vonda

93 Marion Zimmer Bradley, letter in *Future Retrospective* #12 (1977), reprinted in *Science Fiction Review* #23 (November 1977), p. 83.

94 Vonda McIntyre interviewed by Paul Novitski in *Starship* #34 (Spring 1979), p. 26.

McIntyre, Lisa Tuttle, Joan Vinge, and compiling the special women's issue in 1977; and to James Baen's work at *Galaxy* in 1975–76, running the works of Lisa Tuttle, Nancy Kress, Pat Murphy, C. J. Cherryh and serializing Joanna Russ's, 'We Who Are About To…'. *F&SF* had continued to run many feminist stories, including Tiptree's landmark story 'The Women Men Don't See' in 1973. Nor should we forget the works of John Varley, many of whose stories are told from a female perspective. Vonda McIntyre regarded his work as 'amazing'.[95] In his future-history setting it is common practice for individuals to change sex so that in any one story a female character may well have previously been male, or vice versa, which enriches their outlook and experience and creates a stronger character. Nevertheless, Varley still had to work hard at it:

> I've wondered if that's cheating in a way, it's ducking issues of feminism, which I want to confront, but I don't feel that I'm politically sophisti-cated enough in so many ways to confront certain things. I'm learning things as I go along in my writing, working out my feelings about things. So I thought, as far as feminism goes, what would people be like if they could change; see it from both sides, so that the person's sex was not an overriding issue in their lives.[96]

It was the magazines – and especially the editors Edward Ferman and James Baen – that had allowed Varley to experiment and learn. Yet because the magazines had been achieving this steadily over several years it was passing unnoticed by many, and it was only when these various stories were anthologized and wrapped up as something special in the mid-seventies that it seemed as if a revolution had happened overnight.

Part of this 'revolution' was also developing in the amateur magazines, which almost served as a feminist 'underground' for much of the decade. These magazines ran some fiction, but their major purpose was allowing room for discussion of feminist issues and gaining a greater understanding of what was happening.

When Jeffrey Smith began *Khatru* in February 1975, it was not intended to explore feminist issues. It was a general magazine discussing current trends in science fiction, which it did for the first two issues. But all through 1975 Smith was sending ever-heavier bundles of letters around a group of writers developing an interactive symposium on 'Women in Science Fiction'. This appeared as a double issue in November 1975, and I have already quoted from it extensively. The final typed copy ran to 120

---

95 Vonda McIntyre interviewed by Paul Novitski, p. 23.
96 John Varley interviewed by Daniel DePrez, *Science Fiction Review* #22 (August 1977), p. 10.

quarto pages and remains the biggest single discussion on the subject. The main contributors were Suzy McKee Charnas, Samuel R. Delany, Virginia Kidd, Ursula K. Le Guin, Vonda McIntyre, Raylyn Moore, Joanna Russ, James Tiptree, Kate Wilhelm and Chelsea Quinn Yarbro, each responding to Smith's questions and then reacting to each other's responses. For the first time in print these authors fully and openly expressed their feelings about how they perceived male-dominated science fiction and how they wanted to rectify the balance. They did not all agree, and there was considerable anger and frustration amongst some of the responses, but it was clearly not only an informative but also a therapeutic process, and the magazine issue has remained something of a landmark ever since.

The first feminist amateur magazine appeared in Canada. This was *The Witch and the Chameleon* (often abbreviated to *WatCH*), published and edited by Amanda Bankier of Hamilton, Ontario. It ran for five issues (the last one a double) from August 1974. Bankier opened the first issue with the observation, 'There seem to be a lot of changes in the science fictional air these days, now that women are around.'[97]

In preparing the magazine, Bankier had placed an advert in the Worldcon Progress Report, which yielded several responses. The first was from Vonda McIntyre who became a regular contributor and whose voice set the tone for the magazine. Amongst her contributions was a fascinating analysis of a year's worth of short fiction, 'About 2,675,250 words' (#3, April 1975), which showed how long it was taking for attitudes to change amongst most of the male writers in the sf magazines.

Bankier encouraged feedback and discussion, leading to a number of exchanges in the letter and review columns. The most heated began in issue #2 (November 1974) with Vonda McIntyre's review of Marion Zimmer Bradley's *Darkover Landfall*, where McIntyre accused Bradley of being anti-feminist. This led to a fascinating exchange between Bradley and Joanna Russ, their letters running through the remaining three issues and forming significant articles. Russ had the last word, purely because the magazine folded, and in her letter in issue #5/6 Russ explores the very basis of cultural behaviour that encourages not only sexism but racism and other prejudices, and recognizes that change can only be made one step at a time, provided we're all moving in the same direction.

Jennifer Bankier, Amanda's sister, contributed a criticism of a panel discussion at the 1974 World SF Convention held in Washington in late August 1974 on 'Women in SF: Image and Reality' (#2). Katherine Kurtz had dominated the panel with her view that science fiction was not expressing discrimination against women, rather that it was poor writing.

97 Amanda Bankier, 'Editorial', *The Witch and the Chameleon* #1 (August 1974), p. 2.

Bankier, who was a lawyer, refuted Kurtz's view and argued cogently about what constituted discrimination. Her article brought a wave of responses, including a four-page letter from Kate Wilhelm who looked at the prejudices and hurdles throughout life that work against women becoming writers. 'I do find it fascinating and intriguing', she wrote, 'that there are a number of women, growing all the time, who have managed to pick their way through the maze of obstacles, and that so many of them are relatively sane.'[98] Wilhelm's response was the first time she had proactively responded to a fanzine, regarding *WatCH* as the first proper forum in which to allow a sensible discussion of feminist issues.

WatCH ceased with issue #5/6 owing to pressure of work and other commitments, but its place as the leading feminist fanzine was soon taken by *Janus*, launched in Fall 1975 by the Madison Science Fiction Group in Wisconsin. It was edited by Jan Bogstad, assisted by Jeanne Gomoll, who later became co-editor. Although it had a feminist perspective from the outset, it was a general fanzine, like so many, with articles and reviews on all aspects of the sf scene, including an interview with local writer Clifford Simak in the fourth issue (June 1976). Its feminist slant, though, soon attracted interest and the magazine became a focus in organizing the first feminist science-fiction convention, dubbed WisCon, in Madison in February 1977, now held annually. Katherine MacLean and Amanda Bankier were guests of honour at the first, since when all the major players have appeared. It was at WisCon that plans for the Tiptree Award were announced in 1991 for 'science fiction or fantasy that explores and expands the roles of women and men'. *Janus* served as a beacon amongst feminists during the 1970s, providing a forum for discussion and ideas. It was shortlisted for the Hugo Award in 1978, 1979 and 1980, and both Bogstad and Gomoll won the Fan Activity Achievement Award in 1978 and 1979. *Janus* changed its name to *Aurora* in 1981 and continued until issue #27 in 1987.

While *Janus* was the primary discussion magazine for the feminist movement, *Pandora* became the principal fiction magazine. It first appeared in October 1978, edited by Lois Wickstrom, then an analytical chemist in Denver, Colorado. The first issue was a standard quarto-size fanzine but Wickstrom secured a $700 grant from a local Women's Institute and this allowed her to produce the magazine by offset-litho, in octavo booklet format, and to pay a basic cent a word. With a thousand copies printed, it made *Pandora* a semi-professional magazine. By issue #3 (April 1979) it was fully typeset with colour covers.

Pandora ran the motto 'If Pandora hadn't been curious, there would be

98 Kate Wilhelm, 'Women Writers', *The Witch and the Chameleon* #3 (April 1975), p. 22.

nothing to write about.' In Greek mythology Pandora was the first woman sent by the gods to bring misery to all men. Hermes later delivered a large box but gave no details of the contents. Although advised by her husband, Epimetheus, to leave the box alone, Pandora's curiosity got the better of her and she opened the box. Out came all the ills of the world. The story is similar to that of Eve and the apple in the Bible. It is a strange motto and name for a feminist magazine, as it admits a female failing of curiosity and temptation, though it served as a basis for reworking negative images. The motto is very apt as regards fiction in general, because all stories arise from those ills.

Each issue of *Pandora* sought to include at least one story 'that only *Pandora* could print', which led to some interesting examples. In the second issue, Lili Winkler contributed 'My Friend Shirley' about human embryo transplants. The original version of the story was told from Winkler's pro-abortion viewpoint but, after advice from William Tenn, Winkler rewrote the story from the viewpoint of an anti-abortionist, leading to a sharper, more intense story.

Pandora ran several such challenging stories. 'Violation' by Al Sirois (#5, 1980) takes us into the psyche of a sex offender whose punishment is to undergo a sex change. 'In a Bed of Stone' by Jean Lorrah (#6, 1980), a tale of alien sexual manipulation, had previously appeared as a *Star Trek* story in *The Rooster and the Raven* (#2, Winter 1976) but was revised for *Pandora*. 'The Resurrection of Raoul T. Harper' by Connie Kidwell (#7, March 1981) is a moving account of a woman awaiting the return of her once-dead husband who had been saved by cryonics. Wickstrom also bought a story by Lyn Schumaker, which dealt with a victim of rape. It had arisen out of a Clarion workshop, but Damon Knight was so impressed by the story that he acquired it, reimbursed Wickstrom, and ran it in *Orbit 21* (1980). The title, 'And the TV Changed Colors When She Spoke' had been one suggested by Wickstrom.

Pandora attracted many women writers. 'Nuns and Chimneysweeps' in issue #3 (April 1979), illustrated by Victoria Poyser, marked the first appearance in print of Lisa Goldstein, and later served as the first chapter of her debut novel, *The Red Magician* (1982). There was work from Jayge Carr, Phyllis Ann Karr, Margaret 'Steve' Barnes, Janet Fox and Janrae Frank, whose stories about the Amazon warrior Chimquar appeared in several issues. But the magazine also attracted many male writers, including Larry Teufner, Steve Eng, Jim Aikin and Ralph Roberts, and Thomas Disch contributed some poetry. The magazine was effectively illustrated with work by Victoria Poyser, Cynthia Weinberg and Vance Kirkland, and the whole package was an attractive and often thought-provoking magazine.

Despite its print run, *Pandora* only had around two hundred subscribers plus sales or distribution of a further five hundred. Wickstrom recently told me that she never received the major breakthrough story that she had hoped for, though she worked hard with her contributors getting stories into shape. She did believe that the stories gave rise to insightful discussions at various conventions. Wickstrom was pleased at how many male writers contributed to the magazine but became alarmed at how many new female contributors continued to use their initials only, rather than identifying themselves. Even after a decade, it seems that old prejudices still held sway.

Not all women wanted to write fiction labelled feminist sf, since it rather spoiled the intent. In 1975, before she had seen Pamela Sargent's first anthology, Raylyn Moore commented, 'And most depressing of all to me … would be the concept of a sf anthology or magazine on the woman theme, restricted to women sf writers. … That would be rank segregation, guaranteed to exacerbate all our differences'.[99] Inevitably the feminist movement had drawn attention to itself and had resulted, in a few instances, to an exaggeration of the issues. Over time these would settle down and it was hoped that women writers would be treated on equal terms and that stereotypical images of women in sf would cease. Ursula K. Le Guin expressed this perfectly in her guest of honour speech at the 1975 World SF Convention held in Melbourne, Australia:

> When you undertake to make a work of art – a novel or a clay pot – you're not competing with anybody, except yourself and God. Can I do it better this time? Once you have realized that that is the only question, once you have faced the empty page or the lump of clay in that solitude, without anyone to blame for failure but yourself, and known that fear and that challenge, you aren't going to care very much about being ladylike, or about your so-called competition, male or female. The practice of an art is, in its absolute discipline, the experience of absolute freedom. And that, above all, is why I'd like to see more of my sisters trying out their wings above the mountains. Because freedom is not always an easy thing for women to find.[100]

By making it happen and by producing quality science fiction, women had been competing with their male counterparts for over thirty years. The new freedom of the seventies gave them the scope to portray women in an equal role in society. The magazines and anthologies developed their work, without forcing it, so that by the end of the decade Virginia

---

99 Raylyn Moore, *Khatru* #3/4 (November 1975), p. 58.

100 Ursula K. Le Guin, 'The Stone Ax and the Muskoxen', *Vector* #71 (December 1975), reprinted in Le Guin, *The Language of the Night*, p. 222.

Kidd – a science-fiction fan since the thirties and a literary agent and occasional writer since the sixties – could compile *Millenial Women* (1978), an anthology of new fiction all by women writers presenting strong characters in human situations. Kidd writes in her introduction:

> … what seems to me one of the most impressive aspects of the collection is that all of these science fiction writers avoid hard-core science fiction for sociology, soft-pedal radical feminism for humanism, and write about women simply as women.[101]

And all these writers – Ursula K. Le Guin, Joan Vinge, Cynthia Felice, Cherry Wilder, Elizabeth Lynn and Diana Paxson – had entered science fiction through the magazines or anthologies. Without fuss, *Millenial Women* presented true liberated fiction. Marilyn Hacker contributed an introductory poem looking forward to how her daughter might be perceived in the year 2000, and ended it with the words 'The war is over.'

There were still battles to be fought. In the penultimate issue of *Aurora* (Winter 1986/7), Jeanne Gomoll wrote an 'Open Letter to Joanna Russ', taking issue with Bruce Sterling's comment, in his introduction to William Gibson's *Burning Chrome* (1986), that 'SF in the late Seventies was confused, self-involved, and stale.' In one sentence, Sterling had dismissed the feminist movement and the quality of groundbreaking work that had appeared. Gomoll spent some time highlighting the achievements of the 1970s, including the following: 'From 1953 through 1967 there had not been one single woman to win a Hugo award for fiction. Between 1968 and 1984 there were eleven.'[102]

That record would continue, though equality was still some way away. From the seventies to date 26 per cent of the Hugo Awards in the fiction categories have gone to women writers, the greater proportion of those for novels and novellas. Interestingly, though, the proportion amongst the John W. Campbell Award for Best New Writer is almost evenly matched with 17 to women and 18 to men as of 2006.[103] It is an irony that would have pleased Campbell enormously.

The Elwood Factor

If everything covered so far had been all that happened in the early seventies then the original anthology would have had an honourable and

---

101 Virginia Kidd, 'Introduction', *Millennial Women* (New York: Delacorte, 1978), p. 3.
102 Jeanne Gomoll, 'Open Letter to Joanna Russ', *Aurora* 10:1 (Winter 1986/7).
103 My thanks for Amanda Bankier for drawing my attention to this.

rewarding history. Unfortunately, the field suffered a blight in the mid-seventies from which it took a while to recover, and that blight is blamed on one person, Roger Elwood. Elwood compiled so many anthologies in such a short time it is claimed that he saturated the field and, because the books did not sell well, it turned publishers against anthologies. It seems hard to imagine that one person could cause such a blight so, before passing judgement, we ought to consider this Elwood phenomenon in some detail and see what effect it had on the course of sf publishing during the late seventies.

Roger Elwood was born in January 1943 in Atlantic City, New Jersey. He left school at 18 and was soon selling material to a wide range of magazines, such as *Lady's Circle*, *Woman's World* and various film magazines. Most of these were short articles. He wrote very little fiction. Two known stories were 'I See Death in a Shadow' in the June 1964 issue of *Mike Shayne Mystery Magazine* and 'How to Murder Your Boss' in the first, and only, issue of the American edition of *Edgar Wallace Mystery Magazine* in March 1966.

Elwood had discovered science fiction in his early teens. His father had read sf back in the Gernsback days. Although Elwood had a great affection for the field, he had little propensity to write it. He did, though, want to compile anthologies, and tried to sell various proposals without success. In the end, he turned to Sam Moskowitz for help. Moskowitz told me:

> I ghost-edited the first anthologies of Roger Elwood; no one would take them until they knew I would put them together. His *Alien Worlds* and *Invasion of the Robots* were both done by me as are all those listed in collaboration. He wrote the introduction to *Strange Signposts*, but I did everything else.[104]

Elwood had become entrepreneurial early on. He discovered that with Moskowitz's help he could sell the anthology, pay Moskowitz to compile them, and then publish them either wholly under his name or jointly. Moskowitz compiled eight anthologies for Elwood from *Alien Worlds* (1964) to *Other Worlds, Other Times* (1969). All were reprint anthologies and ran mostly classic science fiction. There was no new material.

These volumes gave Elwood access to various publishing offices and he developed his output by making a similar arrangement with Vic Ghidalia. Ghidalia was a public relations officer who had a deep interest in supernatural and weird fiction and an extensive collection of material, but had been unable to interest a publisher in any anthologies. Ghidalia told me:

104 Personal letter, Moskowitz/Ashley, 12 November 1976.

Roger Elwood and I collaborated, he as my agent and I as the creative force for which Mr. Elwood took on co-editor credits, though he strictly handled sales of projects to publishers and cleared titles for permission.[105]

Elwood was acting more as a packager than an editor. It's a role adopted today in similar form by Martin H. Greenberg and has been used by Lyle Kenyon Engel and Byron Preiss, so is not unusual.

Ghidalia compiled and Elwood 'agented' another eight volumes, starting with *The Little Monsters* (1969) and ending with the much-delayed *Beware More Beasts* (1975). All of these were reprint anthologies although *Androids, Time Machines and Blue Giraffes* (1973), aimed at younger readers, did include a few new stories.

Elwood now had his name on 16 anthologies, though he had done little work in actually compiling them. Had he stopped there no one would remember his name, but he had the bit between his teeth. Ghidalia explained, 'He struck out on his own while clearing titles on *The Venus Factor* [1972], when he came in contact with authors' agent Virginia Kidd who interested him in editing anthologies utilizing new stories, many from authors she represented.'[106]

In fact, just before this, Elwood had sold his first all-original solo effort. This was *Signs and Wonders* published in April 1972 from the small family company of Fleming H. Revell in Old Tappan, New Jersey. Revell concentrated on religious books and Elwood was a devout Christian. He was particularly interested in how religious themes could be explored via science fiction. It was dangerous territory for Elwood, since his beliefs would not allow him to publish anything blasphemous or insulting to his religion. His approach was to present anthologies that showed the wonder and glory of God in various ways.

The premise that inspired this anthology was that as God had given man dominion over all of God's creation, this must extend to all the planets, so it was our duty to ensure that all alien souls were saved. *Signs and Wonders* was thus full of missionary sf. This wasn't new to science fiction – there had been several stories of this nature in the early fifties, such as Ray Bradbury's 'In This Sign' (*Imagination*, April 1951) and James Blish's 'A Case of Conscience' (*If*, September 1953). But it required skilled writing so as not to proselytise. Elwood had approached seven writers, of whom only a few – Farmer, Malzberg, perhaps Tom Godwin – had the skill to treat the subject wisely but who, for individual reasons, wrote the stories their way. Farmer's 'Towards the Beloved City' considers the apocalypse

---

105 Personal letter, Ghidalia/Ashley, 12 April 1977.
106 Personal letter, Ghidalia/Ashley, 12 April 1977.

happening as described in the Book of Revelation and questions how you would know good from evil. Malzberg's 'In the Cup' treats a belief in God as a mental disease that must be cured. In 'Terrible Quick Sword', Emil Petaja has aliens invade Earth by using religion against us.

Elwood had also approached old-timers Edmond Hamilton and Otto Binder, who must have been surprised to receive such a commission at this time. Binder sent in two stories, resurrecting his long-dead alias Gordon A. Giles (spelled Gyles here) for the occasion. 'All in Good Time', as Binder, shows a future society where religion is a crime and to defend himself a man must prove that God exists. Hamilton's story is the only one that follows Elwood's premise and considers how a missionary would tackle evangelical work amongst an alien species.

The appearance of both Binder and Hamilton in an anthology of new stories in the early seventies, when so much was happening in the sf field, was a sign that Elwood might not be seeking the most cutting-edge material. For this early book, Elwood's interpretation of his vision did not readily translate into fiction, and he was having problems finding what he needed. As he progressed, he became less restrictive. Nevertheless, although *Signs and Wonders* is a weak anthology, the fact that it came from a publisher of religious books meant that it was aimed at a different readership, unaware of the current state of sf, most of whom may have seen the book as bold and original. The science-fiction world, by and large, overlooked the book, although Samuel Mines reviewed it for *Luna Monthly* and summed it up as 'dreadful'.[107]

Elwood, though, was only just getting going. If he could sell an anthology of Christian fiction to one religious publisher, he could sell it to others. His next two anthologies were also promoted as religious. *And Now Walk Gently Through the Fire…* came from Chilton in February 1973 and *Flame Tree Planet* from Concordia in March 1973. The ball had started to roll and it was now that Elwood's entrepreneurial skills and his remarkable ingenuity revealed themselves. Working from his office at home and operating almost entirely by telephone, he contacted a wide range of publishing houses and convinced them to publish an anthology based on a topical or religious theme. He then contacted a selection of contributors, again by telephone, and within hours the volume was filled. He then had only to wait for the stories to arrive and compile the anthology. He had started this process in the summer of 1971 and over the next 12 to 15 months he secured contracts for 40 anthologies. Delivery dates and publishing schedules meant that rather than these books appearing gradually, over a period of time, they all came together during 1973 and 1974.

107 Samuel Mines review in *Luna Monthly* #49 (Autumn 1973), p. 26.

I have no reason to doubt that when he started Elwood checked the stories thoroughly and certainly rejected some. As the contracts built up and as the work became time-consuming, the opportunity to check all of the stories thoroughly or critically may not always have arisen. Here are just two examples of Elwood's working practices, which highlight both his facility for placing new anthology ideas and his less-than-cautious way of accepting manuscripts.

Theodore Sturgeon recalled how (in 1973) Elwood phoned him to request a new story. Sturgeon was becoming perturbed over the volume of Elwood anthologies and so declined. Elwood was persistent and, during the conversation, Sturgeon mentioned that he had recently acquired a tape recorder and had carried out interviews with various sf writers, during which he had posed the question, 'How come we're all white?' Sturgeon continues:

> In this instance, however, when I chattily mentioned this preoccupation of mine and mentioned the tapes I have, he [Elwood] rose to bait like a speckled trout in Wormsville, hung up, checked with a publisher and called me back. How about an anthology of sf stories by and about blacks – would I then write one?[108]

Sturgeon declined again, but agreed to write an introduction. That anthology came to nothing in the end, but it demonstrates how quickly Elwood could sell a project and harness it to a major name.

As for his dealings with authors, David Gerrold recalled the following:

> My agent told me to stay away from Roger Elwood, so when Roger asked me for stories, I took two stories out of the trunk. They were the worst stories I ever wrote. They hadn't worked out so I put them in the trunk. So I thought I would send them to Roger, and he would reject them, and then the next time he asked me for stories, I'd say, 'Well, I sent you some stories. You didn't like them.' Right? The son of a bitch bought both stories and published them, and I realized I could not even send him bad stories or he'd buy them. That was it with Roger Elwood for me.[109]

Those stories were 'An Infinity of Loving' in *Ten Tomorrows* and 'Skinflowers' in *The Berserkers*. *Ten Tomorrows* was Elwood's ninth original anthology, so he was amassing stories uncritically from an early stage.

Once the flood of Elwood's books appeared, it was impossible to ignore them. Sixteen anthologies bearing his name appeared in total in 1973

---

108 Theodore Sturgeon, 'Galaxy Bookshelf', *Galaxy* 34:6 (March 1974) p. 84

109 David Gerrold in interview with Darrell Schweitzer, *Amazing SF Stories* 59:3 (September 1985), pp. 74–5.

(including two with Vic Ghidalia), with another twenty-four during 1974, and more promised in 1975.

But this wasn't all. His anthology *And Now Walk Gently Through the Fire...* from Chilton had been picked up by the Science Fiction Book Club and generally received good reviews and good sales. It was certainly a better book than *Signs and Wonders*, with a wider choice of writers and a less-evangelistic approach. This gave Elwood greater credibility within the field, especially amongst publishers who had not previously had any experience with science fiction but who now saw it as a new opportunity. Chilton appointed Elwood as their consulting SF editor in June 1973. A few months later Pyramid Books did the same (for six books a year) and by December 1973 so had Bobbs-Merrill (for twelve books a year). Elwood's greatest coup (and his downfall) was to establish a science-fiction line with Harlequin Books, in March 1974, for 48 books a year. Harlequin were noted for their romance titles and Elwood convinced them to run a new series of paperback sf novels, four a month, in what became Laser Books.

Elwood was everywhere. People did calculations and reckoned that Elwood was now controlling 40 per cent of the sf market.[110] Barry Malzberg estimated in 1973 that since Elwood had 'entered the field in mid-1971, [he had] already purchased and paid for seven million words and, with increasing editorial responsibilities, [may] be buying three million words a year through 1974 and subsequently.'[111] To put that in perspective, Malzberg believed that in 1974 Elwood would buy more fiction than was appearing in all the current sf magazines combined.

Questions were asked. Firstly, should one individual have such control over so much of the field? And secondly, should *this* individual have such control? What experience did he have? What knowledge of the field did he have? And, how much would his strong religious beliefs influence what he bought. Elwood stated that he did not like profanities in his books, or anything that encouraged permissiveness. In other words, he would only acquire material that fitted in with his personal doctrine.[112]

110 Elwood challenged the 40 per cent figure in an interview with Richard A. Lupoff in *Algol* #22 (May 1974), p. 20, but after some calculations came to accept it. The figure was also agreed by Elwood in an interview by Denis Quane in *Notes from the Chemistry Dept.* #8 (October 1974), p. 5. In 'A Personal Reaction', *Science Fiction Review* #13 (May 1975), p. 14, Bruce D. Arthurs restated that figure as applicable in mid-1974 but that it was now closer to 20 per cent. By November 1975, Elwood was stating the figure was closer to 25 per cent (see *Vector* #79, January/February 1977), p. 11.

111 Barry N. Malzberg, 'The Case of Roger Elwood', *Analog* 93:3 (May 1974), p. 164.

112 In his interview with Lupoff, Elwood said that he would not accept a story involving incest or with unnecessary profanities like 'Oh Christ' or 'Oh Jesus' or with the word 'fuck'.

Some writers regarded this as tantamount to censorship and challenged the circumstances that allowed someone with this attitude to have such an influential role over the field.

This was the debate that raged, and one that inevitably had two opposing sides. There were those who were concerned that the field had only been liberated in the last decade but was now in danger of closing in on itself again. Should this be allowed? On the other hand, there were some writers and certainly some readers who felt that all editors would have their personal requirements and that the field had coped with these over the years without suffering unduly. Why worry about that when Elwood was opening up many new markets? The issue became one of scale versus influence.

Elwood's response was consistent in all the interviews he gave. First regarding his tastes:

> I am not an idiosyncratic editor, despite a few taboos on sex and religion. I've taken a wide spectrum of stories and approaches to stories. If you don't narrow down and take *only* experimental, I don't see how editorial preferences and prejudices can play a large part – since you have no prejudices as far as *type* of story.[113]

And as regards the size of the field he controlled:

> Harlequin and Bobbs are *new* markets. [...] These new markets are in *addition*, so we have what amounts to an expansion of markets. If I were to take over somebody else's job, that would be a contraction. So I see no danger of Roger Elwood controlling any large percentage of the field.[114]

The science-fiction field had seen several periods of expansion and decline, which I have already chronicled in these books. In all cases, it was the opportunist publishers jumping on the bandwagon and saturating the field. Bookstalls and news-stands could only stock so much and it reached a point when boxes of magazines were being returned unopened because the dealer had never got round to displaying them. This had happened less than twenty years before so most of the older sf writers and fans would recall it, and this was their cause for concern.

In addition, they knew that when a field becomes saturated, it is usually with poor material. Writers can only produce so much good material, and even if this was an expansion of the field, allowing scope for new writers, those new writers needed good editors and strong guidance. Elwood had

---

113 Elwood in interview with Richard Lupoff, p. 22.
114 Elwood in interview with Richard Lupoff, p. 22.

yet to prove that he was a good editor. The evidence to date was suggesting the opposite. Most of the anthologies bearing his name had been edited by others, so he had no real track record of selecting quality material, and the new books appearing under his name included work by such old-timers as Otto Binder and Arthur Tofte. Neither Binder nor Tofte had written any adult sf for twenty years or more. No matter what good intentions Elwood had, he was not endearing himself to the sf community.

So let's check the evidence. The final evidence should rest with the quality of his work, but we need to consider all of the charges made against him. These fall into the following:

1. Elwood had too great a control owing to the quantity of the material he was buying;
2. Elwood's output saturated the market causing a downturn in sales;
3. Elwood's religious views caused him to dictate too closely the content of work;
4. Elwood's anthologies were of poor quality, which also caused a downturn in sales.

First let's try and get a handle on the statistics, particularly as regards the number of stories Elwood was buying and the number of books he produced. Table 2.3 is a complete list of Elwood's original anthologies in the order in which they were published between 1972 and 1977. This shows only the first edition, but most of the hardbacks listed also had paperback editions, doubling the number of titles visible on the shelves.

Table 2.3 enables us to see that in total Elwood compiled 48 original anthologies. I've noted in the list the two issues he edited of *Odyssey* magazine, of which more later. So we could argue that Elwood bought material for 50 separate publications. If we count the new stories in these anthologies (that is, excluding the few reprinted stories noted above) then we can see that Elwood acquired 414 stories (plus another 14 for the magazine), the vast majority of which appeared in 1973 and 1974.

Let's compare this against all of the other original anthologies. I've separated out the three other primary editors of original anthologies – Terry Carr, Damon Knight and Robert Silverberg – for comparison. I have also shown separately the professional magazines, as these were major markets for the short story. The figures are shown in Table 2.4.

Based on original anthologies alone, it shows that at his peak in 1974 Elwood was publishing over 56 per cent of all stories appearing in the original anthology market. For the two years 1973/74 it averages to 52 per cent, over half the share. However the short-story market included the magazines in which Elwood had little if any influence (just the two

Table 2.3 *Schedule of original anthologies and magazines edited by Roger Elwood, 1972–77*

1972
(1 volume, 8 ss)
Apr.   *Signs and Wonders*, Fleming H. Revell, hb, 157 pp., 8 ss.

1973
(14 volumes, 149 ss)
Feb.   *And Now Walk Gently Through the Fire...*, Chilton, hb, 185 pp., 10 ss.
Mar.   *Demon Kind*, Avon, pb, 192 pp., 11 ss.
        Flame Tree Planet, Concordia, pb, 159 pp., 10 ss.
Apr.   **Children of Infinity*, Franklin Watts, hb, 172 pp., 10 ss.
Jun.   *Showcase*, Harper & Row, hb, 191 pp., 12 ss.
Jul.   *Future City*, Trident Press, hb, 256 pp., 19 ss plus other material.
        Saving Worlds, hb, Doubleday, 237 pp., 16 ss. plus other material. Pb
        edition as *The Wounded Planet* (Bantam, Aug. 1974). Edited jointly
        with Virginia Kidd.
Sep.   *Ten Tomorrows*, Fawcett, pb, 224 pp., 10 ss.
        Future Quest, Avon, pb, 192 pp., 8 ss.
        The Other Side of Tomorrow, Random House, hb, 207 pp., 9 ss.
Oct.   **Monster Tales*, Rand, McNally, hb, 117 pp., 6 ss.
        *Science Fiction Tales, Rand, McNally, hb, 124 pp., 7 ss
Nov.   *Tomorrow's Alternatives (Frontiers #1)*, Macmillan, hb, 198 pp., 12 ss.
        The New Mind (Frontiers #2), Macmillan, hb, 180 pp., 9 ss.

1974
(24 volumes, 175 ss)
Jan.   *The Berserkers*, Trident Press, hb, 217 pp., 14 ss.
        Vampires, Werewolves and Other Monsters, Curtis Books, pb, 205 pp., 12
        ss.
Feb.   *Omega*, Walker, hb, 190 pp., 13 ss.
Mar.   *Crisis*, Thomas Nelson, hb, 176 pp., 9 new ss. (1 reprint)
        The Far Side of Time, Dodd, Mead, hb, 235 pp., 13 ss.
        *The Learning Maze and Other Stories, Julian Messner, hb, 191 pp., 4
        new ss. (3 reprints)
        *Science Fiction Adventures from Way Out, Whitman, 212 pp., hb, 8 ss.
        *Survival from Infinity, Franklin Watts, hb, 174 pp., 8 ss.
Apr.   *Continuum 1*, Putnam's, hb, 246 pp., 8 ss.
May.   *Long Night of Waiting and Other Stories*, Aurora, hb, 212 pp., 14 ss.
Aug.   *Continuum 2*, Putnam's, hb, 250 pp., 8 ss.
Sept.   *Future Kin*, Doubleday, hb, 180 pp., 7 new ss. (1 reprint).
        Strange Gods, Pocket Books, pb, 192 pp., 11 ss.
Oct.   **Horror Tales*, Rand, McNally, hb, 123 pp., 7 ss.

More Science Fiction Tales, Rand, McNally, hb, 124 pp., 7 ss.

Adrift in Space and Other Stories, Lerner SF Library, hb, 47 pp., 3 ss.

The Graduated Robot and Other Stories, Lerner SF Library, hb, 47 pp., 3 ss.

Journey to Another Star and Other Stories, Lerner SF Library., hb, 47 pp., 3 ss.

The Killer Plants and Other Stories, Lerner SF Library., hb, 47 pp., 3 ss.

The Mind Angel and Other Stories, Lerner SF Library., hb, 47 pp., 3 ss.

The Missing World and Other Stories, Lerner SF Library, hb, 47 pp., 3 ss.

Night of the Sphinx and Other Stories, Lerner SF Library, hb, 47 pp., 3 ss.

The Tunnel and Other Stories, Lerner SF Library, hb, 47 pp., 3 ss.

Dec.   *Continuum 3*, Putnam's, hb, 182 pp., 8 ss.

Note: in addition in 1974 Elwood compiled two single-author reprint collections, *The Many Worlds of Poul Anderson* and *The Many Worlds of Andre Norton* for Chilton.

1975
(6 volumes, 70 ss)
Jan.   *Future Corruption*, Warner, pb, 189 pp., 12 ss.
Apr.   *Continuum 4*, Putnam's, hb, 186 pp., 8 ss.
Aug.   *In the Wake of Man*, Bobbs-Merrill, hb, 229 pp., 3 ss (all novellas).
Nov.   *Tomorrow: New Worlds of Science Fiction*, Evans, hb, 218 pp., 10 ss.
Dec.   *Dystopian Visions*, Prentice-Hall, hb, 197 pp., 13 ss.
        Epoch, Berkley, hb, 623 pp., 24 ss. Edited jointly with Robert Silverberg.

1976
(1 volumes, 6 ss)
Sep.   *The 50-meter Monsters and Other Horrors*, Pocket Books, pb, 134 pp., 6 ss.

Note: in addition this year Elwood compiled two issues of the magazine *Odyssey*, containing 14 ss. in total.

1977
(2 volumes; 6 ss)
Mar.   *A World Named Cleopatra* (credited to Poul Anderson), Pyramid, pb, 192 pp., 3 ss. (plus 2 reprints)
        Futurelove, Bobbs-Merrill, hb, 181 pp., 3 ss. (all novellas)

Note: Titles asterisked (*) were published for the juvenile market; 'hb' = hardback, 'pb' = paperback; the number of pages are shown, e.g. 192 pp., and the number of stories e.g. 10 ss.

Table 2.4 *Total number of new short stories acquired by Elwood and other major markets.*

	1972	1973	1974	1975	1976	1977	Total
Elwood	8	149	175	70	6	6	414
Carr	13	10	29	0	16	8	76
Knight	31	14	38	26	11	13	133
Silverberg	14	20	13	42	15	15	119
Others	139	118	57	49	121	121	605
Subtotal original anthologies	205	311	312	187	183	160	1,358
Elwood as % of original anthologies	3.9%	47.9%	56.1%	37.4%	3.3%	3.8%	30.5%
Analog	60	57	56	52	50	64	339
F&SF	79	87	87	82	70	80	485
Amazing/Fantastic	59	47	65	67	64	55	357
Galaxy/If	61	65	96	48	41	46	357
Vertex/Cosmos	0	37	77	52	0	27	170
Subtotal major magazines	259	293	381	301	225	272	1,731
Total magazines + original anthologies	464	604	693	488	408	432	3,089
Elwood as % of magazines + anthologies* (* includes 14 ss. in *Odyssey*)	1.7%	24.7%	25.3%	14.3%	4.9%	1.4%	13.9%

issues of *Odyssey*). If we include all of the major magazines as well as the original anthologies, we find that Elwood's share of the market in 1973/74 was 25 per cent – a quarter of the entire market. This is certainly considerable, but it only remained at that peak for two years. We might also note that between them Carr, Knight and Silverberg had a 24 per cent share of the original anthology market over the same period, and their involvement continued beyond 1977.

If we take Elwood's impact over the full period of his involvement in the anthology market, we find that his overall share was 30.5 per cent

Table 2.5 *Total number of short-story volumes published, 1972 to 1977**

	1972	1973	1974	1975	1976	1977	Total
Hardcovers							
Original anthologies	7	20	31	10	13	7	88
Reprint anthologies	15	22	20	19	14	22	112
Story collections	15	10	17	28	25	15	110
Total	37	52	68	57	52	44	310
Number edited							
by Elwood	1	10	22	5	1	1	40
Elwood's %	2.7%	19.2%	32.4%	8.8%	1.9%	2.3%	12.9%
Paperbacks							
Original anthologies	7	11	6	6	11	16	57
Reprint anthologies	18	29	28	22	23	16	136
Story collections	12	16	13	11	22	24	98
Total	37	56	47	39	56	55	291
Number edited							
by Elwood	2	7	4	3	2	1	19
Elwood's %	5.4%	12.5%	8.5%	7.7%	3.6%	1.8%	6.5%
Total all anthologies	47	82	85	57	51	61	383
Number edited							
by Elwood	3	17	26	8	3	2	59
Elwood's %	6.4%	20.7%	30.6%	14.0%	5.9%	3.3%	15.4%

*Figures for total hardcovers and paperbacks provided courtesy of William Contento based on *Locus* data.

of original anthologies, and nearly 14 per cent of the full sf short-story market.

We should also note that Elwood's figures include stories he purchased for young-adult anthologies, essentially a different market. These totalled 23 stories in 1973 and 58 in 1974. If those figures are excluded, then Elwood's share of the anthology market becomes 43.8 per cent in 1973 and 46.1 per cent in 1974, and 26.1 per cent overall. In simple terms, Elwood had influence on just over a quarter of the original anthology market during the period 1972–77, almost exactly the same figure as that shared by Carr, Knight and Silverberg.

However, when we take the whole adult short-story market into

account, Elwood's share over the same period was 11 per cent, while
Edward Ferman's, as editor of *F&SF*, was nearly 16 per cent. Ferman
also edited two original anthologies jointly with Barry Malzberg, and if
we include the totals for those two anthologies (15 stories), it nudges
Ferman's impact to just over 16 per cent. Ferman's equivalent figure for
Elwood's peak years of 1973 and 1974 was 14.3 per cent (when Elwood's
share was 25 per cent).

Before considering the significance of this, let's look at the other related
concern, that Elwood's books were flooding the market and affecting sales.
This is a more complicated problem, much harder to define. After all, not
all bookstores order all books. Was the problem related more to paperbacks or hardbacks? More pertinently, did the book dealer or the public
distinguish between original anthologies, reprint anthologies and author's
short-story collections when looking at a row of books? These are qualitative questions that statistics cannot answer, but we can make a stab at the
scale of the problem. I am, once again, only considering first editions in
Table 2.5 and so I do not include paperback reprints of hardcover editions.
Neither do I include reprints of British anthologies. I am looking solely at
Elwood's penetration of the first-edition market.

Treating reprint and original anthologies together (as I am sure most
dealers and purchasers would), Elwood controlled just over 30 per cent
of them during his peak year of 1974. This includes the 13 young-adult
volumes issued in 1974 (and three volumes in 1973). If we exclude those,
then his share in 1974 was 18 per cent, and over the two years 1973/74
this share was 13.8 per cent. I think it is reasonable to exclude the juvenile
volumes, or at least the eight-volume Lerner SF Library. This was a series
of slim books (47 pages) with just three stories per volume. They all shared
the same editorial by Isaac Asimov, so one could argue that this formed one
large book split into eight parts. I have included them because they appear
in all lists of Elwood's anthologies, but they inflate Elwood's output out of
proportion. Table 2.5 shows that he controlled just over 15 per cent of the
anthology market during the period 1972–1977 but again if we exclude all
juvenile anthologies (including two by David Bischoff published in 1977
and included above), we find that Elwood's share drops to 11.8 per cent.

If we add short-story collections into the equation then his share
becomes 10.1 per cent over the six-year period, including juveniles, and
7.7 per cent excluding juveniles. These figures no longer seem so high.
In fact, during this same six-year period Robert Silverberg published 19
reprint anthologies, 15 original anthologies and 12 collections, a total of
46 books (adult), compared to 43 by Elwood. So, in terms of metres of
shelf space, Silverberg's books took up just as much room.

The scale of Elwood's production is only one part of the problem. His remarkable industry caused a huge spike to appear on the graph during 1973–74 that made everyone notice his books. Had their publication been spread evenly over the six years, the production rate would not have appeared so alarming. It was the expectation that he would sustain the rate of these two years that caused everyone to panic, especially as he was also contracted to purchase over sixty-six books per year for four separate publishers.

The production rate of his anthologies would not have been sufficient for Elwood's work to be detrimental to the field. Had his books been of a high quality, and sold well, I doubt whether any one would have worried. After all, it does not matter that Silverberg's collections and anthologies (plus his novels, of course) were taking up an equal or greater amount of shelf space because these were quality works and they sold.

The only sales figures I know of for Elwood's books are the few he reported himself. In an interview conducted in 1975, he reported, 'sales have gone as high, in hardcover, as 25,000 – 20–25,000 per title … They've gone as high in paperback as 125,000.' There is some confusion in Elwood's comments. He stated that he had been dropped by Putnam/Berkley because of poor sales. Putnam published the *Continuum* series. However, elsewhere in the interview Elwood stated, 'The *Continuum* series started out very poorly, is building up now, and my conjecture is that these books will earn the writers and myself from $4-$10,000 dollars in additional royalties.' He also said that the Dodd, Mead volume *The Other Side of Time* had poor sales, but the only anthology published by Dodd, Mead was *The Far Side of Time*.[115] One might excuse Elwood confusing the titles of his anthologies but not mistaking whether Putnam had dropped him because of poor sales. We have to be cautious about Elwood's statements, but they would still suggest that at least some of his anthologies sold well, perhaps even very well, while others had steady sales.

Elwood also claimed that 70–80 per cent of reviews of his books in a wide variety of trade and genre magazines were favourable.[116] I have read as many as I could find both within the field and in general and trade magazines and it is true that the majority of trade reviews are either favourable or non-committal, while those within the genre are mixed, often going between extremes. Here are a few by way of evidence. First the favourable ones:

115 Interview conducted by Christopher Fowler and published in *Vector* 79, January/February 1977, p. 14.

116 See *Notes from the Chemistry Dept.* #8, p. 7.

- P. Schuyler Miller in *Analog* (August 1973) on *And Now Walk Gently Through the Fire…*: 'You'll find some more conventional science fiction here, and very good stuff too' (p. 163).
- Theodore Sturgeon in *Galaxy* (December 1973): 'the fact remains that when Elwood comes up with a good one, it's very good indeed, viz. *Future City*. […] let no one, at any stage of argument, say Elwood can't put together a big one' (pp. 70–71).
- Barry Malzberg in *Analog* (May 1974): 'The indisputable fact is that almost all of the Elwood anthologies are at least adequate relative to the market, and some – *Showcase, Future City, The Berserkers* – are above average' (p. 165).
- Paul Walker in *Luna Monthly* (May 1974): 'the consistent quality of the stories I have read in his past four books is really impressive. […] Elwood's anthologies … have an abundance of stories I have actually *enjoyed*, and *The Far Side of Time* and *Flame Tree Planet* are no exceptions' (p. 18).
- Charles N. Brown in *Locus* (3 June 1975) on *Continuum 1*: 'This book, probably the best of Elwood's original anthologies … contains eight stories. All are very good or better, making this an outstanding buy' (p. 5).

There are others like that, but these show that on an individual basis Elwood was publishing some material worthy of consideration. Of course, one can match the above like-for-like with adverse comments:

- Charles N. Brown in *Locus* (3 June 1975) on *The Wounded Planet*: 'Writing warning stories about current problems is usually a wasted effort. The one exception is Robert Silverberg's "The Wind and the Rain", but one story isn't enough to save this disaster' (p. 5).
- Richard Delap in *The WSFA Journal* (December 1974) on *Omega*: 'Not much in this one. Elwood is after "name" writers again and doesn't seem to care much what they give him, while the new writers fill in the holes with toss-off items of equal disinterest. Five stories are at best readable … but even they have a fill-up quality, like something rushed out to feed a hungry magazine at deadline time. I can't even recommend the paper edition of this one' (p. 23).
- Joanna Russ in *F&SF* (March 1975): 'a well-meaning steam dynamo named Roger Elwood has been diluting the anthology market to death lately, innocently unaware that an increase in titles published may not mean reaching a new audience, but only overloading the existing one, and that good fiction can't be cranked out like haggis' (p. 45).
- Charlotte Moslander in *Luna Monthly* (August 1975) on *Children of*

Infinity and *Survival from Infinity*: 'To judge by these two anthologies, Elwood is trying hard to live up to his reputation for mediocrity – they are composed for the greater part of juvenile fiction of little merit' (p. 28),

- Bruce Gillespie in *S.F. Commentary* (Oct–Dec 1976) on *Dystopian Visions*: 'It has nothing to recommend it at all. Surely only Roger Elwood could achieve *nothing* on a subject like "dystopian visions"' (p. 133).

None of the stories in an Elwood anthology won any award, though several appeared amongst the top ten in the annual *Locus* poll and a few were nominated for a Nebula or (once) a Hugo. The one anthology by Elwood to win an award (it topped the Locus poll as that year's best anthology) was *Epoch*, which he co-edited with Silverberg. Four stories from that volume were also nominated for a Nebula or Hugo.

If you read all of Elwood's adult anthologies, a certain pattern emerges. There are those he was clearly passionate about and put time into getting right and there are others where you feel it was a quick commission, carelessly assembled. There's no way to tell one from the other without reading them, and that is part of the problem. Anyone who started delving into Elwood with a dud is likely to avoid all future volumes, and the law of averages will mean that even if you started with a good one and came back for more, you would soon find a bad one and from then on become hesitant.

Of Elwood's 33 adult anthologies, I would rate ten as worthy of investigation, but only six of those as above average quality, and that's a qualified six because four of them are the *Continuum* sequence of books which should be read as one unit. The other two titles of merit are *Future City*, which was one of Elwood's own favourites, and *Epoch*, compiled with Silverberg. The other four are *Showcase*, *Ten Tomorrows*, *The Berserkers* and *Omega*.

Future City, as the title implies, is a themed anthology looking at how the urban nucleus may evolve over time. Elwood seems on a mission here. His Christian beliefs made him feel that the city was the seat of corruption – a view that he expounds in detail in his preface, one of the few that he wrote for his books. When he commissioned the stories, he asked the authors to be as downbeat as possible, as he wanted a volume that showed the city at its worst. He presented the stories in chronological order so that the reader could watch the inevitable degradation of the city. The volume opens with Ben Bova's 'The Sightseers', set in the near future when New York has become so polluted that it has been closed down and is only visited for two weeks of the year as a tourist attraction. It ends with '5,000,000 AD' by Miriam Allen de Ford, which traces the last days of the planet. In between are stories by Barry Malzberg (three of them), Robert Silverberg, George Zebrowski and a particularly moving one by Harlan Ellison, the rather overlooked 'Hindsight: 480 Seconds', set in the last city on earth.

Continuum was one of Elwood's more inspired ideas. He brought together eight authors and asked them to produce either a series or an episodic novel that could be presented in four parts. Although each episode had to be self-contained, the overall intent was for continuity between each volume, hence the title. Like all inspired ideas, it needed more inspiration to see it through and that was lacking, but there's enough to make this more than just a novelty item. The eight authors were, at the start, Philip José Farmer, Poul Anderson, Chad Oliver, Thomas Scortia, Anne McCaffrey, Gene Wolfe, Edgar Pangborn and Dean R. Koontz. Farmer's stories formed the core of his novel *Stations of the Nightmare* (1982), a guaranteed Elwood plot, involving a man infected by an alien organism that makes him both a healer and a killer until he masters his powers. Anne McCaffrey's sequence introduces us to Killashandra, a girl training to be a crystal singer. They formed the basis of *Crystal Singer* (1982), the first volume of what became a trilogy. Edgar Pangborn provided further stories in the post-nuclear world of *Davy*, these ones forming the core of *Still I Persist in Wondering* (1978). Of the others, only Dean Koontz chose not to contribute to each volume. Instead, he established a scenario in the first volume with 'Night of the Storm' in which four robots who have hitherto not seen a human now encounter one. Thereafter each story follows their beliefs and reactions. The authors who continued the series, based on Koontz's outline, were Gail Kimberly, Pamela Sargent and George Zebrowski in collaboration, and Barry Malzberg, who brought the series to a typically violent conclusion. The first volume of *Continuum* is very good, but each successive volume pales slightly, so that the total value is less than the sum of the parts.

The idea for *Epoch* was devised by Elwood and he asked Silverberg to collaborate with him. Silverberg told me that the two of them drew up a list of contributors between them and divided them between those with whom Silverberg worked closely and those with whom Elwood did. The two then commissioned and acquired material individually but agreed on the final line-up. The book was promoted as representing the state-of-the-art in science fiction as of the mid-seventies and in that sense some compared it to bringing an end to a period of resurgence that Ellison had started with *Dangerous Visions*. I don't see it quite like that, though the sheer size of the book causes it to make a statement. In fact, the size has more to do with the fact that Larry Niven's opening story, 'ARM', and Jack Vance's closing short novel, 'The Dogtown Tourist Agency', curiously both sf detective stories, take up nearly a quarter of the book by themselves. The other 22 stories are all relatively short – a trademark of Elwood's books – but include some polished work by Michael Bishop, Jack Dann, Frederik Pohl, R. A. Lafferty (one of Elwood's consistently original contributors) and an especially labyrinthine piece by Brian Aldiss. Both George R. R. Martin and Greg Benford contributed superior time-travel stories, each utterly individualistic, and Joseph Green penned a wonderful tribute to the space opera, even calling his hero Neil Jones (after the creator of Professor Jameson). Each author contributed an after-word to their story, saying something about its origins or significance. The whole package hangs together well and, unlike *Dangerous Visions*, which was picking up the gauntlet and saying, 'Here's what we're going to do', *Epoch* was saying, 'We know where we're going, now, and we're going to have fun on the way.' It's a positive anthology that shows that the field had gained strength and confidence over the previous few years.

I suspect that much of that strength and confidence came from Silver-berg's involvement with the project, as the book reads unlike almost any of Elwood's other volumes. But I also expect that Elwood tempered the more extreme works that Silverberg enjoyed, giving the final selection a pleasing balance.

Of the 333 stories published in Elwood's adult original anthologies I would estimate that about 10 per cent are of particular merit, perhaps enough to fill two good-size volumes. Perhaps another 25 per cent are entertaining but of no great significance. The remainder, almost two-thirds, are minor. The top 10 per cent are scattered through a dozen anthologies, which is why so many of Elwood's books appear to be of only average quality. He just did too much with too little or, as Jerry Pournelle summarized it, 'I believe he's bought more stories than there were good stories around to be bought.'[117]

The final charge was one of censorship, but this one seems the weakest charge of all. Every editor and every market has its own set of criteria. One would write to a certain level or within certain limitations for the romance market, the children's market, or even the avant-garde market. Most writers knew, or soon came to know, Elwood's criteria, which were set by his own high moral standards. Most writers could also write within that and only a few lambasted Elwood as being too censorious. In fact, some writers, notably Barry Malzberg, succeeded in selling Elwood several extreme stories. 'Culture Lock' in *Future City* involves active homosexu-

---

117 Jerry Pournelle, 'Concerning Roger Elwood', *Notes from the Chemistry Dept.* #10 (March 1975), p. 6.

ality and drugs, but Elwood still ran it because Malzberg did not sensationalize the subject but treated it fairly within the context of the story. Anne McCaffrey likewise sold Elwood a story which was sexually explicit and which her agent, Virginia Kidd, did not believe that Elwood would buy. 'But he did,' McCaffrey recalled, 'And he wanted more.'[118]

Elwood was quite prepared to run risqué stories – stories for which his own Church would criticize him – provided they were skilfully written. The top-quality authors could do this. The problem was that, as time went on, the stories about Elwood's taboos spread, writers became wary rather than trying to write something challenging, and those who did contribute moderated everything to the point of blandness. Elwood, as editor, was never the villain that so many made him out to be. He was ambitious, careless, naïve, overzealous and rather too full of himself to take heed of his mistakes. As a result he harmed his own reputation irreparably, but I see no firm evidence that he harmed the reputation of science fiction, certainly not in the way that the imprudent boom-publishers of the mid-fifties did, or the pulpsters of the thirties. Or, for that matter, the atrocious magazine *Skyworlds*, which I shall cover briefly later.

But neither did Elwood advance science fiction in any way, unlike Knight, Carr and Silverberg. Elwood simply bloated the field for a couple of years, provided a quick-fix market for many writers, and then moved on.

In March 1975, Elwood announced that he was leaving the original anthology market to concentrate on purchasing novels. This was essentially because of the workload arising from the Laser Books deal with Harlequin and a new deal that he was negotiating with Transworld Publishing in Britain. Elwood anticipated he would be commissioning over eighty novels during the next two years and that, along with other projects, left no time for the workload arising from short-story commissions and assembling anthologies. Elwood's other commitments grew. He became involved in the comic-book field, in acquiring material for spoken-word records, and in preparing audio-visual packs for teaching science fiction. But he had not left the short-story field entirely.

The first issue of his magazine *Odyssey*, dated Spring 1976, appeared on 1 February 1976. It was in the large-flat format, which was becoming the vogue in the mid-seventies, with a striking cover by Kelly Freas in the same style he would use on Laser Books. The magazine was printed on cheap book paper, so it was not a slick. In fact the whole magazine looked cheaply produced, with little care or attention. It was filled with lurid

118 See interview with Anne McCaffrey by Chris Morgan, *Science Fiction Review* #44, Fall 1982, p. 23.

adverts that one normally sees in confession magazines. The contents page was full of hype and difficult to follow. The internal illustrations were bland wash. The magazine was poorly proofread, including names misspelled ('Federik' Pohl, for instance), and did nothing to inspire confidence.

The publisher was Gambi Publications, a division of Web Offset Industries. They were thus both publisher and printer, which is usually an advantage. However, Gambi were used to publishing cheap, sensational magazines. They had taken over the men's magazine *Saga* in 1966 and it had rapidly lowered in tone from its days under Macfadden in the fifties. They also produced a quarterly *UFO Report*, compiled by Martin Singer, who was Elwood's editorial director. Their production and distribution were geared towards the men's magazine market with no attempt to produce a quality product.

In the first issue, Frederik Pohl's 'The Prisoner of New York Island' is a bleak portrayal of urban America, a story that seemed straight out of Elwood's *Future City*. Pournelle's 'Bind Your Sons to Exile' looks at the human angle of the move towards space colonization and the mining of the asteroids. The story reads as if it were written for a less-discriminating readership. Fred Saberhagen's 'Beneath the Hills of Azlaroc' is a supposed account of how an explorer survived an encounter with a neutron star. Most of these stories are bleak and downbeat, a mood that was even more prevalent in the second issue, with stories by Robert Hoskins, Lee Harding, Kathleen Sky and R. A. Lafferty. Larry Niven's 'The Magic Goes Away', a key story in his Mana sequence, was the best content, albeit fantasy with a scientific logic, but was also slightly depressing. Most of the fiction was very readable, but did not leave the reader overly ebullient. Elwood also mistakenly tried a few novelty items. Robert Bloch's 'ETFF' is no more than fan fiction, a spoof on TAFF (Transatlantic Fan Fund, set up so that British fans could attend World Conventions in America, and vice versa). Ray Russell's 'Captain Clark of the Space Patrol' was the ultimate in deep-trunk stories: four micro-tales written by Russell in a school notebook when he was nine or ten. This might be something to include in an established magazine as a one-off novelty, but not in what should be a showcase issue for the magazine launch. The magazine also ran a book review column by Robert Silverberg, coverage of the fan scene by Charles N. Brown, and a film column by Forrest Ackerman.

Elwood had high hopes for *Odyssey*. In his November 1975 interview he had said, 'I want this magazine to show what a Roger Elwood magazine can be, as representative of the best. Because here I have no restrictions whatsoever from the publisher. None. Total, absolute.'[119]

119 Elwood, *Vector* #79, p. 14.

Perhaps Elwood was being naïve again. He said in the same interview that the distribution would be 'top notch', as the publisher had a good relationship with Kable, the distributors. Yet, just six months later, *Odyssey* was in trouble. The third issue was delayed until problems were resolved. These included poor sales, poor production values and slow payments.[120] Reading between the lines, when Charles N. Brown referred to Elwood's 'editing' (in quotes) of *Odyssey* in *Locus* 200, Elwood's freedom was probably not as total as he had believed and since he had such hopes for the magazine, it made the failure even more disappointing. Distribution may not have been the problem but rather retailer display time. Dick Geis reported that in his local store in Portland, Oregon, the first issue was on display for just two weeks and the second issue for only a week, and the single copy of each that Geis bought were the only ones sold.[121] The cheap appearance of the magazine but with a $1 cover price, would not have helped. Final sales figures are not known. Elwood believed that 150,000 copies were printed.[122] This figure was close to the print run of *Analog* which had a sell-through of just over 60 per cent, with about half of that being via news-stand sales in 1976. Sales of other magazines were close to 50 per cent of the print run, with again half sold on the news-stands. On that basis, *Odyssey* is unlikely to have sold more than 37,000 copies, but if Geis's example of on-sale display time was in any way typical, sales may have been perhaps a third or a quarter of that, around 10,000–15,000 copies. Gambi were used to sales of around 200,000 with *Saga*. No wonder they pulled the plug. The third issue was never published and plans for a companion magazine were scrapped.

That was not the end of Elwood's problems. He had been having difficulties with authors contributing to the Laser Books series published by Harlequin. Books were not being delivered in accordance with what Elwood believed to have been his requirements; some were even rewritten without the author's consent. There were disputes over payment. In fact, just about everything that could go wrong did.[123] The books, like Elwood's anthologies, were of variable quality. They had been aimed at a general readership but were not being taken up and were only being read by the sf readers, who were used to much meatier material. Laser Books had fallen between two markets and failed. Sales were reported to be as low as 20,000, which would be good today but at that time was very much

120 See news report in *Locus* 191, 31 July 1976, p. 2.
121 See *Science Fiction Review* #17, p. 45 and #18, p. 30.
122 See news story in *Luna Monthly* #59 (November 1975), p. 9.
123 Almost every author of that day has a Laser Books anecdote, far too many to cite here. Two examples will be found in Piers Anthony's *Bio of an Ogre*, pp. 199–200 and Tim Powers's introduction to the 1989 NESFA Press edition of *An Epitaph in Rust.*

the lower end of the scale. The series was stopped with the February 1977
titles after 57 books. Elwood had already severed his connection with
Harlequin and soon after did so with all his New York publishers. He soon
had a new project, though, as consulting editor and packager for a new sf
series for Pinnacle Books. Pinnacle were relocating their operations from
New York to Los Angeles, and Elwood moved there in May 1977. Thereafter Elwood's presence faded from the scene and he turned to other fields
and to writing religious novels, though we will encounter him again with
the comic *Starstream* and the horror magazine *Chillers*.

Ever since, though, Elwood's name has become a byword for all that
was bad in sf editing. Did he deserve it?

There is no doubt that his business practices left much to be desired.
Because he was so industrious, working as much as possible by telephone,
he maintained few written records. He would commission a story over
the phone, often with a prescriptive outline of dos and don'ts, but he
would also ask the author to make a record of that and copy it to Elwood.
This was a presumption in itself, and few authors kept detailed notes. As a
consequence, Elwood often forgot what he had asked for, with the inevitable consequences that some stories would be rejected because they were
not what he was expecting or because there was confusion over deadlines,
payments, or any of a number of other details. Authors complained to the
SFWA Grievance Committee, and its chairman, Jerry Pournelle, had the
task of resolving the problem. Pournelle and Elwood came to a 17-point
legal agreement between Elwood and the SFWA which, through Elwood's
own disorganization, he returned to Pournelle unsigned![124]

Elwood's problem was that he was overambitious, overzealous, and
inexperienced. He was naïve but well-intentioned, but was so blinded by
his own self-belief, that he had no concept of the potential problem that
he was causing. He believed that all of his contributors would deliver
what he asked for – and more often than not they didn't. He believed
that his religious views allowed him to use science fiction as a medium to
promote Christian values, which was fine for some readers, but intoler-
able to many writers. He was actually remarkably tolerant of what he was
sent and although he did request revisions, these were seldom significant.
Ironically it was this rather bland acceptance of anything other than a few
strict taboos that led to equally bland anthologies.

Within all this chaos, Elwood did some good. He opened up new
markets, some of which continued to publish science fiction after Elwood
left. Bobbs-Merrill and Chilton in particular published some good books

---

124 Pournelle, 'Concerning Roger Elwood', p. 6.

Table 2.6 *Original anthologies, 1970–83*

Year	Number	Year	Number
1970	8	1977	18
1971	11	1978	12
1972	12	1979	13
1973	27	1980	22
1974	23	1981	15
1975	13	1982	6
1976	16	1983	1

that might not otherwise have existed.[125] He secured good wordage rates for his anthologies, usually between three and five cents a word. He also negotiated a high share of future royalties to his contributors, rising from a share of 60 per cent to 70 per cent. And he gave new writers an opportunity to experiment, though he otherwise offered little guidance or discipline.

In a speech delivered in 1983 Michael Bishop proclaimed that, 'Roger Elwood single-handedly killed off the original anthology market – with one or two exceptions – for the late 1970s and early 1980s and maybe the foreseeable future as well.'[126]

Did he? Can we accuse him so blatantly of achieving this all by himself?

Let's first check out the statistics. Table 2.6 is the number of original anthologies published from 1970 until 1983, six years after Elwood's last anthology. I've stripped out from these figures all juvenile/young-adult volumes and have counted first editions only, no reprints, and no non-US titles. The figures become complicated from 1979 on because of the growth in fantasy volumes, particularly shared world. I've excluded all fantasy and horror volumes for the moment,[127] although they are a factor in the recovery of the market during the 1980s. At this stage I want to concentrate solely on original anthologies of adult sf.

125 These include, from Bobbs-Merrill, *Guernica Night* and *Conversations* by Barry Malzberg, *Science Fiction of the 30s* by Damon Knight, and the continuation of the US edition of the *Best SF* series by Brian Aldiss and Harry Harrison. From Chilton they include *The Starcrossed*, Ben Bova, *Inheritors of Earth*, Poul Anderson and Gordon Eklund, *Infinite Jests* an anthology by Robert Silverberg, and Philip Jose Farmer's *Mother Was a Lovely Beast*, an anthology of 'feral fiction'.

126 Michael Bishop, 'Light Years and Dark', speech delivered at the Third Annual Emory SF and Fantasy Symposium, Emory University, Atlanta, 12 February 1983, printed in *Asimov's SF Magazine*, April 1984.

127 Fantasy and young-adult volumes are included in Table 2.5, which explains any variances.

At this level, the figures remain reasonably consistent. There is a drop in 1978 and 1979 but it recovers in 1980. The real drop comes in 1982 when the fantasy anthology takes over and the growth starts in the horror anthology market. This had nothing to do with Roger Elwood. The mean average of all these years is 14 (the median is 13) and we can see that for most of these years the output was close to those averages. The two years of Elwood's high production are a blip, but no more than that. While there may have been some reaction amongst publishers to the impact of Elwood's output, it does not seem significant. Elwood had opened up new markets and it was those markets which turned away again from sf (though not all). The regular publishers no doubt paused, took stock, and carried on.

The original anthologies, especially *Orbit*, *New Dimensions* and *Universe*, had proved themselves and encouraged changes at the sf magazines, which had revived reader interest. Circulation of the major magazines had risen during the mid-seventies. The fact that Harper & Row dropped *Orbit* in 1977 had far more to do with the growing reader dissatisfaction with *Orbit* and the fall in sales than with a reader reaction to Elwood. Silverberg had grown tired of editing *New Dimensions* by the end of the seventies and handed the series to Marta Randall, who produced two more volumes. The series ended with Volume 12 in 1981. *Universe* carried on until Carr's death in 1987, reaching 17 volumes, so there was no lack of support for the series. Judy-Lynn del Rey continued *Stellar* at Ballantine. Roy Torgeson began *Chrysalis* for Zebra Books in 1977 and, more significantly, James Baen launched *Destinies* at Ace Books in 1978, which I shall discuss later. The original anthology continued, but at a more moderate pace. Elwood had certainly not killed it off.

The economic climate and changing attitudes were also factors in the rise and fall of the original anthology. Publishers were still recovering from the recession of the early seventies and were clearly more cautious as the seventies progressed. They opted for greater certainties. The number of reprint anthologies, for instance, continued much the same throughout this period, averaging four volumes a month.

Rather than point at Elwood's anthologies and blame him for the change in the original anthology market, we need to look at what else was filling the shelves at that time. If the majority of Elwood's original anthologies were the low point of that market, then he was not alone.

Heroes and Villains

In July 1963 Ballantine Books had launched its new paperback edition of Edgar Rice Burroughs's Tarzan novels. The Tarzan books had seldom been out of print, but this quality paperback printing from a prestigious publishing house, and a tie-in to the new TV series, revived popularity in Tarzan for a new generation. Before long Ballantine and Ace Books were rivalling each other for whichever Burroughs's books they could get back into print. It was a major publishing programme that reintroduced pulp characters to a new readership.

Publishers looked for other pulp heroes to resurrect. In 1964 Bantam Books began to reprint the adventures of Doc Savage. These had originally appeared in the magazine *Doc Savage*, starting in 1933. The novels were written chiefly by Lester Dent under the house-name of Kenneth Robeson. Bantam released the first three novels in October 1964 and the next three in April 1965. Sales were positive and each new novel was released first quarterly, then bi-monthly, and then on a monthly basis from March 1968. The monthly schedule continued until September 1971 when they shifted back to bi-monthly, then quarterly. It was not until 1975 that the schedule became erratic but there were still three or four volumes per year throughout the seventies and eighties. It was a clear sign that the old pulp heroes were still popular and that they had a new lease of life in paperbacks.

In 1969, Bantam took over reprinting The Shadow novels in sequence. There had been earlier attempts at reprinting The Shadow without much success, and Bantam's flirtation also failed. Pyramid Books picked it up in 1974 and sustained it until their demise in 1977 when it passed to Jove Books for the next year. Warner Books had more success with The Avenger, which had also appeared under the Kenneth Robeson house name. They reprinted all of the original novels on a monthly basis from June 1972 to May 1974, and then commissioned Ron Goulart to provide further novels, which continued on a monthly basis until May 1975.

Other pulp characters were revived by various publishers on an experimental basis. Ace resurrected Neil R. Jones's Professor Jameson in a series of five books during 1967–68, while Popular Library reprinted some of Edmond Hamilton's Captain Future novels in 1969. There was a sudden and rather surprising revival of E. E. Smith's Skylark series in Britain in 1974–75. In fact, all of 'Doc' Smith's works came back into print, and other writers were commissioned to continue some of Smith's lesser series.

The early/mid-seventies saw paperbacks overtaken by series heroes. Most of these were not science fiction. They were an outgrowth of the all-action espionage hero, a more violent and macho version of James Bond or The Man from UNCLE. The first major hit was The Executioner, the name given to Mack Bolan created by Don Pendleton. That series began with *War Against the Mafia* in 1969 and Pendleton continued them for three or four books a year before other authors took over. Perhaps the biggest of all these series was The Destroyer by Warren Murphy and Richard Ben Sapir which began with *Created, the Destroyer* in 1971 and continues to this day with over a hundred and forty titles. These series led inevitably to the creation of the best-known such character, John Rambo in David Morrell's *First Blood* (1982).

Philip José Farmer revelled in all these pulp and superheroes. In his books *Tarzan Alive* (Doubleday, 1972) and *Doc Savage: His Apocalyptic Life* (Doubleday, 1973), Farmer created the vast, interlinked Wold Newton family which connected just about every major fictional character from Tarzan to Sherlock Holmes to Doc Savage to Professor Challenger to A. J. Raffles, and so on. It was great fun and all part of a process of exploring shared worlds that was developing in science fiction in the seventies, something that would emerge as a significant force in the eighties.

Another major factor was the influence of *Star Trek*. Bantam Books had secured the rights to the novelization of the original *Star Trek* TV series. James Blish adapted the teleplays into a sequence of short stories collected in 12 volumes published between 1967 and 1977. The last volume was completed by Blish's widow, Judith Ann Lawrence, after his death, and Lawrence compiled a thirteenth volume, *Mudd's Angels* (1978). Blish also wrote the original novel, *Spock Must Die!*, published by Bantam in February 1970. Although the original *Star Trek* TV series had finished in 1969, after only three seasons, fans would not allow it to die. A Star Trek convention was held in New York in January 1972 with over three thousand attendees. Another was held in Los Angeles in April 1973 with over ten thousand attending. To meet the demand, Paramount Pictures produced an animated series for TV which ran for 22 episodes from September 1973 to October 1974. Alan Dean Foster wrote adaptations of this series, from *Star Trek: Log One* in 1974 to *Log Six* in 1976. Thereafter the series became full-length novels, and other new, authorized novels were also appearing, starting with *Spock Messiah!* by Thomas N. Scortia and Charles A. Spano, Jr. in September 1976.

Fan fiction also proliferated, of which more later. Gene Roddenberry eventually gave approval to an anthology of stories reprinted (and revised) from the major fanzines: *Star Trek: The New Voyages*, which was edited by Sondra Marshak and Myrna Culbreath and also published by Bantam Books in March 1976. It contained stories by Juanita Coulson, Ruth

Berman and Eleanor Arnason, amongst others, showing how much *Star Trek* appealed to women. A second volume appeared in January 1978.

Donald Wollheim of Ace Books knew the sales potential of series characters, which remained as effective in paperbacks as it had in the original hero pulps and comic books. He had reprinted many at Ace Books, including various Burroughs characters and, before Lancer Books officially published the series, some of the original Conan books. Wollheim commissioned several new series for Ace, including E. C. Tubb's Earl Dumarest. Dumarest was a cunning adventurer in the far-distant future. He had been born on Earth and, after adventures on many planets, was trying to find his way back home. No one seemed to know anything about Earth any more; all records had been deleted from the databases. The series began with *The Winds of Gath*, published in October 1967. Wollheim took the series with him when he established his own new publishing imprint, DAW Books, in April 1972, and continued to publish it through to Book 31, *The Temple of Truth* in July 1985.

Wollheim made DAW Books as close to a paperback magazine series as he could. Every book had a uniform design and logo, all with yellow, stylized covers and each with a unique book number, in addition to the statutory ISBN. He commissioned several new character series. British writer Kenneth Bulmer produced an imitation John Carter of Mars series, featuring Dray Prescot of Antares. The first book, *Transit to Scorpio*, appeared under the alias Alan Burt Akers in December 1972 and continued regularly with two or three books a year until 1985. From 1979 the books appeared under the Dray Prescot name The last that Wollheim published was *Omens of Kregen* in December 1985.

Writing as Gregory Kern, E. C. Tubb began a new series for Wollheim, running alongside the Dumarest quest. This featured Cap Kennedy, 'Free Acting Terran Envoy', a kind of Galactic troubleshooter and initially based on Hamilton's Captain Future. The series began with *Galaxy of the Lost* in September 1973 and DAW published them on almost a monthly basis (although there was some slippage at the end) until Volume 16, *Beyond the Galactic Lens* in December 1975.

Wollheim published many more regular series: the Darkover novels by Marion Zimmer Bradley, the Diadem series by Jo Clayton, various fantasy heroes by Lin Carter, and most notorious of all, the Gor books by John Norman. This was another Burroughs-imitation series tracing the adventures of Tarl Cabot on the world of Gor, Earth's orbital twin, which is always on the other side of the Sun. The series had originated at Ballantine Books with *Tarnsman of Gor* in 1966 but had lapsed after five volumes until Wollheim picked it up with *Huntsmen of Gor* in March

1974. It was dropped in 1977 but reappeared in 1982. The series was notorious because of its violent, male-chauvinist stance in which women were treated only as sex objects. With the rise of feminism, the series was hated by many, and John Norman (the alias of John Lange) did himself no favours when he brought out a spin-off book from the series called *Imaginative Sex*, which Wollheim published as a non-sequential DAW Book in December 1974.

There was one other series that Wollheim had initiated when still at Ace Books and which remained at Ace after Wollheim left. It's one that is often overlooked and yet it was the closest there was at the time to a merger of the paperback with the magazine format. This was *Perry Rhodan*. Rhodan is an American astronaut who discovers an abandoned alien craft on the Moon. Using the alien technology, Rhodan is able to establish a New Power group (interpreted by some as a Fascist organization) which grows into a Solar Empire and becomes a potent force throughout the Galaxy.

As noted in *Transformations*, the character was created by Walter Ernsting in Germany, with the first adventures appearing in a series of weekly booklets in September 1961. The series has continued non-stop in Germany, passing through the 2,300 mark in 2005. Despite its popularity there and in other European countries (except Great Britain), there was a problem establishing a regular US edition.

Translations are always a problem because besides purchasing the rights to the original book (and in the case of the Perry Rhodan series this includes the cost of the licence), there is also the cost of the translation, and good translators, who also have a feel for the idiom of the book, are not easy to find. Moreover, the original weekly stories are only of novella length, and to begin with Wollheim agreed that Ace should run two novels per book, which means double the rights fee and double the translation costs. Ace had secured the series through the auspices of Forrest J Ackerman. Ackerman's wife Wendayne, who was German by birth but also fluent in English, provided the translation. It worked well. The first two novellas, 'Enterprise Stardust' and 'The Third Power' were issued as one volume in May 1969, followed by four more double volumes until May 1970. Ace then took stock of the position, and realized that the series would be more profitable if they ran just one novella per volume and padded the book out with additional material. The series was relaunched with Book 6 in August 1971, which featured story 12, 'The Secret of the Time Vault'. The book had now shrunk from 192 pages to 128. Ackerman filled the remaining pages with an editorial, a letter column, 'The Perryscope', and a column on sf films. The series ran monthly, with a couple of breaks, until July 1973 when it appeared twice a month and even occasionally three times a month, until October 1976, when it began to slow down a little.

Ackerman, usually known as Forrie or 4e, had the reputation of being science fiction's 'No. 1 Fan', because he had been the first fan to join the Science Fiction League run by Hugo Gernsback in 1934. He had coined the term 'sci-fi', a neologism loathed by all purist sf fans who equate it with the worst of all science-fiction shlock. It certainly applied to the formulaic pulp space opera of Captain Future and Professor Jameson, and although there were attempts to make Perry Rhodan a cut above that, Ackerman happily dragged it back down again. He knew that the Perry Rhodan adventures would appeal more to younger readers so he pitched the *Perry Rhodan* 'maga-book', as he now termed it, at an adolescent level. Of course, the general reading public wouldn't know the difference, and with the proliferation of Perry Rhodan titles, the term 'sci-fi' soon became synonymous with all that was bad about the genre, which was unfair to both.

From Volume 16 (August 1972), Ackerman supplemented the Rhodan novella with a very short story and an episode from Garrett P. Serviss's 1898 newspaper serial 'Edison's Conquest of Space'. This was of interest to old-guard sf fans but must have been puzzling to young readers. The short stories were usually also reprints from either old fanzines or magazines of the fifties, mostly from clients of Ackerman's former literary agency. Very few of the reprinted stories are of interest but once in a while Ackerman published a new story. 'Ranger of Eternity' (#17, September 1972) was an early short story by Donald F. Glut, a fellow enthusiast of Ackerman's in monster movies, who has written many books on dinosaurs and adapted several films into novels, including the novelization of *The Empire Strikes Back* in 1979. Volume 20 (December 1972) published the first story by Steven Utley, 'The Unkindest Cut of All', a parody of Gernsbackian sf which was well suited to Ackerman's sense of humour. Another Rhodan debutant was David Bischoff with 'The Sky's an Oyster, the Stars are Pearls' (#66, March 1975), with George W. Proctor and Gerald W. Page amongst other contributors.

Amongst the serials that Ackerman reprinted are some of historical interest. Richard Vaughan's 'The Exile of the Skies', had been one of the most popular serials in *Wonder Stories* in the early thirties but had not been reprinted in any form until Ackerman ran it in books 23–31 in 1973. He also reprinted the round-robin story 'Cosmos', which had been serialized in the fan magazine *Science Fiction Digest* in 1933 but not reprinted in a complete form outside the fan scene. Although it had little literary merit, it was a true novelty item, with episodes written by Ralph Milne Farley, John W. Campbell, Abraham Merritt and E. E. Smith amongst others.

Perhaps the most interesting item run in *Perry Rhodan* was the serialization of a new Lensman novel, based on the series by E. E. Smith. This was 'New Lensman' by William B. Ellern, which ran from books 61–74 (January–July 1975). It was set early in the Lensman universe, around the time of the founding of the Galactic Patrol. *Perry Rhodan* also serialized Ellern's short novel 'Triplanetary Agent' (#100–105, August–November 1976).

The size of the *Perry Rhodan* magabook increased to accommodate all these extras, eventually returning back to the original 192 pages, but still featuring only one Rhodan adventure. Despite the genuine novelty factor of some of these additional items, much of the padded material was very minor and added nothing of value or interest to the Rhodan serial. 'The Perryscope' had become quite a lively forum and there was a regular feature on the Perry Rhodan universe in 'The Rhodanary' and, for a brief while, an 'Encyclopedia Rhodania'.

Tom Doherty became the head of Ace Books in 1975 and disliked the Perry Rhodan series because he thought it was too juvenile, even though it was profitable. He wound the series down and ended it with several large double volumes of 256 pages, the last being #117/8 in August 1977. They were followed by five Atlan novels, a spin-off series to Perry Rhodan, to complete subscriptions, but the series ended by Christmas 1977.

Ackerman established Master Publications to continue the series which were now issued in a dime-novel magazine format similar to that of the original German editions. They were released in groups of five every other month, but negotiations over renewing the licence failed and the series stopped. For many it was not soon enough. Although the story-line had developed considerably as the series progressed, at the outset there was not much action and the series was far removed from the sophisticated form that US sf had reached by the early seventies. When P. Schuyler Miller reviewed the early books he called them 'bland', and that was from an author who grew up with space opera. It clearly appealed to enough readers to sustain the series through to the late seventies, but to many it was an embarrassment.

So, in 1974 the shelves were not really overloaded with Roger Elwood anthologies. It's amazing that he could get any books on the shelves at all alongside all those copies of *Perry Rhodan, Cap Kennedy, Dumarest, Doc Savage, The Avenger, Dray Prescot, The Destroyer, The Exterminator, Gor, John Carter, Star Trek* and many, many more. These books, resurrecting the pulp glories of the thirties, were pushing science fiction backwards, not forwards. In fact, there was a great nostalgia boom in the early seventies. Isaac Asimov compiled a huge 986-page retrospective anthology of early science fiction, *Before the Golden Age* (1974), Frederik and Carol Pohl assembled *Science Fiction: The Great Years* (1973) and Damon Knight compiled *Science Fiction of the 30s* (1975). It was at the same time that I compiled my original *History of the Science Fiction Magazine* for New English Library. Brian Aldiss's history of science fiction, *Billion Year Spree*, also appeared at that time (1973) and, with Harry Harrison, Aldiss produced several anthologies of stories from the thirties and forties.

Some of this was a reaction to the new academic interest in science fiction, providing an opportunity to make old texts available again, but some of it was also the start of a fascination with early science fiction as providing more of that sense of wonder than the current range of fiction. Despite the quality of the new material appearing, much of it was experimental or bleak, and was driving some readers back to the past.

There was one editor who took advantage of this nostalgia for the old days and tried to turn it into something constructive and positive. Byron Preiss put together a series of anthologies under the collective title *Weird Heroes*, called 'A New American Pulp'. He wrote in his introduction, '*Weird Heroes* is a collective effort to do something new: to approach three popular heroic fantasy forms – science fiction, the pulps and the comics – from different and exciting directions.' He added, '*Weird Heroes* is a collective effort to give back to heroic fiction its thrilling sense of adventure and entertainment – the heartbeat of the old pulps.'[128]

Preiss was a writer and editor with a vision. He was only 22, but he could see the direction publishing should take. He believed that there should be a merger of artforms but that this should be treated creatively and should not talk down to adolescents. He created Byron Preiss Visual Publications in 1974 to package books for publishers. *Weird Heroes* was one of the first of these. Preiss developed ideas for new heroes and new concepts and commissioned writers to develop them. He also sought to have those works illustrated by the best of the modern graphic artists.

The first two volumes of *Weird Heroes* had been put together as one book, but it was too big, so Pyramid published it as two books in October and December 1975. Ron Goulart introduced the Gypsy, a mysterious itinerant traveller who finds clues to his identity dotted across a transformed twenty-first-century Europe. Archie Goodwin presented the Stalker, a Vietnam veteran who combats evil forces in Oklahoma. Preiss's own character, Guts, in the guise of a fifties rock'n'roll greaser, travels

---

128 Both quotes are from Preiss's 'Introduction' in *Weird Heroes* #1, Pyramid Books, October 1975.

through time, foiling villains. Philip Jose Farmer created Greatheart Silver, Zeppelin captain and adventurer-detective in a spoof of all pulp heroes. The one reprint in the first volume was an unusual one. 'Rose in the Sunshine State' by JoAnn Kobin first appeared in *Aphra* (Spring 1974), a small-circulation feminist literary magazine. Kobin's character, Rose, is a 68-year-old retired woman in Florida who finds herself having to stand up for the rights of her fellow pensioners. She seemed a most unlikely hero, but was a refreshing one.

In the second volume, Ted White presented Doc Phoenix, called the logical successor to Doc Savage. Steve Englehart's Viva is a society-scarred ex-prostitute turned jungle woman! Charlie Swift lampooned the western genre with the Camden Kid. Elliott Maggin had three female ex-cons operating a detective agency from deep in the New York subway. Finally, Harlan Ellison breathed life into his pseudonymous anti-hero Cordwainer Bird.

All these stories were illustrated by artists Jim Steranko, Jeff Jones, Alex Nino, Esteban Maroto and Stephen Fabian amongst others, most of them better known for their comic-book work.

The result was a fascinating package of new, often unlikely heroes for the new age. It was Preiss's hope that these characters could be developed through new stories and novels. Pyramid Books were interested and they commissioned a series. Ron Goulart delivered two Gypsy novels, *Quest of the Gypsy* (#3, September 1976) and *Eye of the Vulture* (#7, October 1977), both beautifully illustrated by Alex Nino. Beth Meacham and Tappan King created the heroine Nightshade, a female, updated version of The Shadow, in 'Terror, Inc'. (#4, October 1976). *The Oz Encounter* (#5, January 1977), was a new Doc Phoenix novel developed by Marv Wolfman from an outline which Ted White was unable to complete because of a fire at his home.

There were two more anthologies in the series, Volume 6 in April 1977 and Volume 8 in November 1977. Here the emphasis was on supersleuths. Ron Goulart created Shinbet, half-man, half-serpent and a very slippery interplanetary sleuth. Arthur Byron Cover created Franklin Davis, known as the Galactic Gumshoe. Ben Bova rectified the superhero balance with Orion, a mere mortal suddenly projected through time to become the leader of demi-gods. J. Michael Reaves created Kamus of Kadizhar a fantasy hero with more than a dose of Philip Marlowe. And, finally, Philip José Farmer, masquerading as Maxwell Grant, turned Kenneth Robeson into a real character in another of his labyrinthine metafictions.

These stories were tremendous fun and had huge potential. Unfortunately, the series became lost during the takeover of Pyramid Books by Harcourt, Brace, Jovanovich, the last two volumes appearing under the imprint of Jove Books. Preiss knew the contract was not going to be renewed and wrote a farewell in the final volume. Thankfully, not all of the heroes vanished. Ben Bova's Orion in particular has gone on to appear in five volumes, starting with *Orion* (1984). Michael Reaves put together four Kamus adventures in *Darkworld Detective* (1982), and John Shirley continued the character in *The Black Hole of Carcosa* (1988). Byron Preiss had his full-length novel *Guts* published by Ace Books in 1979 and Philip Farmer collected together his Greatheart stories in *Greatheart Silver* (1982). So, *Weird Heroes* had its offspring, but did not otherwise survive the retro-pulp nostalgia of the seventies.

The swamping of the shelves with cheap 'sci-fi' or bland space adventures and anthologies became too much for some writers. Robert Silverberg led the retaliation. In February 1975, at a convention in Vancouver, Canada, and again at a meeting of the newly established Science Fiction Research Association's regional conference on 11 April 1975, Silverberg announced that, when he had completed his latest novel, *Shadrach in the Furnace*, at the end of the month, he was going to retire from writing sf. He would still attend conferences and would still edit anthologies, but he had no intention of writing any more sf for at least two or three years, and possibly forever. The farewell kiss blown to the world at the end of *Shadrach* was Silverberg's parting wave.

The gist of the reasoning behind this announcement was captured by Donald C. Thompson:

> We have tried to upgrade this field; we have provided it with quality material that it can be proud of, but our efforts have been rejected. Science fiction readers don't want literary quality, they want space adventure – Perry Rhodan and Cap Kennedy. That's what the public thinks when you say 'science fiction', and that's what science fiction *is*. And High School teachers of science fiction may argue that Perry Rhodan serves a useful purpose by getting kids interested in sf and that once they get hooked on that they will eventually develop enough taste to prefer the better fiction. But it isn't so. Most of them never get beyond Perry Rhodan. We have suffered by having our stories labelled science fiction, and so we reject that label.[129]

It has always been a sad fact of artistic creation that most people enjoy the lowest common denominator. Sturgeon stated that 90 per cent of every-

---

129 Donald C. Thompson, 'Spec Fic and the Perry Rhodan Ghetto', originally published in *Don-o-Saur* #41 and reprinted in *Science Fiction Review* #15, November 1975.

thing is crap, and 90 per cent of the 'reading' public enjoy 90 per cent of the crap. The word 'reading' is in quotes because this statement applies just as much to all media, probably more so to television and cinema and certainly to the comic-book medium. This isn't new. In the nineteenth century the 'penny dreadfuls' sold in their hundreds of thousands, while the literary works of Thomas Hardy and Anthony Trollope struggled for years to reach even a few thousand. The major literary magazines of *Blackwood's* and *The Cornhill* had circulations seldom exceeding 10,000 copies, while the lurid cheap weeklies sold ten times that amount.

Silverberg, of course, knew this, and like all writers, accepted and suffered it. But in 1975 his frustration boiled over. The problem was not just being surrounded by a seemingly unstoppable mass of uninspiring formulaic dreck, but it was the fact that the dreck was crowding out almost everything else; the good material was not being kept in print, except for those few long-established top-sellers, such as Heinlein and Bradbury. Silverberg's early work, which he was only too ready to admit was mostly potboiler material, remained in print, but his more recent groundbreaking material was all too rapidly vanishing into oblivion. It was one thing when readers showed their ignorance by buying literary junk food, but quite another when publishers failed to support the quality work.

Barry Malzberg stated the position succinctly in his essay 'The Engines of the Night':

> Science fiction is the only branch of literature whose poorer examples are almost invariably used by critics outside the genre to attack all of it. A lousy western is a lousy western, a seriously intended novel that falls apart is a disaster ... but a science-fiction novel that fails illustrates the inadequacy of the genre.[130]

Like Silverberg, Malzberg had grown dissatisfied with the general reception and treatment of science fiction and his place in it. So he also decided to retire. In his resignation essay, 'Rage, Pain, Alienation and Other Aspects of the Writing of Science Fiction' (*F&SF*, April 1976), Malzberg explained that he had chosen to write science fiction because it was a field where one could produce literary fiction and almost earn a living from it and pretty much be left alone. But of course no writer wants to be left entirely alone. They want some recognition for their efforts. Malzberg had won the first John W. Campbell Memorial Award in 1973 for his novel *Beyond Apollo* but this had been criticized by many fans. They believed that *Beyond*

130 Barry Malzberg, 'The Engines of the Night', *Science Fiction Review* #40, Fall 1981, p. 21.

Apollo was not the kind of book that Campbell would have published. That may be true, but the purpose of the award was not to perpetuate Campbellian fiction but to honour advances in the field by presenting the award to the novel that truly reflected excellence in writing and a contribution to the development of sf. The resentment amongst a certain faction of the sf fraternity to Malzberg's honour was just one example of how the sf readers themselves were reluctant to change. Campbell had recognized this. He had cause on several occasions to criticize his readers for their inability to move with the times and their determination to cling to the past.[131]

Malzberg moved on to produce a remarkable body of work, but by January 1975 had come to realize that he had written himself into a corner. As he wrote in his essay, 'I had discovered I was *invisible* outside of the confines of the sf market itself', and 'I was getting knifed up pretty good *inside* sf.' To Malzberg the academic/literary nexus 'either does not know we exist or patronizes us as pulp hacks for escapist kids'.[132] So, unable to achieve any longer what he had wanted to achieve, he quit. His story, 'Seeking Assistance', published alongside his essay in the April 1976 *F&SF* was 'the last s-f story ... I will ever write'.

It wasn't, of course. No creative artist, certainly not one with as much passion as Malzberg, just stops. Malzberg's backlog of material with other editors was sufficiently huge that it was difficult to tell when his old output ceased and his new output began. There was perhaps an identifiable period of a year or two when most of Malzberg's energies were directed towards other writings, but he was certainly back in the sf field by 1979. Silverberg also returned after a four-year absence, motivated by the financial pressures of an expensive divorce.[133]

Harlan Ellison, who held views similar to those of Silverberg and Malzberg, soon had his resignation speech ready. Ellison's vitriol, expressed in a talk given at the meeting of the Science Fiction Writers of America (SFWA) in April 1977,[134] was not aimed at the reading public, most of whom he had long since accepted as a lost cause.[135] His anger was aimed at the writers themselves, or more specifically the SFWA. To Harlan, the

131 See my discussion of this in *Transformations*, p. 202.
132 Barry Malzberg, 'Rage, Pain, Alienation and Other Aspects of the Writing of Science Fiction', *F&SF* 50:4 (April 1976), pp. 106–7.
133 Personal e-mail, Silverberg/Ashley, 5 October 2006.
134 Published as 'How You Stupidly Blew Fifteen Million Dollars a Week, Avoided Having an Adenoid-Shaped Swimming Pool in your Back Yard, Missed the Opportunity to have a Mutually Destructive Love Affair with Clint Eastwood and/or Raquel Welch, and Otherwise Pissed me Off', *Algol* #31, Spring 1978, pp. 9–14.
135 In his speech, Ellison commented, 'Tragically, the illiterate keep multiplying, and the audience for books must be kept alive!'

SFWA spent its energies advising its members on minor issues and not facing the major issues, namely that the film and television industries were happily plundering sf writers of their ideas and handing them over to robots to type, and that no professional sf writer was receiving any benefit. The organization that advised and supported the top professional sf writers in America, who had done so much to develop the quality and respectability of published sf, was doing nothing to contribute to or gain benefits from the cinematic equivalent. It was evident to Ellison that the SFWA liked it that way. They liked their own little world, and did not want to acknowledge anything beyond it. He saw that as a death wish and wanted nothing to do with it, so he resigned his membership.

Unlike Silverberg and Malzberg, Ellison did not retire from sf. For a start, he had long maintained that he was not a science-fiction writer. He was a creative writer who occasionally wrote sf. He was not about to retire as a writer, but he could no longer remain part of an organization that ignored the biggest market for sf. Ellison's resignation was therefore not the same as the others, but it was part of a general dissatisfaction that ran through sf in the seventies. Here were writers doing their best to improve the quality of science fiction and to have it recognized as an equal on the stage of literature, but their voice was not being heard by publishers, by the reading public or by the film industry.

There was another who held similar views to those of Ellison and Malzberg and who expressed himself in no uncertain terms, but this was not an American, but a Pole: Stanislaw Lem, and his attitude towards American science fiction was yet another wake-up call.

The Threat from Without

In 1971 Donald A. Wollheim published *Science Fiction: What's It All About* (1971), translated by Sam Lundwall from his own book first published in Sweden in 1969.[136] This provided a history and overview of science fiction from a European perspective. In an introduction to the US edition, Wollheim commented on an all-too-apparent Anglo-American provincialism:

> We tend to think that all that is worth reading and all that is worth notice is naturally written in English. In our conventions and our awards and our discussions we slip into the habit of referring to our favourites as the world's best this and the world's best that. The annual American science

136 Originally published as *Science Fiction – Från begynnelsen till våra dagar* (Stockholm: Sveriges Radios forlag, 1969).

fiction convention calls itself the World Science Fiction Convention, though every now and then it deigns to allow itself to meet overseas, but always with a strong cord attached so that it will return the next year to its 'natural' heliocentric American habitat.[137]

The World Science Fiction Convention had been held outside of North America only three times since the first in 1939, and two of those had been in London. The 1970 convention was in Heidelberg, Germany, as if recognizing a new European awareness. Yet when the Hugos were awarded, not one went to anyone outside of the United States or Britain, not even amongst the artists, where language was no barrier to appreciating quality. There was a German (or, more accurately, Austrian) guest of honour, Herbert W. Franke, but he was alongside the US and British guests, Robert Silverberg and E. C. Tubb. Although Franke had been writing fiction since 1960, he had had no books translated into English and, so far as I can find, only one short story, 'The Man Who Feared Robots', in *F&SF* in 1963.

At the time that Heidelberg was bidding for the Worldcon, there was some opposition from US fans. Ted White, who supported a genuine 'world' convention, summed up the views of the anti-brigade who believed that the Worldcon was 'ours, we made it, we have the right to call it anything we like and too bad for the rest of them if they don't like it'. White added:

> which is really an arrogant position but one which is certainly not uncommon in fandom and one which we have encountered at past Worldcon business sessions... Somebody will stand up and say there are only half-a-dozen fans in the rest of the world and they certainly have no business letting those inferior morons take over.[138]

Thankfully, changes were happening to prise Britain and the United States out of their parochialism. There had already been a flurry of anthologies presenting stories from the Soviet Union. The Foreign Language Publishing House in Moscow had published *The Heart of the Serpent* as far back in 1961, followed by *Destination Amalthea* edited by Richard Dixon in 1963. Robert Magidoff compiled *Russian Science Fiction* for New York University Press in 1964 with two more volumes in 1968 and 1969. Mirra Ginsburg compiled *The Last Door to Aiya* (Phillips, 1968) and *The Ultimate Threshold* (Holt, 1970). The British publisher MacGibbon & Kee

---

137 Donald A. Wollheim, 'Introduction', *Science Fiction: What's It All About* (New York: Ace Books, 1971) p. 7.

138 Ted White speaking in a panel discussion at the 12th Annual Lunacon held in New York on 13 April 1969, printed as 'Whither Wordcons?', *Luna* #7, 1969.

issued the anonymously compiled *Path Into the Unknown* (1966),[139] plus *Vortex* (1970) compiled by G. C. Bearne. In addition, in 1967 the Russian publisher, Mir, had issued an English-language edition of *Far Rainbow* by Arkady and Boris Strugatsky, their first book appearance in English. All of these books were there if you looked for them, but they did not attract much attention. P. Schuyler Miller was one of the few to review them but he found many of the translations poor, citing those by Mirra Ginsburg as the best. He concluded, 'Russian offerings are still at the stage that English and American SF passed through in the Twenties and Thirties.'[140] He revised that estimate two years later when he read Ginsburg's *The Ultimate Threshold*, where he saw a degree of satire and social commentary creeping into the fiction – a Soviet 'New Wave' he called it – and judged that perhaps Russian sf had reached the stage that *Astounding* was at when Campbell took over in 1937.

The year 1970, though, was something of a watershed, with a wave of translated books from several publishers: from Japan came *Inter Ice Age Four* by Kobo Abe;[141] from France, *Future Times Three* and *The Ice People*[142] by René Barjavel; from Czechoslovakia, a story collection, *In the Footsteps of the Abominable Snowman* by Josef Nesvadba; from Russia came *Notes from the Future* by Nicolai Amosoff,[143] and most significantly from Poland, *Solaris*[144] by Stanislaw Lem.

This was but the tip of the iceberg, with much more to come. By way of preparation, Darko Suvin produced a volume of Eastern European sf, *Other Worlds, Other Seas* (1970), with the first appearance of Stanislaw Lem in book form in the United States, while Lem's agent, the Austrian author Franz Rottensteiner, similarly assembled an anthology of European sf, *View from Another Shore*, for Seabury Press in 1973. Rottensteiner was arguably Europe's foremost critic and authority on science fiction and had, since 1963, been producing the studious fanzine, *Quarber Merkur*. Although described by Peter Nicholls in the *Encyclopedia of Science Fiction* as 'one of the longest running and most impressive of its type', *Quarber Merkur* has never won or been nominated for a Hugo, not even in 1970 (or, for that matter, 1990, when the Worldcon returned to mainland Europe). Another European expert, Pierre Versins, published *Encyclopédie*

139 The US edition from Delacorte Press in 1968 included an introduction by Judith Merril.

140 P. Schuyler Miller, 'More From the Soviety', *Analog* 82:2 (October 1968), p. 160.

141 Originally published as *Daiyon Kanpyooki* in Tokyo in 1959.

142 Originally published as *Le Voyageur imprudent*, in Paris in 1944, and *La Nuit des temps* in Paris in 1968.

143 Originally published as *Zapiski iz budushchego* in Russia in 1967.

144 Originally published in Warsaw in 1961.

de l'utopie et de la science fiction in Lausanne in 1972, a massive 1,000+-page encyclopedia that covered all aspects of science fiction with entries on many European writers totally unknown in the West. Unfortunately, this volume has never been translated into English, much to the frustration of US and British scholars. Prompted by all of this and Lundwall's *Science Fiction: What It's All About*, it began to dawn on US and British readers that there were many other worlds out there. Of all these European writers, Stanislaw Lem dominated the seventies, and his views on US and British science fiction cannot be ignored.

Lem's first story to appear in an English-language sf magazine was 'Are You There, Mister Jones?'[145] in the Anglo-Australian *Vision of Tomorrow* for August 1969. Apart from 'Trurl's Electronic Bard', reprinted in the September 1975 *Science Fiction Monthly*, Lem had no other fiction in any English-language sf magazine, though he did have a story printed in the special sf issue of *Antaeus* in 1977. He also had stories reprinted in *Omni*: 'The Test' (October 1979), 'Return From the Stars' (June 1980) and 'The Accident' (June 1982), but, as we shall see, *Omni* was a high-paying science magazine and not really an sf one. In other words, Lem, one of the best-selling sf writers of the twentieth century, had no stories published in any US genre sf magazine. Yet his work was appearing in sf magazines in Japan and Europe.

Readers of the US magazines would have been aware of him because his books were frequently reviewed, and there were many articles by and about him in the amateur magazines and academic journals. His articles from Rottensteiner's *Quarber Merkur* were translated for Bruce Gillespie's *SF Commentary* in Australia and for *Science Fiction Studies* where it became apparent that Lem had a good grasp of US and British sf.

His first book to be published in English was *Solaris* (1970), and it remains his best known, partly because of the film version in 1971. But he had been writing for 20 years and had produced a substantial body of work, much of it translated throughout Europe and beyond. In 1969, Franz Rottensteiner had reported that Lem was 'the most popular foreign author in the USSR, with a sale of about 3 million copies'.[146] His first sf novel had been *Astronauci* (1951), a relatively straightforward story of a voyage to Venus and the discovery of the fate of the inhabitants, but his works soon became denser, more philosophical and, apart from occasional brief satirical tales, more metaphysical. Although he had trained in medicine,

145 Originally entitled 'Czy pan istnieje, Mr Johns?' and published in the Polish weekly *Przekrój* in 1956.
146 Franz Rottensteiner, 'Authoritatively Speaking', *Luna Monthly* #3, August 1969, p. 6.

Lem became fascinated by cybernetics and its effects upon society and the human condition. He set out to explore how humans would react to significant changes in society brought on by technological advances. That is, of course, what the majority of science fiction does, but Lem was not aware that he was writing science fiction until he had already completed several novels. His interest was in futurology and that's how he saw his work. He disliked the phrase 'science fiction', seeing it as meaningless.

Lem's route into science fiction had not followed any traditional path. He was widely read in literature and philosophy but his grounding in science fiction had been through the works of Olaf Stapledon, another literary philosopher of his day whose work stood apart from the main trunk of science fiction, despite its influence on Arthur C. Clarke. For Lem, the storyline was incidental, there to provide a framework in which to explore various concepts and ideologies.

Lem's neologisms, narrative structure and philosophical outlook all broke new territory, making it difficult to translate into English. It was not until Michael Kandel's translations appeared from Seabury Press that one could put faith in their accuracy. Earlier translations were weak and did Lem no favours. *Solaris*, for instance, was translated via a French version and not directly from the Polish. Even so, Lem's approach to science fiction should have made his work ideally suited to US and British readers emerging from the New Wave revolution. Yet his work was not immediately welcomed in the United States as it had been in Europe. Theodore Sturgeon, when considering *Solaris* and Lem's enigmatic style, commented:

> Lem's unique gift to the kind of science fiction written by classicists, then, apparently is no more than an infusion of the same lack of logical rigor as that which distinguishes much 'New Wave' commercial sf of the sixties, in which illusions of profundity are generated by imprecise references, paradoxic exposition and a ruthless unwillingness to let the characters act as smart as they say they are.[147]

In Lem's view the New Wave was a wasted opportunity, 'The New Wavers knew that they should look for something new but they did not have the slightest idea what it could be.'[148]

Lem believed that the New Wavers should have used Philip K. Dick as their 'guiding star' rather than, as he believed, Norman Spinrad, Samuel Delany or Michael Moorcock. He seemed unaware of the impact of the

147 Theodore Sturgeon, 'Galaxy Bookshelf', *Galaxy* 31:6 (May 1971), p. 102.
148 Stanislaw Lem, 'SF: A Hopeless Case – With Exceptions', *SF Commentary* 35/6/7 (July/September 1973), p. 31, translated by Werner Koopmann from the original article in *Quarber Merkur* #30, 1972.

work of William S. Burroughs upon the New Wave. In Lem's view, 'Until now the New Wave has succeeded well in making sf quite boring.'[149]

Lem thought that his strength as a writer lay in the fact that he was uncluttered by the past. 'The lack of a strong influence of standard sf has led me to creative independence', he reflected in 1978.[150] George Zebrowski, one of Lem's primary advocates in America, also agreed:

> Lem writes according to his own convention; fantastic elements are not present in his work only for their own sake, for the sake of a sense-of-wonder high. Lem's approach, if we don't want to talk in terms of better or worse, is different and adequate to *his* aims.[151]

As Lem became more acquainted with US sf, he felt that it was being governed by the wrong 'rules', derived from the gutter of popular fiction that had set science fiction on the wrong path. He perceived that all literature fell into two groups, which he defined as the Upper Realm and the Lower Realm, the distinction being between quality fiction and trivia. His criterion was that if an author's name was critically respected, then his or her work would automatically be in the Upper Realm. All formulaic and genre fiction fell into the Lower Realm. Lem regarded all his work as variations upon the mainstream and not as science fiction.

Lem saw science fiction as unusual amongst literary forms, as it had all the qualities of the Lower Realm but strove, unsuccessfully, to be regarded as part of the Upper Realm. This was the dilemma that always annoyed science-fiction enthusiasts. The moment a work of science fiction is regarded as being of high quality, it ceases to be science fiction. The classification 'science fiction', by its very existence, condemns any literature so defined. It was his essay, 'SF: A Hopeless Case' (1972), cited above, that effectively defined the science-fiction 'ghetto'.

He also distinguished between US and British sf. British sf had the 'better manners and customs' and the language was 'more cultivated', while US sf had started 'in the slums of the Lower Realm' and lacked all courtly manners. To Lem most US sf had no redeeming features at all. It was, to him, all 'trash', with the exception that some of the work of Philip K. Dick and, more recently, Ursula Le Guin had qualities of the Upper Realm.

This view was obviously going to alienate Lem from many science-fiction fans, while at the same time endearing him to the literary establishment. When Theodore Solotaroff came to review Lem in the *New York*

149 Lem, 'SF: A Hopeless Case – With Exceptions',
150 Stanislaw Lem, 'The Profession of Science Fiction', *Foundation* #15 (January 1979), p. 46.
151 George Zebrowski, 'International Science Fiction', *F&SF* 53:2 (August 1977), p. 77.

Times in 1976, he called him 'a major writer and one of the deep spirits of our age'.[152] At the same time, Spider Robinson, in reviewing *The Invincible* (another poor translation), found it 'unoriginal, stereotyped and dull'.[153]

It is difficult to know how much sf Lem had read – and in what form – but from his writings on the subject, which were many and detailed, he had clearly made an effort to explore what he could find. He deduced the following view of science-fiction fandom 'from western fanzines and SF magazines': 'I think fandom to be the gilded cuffs of SF. It diminishes the manoeuvring space of writers, is intellectually passive, lazy, opportunistic, and very low-brow artistically; that is with bad taste, scientific ignorance and so on.'[154]

Lem could not understand why US readers accepted such poor fiction and did not demand better work. He understood that writers needed to earn a living, but could not understand why they would produce such poor material for a meagre return. He saw the commercialization of fiction and the belief that there was an inverse link between popularity (= sales = profit) and quality as a virus affecting Western literature. He believed that in Eastern Europe there was still respect for literature as a 'form of service to society, as an activity which has its own didactic, ethical component. In the West, generally speaking, they don't feel this way.' He concluded that 'Literature is sick, there's no doubt about it, and that's very sad.'[155]

Lem's viewpoint on US science fiction resulted in a sordid episode with the SFWA. Lem had been made an honorary member of the SFWA in May 1973, although in fact he could have become a full active member because by then his work had been published in the United States. In February 1975 Lem wrote an article for a German magazine that was translated under the title 'Looking Down on Science Fiction' in *Atlas World Press Review* for August 1975.

In this article Lem took US sf writers and fans to task, calling them 'a kind of Anti-Establishment challenging the hegemony of "normal" litera-ture, derisively or enviously referred to as the "mainstream".' He regarded most sf as 'elementary' and recognized that he was being perceived as a pariah because he had tried to 'alert readers to how awful the writing was, how hackneyed were its stereotypes, and how many opportunities

152 Theodore Solotaroff, 'A Master of Science Fiction – and More', *New York Times*, 29 August 1976, p. 218.

153 Spider Robinson, 'Galaxy Bookshelf', *Galaxy* 37:4, May 1976, p. 124.

154 Interview with Lem by Daniel Say, with responses written by Lem in English. It was first published in *Entropy Negative* #6 (1973) and reprinted with revisions in *The Alien Critic* #10, August 1974. Quote from p. 9.

155 Interview with Lem by Konstantin Dushenko, *Knizhnoe Obozrenie*, 8 September 1989, translated by John Costello, *Science Fiction Review* 1:3, Autumn 1990, p. 33.

are missed by the authors'.[156] Lem criticized the SFWA for allowing this to happen and for rewarding writers with the Nebula. He said that he had originally accepted the honorary membership because he believed he might be able to work toward some reform 'from within' but that he now wondered why he bothered.

Needless to say, some members of the SFWA saw Lem's article and questioned why he was an honorary member. It was soon pointed out that the honorary membership must be unnecessary because Lem was eligible for active membership and, using this as a loophole, Lem's honorary membership was withdrawn in March 1976, with an invitation that he could reapply as an active member. Lem declined.

The whole affair left a bad taste amongst those SFWA members who felt that Lem had been treated poorly and that his ousting had given the impression that the United States did not support free speech. There was a wave of protests and sabre-rattling, but the affair was left to fade away.

But Lem's views could not be entirely ignored because they contained much that the literary establishment itself claimed against science fiction. Indeed, it echoed some of the views of Silverberg, Malzberg and Ellison and also the sentiments of the feminist movement. Russ, Wilhelm and Lem were all looking to sf to mature, and Silverberg was angry at the commercialization of lesser fiction at the expense of better work. Lem held these same views, though he went further, expecting sf to cast off its roots and reshape itself entirely. Despite science fiction being a literature of change, the average sf reader does not readily respond to change, preferring a comfortable, almost predictable form of escapism. Publishers pander to the popular end of the market with repetitive formulaic adventure fiction, such as *Doc Savage*, while Damon Knight's *Orbit* or Samuel Delany's *QUARK/* is laid to rest.

Ursula Le Guin, who, alongside Dick, was the only US writer whom Lem saw as having any true grasp of his 'Upper Realm', echoed Lem's views precisely when she wrote:

> Science fiction has mostly settled for a pseudo-objective listing of marvels and wonders and horrors which illuminate nothing beyond themselves and are without real moral resonance: daydreams, wishful thinking and nightmares. The invention is superb, but self-enclosed and sterile. And the more eccentric and childish side of science fiction fandom, and the defensive, fanatic in-groups, both feed upon and nourish this kind of triviality, which is harmless in itself, but which degrades taste by keeping publishers' standards, and readers' and critics' expectations,

156 Lem's article, together with a summary of events chronicled by Pamela Sargent and George Zebrowski, is to be found in *Science Fiction Studies* #12, July 1977, pp. 126–44.

very low. It's as if they wanted us all to play poker without betting. But the real game is played for real stakes. It's a pity that this trivial image is perpetuated, when the work of people from Zamyatin to Lem has shown that when science fiction uses its limitless range of symbol and metaphor novelistically, with the subject at the centre, it can show us who we are, and where we are, and what choices face us, with unsurpassed clarity, and with a great and troubling beauty.[157]

In Lem's view, science fiction would not mature as long as it clung to its roots and related to its fans. This was evidenced by the comments of L. W. Michaelson who interviewed Lem in 1979. Lem had observed that US sf writers were too interested in mass markets and mass sales 'and use violence and bug-eyed monsters to gain readers', to which Michaelson commented, 'It is pretty much true what you say, but even so I was disappointed in your *Travels of Pirx*. I was hoping a monster would appear and satisfy my acquired taste for violence and excitement.'[158]

This comment was not from a comic-book fan but from a teacher of science fiction at Colorado State University, who was echoing his students' views as much as his own.

Readers' tastes and demands needed to change. The best place for writers to experiment and influence readers' needs was within the magazines and anthologies. Lem did not comment about the sf magazines specifically, grouping them instead with fanzines, so he may not have been aware of the innovative fiction that was appearing there in the seventies, particularly the works of Robert Silverberg, Michael Bishop, George R. R. Martin, Harlan Ellison, R. A. Lafferty and James Tiptree, Jr., some of which should have demonstrated to Lem the medium's higher potential. Science fiction was undergoing a change in the seventies, but whether for good or for ill had yet to be seen.

157 Ursula K. Le Guin, 'Science Fiction and Mrs Brown' in Le Guin, *The Language of the Night* (1982 edition), pp. 108–9.

158 L. W. Michaelson, 'A Conversation with Stanislaw Lem', *Amazing* 27:10 (January 1981), p. 117. The book he refers to is better known under its full title *Tales of Pirx the Pilot*.

3

Small but Dangerous:
The Alternate Gateways

So far, this history has concentrated on the professional science-fiction magazines. But always in the background, sometimes making enough of a disturbance to be noticed, is a wide diversity of 'little' magazines, ranging from fanzines to semi-professional, some of the latter so good that they not only rival the professional magazines, they dictate trends.

During the seventies, these little magazines took a stronger hold on the fields of both science fiction and weird fiction, so much so that by the end of the seventies they were starting to have a significant impact. This section looks at these 'little' magazines in all their forms, including the academic press.

First, though, we need to be clear what is meant by such terms as 'small-press', 'semi-professional' and 'amateur' magazines. There are no simple definitions to distinguish one from another and they are not necessarily mutually exclusive.

At the top level are the professional magazines produced by a commercial publisher for profit. The publisher is almost always a corporation, the magazine pays its contributors, seeks national news-stand distribution and publishes some level of advertising. The publisher may produce the magazine because it feels it is important and therefore may sustain it through periods when it is making a loss, but essentially it is a commercial product. That means it must have a certain level of circulation. That level may vary depending on the size of the firm. The Hugo Award committee defines professional as having a press run above 10,000 copies and I shall keep to that rather than add to the confusion, though it seems a low figure, even today. Magazines that fall into that category include all those discussed in Chapter 1, such as *Analog, Galaxy, F&SF, Vertex* and *Amazing Stories*.

At the other extreme is the fan magazine or amateur magazine. This is something produced for pleasure. It may be sold but is more often distributed free or in exchange for other magazines. It does not pay its contributors, runs no advertising to speak of, has no news-stand distribution, and may have a print run of only a few hundred copies, if that. I tend to distinguish between a fanzine and an amateur magazine. A fanzine I regard as something for and about fandom: much of the content is non-fiction, and relies heavily on reader feedback, letters, commentary and reviews. An amateur magazine I regard as something that is the amateur version of a professional magazine (or prozine), in that it runs predominantly fiction and tries to mimic everything you'd expect to see in a prozine.

Between these two extremes is a vague area termed 'semi-professional'. The Hugo Award committee states that to fit into this category it has to meet at least two of the following criteria[1]:

1. it must have an average press run of at least a thousand copies per issue;
2. it must pay its contributors and/or staff in other than copies of the magazine;
3. it must provide at least half the income of any one person;
4. it must have at least 15 per cent of its space occupied by advertising;
5. it must announce itself to be a semi-prozine.

The last criterion seems a red herring to me. The crucial ones are that the magazine has sufficient income (whether through sales or advertising or both) to contribute to the livelihood of its publisher and that it pays its contributors and any others associated with the magazine.

Notice that these criteria do not include the appearance of the magazine. In these days of desktop publishing it is easy for a magazine to look very professional, yet it may still be produced on a shoestring, have a very low print run, and not pay for its material. In pre-computer days the expense of printing a magazine usually meant that it had a circulation sufficiently high to cover the costs, unless the publisher was also a printer by profession.

If the publisher of the semi-prozine also issues other material (books, pamphlets, other magazines) under an imprint, such as Whispers Press, and that press is self-sufficient (or nearly so), even without the magazine, then that magazine could also be called a small-press magazine. The terms are almost synonymous, except that some semi-prozines are not produced by an independent press, but solely by an individual who works from

---

1 These criteria were first applied at the 1984 World SF Convention but had been approved by the World SF Committee in 1982 following representation from fans Marty and Robbie Cantor and Mike Glicksohn.

home. Conversely, the circulation of some small-press magazines may be sufficient to be classified as professional. This happened with several titles in the 1980s, such as *Cemetery Dance* and *The Horror Show*.

The phrase 'little magazine' has a far older origin, and usually means a literary magazine (as distinct from a popular one) which is produced on a not-for-profit basis and which has the primary purpose of publishing and studying literature as an art form. Since, until relatively recently, few would have considered science fiction as a literary art form, there was no confusion between 'little' magazines and 'semi-professional' or 'small-press' magazines, but in fact there is considerable overlap. Once again the terms are almost synonymous, but not quite. I would argue that some little magazines cross that divide between amateur magazines and semi-professional magazines, in that they have a small circulation and are not produced for profit, but have a high literary focus. They tend to publish more non-fiction than fiction, but there is no hard-and-fast distinction there. A magazine that I would define as both a 'little' magazine and a 'small-press' magazine is August Derleth's *The Arkham Sampler* and its successor, *The Arkham Collector*. Both were designed for the serious study of literature, both were produced by a small, independent press, Arkham House, and both had small circulations. Both were also semi-prozines as they made small payments to their contributors and the income contributed, albeit marginally, to the upkeep of Arkham House, though this seldom contributed much to the livelihood of August Derleth.

There are a large number of magazines devoted to the study and analysis of science fiction. Many are produced by the fans themselves and are the major source of primary material on the writers, editors and publishers of science fiction and their output. They occasionally, though rarely, publish fiction. These include such magazines as *Algol, Thrust, Riverside Quarterly, Science Fiction Review* and others, all of which I discuss later in this section. Some of these have a circulation high enough to make them semi-professional and most of them are intent on a serious discussion of science fiction as literature, so they ought to qualify as literary 'little' magazines, but generally they are ignored by the literary establishment who consider such things.

Since the 1970s (and earlier in a few cases) there has been a growth in academic magazines, such as *Extrapolation, Science Fiction Studies* and *Foundation*. These are all produced by academic foundations and rarely, if ever, publish fiction. They run serious analyses and studies of sf as literature. They are, strictly speaking, also 'little' magazines, but are distinct from small-press or semi-professional magazines, as there is no commercial motive as such. They are more like the literary reviews of other media.

I do not intend to discuss them in detail, but because the early days of academic interest in sf had an impact on the wider world of sf publishing, I will explore their origins.

These, then, are the material for discussion in this section, and I shall turn first to the semi-professional magazines.

Little Wonders

Writing in 'The Clubhouse' column in the November 1969 *Amazing Stories*, John Berry remarked:

> Something new is happening in science-fiction fandom; a new kind of fanzine is emerging. It is a large-scale, large-circulation fanzine, often with a near-professional quality of appearance, and deals with the entire science fiction world of prozines, fanzines, conventions, movies, paperbacks, and tv shows as a single whole. [...] The lines between 'fan' and 'pro' are breaking down. The dynamic changes in sf are now taking place as much in the pages of fanzines as in professional circles.[2]

The magazines that Berry cited included Richard Geis's *Science Fiction Review*, Ray Fisher's *Odd*, Leland Sapiro's *Riverside Quarterly*, Andrew Porter's *Algol* and John Bangsund's *Australian Science Fiction Review*. These were taking the role of the 'little' magazine, providing serious discussion of science fiction and treating it as any other branch of literature. Some, like Geis's *Science Fiction Review*, had a circulation in excess of two thousand copies, and rising. These magazines were reaching beyond the core of active sf fans to a wider readership, including the growing academic market, who did not just want to read sf for enjoyment, but wanted to understand the medium and what it was telling us. Science fiction had matured dramatically in the previous ten years, thanks to editors Frederik Pohl, Harlan Ellison, Damon Knight and Michael Moorcock in particular, and to a whole new generation of writers. The readers had similarly matured and science fiction was no longer just escapist literature. It was a literature that had a voice about the world and our future. It was a literature that spoke not only for the new Space Age, but for the age of the environment, the age of feminism, the pro- or anti-war factions, and so much more.

Alongside this growth in science-fiction awareness, the amateur fiction magazine also tried to mature, but this was viewed with rather more scepticism. In the past the 'amateur' magazine had made a mark. In the thirties, when science fiction was passing through a difficult stage, William

2 John D. Berry, 'The Clubhouse', *Amazing Stories* 43:4, November 1969, p. 109.

Crawford published and endeavoured to sustain *Marvel Tales*, a magazine intended to restore some of the creativity and originality to the field. This and similar magazines are discussed in *The Time Machines*. In the fifties and sixties a few such magazines continued but on the whole they had died out. The profusion of professional science-fiction magazines meant that there was little demand for amateur magazines devoted solely to fiction. Why read 'amateur' fiction (in its pejorative sense) when there was an abundance of better-quality fiction?

Nevertheless, there were attempts. One of the first was *Perihelion*. This had started as a standard mimeographed fanzine called *Seldon Seen*, produced by Sam Bellotto, Jr. for a science-fiction club he had organized while attending Long Island University. Two issues were published in April and July 1967 in this form, providing a range of articles and stories. Bellotto was a senior journalism major and the university allowed the club an annual publication budget provided that the magazine was freely available to the students. Bellotto recalls:

> Having the resources of the school's journalism department at my disposal, and several like-minded associates, we transformed the ugly duckling fanzine into a real semi-pro magazine. The title, *Seldon Seen* (after the Isaac Asimov hero Hari Seldon), just didn't fit anymore, so that was changed to *Perihelion*. Asimov didn't mind at all.[3]

Perihelion retained the original numbering, so began as issue #3, dated November/December 1967. It was printed offset from typed originals, running to 40 quarto-size pages on good-quality coated stock with heavier cover stock. It included screened artwork and photographs. The first new-style issue, like its predecessors, presented a mixture of fannish news, articles and fiction, including a heroic-fantasy comic strip, 'Alaron', by art editor, William Stillwell. Amongst its fiction was work by writers who would soon be selling professionally, including Robert E. Toomey and Evelyn Lief. At this stage, *Perihelion* still regarded itself as an amateur production. A notice in the issue, requesting material from writers and artists, 'not necessarily professionals', stated, 'After all, we are a fanzine, and if we wanted only pros, we'd have to pay.' Nevertheless, the magazine was clearly modelling itself on the professional magazines rather than fanzines. Its layout and approach were professional in outlook, including the acquisition of some advertisements.

Issue #4 (February/March 1968) reduced the number of 'fan' departments and increased the fiction. Issue #5 (May/June 1968) began a new comic strip by Vaughn Bodé, 'Tubs'. Issue #6 (January/February 1969)

3 Personal e-mail, Bellotto/Ashley, 5 April 2006.

included an interview with Edward L. Ferman and the start of a two-part novelette by Dean R. Koontz, 'The Face in his Belly'. It was this issue that came to the attention of John D. Berry, who reviewed it in 'The Clubhouse' in the September 1969 *Amazing*. He approved of Bodé's comic strip but otherwise felt that the presentation and fiction were of poor quality. The gist of Berry's review was that *Perihelion* had pretensions of grandeur, bringing a vehement response from Bellotto, annoyed that reviewers should feel that fanzines could not aspire to greater things. Bellotto was firm that *Perihelion* was no longer a fanzine, calling it 'a semi-professional magazine of "new wave speculative literature"'. [4]

By the Hugo Committee criteria, *Perihelion* was not semi-professional, qualifying only in relation to clause 5. It did not pay for its material, it was supported by the college, and its circulation was under a thousand. Bellotto told me that, so far as he could recall, a typical print run was between 500 and 1,000 copies. Issues were provided free to students and any remaining stock was sold at local sf conventions. He believed there were only about a dozen subscriptions. *Perihelion* was therefore an amateur magazine, but with the soul of a prozine. Had finances allowed, it might have gone further.

The college sf club folded just before Bellotto graduated. He took the magazine with him and produced a seventh issue (Summer 1969), which he financed entirely. This was well-produced with good printing, improved artwork and a respectable line-up. The Bodé comic strip continued, along with the conclusion of Dean Koontz's novelette, fiction from David R. Bunch and Gregory FitzGerald, and articles on dreams and cryonics. Bellotto used the issue to attract finance, but felt that he did not have the right marketing skills. The only investors who showed interest told him to come back after he had produced a few more issues, but he did not have the finances to do that. *Perihelion* thus folded, though the final issue had some benefit. It secured Bellotto his first job as the editor of a management magazine, his employer telling him it was the best resumé they had seen in years.

What let *Perihelion* down was trying to run before it could walk. Finances aside, the magazine still had weaknesses in its artwork and fiction content, and no amount of professional-quality production would hide that. A magazine had to set its standards high if it was to take on the wider world. Fandom enjoyed fannish things, but the moment you dressed in a veneer of professionalism, it would unsheath its critical claws.

Few in the science-fiction world attempted to run this difficult gauntlet and it was usually those with the ignorance and bravado of youth. Soon

4 Sam Bellotto, Jr., letter, *Amazing Stories* 43:5, January 1970, p. 137.

after *Perihelion* died, 18-year-old South Carolina fan Stephen Gregg endeavoured to start a semi-professional magazine. He spent well over a year on the planning and organizing, so that when *Eternity* eventually appeared, dated July 1973, it was clear that much care and thought had gone into it. Its appearance was let down by its typesetting, which was offset from typewritten sheets. It was in octavo format, ran to 40 pages (including covers) and sold for $1. Gregg printed over a thousand copies of the magazine and managed to secure some news-stand distribution, though sales for the first issue were low. He also paid one cent a word for material, so the magazine was genuinely semi-professional even though it looked only a little above fanzine level.

Gregg argued in his editorial that the professional magazines tended to ignore poetry and graphic art, citing for the latter the fate of Vaughn Bodé in *Galaxy*. For *Eternity*, Gregg secured a series of cartoons by Jack Gaughan, 'Genii', not one of his best efforts, and a short graphic story, 'Punchcap' by Dan Osterman, which was also poorly executed. The poetry was mostly short, but included pieces by Roger Zelazny and *Eternity*'s assistant editor, Scott Edelstein. Far better were the interior story illustrations by Ed Romero, and the back-cover sampling of work by Darrell Anderson. Stephen Fabian provided a fine black-and-white cover.

Eternity's strengths were not in its art or poetry but in its fiction and essays. Gregg had secured a short introspective piece by Philip K. Dick, 'Notes Made Late at Night by a Weary SF Writer', written in 1968 when Dick was clearly in a depressed state, and revealing much about his views of his own fiction. Dennis O'Neil looked at the Comics Code and self-imposed censorship in comics, and Scott Edelstein paralleled this in his article on sf in the cinema and the potential of the video. Barry Malzberg contributed his own version of Ballard's condensed-novel technique in his Vietnam-inspired 'Report of the Defense'. Joseph Green appeared with a fable on truth and lies and how we perceive the world about us. These and other stories by Edward Bryant, Robert E. Margroff and Andrew Offutt showed that Gregg was interested in stories that did not fit easily into a traditional mould. They were stories that, with some extra polish, would have worked well in the more experimental anthologies such as *QUARK/* or *Orbit*. Despite *Eternity*'s physical shortcomings, it was a magazine that held promise.

Gregg was learning the hard way. Although *Eternity* was planned as a quarterly, it took almost a year to finalize the second issue, and the remaining two issues also appeared roughly annually. Gregg revealed that most of the income from the news-stand sales of the first issue had still not been received from the retailer. Producing *Eternity* was costly, about a tenth of Gregg's salary per issue. It was a problem faced by all those who sought professional production and distribution in the days before the internet and desktop publishing.

Considering those problems, Gregg did a good job with *Eternity*. The second issue was far better produced, though the graphics sections still looked amateurish. Gregg began a feature interview, starting with Thomas M. Disch followed by Kate Wilhelm in issue #3 and Damon Knight in issue #4. Otherwise, non-fiction took a back seat to the fiction which was always challenging and unsettling. *Eternity* was picking up several experimental items by Clarion alumni including Arthur Byron Cover, Glen Cook and Robert Wissner plus equally infusive material by Barry Malzberg, David R. Bunch and Pg Wyal. The combination of poetry, graphics and challenging fiction caused Richard Geis to comment that the magazine 'was aimed at the young, literate, wide-interest sf and fantasy reader', and to ask, 'How many of them are around, Stephen?'[5] Geis was of the view that by the third issue the art and graphics were superior to those in most sf prozines, and judged that *Eternity* was 'more than simply a "semi-pro"' magazine, but his question makes the point that such a literate magazine had a limited market.

Geis's question puzzled Gregg and he used it as the basis for his editorial in the fourth issue. The third issue had brought considerable reader comment, mostly supportive, but with extreme views for and against the publication of poetry. Poetry formed a significant part of the third issue, along with an article by Peter Dillingham looking for a definition of sf or speculative poetry. Gregg was reconsidering the future of *Eternity* in the light of the interest in poetry, and asked for reader feedback.

Poetry was always an overlooked form in the sf magazines, but there was a growing interest in the medium, and the small-press and semi-prozines became its primary market. Mark Rich issued the two earliest amateur magazines devoted to sf poetry at this time, *The Silent Planet* (October 1973) and *Treaders of Starlight* (2 issues, October 1974–August 1976). These were followed by Robert Frazier's *Speculative Poetry Review* in 1977, on which Stephen Gregg also worked,[6] and Steve Rasnic Tem's *Umbral* in 1978. It was in 1978 that Suzette Haden Elgin established the Science Fiction Poetry Association, with its newsletter *Star*Line*, and inaugurated the Rhysling Awards. The first winners of the award, in 1978, were Gene Wolfe in the long-poem category, and Duane Ackerson, Sonya Dorman and Andrew Joron, who tied in the short-poem category. Sf

---

5 Richard E. Geis in *The Alien Critic* #10, August 1974, p. 31.

6 Gregg compiled the first issue of *Speculative Poetry Review* which Frazier published, and it was sent to subscribers of *Eternity* to honour subscriptions.

Poetry came out from the shadows during the seventies thanks to people such as Stephen Gregg taking the opportunity to promote the medium that helped give it this impetus. Increasingly sf poetry would feature in the major sf magazines.

Eternity was a worthy magazine that had its sights set on a level of quality and creativity that was limited only by personal finances, which made it difficult for Gregg to continue publishing the magazine. In November 1975 Gregg succeeded in selling the idea of an anthology series based on the magazine to New Hope Publishing of Pennsylvania. The first volume was to consist of the contents of *Eternity* #5 plus selected reprints from earlier issues. Unfortunately, before the book appeared, New Hope suffered a financial setback and the project was dropped. After *Eternity* folded, Gregg established a bookshop in his new home town of Clemson. It became one of the major specialist shops in South Carolina. In 1979, having secured some financial backing from a co-publisher, Henry Vogel, Gregg made a second attempt to publish *Eternity*, still in quarto format but running to 80 pages (for $1.75) and with better-quality printing and graphics. It retained much the same mix of poetry, fiction and interviews, though it added a science column by Karl T. Pflock. The first issue reprinted some material from the original series but the second issue, in early 1980, was almost all new material, including Orson Scott Card's early Worthing story, 'Tinker', and the first of John Shirley's wonderfully comic stories, 'Undermuck with Quill Tripstickler', about his eponymous galactic agent. A third issue was assembled but then a whole series of catastrophes, including the theft of the manuscripts and the typeset copy, caused Gregg to call it a day. Gregg continued to run the Clemson Bookshop until his death of Pick's Disease when still only 50, in January 2005.

Another method of developing a semi-professional magazine was to take it one step at a time. The only all-fiction fanzine to do so is also the longest-surviving on record, *Space and Time*. It had started as a bit of fun amongst three school friends, John Eiche, Larry Lee and Gordon Linzner, who acquired a cheap mimeograph and produced a crudely duplicated magazine of a few copies with material by their high-school friends. That first issue was dated Spring 1966. Gordon Linzner could have had no idea that 40 years later he would eventually edit the one hundredth issue.

The early issues, published at the rate of one or two a year, contained the usual fannish mixture of adolescent stories, comic strips and poetry, with nothing of any lasting merit. Interest waned in the magazine amongst his friends but Linzner, who had now also discovered sf fandom, persevered.

With the fifth issue, dated Spring 1969, Linzner switched it to a neater, octavo-size, 20-page booklet which he promoted more widely, selling it for 25 cents. Circulation remained small, around a hundred copies, but awareness of it grew steadily. Linzner had broadened the remit so that the magazine published as much weird fiction as it did science fiction. The eighth issue (February 1970), printed the very first appearance by Darrell Schweitzer, who became a regular contributor. Issue #11 (April 1971) ran the first of Robert Weinberg's Lovecraftian series about investigator Morgan Smith. That issue also doubled in both price and pagination and for the first time started to look like a serious magazine. It was rare for an amateur sf magazine to run nothing but fiction, and new and upcoming writers began to view it as another potential (though as yet unpaying) market. Issue #12 (June 1971) ran a story by Janet Fox, who had been appearing regularly in other amateur magazines and had also sold to the *Magazine of Horror*. David C. Smith's first appearance in print was with 'The Apach' Curse' (#17, November 1972). 'Twilight' (#16, August 1972) was one of the earliest pieces of fiction by Gustav Hasford, who became best known for the Vietnam War novel, *The Short-Timers* (1979), the basis of the film *Full Metal Jacket*.

With issue #23 (March 1974), Linzner began to make small-token payments to contributors and, though circulation remained small – in the low hundreds, it was from that issue that Linzner regarded the magazine as semi-professional. One of Linzner's more remarkable achievements was that from the May 1973 issue (#18) he kept the magazine to a regular bi-monthly schedule and that alone attracted contributors, knowing that their work would appear within a reasonable period. Linzner produced several special issues. Those for May and November 1973 focused on swords and sorcery, those for September 1973, November 1975 and September 1977, were labelled 'Harvest of Horror' issues, and that for September 1974, was a space-opera issue. Otherwise the content was a mixture of fantasy, sf and horror of variable quality.

Linzner was especially pleased when Andrew Offutt selected three stories from *Space and Time* to include in the third volume of his otherwise all-original anthology series *Swords Against Darkness*, published in March 1978. These were 'Descales' Skull' by David C. Smith (July 1973), 'Tower of Darkness' by David Madison (January 1975) and 'Servitude' by Wayne Hooks (January 1976). The quality of the fiction had certainly improved during the mid-seventies. With issue #45, dated November 1977, the size increased again, this time to 60 pages (for $1.50) and the print run rose to around four hundred copies. He also switched to a quarterly schedule from January 1978. It was now running stories by professional writers, including Offutt himself, Charles R. Saunders, Charles de Lint, Eric Vinicoff with Marcia Martin, plus artwork by Charles Vess, Gene Day, Gary Kato and others. There was still a feeling that *Space and Time* wasn't quite taking itself too seriously, as it ran a number of spoof stories, such as Linzner's own James Bond parodies featuring James Blood, but the quality and tenacity of the magazine was sufficient for it to be treated respectfully. Linzner would continue to improve the magazine's appearance and content to make it one of the most reliable semi-prozines of the last 30 years, as we shall discover in the next volume.

One sf semi-prozine that appeared at this time does not fall naturally into any group, though it was clearly inspired by the Perry Rhodan books and *Star Trek*. This was *Stardust*, the only English-language Canadian magazine of the seventies devoted entirely to science fiction.[7] The editor was Forrest Fusco of Toronto. The magazine's title came from the name of Perry Rhodan's first starship. The first issue, undated but released in August 1975, looked unprepossessing. Another octavo, saddle-stapled magazine, it was printed offset from typed pages which, though reasonably well typed, looked cheap. It did not help that the pages were collated in the wrong order. It contained only two stories, the lead, 'Green Goddess' by Adele Gorman, being an attempt at some kind of sexual Olympics, while the other was weak in every respect, including scientific knowledge. Fusco noted that he hoped to produce the magazine quarterly, but in effect it appeared when finances made it possible. Even so, Fusco promised to pay a cent a word for fiction, the same rate paid by *Amazing Stories*.

There was a sudden change in format with the second issue, which dropped to pocketbook size, with 80 pages selling for $1.50. Although still typed, the smaller size looked neater and easier to read, although the stories, apart from a reprint of Darrell Schweitzer's 'The Story of Obbok', remained amateurish. The third issue, in the same format, and with a *Star Trek* cover, included an original (though probably unauthorized) *Star Trek* story, 'Combination' by Constance Reinl and Conrad Jakob, plus a review of the anthology *Star Trek: The New Voyages*, but the magazine was still struggling to publish material of any quality.

That happened with the fourth issue, which returned to octavo size but now neatly printed and bound and with a much sharper typeface. Fusco had changed printers and set up Stardust Publications which brought with it a new respectability. The contents improved sharply. Stories included the original version of 'The Night the Arcturians Landed' by Chris Dornan

---

7 The French-language magazine *Solaris* was launched in September 1974 (as *Requiem*) and though predominantly sf it also runs fantasy and weird fiction. See Appendix 1.

which had been published in a revised version in *Unearth*. Dornan and
Dena Bain, also in issue #4, were both present again in issue #5, which
also included a clever robot story, 'Quest' by Julian Dust. From there on,
Stardust retained a reasonably good quality of fiction, nothing remarkable
but nothing as bad as the first few issues. It also attracted better artists.

Fusco struggled to maintain a quarterly schedule and deadlines slipped,
but he put out three more fairly regular issues, the price rising to $1.95 on
the eighth. The magazine received some news-stand distribution, though
most was local to Toronto. There was a gap of nearly two years before the
final issue, dated Spring 1981. Fusco was trying to appeal to a wider readership. He had the whole magazine professionally typeset but retained the
$1.95 cover price. In addition to five new stories, it reprinted a story by
Phyllis Gotlieb and printed a recent talk given by John Robert Colombo,
'Four Hundred Years of Fantastic Literature in Canada'. However, despite
his efforts, Fusco was unable to go any further and this was the last issue.
It was a valiant effort that took a while to get going. It was not able to
advance Canadian English-language sf, which would have to wait for
nine more years before it had a regular magazine.

Stardust was just one example of where amateur and small-press
magazines were appearing in countries that had no professional magazine
of their own. This was true throughout much of Europe and beyond, as I
explore in Appendix 1, and it was equally true in Australia.

Australia's last professional sf magazine was *Vision of Tomorrow*, a joint
Anglo-Australian venture, financed by Australian businessman Ron
Graham but published and edited in Britain. It was supposed to allow
room for at least 40 per cent Australian material, a figure the editor
Philip Harbottle struggled to meet, but it was at least a genuine market.
After it ceased publication in September 1970, Australia was devoid of
any professional sf market. That same year Leith Morton, then a student
at the University of Sydney, produced an amateur magazine, *Enigma*,
for the University SF Association. With the fourth issue in 1972, it was
taken over by Van Ikin, another student later to become an associate
professor of English and cultural studies. He made the magazine his own
and continued it during his postgraduate years, remaining as editor until
1979. After the early spirit-duplicated issues, it became a neatly produced
offset magazine with colour art and a creative format. It never paid for
contributions and its print run averaged about 400-500 copies, so it never
broke through into the semi-professional ranks, but in all other requirements it was highly professional. It sold some advertising space and had a
healthy subscriber list which just about covered the cost of production. It
published the first stories by Terry Dowling (the mistitled 'The Illusion of

Motion', October 1975) and Rick Kennett ('Troublesome Green', January 1979), and early artwork by Nick Stathopoulos. It was the only 'regular' sf periodical in Australia during the seventies. It won the Australian Ditmar Award in 1978 as the best amateur publication. It continued briefly after Van Ikin left Sydney, but was a mere shadow and folded in 1981.

While *Enigma* was dipping into the shallows, another magazine appeared, seeking to make a splash. Paul Collins had been born in Canvey Island, in Britain, in 1954, but emigrated with his family to New Zealand when he was nine. Though they returned briefly to Britain, they settled in New Zealand and Collins later moved to Australia in 1972. He undertook various jobs, including working as a stunt man, before he tried to make a career as a writer. He decided to publish a magazine in the hope that this would finance his writing career and, in August 1975, launched the digest format *Void*. He discovered at the last moment that the World SF Convention was being held in Melbourne that September, where he was able to promote the magazine. Fully typeset, with a few minor illustrations, *Void* ran to 82 pages, and sold for $1. It was unnumbered and not designated as a magazine, but rather ran an ISBN number and called itself a 'collection' on the contents page, a terminology it retained throughout. It could easily pass as a digest-size book, and 5,000 copies were printed, extremely ambitious for a first issue.

Collins was new to the sf world and had not yet connected with Australian fandom. He filled the issue primarily with US writers, four stories being reprints from Roger Elwood's anthology *Crisis*, plus an even older, 'classic' reprint by Ralph Milne Farley. The only Australian items were short fillers. This did not endear Collins to Australian fans. He rectified it with the second issue which, apart from one remaining US reprint, contained work chiefly by Australians or (in the case of A. Bertram Chandler) those long-resident in Australia. These were also mostly new stories, and Collins steadily developed *Void* as a market for Australian sf, sustaining a quarterly schedule for the first year, though the fifth issue was delayed.

The presence of *Void* encouraged three authors back to writing – Jack Wodhams, Frank Bryning and Wynne Whitford. *Void* also provided a vehicle for Van Ikin, who had previously sold to non-sf markets. Nevertheless, Collins still found trouble getting sufficient Australian quality material and ran a number of reprints and some US material. Despite the large print run and serious efforts by Collins, *Void* never quite clicked with the Australian market. You have a feeling that Collins was holding the stalls until the real trading commenced.

After the fifth issue in February 1977, Collins changed tactics. He secured a grant from the Literature Board of Australia and converted *Void* into a hardcover anthology series. For the purpose of fulfilling subscriptions Collins treated his first volume, *Envisaged Worlds*, released in April 1978, as issues #6–#8 of *Void*. The same applied to two more 'triple' volumes, *Other Worlds* and *Alien Worlds* issued at six-monthly intervals, and the delayed *Distant Worlds* (1981) and *Frontier Worlds* (1983). These ran far more works by local writers, and it was only with these books that you felt that an Australian scene was stirring. Even then the anthologies favoured a more traditional sf and the quality of the fiction was variable.

Apart from the amateur magazine *Boggle* (1977-78), published by Peter Knox of Randwick, New South Wales, which called itself 'a forum for the development of Australasian science fiction writing', but which had problems over finance and folded after three slim issues, the only other market at the end of the seventies was *The Cygnus Chronicler*. It began in October 1977 as a single-sheet fanzine produced in Canberra by Neville Angove for an amateur press group. With the third issue in December 1979 it became fully typeset and ran to eight pages, with a lead story by A. Bertram Chandler. By issue #7 (December 1980) it had grown to 24 pages and featured quality artwork, mostly by Michael Dutkiewicz, who also served as art editor. It ran fiction by Cherry Wilder ('Gone to Earth', March 1981), Jack Wodhams, Paul Collins and Steve Paulsen, amongst others. Its print run was only 250 copies but Angove managed to pay a cent a word for contributions, making it one of the few paying markets in Australia at that time. In its semi-professional form it ran for 17 issues until December 1983 when pressure of work forced Angove to cease publication. By then it had served well in holding the fort for Australian sf until a new market emerged in the eighties.

In Britain there were plenty of amateur magazines, including many good critical ones such as *Cypher* and *Arena*, but no true semi-professional fiction magazine. The revival of *New Worlds* filled that gap, though idiosyncratically. Now in its fortieth year, counting from the original fanzine founded by John Carnell in March 1939, *New Worlds* had been just about everything from fanzine to prozine to slick to anthology and now to semi-prozine. *New Worlds* had arguably already been a semi-prozine in its last days as a magazine in 1971, if circulation is the primary criterion. The last anthology edition, *New Worlds 10*, had appeared in August 1976.

Moorcock would not let the title fade away though. In March 1978 he cobbled together a photocopied set of two A3-size pages, folded in half to A4 size, which he labelled issue #212, dated Spring and distributed to a few interested parties. The central pages, unfolded into tabloid size, were a mock edition of *The Guardian* as if from some alternate timeline in May 1948, full of news stories of the continuing war. These were all written by Moorcock under such aliases as Oswald Bastable, James Colvin and Roy Kipling, plus – on the 'back page' – a scoop by M. John Harrison on the sentencing of various writers and visionaries on their fraudulent concept of Space. The piece, which was very cleverly assembled, had originally appeared in the underground paper *Frendz* in 1971.

With the next issue (Summer 1978), which ran to 32 pages, production was more formalized. The issue was assembled by Moorcock with help from Jill Riches, whom Moorcock had married in May 1978 and who served as art editor. It was published in Manchester by Charles Partington and Harry Nadler. Besides artwork and poetry reprinted in facsimile form from Moorcock's collection of old magazines, the magazine again consisted of mock newspaper stories, making *New Worlds* a genuine 'alternative' magazine. By the next issue the collective who were compiling *New Worlds* – which included Robert Meadley, Michael Butterworth, Barrington Bayley, Charles Platt and Richard Glyn Jones – were really starting to have fun with the concept of mock stories and parodies, not all in good taste, but always original. *New Worlds* had reinvented itself yet again and now felt like the kind of magazine you might have been reading had you lived in some alternate time.

Issue #215 (Spring 1979) was guest-edited by David Britton with Michael Butterworth of Savoy Books in Manchester and was filled with their own fascinations. Some mock stories remained, but, hard though it was to imagine, the issue seemed more conventional, albeit at the far end of an indulgent scale. There was a Jerry Cornelius story by Charles Partington, an article about M. John Harrison, a feature by Butterworth on the shape of the 'New Literature', and an item by Heathcote Williams on Kirlian auras. None of these items was presented in a standard way, though, and the magazine was imbued with a sense of pretence, as if everything could be a hoax. The final issue in this incarnation (#216, September 1979) was compiled by Charles Platt with Moorcock and reverted to the mock news stories and experimental fiction, though it was labelled by Platt as a 'Normal Issue', recognizing that previous issues had become rather obscure. In fact the magazine was now poking fun at itself and rounded out rather neatly these hedonistic but genuinely clever issues. Once again, *New Worlds* proved that it could not be categorized or pigeonholed. It was a genuine magazine of alternates.

Although after issue #216 *New Worlds* went into another hiatus for a decade, Charles Partington, who had printed the issues, produced his own magazine along similar lines which appeared in March 1980 and which was called, rather appropriately, *Something Else*. The magazine was A4 size, printed on glossy paper and ran to 40 pages. It featured several full-page colour illustrations including a centre-page spread by James Cawthorn of Moorcock's Elric. Although it ran some graphics, *Something Else* consisted mostly of fiction, some of it relatively conventional. Brian Aldiss, who had started to experiment with the form of 'enigmas' for his fiction contributed 'Three Evolutionary Enigmas'; there were extracts from Moorcock's *The Russian Intelligence* and M. John Harrison's *A Storm of Wings*, but the major contribution was Partington's own 'Nosferatu's Ape', which uses images from the silent cinema and Lovecraft's oeuvre to tell an ingenious tale of the true nature of Nosferatu in Murnau's 1922 film.

Partington produced a second issue later that year which had lost some of the gloss of the first and looked rather more hastily prepared. It contained fiction by Brian Aldiss, John Brunner, Hilary Bailey (a Una Persson story) plus an overview of Bob Shaw's career, a retrospective piece by Charles Platt on the *New Worlds* literary movement, and an excerpt from a planned biography of Moorcock. Enjoyable though the contents were on an individual basis, the issue felt like a deflated *New Worlds*. It was a good time to stop. In fact Partington always intended to produce further issues of *Something Else* but life got in the way and only one more appeared, nearly four years later in Spring 1984, an attractive issue but one that by now looked like a relic. The *New Worlds* experiment was long over, as Moorcock and Platt themselves knew, and only *New Worlds* could reinvent itself, as it would continue to do.

One fact that all these magazines made evident was that if the professional magazines did not satisfy a need, a semi-professional or amateur magazine would try to fill the gap. Although the needs of the sf readers were primarily met by the professional magazines, this was not the case for the fans of either fantasy or weird fiction.

The Fantastic Dimension

Publishers like categories so that books can be labelled. Science fiction had been a genre since 1926 and most publishers were convinced that they knew what that was, regardless of what was being written. Fantasy had also become a marketing genre by 1967, thanks to the success of *Lord of the Rings* and Robert E. Howard's Conan books, which rather limited the scope of fantasy and confined what had once been the greatest domain of literature to 'heroic' or 'high fantasy'.

Fantasy had long played second fiddle to science fiction. Publishers who ran both science fiction and fantasy magazines – such as *Astounding* with *Unknown*, *New Worlds* with *Science Fantasy*, *Galaxy* with *Beyond* and *Amazing Stories* with *Fantastic* – found that the fantasy companion always sold fewer issues, even though it might contain superior material. On the whole, fantasy magazines were shorter-lived, *Weird Tales* and *Fantastic* being the only ones that had a significant lifetime. There were occasional semi-professional fantasy magazines, but most of these tended to be slanted towards horror fiction, like Manly Banister's *The Nekromantikon* in the early fifties.

There was, though, a significant crossover readership. When *Locus* asked its readers in 1975 what other 'sf associated subjects' interested them, 30 per cent said weird fiction and 39 per cent said sword and sorcery, and those figures remained fairly constant for the rest of the decade. A survey by *Algol* at the same time had similar figures: 33.3 per cent for weird fiction and 41.7 per cent for sword and sorcery.[8] Evidently a high proportion of sf readers would also follow fantasy and weird fiction magazines, with possible crossover influences, as attested by the continuing success of *F&SF*.

The most significant of the fantasy 'little' magazines in the sixties was *Amra*. Just as H. P. Lovecraft had his followers, so did Robert E. Howard, and in 1956 Fritz Leiber and fellow Howard devotees established the fan organization, the Hyborian Legion or League. *Amra* was its newsletter, edited initially by George R. Heap, but from January 1959 it was taken over by George Scithers who turned it into a magazine in its own right. Over time far more people read *Amra* than ever belonged to the Hyborian Legion. It was a surprisingly attractive magazine for those days, produced by offset-litho from very neatly typed and laid-out originals. It was slightly larger than octavo and usually ran to between 20 and 30 pages. It featured mostly articles, but also the occasional fiction, and its contributors included L. Sprague de Camp, Lin Carter, Poul Anderson, Michael Moorcock, John Brunner and Leiber himself, as well as artwork by George Barr, Jeff Jones, Jim Cawthorn and, most notably, Roy Krenkel. There were early contributions by Jerry Pournelle (on weapons in fantasy in the March 1967 issue), Howard Waldrop (commentary in the October 1967 issue) and Tim Powers (four limericks in the May 1969 issue). Scithers sustained it for 71 issues, initially producing four or five a year, six some years, but the magazine had all but ceased by 1976 and only five more issues appeared, closing in July 1982. It won two Hugos as best fanzine in 1964 and 1967.

8 See *Locus* #173 (10 May 1975), p. 5 and *Algol* #25 (Winter 1976), p. 48.

The work of Robert E. Howard continued to have an influence on the magazines. Glenn Lord had been publishing *The Howard Collector* since Summer 1961, but it was not until the 1970s, following the success of the Conan stories in paperback and, the growth of Conan comic books, starting with *Conan the Barbarian* in October 1970 and *Savage Tales* in May 1971, that Howard-related fanzines began to take off.

During the seventies, there was a rash of small chapbook-size magazines on the borderline of amateur/semi-professional status, not unlike *Space & Time*. They concentrated mostly on fantasy and horror, and were useful markets for developing writers. Titles included the Canadian *Dark Fantasy* (began Summer 1973), *The Diversifier* (began June 1974), *Midnight Sun* (began late 1974), *Evermist* (began December 1974), *Astral Dimensions* (began Winter 1975), *Black Lite* (began August 1976) and *Phantasy Digest* (began late 1976). These magazines ran material by many of the same writers but each had a distinctive enough character.

The best of them was *Midnight Sun*. This was a highly attractive magazine produced by Gary Hoppenstand of Columbus, Ohio. It was started to support the work of Karl Edward Wagner, especially his dark hero, Kane, and other 'serious epic fantasy'. The first issue, priced at an extreme $4, ran three of Wagner's stories plus the first half of the serialization of the full version of his Kane novel 'Darkness Weaves', along with an appreciation of his work by Manly Wade Wellman. Wagner dominated the second issue, but there were also fantasies by David Drake and Robert Weinberg, plus an art portfolio by George Chastain inspired by William Hope Hodgson's *House on the Borderland*.

Both of these issues were perfect bound with 122 and 96 pages respectively. The first suffered from being badly typed, despite the quality presentation, but the second was formally typeset on standard book paper and sold for $3.98. The third issue, dated April 1976, saw a sudden change. Hoppenstand had decided to switch to a bi-monthly schedule and slimmed the magazine down to 28 pages, saddle-stapled on coated stock and selling for $2.50. This issue concentrated on the works of H. H. Hollis, the alias of lawyer Neal Ramey, Jr., who had sold several stories to *Galaxy* and *If*. His stories all feature the cases of space lawyer Gallegher but they are comparatively minor pieces lacking much plot development. Moreover, a composition error led to three pages being bound in the wrong sequence. Problems continued to dog Hoppenstand. The next issue cost him twice as much as budgeted to print and then over half the run was lost by the postal services. Hoppenstand had to reprint the issue to meet orders but it left him seriously in debt. Yet this fourth issue, dated August 1976, was the best so far. Beautifully laid out and printed, it ran to 44 pages on coated stock and sold for $2.50. Its dark, ominous cover heralded a return to dark fantasy, featuring two stories by Charles L. Grant plus fiction by Joseph Payne Brennan, Richard K. Lyon and Basil Copper.

Since Hoppenstand was unable to finance further issues, that would have been the last, but three years later Harlan Ellison, curious as to the magazine's fate, generously donated to Hopperstand one of his unpublished stories, 'In the Fourth Year of the War'. Charles L. Grant also donated two stories and there were further tales by Carl Jacobi and H. H. Hollis (who, alas, had died in May 1977). This final issue, released in 1979, allowed Hoppenstand to recoup his losses, but he decided to produce no more, which is a shame as Hoppenstand was a talented editor. He has, though, gone on to become a professor of American popular culture and has written several books about the works of Stephen King, Anne Rice and Clive Barker.

Of the other magazines listed above, *Dark Fantasy* was also of some interest. It was published by Howard E. Day (who used the variant Gene Day for his artwork) of Gananoque, Ontario. It was a neat, octavo-sized magazine of 40-48 pages, selling for $1 (Canadian). It published mostly heroic fantasy and supernatural fiction. Day is usually attributed with coining the phrase 'dark fantasy', which has since gone on to stand for a blending of the more dark and brooding aspects of fantasy with supernatural horror.

Dark Fantasy is best known today for having published the first work by Charles R. Saunders. Although American by birth, Saunders had settled in Canada in 1969 and became a Canadian citizen. He was one of the few black writers of fantasy and sf. He found fantasy more liberating and began to write a series featuring a black fantasy hero, Imaro, which he called an 'antidote to Tarzan'. The first of these, 'M'Ji Ya Wazimu' appeared in *Dark Fantasy* #4 (July 1974). Lin Carter read that issue and selected the story for the first volume of his *Year's Best Fantasy Stories* for DAW Books in 1975. That in turn attracted the interest of publisher Donald Wollheim, who commissioned Saunders to rework his Imaro stories into a novel, resulting in *Imaro* (1981). It's a simple example of how the amateur magazines could launch a writer's career. Saunders was a prolific and popular contributor to most of the small magazines during the seventies and yet, despite it being collected into book form, no professional magazine published any of his work until *Twilight Zone* in 1988, by which time Saunders was at the end of his first phase of writing. Saunders edited his own amateur magazine, *Stardock*, which was published on behalf of the Ottawa Science Fiction Society and which saw four issues from Summer 1977 to Fall 1979 (the last one edited by Jeff Cohen). Saunders's interest in the small-press movement led to him and Gene Day founding the Small Press Writers and Artists Organization (SPWAO) in 1979, and he served as its first president.

He also wrote a groundbreaking essay, 'Why Blacks Don't Read Science Fiction', published in the feminist magazine *Windhaven* #5 in 1977. The article was a reaction to Theodore Sturgeon's puzzlement over why there were not more black writers. Sturgeon had repeated the comments he had made in his *Galaxy* column (cited in the previous chapter[9]) in an interview in the comic *Unknown Worlds of Science Fiction*. Saunders reacted to Sturgeon's comment, arising from a conversation with a black fan, that 'the average black, especially the ghetto black, is far too concerned with reality to try to escape from it'.[10] Saunders argued that sf was so dominated by the white man that, when read from a black reader's viewpoint, it offered no escape at all. Saunders believed that most sf was more likely to feature a sympathetic alien than a heroic black man. Unfortunately, Saunders's essay appeared in the last issue of *Windhaven* so there was no opportunity to check reader feedback, and it would be over twenty years before we would discover the sequel.

In 2000 Saunders contributed an update to his article, 'Why Blacks Should Read (and Write) Science Fiction', for the anthology *Dark Matter* edited by Sheree R. Thomas. Saunders noted the changes of the intervening 20 years with a small but notable increase in the number of black writers and the change in attitude toward non-white racial groups in fiction. Saunders's article was a wake-up call to writers, just as the essays by Joanna Russ and others had been with regard to feminist issues. The advances in both subjects will be tracked in the next volume.

Dark Fantasy was a friend to other new writers. It published the first work by Galad Elflandsson and early work by Ardath Mayhar and Charles de Lint. Gene Day had sent copies of the early issues to James Warren's magazines *Creepy* and *Eerie* and had received favourable reviews, which had boosted interest in the magazine. Day published artwork by several comics artists, including Neal Adams, Larry Dickison and Tim Hammell, as well as the work of Stephen Fabian.

Like *Midnight Sun*, *Dark Fantasy* also had its problems with printers, this time a California printer who offered tempting prices but then pocketed the money and claimed that the magazine had been lost. Both issues #12 and #13 suffered this fate and though a revised issue #12 was eventually released out of sequence in April 1979, issue #13 never did appear. That

---

9 See Theodore Sturgeon, 'Galaxy Bookshelf', *Galaxy* 34:6 (March 1974), p. 84.

10 Theodore Sturgeon interviewed by Alan Brennert, *Unknown Worlds of Science Fiction*, #1 (1976), pp. 19, 88.

means that the later issue numbering of *Dark Fantasy* is one more than the actual number. The magazine ran for 22 issues, finishing with issue #23 in November 1980. By then Day had carved out a career in the comics business and adapted *Star Wars* for Marvel Comics. Tragically, he died of a heart attack in October 1982 aged only 31. Two years later Gordon Derevanchuk published a commemorative double issue of *Dark Fantasy* (#24/5, August 1984) as a tribute to Day.

Dark Fantasy was not the only Canadian small magazine. Dale Hammell of Richmond, British Columbia, issued *The Copper Toadstool* in September 1976 on a twice-yearly basis under the imprint of Soda Publications. The magazine was primarily light fantasy, as opposed to dark, and published some of the early eccentric tales by Albert Manachino, early work by Galad Elflandsson and Lovecraftian tales by Randall Larson, Phillip C. Heath and G. N. Gabbard. After the first issue, the magazine increased its page count to around a hundred. The final double issue, dated July 1979, was in handsome trade-paperback format and retitled *The Storyteller*.

Before he became a professional writer, Charles de Lint published four issues of a magazine under various titles. This was under the imprint of his Triskell Press, in Ottawa, which was originally initiated with Charles Saunders and which de Lint still maintains for his annual chapbooks. His publications were also of light fantasy, arguably more high fantasy than the basic sword-and-sorcery of most magazines, with contributions from Tanith Lee, David Madison, Andrew Offutt, Diana L. Paxson, Marion Zimmer Bradley, Darrell Schweitzer, Thomas Burnett Swann, Galad Elflandsson and Joy Chant. The first issue, published in Spring 1978 was called *Dragonbane*. It was edited by Saunders and went for the darker elements of fantasy. It was followed that autumn by the Dunsanian *Beyond the Fields We Know*, which de Lint compiled and which was in a lighter vein. They then merged the titles as *Dragonfields* for two last issues in Summer 1980 and Winter 1983.

The other extreme from these small 'chapbook'-style magazines were those where the publishers cast off all financial care and produced the most beautiful magazines they could afford.

The most revered of all amateur magazines of the late sixties was *Trumpet*, produced by Tom Reamy from Plano (later Dallas), Texas. Reamy had been at the heart of Texas fandom for many years and was not a newcomer like Bellotto. He had published an earlier fanzine, *Crifanac*, in the mid-fifties, and in June 1965, when Reamy was a seasoned 30-year-old, he launched the first issue of *Trumpet*, ostensibly as a journal for New Dallas Fandom. It appeared as and when Reamy had the time and money, and ran, under Reamy, for 11 issues until 1974. Harry Warner, the historian of sf fandom, regarded *Trumpet* as 'one of the finest looking fanzines in history'.[11] Reamy worked in the aerospace industry (and much else) but he was by training a graphic designer and his skills allowed him to print a magazine with high-quality production values. It was on slick paper, quarto format, side-stapled and running to between 40 and 52 pages. The cover price of 50 cents was believed exorbitant at the time.

It was not designed as a fiction magazine. Reamy published a few squibs each issue and reprinted two stories by Leonora Carrington. The sixth issue (June 1967) ran the most fiction, with contributions by Andrew Offutt, John Boardman and Don Hutchison, amongst others. But no one bought the magazine for the fiction. The main features were the articles on a wide range of topics (with contributions by Ray Bradbury, Marion Zimmer Bradley, Robert Bloch, Harlan Ellison, Ray Nelson, Larry Niven and Jerry Pournelle), the book and movie reviews and, in particular, the artwork. *Trumpet* published work by Vaughn Bodé, D. Bruce Berry, Stephen Fabian, Berni Wrightson and Hannes Bok. The ninth issue, released in the spring of 1969, not only had a full-colour cover by Bok, but ran a portfolio of his poems. Another feature was the adaptation into comic-strip form of Poul Anderson's novel 'The Broken Sword', illustrated by George Barr with continuity by Reamy, which began in issue #4 (April 1966). Everybody loved *Trumpet*. It was a joy to behold, had no pretensions, and embraced the core of fannish delights. It would also have appealed to comics and movie fandom, making *Trumpet* closer to the media and graphics magazines that followed, rather than to the traditional science-fiction magazine. It was nominated for the Hugo Award for Best Fanzine in 1967 and 1969, though did not win, perhaps because fans could not view it as a 'fanzine'. The magazine was one of the first that should have qualified as 'semi-professional' but no such category existed then.

In fact, *Trumpet* did turn semi-pro. Reamy had effectively dropped it with issue #10 in Autumn 1969. With the running down of the aerospace industry, Reamy found himself without a job and in the summer of 1971 headed west to the lure of Hollywood, returning after 18 months a wiser but not a wealthier man. Soon after, he was tempted back into publishing by his friend Larry Herndon who ran the comic-book publisher Nostalgia, Inc. Herndon's outfit produced magazines wallowing in nostalgia such as *Remember When* and *Yesterday's Comics*, and for some reason he believed that *Trumpet* would work within his set-up and be a profitable venture. Reamy went along with it. Nostalgia, Inc. became the publisher of the

11 Harry Warner, Jr., *A Wealth of Fable* (Van Nuys: SCIFI Press, 1992), p. 224.

magazine, and took over the title, with Reamy as editor, assisted by Ken Keller. However, Reamy soon found that he had problems with the firm. Despite the large print run, Nostalgia, Inc. was reluctant to send out review copies, and there were delays in publishing the issue, which did not appear until 1974. The issue was one of the smallest, only 32 pages, yet sold for $1. It had two minor pieces of fiction and reprinted Ellison's '"Repent, Harlequin!" said the Ticktockman'. There was the usual mix of letters and articles plus art portfolios by Robert Kline and Stephen Fabian (who also did the cover), but the issue lacked the soul of the earlier ones. Its most interesting content was Reamy's account of his time in Hollywood working on the film *Flesh Gordon*.

Having effectively lost control of *Trumpet*, and having moved to Kansas City, Reamy set up the Nickelodeon Graphic Arts Service and began a new magazine, the rather audacious *Nickelodeon*, to all intents 'son of *Trumpet*'. It looked exactly the same, with the same mix of chat, articles, poetry, artwork and fiction. It had the rather dubious addition of a full-frontal nude centrefold: Stephen Utley in the first issue, and Jim Thomas and Fran Calhoun in the second. Reamy believed that fans favoured the photographs,[12] but Ken Keller, who co-produced the magazine, thought that readers found them of little merit and that their presence harmed sales.[13]

The fiction was of some interest. The first issue included 'The Very Old Badger Game' by Wilson Tucker, which was the original ending of Tucker's novel *The Long Loud Silence*. There was also a spoof Lovecraft story, 'Riders of the Purple Ooze', by Joe Pumilia and Bill Wallace writing as 'M. M. Moamrath'. The second issue ran Howard Waldrop's poignant tribute to the Golden Age of Hollywood comedy, 'Save a Place in the Lifeboat for Me'.

There was plenty of beautiful artwork. The first issue featured a cover by Richard Corben and there was work in both issues by James Odbert, Roger Stine, Tim Kirk, George Barr, Vincent di Fate and William Rotsler. Reamy had planned to issue *Nickelodeon* quarterly but by the time of the second issue, he was so busy writing professionally that he could no longer sustain it and the magazine lapsed, although most of the third issue had been prepared. Reamy died before he could publish it.

Ken Keller salvaged that third issue and eventually published it as *Trumpet* #12, in the summer of 1981.[14] It featured another Lovecraft spoof

---

12 See interview with Reamy, *Shayol* #1 (November 1977), p. 40.

13 See Ken Keller's editorial to *Trumpet* #12 (Summer 1981), p. 3.

14 In fact, Keller had all but completed the magazine a year earlier, as he reported in *Science Fiction Chronicle* #8 (May 1980) that the issue was being printed and that a thirteenth issue was in preparation.

by Moamrath, and the usual mix of art and articles, but this was more of a tribute issue. *Trumpet* had long since passed into nostalgia but it had left its mark by showing what production values could be achieved by amateurs, even with limited budgets, and served as a model for other aspiring publishers of the seventies. Amongst these was arguably the most beautiful semi-pro fantasy magazine of the period, *Shayol*.

In 1972 the Robert E. Howard amateur-press organization, REHupa, was founded by Tim Marion and led to an explosion of Howard-related magazines. In 1974, teenage Howard fans Arnie Fenner and Byron Roark of the Shawnee Mission in Kansas, believing they could do more with a Howard magazine than *Amra*, brought out *REH: Lone Star Fictioneer*, the first issue dated Spring 1975. It was published in large-flat format on good-quality paper, running to 48 pages for the first issue, and more for later issues. It was devoted to the works of Robert E. Howard, including articles about his writings or what they inspired, especially artwork, with full-colour covers and portfolios by John Severin, Alan Weiss and Marcus Boas, and interviews with Roy Thomas, Barry Smith and others. It reprinted some Howard material from lesser-known sources, but is most collectable today because it ran several previously unpublished historical stories by Howard, including the novellas 'Sword Woman' and 'Three Bladed Doom'. The first two issues had print runs of only 500 each, but it shot up to 2,500 with issue #3 and 3,000 for issue #4. Those issues were typeset by Pat Cadigan, Fenner's future wife, who worked at Tom Reamy's Nickelodeon Graphics business in Kansas.

The magazine ran for four quarterly issues until Spring 1976, but had clearly already outgrown itself. Fenner wanted to broaden the magazine's appeal and not focus solely on Howard. So, *REH: Lone Star Fictioneer* was retired and *Chacal* was born, its first issue dated Winter 1976. *Chacal* retained some Howard material, either by him or imitative work by David C. Smith and Karl Edward Wagner, but also ran a greater variety of material. This included Howard Waldrop's extravagant 'Der Untergang des Abendlandesmenschen', an eccentric, expressionist vampire detective story. There were art portfolios by Tim Kirk and Jeff Easley, an interview with C. L. Moore, Tom Reamy's story 'Mistress of Windraven' and an article on Hannes Bok. *Chacal* was nominated for the World Fantasy Award and Waldrop's short story short-listed for the British Fantasy Award.

Thereafter Roark and Fenner disagreed on the direction of the magazine. *Chacal* #2 (Spring 1977) was produced by Fenner with Pat Cadigan, now under the Daemon Graphic imprint. It was superficially similar to the first issue with another eccentric story by Waldrop, a Kane story by Wagner, portfolios by Kirk and Jim Fitzpatrick, an interview with Manly Wade

Wellman, and a new M. M. Moamrath story, 'The Next to the Last Voyage of the Cuttle Sark', this time under the writers' real names of Bill Wallace and Joe Pumilia. But Fenner had brought a focus to his creative vision with the format and overall design, resulting in a more professional gloss. Pat Cadigan came on board as associate editor, bemoaning the lack of women in past issues and hoping to change that. The issue ran her first published story, 'Last Chance For Angina Pectoris at Miss Sadie's Saloon, Dry Gulch', an amusing forecast of one way of dying happy amongst the asteroids.

Fenner felt that *Chacal* was being overlooked because it was still viewed as a Howard-zine, and it needed a greater circulation to meet the cost of production. So, another change occurred. *Chacal* folded and *Shayol* was born, with a new imprint, Flight Unlimited, in Kansas City. The first issue was dated November 1977. Tom Reamy was listed as art director and consultant. Cadigan was listed as editor but, as she later commented, it was all Fenner's vision:

> I left all the design and art decisions to Arnie, and we looked at the fiction together, but really Arnie should get just about all the credit for *Shayol*. He put the most sweat and thought and everything into it. I just picked some of the fiction, and he'd hold up designs saying, 'How's this?' I was the editor, and I did editing, but we did pick fiction together.[15]

Shayol was a beautiful slick magazine, printed on quality, coated stock with artwork or photographs on almost every page. Fenner had hoped to sell the 64-page package for $2 but the smaller print run they did for the first issue (2,500 copies) pushed the price to $3. Gardner Dozois regarded Roger Stine's cover, 'Flight', which depicted a tethered creature trying to capture a butterfly while balloons vanish into the distance as 'the most beautiful cover of the year'.[16] There was little remaining of the Howard content of past incarnations, though Karl Wagner contributed an article on the origins of his doomed character Kane. There was a Hobbit portfolio by Jeff Easley, and a Celtic portfolio by Jim Fitzpatrick, an interview with Tom Reamy and an article by Michael Bishop on book reviews, but otherwise the issue was predominantly fiction. This format remained steady for all issues of *Shayol*: beautiful covers, internal art portfolios and artist or author interviews. Prominent artists were Tim Kirk, Clyde Caldwell, Robert Haas, Vikki Marshall, Hank Jankus and Thomas Blackshear.

The quality of the fiction was variable, but it was always different and exciting. Perhaps their star contributor, certainly the most unconventional,

15 Interview with Pat Cadigan, *Nova Express* 3:1 (Fall 1989), p. 13.
16 See *Shayol* 3:1, 1985, p. 29.

was Howard Waldrop. Waldrop's fiction was always unclassifiable, which is why so little of it appeared in the professional magazines at the time but instead was to be found in the specialist anthologies or semi-professional magazines. Frequently spoofing sf and movie icons, Waldrop's work, rather like Lafferty's, ranged from surreal to eccentric, but was never dull. His contributions included 'Dr. Hudson's Secret Gorilla' (November 1977), 'All About Strange Monsters of the Recent Past' (Winter 1980) and his potent attack on racism, 'Horror, We Got' (#3, Summer 1979). Waldrop acknowledged his debt to *Shayol* in his collection *Howard Who?* where he commented that the magazine paid promptly, that his work was respected and that it was presented in an attractive and beautiful form. Moreover, he remarked that the contributors to *Shayol* were 'a Who's Who of everyone who was trying to do something with the SF or fantasy short story'.[17]

Other important contributors included Harlan Ellison, Tom Reamy, Michael Bishop, Lisa Tuttle and Steven Utley (often pseudonymously), making the most of an active circle of Texan writers of the seventies.[18] Reamy's 'Wonder Show' in the first issue was an excerpt from his first novel, at that time unpublished, *Blind Voices*, while 'Blue Eyes' (#3, Summer 1979) was the seed for what was hoped to be a new novel set in a post-apocalypse native culture. *Shayol* paid a variable rate for fiction, starting at around one and a half cents a word in the early issues but rising for some of the big-name authors and averaging 4 cents a word over its run. For cover art he paid around $300, a respectable professional rate for the period.

Shayol was the peak of semi-professional magazine publication in the seventies and has scarcely been bettered since, even with desktop publishing. It showed what could be achieved when those with artistic vision and creative imagination combined their talents. Fenner told me, 'we didn't know what we were doing; we just learned as we went. If we'd really known what we were doing we would have either been much more successful, or been smart enough not to do it at all and save ourselves a lot of work and money!'[19]

The cost of producing *Shayol* was steep and it only just broke even, but Fenner was not in it for the financial return, but for producing a quality product, and *Shayol* was that in every way. It allowed writers and artists a forum in which to experiment and to see their work in a visually stunning context.

17 Howard Waldrop, *Strange Things in Close Up* (London: Legend, 1989), p. 35.

18 George W. Proctor and Steven Utley compiled a showcase anthology of Texan sf and fantasy, *Lone Star Universe* (Austin, TX: Heldelberg Publishers, 1976), which included Bruce Sterling's first professional sale.

19 Personal e-mail, Fenner/Ashley, 23 July 2006.

The print run varied from issue to issue, peaking at 10,000 for issue #6 (Winter 1982), which ran Ellison's story 'Prince Myshkin, and Hold the Relish'. With that number, it verged on professional status. *Shayol* was distributed by Bud Plant whose positive promotion managed to shift the majority of copies in time. There were very few subscriptions to the magazine.[20]

Usually Fenner waited until the previous issue sold out before producing the next, so the magazine appeared on an erratic schedule, at the rate of approximately one a year, with a much delayed seventh and final issue in 1985. By then Fenner, who worked full-time for Hallmark Cards, was also spending more time on design work for others, and Pat Cadigan was developing her writing career. It was an end to an era that had started with *Trumpet* 20 years before.

Graphic Developments

There were other magazines, like *Shayol*, that emphasized the shift towards the visual exploration of sf and fantasy images. We have seen how this interest manifested itself in Britain with *Science Fiction Monthly*. The development in America was, not surprisingly, more dramatic and more effective. In the autumn of 1976 Thomas Durwood's Morning Star Press, also in Kansas, produced the first issue of *Ariel*, at this time labelled 'a fantasy magazine'. It looked more like a large-format, soft-covered coffee-table book, with the emphasis on art and illustration.

The feature artists in this issue were Burne Hogarth, Frank Frazetta (the subject of an interview) and Richard Corben. Corben provided the cover, plus the start of a comic strip, 'Den', and an extract from his graphic novel, *Bloodstar*, just published by Morning Star Press. Though not the first graphic novel to be published, *Bloodstar*, adapted from Robert E. Howard's 'Valley of the Worm', from *Weird Tales*, was one of the first books to label itself as such on the cover. Graphic novels, sometimes called visual novels, were not exactly new. They were essentially an outgrowth of some of the more mature comic-book novels and underground comics that had appeared as a way of circumventing the Comics Code of 1954 by converting comics into magazines or books.

Ariel worked as a showcase for the graphic novel scene, with the emphasis on fantasy and science fiction. With the second volume, now subtitled 'the Book of Fantasy', there was new work by Harlan Ellison

---

20 In a personal e-mail, 23 July 2006, Fenner believed there were never more than fifty subscribers, and those to the first four issues only.

and there were reprints by Ray Bradbury and Michael Moorcock and the transcription of a talk by Ursula Le Guin, 'Science Fiction Chauvinism'. The latter showed that *Ariel* sought to have a mature appreciation of sf and fantasy, rather than simply excellent graphics. The final two volumes, which were co-published and distributed by Ballantine Books in April and October 1978, were even larger and more extravagant, taking fantasy artwork to new heights. It ran artwork by Barry Windsor-Smith, Michael Hague, Bruce Jones, Tim Conrad and Al Williamson plus a new Elric story by Michael Moorcock and other stories, poems and vignettes by Larry Niven, Roger Zelazny, Harlan Ellison and Jane Yolen.

The cost of reproducing colour art at that time was expensive and *Ariel* needed good sales and a high price to cover costs, but even selling at $7.95 on the fourth and final volume,[21] sales were not sufficient and the series was dropped. Its presence had been highly visible, though, and had introduced to a wider fantasy market some of the artists who had been making a name for themselves in the underground comics, in particular Richard Corben.

Corben's artwork was always adult in nature, and the 'graphic novel', a term which is descriptive in both interpretations of the adjective, was one route by which the growing mass of underground comics surfaced. The underground comics press had been growing since the mid-sixties and had been predicted by Harvey Kurtzman in *Mad* back in 1954,[22] as a result of the Comics Code. The Comics Code had been introduced (or more accurately considerably revised from an impotent 1948 version) in 1954 following a report by Dr Frederic Wertham on the harmful nature of some of the imagery depicted in crime and horror comics. The background to this was discussed in *Transformations*. The Code actually forbade any depiction of ghouls, vampires, zombies and werewolves or any graphic or glorified violence. Overnight the horror comics vanished, taking with them most of the more lurid science-fiction comics. Only those depicting the clean-cut crime-fighting superheroes continued, provided that there was no excessive violence.

The Code, though, only applied to comics intended for sale to children. It did not apply to adult magazines. So it was possible to circumvent the Code by producing comics to be sold only to adults. This usually meant that they carried a higher cover price and were bigger than traditional comics in both their dimensions and their pagination. Comic magazines tended to be standard A4 size, the same size as standard slick magazines. The more adult comics tended to be sold privately or kept beneath the

21 The first volume had been $5.95, and the next two $6.95.
22 Harvey Kurtzman, 'Comics Go Underground', *Mad* #16 (October 1954).

counter and they soon became known as underground comics, or 'comix' for short.

The magazine that did most to establish the adult underground comic was *Zap*, from Robert Crumb, which appeared in early 1968 and which popularized the spelling of 'comix' for the alternative press. But the magazine more closely associated with the sf scene was Wally Wood's *Witzend*, which appeared in the summer of 1966. Wood was one of the master comic artists. He had worked for EC's *Weird Science* and *Weird Fantasy* from the start, in 1950, and was later one of the mainstay talents in *Mad*. He also illustrated some of the sf pulps, including *Planet Stories* in its last days, and was a regular contributor to *Galaxy*.

Witzend was one of a number of independent amateur magazines which emerged during a growing turbulence in the comic-book field, and though *Witzend* grew out of that it was sufficiently professional to be regarded as a fully independent 'prozine', despite a print run of only a few thousand. Wood championed the artists, allowing them to keep the copyright in their work (which was normally owned by the publisher), and giving them artistic freedom. The magazine's emphasis was on science fiction. The first issue salvaged Al Williamson's post-holocaust comic-strip 'Savage World', which had been drawn in 1954 for the comic *Buster Crabbe* but had not been used because the magazine had failed. Wood updated the strip with a new script. The magazine appeared whenever Wood could finance it, with just two issues in 1967 and a fourth in 1968. These issues contain work by Steve Ditko, Roy Krenkel, Frank Frazetta, Art Spiegelman, a portfolio of Edgar Rice Burroughs characters by Reed Crandall, and Gray Morrow's incomplete serial, 'Orion'. Wood contributed his own strip featuring Animan and, more importantly, from issue #4, his narrative story 'The World of the Wizard King', a fantasy inspired by *Lord of the Rings*.

Wood, needing to return to full-time work, sold *Witzend* to his friend Bill Pearson after issue #4, with the condition that it honour existing subscriptions for at least four more issues. Pearson's first issue, dated October 1968, of which he printed 5,000 copies, promised a new Conan-like strip, Talon, illustrated by Jim Steranko, but the full story was never completed. Over the next few issues Vaughn Bodé, Berni Wrightson, Jeff Jones and Howard Chaykin were added to the contributors. *Witzend*'s irregular schedule became even more irregular after the eighth issue in Summer 1971, and only five more issues appeared over the next 14 years, with increasingly less fantasy content.

Running parallel to the underground magazines was the emergence of comics in magazine format. It was James Warren, the publisher of *Famous*

Monsters of Filmland who made this simple and very profitable move in January 1965 when he launched *Creepy*, followed by *Eerie* in March 1966 and *Vampirella* in October 1969. *Creepy* and *Eerie* were magazine versions of the fifties *Vault of Horror* and similar titles, with a 'host', Cousin Creepy or Uncle Eerie, introducing a series of stories, all illustrated in black-and-white rather than colour. Although the first issue of *Creepy* focused on the usual popular monsters – vampires, werewolves and the Frankenstein monster – from issue #2 it began the serialization of Otto Binder's Adam Link series, starting with 'I, Robot', illustrated by Joe Orlando. Archie Goodwin adapted a number of classic weird tales by Edgar Allan Poe, Ambrose Bierce and Bram Stoker, usually illustrated by Gray Morrow, with other adaptations of work by Robert Louis Stevenson, Rudyard Kipling and Sheridan Le Fanu, illustrated by Frank Frazetta, Reed Crandall or Dan Adkins. Warren suffered a financial setback during 1968, which caused the magazines to reprint items from other Warren publications, and it was not until 1970 that *Creepy* and *Eerie* were back on their feet, now supported by *Vampirella.*

Vampirella, like Cousin Creepy, was the host of her magazine. The character had been created by Forrest Ackerman. She came from the planet Drakulon where blood flows like water. The planet, though, is frequently in peril from its unstable sun, but Vampirella manages to escape in a spaceship from Earth. Once on Earth, Vampirella becomes a heroine fighting Earth's evil vampires, a prototype Buffy. Ackerman and Donald F. Glut wrote most of the early storylines, with art by Tom Sutton and Mike Royer, and covers by Frazetta, Bodé, Ken Kelly and Bill Hughes before the clique of Spanish artists took over. *Vampirella* proved extremely popular and was the longest-surviving of the magazines, reaching 112 issues in March 1983. It was sold to Harris Publications and revived in 1988.

The success of Warren's black-and-white comic magazines caused other publishers to try the same. The most experimental of the leading comic-book publishers was Marvel Comics, who established their own black-and-white competitor with *Savage Tales* in May 1971. Marvel's publisher, Martin Goodman, who had founded *Marvel Comics* in 1939, named after his successful sf pulp, *Marvel Science Stories*, had retired[23] in 1972 and his wife's nephew, Stan Lee, the editor-in-chief, had taken over. While Lee sustained the core money-earning comics, he was always prepared to try something new.

23 Goodman continued to publish magazines and produced one of the worst of all sf magazines, *Skyworlds*, published by his company Humorama, Inc., with his brother Abraham. *Skyworlds*, edited by Jeff Stevens, lasted four quarterly issues from November 1977 to August 1978. It was an 80-page digest, looked cheap (though sold for 75 cents) and reprinted material mostly from early-fifties issues of *Marvel Science Fiction*.

Marvel Comics had already breached the Comics Code with three special issues of *Spider-Man* running May to July 1971. These were published in response to a request from the Department of Health, Education and Welfare asking whether Marvel could run a story dealing with the dangers of drugs. While the 1954 Code did not refer explicitly to drugs, the implication remained that they could not be glorified or shown to be good. Lee, however, felt that there was good reason to develop the story. This became a major factor in the revision of the Comics Code in 1971, which now made any reference to drugs explicit. If anything, the 1971 Code was more restrictive, but it now allowed references to drugs if it was in order to emphasize a moral code. The same applied to attitudes to sex and violence. Comics, therefore, continued on their puritan way, and the lack of any other relaxation in the Code led to more underground comix and to 'adult' magazines.

Several publishers followed this route in the early seventies. Of these, the most relevant to this history is Marvel's attempt to produce an adult science-fiction comic-book magazine. It took a circuitous route. Initially Marvel published a standard 36-page, 20-cent colour comic, *Worlds Unknown*, starting in May 1973. It adapted several important short sf stories. These included 'The Day After the Day the Martians Came' by Frederik Pohl and 'He That Hath Wings' by Edmond Hamilton in issue #1, 'A Gun for Dinosaur' by L. Sprague de Camp in issue #2, 'Farewell to the Master' by Harry Bates in #3, 'Arena' by Fredric Brown in #4, 'Black Destroyer' by A. E. van Vogt in #5 and 'Killdozer' by Theodore Sturgeon in #6. The adaptations were chiefly by Gerry Conway and Roy Thomas, with art mostly by Angelo Torres, Dan Adkins and Dick Ayers. The magazine ran for eight bi-monthly issues and folded in August 1974. Some issues sold better than others, and editor Roy Thomas believed that the format was too constricting, as they could only focus on one or two stories per issue. He concluded, 'if the casual reader didn't happen to like that particular theme, it was no go for the entire package – and no sale on the *next* ish, in all probability'.[24] He believed that the real answer was to adopt the larger magazine format, selling for 80 cents or $1, which allowed more scope and variety and was likely to engage more interest.

So *Worlds Unknown* was revamped and became *Unknown Worlds of Science Fiction*, issued as an 80-page magazine selling for $1, with the first issue dated January 1975. Hoping for a more sophisticated readership, Thomas, and his associate editor Gerry Conway, tried an experiment. As their 'host', they adapted Bob Shaw's slow-glass concept as the framing device through which to view the various stories. Bob Shaw was delighted

24 Roy Thomas, 'Editorial', *Unknown Worlds of Science Fiction* 1:1 (January 1975), p. 4.

with the idea[25] and Marvel further developed slow glass (in a storyline by Tony Isabella) to make it of extraterrestrial origin, introduced to Earth by the mysterious character of 'the Peddler'.

Unknown Worlds not only adapted several well-known sf stories and novels, including John Wyndham's 'The Day of the Triffids', Alfred Bester's 'Adam and No Eve', Harlan Ellison's '"Repent, Harlequin!" said the Ticktockman', Robert Silverberg's 'Good News from the Vatican', Larry Niven's 'All the Myriad Ways' and Michael Moorcock's 'Behold the Man' (which yielded a striking if inaccurate cover by Frank Brunner), it also ran several new stories plus author interviews. Those interviewed included Ray Bradbury (#1), Alfred Bester (#2), Frank Herbert (#3), A. E. van Vogt (#4), Larry Niven (#5) and Bob Shaw (#6). Amongst the new stories were Tony Isabella's 'War Toy' (#1), which considered what you do with robots built for war in peacetime, and 'Addict' by Donald F. Glut (#5), about the need of man still to be able to dream in a regimented future.

Unknown Worlds was an excellent magazine, taking new sf seriously and trying to bring it to a wider audience. Unfortunately, the way in which such stories were interpreted made them less appealing to younger readers than the usual superhero fare. Ted White was of the view that the magazine was 'condescending' and that it 'failed to approach even the standards set down in the early fifties by EC – in either art or story'.[26] Although sales were good, they were not good enough. The magazine was dropped after its sixth issue, in November 1975. Even then, Roy Thomas and Stan Lee felt that it should have one more chance. An enlarged 92-page annual was issued for Christmas 1976, selling at $1.25. It was dedicated to the memory of Stanley G. Weinbaum and ran an adaptation, by Donald Glut, of 'A Martian Odyssey'. It also reran Gerry Conway's adaptation of Fredric Brown's 'Arena', plus several stories by Bruce Jones and an interview with Theodore Sturgeon. Had this issue sold sufficiently well, the magazine might yet have been revived, but apparently it didn't, as nothing more was seen. In his editorial, Thomas had observed that generally sf comics did not sell well unless cast into the superhero or fantasy mould. The gulf between the sf comic and the traditional sf magazine thus seemed as wide as ever, so far as the readership was concerned.

The same fate befell *Starstream*, which was Roger Elwood's attempt to edit a science-fiction comic. It was published by the Western Publishing Company, an imprint of Whitman, a company owned by Dell Publishing. It was an all-colour comic, its 64 pages selling for 79 cents and it ran

25 Bob Shaw, letter in *Unknown Worlds of Science Fiction* 1:3 (May 1975), p. 80.
26 Ted White, 'My Column', *Thrust* #9 (Fall 1977), p. 13.

for just four issues, starting August 1976. Elwood acquired the rights to several excellent stories, well suited to adaptations. The headline stories over the four issues were John W. Campbell's 'Who Goes There?' (#1), Larry Niven's 'Flight of the Horse' and Dean Koontz's 'Night of the Storm' (both #2), Jack Williamson's 'Born of the Sun' and Theodore Sturgeon's 'Microcosmic God' (both #3) and Poul Anderson's 'Call Me Joe' (#4). Unfortunately, the adaptations were often too drastic and the artwork, mostly by Frank Bolle and Alden McWilliams too basic, even dated, so that *Starstream* fell between two camps – being perhaps too advanced for younger readers but too immature for older ones. It was also very expensive to produce and the cover price was too low, so its failure seemed inevitable.

Something very different was needed.

One of the great discoveries in Warren's magazines was Richard Corben, who first appeared in the November 1970 *Creepy* with the story 'Frozen Beauty', a fairy-tale of a countess who steals a young girl's beauty. Corben, who had studied at the Kansas City Art Institute, had previously produced some artwork for underground comics, starting with 'Monsters Rule', an sf story serialized in the tabloid newsletter of comic fandom, *Voice of Comicdom*, during 1968. This early work, including his material for Warren's magazines, was in black-and-white but it was his colour work that would establish his name. His first colour strip was 'Cidopey' in the first issue of *Up from the Deep* (1971) and this reappeared in 1974 in the magazine that brought him worldwide acclaim, *Métal Hurlant*.[27]

Métal Hurlant was created by the French artists Jean Giraud, Philippe Druillet and Bernard Farkas and the writer Jean-Pierre Dionnet, who together formed the collective Les Humanoïdes Associés in 1974. The first issue appeared just before Christmas 1974 with 68 pages, 18 in colour, selling for 8 francs.[28] Originally planned on a quarterly basis (the first issue effectively Spring 1975), it switched to bi-monthly in January 1976 and monthly from October 1976. Featured in the first four issues was Jean Giraud's enigmatic, wordless, surreal graphic story 'Arzach'. Drawn under the alias 'Moebius', which Giraud reserved for his fantasy work, 'Arzach' is set in a dream-like world where the eponymous hero flies on the back of an ancient reptilian creature and undergoes various (often sexual) adventures. The lack of a script leaves 'Arzach' open to endless interpretation, which is one of its strengths, and it can be read as an allegory, a satire or a plain but unexplained adventure.

27 Data for publication sources of Corben's early material is drawn from the website, 'The Most Complete Comicography of Richard Corben' at http://www.muuta.net/.
28 At that time roughly $1.78 or about £0.75.

The graphic story had a significant profile in Europe, especially amongst French-speaking countries, where it was treated as serious adult entertainment and not juvenile cartoons as in the United States. The best known of the continental graphic stories have been *The Adventures of Tintin*, created by the Belgian artist Georges Remi, working under the alias Hergé, in 1929, and *Astérix the Gaul*, created by René Goscinny and Albert Udozo in 1959. The latter series began in the magazine *Pilote*, launched by Goscinny, Udozo and others as a showcase for French graphic artists. It was here that Jean Giraud established his reputation with his western hero, 'Blueberry', which started in 1963. Philippe Druillet was another regular in *Pilote* where he developed his character of Lone Sloane, which also transferred to *Métal Hurlant*. Set far in the future, Lone Sloane, who is adrift in space after an accident, is suddenly whipped into an alternate alien universe where he battles for survival and understanding.

The works of Druillet and Giraud set the standard for *Métal Hurlant*. In addition to 'Azrach', Giraud created a new series, 'Le Garage hermétique' ('The Airtight Garage'), which included Michael Moorcock's character Jerry Cornelius. It is set in a huge hollow asteroid which houses a variety of odd societies and which is under constant threat from outside forces.

This magazine was ideal for Corben. His work was featured on the cover of the third issue (Autumn 1976), which also began his series about Den. Den is a weak adolescent boy who is transported to a Burroughsian-style world where he becomes a muscular man, bald and always totally nude, who undergoes various fantasy and sexual adventures. Den had been created by Corben for a short animated film, *Neverwhere*, in 1968 and adapted for the magazine *Grim Wit* in 1973, but the appearance in *Métal Hurlant* was the first full version, serialized over four issues. It was these abstract, surreal, erotic works by Giraud, Druillet and Corben that gave *Métal Hurlant* its character and appeal and caused it to stand apart from other magazines on the market.

In the meantime, *Pilote* had licensed a comic page from *National Lampoon*, the US humour and satire magazine, which had been published since April 1970. When *Pilote* sent through a published copy, it alerted the publishers to the nature and content of the French comic magazines. When *Métal Hurlant* was launched, Sean Kelly, senior editor of *National Lampoon*, saw its potential and recommended to *National Lampoon*'s owner, Matty Simmons, the idea of producing a US edition. They saw its wider potential, its mixture of eroticism, satire and fantasy imagery being well suited to the growing market for US adult 'comix'.

Simmons acquired the licence and the first US issue, now renamed

Heavy Metal,[29] went on sale in mid-March 1977 (dated April), with Sean Kelly as editor. The first issue led with a reprint of Corben's 'Den', now as a 13-part serial, which was followed almost immediately by Corben's adaptation of 'New Tales of the Arabian Nights', scripted by Jan Strnad (June 1978–July 1979). Corben was represented in almost every issue of *Heavy Metal* during its first decade, including serialization of the first colour version of 'Bloodstar' (December 1980–July 1981) and a new 18-part Den serial, 'Den II' (September 1981–March 1983), and his imagery became almost synonymous with the magazine.

At the start, *Heavy Metal* drew most of its material from the French edition, but it also included some home-grown material. The first issue began a complete serialization of Vaughn Bodé's 'Sunpot' (April–July 1977), which had suffered so egregiously in *Galaxy*. It also ran an excerpt from Terry Brooks's novel, *The Sword of Shannara*, and over the next few months there were text stories by Roger Zelazny and Harlan Ellison. Gray Morrow's 'Orion', which had remained incomplete in *Witzend*, now appeared in full (December 1978),[30]. and there was new work by artists Howard Chaykin, Tom Barber, Angus McKie, Marcus Boas, Steve Fabian and Clyde Caldwell.

The first issue of *Heavy Metal* had guaranteed advertisers a sale of 150,000 copies and very soon it was selling 200,000 copies.[31] It paid authors ten cents a word,[32] twice that of any of the standard sf magazines. However, after a year its circulation seemed to have hit a ceiling and the publishers did not think that that was high enough.[33] Their view was

---

29 *Métal Hurlant* translates as 'screaming metal' but 'heavy metal' was a more suitable name because of its associations with the American pop culture, especially the drug scene and hard-rock music. The phrase may have originated with William S. Burroughs, who coined the nickname 'the heavy metal kid' for one of his characters in *The Soft Machine* (1962) and used it as a metaphor for addictive drugs in *Nova Express* (1964). The phrase was used by the graphic designers Michael English and Nigel Waymouth, who operated as Hapshash and the Coloured Coat, and released a psychedelic-music album in 1967 as *Featuring the Heavenly Host and the Heavy Metal Kids*.

30 Morrow's 'Orion' had also appeared in the magazine *Hot Stuf'*, which was remarkably prescient of *Métal Hurlant*. It was published by Sal Quartuccio and saw eight issues from Summer 1974 to Winter 1978. Its print run rose from 2,500 for the first issue to 15,000 for the last three.

31 This is the figure reported in *The Comics Journal* #59 (October 1980), p. 17. Locus #223 (July 1979), reported the figure as 300,000, but the total paid circulation reported for the year 1977/78 was 202,818.

32 That was the wordage rate reported in *Locus* #199 (February 1977), p. 1. Ted White reported that he paid an average of 15 cents a word (see *Thrust* #43/4, Spring/Summer 1993, p. 28), while Henry Morrison reported that Richard Lupoff was paid 20 cents a word (see *Thrust* #10, Spring 1978, p. 10).

33 The average paid circulation in the first year (1976/7) was 144,232 and for the next two years was 202,818 and 204,015.

that the magazine lacked depth for US readers. It could be read relatively quickly and it needed something extra to sustain reader interest. Sean Kelly had been unable to devote as much time to the magazine as originally planned and the work had fallen, by default, to Simmons's daughter, Julie. However, in August 1979, Leonard Mogel, the magazine's publisher, brought in Ted White as editor, mostly on the recommendation of David Hartwell. This was just six months after White had stepped down as editor of *Amazing* and *Fantastic*.

White was delighted to become editor. 'If there is one magazine in the world that I want to edit, it is *Heavy Metal'*,he wrote.[34] His editorship became effective from the January 1980 issue. His answer was to remove all of the text stories, continue to develop the graphic art as stories rather than 'comix', and to introduce further text, which he did by way of columns covering science fiction (by Steve Brown), films (Bhob Stewart), music (Lou Stathis) and underground comics (Jay Kinney), with additional features on rock music. He toned down some of the more extreme, sado-masochistic material from *Métal Hurlant* and aimed for a good mix of light and dark:

> My mandate, when I was hired, was to *increase* the amount of printed text in the magazine. It was thought this would bring in more advertising. My notion was to integrate the text with the comics. This was, in fact, a modification of the design I'd presented to Sol Cohen years earlier for a larger-sized *Amazing* – and used again in *Stardate* to integrate articles and fiction – which I worked out in execution with art director John Workman. My ideas excited John and we worked closely to redesign *Heavy Metal*. Some of the strips ran vertically or horizontally through the text where it was continued to the back of the magazine. The artists, once they learned about this idea, loved it and kept coming up with new ways to exploit it. The end result was a *magazine* rather than a scrapbook of comics, which had been the case with the late 1979 issues.[35]

White revised translations of the scripts from the French edition, casting them in an American idiom. Steve Stiles illustrated a new strip, 'The Adventures of Professor Thintwistle and his Incredible Aether Flyer' (from February 1980), a wonderful steampunk yarn scripted by Richard Lupoff. There was art by Tito Salomoni, Angus McKie, Chris Achilleos, H. R. Giger, Jim Burns and Guido Crepax, plus a series on eroticism by Jean Giraud. Martin Springett's detailed, surreal artwork for his own story 'Awaken' (November 1980) is especially notable.

34 Ted White, 'My Column', *Thrust* #14 (Winter 1980), p. 9.
35 Personal e-mail, White/Ashley, 4 September 2006.

There was an inevitable reaction to White's changes from readers. The May 1980 letter column was full of howlings from readers who, from their general tone, seemed almost unable to read text and only ever looked through *Heavy Metal* for the pictures when they were stoned. A more literate sample of the readers responded with more positive comments in the October issue but there was still an underlying feeling that the majority of readers did not like the changes. Towards the end of the year, White was told that sales had not improved and that management were uncertain about the value of the new columns. Whereas they felt that the magazine should be tapping into the interest in popular media events, White was all for pursuing lesser-known material. White felt that *Heavy Metal* should be leading, not following, whereas management wanted the popular not the esoteric. According to White, no one in management had spoken to him about tapping into popular media events, something he was in fact planning.

Although White told me that he later learned that sales had not fallen but had actually peaked during his editorship, this is not borne out by the Annual Statement of Circulation, which shows a drop to 183,886 in 1979/80 and to 172,116 in 1980/81. White believes he was fired for more personal reasons concerning problems between the publisher, Leonard Mogel, who had been demoted as president of the company, and the company's owner, Matty Simmons. Mogel thereafter assumed the editorship from the December 1980 issue, though most of the work fell to Julie Simmons. White was bitterly disappointed: 'It was easily the best editorial job I've ever had; one I'd been born to.'[36]

White's changes had improved the overall quality of a magazine that was otherwise superficially attractive but had little substance, but the evidence suggests that this was not what readers wanted. So while *Heavy Metal* may have attracted a significant readership, greater than any of the traditional sf magazines, it was not likely to take away many of their readers.

It was a period of uncertainty. *Métal Hurlant* was in a financial crisis and *Heavy Metal* seemed to have lost direction. Both would recover, though *Métal Hurlant* ceased publication in July 1987, and *Heavy Metal*, which reached a peak of sales in 1981/2 of 234,000 before a rapid fall-off, reduced its schedule in 1986. It has survived, but it has ceased to have the impact or influence of its early years. Nevertheless, it had shown what the marriage of graphic art and sf/fantasy could achieve, something that White and others had wanted to do years before. White had mused over the fact that his budget for each issue of *Heavy Metal* had been as much as

36 Ibid.

all 12 issues of *Amazing* and *Fantastic* for a year, and that he earned more in one year with the magazine than he had in all the ten years working for Sol Cohen. Even then, though, White had not been able to progress *Heavy Metal* beyond its original template because of differences of opinion. All too often in the story of the sf magazine, vision and business don't mix.

But sometimes they do. At the same time that *Heavy Metal* was following the erotic and graphic, a new comix magazine emerged in Britain that followed the traditional route but with a more adult and violent content. This was *2000 AD*, published by IPC Magazines and developed by editor Pat Mills and writer John Wagner. Its first issue, dated 26 February 1977, was in the traditional quarto-sized, 32-page, British-weekly-comic format, selling for 8 pence.

The team had already had much success but equal notoriety with their comic *Action*, which had been running for just a year when *2000 AD* appeared. *Action* had contained, in the eyes of many, excessive violence and gore, especially the serial 'Kids Rule OK', scripted by Jack Adrian and illustrated by Mike White. It is set in London in the mid-1980s after a plague has wiped out all adults, and children are running wild. The outcry against the magazine led to the 23 October 1976 issue being pulped, and the magazine was hastily revised and relaunched in a toned-down manner the following month. Sales soon diminished, though, and the magazine folded.

When developing *2000 AD*, Mills and Wagner wanted to retain the anti-authoritarian tone with as much violence as they could reasonably sustain without causing controversy. One route was to bring back a comic strip featuring a clean-cut hero who had saved magazines before in moments of strife and that was Dan Dare, which had run in *The Eagle* during the fifties and sixties. For this series, Dan Dare had been placed in suspended animation and revived two centuries hence. The initial reincarnation had little in common with the original Dan Dare and did not prove popular, but was soon revamped into a space-opera series, not unlike *Star Trek*, with Dan Dare on various deep-space missions. Mills and Kelvin Gosnell, who became the first editor of *2000 AD* after its launch, also devised the gimmick that the magazine was edited by an alien, Tharg the Mighty, about whom occasional story-lines also appeared. This rather limited the age appeal of some of the material to pre- or early teens, although the various series used in the comic had a high level of adult appeal.

These included a future sports series, 'Harlem Heroes', a super-special-agent series, 'MACH 1', a violent but original series, 'Flesh', where cowboys of the future farm dinosaurs in the past, a series about the communist invasion of Britain, 'Invasion' – the only series actually set around the year 2000 – and, most famously of all, a series about a violent future lawman, 'Judge Dredd'.

The character of Judge Dredd had been created by Mills and Wagner and visualized by Spanish artist Carlos Ezquerra, although initial differences meant that the first strip, delayed to the second issue, was drawn by Mike McMahon. The series is set at the close of the twenty-first century, in a post-nuclear North America dominated by a handful of giant cities. Here law is enforced by a number of judges who have the power to arrest, try and execute criminals on the spot. All of the judges are clones of an original judge, but each has his own personality. Dredd is human but takes advantage of all the latest technology, making him a superhero by true sf means. Judge Dredd soon became the most popular character in *2000 AD* and eventually had a comic of his own from October 1990.

The popularity of Judge Dredd also meant that there were considerable financial benefits in the spin-off merchandise, something that was limited in *Heavy Metal*. These included novels, a film, role-playing games and video games, which were becoming the new popular medium.

Rival Roles

War-games had been a popular form of entertainment for centuries – chess is, after all, a form of war game. Battlefield board games have been around since at least 1780,[37] and H. G. Wells wrote an instruction book on war-games, *Little Wars*, in 1913. Fritz Leiber and Harry Fischer had created their own fantasy war-game when they developed the world of Nehwon for their stories about Fafhrd and the Grey Mouser in 1937,[38] but the real interest in role-playing fantasy games did not establish itself until the 1970s, in the wake of the success of *Lord of the Rings* and other fantasy novels.

The best-known of them, and the one that has come to symbolize fantasy role-playing games, is *Dungeons and Dragons*, created by Gary Gygax and Dave Arneson in 1974 and produced by the company Tactical Studies Rules, better known as TSR, that Gygax established with Don Kaye in 1973. The game had a predecessor in Gygax's *Chainmail*, which he had

---

37 For those interested in the history and development of war games, I would recommend *Introduction to Battle Gaming* by Terence Wise (London: Model and Allied Publications, 1969), *Wargames* by David Nash (London: Hamlyn, 1974), *The Ancient War Game* by Charles Grant (New York: St Martin's, 1974) and the four-volume *War Games Through the Ages* by Donald F. Featherstone (London: Stanley Paul, 1974–76).

38 Suitably revised, their game was released by TSR in 1977 as *Lankhmar*.

developed in 1971 and which was the first war-game to introduce fantasy creatures. Arneson's *Blackmoor*, developed in 1970, was the first to have a fantasy setting. *Dungeons & Dragons* was drawn entirely from fantasy fiction and legend. The primary inspiration was the works of Robert E. Howard, L. Sprague de Camp, Fritz Leiber and Jack Vance, rather than Tolkien. The system of magic included in the game was based on that in Vance's *The Dying Earth*.[39]

The first commercial war-game was *Tactics*, designed by Charles S. Roberts in 1953. Roberts founded the firm Avalon Hill, in Baltimore, Maryland, which developed the very popular boardgame, *Gettysburg*. In 1964 they launched the magazine *The General*. Its great rival was *Strategy & Tactics*, an independent magazine founded by Chris Wagner in 1966 and taken over by Jim Dunnigan in 1969 when he created the company SPI (Simulations Publications, Inc.).

Both magazines were popular but it was *Strategy & Tactics* that took the lead and it was from the many war-games that it published – a new one each issue – that devotees began to develop their own games, mostly from military history but increasingly with fantasy or sf elements. By the mid-seventies, many sf and fantasy board-games existed,[40] including *Triplanetary* (1973) from Game Designers Workshop (not based on E. E. Smith's novel), *Infinity* (1973) from Gamut of Games, *Second Galactic War* (1973) by Third Millenium, Inc., *Starforce* (1974) from SPI, and *Stellar Conquest* (1975) from Metagaming. However, after *Dungeons & Dragons* (1974) from TSR, such games were increasingly developed to be suitable for role-playing. These included *Tunnels and Trolls* (1975) from Flying Buffalo, an imitation of *Dungeons and Dragons* but adapted so that it could also be played by mail, *White Bear and Red Moon* (1975) from Chaosium, *Traveller* (1977) from Game Designers Workshop, *Chivalry and Sorcery* (1977) from Fantasy Games Unlimited and, almost inevitably, *Starship Troopers* (1976), based on Robert A. Heinlein's novel, and *Dune* (1979), based on Frank Herbert's novel, both from Avalon Hill. The appeal of the role-playing game is that while it still follows a set of rules and instructions, there is scope for improvization, with the participants being able to create a story within a game. Thus, in a very real sense, these games were bringing fantasy and sf alive.

The games were accompanied by booklets and instructions and, with the need for updates and new developments, some companies soon issued

39 See online interview with Gygax at http://uk.pc.gamespy.com/articles/538/538817p3.html.

40 In 1979 David Nalle assessed that there were 400 different games from 40 different companies and that one-third of the wargaming industry was devoted to sf and fantasy games. See 'Paper Warriors', *Thrust* #13 (Fall 1979), p. 31.

their own magazines. By chance, the first two appeared at the same time, in March 1975: *The Space Gamer* from Metagaming and *The Strategic Review* from TSR.

Of the two, only *The Space Gamer* looked like a proper magazine, though it was only a slim, 16-page, digest-sized booklet, selling for $1 and published quarterly. It looked no different from other similar amateur magazines, printed offset from typed pages. It was edited by Howard Thompson, the mastermind behind Metagaming's *Stellar Conquest* and new games *Godsfire* and *Ogre*. Although some of its contents were given over to news about fantasy and sf games (and not just those from Metagaming) there were various articles which showed that those who worked at Metagaming, most notably Steve Jackson, were well acquainted with science fiction and the sf magazines. In issue #9 (December 1976), for instance, Steve Jackson wrote about how he wanted to include an intelligent armoured tank in the game *Ogre*, and during his research had checked out Colin Kapp's story 'Gottlos' and Keith Laumer's Bolo stories. Ben Ostrander, who took over as editor from issue #9, contributed a book review column which occasionally looked at different themes in sf. Most significantly, the magazine ran fiction which was independent of stories related to the games. From issue #1, Howard Thompson contributed a six-part series on the space adventures of Eldon Tannish. The magazine ran the first stories by Glenn Arthur Rahman, who was soon appearing in many of the semi-prozines, and early work by Lawrence Watt-Evans and Timothy Zahn. Most of the fiction in *The Space Gamer* was weak and formulaic, but there were occasional surprises. Timothy Zahn's story 'The Challenge' (#34, December 1980) conceived a game played through a series of computerized worlds, not unlike the internet, which created a fragmented view of the Earth to aliens who were monitoring humans from space.

The Space Gamer shifted to full large-flat format from issue #15 (January/February 1978), at which stage it may be treated as semi-professional. It was taken over by Steve Jackson when he set up his own gaming company in 1980, becoming monthly from July 1980, and adopting slick paper from October 1982, when it had grown to 44 pages. From here on it was a fully professional magazine, paying 3 cents a word for fiction. For a period from August 1983 to July 1984 it split in two, alternating monthly as *Space Gamer* and *Fantasy Gamer*. It eventually ceased publication in September 1985 after 76 issues.

TSR's *The Strategic Review* had a more significant future. It began as a brief quarterly newsletter, becoming bi-monthly from December 1975 and, after a brief name change to *Strategic Preview* in May 1976, it was completely revamped and, under the editorship of Tim Kask, was relaunched as *The*

Dragon from June 1976. It now looked the part of a professional magazine and, alongside the gaming material, it ran new fiction. Initially this was game-related, including a serial by Gygax himself, 'The Gnome Cache', under the alias Ernst Garrison. But it soon ran new fiction by professional writers of fantasy. Gardner Fox, who had recently returned to writing novels and short stories after most of a lifetime in comics, began a series about a barbarian mercenary, Niall of the Far Travels, with 'Shadow of a Demon' (August 1976). Fritz Leiber contributed a new Grey Mouser story, 'Sea Magic' (December 1977), and his friend Harry O. Fischer appeared with a rare new story, 'The Finzer Family' (July–September 1977). Fischer also contributed a piece on his early days with Leiber, 'The Childhood and Youth of the Grey Mouser' (September 1978). It also reprinted, as a serial, Fletcher Pratt and L. Sprague de Camp's Harold Shea story, 'The Green Magician' (June–July 1978). There was not fiction in every issue, but there was enough to make this a viable market, especially after it went monthly in May 1978. Kim Mohan, who would later edit *Amazing Stories*, joined the staff of *The Dragon* as an assistant with issue #30 (October 1979) and became full editor with issue #68 (December 1982). Circulation rose rapidly from a few thousand to around thirty thousand by 1979 and continued to climb, hitting the 100,000 mark by the end of the 1980s.

As the role-playing phenomenon gathered pace, further magazines appeared. *White Dwarf* was the British contender, started in June 1977 by Games Workshop and edited by Ian Livingstone, though this rarely ran fiction outside the games scenarios themselves. There was *Different Worlds* from Chaosium, which began in January 1979, but this also ran virtually no fiction. The two major markets for fiction were *Sorcerer's Apprentice* and *Ares*.

Sorcerer's Apprentice came from Flying Buffalo, Inc., of Scottsdale, Arizona, and was the official magazine of the *Tunnels and Trolls* game. Its editor was Ken St Andre. It was a slick, quarto-sized magazine, its first issue (Winter 1978) running to 28 pages, selling for $2, but it soon expanded to 40 pages for $2.25. It ran one or two stories in each issue, mostly originals, starting with 'Brother to Ghosts' by Robert E. Vardeman. Later issues included a new Dilvish story by Roger Zelazny, 'Garden of Blood' (Summer 1979), several new stories by Tanith Lee and Charles de Lint, and other contributions by L. Sprague de Camp, C. J. Cherryh and Manly Wade Wellman. *Sorcerer's Apprentice* was an attractive magazine, and was expensive to produce. Flying Buffalo never had the capital of TSR or similar companies, though it still paid around 3 cents a word for fiction, and the magazine was eventually wound up after 17 issues in 1983, the final one running a new Kane story by Karl Wagner.

Ares came from SPI, based in New York, and was the fantasy and sf companion to their military history magazine *Strategy & Tactics*. Its editor and creative director was Redmond Simonsen, with Michael Moore and Robert J. Ryer as managing editors from issue #9 (July 1981). It began in March 1980, in the same slick-flat format as *Sorcerer's Apprentice*, but running with 40 pages from the start and costing more, at $3 per issue, which rose to $4 after nine issues. It also paid top rates, up to 6 cents a word. It appeared bi-monthly at the outset and it also published a new game in each issue, along with one or two stories and occasional articles of fantasy interest. It was more sf-orientated than either *Sorcerer's Apprentice* or *The Dragon* and generally ran a greater variety of fiction, along with some excellent covers by Howard Chaykin, Barclay Shaw and John Butterfield. John Boardman contributed a regular column on 'Science for Science Fiction', while Susan Shwartz wrote a similar 'Facts for Fantasy', and both contributed other articles on specific sf or fantasy themes. L. Sprague de Camp appeared with a piece on Conan in issue #2 (May 1980) and David J. Schow contributed a column on films and media as well as several horror stories. Other fiction was by M. Lucie Chin, Timothy Zahn, Jayge Carr, Harry Harrison (who contributed a new Stainless Steel Rat story) and Poul Anderson. It was a very readable magazine, even for those not interested in the games, but the production costs were high and SPI were in financial difficulties by the end of 1981, filing for bankruptcy in 1982. The last issue under their management was #12 (January 1982). Their assets were acquired by TSR, who recommenced publishing *Ares* after the lapse of a year and produced five quarterly issues before they dropped it. Simonsen stepped down as overall director with the change-over and Michael Moore was editor-in-chief for two issues, but Kim Mohan, editor of *Dragon*, edited the last three. By then, TSR's *Dragon* was the only major gaming magazine market in the US for fiction, but the games themselves were flourishing.

By this time the role-playing board games had their rivals in computer-based games. The first computer game had been *Spacewar*, invented as far back as 1962 by Steve Russell, then a young computer programmer at MIT, who was fascinated by the work of E. E. Smith. It was not until 1971 that the first commercial arcade video game, *Computer Space*, was marketed. It was invented by Nolan Bushnell, who established Atari the following year. It was Atari that developed the first commercially successful home video-games system in 1977. It is significant how many of these early computer games were based on science-fiction or fantasy motifs, for while these did not generate the same magazines as the board-games, they did attract those who might otherwise have been interested in the magazines.

Playing these games had the potential to drain away new talent, as it was almost a substitute for writing. John M. Ford commented: 'Gaming SF offers many of the pleasures of creation – *you* plot the story, *you* make the decisions – and all without the fear of rejection. Well, you *can* lose, of course. But as with any good writer, next time's another story.'[41]

Role-playing games and computer games were the first major rival to the fiction magazines since the pocketbook and television.

Spawn of the Weird

If 1971 had seen shock waves reverberate through the science-fiction community following the death of John W. Campbell, Jr., the year was arguably worse for the weird-fiction community, which saw not only the death of August Derleth, just a week before Campbell, at the age of 62, but also the passing of six horror-fiction magazines.

To be strict, there is no such genre as 'horror'. Horror is a mood, not a subject, and can be applied equally to science fiction, fantasy or crime fiction (where it is usually called 'suspense'). What was originally meant by horror fiction was supernatural horror, rather than physical horror, though the latter, in the form of the *conte cruel*, had never gone away. Despite the popularity of ghost stories, they had fallen out of favour with publishers, and the field of supernatural fiction, or weird fiction, languished.

August Derleth had almost single-handedly kept weird fiction alive with Arkham House, the grandfather of all specialist sf and fantasy small presses, which had started out in 1939 with the idea of bringing all of H. P. Lovecraft's fiction into print in hardcover form to avoid it being lost in rare magazines. Arkham House was essentially a book publisher, and Derleth was one of the first to develop original anthologies of weird tales, long before they became popular in the science-fiction field. Starting with *Dark Mind, Dark Heart* (1962), Derleth encouraged a new generation of writers while sustaining the old school of *Weird Tales* contributors. Robert Bloch, Carl Jacobi and Joseph Payne Brennan happily rubbed shoulders with Ramsey Campbell, Basil Copper and James Wade. His other all-new anthologies, all from Arkham House, were *Over the Edge* (1964), *Travellers by Night* (1967) and *Dark Things* (1971), plus the mixed new/reprint *Tales of the Cthulhu Mythos* (1969). After Derleth's death, Gerald W. Page assembled *Nameless Places* (1975) and others would take the Cthulhu

---

41 John M. Ford, 'On Tabletop Universes', *Isaac Asimov's Science Fiction Magazine* 3:4 (April 1979), p. 109.

Mythos further, starting with *The Disciples of Cthulhu* (1976) compiled by Paul Berglund.

Derleth had experimented with magazines. During 1948–49 he issued a small review, *The Arkham Sampler*, and again in 1967 he began an even smaller, chapbook-style house magazine, *The Arkham Collector*, which grew out of his catalogue. It not only provided publishing news but ran new stories and poetry. Alan Dean Foster, Brian Lumley and James Wade all saw their first stories in print in *The Arkham Collector*. It appeared twice yearly for ten issues, folding with Derleth's death in the summer od 1971.

Another small-press magazine, *Mirage*, also saw its last issue in 1971. It was published irregularly by Jack Chalker from his own Mirage Press, and had seen only eight issues by its last in 1971, but they were exceptional issues, rising to a circulation in excess of a thousand copies. *Mirage* ran some of the earliest appearances by Ramsey Campbell, Edward Bryant, Ray Nelson and (with poetry) Tim Powers. It also ran some of the last completed stories by David H. Keller and Seabury Quinn.

It was also in 1971 that Robert Lowndes's weird-fiction magazines ceased. *Magazine of Horror* had started in August 1963, its publisher Louis Elson inspired by the success in Britain of the *Pan Book of Horror* series. It eventually begat various companion titles, including *Startling Mystery Stories*, *Weird Terror Tales* and *Bizarre Fantasy Tales*. These magazines were all predominantly reprint, Lowndes judiciously selecting material that was either out of copyright or came relatively cheap. He reprinted much from the magazines *Weird Tales* and *Strange Tales* to a readership that had not known the original magazines and welcomed the opportunity to read seldom-reprinted material. He also ran some new material, most famously the first two professionally published stories by Stephen King. However, the magazines had patchy distribution and, though popular, sales always kept them on the borderline. When the publisher was taken over by a new company in 1971, all of the titles were dropped.

Forgotten Fantasy, a very neat digest magazine edited by Douglas Menville, also folded at that time after just five issues in June 1971. It had been all reprint, and thus not a market for writers, but reprinted some rare material, a mixture of supernatural fiction, fantasy and scientific romance.

The passing of all these magazines, coinciding with the death of August Derleth, left the United States with no regular professional magazine of weird fiction[42] and no champion of the cause. As the fields of science

42 One cannot include in this category the magazine *Gothic Romances* from Dell Publishing, which ran from November 1970 to September 1971, or *Gothic Secrets* from Stanley

fiction and fantasy have shown in the past, when the commercial world deserts the genre, the fan world responds.

One publisher who hoped to fill the gap was the valiant William L. Crawford. Crawford had to all intents started the small-press sf-magazine field with *Marvel Tales* and *Unusual Stories* in 1934 and had always had aspirations beyond his capabilities. During the late forties and early fifties he had published a number of books under his FPCI imprint. Most were of minor interest and few sold well because Crawford was lacklustre over his promotion and marketing of the books. Between 1954 and 1968 he published nothing, but came alive again in 1969 when he revived his fifties magazine *Spaceway*. Unfortunately, like his books, *Spaceway* was an inferior product, cheaply produced with minor material, most of it either reprinted from Crawford's earlier magazines or held over in the inventory. One item of interest was the start of Andre Norton's serial 'Garan of Yu-Lac' which Norton had submitted to Crawford in 1936. Even now the serial remained incomplete as, unable to secure a distribution deal, Crawford folded *Spaceway* after four issues in May 1970.[43]

At that same time, the Los Angeles magazine *Coven 13* folded after only four issues because it too had not been able to secure national distribution. *Coven 13* had been a handsome digest magazine, with some good-quality contributions from Harlan Ellison, Alan Caillou, Ron Goulart and others. It published mostly light fantasy in the style of *Unknown*. Crawford agreed to buy the title and subscription list and planned to continue it in the same format, but again he encountered distribution problems. One distributor suggested that sales would be better if the magazine were published in the large-flat format and with a different title. The final choice was *Witchcraft & Sorcery*. These changes caused delays, because the fifth issue had already been set ready for the digest format, so that when the fifth issue appeared, dated January/February 1971 (though released in November 1970), it had not only lost impetus from the original magazine, but was no longer a recognizable continuation. To all intents, *Witchcraft & Sorcery* was a different magazine.

Crawford had been assisted on *Spaceway* by Gerald Page, who had been trying to interest Crawford in issuing a companion fantasy magazine.

Publications, which saw just two issues, August and September 1971, or *Adventures in Horror* (retitled *Horror Stories* from its third issue), also from Stanley Publications, which saw seven issues from October 1970 to October 1971. These were large format, low-grade, confession-style magazines boasting such titles as 'The Naked Slaves of the Master of Hell' and 'Fangs of a Fiend for the Girl Who Died Twice'.

43 Norton's novel eventually appeared in print complete as *Garan the Eternal* in 1972, though because of binding problems Crawford's hardcover edition appeared after the paperback edition from DAW Books.

When Crawford acquired *Coven 13*, he asked Page if he would join him in the venture. Page became editor, and his friend Jerry Burge became art director. Burge was responsible for converting the magazine to the new format and securing new artwork. The new format looked good, running to 64 pages for 60 cents and with bright attractive covers, though the small internal print became tiresome when not broken up by artwork. Burge published work by several popular fan artists such as D. Bruce Berry, Jeff Jones, Denis Tiani and Tim Kirk, along with the first professional art by Stephen Fabian, who provided the Finlayesque frontispiece to the first issue. R. Edward Jennings produced an illustrated feature, 'Witchways', similar to Lee Brown Coye's 'Weirdisms' in *Weird Tales*.

Witchcraft & Sorcery called itself 'the Modern Magazine of Weird Tales', an overt link to the venerable pulp *Weird Tales* that had left such a void when it folded in 1954. Of particular interest to nostalgia buffs was E. Hoffmann Price's series of reminiscences, 'Jade Pagoda', where he looked back to his friendships amongst the *Weird Tales* coterie. Price was the only author to have personally met all three of *Weird Tales*'s major contributors, Robert E. Howard, Clark Ashton Smith and H. P. Lovecraft. All of these were represented in the first issue by poems, fiction or letters, and Price had the lead story, an Oriental fantasy, 'Dragon's Daughter', in the second issue (May 1971). Between them Page and Burge did a good job in evoking the spirit of *Weird Tales*. Page was also the major contributor, completing a Robert E. Howard story and contributing four others under the pen names Carleton Grindle, Edmund Shirlan, Leo Tifton and Kenneth Pembrooke. There was also work by David A. English, Leo P. Kelley, Lin Carter, August Derleth, Brian Lumley, Glen Cook and Emil Petaja, all in the *Weird Tales* tradition. The emphasis was on strange tales and supernatural horror, with some sword and sorcery, but no science fiction.

Sales of these first two issues were good, around twenty-thousand according to Page, but then the distributor removed his support and Crawford had to rely on sales by subscription and through specialist shops. *Witchcraft & Sorcery* had to tighten its belt, reducing its page count by half to 30 with the resultant loss of features and fiction. It still sought to run long stories but this led to only three or four stories in total per issue. Although Crawford and Burge tried to sustain production values, these inevitably suffered, though the issues looked good and compare favourably with those produced today with the advantage of desktop publishing. Issues appeared as and when funds were available: the third and fourth issues in February and July 1972, the fifth a year later in July 1973 and the sixth in September 1974. The final issue contained a round-robin story, 'Othuum', with chapters written in turn by Brian Lumley, David Gerrold,

Emil Petaja, Miriam Allen deFord and Ross Rocklynne. Few such experiments are successful, though this one worked surprisingly well, perhaps because the Lovecraftian style in which it was written was so imitable. That final issue also included one of R. A. Lafferty's eccentric stories, 'The Man with the Aura'.

Sales were no longer sufficient to make a financial return, and Page and Burge, who owned a quarter each of the title, were finding it difficult to spare the time. Crawford long hoped to continue the magazine. When he wrote to me in March 1975 he commented that they were 'marking time', waiting for some chance benefactor. But none came and the magazine expired. Crawford had initiated a witchcraft and sorcery convention in Los Angeles in 1971, a suitable venue for selling the magazine, and this continued under several names such as Fantasy Faire or Science Fantasy Faire until his death in 1984. The following year the International Association for the Fantastic in the Arts inaugurated a William L. Crawford Award, sponsored by Andre Norton, for the author of the best first fantasy novel published in the preceding 18 months.

Witchcraft & Sorcery made a creditable job of emulating *Weird Tales* albeit it in only six issues spread over four years. Ever since *Weird Tales* had folded in 1954, various devotees had sought to perpetuate its memory. One of its latter-day contributors, Joseph Payne Brennan, of New Haven, Connecticut, felt the urge to fill the gap with a little magazine called *Macabre*. He knew he could not replace *Weird Tales* but, as he stated in his first editorial, in the summer of 1957, 'it can do two things: it can work for the revival of that unique magazine and it can, meanwhile, serve as a rallying place for all those devoted to horror and the supernatural'.

Such has been the determination of many 'fan' magazines. A modest publication, a small booklet of 24 pages or so, appearing at first twice-yearly but then irregularly, *Macabre* kept one small candle alight until the day that the weird-fiction magazine would return. He attracted contributions from August Derleth and Robert F. Young, Kit Reed and Lilith Lorraine, Richard L. Tierney and the poet Sydney King Russell. And there were plenty of items by Brennan himself. It was a struggle to keep the magazine going, and it became irregular after 1966, ceasing altogether with its twenty-third issue in 1976. One of its contributors in those last few years was W. Paul Ganley of Chambersburg, Pennsylvania (he moved to Buffalo, New York in 1973) who, in 1968, began his own little magazine, *Weirdbook*.

Weirdbook looked rather shoddy at the outset. Issued in large-flat format, reproduced offset from typed pages, it had only 32 pages but sold for 75 cents. Ganley did pay for contributions, but only $1 per page for fiction and artwork, with a small bonus for what was voted the best story or poem per issue. He acquired material from old-timers H. Warner Munn and Joseph Payne Brennan plus stories from the bottomless trunk of Robert E. Howard and filled the rest of the issue with his own pseudonymous stories. The early issues were not inspiring, the stories for the most part being routine and unmemorable. Ganley remarked that having mailed out 500 copies of the first issue he received only two responses in the first month.[44] Ganley was tenacious, though, and steadily the magazine improved in both contents and appearance. *Weirdbook* was intended as a quarterly but appeared usually every ten or twelve months, so took a while to develop, but its reputation spread by word of mouth. As a rare market for new weird fiction, it attracted pieces from new writers and he was soon publishing Darrell Schweitzer, Janet Fox, Eddy Bertin, James Wade, Gerald Page, William Scott Home, Wade Wellman (son of Manly Wade Wellman) and Ardath Mayhar. In issue #7 (October 1973) Ganley reported that *Weirdbook* now had a 1000-copy print run but only 288 subscribers and that the magazine was financed primarily by sales of back issues. From issue #8 (December 1974) Ganley achieved limited news-stand distribution. Soon after, Ganley issued an occasional companion magazine, *Eerie Country*, as an overflow for material not quite suitable for *Weirdbook*, though this did not really get into its stride until the eighties.

Weirdbook came into its own when it entered a second series from issue #11 (March 1977). It doubled in size to 64 pages, with a price rise to $3 and a rise in payment rates to $2 a page! *Weirdbook* was now running longer stories per issue, which had started with 'The White Isle' by Darrell Schweitzer (#9, 1975) followed by 'Silver Mirror, Red War' by Robert D. San Souci (#10, 1976) and 'Within the Walls of Tyre' by Michael Bishop (#13, 1978). *Weirdbook* also became the primary market for arch-Lovecraftian Brian Lumley. Ganley sustained *Weirdbook* for a remarkable 30 years, winning two World Fantasy Awards for his efforts.

The early seventies saw several new semi-prozines in the wake of *Weirdbook*, including *HPL, Moonbroth, Spoor, Etchings and Odysseys, From Beyond the Dark Gateway, Kadath, Wyrd* and *Nyctalops*, all inspired by *Weird Tales* and, in particular, the works of H. P. Lovecraft and Clark Ashton Smith. *Nyctalops*, produced by Harry O. Morris in Albuquerque, New Mexico, first appeared in May 1970 and provided a forum for the serious study of the work of Lovecraft and Smith. It was also a source for the early work of Thomas Ligotti, one of the great discoveries of the small press in the seventies. Ligotti is a perfect example of the type of writer who might never have established his reputation had it not been for the semi-

44 See *Weirdbook* #3, p. 2.

professional magazines. For the first ten years, all of his stories appeared in little magazines, primarily *Grimoire, Fantasy & Terror, Fantasy Macabre, Grue* and *Dagon* before eventually he sold to *F&SF*, and by then he was regarded as one of the best new writers of surreal weird fiction, and the small press's best-kept secret.

The one-off *HPL*,[45] produced by Meade and Penny Frierson in Birmingham, Alabama, and dedicated to the life and work of H. P. Lovecraft, sold out its 1000-copy print run in a matter of weeks. It marked the first appearance in print of A.A. Attanasio (as Al Attanasio) with 'The Elder Sign'. Lin Carter also tried to create a fantasy magazine, called *Kadath*. It was promised for a long time, with Carter requesting $5 a copy in advance subscriptions, but was exceedingly short on delivery, a slim 28-page quarto-size booklet, released in the summer of 1974. It consisted mostly of fragments of material by Robert E. Howard, H. P. Lovecraft and Clark Ashton Smith, and a new story by Carter, though its highlight was a previously unpublished novelette by Hannes Bok, 'Jewel Quest'. Carter had already spent most of the subscription money and had no funds to pay for the full print run or distribution of the magazine, so only a few copies were produced. While of no great importance, it is one of the rarest magazines of the seventies.

One professional magazine that appeared at this time is something of an anomaly. *The Haunt of Horror* was a digest-sized fiction magazine issued by the Marvel Comics Group. Editor Gerard F. Conway admitted in his editorial that it was an experiment by Marvel, and they were all slightly nervous about it. Its first issue, dated June 1973, appeared on 15 March, allowing a long on-sale time for maximum effect. Its 160 pages sold for 75 cents. Despite using the old digest format, it was attractively presented, with an effective cover by Gray Morrow and interior art by Frank Brunner, Mike Ploog and Walt Simonson amongst others. In many ways it resembled *Coven 13*, a mixture of light and dark fantasy in the *Unknown* tradition. It ran predominantly new material, though its one reprint, a two-part serialization of Fritz Leiber's 'Conjure Wife', which had first appeared in *Unknown*, took up almost a half of each issue and had only recently been available in paperback. George Alec Effinger was associate editor as well as a contributor under the alias John K. Diomede, starting a pulp-hero-inspired series about Dr. Warm. Other contributors included R. A. Lafferty, Ramsey Campbell and Harlan Ellison (whose story 'Neon' had its final pages presented in the wrong sequence; the whole story was reprinted in the second issue with new artwork). 'Loup Garou',

45 There were also three *HPL Supplements* issued in standard fanzine format between 1972 and 1975.

in the first issue, saw A. A. Attanasio's first professional sale. The second issue (August 1973) included early work by Howard Waldrop and Arthur Byron Cover, plus work by more-seasoned writers Ron Goulart and Anne McCaffrey. It was an entertaining magazine, which held promise for the future. Alas, the powers that be at Marvel let their nerves get the better of them, and warnings of poor sales caused them to pull the plug before firm sales figures were in. The third issue was almost ready to run (dated October 1973), with stories lined up by Ramsey Campbell, Alan Brennert, George Zebrowski and John Jakes, as well as another Dr Warm story. Had Marvel persevered, *The Haunt of Horror* might have appealed to the new converts to horror following the success of *The Exorcist*, released on 26 December 1973, but it wasn't given the chance. Instead it was converted into a black-and-white comic magazine under the editorship of Tony Isabella, and ran for five more issues from May 1974 to January 1975, each issue using up one of the stories for the lost third issue in text form. Isabella had little interest in the magazine and, once the inventory was exhausted, it was dropped.

Meanwhile, *Macabre*, *Weirdbook* and *Witchcraft & Sorcery* had achieved their task of holding the fort until *Weird Tales* returned, which it did in 1973. Leo Margulies, who ran Renown Publications, had acquired the rights to both *Weird Tales* and its senior partner, *Short Stories*, in August 1957. At that time, he was building a new stable of magazines and had launched *Michael Shayne Mystery Magazine* in September 1956 and *Satellite Science Fiction* in October 1956. He relaunched *Short Stories* in December 1957 and marketed it as a men's magazine, like *Argosy* had become. Sales were poor because of the general blight that fell over the digest magazine field at the end of the fifties, and *Short Stories* folded in September 1959. Margulies chose not to relaunch *Weird Tales* at that time, though he was itching to do so, and experimented with two anthologies reprinting from *Weird Tales* in 1961, *The Unexpected* and *The Ghoul Keepers*. Margulies planned to revive *Weird Tales* as a reprint magazine in 1962 but was talked out of it by Sam Moskowitz who argued that the time was not right. Two more reprint anthologies followed, *Weird Tales* (1964) and *Worlds of Weird* (1965), this time edited by Moskowitz. Sales were satisfactory but Margulies held off reviving the magazine until the market improved. It was still his intention to fill it with stories from *Weird Tales* but Moskowitz argued that he could include far rarer reprints from obscure sources, which were as good as using new material and would save the budget for selected new material.

Margulies agreed and the revived *Weird Tales* appeared in April 1973, the first issue dated Summer. It was published in a semi-pulp format on newsprint rather than pulp paper, with 96 pages selling for 75 cents. The first issue was typical of the short run. Stories were predominantly reprint, some from *Weird Tales* but most from earlier pulps and magazines like *The Black Cat* and *Blue Book*. Most of these stories had not been reprinted since their original appearance, or only in equally obscure places, so they would have been new to most readers. The stories were not Lovecraftian, but most would have been ones that Lovecraft appreciated, as was evident from references in a revised version of his essay 'Supernatural Horror in Literature', run in the second issue (Fall 1973). Lovecraft had completed this in 1936 but it had remained unpublished. Such new stories as were published, one or two per issue, were minor and rather pedestrian. The centrepiece of the first three issues was Moskowitz's biography of William Hope Hodgson, accompanied by reprints of little-known stories by Hodgson.

Most correspondents were appreciative of the revived magazine, since it made available little-known material, but it had the feel of a museum piece with nothing new or progressive. Distribution was also poor and sales averaged 18,000, when the break-even point was 23,000.[46] Margulies might have kept it going had his other titles been successful but only *Mike Shayne Mystery Magazine* was selling well. Two other titles, *Zane Grey's Western Magazine* and *Charlie Chan Mystery Magazine* also had poor sales and Margulies wound up both of those along with *Weird Tales* after its fourth issue, dated Summer 1974. Moskowitz had also had enough because Margulies still operated as if he were running his pulp empire at Standard Magazines in the thirties and forties, meddling with manuscripts and rewriting Moskowitz's introductions. Margulies was, in any case, in poor health and died the following year, on 26 December 1975, aged 74.

Margulies's widow, Cylvia, looked for potential buyers for the various titles. Illinois fan, collector and writer Robert Weinberg had been in contact with Margulies when compiling his tribute to *Weird Tales*, *WT50*, which he self-published in 1974. Weinberg and a colleague, Victor Dricks, went into negotiations with Cylvia Margulies and eventually acquired the title in 1976, beating out Forrest Ackerman, who was also keen. I'll return to its subsequent revivals in the next volume.

Although *Macabre*, *Weirdbook* and others had looked for a revival of *Weird Tales*, the Margulies version, while of interest, was not really what had been envisaged. *Weird Tales* had, after all, earned the sobriquet 'the Unique Magazine' in its day, and the value of the title was its ability to publish material that was different. Amongst the small press most of the

---

46 Data from personal correspondence with Sam Moskowitz, letter dated 12 November 1976.

Weird Tales school of magazines were essentially Lovecraftian,[47] but the horror field was about to be blown open with a whole new generation of writers. The magazine that did the most to promote the new generation and established the benchmark of quality amongst small-press magazines was *Whispers*.

The title was going to be *Whispers from Arkham*. The editor, an army dentist called Stuart David Schiff, along with David Hartwell, after Derleth's death, had conceived the idea of continuing *The Arkham Collector*. Schiff was unable to obtain permission from Arkham House, but by then his ideas had grown further and *Whispers* was launched as a magazine not only of news and reviews of weird fiction, but of bibliographic interest, with articles and studies of the field, and as a paying market for new short fiction.

The first issue was dated July 1973. It was a neat, digest-size magazine, saddle-stapled, running to 64 pages and selling for $1.50, a high price but one that many collectors felt worth paying. It was bound in black card covers with the logo in white and a black-and-white cover illustration by Tim Kirk, a format that was striking and effective. The magazine contained all that Schiff promised. There was a round-up of latest developments, which was kept current by Schiff and included an additional supplement page tucked loose into the issue. There were articles which were learned without being overly academic. The first issue included Professor Dirk W. Mosig's 'Toward a Greater Appreciation of H. P. Lovecraft'. Mosig was a key figure in the re-evaluation of Lovecraft's work, occupying a pivotal point between the days of August Derleth and the subsequent investigations by L. Sprague de Camp, S. T. Joshi and others. Mosig contributed several perceptive articles over the first few issues of *Whispers*, including the ground-breaking 'Myth-Maker' (#9, December 1976), which sought to distinguish between Lovecraft's various story cycles and the emergent Cthulhu Mythos.

The stories in the first issue were a mixture of Lovecraftian sorcery in Brian Lumley's 'House of Cthulhu', more tempered Lovecraftiana in David Riley's 'The Urn', and traditional weird fiction in Joseph Payne Brennan's 'The Willow Platform', which proved the most popular story of the issue. There was art by Denis Tiani, Steve Fabian, Lee Brown Coye and Harry O. Morris. The magazine managed to evoke some of the atmosphere of *Weird Tales* without wallowing in its memory, but rather teased that memory to see what else might emerge.

---

47 Another that emerged at this time was *Eldritch Tales* (first issue titled *The Dark Messenger Reader*) in December 1975, with stories that were solely Lovecraftian, though later issues broadened in scope.

Schiff sustained the same format and formula through the first nine issues. Although he intended to publish *Whispers* quarterly, it rarely met that schedule because of Schiff's other commitments, and, after occasional lapses, Schiff put out a double-issue, perfect bound with 130 pages at twice the price. These issues counted as double against subscriptions and so received a double number, as a consequence of which *Whispers* ended up with 24 numbered issues but only 16 physical copies. The second double issue (#11/12, October 1978) was the first to be typeset and from the following issue (#13/14, October 1979) the covers became full-colour and usually wraparound. In 1977 Schiff also began Whispers Press, producing quality books in special editions which became sufficiently profitable to help subsidize the magazine. This all added to the demands upon Schiff's time, making the magazine even more irregular, despite having employed David Drake as an assistant editor and general anchorman.

Whispers published some fine first-run fiction, including many by *Weird Tales*'s luminaries Fritz Leiber, Carol Jacobi, Hugh B. Cave and Manly Wade Wellman. The third issue (March 1974) ran Karl Edward Wagner's 'Sticks', which went on to win the British Fantasy Award. Later issues included material by R. A . Lafferty, Dennis Etchison, William F. Nolan, David Drake, Robert Aickman, Roger Zelazny, Brian Lumley, Glen Cook and Richard Christian Matheson (his first sale). Most of the later double issues had sections dedicated to specific authors, including Manly Wade Wellman (#11/12, October 1978), Fritz Leiber (#13/14, October 1979), Ramsey Campbell (#15/16, March 1982), Stephen King (#17/18, August 1982) and Whitley Strieber (#19/20, October 1983). These later issues were predominantly fiction, the general essays being replaced by studies of or interviews with the selected author.

Whispers was ideally placed to take advantage of the new interest in horror fiction following the release of *The Exorcist* in December 1973 and the popularity of Stephen King with the publication of *Carrie* in March 1974. Although *Whispers* remained firmly linked to the *Weird Tales* tradition, it embraced the emerging generation of new writers.

The success of *Whispers* allowed Schiff to assemble a showcase anthology of the best from the magazine plus some new material as *Whispers*, published by Doubleday in August 1977. It sold well and started a series of original anthologies that ran for six volumes until July 1987 alongside the increasingly erratic magazine. A seventh volume was completed and paid for but was then cancelled when sales of horror fiction dipped in the late eighties. Schiff was able to use the material from that volume in *The Best of Whispers* (Borderland Press, 1994), which also included the original version of Lucius Shepard's short novel, 'The Golden', planned for a special Shepard issue of *Whispers* in 1992.

The pressure of Schiff's workload and other personal commitments eventually took their toll and he was forced to stop his publishing enterprises in 1987, though there was a 'final' issue of *Whispers* released jointly with the final *Weirdbook* in 1997, which managed to clear Schiff's backlog of material. *Whispers* had by then long achieved its purpose of providing a forum for the serious discussion and promotion of weird fiction at a time when interest was reviving. With no professional magazine meeting the need, *Whispers* provided a quality if irregular market that gave some status to its contents. Schiff won the World Fantasy Award four times between 1975 and 1985 for *Whispers* and his other small-press activities, and the magazine was regarded as the flagbearer for the new generation.

Britain's answer to *Whispers* was *Fantasy Tales*. Despite colour covers and considerable time and effort in its production, the magazine never looked as sophisticated as *Whispers* but was rather like a glorified amateur magazine, at least at the outset. It was in digest-size form, its 48 pages selling for 60 pence,[48] with a print run of about a thousand. It was produced by Stephen Jones and David A. Sutton, both of whom had already established a reputation in Britain amongst fantasy fandom. Sutton had published the amateur magazine *Shadow*, which ran for 21 issues between 1968 and 1974 and was, at the time, the only British magazine to consider weird fiction seriously. He had also edited several original anthologies of weird fiction, starting with *New Writings in Horror and the Supernatural #1* in 1971. Jones had already proved himself a capable artist, contributing to *Shadow* and other magazines, and in 1974 had taken over producing *Dark Horizons*, the official journal of the British Fantasy Society, which had been in existence since 1971. Jones transformed the magazine from a readable but poorly produced publication to one that was neat, attractive and interesting.

These combined talents of artistic vision and a knowledgeable overview of weird fiction came together in *Fantasy Tales*. The title was slightly misleading, giving the impression that it dealt solely with Conanesque fantasy, a belief aggravated by the cover artwork by Jim Pitts, but it was the closest they could get without being able to use *Weird Tales*. The magazine was a deliberate attempt to emulate and evoke the feeling of the American pulps of the thirties and forties, primarily *Weird Tales*, *Strange Tales* and *Unknown*. It ran predominantly new fiction, and such reprints as

---

48 This was the equivalent of $1, but to allow for extra postage the US cover price was $2.

it used came from obscure but fairly recent sources, very little being used from the old pulps. *Fantasy Tales* was really a nostalgia trip. There were the inevitable Lovecraftian and Conanesque stories but also a good mix of the unusual and strange, such as Brian Mooney's Wellsian 'The Dream Shop' and Eddy Bertin's vampire story 'The Price to Pay'. The magazine was well supported and the first issue boasted the names of Ramsey Campbell, Brian Lumley, Michael Moorcock and Kenneth Bulmer. That first issue won *Fantasy Tales* the British Fantasy Award in the small-press category.

The cost of producing colour covers proved too high and with issue #5 (Winter 1979) Jones and Sutton cut back to using black-and-white art on thicker card covers. Bizarrely, this improved the magazine's image, giving it a starker atmosphere, closer to *Whispers*. By now the magazine had established itself and was attracting material from a wide range of new and old-time writers, including Manly Wade Wellman, H. Warner Munn, Karl Wagner, Darrell Schweitzer, Lin Carter, Hugh B. Cave, Dennis Etchison, Clive Barker and Thomas Ligotti.

Fantasy Tales was far ahead of anything else produced in Britain at that time, although, in all honesty, there was not much else. Nevertheless it was almost solely due to Stephen Jones's vision and drive that the quality of British small-press magazines improved. It was primarily through *Fantasy Tales* that a paying market for weird fiction re-emerged in Britain. In total the magazine would win six British Fantasy Awards and one World Fantasy Award. In the eighties it would transform into a professional magazine..

Under Scrutiny

Perhaps the most surprising rift to hit the science-fiction world in the 1970s was not the threat of rival publications or of dwindling magazine circulations, but the threat that science fiction was being taken seriously. Within the sf world, science fiction has always been taken seriously, but it has been subject to so much ridicule by critics and academics over the years that when those same people started to study sf seriously and teach it at college, the sf fraternity became suspicious. James Gunn summed it up in a guest editorial in *Analog* in 1974: 'The ghetto 'us-against-them' attitude, which gave science fiction fandom its strength and science fiction writers their feelings of brotherhood, erupts today in concern about the teaching of science fiction.'[49] That concern had been expressed by Ben Bova in his

49 James Gunn, 'Teaching Science Fiction Revisited', *Analog* 94:3 (November 1974), p. 6.

editorial in the June 1974 *Analog* where he believed that far too many courses were being taught by those who had only a superficial knowledge of science fiction and that this might well disillusion the students and turn them away from sf. Bova's view on the subject did not change. In one of his last editorials in the July 1978 *Analog* he wrote:

> There are hundreds – perhaps thousands – of teachers giving science fiction courses in the nation's schools who know sf intimately and love it well. But there are even more of them who don't know the subject, yet loudly maintain that *it is not necessary to know something in order to teach it!*[50]

He was particularly incensed that none of the college professors or teachers he spoke to realized that the sf magazines were still being published and were aghast at the idea that any of them, even *Analog*, be used as part of a college course, because they were too current.

He was right to be concerned. The first science-fiction course that had formed part of the official curriculum of a college had been created in 1962 by Mark Hillegas at Colgate University, at Hamilton, New York, but five years later his colleagues at the University still viewed the course with scepticism. He was frequently asked, 'You don't *really* think that science fiction is literature?', as a consequence of which, in order to make the course more academically respectable, he concentrated purely on mainstream texts (works by Aldous Huxley, H. G. Wells, George Orwell, E. M. Forster, and so on) and dropped any works of popular or, as he called it, 'professional', science fiction. Hillegas could see little prospect of change: 'the reason there is no future for a course in science fiction is not that science fiction cannot be literature. The values of literary intellectuals and the nature of English Departments are the reason.'[51] Hillegas went on to explain firstly that English Departments are intellectually conservative, by the very nature of the beast, and hold dearly – and quite rightly – a set of values within literature, and secondly that there is a deep 'hatred', as Hillegas termed it, for science and technology. Both Thomas Clareson and Lester del Rey agreed with those attitudes,[52] though Clareson believed that at least one of those barriers was changing. Some science fiction, in the late sixties, had turned against science, and dystopias (and indeed utopias) proved a more valid subject for study than the more protean science fiction, which was difficult to categorize. Jack Williamson, writing

50 Ben Bova, 'Dark Age', *Analog* 98:7 (July 1978), p. 5.
51 Mark Hillegas, 'The Course in Science Fiction: A Hope Deferred', *Extrapolation* #9 (December 1967), pp. 19–20.
52 See 'SF: The Academic Dimensions' by Thomas Clareson, *F&SF* 42:5 (May 1972), p. 118 and 'The Siren Song of Academe' by Lester del Rey, *Galaxy* 36:3 (March 1975), p. 78.

in 1971, was of the view that soon after Hillegas wrote his comments the tide turned and that by that year there were some two hundred courses being taught.[53]

Quite what caused that change in attitude is difficult to determine. Clareson may have been right with regard to the anti-science shift. William Tenn thought there were probably many reasons, driven as much by demand amongst students and the realization amongst colleges that here was potential for popular courses that were (at the time) high-profile.[54] The student demand was almost certainly driven by the social, political and technological changes of the sixties, including the space race, improved telecommunications and civil rights, all of which highlighted the accelerating development of society, bringing with it a need to be prepared – the philosophy behind Alvin Toffler's *Future Shock*. Moreover, science fiction, by its very nature, was anti-establishment, which was much of its appeal to the rebellious young, though this factor alone made it difficult for the orthodox establishment to address.

Whatever the causes, the demand for courses in science fiction (not just teaching the subject, but also teaching how to write it, as we have seen with the Clarion Workshops) had arrived like a tidal wave at the start of the seventies, and colleges struggled to meet it. P. Schuyler Miller considered this crisis in its early stages:

> Where teachers who enjoy science fiction – or who write it (Gunn, Williamson, Klass, and others in special courses) – are giving SF courses, they seem to be sound, valid and meaty. But too many young instructors are assigned the job of teaching about something they have never read, don't understand, and can't find out about through normal academic channels. The journals of SF scholarship help (the SFRA's *Extrapolation* and others). The academic world is becoming aware of the very tough and valid – and informed – SF criticism in such non-professional journals as Canada's *Riverside Quarterly* and Australia's *Science Fiction Commentary*. Some university libraries are assembling reference collections of science-fiction magazines and books, so that instructors don't have to limit themselves to Wells, *Brave New Worlds*, *1984* and Zamiatin's *We*. But *the colleges need help*.[55]

The SFRA that Miller referred to was the Science Fiction Research Association, which had been established in October 1970 to encourage

53 Jack Williamson, 'Science Fiction Comes to College', *Extrapolation* 12:2 (May 1971), p. 67.

54 William Tenn, 'Jazz Then, Musicology Now', *F&SF* 42:5 (May 1972), pp. 113–14.

55 P. Schuyler Miller, 'Men of Many Worlds', 'The Reference Library', *Analog* 93:2 (April 1974), p. 165.

and develop the teaching of science fiction and scholarship throughout the field.[56] Its founding chairman was Thomas D. Clareson, who was undeniably science fiction's greatest ally in the world of academe. Robert Reginald called him 'the father of science fiction criticism', adding that 'His stature and influence were in many ways comparable to that of John W. Campbell, Jr.'s contributions to the Golden Age of sf literature.'[57]

Clareson was professor of English at the College of Wooster, Ohio. His Ph.D. thesis in 1955 had been on 'The Emergence of American Science Fiction', a subject which served as the basis for two of his major works, *Science Fiction in America, 1870s–1930s* (1984) and *Some Kind of Paradise* (1985). In 1958 Clareson chaired a science-fiction conference at the Modern Language Association convention and out of that grew *Extrapolation*, which served as the newsletter to that conference from 1959 onwards. 'Newsletter' is scarcely an apt description for this twice-yearly review, which often ran to 40 or 50 pages and included valuable bibliographies, studies and analyses of authors and their works. *Extrapolation* was also made available to members of the SFRA from 1971. Clareson also compiled one of the first critical anthologies which doubled as a teaching aid, *SF: The Other Side of Realism* (1971).

Clareson's work was of crucial help to the emerging teachers and students of science fiction, but he could not do it alone. In 1973 Richard Dale Mullen of Indiana State University and Darko Suvin of McGill University, Montreal launched *Science-Fiction Studies* as another academic journal. While it published much the same material as *Extrapolation*, there was a degree of rigour and thoroughness about *Science-Fiction Studies* which gave it an authoritative air, while Clareson's *Extrapolation* was more relaxed and open to more bibliographical work. *Science-Fiction Studies* provided considerable research into early science-fiction texts and the international scene. Mullen imbued it with an atmosphere that combined dedicated research and a degree of fascination at what was being uncovered.

In Britain, George Hay was instrumental in establishing the Science Fiction Foundation (SFF) at the North-East London Polytechnic in 1971. The SFF was to serve as a centre of excellence providing research facilities for the study of sf, to promote and publicize the benefits and an understanding of the medium, and to pursue the educational value of sf. As a consequence, the administrator of the SFF also served as a senior lecturer. The first administrator was Peter Nicholls, who served from 1971–77, followed by Malcolm Edwards. In March 1972 they started the journal *Foundation*, edited by Charles Barren (#1–#4), followed by Peter Nicholls.

---

56 Its full original aims are listed in *Extrapolation* 12:2 (May 1971), p. 63.
57 Roger Reginald, *Locus* #391 (August 1993), p. 59.

It was intended as a quarterly but soon became twice-yearly (though under Malcolm Edwards's editorship in the later seventies it saw three issues a year).

The contents of these three scholarly journals had a degree of consistency. It was evident from the articles published in the early issues of *Extrapolation* and *Science-Fiction Studies* that an embarrassing number of the academic contributors had little knowledge of genre science fiction and focused purely on mainstream sf, with articles on Jules Verne, Eugene Zamyatin, Edgar Allan Poe, Jorge Luis Borges, Olaf Stapledon and, most frequently, H. G. Wells. Stanislaw Lem also received much attention, as we have seen, and *Science-Fiction Studies* provided a platform for his own views. A few noted genre writers somehow escaped the pit and were open for discussion, including Ray Bradbury, Ursula Le Guin, Arthur C. Clarke, John Wyndham and Philip K. Dick, but, apart from occasional book reviews or contributions by writers from within the field (notably Brian Aldiss, Ian Watson and Le Guin herself), little regard was given to popular sf.

This was not surprising and not necessarily bad in itself. It was better that contributors should start in an area where they were knowledgeable and then broaden their coverage once they had gained understanding and confidence. It was all a process of growing, but it was important that it should grow and not remain limited to the study of a select few writers who had somehow acquired academic acceptability.

Foundation had a more liberal scope than the other two magazines, seeking not only academic studies but also essays by authors about their work or careers. The series 'The Development of a Science Fiction Writer', included reflections by John Brunner, James Blish, A. E. van Vogt, Ursula K. Le Guin and L. Sprague de Camp in the first five issues. It then became 'The Profession of Science Fiction', with contributions by Poul Anderson, Brian Aldiss, Samuel R. Delany, Robert Silverberg, Richard Cowper, Bob Shaw and many others. These, at least, acknowledged the existence of genre sf and gave opportunity for academics to familiarize themselves with it.

The science-fiction magazines considered the subject on several occasions. Alexei Panshin, in his 'SF in Dimension' column for *Fantastic*, wrote an essay 'SF and Academia' (December 1971). *F&SF*, with the help of Philip Klass (well-known as an sf writer under his alias William Tenn), assembled a special feature in the May 1972 issue 'Science Fiction and the University', with contributions from Thomas Clareson, Darko Suvin, Isaac Asimov and Klass himself. Perhaps the most vocal of all was Ben Bova, who discussed sf teaching in two of his editorials in *Analog*, and gave space to James Gunn and Lloyd Biggle, Jr. for two essays on the subject.

All were much of the same opinion. They accepted that rigorous sf criticism was good for the field, and that if the attention fostered interest amongst a wider circle of students and teachers, the field would grow. But their main concern was that all too few teachers had a sufficiently wide appreciation of the field to provide adequate discussion and understanding, with the consequence that any course would be limited and would disillusion the students. That would doubtless change over time, but these first few years were crucial.

Those academics who went beyond the safety of a few standard texts and explored the sf pit did so at their own risk. In his 1971 essay, 'SF: A Literature of Ideas', Robert J. Barthell considered how pulp sf's desire to explore technology caused it to sidestep characterization. His research, which his notes show was based on reference books produced within the sf field, reveals his otherwise limited knowledge. At the start of the essay he says, 'Since many of the early science-fiction stories during the pulp days were written by mainstream writers, it is difficult to believe that these people could not have developed good characterisation and a fine literary story.'[58]

As I explored in *The Time Machines*, none of the contributors to the early sf magazines wrote for the mainstream, unless one counts some of the general-fiction pulps such as *Argosy* as mainstream. The contributors to Gernsback's magazines were, for the most part, gadgeteers and experimenters who wrote fiction to consider the potential of a new invention, while the contributors to Bates's *Astounding* were pulpsters who placed an emphasis on action and adventure. Literary style and characterization had nothing to do with it, and anyone acquainted with the magazines first-hand would know that.

This kind of misunderstanding was not isolated. In his essay, 'The Morasses of Academe Revisited' (*Analog*, September 1978), Lloyd Biggle, Jr. chose at random two essays from *Science-Fiction Studies* and *Journal of Popular Culture* and found scores of errors in each, errors which for the most part could have been avoided by a small amount of extra research. Likewise Samuel Delany was frustrated by the ignorance of many academics about the authentic history of science fiction, preferring to create their own or ignore it completely: 'The working assumption of most academic critics ... is that somehow the history of science fiction began precisely at the moment they began to read it – or as frequently in the nebulous yesterdays of sixteenth or seventeenth century utopias.'[59]

58 Robert J. Barthell, 'SF: A Literature of Ideas', *Extrapolation* 13:1 (December 1971), p. 56.
59 Samuel Delany, 'Science Fiction and "Literature"', *Analog* 99:5 (May 1979), p. 63.

In the views of some, notably Ben Bova, the teachers had little ability or inclination to undertake the research. In the October 1974 *Analog*, a reader wrote in to say how disappointed he had been with an sf course that he attended, because the instructor had less knowledge of the field than he did. Bova's response was that teachers prefer to work with old and trusted books, 'because they don't want to do the work necessary to keep up with the field' (p. 177). Perhaps a harsh view, but one that was not surprising in the light of Bova's experiences.

It was to meet the demands of colleges that Martin H. Greenberg's anthology machine stirred into action. At the time, Greenberg was a professor of political science at the University of Wisconsin and a colleague suggested to him that it might be rewarding to assemble a volume of science-fiction stories to illustrate certain political themes and concepts. Greenberg worked in collaboration with various academics – mostly Patricia S. Warrick, Joseph Olander and Charles G. Waugh at the start, with occasional other experts – and his books appeared at the rate of four or five a year. The first batch, all in 1974, included *Political Science Fiction*, from Prentice-Hall, *American Government Through Science Fiction*, *Introductory Psychology Through Science Fiction* and *School and Society Through Science Fiction*, from Rand, McNally, and *Sociology Through Science Fiction* and *Anthropology Through Science Fiction* from St Martin's Press. The anthologies explored not only social and political issues but also religious and moral problems, and *The New Awareness* (1975) was an especially powerful volume.

Greenberg and his colleagues produced 15 of these anthologies between 1974 and 1978, the early years coinciding with when original anthologies and the Elwood phenomenon were at their height. There were big differences though. For a start, all of Greenberg's volumes reprinted material and had only a smattering of new fiction. The reprints were selected not only for their quality but also for their relevance to the theme and for their importance in exploring difficult issues and raising moral dilemmas. They were stories that few, if any, colleges running sf courses would otherwise have had knowledge of or access to. They served an important function, especially in highlighting the role which science fiction has played in exploring complex issues. The anthologies included lengthy introductions by Greenberg and his collaborators, which provided enough discussion material for a whole course. Greenberg has since gone on to publish over a thousand anthologies of varying degrees of quality, on rather more populist themes, but few have improved on these early volumes.

A host of other publishers and commentators turned to producing science-fiction books for colleges, but they were met by various levels of approval or resentment within the sf fraternity. Take, for instance, *Science Fiction: An Introduction* (1973) by L. David Allen of the University of Nebraska, one of the 'Cliff's Notes' teaching aids. Lester del Rey, who had previously expressed several anti-academic views, was supportive of this volume, remarking, 'This is the first academic work meant to explain our field which I can genuinely applaud.'[60] James Gunn likewise called it 'a useful book with some illuminating concepts and some insightful analyses'.[61] Conversely, Joanna Russ, who was then an assistant professor of English at the State University of New York, tore the book to shreds in her review, which focused more on the poor use of English than on the information that it contained. Her final comment was 'This is not merely a useless book; it is obscene, exploitative, and part of the obscure reasons why Americans cannot read.'[62]

One reason for this resentment was that some academics appeared to believe that the sf field was only now being opened up to rigorous scrutiny and that the readers and writers of sf had done nothing to assess their own field, but this was far from true. Robert Lowndes had encouraged articles evaluating science fiction in his magazines in the early fifties, including work by James Gunn, Robert Madle, Sam Moskowitz and Tom Clareson. During the sf boom of the fifties several reference books had appeared by writers of sf, most notably *Modern Science Fiction: Its Meaning and its Future* (1953) by Reginald Bretnor and *The Science-Fiction Handbook* (1953) by L. Sprague de Camp.

The sf field had also been publishing its own reference works, many of academic rigour. The most noted publisher was Advent which had been established as far back as 1956 by a group of fans that included Earl Kemp, Ed Wood and Robert E. Briney, with George Price joining in 1960. Their first book had been a collection of some of Damon Knight's trenchant book reviews, *In Search of Wonder* (1956), while their first book with academic connections was *The Science Fiction Novel* (1959). Assembled by Earl Kemp, with an introduction by Basil Davenport, this brought together four talks given by Heinlein, Kornbluth, Bester and Bloch in 1957 at the University of Chicago's night-school course in sf. Other works of academic or bibliographic interest included *A Requiem for Astounding* (1964), Alva Rogers's affectionate study of that magazine's glory days, *The Issue at Hand* (1964), literary criticism by James Blish under his William Atheling, Jr. alias, *Heinlein in Dimension* (1968) by Alexei Panshin, and *The*

60 Lester Del Rey, 'The Reading Room', *Worlds of If* 22:7 (September/October 1974), p. 132.

61 James Gunn, 'Teaching Science Fiction Revisited', *Analog* 94:3 (November 1974), p. 10.

62 Joanna Russ, 'Books', *F&SF* 48:4 (April 1975), p. 60

Encyclopedia of Science Fiction and Fantasy by Donald H. Tuck (3 volumes, 1974, 1978, 1982), a most meticulous and thoroughly annotated bibliography of the field through to 1968.

With the growth of academic interest, the science-fiction field found it easy to respond to the demand. Robert Silverberg, quick off the mark as always, compiled *The Mirror of Infinity* (1970), an anthology of key stories where each story had a critical introduction by an expert either within or outside the field. Thus Jack Williamson commented on H. G. Wells's 'The Star', Harry Harrison on Asimov's 'Nightfall', Kingsley Amis on Cordwainer Smith's 'The Game of Rat and Dragon', H. Bruce Franklin on Ballard's 'The Subliminal Man' and Willis McNelly on Ellison's 'I Have No Mouth and I Must Scream'. Almost all of the stories came from within the magazine-sf field. Reginald Bretnor compiled a new volume of critical essays, *Science Fiction, Today and Tomorrow* (1974), which brought together articles assessing the state of the art by 15 sf writers, including Poul Anderson, Ben Bova, Hal Clement, Anne McCaffrey, Gordon R. Dickson and Frank Herbert. It was also now that Brian Aldiss published the first edition of his history of the field, *Billion Year Spree* (1973).

The science-fiction fan press had been a source of discussion and analysis of the field for some forty years. Lloyd Biggle, following his highlighting of the errors in two essays published in academic journals mentioned above, remarked, 'I've seen articles in fanzines, by fans with no training in scholarship, that were vastly superior to the two articles I have discussed here.'[63] In fact, the fan press had been developing a more scholarly approach to science fiction before college courses started in earnest, and both were probably encouraged by the same interest among fans and students in the maturing of the sf field and its increased relevance as a conscience of society.

Biggle's article had been a follow-up to a talk he gave at the Nebula Awards banquet in April 1973, which was then published in *Riverside Quarterly* as 'Science Fiction Goes to College: Groves and the Morasses of Academe' (#22, April 1974). *Riverside Quarterly* was the first of the amateur magazines to profess this academic rigour. It grew out of another serious amateur magazine, *Inside*, a fifties fanzine that had re-emerged in 1962, edited by Jon White, with Leland Sapiro as an assistant editor. White soon tired of the venture and Sapiro took over, changing the name to *Riverside Quarterly* (*RQ*)[64] and starting over again from Volume 1. The first

---

63 Lloyd Biggle, Jr., 'The Morasses of Academe Revisited', *Analog* 98:9 (September 1978), p. 162.

64 The title came from Jon White's address in the fifties, Riverside Drive in New York, which had been a popular fan haunt.

issue was dated August 1964. It was in small-digest format and it initially had 40 pages but would soon grow to around 80 pages, and topped 96 in 1973. Sapiro published it twice a year (three times in 1966), a schedule he maintained for 23 issues until 1974, despite several changes of address. Although the first issue was produced in Los Angeles, by the second issue Sapiro had relocated to Saskatoon in Canada, moving to Regina in 1967 and eventually returning to the United States, to Gainesville, Florida, in 1974.

Sapiro was a university lecturer (in mathematics) and wanted the magazine to feature serious articles about science fiction and fantasy. Though some fans shunned its overly academic nature, there were sufficient who supported it for it to establish itself. It was most noticeable for serializing Alexei Panshin's long study of the work of Robert A. Heinlein, 'Heinlein in Dimension' (May/June 1965–March 1967). Heinlein was opposed to anyone writing a book about him or his work and threatened to sue if it were published. As a consequence, Advent, to whom Panshin had sent the work, held back, but Sapiro decided to print it. When there was no response from Heinlein, Advent then published the book. Another notable work to be serialized in *RQ* was Jack Williamson's 'H. G. Wells, Critic of Progress' (August 1967–August 1969), which had been Williamson's Ph.D. thesis and which subsequently appeared in book form from Chalker's Mirage Press in 1973. Sandra Miesel also contributed several of her early articles which formed the basis for her critical studies of *Lord of the Rings* and Poul Anderson.

Many leading writers read *RQ* and often wrote long letters or articles, amongst them Fritz Leiber, James Blish, Poul Anderson, Ursula Le Guin and Sam Moskowitz. One of Campbell's epistles, in response to a piece on parapsychology, was converted into the article 'Voluntarism' in the March 1968 issue. R. D. Mullen submitted several articles before he began *Science-Fiction Studies*, including pieces on James Blish, van Vogt, Edgar Rice Burroughs and H. Rider Haggard.

Occasionally *RQ* ran fiction, seldom anything of note, but there were a few amusing parodies or brief experiments by the likes of Algis Budrys, Reginald Bretnor and Kris Neville. Worthy of mention is 'Edward Lear's Visit to the Moon' by Joe Christopher (#18, February 1972).

RQ was often in financial difficulties and Sapiro appealed in issue #22 (April 1974) for renewals of subscriptions, his editorial implying that the current paid circulation (or at least subscription level) was around a thousand copies, a level boosted following an advert he placed in *Galaxy*.[65] This was a large circulation for an amateur magazine with high

---

65 See Sapiro's editorial in issue #22, April 1974, p. 99.

upfront costs for paper, printing and postage. Without a regular renewal of subscriptions it would be difficult to sustain, and indeed *RQ* went into limbo after the following issue. Sapiro revived it in 1977 and published an issue roughly every eighteen months until #35 in June 1995.

The magazine received three Hugo nominations but never won the award. While highly respected it was always viewed cautiously by the core of sf fans, who were dubious of taking sf too seriously, and, despite a library sale of 200 copies, it was not an academic magazine, so it rather fell between two camps. Nevertheless, it published some of the most interesting critical articles of the sixties and early seventies.

By the early seventies a new breed of semi-professional fan magazine was emerging. Though they retained an essentially fannish base, with long letter columns and insider jokes and discussion of fan activity, they also ran long, sometimes passionate articles or bibliographies of considerable value. One of the largest such magazines of the period was *Niekas*, produced by Ed Meskys from New Hampshire, which had first appeared in June 1962. After the first year, issues were frequently in excess of fifty pages and twice topped a hundred – a huge amount of work to type and distribute two or three times a year. One of its most noted contributions was an encyclopediac series by Robert Foster on the characters and places in Tolkien's *Lord of the Rings* and *The Hobbit* and this was subsequently published by Mirage Press in book form as *The Guide to Middle Earth* in 1971.

There was a large number of serious fan magazines around by the end of the sixties, and fandom had grown to a sufficient size that a few editors could see opportunities for expanding and making some money from publishing. Opportunities improved when editors started to shift from the standard duplicated or mimeographed magazine to using offset lithography from typed sheets and some even went so far as to be formally printed. One of the first important ones to shift to the litho process was *Odd*, published by Ray Fisher in St Louis, Missouri. This had been an early-fifties magazine revived in the mid-sixties and which switched to litho with the Summer 1968 issue. At the same time, the journal of the Los Angeles SF Society, *Shangri L'Affaires*, also switched to litho. These remained essentially fan magazines, but the one that made a noticeable shift was Richard Geis's *Science Fiction Review*. This magazine had started life as *Psychotic* in July 1953, changing its name to *Science Fiction Review* in August 1955 before ceasing publication two months later with issue #23 when Geis was 'burned out'. Geis revived it in 1967 as *Psychotic*, continuing the original numbering, and then renamed it *Science Fiction Review* from November 1968 (#28). That was his first lithoed issue and he switched from a slim quarto magazine to a thick (68-page) octavo format, selling for 50 cents. John Berry, reviewing in *Amazing Stories* remarked on the change:

> the magazine has found a new and different vitality. It is becoming less of a fanzine and is leaning more toward professional interests – sort of a 'little' magazine of the science fiction world. The meat of the magazine has shifted from its letter column to the articles and reviews appearing in it.[66]

Geis also increased the print run to 1000 copies, making the magazine a serious venture. Geis's personality was always a central element of his magazine and he was able to sustain both a friendly, chatty atmosphere and an open, serious discussion of science-fiction issues. For instance, issue #28 ran Philip Jose Farmer's guest of honour speech, entitled 'REAP', presented at the 28th World SF Convention in San Francisco, which looked at the state of the science-fiction field and where it had failed in serving as an early warning system for society's failings. Later issues, notably #30 (April 1969), served as an arena for the arguments for and against the New Wave.

Geis sustained *Science Fiction Review* with exhausting regularity, a 48/52-page issue appearing every other month, and occasionally monthly. He slipped back to a quarto mimeographed magazine from June 1969, which may have made the magazine look less professional, but the content remained pertinent, current and vibrant – the best way of keeping track of the current thinking in the sf field. The magazine won the Hugo as best 'fanzine' in 1969 and 1970.

The regular production of the magazine was hard work and Geis felt he had lost the enjoyment that he had once gained from it. Much of the pleasure of the magazine was in allowing Geis an outlet for his own views as well as exploring those of others and there were times when Geis wanted to get back to the 'personalzine', that he once produced. The March 1971 issue (#43), which switched back to the octavo-size, lithoed format, proved to be the last, at least of that series. Geis re-emerged a year later with the eponymous magazine, *Richard E. Geis*, filled with his own thoughts and ramblings but after three issues (all in 1972) it mutated back into a review, now called, from January 1973 (#4), *The Alien Critic*, with the old title of *Science Fiction Review* restored from issue #12 (February 1975). Geis once again played around with size, content and printing, but from August 1975 it settled down in a standard quarto format, fully lithoed and generally running to 64 pages, but sometimes

66 John Berry, 'The Clubhouse', *Amazing Stories* 43:2 (July 1969), p. 130.

as high as 80. Geis sustained a bi-monthly schedule, slipping to quarterly in 1979. His print run in 1973 was 2,000 copies, but the demand for copies caused him to issue a reprint in 1976 of another 3,000 copies. As Geis handled all collation and mailing himself, any more than 3,000 became all-consuming. But he found that 3,000 copies selling at $1 an issue (increasing steadily through the decade), six times a year was sufficient to make a moderate profit and allow him to pay contributors. *Science Fiction Review* was thus a genuine semi-professional magazine, but the Hugo Award did not recognize that category until 1984 so the four further Hugos which the magazine won (in 1973, 1974, 1977 and 1979) were all as 'fanzine' or 'amateur magazine'.

Science Fiction Review was an open forum for all comers. It ran articles, interviews and several regular columns (including ones by Ted White and John Brunner), but its strength lay in its apparent randomness. Much of the magazine was Geis's commentary upon the current state of sf through reviewing books and magazines, responding to feedback from fans and writers, and arguing with his 'alter ego', the feature that became so prominent in Geis's column in *If* and *Galaxy*. Many professional writers took part in this repartee, which was frequently informative, sometimes acerbic, but always fascinating. The magazine was the closest equivalent in the 1970s of a chat group on the internet today.

Science Fiction Review gave science-fiction fandom a voice beyond the hard core of fandom. There was more honest opinion and critical analysis of science fiction in a single issue than in a whole year of the academic magazines, plus a mass of information, all of which allowed for a greater understanding of the field. It happened at a time when the market for science fiction was growing and this gave a boost to other fan editors and publishers.

Although it might not have been recognized by the Hugo Award committee, a new tier of amateur magazine appeared which was above the basic fannish level, and which catered for the serious sf reader and writer. These were true 'little' magazines. They fell into two groups. One was the news magazine and the other was the serious critical magazine (called 'sercon').

The grandfather of the news magazine was James Taurasi's *Science Fiction Times*. Taurasi had first published *Fantasy News* in June 1938 but from September 1941 this was superseded by *Fantasy Times*, which became *Science Fiction Times* in May 1957. It continued for 465 issues, most of them edited by Taurasi, and the last appeared in April 1969.[67] Throughout, it was a simple mimeographed newsletter of just one or two sheets. Its place

67 A German edition, which had started in 1958, continued through until 1994.

was taken by *Locus*, produced by Charles Brown, initially with Ed Meskys and Dave Vanderwerf. It first appeared on 27 June 1968 as a single-sheet, mimeographed newsletter. It continued with reliable regularity, usually weekly, its page count increasing, but it did not switch to an offset litho format until issue #155, dated 12 February 1974. By then it had already won the first of the many Hugo Awards it would receive, but it was not really until 1976, when Brown decided to work full-time on its production, that *Locus* moved up a gear. Thereafter it became more than simply a newsletter and included interviews, articles and other features, including a healthy amount of publishers' advertising. Circulation, which had been around 800 in 1971 had risen to 3,600 by 1980. *Locus* had in effect become the trade journal of sf publishing and remains the essential magazine for anyone wanting to know about news and developments in the science-fiction field.

Between the demise of *Science Fiction Times* and the increased status of *Locus*, one other news magazine held sway and that was *Luna Monthly*. In fact there were two magazines of this name, both produced by Frank and Ann Dietz. Frank Dietz had been an active fan since 1947 and (since 1957) president of the New York Science Fiction Society, the Lunarians. He organized the annual local convention, known colloquially as the Lunacon, from 1957 to 1971. *Luna* was originally an offshoot of this, a standard, mimeographed, quarto fanzine which saw five issues from 1962 to 1966. It presented transcripts of speeches from conventions, not just Lunacon. In 1969 *Luna* was revived as a neat, octavo, lithoed magazine. It ran speeches by Willy Ley, Frederik Pohl, E. E. Smith and Joanna Russ amongst others.

At the same time, Dietz and his wife Ann began a news magazine, which they called *Luna Monthly*. Its first issue was June 1969, also in a neat octavo format running to 32 pages for 25 cents. It was a true magazine, as distinct from a newsletter, with news interspersed between reviews and short articles, many betraying an interest in *Star Trek*. The original *Luna* soon seemed superfluous. It ran for at least five more issues and then merged with *Luna Monthly*. Frank and Ann Dietz acquired a new typesetting machine in 1970 and *Luna Monthly* became fully typeset from issue #20 (January 1971). By then it had become far more than a news magazine – in fact news had never been a major feature. It was most notable for its book reviews, its coverage of the international scene and its series of interviews with prominent writers by Paul Walker, which were later collected as *Speaking of Science Fiction* and published by Luna Books in 1978. The magazine continued for 67 issues, becoming increasingly irregular, the last dated Spring 1977.

There were other news magazines. In June 1978, Paul C. Allen started *Fantasy Newsletter* for the fantasy-fiction field, and this rapidly evolved into a magazine in January 1980. It soon outgrew Allen's ability to cope with the production, 'too big for a hobby but not big enough for a business',[68] as he saw it. He folded the magazine with issue #41 (October 1981) but it was promptly acquired by Robert Collins of the College of Humanities at Florida Atlantic University who continued the magazine without a gap, but now as a more 'popular' and open academic journal, subsequently retitled *Fantasy Review* in 1984. Andrew Porter also began *Science Fiction Chronicle* as a separate news magazine in October 1979, the closest there was to *Locus*. It had started as a supplement within his magazine *Algol*.[69]

Algol was the best example of the new-style, slick 'sercon' magazine. It was produced by Andrew Porter in New York and had originated as a fanzine in November 1963. Its first few slim issues were produced at High School and contained nothing of interest, but he soon sidelined his fan writings into *Degler* (which later became the news magazine *S.F. Weekly*) and *Algol* became a more serious, considerably larger and less regular magazine. This coincided with Porter becoming an assistant editor at *F&SF*, a role he held from June 1966 to May 1974.[70]

Algol attracted contributions by major writers. Authors provided articles on the background to their work, including Piers Anthony on the origins of *Chthon* (#14, Fall 1968), Norman Spinrad on *Bug Jack Barron* (#15, Spring 1969), Alfred Bester on *The Demolished Man* (#18, May 1972) and Marion Zimmer Bradley on the importance of anguish in science fiction (#19, November 1972). The last three essays were reissued by Porter under his Algol Press imprint in 1976 as *Experiment Perilous*.

There were several special issues with a section focusing on the works of certain authors. Issue #12 (March 1967) featured Harlan Ellison, including his controversial convention speech, 'A Time for Daring', where he attacked sf coteries such as Milford, and challenged editors to be more daring in their choice of fiction. This and other contributions by and about Ellison were included in *The Book of Ellison*, from Algol Press, when Ellison was guest of honour at the 1978 World SF Convention. Other special issues featured were Cordwainer Smith (#20, May 1973), Ursula K. Le Guin (#21, November 1973) and Arthur C. Clarke (#23, November 1974).

Ted White and Richard Lupoff became regular columnists, Lupoff's book-review column being the magazine's most popular feature. Susan Wood,

68 See news story *Locus* #249 (October 1981), pp. 3, 23.
69 It began in issue #33, Winter 1978/9.
70 Credited on the magazine's masthead as April 1967 to October 1974.

Vincent Di Fate and Frederik Pohl joined the ranks in later issues. Pohl joined after Ted White was rather unceremoniously dropped following a disagreement over the content of a column on art directors.

There were also many learned articles, the equal of any academic studies. R. D. Mullen remarked that he was 'astonished and overwhelmed by the overall excellence of *Algol*'. Such pieces included Wolf Rilla's study of the parameters of science fiction as viewed by film directors, 'The Boundary of Imagination' (#22, May 1974), Brian Stableford's 'The Social Role of SF' (#24, Summer 1975) and James Gunn's study of the evolution of sf, 'From the Pulps to the Classroom' (#27, Fall 1976). Interestingly, when Porter surveyed his readers in 1975, these more critical articles were the ones least appreciated by readers.[71] When he took another survey three years later the question was asked in a different way, but that time the main feature articles were rated the most popular.

From issue #16 (December 1970), which appeared after a hiatus of some eighteen months, *Algol* switched to photo-offset printing. Issue #19 was partially typeset (by Ann Dietz at Luna Publications) and from issue #22 (May 1974) it went fully typeset on quality coated stock, and carried a number of paying adverts. With issue #24 (Summer 1975) it adopted full-colour covers.

Porter strove to make *Algol* an attractive magazine. It contained a profusion of photographs and illustrations, some of the latter still rather fannish. Jack Gaughan, Vaughn Bodé, Jim Steranko, Stephen Fabian, Jay Kinney, Mike Hinge and Mike Gilbert were amongst the many artists who featured in the magazine. The covers were always impressive, shifting to coated stock from issue #21 and to full-colour from #24. All of this was expensive and the heavier coated stock increased postal charges. Porter noted in November 1973 that the cost of mailing a single issue had risen from 14 cents to 32 cents over the previous couple of months. Porter was subject to the same price rises for paper, printing and postage that affected the major magazines, and in his case he had nowhere else to spread the costs. The price of *Algol* therefore rose from 80 cents with issue #20 (May 1973) to $2.25 by the end of the decade. Yet during all that time *Algol's* sales continued to rise as Porter was able to achieve a greater penetration of the market and present a quality product. Print runs rose from around five hundred copies for issue #16 (December 1970) to over six thousand by #33 (Winter 1978/9).

By issue #19 *Algol* was classed as semi-professional. Porter was paying for all contributions by then and that was the first issue with a print run of 1000 copies. By issue #20 (May 1973) he reported that most back issues

---

71 See '*Algol* Reader Survey Results', *Algol* #25 (Winter 1976), p. 48.

had sold out and that he was now printing 1,500 copies. These facts are relevant because the committee organizing the 1974 World SF Convention had concerns that certain magazines, notably *Algol* and *The Alien Critic*, were no longer eligible for the 'fanzine' award because they paid contributors and were seeking to make a profit. In fact, since 1972 the category had been for best 'amateur magazine' and Porter argued that it did not matter if he made a slight profit and chose to pay certain contributors, the magazine was not produced to earn a living – it had only crept into profit because Porter had sold books and magazines to fund it. In the end *Algol* was treated as eligible and it tied with *The Alien Critic* for that year's Hugo, though Porter subsequently withdrew it as a protest.

Thereafter Porter continued to upgrade *Algol* and move away from a fan base. By issue #23 (November 1974) he said it was 'evolving toward a trade magazine', aimed at 'the general SF reading public' as distinct from the core fans. By the second half of the seventies, with the print run at over six thousand copies, *Algol* was selling twice as many copies through bookstores than through subscription. This wider appeal led Porter to change the magazine's name to *Starship* with effect from issue #34 (Spring 1979), a name that he believed meant more to the general reader. By then Porter stated that he regarded the magazine as 'very much a professional publication'.[72] He also experimented with short fiction, running a Berserker story by Fred Saberhagen in issue #29 (Summer/Fall 1977) to accompany an article by Saberhagen about the Berserkers, but there was less support for fiction and it was dropped.

Algol was the pre-eminent critical magazine of the field in the seventies and early eighties, with no real competitors for the quality of its presentation or its content. There were other high-quality amateur magazines that served as a valuable forum for the discussion and evaluation of science fiction, such as Bill Bowers's *Outworlds*, which was also popular with professionals because of the freedom it gave them, but *Outworlds* was always at heart a fanzine. It was the same for other serious fanzines around the world, mostly notably Peter Weston's *Speculation* and the British Science Fiction Association's *Vector* in Britain, and Bruce Gillespie's *S. F. Commentary* and Van Ikin's *Science Fiction* in Australia. Only one other editor in the seventies had enough gall to try and beat *Algol* at its own game and that was Doug Fratz with *Thrust*.

Doug's entry into science-fiction fandom had been via comics fandom rather than sf. In his teens, he had produced several issues of a comics fanzine, *Comicology*, but his interest in science fiction grew and, once at the University of Maryland, he became involved in the fledgeling student

---

72 See Porter's editorial, *Starship* #34, Spring 1979, p. 5.

sf society, volunteering to produce their magazine with help from Steven Goldstein. *Thrust*'s first issue appeared in February 1973 in standard quarto format, produced offset from typing. It was a fairly typical student fanzine filled with relatively minor fiction, reviews and a *Star Trek* article. Fratz did use a cover by Morris Scott Dollens from a painting he had acquired at a convention and he secured some art by Berni Wrightson via his comics contacts. The plan was to issue it bi-monthly and the second issue appeared on time in April 1973. It still ran fiction, but this time had a news column and an interview with Roger Zelazny and Poul Anderson. Fratz used another Dollens cover, plus artwork by Dan Adkins. It was clearly produced by someone who knew what he was doing, but was a long way from being anything other than average. It continued in this manner through five more issues, the sixth edited solely by Steven Goldstein. Each issue showed a steady improvement, issue #4 (January 1974), running the story 'The Most Dangerous Man in the World' by Chris Lampton and David Bischoff, which later resurfaced in *Void*. Issue #5 (April 1974) ran Frederik Pohl's guest of honour speech and an interview with him by Roger Zelazny. Issue #7 (Spring 1976) was the last to appear under the auspices of the University of Maryland. It was edited primarily by Dennis Bailey, but he asked for Fratz's help to complete it. It contained an interview with Harlan Ellison by Bischoff and Lampton plus an article by Bischoff on his relationship with Ellison, both his work and the man. It ran a good selection of critical book reviews, but it still looked every inch a fanzine. However, it no longer ran any fiction. Steven Goldstein instead put out an alternative issue for stories, *Counter Thrust*, a rather shoddily produced 20-page A4 magazine which concentrated on fantasy fiction. Its only contents of note were a story by Damien Broderick and an interview with Roger Zelazny. It was planned as an annual, but saw just one issue, undated, in the late spring of 1976.

Thereafter, everything changed. Fratz had left college, qualified as a chemist, and was busy in other activities when the urge returned to continue *Thrust*. He announced that he was resuming publication of the magazine separate from the university, causing some difficulties which were eventually resolved, and he set his sights on establishing a quality science-fiction review that challenged the other leading magazines, especially *Algol*. The opportunity came when Porter decided not to run Ted White's column on artwork, and Fratz snapped it up. Thereafter White's 'My Column' moved permanently to *Thrust*. This led to an altercation between Fratz and Porter, especially after Fratz posted an advert for *Thrust* in *Locus*, using as the hook the question of why Porter had dropped White's column. Porter took objection to this and refused to run Fratz's advert for *Thrust* in *Algol*. In a somewhat petty reaction, Ted White and Dan Steffan drew a spoof cover for a magazine called *Algon*, 'the magazine about bland stuff', which featured on the back cover of *Thrust* #9.

Fratz's first separate issue was #8, dated Spring 1977. Despite a substantial increase in size (38 pages) plus a two-colour cover and advertising, it still looked like a fanzine, printed offset from typed sheets, but it was a giant leap from issue #7 and showed Fratz's determination. Its one weakness was a comic strip, 'War Mind', by Matt Howarth, but it ran a good selection of reviews and criticism. The magazine continued to improve both in content and production values. Issue #9 (Fall 1977) featured an article by and interview with Norman Spinrad, plus an article on *Star Wars* that included film stills. Issue #10 (Spring 1978) was the first to feature a slick cover, though the remaining paper was of poor newsprint quality and did not improve until issue #13 (Fall 1979). That upgrade further helped sales and by 1980 *Thrust* had a paid circulation of 1,700 (out of a print run of 2,200).

Between issues #10 and #13 *Thrust* acquired several regular columnists. In addition to Ted White, there was Charles Sheffield, Lou Stathis, John Shirley and Michael Bishop. David Bischoff and Chris Lampton were also regulars. Dan Steffan took over the art direction. Darrell Schweitzer and Jeffrey Elliot contributed regular author interviews and there was a growing number of perceptive book reviews and commentary. It continued to run occasional graphic stories, but these were an improvement on the earlier comic strips These issues in 1979 earned *Thrust* the first of its five Hugo nominations, though it would never win the award.

Thrust completed a neat triangle of critical 'fan' magazines, with the more widely appealing *Algol* at the apex and the highly personal and often frenetic *Science Fiction Review* at the other base corner. Fratz sought to be challenging and demanding, seeking a rigorous scrutiny of science fiction, even beyond the academic autopsy of *Science-Fiction Studies*. *Thrust* published several exposé articles revealing the behind-the-scenes facts about certain events. White did this on several occasions in his column, Lou Stathis wrote about his experiences in the book and record business and John Shirley likewise bemoaned how book and magazine editors were increasingly overruled by accountants and salespeople. So, while it was never as critically astute as *Algol*, *Thrust* knew where to turn the stones and see what crawled out.

While there would have been some considerable overlap in the readership of *Algol*, *Thrust*, *Locus* and *Science Fiction Review* (whose circulations peaked respectively at around 6,000, 1,700, 3,400 and 5,000 during the seventies) it is probably not too far adrift to suggest that there were of the order of ten thousand readers who were as interested (possibly more interested) in reading about science fiction as in reading the fiction itself. It's a number to be of sufficient importance to sf publishers in promoting their books, hence the ability for the leading review magazines to secure the advertising which they needed to help finance themselves. But it's also of sufficient size to foster a wide range of feedback and comment upon the works of individual authors, indeed by far the greatest source of feedback that writers receive. It is little surprise, therefore, that many of the professional sf writers contribute to the amateur or semi-professional 'little' magazines, paid or unpaid, not just for the personal gratification, but because it is instructive and rewarding.

The diversity of markets that developed in the seventies would continue to grow into the eighties and nineties, as I shall explore in the next volume. Although there was a significant crossover interest, it was also inevitable over time that readers might become drawn towards a more select number of subjects, such as role-play games or adult comics, with a greater chance of splitting the field and reducing further the readership of the sf magazines.

Yet, despite these rival markets, the two greatest challenges – media magazines and the internet – were yet to come. The science-fiction magazines might have survived the onslaught from the original anthology series and the sf comics, but their problems had only just started.

4

Back to the Future:
The Final Gateways

The previous three chapters have dealt primarily with the period 1970 to 1977, passing occasionally beyond those years to complete discussion of a few individual threads. The period coincided with the economic depression in the United States and Britain but also coincided, give or take a year, with Ben Bova's editorship at *Analog*, the rise and fall of Roger Elwood, and most of the original anthologies, and the fall from grace of *Galaxy*. There was too much that continued on beyond these years to treat it as a self-contained period, but there was enough that began and ended during that time to see it as a distinct period of transition.

The years 1976 to 1978 saw a recovery in the economic situation and with it a change in the fortunes of the science-fiction magazines. With the economy it was a false dawn – the light at the end of the tunnel extinguished again after a few years – but with the sf magazines it was the start of a new era, one that was almost as complicated as the previous era, but now squeezed into four or five years. The period from 1977 to 1982 would see the rise and, in some cases, fall of a surprising number of new magazines, all of which underwent a variety of rapid changes. It was as if, following the transitional post-Campbell years, the field felt ready to regenerate itself. In this chapter we shall see how well it managed.

The Rise and Fall of Galileo

As the American economy began to recover in the second half of the seventies, and as the spate of original anthologies ran their course, so the sf magazines showed signs of resurgence. In late 1975 there had been plans from publisher Ed Goldstein, with his editor Larry Shaw, for a new magazine, originally called *Alpha*, to appear in January 1976. At the last minute, plans fell through because of distribution problems and Goldstein subsequently satisfied his desire for an all-fiction magazine by acquiring *Mike Shayne's Mystery Magazine* from Cylvia Margulies. There had also been two issues of Elwood's *Odyssey* in 1976, but the two important magazines appeared towards the end of the year – *Galileo* in September and *Isaac Asimov's Science Fiction Magazine* in December. With plans also in hand for a third new magazine, *Cosmos*, which went on sale on 4 March 1977, the appearance of *Heavy Metal* ten days later, and the rumours that Bob Guccione of *Penthouse* was considering something new, the magazine scene was looking promising.

Galileo would prove to be both the success story of the late seventies and its worst disaster, and became an object lesson to everyone in the trade.

It had been launched by Vincent McCaffrey who, since 1974, had been running a second-hand bookstore in Boston, Massachusetts, called Avenue Victor Hugo. Its relaxed air and wide selection of books made it a popular venue and McCaffrey always had a complement of volunteers happy to help out. McCaffrey had been publishing the occasional issue of a short-story magazine called *Fiction* since June 1972, which was in quarto format, printed on newsprint. He devoted some issues to particular genres and was planning to make the tenth issue a special science-fiction issue in 1975. Requests were sent to a number of major writers and the response was so good that McCaffrey felt it worth experimenting with an all-sf magazine. The ninth issue of *Fiction*, which had been a special western issue, had sold poorly, and McCaffrey decided to wind up *Fiction* and issue *Galileo* in its place.

The name *Galileo* was chosen, according to the editor, to represent that mix of an 'undying quest for knowledge and sense of wonder that motivates all scientists'. As editor, McCaffrey chose Charles C. Ryan, a reporter and newspaperman then working for the *Daily Times Chronicle* in Woburn, Massachusetts. Ryan had been involved in the anti-Vietnam peace movement and had New Age leanings, and was sensitive towards exploitation and capitalism. There was a strong feeling, through his editorials and his choice of fiction and articles, that Ryan wanted *Galileo* to be a magazine that cared for the Earth and its future. He was pro-technology, but only so far as technology helped the Earth and its peoples. The magazine carried a variety of articles promoting nuclear power and the space programme, living up to its cover tag as the 'Magazine of Science & Fiction'. Ryan was of the firm belief that an all-fiction magazine would soon flounder, but that one which presented its views through a variety of forms, would have greater appeal.

Like *Fiction*, *Galileo* was in quarto format, side-stapled, running to 80 pages and printed on newsprint. It increased to 96 pages with the second issue. The font size allowed *Galileo* to run more wordage than any of the digest magazines which gave good value for money, even though the early issues were priced at $1.50, at a time when *Analog* was still $1.

The paper was not the best for the reproduction of pictures, though the production team persevered. They ran many photographs of the contributors, not always showing them to best effect, but the inside back cover of each issue featured a full-page professional photograph of a writer. These included Poul Anderson, Marion Zimmer Bradley, Hal Clement, Harlan Ellison, Larry Niven and Robert Silverberg. The size allowed for a good display of art on the front and back covers, used to advantage by artists Tom Barber, Carl Lundgren, Ron Miller, Jeff Jones and John Schoenherr. However, internally there were insufficient illustrations to break up the wall of text, and such illustrations as did appear were often bland and uninspiring.

The first issue, quarterly at this stage, was rather cautious in content, with only a limited budget. Eight thousand copies were printed and sold primarily through specialist bookshops and by charter subscriptions. There was no general news-stand distribution. The cover bore no date so that issues could be displayed for as long as possible.

The issue included the transcript of a speech by Arthur C. Clarke on the advance of telecommunications, and the reprint of an article by Ray Bradbury on a conjectural meeting with Jules Verne. *Galileo* also picked up Peter Weston's series on sf themes from the defunct *Science Fiction Monthly* with a piece on robots. Besides the usual editorial features, the one other piece of non-fiction was 'The Aleph', an astonishing listing of current books compiled by the industrious Andrew Whyte, complete with detailed bibliographic comments. Whyte sustained this throughout *Galileo*'s existence and it remains a useful compendium.

The fiction was more traditional than experimental, mostly by new and developing writers, and written from the more-aware seventies viewpoint on ecological and technological matters. One of the more prolific contributors of fiction, with five stories in the first ten issues, was Kevin O'Donnell. He, like Robert Chilson, who also appeared in the first issue, was from the *Analog* school of writing. Chilson had been a Campbell discovery and O'Donnell had worked under Bova. Like Varley, O'Donnell had been encouraged by Robert Heinlein's Annapolis speech, published in *Analog*, which gave his five rules to become a published writer (see page 96). Yet despite this *Analog* pedigree, their work for *Galileo*, as with the other contributors, was more in the vogue of *Galaxy*, exploring social aspects of the future.

O'Donnell's stories are good examples of the balance Ryan wanted to achieve, blending the human with the alien and the mundane with the imaginative. 'Next Door Neighbor', in the first issue, is the poignant story of an alien seeking refuge on Earth, while 'Do Not Go Gentle' (March 1978) is an evocative story of a nurse with the power to control the human life-force. It became the runner-up in *Galileo*'s prize competition for that year's best story under 3,000 words, as judged by Poul Anderson. The winner was 'Django' (January 1978) by Harlan Ellison, a parable of the power of art over mortality. Ellison had written the story as one of his promotional stunts, sitting in the shop window at Avenue Victor Hugo.

As the magazine developed, so greater names appeared: articles by Carl Sagan, Hal Clement and David Gerrold, stories by Brian Aldiss, Jack Williamson and Marion Zimmer Bradley, and features by or about Kelly Freas, John Schoenherr, A. E. van Vogt, Frederik Pohl, and so on. *Galileo* was where Robert Silverberg's column 'Opinion' first appeared, in issue #9 (July 1978), and which has continued to appear in various magazines to this day (later retitled 'Reflections'), the second-longest-running column after Asimov's 'Science' in *F&SF*. With the fifth issue, as it prepared to go bi-monthly, *Galileo* had the confidence to run a serial, and a long one, 'The Masters of Solitude' by Marvin Kaye and Parke Godwin, set in a post-nuclear America where witchcraft has become a potent force.

Importantly, *Galileo* became a market for new writers and here Ryan's skill at identifying talent was good. He launched (or in a couple of cases relaunched) the sf careers of several writers, including M. Lucie Chin, Cynthia Felice, John Kessel, David Schow, Lewis Shiner and Connie Willis. He also published the first science article by James P. Hogan.

After her first sale to Ejler Jakobssen, seven years earlier, Connie Willis had been writing material mostly for the confession magazines when she at last found a way back into the sf magazines with 'Capra Corn' (March 1978), a tribute to the Hollywood romantic comedies of the thirties and forties. Her next story was a major shift. 'Samaritan' (July 1978), one of the best stories to appear in *Galileo*, questions the nature of humanity through the eyes of an orang-utan. Amongst her other contributions, 'Daisy, in the Sun' (November 1979), a beautiful coming-of-age/loss-of-innocence parable set against the death of the Sun, earned the first of her many Hugo nominations, and was the only story from *Galileo* to find its way on to the Hugo ballot. *Galileo*, the only sf market to accept Willis's stories at that time, allowed her to experiment, which led to a rapid maturing of her talent. Willis told me:

> Beginning writers are extremely vulnerable to criticism and/or career advice, and if Charlie had told me there was no place in science fiction

for screwball comedy, I'd probably have stopped writing them. Instead, he encouraged me to do pretty much anything I wanted, even if it was a story about a toddler's mother attending an eclipse or an ape who wanted to be baptized. He even published a dark little story I didn't think I'd be able to sell *anywhere*. It was called, 'Daisy, in the Sun', and when it was nominated for the Hugo Award, Charlie kindly offered to let me stay with his family during the Boston World Science Fiction Convention.[1]

John Kessel first appeared with the nightmarish neo-doppelganger story 'The Silver Man' (May 1978).[2] Ryan asked for two revisions before he accepted the story. Ryan bought three other stories from Kessel, although the third, 'Just Protoplasm', which had been another sold earlier to one of Edelstein's abortive anthologies, was in the fated seventeenth issue of *Galileo*, which was never published. Ryan also bought a comic strip, 'Crosswhen', which Kessel had developed with artist Terry Lee and had originally hoped to have syndicated in a daily newspaper. Whereas comic strips don't, as a rule, appeal to readers in sf magazines, there seemed to be no significant anti-lobby for this one. Perhaps the growth in adult and underground comics was at last having an effect, but this one worked and remained in *Galileo* until the magazine's demise.

Lewis Shiner's experience was not quite as rewarding as Kessel's. Ryan asked for a rewrite of Shiner's 'Tinker's Damn', but was dismayed by the outcome so he reworked a third version from the previous two. Although Shiner was paid for the story, he was unaware that it had been published (October 1977) and was disappointed with the result. Shiner told me, 'I don't feel Charlie made much of an effort to work with me on getting a story we would both be happy with, and I didn't want to risk losing the sale by being pushy.'[3]

Kessel's view, however, was:

> [Ryan] was extraordinarily hardworking and solicitous to someone who he might simply have rejected (at the time nobody else seemed to have any trouble rejecting my stories). He deserves a place in SF history for spotting some writers in the slush pile whom other editors were passing over, writers who went on to have long and notable careers.[4]

These experiences reveal an editor determined to get things right on his own terms. The fact that he developed so many new writers shows that

1 Personal e-mail, Willis/Ashley, 22 September 2006.
2 He had previously sold a story to Scott Edelstein for an anthology that never appeared because the publisher went bankrupt. That story, after many rewrites, later appeared as 'The Pure Product' in *Asimov's*, March 1986.
3 Personal e-mail, Shiner/Ashley, 5 August 2006.
4 Personal e-mail, Kessel/Ashley, 4 August 2006.

Ryan recognized talent when he saw it and did not want it lost. Without setting them apart, Ryan explored feminist and humanist issues and encouraged many women writers. Besides Connie Willis, Cynthia Felice and M. Lucie Chin, he published work by Alice Laurance, Dona Vaughn, Cherry Wilder (giving the first US publication to her sf debut from *New Writings*), Mary Schaub and Susan Lull.

Throughout the first two years, *Galileo*'s sales improved. The first issue's print run of 8,000 copies sold out; by issue #5 they were printing 32,000 copies[5] and Ryan was reporting that the circulation had 'more than tripled'.[6] This would imply sales of around 24,000, though in an interview that year Ryan stated, 'we hope to reach about 20,000 by the October issue'.[7] A few months later, assistant editor Floyd Kemske was reporting that subscriptions had grown by 11,000.[8] The first hard evidence we have is the legal Statement of Ownership and Circulation published in the March 1979 issue. This covered average sales for the year up to September 1978, which were probably issues #5 to #9 (October 1977 to July 1978). This identified average subscriptions of 32,300 and sales through specialist shops of 2,490. The subscription figure had risen because that average included the results of a major subscription drive with effect from the July 1978 issue where subscriptions had jumped to 52,900.

This success brought with it its own problems. From the start *Galileo* had trouble with issues posted to subscribers. Over 5 per cent of the subscribers' copies of the first issue were apparently lost in the post,[9] a figure Dick Geis found astonishing, remarking that with *Science Fiction Review* only a few were lost that way, around 0.1 per cent.[10] McCaffrey arranged for the second issue, which was ready for mailing in mid-December, to be sent to subscribers at the end of December and that changed the magazine's schedule during 1977. But greater problems lay ahead. In issue #10 (September 1978), McCaffrey reported that the increase in subscribers had caused them to drop their original manual system of recording and

5 Data from personal letter, Ryan/Ashley, 27 November 1977.
6 Charles Ryan, 'Editorial', *Galileo* #6 (January 1978).
7 Charles Ryan interview, *Empire*, November 1977, p. 35.
8 Floyd Kemske, 'Editorial', *Galileo* #10 (September 1978).
9 See 'Editorial', *Galileo* #3, p. 4.
10 See *Science Fiction Review* #21 (May 1977), p. 31. We have also seen that Gary Hoppenstand lost about half his mailing of *Midnight Sun* and that Jack Gaughan had mail problems over artwork. Ted White frequently complained about the deterioration of the postal service and on several occasions material he sent to Cohen was lost (see 'Editorial', *Fantastic*, February 1973). George Scithers commented that maybe 1 in 2000 manuscripts mailed to him were lost (about 0.05 per cent). Stanley Schmidt also spoke of a poorer postal service in his editorial to *Analog*, February 1980. Though McCaffrey's experience was extreme, the postal service did seem to deteriorate during the seventies, with an inevitable effect on magazine subscription sales.

employ a computer company to keep their records. It may seem unbeliev-
able now but at that time Avenue Victor Hugo had no computer. The
computer companies he hired were not especially good. Two were fired
and a third went bankrupt. In this process, data was lost and errors created
and if subscribers received their copies at all they were often several weeks
late. The delays in rekeying all the data and getting the records straight
delayed the eleventh issue by three months and McCaffrey felt obliged to
publish a double issue, #11/12 in late February 1979.

The major consequence of these late mailings was the effect it had on
subscribers. The increase that *Galileo* had during 1978 were cut-price
subscriptions, handled through a mailing agency, and for the first year
very little of that money feeds back to the publisher. The benefit comes
when the subscribers renew after the first year. However, the more the
subscribers were frustrated by delayed mailings the less likely they were
to renew. Worse still, the loss of computer data meant that McCaffrey had
no addresses to allow him to send out renewal reminders. McCaffrey had
to wait to see how many renewed before making any further plans.

And that was when they made their fatal decision. McCaffrey felt that
Galileo was sufficiently robust to risk national news-stand distribution,
and he needed the money from the extra sales to develop his growing
publishing company, including having his own computer.[11] An agreement was reached with Dell Distributing and from issue #13 (July 1979)
Galileo hit the news-stands. To celebrate, Ryan had acquired a new serial,
Larry Niven's latest novel, *The Ringworld Engineers*, the sequel to his
massively successful *Ringworld*. The Ringworld was depicted in a beautiful
wraparound cover by Cortney Skinner. At the same time, the cover price
was raised to $1.95, making *Galileo* the most expensive sf magazine on the
stands. The agreement required that an extra 110,000 copies be printed.
On the assumption of a 40 per cent sell-through, Dell advanced McCaffrey $28,000 per issue to cover the extra cost of printing.[12] This advance
would need to be repaid in due course on top of the money owed to both
the distributor and retailer on each issue (usually 40 per cent of sales).
The budget was tight, but provided that *Galileo's* news-stand sales were
more than 40 per cent of its print run (the equivalent figures for *Analog*
and *Asimov's* that year were well over 50 per cent, with *F&SF* at 40 per
cent), everything should be fine.

However, after four issues, it was discovered that sales were closer to
20 per cent, in addition to the fact that subscribers, either frustrated at

---

11 See letter from Thomas Owen, *Galileo's* assistant editor, in *Science Fiction Review* #31
(May 1979), p. 45.
12 See report in *Locus* #238 (October 1980), pp. 1, 4 for full details.

the mailing problems or perhaps now buying their copies from news-stands, were not renewing in the numbers needed. The peak of 52,900 had dropped to 44,000, with only a proportion of those being at the full subscription rates. McCaffrey found that the magazine was $125,000 in debt, with no money to pay contributors to the last issue (January 1980) or to notify subscribers of the problem. The March 1980 issue was prepared and ready to go, but was never published. It would have started serialization of Joe Haldeman's new novel, 'Worlds'.

The four news-stand issues were of equal quality to the earlier issues in terms of content, with stories by Connie Willis, Joan Vinge, Richard K. Lyon and D. C. Poyer in addition to Niven's serial. There were articles by Robert L. Forward and Hal Clement, plus a symposium looking back at the lunar programme on the tenth anniversary of *Apollo 11* with contributions by sf writers and scientists. The production values, though, did not improve. Despite its high cover price, *Galileo* was still printed on cheap newsprint and had only adequate reproduction of photographs, which did little justice to the steadily improving artwork. Also, *Galileo*'s large format set it apart from the other sf magazines and the casual reader might not have noticed it. Its title may even have worked against it as, at a glance, it may have been misinterpreted as a science magazine. *Galileo* might have been one of the most successful of the new magazines of the seventies, launched like a rocket, but it rapidly burned up on re-entry.

Worse was yet to come. *Galileo* was not the only casualty of its sudden fall from grace. McCaffrey had planned to spread his overheads over a group of magazines. He told me:

> With the full knowledge that there was not sufficient profit in the individual publication of a fiction magazine, it was our foolish thought that we could make a group work by gaining advertising revenue based on the circulation of all, by developing our own distribution network, which was called Offset, and we had built a network of 100+ stores nationwide by the time we signed up with Dell.[13]

Besides a science-fiction news magazine, *Science Fiction Times*, which McCaffrey had started in September 1979 and which struggled on until June 1980, there were plans to establish a western magazine, *Sundown*, a children's magazine, *Now Voyager*, and a mystery magazine, *Baker Street*. On top of this, McCaffrey acquired the rights to *Galaxy*. McCaffrey recalled, 'I got married and went off on my honeymoon, thinking we had a big success, and came back a month later to the first reports of doom.'

13 Personal e-mail, McCaffrey/Ashley, 30 September 2006.

A Fate Worse than Death

When we last saw *Galaxy*, James Baen had departed in August 1977, having completed the October 1977 issue. The new editor was John J. Pierce, aged 36, son of the noted engineer and scientist John R. Pierce (1910–2002) who had sold stories to Gernsback as long ago as 1930, and who was a key figure in the development of the communications satellite. Pierce, Jr. took after his father in a liking for hard technological sf. He was known in sf fandom for his sixties magazine *Renaissance* and for his anti-New-Wave views. In his first editorial he spoke of science fiction as an evolving genre and of the need for an editor to look for new developments and new ideas. He suggested that science fiction's Golden Age was now, the late 1970s, when all that had been science fiction's past was at last coming to fruition in all forms of media. His challenge, of course, was to pull *Galaxy* back into that development and make it once again part of the legacy it had created.

Unfortunately Pierce had far fewer tools to play with. Although Abramson had been making inroads into the money owed to past contributors, there was still a backlog and a reluctance amongst full-time professionals to contribute. Baen had contacts and had earned the trust of writers, but Pierce had yet to prove himself. He was fortunate in that his debut issue started serialization of Zelazny's latest Amber serial, 'The Courts of Chaos', but this had already been secured by Baen. Spider Robinson had left with Baen, dissatisfied over Abramson's handling of the book column,[14] and Pierce brought in Paul Walker as reviewer. Both Dick Geis and Jerry Pournelle continued to contribute their respective columns. Otherwise Pierce was on his own. The majority of stories he acquired were by new writers, few of whom sold any more stories and only two of whom established a career in sf. One was Steve Perry, then writing as Jesse Peel, who debuted with 'With Violet Hands' (December 1977/January 1978), in which future convicts are pitted against each other in gladiatorial contests. The other was Nicholas Yermakov – later to be better known as Simon Hawke – whose first story, 'Writer's Block', appeared in the February 1978 issue. It explored how computers and virtual reality could cure psychoses. Yermakov made one more sale to Pierce, 'The Surrogate Mouth' (November 1978), before moving on to his career as a novelist, selling a few more stories to *F&SF*. Their work was typical of new writers, using well-worn themes but with a slight gloss of originality.

14 See Robinson's letter of resignation and Abramson's response in *Locus* #204 (September 1977).

Pierce attracted a few other writers who were still developing their careers. William Walling, who had been selling to *F&SF* and *Analog* since 1970, appeared with two stories. 'Memo to the Leader', in the combined December 1977/January 1978 issue, was a novel twist on the idea of trying to change history, in this case to stop the Nazis winning, while 'The Norn's Loom' (March 1978) is a suspenseful story of how a spaceship is saved from disaster. Pat Murphy made her second sale to *Galaxy* with the mind-switch tale 'Eyes of the Wolf' (May 1978). Charles Sheffield, who had become a prolific contributor under Baen, appeared just once more with 'Killing Vector' (March 1978), the first of his scientific puzzle stories featuring McAndrew, later collected as *Vectors* (1979), this one showing how mini black holes could be used to propel spacecrafts. Pierce also published the first short story by Tappan King, who had already sold a novel. However King's 'Fearn' (September 1978) is to all intents a fantasy, despite the post-holocaust setting. It was far from the type of material one would expect to find in *Galaxy*.

The biggest surprise in Pierce's issues was the appearance of Cordwainer Smith, who had died in 1966, in the April 1978 issue. Pierce was an acknowledged expert on Smith and had compiled *The Best of Cordwainer Smith* collection for Ballantine in 1975. 'The Queen of the Afternoon' had been started by Smith (real name Paul Linebarger) in 1955 but left unfinished, though a companion story, 'Mark Elf', made it into the May 1957 *Saturn* (as 'Mark XI'). It was one of the earliest stories in his Instrumentality future history. Smith's widow completed the story in 1977.

Pierce performed as good a job as one might have expected in the circumstances. He acquired three more excellent serials, which were the magazine's lifeblood – C. J. Cherryh's 'The Faded Sun: Kesrith', Gregory Benford's 'The Stars in Shroud' and Frederik Pohl's 'Jem', though the last was going to suffer badly in *Galaxy*'s death throes. The short fiction was all readable but little of it gave any feeling of achievement. They were stories that did their job and entertained but did not, as Pierce had wanted, move the field on. Baen had managed to get *Galaxy*'s heart beating again, but under Pierce it was back on the pacemaker. *Galaxy* was particularly weak in its illustrations, of which there were now few in each issue, and most covers lost their spark. From the September 1978 issue, Abramson committed a cardinal sin and changed the familiar *Galaxy* logo from the serif-script form it had featured from the first issue to an all-capital block form which looked bland and uninviting. The next issue saw the last of Pournelle's columns. *Galaxy* was falling apart before the readers' eyes.

A sad picture of the offices at *Galaxy* is portrayed by David Galef, who is now a professor of English at the University of Mississippi but in the summer of 1978 was a young student looking for a summer job who wound up helping out as an assistant to Pierce:

> Starting that June, I found myself working at the UPD offices, doing everything from wading through the slush pile to answering correspondence and occasionally dealing with irate contributors. The editor, John J. Pierce, was a reedy, bespectacled type with a gangly walk and a goofy way of talking, addicted to puns and off-the-wall comments, but he clearly loved what he did and knew what he was talking about. The publisher, Arnold E. Abramson, on the other hand, seemed determined to milk the magazine for whatever it was worth, expending as little as possible on its upkeep. There was also a blousy woman in the office who seemed to do little except keep Abramson happy and care for the cats who prowled around the office and urinated on the carpets. The subscription manager, L. C. Murphy, seemed to do even less. We received complaints from our subscribers who weren't receiving their issues, most of whom eventually cancelled their subscriptions. It's a sobering thought to realize that one reason *Galaxy* finally went under had little to do with the quality of the magazine and a lot to do with issues not being sent out.[15]

We have no further data on *Galaxy*'s sales, the last officially recorded figures being those at the end of Baen's tenure when circulation, or more specifically subscriptions, had risen significantly. *Galaxy*, though, would face the same problem as *Galileo*, because these bargain subscriptions brought in little income unless readers renewed. With the poor state of *Galaxy* and its irregular publication, that was unlikely.

Pierce had hoped that he might make a difference at *Galaxy*, provided that Abramson was able to achieve his part of the bargain and improve the magazine's finances. Unfortunately it did not happen and by June 1978 the position, which had briefly improved, was now worse than before, with debts mounting. Pierce had even resorted to paying authors out of his own pocket and then trying to reclaim the money from Abramson.

Pierce could see no future for the magazine and tendered his resignation on 16 June, agreeing to work through to the end of July. He was overly self-deprecating in his resignation letter to Abramson, saying:

> I am not the best of all possible editors; perhaps someone with more experience than myself could have done better during the last year. But you must surely realize that it is going to be even more difficult now than it was a year ago to find such an editor.[16]

15 Personal e-mail, Galef/Ashley, 6 October 2006.
16 John J. Pierce, letter of resignation, reproduced in *Locus* #212 (July 1978), p. 2.

Although Pierce left on 1 August, *Galaxy*'s irregular schedule meant that his last issue was dated March/April 1979. In total he edited ten issues. The final issue was supposed to carry his parting message but Abramson replaced this at the last minute with an advertisement.

The new editor was Hank Stine. He was known as one of the renegades of the sf field. Now aged 33, Stine had written several perceptive reviews and articles for the magazines since his first publication, *Season of the Witch* (1968), about a man biologically transformed into a woman as punishment for rape and murder. In his first issue Stine promised 'aggressive changes' to restore *Galaxy*'s 'golden days', but these changes would come at a price. *Galaxy*'s word rate was slashed from three cents to one cent, the saving to be put to paying off the backlog owing to writers, but that one cent would be paid promptly on acceptance rather than publication. There is some evidence that payments were made promptly, though the definition of 'acceptance' was dubious, Abramson treating this as meaning once the issue was ready for press.

Stine had little opportunity to put his changes into action. Although he took over at the end of August 1978, Pierce had already completed three further issues and these staggered out during September, December and the following April. The December issue, actually dated November/December, had half of its shipment lost 'due to a computer error',[17] when it was misplaced on a train. The next issue should have appeared in January but was delayed for three months, and even then subscribers' copies were not mailed out till the middle of June.[18] The likeliest explanation is that Abramson was waiting for money received from the distributor for previous issues, which shows that *Galaxy* was existing purely on a hand-to-mouth basis, with no operating capital. During December 1978 and January 1979 Abramson entered into negotiations with Kerry O'Quinn and Norman Jacobs, the publishers of *Starlog*, for them to acquire *Galaxy*. Crucial to the deal was ensuring that UPD's debts were paid. Unfortunately the deal fell through because O'Quinn did not want to inherit the debts or the bad reputation,[19] and *Galaxy* staggered on. Abramson turned to a finance company, The Elm Corporation, which agreed to settle UPD's debts and ensure that authors were paid in full, but effectively this meant that *Galaxy* was mortgaged to Elm.

These behind-the-scenes activities show that, despite his previous mismanagement, Abramson was trying to ensure that all contribu-

17 See interview with Hank Stine by Elton Elliott in *Science Fiction Review* #29 (January/February 1979).

18 See letter from S. John Loscocco, quoted in *Science Fiction Review* #33 (November 1979), p. 5.

19 See *Science Fiction Review* #31 (May 1979), p. 63.

tors would eventually be paid.[20] In this respect one must give credit to Abramson. Stine said of him, 'I've found him to be a man of honor who has lived up to every single agreement we've had so far.'[21]

Not all agreed with that, especially following the cut in wordage rates. Harlan Ellison, whom Stine had ill-advisedly listed amongst those from whom he had material on hand, reacted vehemently, saying in part:

> If I choose to write for shit money, I'll submit my work to the semi-pro magazines that need the boost, not to an alleged 'national magazine' whose prestige went by the boards a decade ago. It is an honor to write for, say, Gary Hoppenstand at *Midnight Sun* for short line; he can't pay much, but he respects the writers and doesn't pretend to be hot stuff while screwing those whose work fills his pages.[22]

Stine had prepared his first three issues long before all of this at the time when it was believed that the magazine would return to a monthly schedule from January 1979, but that never happened. When Charles Platt interviewed Stine in April 1979, Stine remarked how frustrating it had been as, despite the work he had done, none of his issues had been seen after six months' work.[23] The delayed January issue appeared in April (dated March/April) and Stine's first issue did not appear until July (dated June/July). It was not an encouraging issue. The cover illustrated a scene from the new short serial, 'Star Warriors', by Jesse Peel (Steve Perry). It was a none-too-subtle attempt to cash in on the success of *Star Wars* and the imagery of *Star Trek* and was space opera at its most formulaic. It might have worked in *Planet Stories* in the forties or even *If* in the sixties, but for *Galaxy* at the start of the eighties it gave the worst possible message. So too did the 'complete novel' (really a novelette) 'Beneath the Bermuda Triangle' by Jane Gallion, another formula story that pandered to the cultists. The less said about the other stories, including A. E. van Vogt's painfully embarrassing 'Femworld', the better. Stine had put together an issue which was intended to be sensational in every way, but which he hoped would also appeal to a wide range of readers. It did the opposite, pandering purely to the lowest common denominator and contained nothing of merit. His next issue, which appeared in late September (dated September/October), was almost as poor. The only good short story was

---

20 A letter that the Elm Corporation sent to all creditors was printed in *Locus* #221, May 1979, p. 11, where the company's president, S. John Loscocco, emphasised that Abramson had insisted that all contributors to *Galaxy* were to be paid in full.

21 Interview with Hank Stine.

22 Harlan Ellison, letter, *Locus* #215, October 1978, p. 13.

23 See Platt's interview with Stine in C. Platt, *Who Writes Science Fiction?* (Manchester: Savoy Books, 1980), p. 61.

George R. R. Martin's 'A Beast for Norn', though even this was space opera, albeit tongue-in-cheek. Peel's 'Star Warriors' came to a predictable conclusion, while the 'complete novel' was 'The Invasion of America' by Gil Lamont, a weak excuse for a Rambo-style macho adventure. Even the stories by George Alec Effinger and David Bunch did little to appease the disappointment and only Frederik Pohl's serial 'Jem', which still hadn't reached its conclusion even though it had already appeared in book form, injected any quality into the issue.

In the editorial to his second issue, Stine commented that in the nine months since he had been appointed as editor he had read over five thousand manuscripts. If all he could find out of these were the stories in these two issues, it was a poor sign of the state of science fiction and of Stine's editorial skills. Stine's grand plan when he became editor, which was to have work by big-name authors, excerpts from major new novels, and a magazine with wide appeal, had all come to nought, mostly because of *Galaxy*'s financial straits and its atrocious reputation. In the hope of reaching the new market developing with the success of *Star Wars* and *Alien*, Stine had sold to Abramson the idea of two one-shot magazines, *Alien Encounters* and *Wars Among the Stars*, in the large-flat format, but thankfully, these never came to be.

Although Stine had compiled at least two more issues of *Galaxy*, neither appeared. UPD had reached rock bottom. It could not even afford to mail out the subscription copies of Stine's second issue. In December 1979, Arnold Abramson agreed terms to transfer rights in the magazine to Vincent McCaffrey, who set up a separate company, Galaxy Magazine, Inc., to take it over. No money exchanged hands. Instead, as an interim measure, UPD owned 10 per cent of the new company, which allowed a small income to UPD, from a share of all revenues arising, to pay off the remaining debts. The plan was for *Galaxy* to appear bi-monthly, alternating with *Galileo*, starting in February 1980. Whereas *Galileo* was aimed at a more mature readership (the average age was apparently 29), *Galaxy* was to be packaged for a student readership of around 19/20, with the emphasis on adventure. It was going to be in the same large format as *Galileo*. The new editor was going to be Floyd Kemske, who had worked on *Galileo* as the review editor and general co-ordinator. A science editor and reviews editor were also appointed.

All this was agreed in December, before Christmas. Soon after Christmas, McCaffrey discovered the full extent of his problem over sales and the scale of debt. That debt did not affect *Galaxy* directly, as *Galileo* was published by a separate company, Galileo Magazine, an imprint of McCaffrey's Offset Distribution, which was part owned by his Avenue Victor Hugo bookshop.

But the scale of the debt had an inevitable knock-on effect and McCaffrey had to rethink his whole publishing strategy.

The distribution package with Dell was cancelled and McCaffrey returned to the idea of distributing *Galileo* directly, as he had before, for his 40,000 subscribers. The same would happen for *Galaxy* with its 37,000 subscribers[24]. However, McCaffrey's cash-flow problem made it impossible to continue with *Galileo*. Instead the emphasis was placed on honouring commitments for *Galaxy*. It was not until May that they were able to distribute Stine's last issue to subscribers, six months late.

Then in July 1980, against all odds, 22,000 subscribers received a copy of the new *Galaxy*. It looked much like *Galileo* and, thankfully, the original logo and old-style cover format had been restored. Like *Galileo*, it was in large-flat format, on cheap newsprint, though priced slightly lower at $1.50 and, like *Galileo*, it placed a strong emphasis on a package of material, with various science articles, features and reviews, as well as fiction. In fact in almost every way the new *Galaxy* was a duplicate of *Galileo* except that the fiction was toned down, with less sophisticated, all-action fiction – apart from the final episode of Frederik Pohl's 'Jem', which at last reached its long-delayed conclusion. There were only four stories. Raymond Kaminski's 'The Colony' was a textbook traditional story of a derelict spacecraft found at the rim of the solar system. 'In the Shubbi Arms' by Steven Utley and Howard Waldrop dealt with oppressed humans under alien conquerors. 'The Night Machine' by Dona Vaughn concerned how an aged space traveller could live with his young wife. 'In the Days of the Steam Wars', by Eugene Potter and Larry Blamire provided a wonderful evocation of the old Frank Reade dime novels in what was an emerging subgenre of 'steampunk'.

McCaffrey's determination to publish at least one issue of *Galaxy* has to be congratulated, and there must have been hope that new subscriptions might start to regenerate finances. But it was a lost cause. Money was still not coming in to McCaffrey from past news-stand sales of *Galileo* and the debts were not diminishing. An October issue of *Galaxy* was compiled, intended to be a thirtieth-birthday celebration, but it was never published. In October McCaffrey pulled the plug. *Science Fiction Times* was sold to Andrew Whyte, and no further issues appeared, *Galaxy* was put up for sale, and *Galileo* went into cold storage. On 10 December 1980 Avenue Victor Hugo went into Chapter 11 bankruptcy, which allowed the bookstore to continue to operate and repay the debts from store revenues.

---

24 This was the figure quoted in *Locus* #230 (February 1980), p. 1, from figures provided by McCaffrey. The last official figure for *Galaxy*'s subscription level was 51,399, reported in the December 1977 issue in respect of the year ended September 1977.

But it was the last we would see of *Galileo*, though not the last we would see of Charles Ryan, nor, for that matter, of *Galaxy*.

The Cosmos Experience

The deaths of *Galileo* and *Galaxy* were both sad and salutary. They were object lessons in how pride goeth before a fall, and it is possible that neither magazine need have failed had both publishers been cautious. *Galaxy*'s fate had been sealed with the economic crisis of the mid-seventies when Abramson's poor financial decisions left UPD undercapitalized. As Baen reported, *Galaxy* itself, during his editorship, was profitable and had Abramson sold it at that time, as a genuine going concern, it might have survived. But, of course, that was impossible, because *Galaxy* was subsidizing the rest of the company, and in the end UPD drained it dry. *Galileo*, on the other hand, showed what vast potential there was in a subscriber-only magazine and, had McCaffrey been able to sustain that, without the problems that new technology caused, *Galileo* would also have survived. Indeed, both magazines were pointers to the future. News-stand sales were no longer enough to support magazines that were otherwise under-funded. Neither of the companies which ran *Galaxy* and *Galileo* had the wherewithal to finance the costs necessary to support a magazine during its first three to four issues until the money from retail distribution began to flow through. Both magazines, however, almost certainly would have survived had they invested in sales primarily by subscription and specialist stores, because subscriber sales brought in money upfront. Provided subscriber sales grew steadily, and not rapidly as in the case of *Galileo*'s publishers' clearing house drive, the magazine could still be financed, but the extra demand of printing copies for subscribers where the money would not come in for another year was what sealed *Galileo*'s fate.

These lessons were obvious in hindsight, but amazingly difficult to learn at the time. We shall encounter further examples of ambitious magazines overstretching themselves and failing. Against this we need to compare the fate of other new magazines, including the remarkable success of both *Isaac Asimov's Science Fiction Magazine* and *Omni*, as well as the changing circumstances of the existing magazines. Let's deal first with the other important, short-lived victim of the late seventies revival.

Cosmos Science Fiction and Fantasy Magazine, to give it its full title, was published by Baronet Publishing, a new company set up on Madison Avenue in New York in 1976 by Norman Goldfind, until recently the vice-president of Pyramid Books. Baronet was to publish both mass-market paperbacks and illustrated trade-paperback editions, and Goldfind was also interested in publishing a magazine – in fact, two. *Bijou*, a film magazine, was launched in February 1977 (cover date April) followed by *Cosmos* in March (cover date May). Its editor was David G. Hartwell, a former college teacher who was at that time the consulting editor-in-chief of Berkley SF. Hartwell, aged 35, was already well-known and respected for his knowledge of the field. Since 1975 he had been the editor of the Gregg Press science-fiction series of hardcover reprint volumes and since 1965 had produced a nationally distributed 'little' magazine of poetry and fiction called *The Little Magazine*, which had published work by many sf personalities including Joanna Russ, Samuel Delany, Thomas Disch and Ursula Le Guin.

Cosmos was an attractive magazine from the word go. It was in the large-flat format, the same as *Galileo*, and the magazine's art director, Jack Gaughan, took full advantage of that. It not only sported striking colour covers but also a colour centre spread and other coloured artwork. The centre spread featured the work of a specific artist in each issue: Paul Lehr in the first, followed by Will Eisner, Ron Miller and Eddie Jones. The colour art was reproduced on coated stock but the other pages were plain newsprint, so *Cosmos* could be called a semi-slick. Each story was also illustrated by a major artist – Richard Powers, Rick Sternbach, Vincent Di Fate, Alex Schomburg, George Schelling, and many more.

Its 72 pages sold for $1, the same price as the leading digests, but was almost certainly underpriced. There were 150,000 copies printed of the first issue and 125,000 of the subsequent issues, and it needed at least a 20 per cent sell-through to break even. *Cosmos* shared overheads and distribution with *Bijou*, so if *Bijou* sold well it would help subsidize *Cosmos*. With the first issue of *Bijou* sporting a photograph of Clint Eastwood and a feature on the Dirty Harry character, there were high hopes for both magazines.

Unfortunately, *Bijou* failed miserably, its sell-through only around 10 per cent and it promptly folded, leaving *Cosmos* to carry the full burden of costs. Sales of the first four issues remained at around the 35,000–40,000 level which, on its own, was profitable. However, the distribution arrangement meant that *Cosmos* now had to sell 65 per cent of its print run (or over 80,000) in order to make up the loss on the first three issues of *Bijou*, and that would not happen. Had Goldfind continued the magazine in the hope that sales would improve, the losses would have eaten into the book-publishing side, which was Baronet's main business, and so the title was dropped.[25]

---

25 Data provided in personal e-mails by Norman Goldfind and David Hartwell.

This was a bitter blow because, in quality terms, *Cosmos* was an excellent magazine. In presentation and looks it was amongst the best, and certainly better than *Analog* and *F&SF*. Its contents rivalled those magazines, especially *F&SF*, as *Cosmos* also ran fantasy. Its one short serial, Fritz Leiber's 'Rime Isle' (May–July), told the latest adventures of Fafhrd and the Grey Mouser. George R. R. Martin's 'Bitterblooms' (November), though science fiction at the core, is laced with the imagery of fantasy, particularly the Arthurian legend. There is a similar mythic quality in Cherry Wilder's 'The Lodestar' (May). Other stories have that haze of fantasy, blurring the edges of technology to open the reader's perceptions. Richard Lupoff's 'The Child's Story' (September), for instance, creates a beautiful, alien far future, while Thomas F. Monteleone's 'Camera Obscura' (July) reveals an alien world that is all too close. Michael Bishop's 'The House of Compassionate Sharers' (May) is a deeply human story where the technology is a barrier to emotion.

Hartwell attracted an impressive diversity of names, both major contributors, such as Frederik Pohl, Greg Benford, Larry Niven and Norman Spinrad, and new writers. It was good to see a couple of the Clarion alumni making further sales, particular Robert Thurston, whose apocalyptic 'Wheels Westward' (November) was a sequel to his hit Clarion story. Besides the fiction, Hartwell had a centre section, 'a magazine within a magazine', which along with the artwork ran various regular reviews and news, with columns by Robert Silverberg, Charles Brown of *Locus*, Ginjer Buchanan, William Rotsler and, by the last issue, Harlan Ellison. Silverberg's book reviews were perceptive without pontificating and his overview of Philip K. Dick's work in the September column is a lesson in evaluation.

Cosmos was a fine magazine, providing a good range of quality fiction and other material. In its brief existence it was arguably the best sf magazine around and, given sufficient financial backing and better distribution, it should have succeeded. It made good use of the large format, and the only improvement would have been to have used coated stock throughout. However, this would have had an inevitable effect on the price and might have priced the magazine out of the market.

Lessons were being learned from the fate of recent magazines. It was evident from the initial success of *Galileo* and the popularity of such small-press magazines as *Algol* and *Shayol* that magazines could exist adequately by subscription only, even with relatively low circulations, and provided that the overheads were minimal – almost a one-man band – they would survive. Otherwise they needed substantial investment to overcome that initial 'lump' with the cost of development and distribution. Distribution always had been the major problem with magazines, but during the days of the pulps everything was done to such a scale that the problem only affected the small-time publishers. Now, though, distributors were being more selective and the outlets were diminishing. Steve Brown noted that he saw only two copies of *Cosmos* in the entire Baltimore–Washington area.[26] For new magazines there was no middle ground – either they had to be small-scale or large. Of the existing magazines, *Analog* had behind it a large publisher, Condé Nast, though, as we shall see, that would soon change. *F&SF*'s publisher, Mercury Press, had also once had a major presence, but it had since scaled down and, though that name survived, it had effectively turned into a 'cottage industry', as Ferman called it, and opted for the smaller end of the scale.

Ferman's *F&SF* is a case of a magazine that achieved a successful formula and tried not to meddle too much with it, letting it evolve gradually with its market. I have already covered *F&SF* during the seventies and it remained steadfast, the one secure rock within a sea of turbulence. It was the one magazine to benefit from the subscription drives carried out through Publishers' Clearing House. Its subscriptions doubled during the seventies from around eighteen thousand to over thirty-six thousand and continued to rise in the eighties, while their news-stand sales remained fairly static. *F&SF* had sufficient print run to meet the extra demand and once a sufficient number of subscribers renewed after that first year (around 20 per cent), the money began to flow. *F&SF* could do this because it was already established, with sufficient sales, a good distribution network and good printing terms to grant them the flexibility. A new magazine such as *Galileo* had no financial wherewithal to meet the extra printing demands or to anticipate the likely news-stand sales. Undertaking a subscription drive and news-stand distribution at the same time increased the costs too much and too quickly, with no guarantee of sufficient income for at least four months and more likely a year.

It is pertinent that the only truly successful new professional magazines of the seventies both came from established publishers who had an existing track record and sufficient capital to provide the investment necessary to launch a new title. The first of these was *Isaac Asimov's Science Fiction Magazine*.

26 See *Science Fiction Review* #23 (November 1977), p. 69.

Asimov Triumphs

Isaac Asimov records the origins of his eponymous magazine in his autobiography. On 26 February 1976[27] Asimov had dropped off the typescript of a story for *EQMM* at the offices of Davis Publications in Park Avenue, New York when Joel Davis asked to see him. Davis had recently taken over publication of *Alfred Hitchcock's Mystery Magazine* from its March 1976 issue, and was contemplating further expansion into fiction magazines. One of his executive staff had taken his children to a *Star Trek* convention and had been impressed 'by the numbers and enthusiasm of the fans attending'.[28] He suggested that Davis might wish to consider a science-fiction magazine.

The story has echoes of when Leo Margulies was similarly impressed by the sincerity of fans at the first World Science Fiction Convention in New York in July 1939.[29] That had led to Margulies publishing the sf-hero pulp, *Captain Future*, aimed at a teenage readership, and the attitude towards the sf-magazine market did not seem to have altered much, if Davis's executive is any measure.

Davis was no stranger to the science-fiction field. His father, Bernard Davis, had been the partner of William B. Ziff in the Chicago firm Ziff-Davis from 1935 to 1957. That firm had published *Amazing Stories* from 1938 to 1965 and launched both *Fantastic Adventures* and its stepdaughter *Fantastic*, all three close to Bernard Davis's heart. Bernard Davis departed from the company in September 1957 and set up his own Davis Publications, acquiring, as a starting point, *EQMM*, which had hitherto been published by Mercury Press, under Joseph Ferman, and was thus a stable mate to *F&SF*. Davis Publications subsequently developed a stable of over thirty special-interest magazines, many of them relating to either finance or hobbies, and it was only when Joel Davis, who succeeded his father as president of the company in 1972, acquired *Alfred Hitchcock's Mystery Magazine* at the end of 1975 that he gave thought to expanding the digest-size fiction magazines.

In keeping with the two mystery magazines, it was important to have a celebrity's name in the title. Asimov, as one of the most popular and accessible science-fiction writers, was an obvious choice. He was cautious

27 In *In Joy Still Felt*, p. 736, Asimov states that the day he and Davis first discussed the magazine was 26 February 1976 but earlier on that same page he says that he had completed a book on that day and it was the *next* day (i.e. 27 February) that he went to Davis's offices.

28 Isaac Asimov, *In Joy Still Felt*, p. 737.

29 See Sam Moskowitz, *Seekers of Tomorrow* (Cleveland, OH: World Publishing, 1966), p. 82.

to begin with but was soon won over. By the end of April George Scithers had been appointed as editor. Gardner Dozois soon came on board as associate editor. The new magazine was officially announced in June 1976. It was planned as a quarterly at first and the initial issue, dated Spring 1977, was released on 16 December 1976.[30] Some readers assumed that Asimov was the editor, and he soon dispelled that: 'George and I work together. He does the day-to-day work and makes the day-to-day decisions and deserves the credit for whatever success the magazine has. We consult frequently, however, and nothing happens that we don't *both* approve of.'[31] In their combined wisdom, Asimov and Scithers wanted a magazine that people enjoyed. It was not to be one full of stories trying to put the world to rights, nor to be full of experimental or New Wave material. Neither Scithers nor Asimov was against fiction that pushed the barriers, but it had to do it in an entertaining, rather than aggressive way. Asimov set the tone in his first editorial:

> With my name on the magazine, it won't surprise you to hear that we will lean toward hard science fiction, and toward the reasonably straightforward in the way of style. However, we won't take ourselves too seriously and not every story has to be a solemn occasion. We will have humorous stories and we will have an occasional unclassifiable story.[32]

The unclassifiable story in the first issue was 'Kindertotenlieder or Who Puts the Creamy White Filling in the Krap-Snax' by Jonathan Fast, the son of Howard Fast. The story is neither science fiction nor fantasy, but is a macabre little Hansel-and-Gretel-like tale of how big business manipulates children, more suited to *Alfred Hitchcock's Mystery Magazine*. Mystery writer Edward Hoch was similarly present with 'The Homesick Chicken', a lightweight gadget story mixed with a mystery, more suited to Gernsback's magazines of 50 years earlier. Both Asimov's story, 'Think!', about a computer becoming sentient, originally written for a promotional brochure for a laser development company, and Arthur C. Clarke's squib, 'Quarantine', written at the request of George Hay for a series of stories on postcards, were minor pieces of no consequence.

Thankfully, there was more heavyweight material in the issue, most notably two stories by John Varley, one under the alias Herb Boehm and both included at the urging of Gardner Dozois. Varley was on top form and, though 'Good-Bye, Robinson Crusoe', one of his Eight Worlds stories

30 Arthur C. Clarke was quick to remind Asimov that this was his birthday.
31 Isaac Asimov, *Isaac Asimov's Science Fiction Magazine* 1:3 (Fall 1977), p. 190.
32 Isaac Asimov, 'Editorial', *Isaac Asimov's Science Fiction Magazine* 1:1 (Spring 1977), p. 8.

showing how one could not perpetually escape from reality, was good (and incidentally selected by Dozois over twenty years later to lead his anthology *The Good New Stuff* (1999)), it was the pseudonymous 'Air Raid' that caught the public eye. This is a bleak story of a grim future and how time-travellers try to improve their future world by stealing people from the past. It was nominated for both the Hugo and Nebula, and formed the basis of the less-than-successful film *Millenium* (1989), for which Varley wrote the screenplay and the novelization, *Millenium* (1983).

Varley's two stories stood out in the first issue, though there was good material from Fred Saberhagen and Gordon R. Dickson. The latter's 'Time Storm' was an excerpt from his forthcoming novel, *Time Storm* (1977), and other extracts appeared in a later issue of *Asimov's* as well as in *Cosmos*. The extract stood reasonably well on its own, sufficient for it to win the Jupiter Award as that year's best novelette, though it was inevitably inconclusive. Its strength lay in the intriguing concept that Dickson created of a time wave, like a tidal wave, engulfing territory at a rapid rate and of the effect that this had had on individuals. Varley's and Dickson's stories were representative of the more creative end of the spectrum that *Asimov's* would publish.

Asimov had declined to contribute a science column because he was committed to that in *F&SF*, and so this feature became the domain of several contributors, mostly, at the outset, George O. Smith and Milton A. Rothman, both long-time acquaintances of Asimov from the old *Astounding* days. Other regular features included a book-review column by Charles Brown (taken over by Baird Searles from May 1979) and a puzzle column by Martin Gardner, renowned for his books of mathematical problems and paradoxes. He introduced a series of logical or mathematical brainteasers presented in the form of a story and often with a double whammy, so that the solution to the first problem led on to a second or third. There were no prizes for solving them, but they proved popular and were another trademark of the early issues, which were there to exercise the mind in a friendly manner, as well as to entertain.

The humorous items which became another trademark of *Asimov's* were not so evident in the first issue, aside from Arthur Clarke's story, but in his introduction to that story Clarke argued that he was a better punster than Asimov. Asimov naturally rose to the challenge and the second issue carried two extended puns by Asimov, 'About Nothing' and 'Sure Thing'. Asimov assured readers that such puns would not become a permanent feature of the magazine, but the third issue saw the return of Reginald Bretnor's series about Ferdinand Feghoot. This had originated in *F&SF* in 1956, written by Bretnor under the anagram Grendel Briarton. Each brief story had Feghoot in a predicament which led to a punchline that was an excruciating pun, and such stories became known as Feghoots. They had died out in *F&SF* in 1964, but had been briefly resurrected in *Venture* in 1970, and now Feghoot returned for a third time.

This attitude of fun encouraged other contributions, mostly in the form of spoofs or parodies and occasional limericks. In the second issue, Dean McLaughlin resurrected Isaac Asimov's original thiotimoline hoax which had first appeared in *Astounding* in 1948. Thiotimoline has the remarkable property of dissolving just before contact with water. McLaughlin uses this same propensity to reveal the discovery that flares from stars react in advance to striking a match on Earth. In the fourth issue (Winter 1977), Randall Garrett conceived of a Martian conundrum written in the style of a Burroughsian John Carter pastiche and Barry Malzberg resurrected Agatha Christie's Roger Ackroyd, in defiant role, affronted by his rejection as a twenty-fourth-century mysterist. Stanley Schmidt, the new editor of *Analog*, contributed several whimsical stories, including 'Panic' (January/February 1978) which considered the panic caused by the Orson Welles Martian invasion radio broadcast from the viewpoint of the Martians.

This type of literary wordplay became a much-loved feature amongst readers, many of whom submitted their own spoofs and Feghoots. The youngest contributor was Cam Thornley, who was only 15 when 'They'll Do it Every Time' appeared in the January/February 1978 issue. Unfortunately, this type of wordplay threatened to overshadow the more serious fiction. There was a reaction by some readers to 'Bat Durston, Space Marshal' (September/October 1978), a first sale by G. Richard Bozarth. The story was a deliberate parody of the space opera which had so plagued the pulps in the thirties and forties. Though good fun in its own right, there was a fear that the many new readers to *Asimov's* would not understand the parody and would believe that it was serious literature. A far better parody was 'The Last Master of Limericks' (November/December 1978) by Garry R. Osgood, which, while it contained some painful examples, was a cleverly told tale.

The sheer volume of these fun stories, though, did give the impression that the magazine was not only not taking itself very seriously (in itself no bad thing) but also giving the misleading impression that it was okay for sf to be rather juvenile in its outlook. This feeling was further emphasized by some stories which were clearly written for a young readership, the worst of which was Stephen Goldin's 'When There's No Man Around' in the third issue. Although set on Mars, the story could as easily have been set anywhere remote on Earth. It involved a young girl on a return journey across Mars when her vehicle breaks down and, having no way of communicating with home, she finds she has to fix the machine herself. For most of the story she acts like a stereotype of a silly little girl who does not know how machines work until, miraculously, she remedies everything with a hairgrip. Not only was the story insulting to women (and several feminists soon raised objections) but it lacked any credibility as we did not learn what was wrong or how it was resolved. It was written like a children's story but one that not even children would appreciate. In a similar vein, although less condescending, was 'A Simple Outside Job' (Winter 1977) by Robert Lee Hawkins, which has a newly qualified engineer having to find a way out of a difficult spot on Titan. It was written on the level of a boy's adventure story and seemed infuriatingly trite to hard-core sf fans.

That writers regarded *Asimov's* as 'juvenile' was evident in a number of reviews. Orson Scott Card, for instance, identified the business advantage of *Asimov's* having 'tapped a juvenile market that none of the other magazines was reaching'.[33] Darrell Schweitzer told me: 'A lot of writers made up their mind that *Asimov's* was for kids and were not submitting their work, even though it would have been accepted for more than they were being paid elsewhere.'[34] It was an image that *Asimov's* took a while to lose.

One of the notable features of *Asimov's* early years was the number of first-time writers, sometimes as many as four per issue. Scithers always announced a story as a first sale, which doubtless encouraged others to try, and before long *Asimov's* was publishing more first-timers than all the other magazines put together, including *Unearth*. The first of them was Sally A. Sellers in the first issue. 'Perchance to Dream' was a powerful story of a human whose organs could regenerate themselves but who wished for death. It was the result of a writers' workshop held at the University of Michigan by Lloyd Biggle, Jr. Judy-Lynn del Rey was impressed with the story and wrote to the author, care of the magazine, asking to have first sight of any novels Sellers might write. Unfortunately, although Sellers wrote one further story (non-sf), she found the world of writing too tenuous and moved on to other things.

Other writers whose first sales were to *Asimov's* and who went on to establish themselves include J. P. Boyd (Summer 1977), Michael A. Banks (March/April 1978), Sharon Farber (May/June 1978), Diana Paxson (July/August 1978), Barry Longyear (November/December 1978), Al

---

33 Orson Scott Card, reviews in *Science Fiction Review* #29, January/February 1979, p. 30.
34 Personal e-mail, Schweitzer/Ashley, 18 August 2006.

Sarrantonio (March 1979), Sharon Webb[35] (June 1979), F. Gwynplaine MacIntyre (January 1980) and Richard S. McEnroe (May 1980). Scithers also published the first fiction by artist Jack Gaughan, 'One More Time' (November/December 1978). Additionally, other authors who had sold once or twice elsewhere became *Asimov's* regulars during Scithers's editorship. These included Steve Perry (writing as Jesse Peel), John M. Ford, Nancy Kress, Jeff Duntemann, Ted Reynolds, William F. Wu, Juleen Brantingham and Somtow Sucharitkul. All of these names became closely associated with the magazine but none more so than Barry Longyear and Somtow Sucharitkul.

Longyear, a former commercial printer who turned to full-time writing at the age of 35, debuted with 'The Tryouts', which was also the first of his series about the circus folk of the planet Momus. Longyear's back story is that an interstellar circus-ship had crashed on the planet Momus long before and had been forgotten. When they are rediscovered, their descendants have taken their skills to an advanced degree, so that fortune-tellers really do tell fortunes and magicians seem to have mastered real magic, but they now live purely for the show. When a visiting diplomat tries to convince them that they are at the epicentre of warring factions, the circus folk ignore him because his 'act' is unconvincing. It's a lovely idea for a single story, but the popularity of this first tale caused Longyear to continue the series for a little longer than was wise. The first set of stories was collected as *Circus World* (1980), and two other books followed. Even though the idea grew thin, each individual story was cleverly plotted, showing that Longyear was a capable writer but one who needed to stretch himself. That eventually happened with 'Enemy Mine' (September 1979), a finely crafted humanist story of how two enemies, stranded together on a planet, come to respect each other. The story won both the Nebula and Hugo awards for best novella in 1980 and topped the *Locus* poll in the same category. In that same year Longyear won the John W. Campbell Award as best new writer, the first time an individual had won all three awards in the same year. The story was made into a motion picture in 1985.

Somtow Sucharitkul, who now uses the variant form of his name S. P. Somtow, was a Thai composer[36] who was educated in England (at Eton and Cambridge), but who debuted in the United States in *Unearth* in 1977 and also sold a story to *Analog* before his *Asimov's* debut with 'A Day in Mallworld' (October 1979). Mallworld is a hollowed-out asteroid that

---

35 Though under the alias Ron Webb she had sold a poem and a story to *F&SF* in 1963.
36 George Scithers commissioned Sucharitkul to compose 'The Isaac Asimov's Science Fiction Magazine March'. The score for piano was published in the issue for 15 February 1982.

has been converted into a huge shopping mall and contains everything a human could want. As background to the setting, a benign alien race has isolated the human race from the rest of the galaxy until they become more mature, and they use Mallword as an observation post. The stories, which ran occasionally in *Asimov's* over the next two years, were a satire on human (or specifically US) materialism and, though light-hearted, were more ingeniously wrought than other such tales in the magazine. A deeper side of Sucharitkul emerged in his Inquestor series which had started in *Analog* but continued in *Asimov's* with 'The Web Dancer' (December 1979). These stories began to change the frivolous tone of much that had preceded in *Asimov's* as Sucharitkul explored a tyrannical alien race that dominates the universe.

The preponderance of new writers in *Asimov's* contrasts with the surprising dearth of established writers. They were there but not in quantity and rarely in depth, deterred, as Darrell Schweitzer believed, by the magazine's juvenile image. John Varley, who was present in the first issue, contributed one more story under Scithers, the ingenious murder mystery amongst clones, 'The Barbie Murders' (January/February 1978), but did not reappear in the magazine for another six years. Michael Bishop likewise contributed two stories, both atypical, and then contributed no more for six years. Jack Haldeman contributed a series of sf sports stories, starting with 'Louisville Slugger' in the second issue, but they were intentionally light material. F. M. Busby, whose stories of the seventies had displayed great intensity, contributed a surprisingly casual series about a friend called Sam who has the ability to edit time. Brian W. Aldiss contributed the lyrical fantasy 'The Small Stones of Tu Fu' (March/April 1978) about a meeting between a time-traveller and an ancient Chinese poet, but then nothing more for four years. George Alec Effinger appeared with 'The Last Full Measure', a recursive story of an alien trying to discover the secret of Earth's weaponry from a science-fiction reader.

The writers who were less prone to compromise their work were the women, although their fiction was generally less challenging than one would hope. Joan Vinge only contributed during Scithers's editorship – three excellent stories, of which 'To Bell the Cat' (Summer 1977), a first-contact tale that explores human and alien sensitivities, and 'The Storm King' (April 1980), a study in the maturing of character and emotion, are of special merit. Tanith Lee, who had already established a formidable reputation with her novels, produced her first science fiction for the magazines with 'The Thaw' (June 1979) where, two centuries hence, a disenchanted future society decides to rediscover the past by reviving thousands of corpsicles. Jo Clayton, who had also established a following for her novels, contributed a series in the style of Marion Zimmer Bradley featuring a tortured heroine, Gleia, who seeks to rid her world of jewels of legendary evil. The series, which was not altogether convincing, began with 'A Bait of Dreams' (February 1979), under which title the series appeared in book form in 1985. The series was also further evidence that *Asimov's* was not limiting itself to hard sf but including science fantasy and planetary romances.

What was noticeable was that several writers of an older generation contributed stories that felt right at home in the fifties. These included L. Sprague de Camp, Randall Garrett (whose Lord Darcy stories became a regular feature), Jack Williamson, A. Bertram Chandler, Margaret St Clair and Hal Clement.

The only author whose work caused some consternation amongst readers and for which the editors found themselves apologizing was Frederik Pohl. Ironically, the basic premise of Pohl's stories, which began with 'Mars Masked' (February 1979), was tailor-made for *Asimov's*. Pohl was back in his favourite territory of social satire, looking at a near future where the Cold War stalemate has evolved into a Cool War of environmental sabotage. The series, which included *Asimov's* first serial, 'Like Unto the Locust' (December 1979–January 1980), was part of Pohl's forthcoming novel *The Cool War* (1980)and, though not on a par with *Man Plus* or *Gateway*, it was an enjoyable return to the Pohl of old. Except, that is, for Pohl's offensive language. Somehow, neither Scithers nor his new associate editor, Shawna McCarthy, had thought to edit out the four-letter words and, while mature sf readers had found they could live with these in the other magazines, the new readers at *Asimov's* were unprepared for such abuse. Letters of outrage poured into the offices, subsequently countered by letters of support, not dissimilar to the outpouring of offence that had confronted Ben Bova at *Analog* nine years before. While Asimov tried to encourage readers to look beyond the words, both he and Scithers found themselves apologizing. Scithers remarked, 'we want to apologize for not copy-editing this instalment as well as we should. It's not our intention to use language quite that strong when we (and the authors) can avoid doing so.'[37] This whole sequence of stories, along with Scithers's apology, tells us much about the magazine and its readership. Both Scithers and Asimov wanted stories that reflected their tastes and had a wide appeal. As a consequence, they went predominantly for traditional, safe stories and nothing too challenging or revolutionary. This was clearly what readers wanted. The letter column was full of comments from readers who had either given up on the sf magazines but felt they at

37 George Scithers, *Isaac Asimov's Science Fiction Magazine* 4:3 (March 1980), p. 173.

last had a magazine they could read or who were discovering sf magazines for the first time. Scithers's approach was clearly working and attracting a new and, to some extent, unaware readership. When the circulation figures came in for *Asimov's* over its first year, many were surprised at the scale of its popularity. Its average paid circulation for the year 1977/78 was 108,843, which exceeded even that for *Analog*, which stood at 104,612. That was the highest average circulation *Asimov's* would reach, though it came close in 1982/3, by which time subscriptions had doubled. In fact, although news-stand sales steadily fell year by year, that was the same for all of the magazines. What was important about *Asimov's* was that the number of subscribers consistently rose over each of the next five years. *Asimov's* was attracting more and more new readers and, in that light, it should be seen as their gateway into the world of the sf magazine which otherwise had been suffering during the seventies. To achieve this, Scithers had dumbed down some of the fiction and tried to make it accept-able to all, hence the need to avoid any offensive language. He also strove to keep the stories positive and uplifting. This was not unlike the *Analog* of Campbell's last years, except that Scithers avoided overly militaristic stories. In effect, *Asimov's* was a diluted version of *Analog*.

Unfortunately, this approach would only benefit the field if those readers then graduated on to *Analog* or *F&SF*. If they stayed within *Asimov's*, and that magazine did not itself develop, then the field would continue to stagnate. *Asimov's* had to be the base camp, not the final destination. It is true that during the same first six years of *Asimov's* existence (1977–82) the number of subscribers to *Analog* and *F&SF* also increased, but we have no way of knowing what overlap there was amongst readers. The annual *Locus* poll, which of course applies only to readers of *Locus*, showed that the number of readers who also read *Asimov's* dropped from 64 per cent in 1977 to only 39 per cent in 1982, which shows that fewer hardcore fans were reading it. In fact these figures dropped for all magazines, but the smallest drop was *F&SF* (60 per cent down to 53 per cent) while *Asimov's* had the largest drop. So during the period when *Asimov's* readership grew the most, the crossover readership by *Locus* readers dropped the most. This suggests that *Asimov's* was being deserted by the hard-core fans while being embraced by a growing number of new readers who, possibly, were not advancing within the field. The fact that fewer established writers were contributing was further evidence of stagnation.

Gardner Dozois had left after the first year when he realized that there was only partial overlap between his preferences and those of Scithers. Dozois told me: 'I noticed that he was rejecting the stories that I told him I thought he ought to buy and buying the stories that I told him he ought to reject, so it became clear that there was little point in continuing the relationship.'[38] Bearing in mind the impact that Dozois had in discovering new writers when a first reader at *Galaxy*, and the even greater impact when he returned as full editor of *Asimov's* in 1985, we might conjecture that the stories Dozois was recommending were more advanced examples rather than traditional ones. Dozois was replaced by a team of first readers based at Scithers's home in Philadelphia. They included Darrell Schweitzer, Meg Phillips, Alan Lankin, John Ashmead and Lee Weinstein, and became collectively known as 'the Zoo'.

Despite the magazine's popularity, it was not without its critics. The most vocal was John Shirley, who had sold a story to the second issue but did not appear again for another five years. His verdict in 1979 was, 'With the exception of a few stories by Varley and one or two others, the magazine is a fog of predictability, formula and done-to-death techno-bullshit imagery.'[39] A year later his opinion was unchanged and he maintained that Scithers was playing it 'safe':

> And when you're *that* safe, you're schlock. Trouble is, *Asimov's* has a huge and growing circulation. People think that this is science fiction and I fear that it is a major neutralizing influence on the field. It is a sort of convergence point for the field's various banalities and tired conventionalisms. It is influencing the others to be the same way.[40]

The success of *Asimov's*, if viewed in isolation, did seem to suggest this. Delivering a diluted, conventional and homely version of sf would satisfy the masses and sustain a circulation, whereas those magazines and anthologies that had tried to be challenging, unconventional and groundbreaking had wilted and failed. Of course, it was not quite as simple as that. While part of *Asimov's* success was due to a generally acceptable, safe form of sf, we cannot overlook the drawing power of Asimov's name. Many of the readers' letters acknowledge that they picked up the magazine because they were attracted by his name and they felt 'safe' that it would contain material they enjoyed. The following example is typical of many: 'After years of sampling (but never buying) the other magazines, I've found this one to be the first truly satisfying one. At last, here's a magazine to supplement my cyclical rereadings of Asimov! I'm glad I subscribed, sight unseen.'[41] Neither should we forget the abilities of the staff working in Davis's circulation department. They were able not only to draw upon the

---

38 Personal e-mail, Dozois/Ashley, 14 August 2006.

39 John Shirley, 'Paranoid Critical Statements #2', *Thrust* #12 (Summer 1979), p. 26.

40 John Shirley, 'A Final Paranoid Critical Statement', *Thrust* #16 (Fall 1980), p. 23.

41 Letter from Dan E. Williams, *Isaac Asimov's Science Fiction Magazine* 1:3 (Fall 1977), p. 188.

experience of 20 years in marketing *EQMM*, but also to take advantage of that magazine's distribution network. In 1977 *EQMM* had a circulation of over 330,000, and sales of *Alfred Hitchcock's Mystery Magazine* had risen by nearly 10 per cent to almost 125,000 since Davis took it over. *Asimov's* was able to sell a fair percentage of news-stand copies off the back of these, as well as some crossover subscribers. *Asimov's* success was a combination of a shrewd commercial business sense and an understanding of what readers wanted. Having captured that readership, Scithers continued to ply them with more of what they wanted and only slowly raised the level of the magazine's content. This had a lot to do with the fact that the new writers were maturing, and Longyear and Sucharitkul led the way with a greater understanding of their material.

The marketing did not end with the magazine. Stories from the magazine's first year were recycled in two paperback anthologies with the series title *Asimov's Choice*: the first *Astronauts & Androids* followed by *Black Holes & Bug-Eyed Monsters*, assembled by Scithers and published at the end of 1977. The stories in the March/April 1978 issue were then reissued as the third volume, *Comets & Computers*, the May/June issue as *Dark Stars & Dragons* and the July/August issue as *Extraterrestrials and Eclipses*. Davis then tried a new approach. Selections from the first seven issues were repackaged as *Isaac Asimov's Science Fiction Anthology, Volume 1* and published in a 288-page digest form in September 1978. A further four volumes were issued over the next four years, each of which also had a hardcover edition from Dial Press. This not only brought in additional sales revenue at minimal cost, but also attracted further readers.

Davis had been cautious at the outset and had contracted with Asimov and Scithers to produce three quarterly issues. The success meant that the magazine went bi-monthly from the January 1978 issue, monthly from January 1979 and four-weekly from January 1981. It also meant that Davis felt sufficiently confident in the market for fiction magazines that he not only launched two more but also bought another one.

Asimov Expansion

Isaac Asimov recorded in his autobiography that, after five issues, Joel Davis was 'very elated' at how *Isaac Asimov's Science Fiction Magazine* was progressing: 'Apparently its sales and subscriptions were satisfactory and he was talking of going on a monthly basis and of trying out a sister magazine aimed at younger readers.'[42] The sister magazine was *Asimov's*

---

42 Asimov, *In Joy Still Felt*, p. 794.

SF Adventure Magazine. Its first issue, dated Fall 1978, was released on 29 June. It was not issued in digest form but in the large flat-saddle-stapled format, the same as *Cosmos* and *Galileo* but printed on a slightly-better-quality, semi-coated newsprint stock. It ran to 116 pages, larger than either *Cosmos* or *Galileo* but sold for the higher price of $1.75. This was expensive considering it was aimed at younger readers and when compared to the $1.25 of both *Analog* and *F&SF*. There were clearly great hopes as it had a print run of 200,000 copies.

The larger format brought *Asimov's Adventure* on a par with the comic-book magazines and it was hoped that they might sell alongside those. It was clear from Asimov's editorial that this magazine was aimed at a less-discriminating reader:

> We want to fill the void left by the demise of magazines such as *Planet Stories*. We want to meet the needs of at least some of the vast number who discovered *Star Wars* in the movies, who enjoyed it, and who are ready to look for something of the same sort, or better, in print.[43]

Now we really were in the pulp jungle of *Planet Stories* and *Captain Future*. If *Asimov's Adventure* was intended to lead younger readers into the field it needed to stimulate and educate them sufficiently that they could move on to other magazines, not just *Asimov's*. Since *Asimov's* was already a diluted version of *Analog*, to dilute it even further for younger readers was risking a complete washout.

However, that was not Scithers's intention. He told me that *Asimov's Adventure* 'was built on the *IAsfm* inventory – in fact, stacked with the best we had in inventory at the time'.[44] This means that there was no further dilution, but that *Asimov's Adventure* was the best that they had to offer.

In fact that cannot be entirely the case. The lead story in the first issue was 'Captive of the Centaurianess' by Poul Anderson, reprinted from the March 1952 issue of *Planet Stories* and updated for new astronomical data. Nevertheless, the story still reflects the outlook of the early fifties, with a Martian who speaks English like a German and the landscape of Ganymede every bit as we might have hoped a quarter of a century before. The story was enjoyable, knowing its provenance, but was still very dated. More fun, and the best item in the issue, was a slightly abridged version of the new Slippery Jim diGriz novel, 'The Stainless Steel Rat Wants You!', by Harry Harrison, in which our knight in tarnished armour saves the Galaxy from nasty aliens. The remaining stories in the issue were relatively minor, though Jesse Peel's 'Where Now is Thy Brother,

---

43 Isaac Asimov, 'Editorial', *Asimov's SF Adventure Magazine* 1:1 (Fall 1978), p. 8.
44 Personal e-mail, Scithers/Ashley, 13 August 2006.

Epimetheus?' is unusual for the period for its use of martial arts. Asimov's own story, 'Fair Exchange?', is scarcely an adventure, while 'Bystander' by Alan Dean Foster, who was at the start of his career producing novel-izations of blockbuster sf films, was a routine space story. The issue even contained a Feghoot, contaminating the issue with the pun virus.

Apart from Alex Schomburg's work, which was well suited to space opera at comic-book level, the other interior illustrations were poor and unlikely to attract young readers. What may have had some appeal was the *Star-Wars*-style cover, by Paul Alexander, which was reproduced without the lettering as a full-colour centre spread. There were no other departments apart from a letter column, even for the first issue, which contained a dreadfully juvenile letter from Lin Carter, in the style of 1940s letters to *Startling Stories*.

Readers' letters in the later issues generally seemed to approve of the magazine, one or two even claiming it as the best sf magazine around, so it clearly had some appeal, but the first issue was the weakest of the run. Nevertheless, the reception and the sales of around sixty thousand[45] were sufficient for Davis to give the go-ahead for the magazine as a quarterly. The second issue appeared in November 1978, allowing time to acquire better material. It now included a feature on science fiction in Holly-wood, providing an opportunity to reprint *Star-Wars* stills. The second issue contained a new Momus story by Barry Longyear and another sf sports story by Jack Haldeman, but by far the best content was the novella 'Star School' by Joe and Jack Haldeman. Written in the style of Heinlein's juveniles, this is a coming-of-age story of a young farm boy from a high-gravity world who enters a space-cadet school and needs all his strength to survive. There was a further Starschool adventure in the third issue, and both were reworked into the Haldemans' novel, *There is No Darkness* (1986).

By the third issue Scithers had broadened adventure fiction to cover fantasy and though this veered away from the original space-opera approach, the contents improved. It also, curiously, raised the standards because both Roger Zelazny's 'The Last Defender of Camelot' (which won a Balrog award) and Samuel Delany's Nevèrÿon story 'The Tale of Gorgik' were more sophisticated than stories in the previous issues, with subtler levels of meaning which were possibly lost on younger readers. This issue also included the first story sale by Keith Minnion, 'Ghosts', a story of interest not only because it blended science fiction with the supernatural, with ghosts an integral part of a space rescue, but also because it was probably the first sf story to include the new information that Uranus

45 Figure cited in *Locus* #220, April 1979, p. 6.

had rings. The artwork also improved with illustrations by Val Lakey and Frank Borth and this improved still further with the fourth issue which included full-page spreads by Stephen Fabian and George Barr, though this last issue lacked the colour centre spread. The final issue contained a new Circusfolk story by Barry Longyear, 'The Starshow', taking us back to their early days, but more importantly it ran Longyear's novella 'The Jaren', under his Frederick Longbeard alias. This story, rather like 'Enemy Mine', portrays humans through the viewpoint of aliens, but goes further in delineating a perspective of human imperial expansion. Also in the final issue was John Brunner's last Traveller in Black story, 'The Things That Are Gods'. This fine series, which had appeared in four different magazines over 19 years, though set against the vast backdrop of the entropic war between Order and Chaos, focuses on human foibles and weaknesses.

The last two issues of *Asimov's SF Adventure* were considerably superior to the first two and yet their sales were poorer. Although a fifth issue was planned, it was put on hold until the full sales results were through. The magazine relied wholly on news-stand sales, as Davis had chosen not to seek subscriptions, and both distribution and sales were far weaker than envisaged. Scithers recalled:

> I talked with the manager of a comic-book store in Manhattan who happened to like *Asimov's SF Adventure*. He said he put a stack of each issue on the checkout counter – the best conceivable place for a magazine. He said the kids would buy a bunch of the (then) dollar comics, pick up a copy of the *SF Adventure* magazine, turn a few pages, then put it down.[46]

Asimov's Adventure evidently did not appeal to its target readership. At first glance, it had neither the appeal nor the excitement of the comics. Unfortunately, although the later issues contained material of sufficient quality for all ages, the magazine's presentation implied juvenile fiction and so rather than attracting both generations, it appealed to neither. Davis told Scithers that he lost $50,000 on the magazine.

The failure of *Asimov's Adventure* did not dampen Davis's interest in science fiction. In fact, he now brought to fruition a project that he had been planning for two years. On 20 February 1980 he concluded the deal to purchase *Analog* from Condé Nast.

When we last discussed *Analog* we had reached the end of Bova's period as editor. Bova had never considered his editorship of *Analog* as a lifetime job. The income from it made it closer to a hobby. His plan to

---

46 Personal e-mail, Scithers/Ashley, 13 August 2006.

stay for five years, to ensure that the magazine had survived the death of Campbell and was secure, stretched to seven years. By that time he was tiring of the management at Condé Nast who were doing nothing to promote the magazine or expand its market, or indeed to develop other related magazines. In 1975 Bova had suggested to Condé Nast the idea for a large-format slick, full of advertising, that would run some science fiction but would mostly be features about science, technology and the future. His title was *Tomorrow Magazine*. The management were not interested. Over the next few years it became evident that *Analog*'s market penetration was stagnating, and once again management had no interest in expansion or developing promotional ideas. So, at the end of June 1978, Bova resigned, agreeing to stay on until a new editor was found. He recommended Stanley Schmidt, having been impressed by Schmidt's approaches to teaching both physics and science fiction at Heidelberg University in Tiffin, Ohio. Schmidt was then 34. Schmidt was appointed from September 1978 and Bova departed, planning to return to full-time writing, but was instantly hi-jacked as fiction editor of the new magazine from Bob Guccione, *Omni*, of which more later.

Schmidt's first issue was dated December 1978, though there were still stories acquired by Bova in the inventory and, as with the previous handover, it was a few months before Schmidt felt that he was commanding his own ship. Schmidt was no stranger to *Analog*, having appeared there since his very first fiction sale, 'A Flash of Darkness' in September 1968, exactly ten years before. At the outset Schmidt had no intention of rocking the boat. He recognized that *Analog* worked and was successful. He commented:

> My first job is to learn all I can about how it works so I can ensure that it continues to do so. Then, as I gain experience and get feedback from you, I hope to find ways to make it work still better. But gradually, not drastically. I don't plan to come into something which is already working well and immediately make wholesale, sweeping changes.[47]

In one sense Schmidt had an easier task than Bova had had seven years earlier. Campbell had dominated the magazine but, at the same time, his final issues had taken on both a sameness and a quirkiness which irritated many and had been one of the factors which necessitated the New Wave and other revolutions in sf. Bova had to both lay the Campbell ghost and get the magazine back on course, which he did with considerable skill. Schmidt was inheriting a magazine where those wrinkles had been

47 Stanley Schmidt, 'Changing the Guard, But Not too Much', *Analog* 99:1 (January 1979), p. 6.

smoothed out, where new talent had been cultivated and where honour was restored. He had no surgery to undertake.

But in another sense this made Schmidt's job harder. Bova had to do something proactive, but Schmidt didn't. He needed to handle the controls so smoothly that no one noticed the change. But naturally over time he wanted to imprint his personality on the magazine and bring his thinking to it, so there was bound to be some change. Schmidt wanted to do that as calmly as he could.

His main advantage lay in the contributors themselves. The regulars would not want to see things change either; they had only to sustain the quality of their own work and Schmidt was halfway there. Writers who had become associated with the magazine under Bova – Kevin O'Donnell, Jr., Bob Buckley, William E. Cochrane, Donald Kingsbury – and under Campbell – Frank Herbert, Clifford Simak, Gordon R. Dickson, plus a few vital newcomers – John Varley, Orson Scott Card, Michael Bishop – all continued to appear, some more frequently than others, but enough to provide a feeling of similarity and continuity. The scope of their fiction changed little. *Analog*, in other words, continued to deliver what people expected and that kept everyone happy.

Moreover, some of these writers provided novel-length serials or episodes of continuing series, both of which were still the heart of most magazines. Orson Scott Card, for instance, provided 'Songhouse' (September 1979), a long sequel to his highly popular 'Mikal's Songbird', which Bova had published the previous year. Gordon R. Dickson returned, after six years, with the second of his series about the alien Aalaag and their cruel domination of Earth in 'The Cloak and the Staff' (August 1980). John Varley provided one of the year's blockbuster novels, 'Titan' (January–April 1979).

Serials, though, had become a contentious matter in magazines. For a start, they really only worked in monthly magazines, and with so many dropping to bi-monthly or quarterly schedules, serials had become less common. More significantly, rather than wait the month between instalments, readers would buy the novel in paperback or hardback which usually appeared within a month of the serial's final episode and then read it without interruption. Serials no longer had the drawing-power they had once had. Generally, it was only worth running a serial if it was such a major work, usually by a major writer, that the editor knew that it would attract readers, or if it was sufficiently in advance of book publication that it was worth reading in instalments. Varley's 'Titan' was certainly an example of a major work, but Schmidt increasingly moved to publishing serials which at that time had no contracted book publication date. In his first two years, two such serials were 'Class Six Climb' (June–August 1979) by William Cochrane, all about the fight for the survival of an ecologically important planet, and 'One-Wing' (January–February 1980) by Lisa Tuttle and George R. R. Martin, a continuation of their stories set on the planet Windhaven which had started with 'The Storms of Windhaven' in May 1975. In both cases, the book versions did not appear for almost a year after the serials. Bob Buckley's 'World in the Clouds' (March–May 1980), about the first manned landing on Venus, has yet to appear in book form, while 'Dawn' by Dean McLaughlin (27 April–20 July 1981), which develops further the basic idea explored by Isaac Asimov in 'Nightfall', eventually appeared in book form in 2006. Yet both are eminently readable stories. Whether by chance or design, Schmidt was ensuring that *Analog* ran top-quality fiction with a relative exclusivity.

Schmidt did make a few changes, mostly in the non-fiction departments. Since the death of P. Schuyler Miller, the book-review column 'The Reference Library' had been in various hands, though mostly Lester del Rey's. Schmidt continued to rotate the column for a while but then settled down to just two contributors, Thomas Easton providing eight columns and year and Spider Robinson the other four. It was not until October 1982 that Easton became sole proprietor. Schmidt also added a new science feature (May 1979), in addition to the regular monthly article. 'The Alternate View' switched viewpoints each month between G. Harry Stine and Jerry Pournelle, both veterans of the aerospace industry but also both political animals, allowing both to argue their corner on a variety of potentially contentious issues. Their columns frequently prompted a lively debate in the letter column, showing that this feature was both popular and topical. Schmidt also ran an occasional 'State of the Art' essay on issues related to science fiction. Samuel Delany began this (May 1979) with a piece on the lack of detailed knowledge of science fiction by not only college instructors but also publishers and other so-called professionals within the field.

Schmidt also had (and still has) a good reputation for encouraging new and developing writers. His first year saw new or early sales from Somtow Sucharitkul, Michael McCollum, Edward A. Byers (all April 1979), Timothy Zahn (September 1979) and W. T. Quick (October 1979). Zahn would go on to become a nationwide bestseller with his novels based on the *Star-Wars* universe, but before then he was an *Analog* regular. His early stories show a progression of bigger and bigger ideas: in 'Ernie' (September 1979) it's a boxer with a small talent for limited teleportation; in 'The Dreamsender' (July 1980), it's about a man who can communicate through dreams, while in 'A Lingering Death' (December 1980), it's about a virus that imposes longevity. Zahn's stories were always inventive and accessible.

Michael McCollum had previously sold an article to Bova, but began to sell regularly to Schmidt after 'Duty, Honor, Planet' (April 1979). He struck a chord with 'Beer Run' (July 1979), the story that initiated his Paratime series about monitoring the Earth and its parallel universes, which later emerged as the book *A Greater Infinity* (1982). With his first story, 'Pathway' (April 1979), Edward Byers started another popular series dealing with the discovery of a number of stargates, most of which lead humans to garbage worlds rather than Edenic ones.

These new writers delivered material in the traditional *Analog* mode, but they tended to be less militaristic or philosophical. The Campbellian depth was rarely present now. If anything, under Schmidt, the contents grew more humorous. He reintroduced the series of tall stories that Campbell had run during the forties, 'Probability Zero', starting from the August 1979 issue. That also brought Mike Resnick into the sf magazines, writing here with Lou Tabakow. Resnick was already a veteran of scores of erotic novels and a few formulaic sf ones, and his contributions to 'Probability Zero' were far from serious. It would be another decade before Resnick started to produce the material that has since won him many awards.

But there was also pessimism amongst the stories, and a darker side. In 'The Locusts' (June 1979), Steve Barnes and Larry Niven considered whether humans had reached the peak of their evolution and would start to regress. In 'giANTS' (August 1979), Ed Bryant reflected the paranoia about government experiments and what terrors we might unleash. Barry Longyear, now broadening his market from *Asimov's*, further explored the expansionist mindset of humankind from the viewpoint of aliens in 'Savage Planet' (February 1980). George R. R. Martin's 'Nightflyers' (April 1980) is an especially dark story of a spaceship whose computer has become controlled by the spirit of the captain's psychotic and overprotective mother. These stories made us look at ourselves and the world we were affecting. The best of them was 'Can These Bones Live?' (March 1979) by Ted Reynolds, in the mode of a far-future fairy-tale. A woman is resurrected aeons hence by aliens and discovers that she is all that is left of the human race. She is given the choice of reviving the race, but has to prove their value.

There were occasional contributions from an older generation of writers. George O. Smith wrote a clever parody of the space opera, *Star-Wars* style, in 'Scholar's Cluster' (May 1980). Clifford D. Simak contributed not only an intriguing sf puzzle serial, 'The Visitors' (October–December 1979) but one of the best of his latter-day short stories, which swept up all the awards, 'Grotto of the Dancing Deer' (April 1980).

The smooth transition of *Analog* from Bova to Schmidt masked some of the changes that were taking place. The thought-provoking stories were there, as was the state-of-the-art high tech, but many had a lighter, defter touch, authors no longer needing to belabour the point as readers became more keyed in to the rapid changes occurring in technology and society. Campbell's lectures and Bova's stirring rebirth were now giving way to a relaxed confidence in a field where the top writers had raised the standards and were taking the field forward. For once *Analog* no longer seemed the field leader, even though it remained custodian of all that was best in high-tech sf. Under Schmidt, *Analog* felt in safe if less-demanding hands.

The move to Davis Publications, with effect from the September 1980 issue, was thus to Schmidt's advantage. *Analog* had for far too long been the alien in the midst of Condé Nast's magazines, not fitting in with the other glamour, fashion and lifestyle magazines such as *Vogue*, *Mademoiselle* and *House and Garden*. At Davis there was not only a ready-made niche but a publisher keen to support and develop the magazine. There was no doubt that *Analog* would benefit from Davis's marketing and promotional skills, but there was also concern that *Analog*'s individuality might be lost and that it might be expected to follow the route carved out by *Asimov's* in trying to appeal to a less-demanding readership. Schmidt was quick to allay such fears in his first editorial under new management:

> The special expertise and energy Davis can bring to *Analog* lie in the business area: such things as getting *Analog* before the largest possible audience. *Not* by making *Analog* over into a different magazine to appeal to a different audience, but by expanding the audience we already have.[48]

It was a significant time for change. In January 1980 *Analog* had celebrated its fiftieth anniversary and, perhaps more significantly, with the November 1980 edition it reached its 600th issue. Until the recent change, it had had only three publishers: William Clayton, Street and Smith, and Condé Nast, and five editors, Harry Bates, F. Orlin Tremaine, John W. Campbell, Ben Bova and Schmidt. This was remarkably stable considering the upheavals that had affected *Analog*'s only long-surviving rival, *Amazing Stories*, which had even more changes ahead. It was that stability, which had arisen from being supported by major publishers and highly capable editors, that gave *Analog* its confidence and assuredness. Barring major accidents or economic crises, *Analog*'s future should be safe.

---

48 Stanley Schmidt, 'Housewarming', *Analog* 100:9 (September 1980), p. 6.

The only editorial changes were that Shawna McCarthy became managing editor of both *Asimov's* and *Analog*. At the time of the change-over, *Analog*'s associate editor was Marc Kaplan. He was in charge of the day-to-day assembly and production of the magazine. Soon after the move to Davis, Kaplan followed Ben Bova to *Omni* as associate science editor. McCarthy was thereby given the responsibility for the production of both magazines, as well as still serving as in-house editor to Scithers on *Asimov's*. It was a full-time job, made all the more significant with the shift to the four-weekly schedule from the start of 1981. She was assisted by Elizabeth Mitchell on both magazines. Their workload was to grow.

Davis was looking for further expansion, a thread I shall follow briefly, even though it takes us beyond our 1980 cut-off point. With four fiction magazines under his belt, and setting aside the failed experiment of *Asimov's SF Adventure*, Davis launched two more, *Crime Digest* and *Science Fiction Digest*, which I'll consider in the next volume. McCarthy became the full editor of *Science Fiction Digest*. At this same time, Joel Davis brought in Carole Gross, who had previously worked at Doubleday, as a new executive director and vice-president in charge of marketing and production. One of the first changes was to transfer the control of all the artwork and the magazine layout, formerly managed by the editors, to Davis's art department. This led to a complete redesign of both magazines, with a new cover format effective from the April 1981 issues. There was a major restructuring which resulted in a change in most of the senior management. Gross also introduced a new form of contract which expected authors to sign over most of the rights in their stories and brought Davis Publications into conflict with the SFWA. It was an unsettling time. Although Schmidt weathered the storm, Scithers could not contain his displeasure. The result was a parting of the ways. Scithers was given notice to quit with effect from the end of December 1981. The last issue bearing his name as editor was dated 15 February 1982. Scithers planned to return to work on his own publishing house, Owlswick Press, and continue with *Amra*, but within days he found he was once again the editor of a science-fiction magazine. To see how that happened we need to return to *Amazing Stories*.

Amazing Days

The most vulnerable magazines were those trapped in a descending spiral with no significant capital support and a reducing market. Once trapped in that vortex, *Galaxy* was unable to escape and would only have survived had it passed to a new publisher before the rot set in. Both *Amazing* and *Fantastic* were in a similar vortex. When I last discussed them, Cohen had been trying to find a new publisher for them, but without success. One potential buyer had been Roy Torgeson, a bundle of creative energy who, in some people's eyes, was verging on being a new Elwood. Torgeson, though, had higher standards and tried to focus his energies. He had already won a World Fantasy Award with his wife, Shelley, for their work in establishing Alternate World Recordings, a company that had released recordings of works by Harlan Ellison, Robert Bloch and others. Torgeson became the science-fiction editor at Zebra Books and established a strong line in fantasy, horror and occasional science fiction. He was keen to buy the title to *Amazing Stories* because he wanted to change it radically and create a magazine for the eighties. Alas it was not to be. In 1980, via Lin Carter, Torgeson was able to revive *Weird Tales* in pocketbook format. Some concept of what Torgeson might have done to *Amazing* may be seen from the anthology series *Chrysalis* which he started at Zebra Books in August 1977. Torgeson was wide open to experimental fiction but especially loved the idea of doing something exciting and radical with the traditional. *Chrysalis 1* led with a novelette by Richard A. Lupoff, 'Discovery of the Ghooric Zone—March 15, 2337', in which three cyborg astronauts exploring beyond the orbit of Pluto discover Yuggoth, the planet of Lovecraft's pantheon. Harlan Ellison's 'How's the Night Life on Cissalda?' has to be the most audacious sf sex story yet written (and was reprinted, to graphic effect, soon after in *Heavy Metal*). Chelsea Quinn Yarbro's 'Allies' is a suspenseful story of something nasty lurking near a base on an alien world. These were all refreshing and challenging stories and the volume contained other similar ones by Spider Robinson, Theodore Sturgeon, Elizabeth Lynn and Charles L. Grant. The whole *Chrysalis* series, which ran to ten volumes over six years, was as exuberant as its editor, and it leaves one saddened that Torgeson was unable to have the chance to channel that excitement into *Amazing*.

Instead, Cohen passed the whole package to his partner, Arthur Bernhard, and retired to Fort Lauderdale, Florida, where he died in July 1988, aged 77. Bernhard assumed full control on 15 September 1978. He lived in Scottsdale, Arizona, so although the publisher of record remained the same – the Ultimate Publishing Company – the offices shifted from Flushing, New York to Arizona.

Ted White had previously made several approaches to Cohen with ways of improving the magazine:

> I had a good idea for a new and better format, based on the larger size employed by magazines like *Time* and *Playboy*, but one which would

avoid the design and format mistakes of the SF magazines which had tried that size, like *Vertex* and *Odyssey*.[49]

Cohen resisted any suggestions. However, with Arthur Bernhard in control, and with his son Alan as associate publisher, there was a possibility of change. Bernhard told White that he would be more receptive to ideas and so, at the start of October, White met with Bernhard at the distributor's office in New York. White continued:

> My format ideas would not have required much more money, if any, but I also made a pitch for a decent editorial and art budget and a decent salary, so I was turned down flat. 'I'm not going to put money into it until it starts *earning* money!' was the way Arthur put it. He then stopped sending me my salary checks. 'I'll pay you when you turn in an issue,' he said.[50]

That was when White tendered his notice, officially leaving on 9 November 1978. The last issues under his editorial control were the January 1979 *Fantastic* and February 1979 *Amazing Stories*. White returned all new manuscripts to their authors, including those already copy-edited and lined up for the next issues. White maintained that this was under instruction from Bernhard but Bernhard denied this.

For a new editor, Arthur Bernhard turned to Elinor Mavor, aged 42, who, along with her son Scott, had been providing freelance illustration and production work for various sport and astrology magazines that Bernhard also owned. Mavor had been editor of a trade magazine in the restaurant business, *Bill of Fare*, for the previous three years, so she was able to provide both editorial and graphic-design skills. She had been a reader of science fiction since her teens, but had known nothing about *Amazing Stories* or the science-fiction scene, so it was a true baptism of fire. Mavor was the second woman to edit *Amazing* and *Fantastic*, but she was unaware that under Cele Goldsmith the magazines had seen one of their most important periods. Uncertain that the science-fiction field would accept a woman editor, Mavor adopted the alias of Omar Gohagen, though her own name appeared as art director. What attracted Mavor was the opportunity to present the magazines as a package, a marriage between design and fiction. This was a challenge in the digest format, but she had worked in that area before.

Her first issues, the April *Fantastic* and May *Amazing*, showed all the weaknesses of interim issues. With the inventory empty, the stories were once again, for the most part, reprints from the archives, again made

49 Ted White, 'My Column', *Quantum* #43/44 (Spring/Summer 1993), p. 28.
50 Ibid.

without payment. What was most galling about these reprints was that they were not chosen with any distinction of merit, and all of them had been reprinted before within the magazines or one of Cohen's forest of reprint titles. You needed to be a new reader to *Amazing* not to have encountered them already. A couple of brief new stories were squeezed into the issue and these gave Mavor some opportunity to develop her concept for the magazine. One idea was to have a hook to lure the reader into the magazine, so she began a new story on the back-cover which continued within the magazine. Unfortunately few of these stories held much interest and it was only over time, working with artists who presented an attractive back cover illustration to accompany the stories, that they became more appealing. Another unfortunate idea in *Amazing* was to start a graphic story and seek reader contributions to continue it in each issue. Such experiments have always been doomed to failure in the magazines and thankfully, after three excruciating episodes, 'Meccano Sapiens' was seen no more.

Mavor may be excused her first couple of issues. With no inventory, no grounding in science fiction, virtually no budget, a dwindling circulation and with renewed conflict with the SFWA, she was handicapped in every direction. What saw her through was a belief that she could do something and a determination to make it work, and steadily she made progress. She had not known of the previous SFWA boycott or of the acrimony against Ultimate Publishing for the use of reprinted material:

> I caught wind of this early on by reading in the sf trades about the understandable outrage, but when I discussed this with Mr. Bernhard, he brushed the matter aside as unimportant. I finally convinced him that we had to publish only new stories, but he still really didn't under-stand the firestorm, so I took it upon myself to rectify the situation by going to some conventions to meet influential people and try and turn the tide back in our favor.[51]

It took some while to turn the tide. Mavor recalls a confrontation she had with Harlan Ellison at a convention in 1979 where he complained bitterly about how writers had previously been mistreated and how this was being perpetuated. Mavor apologized for the past and promised that the magazines would soon be publishing all new material, and she asked Ellison if he would contribute. He agreed that he would and sent through 'Run, Spot, Run' (January 1981), the sequel – or rather completion – of his award-winning 'A Boy and His Dog' and later 'The Cheese Stands Alone' (March 1982), the latter written specially for Mavor.

51 This and other unsourced quotes in this section are from personal e-mails, Mavor/Ashley, 10 August 2006.

Mavor recalls that Barry Malzberg was another 'whose disdain I suffered early on who reversed himself to the extent of praising one of my new writers, John Steakley, and inviting him to New York to meet a publisher for his novel'. Malzberg was also one of the first established professionals to submit new fiction: 'They Took it All Away' (November 1980), a troubling tale of memory loss and a vanishing world.

Mavor believes that in time she earned the respect of the established writers, 'if slowly and perhaps begrudgingly', and that was due to her hard work and honesty in delivering what she promised. Arthur Bernhard was also appreciative of what she was doing to encourage a new climate of acceptance, and this helped Mavor have more of a free hand in developing the magazine.

Firstly, though, Mavor had to work with what she could find in the slush pile of unsolicited submissions. She began to find promising work by new writers, some of whom rapidly established themselves.

The first was Michael Kube-McDowell, whose first two sales to *Amazing*, 'The Inevitable Conclusion' (August 1979) and 'Antithesis' (February 1980), explored the role of the scientist and served as seeds for his later Trigon Disunity series. Whereas McDowell's stories were in the traditional mould, those by Wayne Wightman, who became a regular contributor after 'The White Ones' (November 1979), were rather more quirky and unpredictable. Wightman sold ten more stories to Mavor, by the end of which he was also selling to *Omni*, *F&SF* and *Asimov's*.

Others whom Mavor discovered include Lawrence C. Connolly ('Cockroaches', May 1980), Sharon Lee ('A Matter of Ceremony', May 1980), John E. Stith ('Early Winter', *Fantastic*, July 1979), Brad Linaweaver ('The Competitor', *Fantastic*, July 1980), John Steakley ('The Bluenose Limit', March 1981), Richard Paul Russo ('The Firebird Suite', September 1981) and Ernest Hogan ('The Rape of Things to Come', March 1982). Bernhard was less impressed with the development of new writers. 'We are not running a school here', he told Mavor.

Because of their low pay rates, *Amazing* and *Fantastic* were regarded as a stepping-stone from the semi-professional magazines to the professionals. They occupied a kind of border zone. They paid the same rates as most of the smaller magazines and sales were likewise not recognized by the SFWA as credentials for membership. A coterie of writers was emerging who were able to sell regularly to the semi-prozines but seldom broke beyond that into the major magazines, rarely going further than *Amazing*. Although Lee, Miller and Stith would later sell novels professionally, and Stith sold a few stories to *Analog*, the bulk of their sales and those of others such as K. L. Jones were to the small press. Some writers, such as Darrell Schweitzer, who already had a strong grounding in the semi-prozines, were able to recycle some of their material. 'Never Argue with Antique Dealers', in the January 1980 *Fantastic*, had first appeared in *Wyrd* (#4, 1975), though no reference was made to this earlier publication.

Many of Mavor's discoveries went on to greater things. Richard Paul Russo, who became a major sf novelist, twice winner of the Philip K. Dick Award, had fond memories:

> We talked on the phone once, and that was another encouraging thing – we had a nice talk about the story, and about writing in general. She was very encouraging to and supportive of newer writers, as I learned later from other writers. She really helped to re-establish the reputation of *Amazing*, which was pretty low before she took over.[52]

Lawrence Connolly, who became better known as a writer of weird fiction, had similar views: 'The field was lucky to have her, and I feel fortunate to have come of age during that brief period during which she served as the editor of science fiction's first magazine.'[53]

In her first issue, Mavor put out an appeal for 'Help Wanted', asking not only for new writers and artists but for those who could undertake reviews, convention news, a fan column and information on college courses. She was soon deluged with offers. Robert Wilcox, a freelance writer who had developed a science-fiction literature course at Glendale Community College in Arizona, became her new editorial consultant. He reopened the magazine's review column, 'The Spectroscope', but used it as a means to explore issues raised in stories published in *Amazing*. Tom Staicar, who had contributed reviews and interviews to various semi-pro magazines and national magazines, introduced a new review column that not only looked at books but occasionally integrated the reviews with interviews and analyses of the writers. His column in the February 1980 *Amazing* provided a good overview of the work of Alan Dean Foster combined with an interview with the author and further feedback from his publisher, Judy-Lynn del Rey. Darrell Schweitzer also returned with his regular 'Amazing Interview', starting with Clifford Simak (February 1980). Other columnists included Steve Fahnstalk, editor of the fanzine *New Venture*, who reviewed fanzines and provided convention news, Tom Easton, who provided a brief science column (later continued by J. Ray Dettling) and, from May 1981, Robert Silverberg, whose 'Opinion' column moved to *Amazing* following the demise of *Galileo*. Mavor also included

---

52 Personal e-mail, Russo/Ashley, 27 August 2006.
53 Personal e-mail, Connolly/Ashley, 12 August 2006.

a couple of new features for each story. Not only did she include a brief biographical introduction by each author, but she also added an afterword 'Why we chose this story', as a guide for contributors. These appeared strained at times, as if searching for an interesting comment, but it was a bold and original move and was occasionally revealing. Even after this feature was dropped in 1981, authors still contributed either biographical or story-background details.

Perhaps most striking about *Amazing* and *Fantastic* was the development in artwork. This was not surprising as that was Mavor's premier skill. Early on she acquired work by Stephen Fabian and Gary Freeman, both with styles similar to her own and that of Scott Mavor. Kent Bash and David Mattingly later provided some excellent covers. Even here, though, where Mavor was at her most skilful, Bernhard would interpose:

> He once stood on a busy street in downtown Phoenix, Arizona, and asked people if they liked dragons, got a bunch of negative replies and then called me and said he wanted to change the cover on the January 1982 issue, after I had already bought the wonderful dragon illustration by Robert Petillo and laid out the cover. I won that argument by saying that I would *quit* if he made me change the cover.

The digest format was still restrictive and gave little scope to present artwork in anything other than a static form, but she made good use of the back cover and occasional full-page spread to give the work as much impact as possible, helped slightly by *Amazing* becoming marginally taller (from 194 mm to 208 mm) – a size that both *Analog* and *Amazing* would later adopt, though *Amazing* reverted to the standard digest size with the January 1982 issue.

These changes took about a year to embed. The reprints were rapidly phased out, and from the February 1980 *Amazing* and April 1980 *Fantastic* all contents were new. At the start of Mavor's control, the original comet-tail logo on *Amazing*'s cover title returned, which appealed to many long-time readers.

It was a remarkable transformation and all credit to Mavor's hard work. The magazines were now a complete package, with a variety of non-fiction features and a good blend of diverse fiction, illustrated in dramatic style. Ted White, who continued to check the magazines, was aware of the change: 'There's a lot of enthusiasm being put into the magazine by its current contributors, and that makes up for a lot. Unfortunately it may not be enough.'[54]

White was alluding to *Amazing*'s dwindling circulation. Mavor believed

---

54 Ted White, 'My Column', *Thrust* #15 (Summer 1980), pp. 36–7.

that a good subscription drive would boost *Amazing*'s flagging sales just as it had, initially, at *Galileo*:

> My suggestions – early on – about investing in a two-and-one-half year campaign to create a subscription list, were never considered important – until it was too late. I had gathered facts and figures during a trip to New York about such a campaign in 1979, when costs would have been feasible.[55]

Instead, Bernhard decided to merge *Amazing* and *Fantastic*. His argument was that while *Amazing* had always been profitable, *Fantastic* had always operated at a loss.[56] Certainly *Fantastic*'s circulation had on average generally been below that of *Amazing*, usually by 3,000–4,000 copies, despite the same print run and distribution, unless it ran a Conan story. The last recorded circulation figures we have for *Fantastic* were for the year 1977/78, which had a paid circulation of 18,370 compared to 22,784 for *Amazing*. Unfortunately, the exact same figures were reported for *Fantastic* in the following year, and we have no figure for its final year, in 1979/80. By then *Amazing*'s had dropped to 17,339 so *Fantastic*'s circulation might have been as low as 13,000.

Fantastic's last few issues had shown a steady improvement in content, including a serialized graphic story beautifully illustrated by Stephen Fabian, 'Daemon', which had started in the July 1979 issue. As the archive reprints were phased out, newer material appeared, sometimes reprinted from other, more recent sources. Marvin Kaye's humorous demon story, 'Damned Funny' (April 1980), had appeared in his anthology *Fiends and Creatures* in 1975. A new serial by Darrell Schweitzer, 'The White Isle' (April–July 1980), written in the style of Clark Ashton Smith, had been revised and expanded from a novelette first published in *Weirdbook* in 1975. Schweitzer also contributed a new story, 'The Headless Horseman' (October 1980), in the same issue in which Marvin Kaye presented a new James Phillimore story, 'The Amorous Umbrella'. *Fantastic* was certainly improving but evidently sales were not, and that proved to be the last issue. It merged with the new, taller *Amazing* from the November 1980 issue. From that point *Amazing* switched from quarterly to bi-monthly and converted the title back to *Amazing Science Fiction Stories*.

The passing of *Fantastic* meant that 1979/80 had seen the loss of four magazines. Both *Galileo* and *Asimov's SF Adventure* were new titles, so their loss did not cut as deep, but both *Fantastic* and *Galaxy* had been published for nearly thirty years. Although *Fantastic* had never been in the same

---

55 Elinor Mavor interviewed by Jeffrey Elliott, *SFWA Bulletin* 18:2 (Summer 1984).
56 See news story 'Amazing/Fantastic Merger' in *Locus* #235 (July 1980), pp. 1, 13.

league as *Galaxy*, it had at the outset, and briefly under Cele Goldsmith and Ted White, published some highly original material. Its passing was yet another sign that the future of the sf magazines was not as rosy as it had seemed only a year or two earlier.

Bernhard had done what he felt necessary, and with *Fantastic*'s title retained in *Amazing*'s masthead, there was always a chance that the magazine might be revived. The focus was now on *Amazing* producing the goods. Bernhard assumed that, with only one magazine to produce, he could reduce Mavor's salary, despite all the hard work she had done. He took no notice of her entreaties that the reason the circulation was falling was because he refused to advertise or undertake a subscription drive.

Despite all these obstacles and the lack of support, Mavor persevered. The May 1980 issue had already shown what she could achieve. Greg Benford appeared with 'Titan Falling', a story written in 1975 and then revised in order to incorporate it into his novel with Gordon Eklund, *If the Stars are Gods*, but which he now presented in its original form. The same issue included a short novel by Wayne Wightman, 'Metamind', featuring the quest for identity by a cyborg, which allowed the author to explore the nature of reality and illusion.

With the combined issue, the fabrication of Omar Gohagen was dropped and Mavor was unmasked as both editor and art director. The last new feature to be added was a variant on the 'Hall of Fame' classic reprint, which began in the January 1981 issue. This time the author wrote a new introduction providing the background to the story and Bernhard paid a proper reprint fee plus extra for the introduction. The first reprint was Silverberg's 'Hole in the Air', and others were by Jack Williamson, Greg Benford, Ron Goulart, David R. Bunch, Theodore Sturgeon, Isaac Asimov and Robert Sheckley.

Mavor also secured new fiction from Robert Adams, Orson Scott Card, George R. R. Martin and Roger Zelazny. Martin's 'Unsound Variations' (January 1982), which draws on Martin's chess expertise, was nominated for both a Hugo and a Nebula. Brad Linaweaver's novelette 'Moon of Ice' (March 1982), the basis of his first novel, set in an alternate timestream where Hitler was victorious, was another Nebula nominee.

Unfortunately, no sooner had Mavor made *Amazing* fly than she had little more than a year in which to flex her wings before Bernhard decided to cut his losses and retire – he was now 70. Mavor had worked wonders against the odds to create an enjoyable and often exciting magazine, one where you could see the enthusiasm sparking. But it was not reflected in sales. Although subscriptions grew, news-stand sales plummeted from nearly 21,000, when Bernhard took over, to under 11,000 by early 1982 – virtually semi-professional level.

Bernhard had been discussing possibilities with a number of parties, including Edward Ferman and Joel Davis, neither of whom was interested. One party, Jonathan Post of Emerald City Publishing in Seattle, was so keen that he started advertising for submissions, believing that he had been successful. Another whom Bernhard had approached was George Scithers, who had just left *Asimov's*. Scithers's Owlswick Press was not in a position to take on either title, though its day as a magazine publisher would come. Soon after, Scithers was contacted by Gary Gygax, publisher of *The Dragon* and a long-time subscriber to *Amra*. He wanted to know whether Scithers could provide any services for TSR which had now grown into a major company. Scithers promptly made the connection and put Gygax in touch with Bernhard.

The deal went through on 27 May 1982, though a letter of intent had been signed nearly two months before, and George Scithers, appointed as the new editor, had already contacted Mavor before she knew of the arrangement. Bernhard had originally tried to secure an arrangement that would see Mavor continue as editor, but such was not to be. Her last issue was that for September 1982, which she compiled but which TSR published. Thereafter Mavor returned to being a freelance artist and graphic designer. In her final editorial Mavor gave some idea of the problems she had encountered but which she felt were all worthwhile, concluding:

> There must remain a place for expression of fresh viewpoints, experimental writing styles and a full range of fantasy storytelling forms. A place where new voices can always be heard, along with older, more seasoned ones. This has been *Amazing*. I hope it always will be.[57]

Whether it always would be is a matter I return to in the next volume.

Hugo Gernsback might have been amused had he known of the fate of his brainchild. When he started *Amazing Stories* 56 years before, his idea had been to encourage experimenters to explore new scientific ideas and create inventions for the future. Now it was going to be published by a company that had emerged out of the popularity of fantasy role-playing games. Readers had moved from creating new technology to creating worlds of magic.

Gernsback, though, would doubtless have left *Amazing* to its own fate because the previous four years had seen two other developments that would have been much closer to Gernsback's heart, one of them the virtual recreation of *Science and Invention*.

---

57 Elinor Mavor, 'Editorial', *Amazing Science Fiction Stories* 28:7 (September 1982), p. 4.

Star Mags

One important aspect of science-fiction publishing during the seventies was that while all but the leading magazines were subject to a downturn in sales, with a disturbing number of casualties, the sale of science-fiction and fantasy books continued to rise, each year bringing a growing number of new titles. *Locus* recorded a 204 per cent increase in new sf books between 1972 and 1979 and a 270 per cent increase if reprints are included.[58] For the first time in 1978 the total number of sf books published in the year exceeded a thousand in the United States alone.

It was horror and fantasy that first made the annual top ten of the *New York Times* bestseller list. *The Exorcist* by William Peter Blatty and *The Other* by Thomas Tryon in 1971, *Jonathan Livingston Seagull* by Richard Bach in 1972 and 1973, *Watership Down* by Richard Adams in 1974. By 1979 Stephen King had made the list with *The Dead Zone*. King had been a top seller from the first, with *Carrie*, and though his works were promoted as 'horror fiction', many of them were science fiction. The basic plot of *Carrie*, about a teenage girl with a powerful psi talent, would have been quite at home in the science-fiction magazines. *The Stand* is an end-of-the-world sf theme with mystical overtones. Through King and fellow writers such as John Saul, Thomas Tryon and especially Dean Koontz, science fiction, repackaged as horror, topped the bestseller charts.

There was also a rise in advances for major authors. The first was Arthur C. Clarke who, thanks to Judy-Lynn del Rey recommending to Ballantine Books the purchase of 'Rendezvous with Rama' after its serialization in *Galaxy*, was able to secure a record $150,000 three-book deal with Ballantine in 1973. The first single-book record advance for a science-fiction writer was $100,000 from Avon Books for Joe Haldeman's *Mindbridge* in May 1976, a deal he was able to make because of the success of *The Forever War*. A year later Larry Niven and Jerry Pournelle secured a $236,500 advance from Fawcett for *Lucifer's Hammer*. These were all deals for paperback editions. In May 1978 Robert Silverberg made a record hardcover advance of $127,500 from Harper & Row for *Lord Valentine's Castle*, the book that marked his return to fiction writing after a three-year abstinence. The next year Robert A. Heinlein pushed the paperback deal higher still with a $500,000 advance from Fawcett for *The Number of the Beast*.

At the same time as the leading sf writers were becoming big business, sf in the cinema exploded with the phenomenal success of *Star Wars*, which premiered on 25 March 1977. It was the success of this film, followed by

58 See '1979 Locus Book Summary', *Locus* #230 (February 1980), p. 8.

Close Encounters of the Third Kind (premiered 16 November 1977), *Superman* (10 December 1978), *Alien* (25 May 1979) and *Star Trek: The Motion Picture* (6 December 1979), that established a new generation of science-fiction films which restored a sense of wonder and awe and, because of the quality of their special effects, brought science-fiction imagery to life as never before.

The connection between fans of written science fiction and those of sf films and TV series had always been close in the past, but after *Star Wars* they began to take on separate existences. Even before *Star Wars*, followers of *Star Trek* had created their own fan base and conventions. The first *Star Trek* convention held in New York in January 1972 had over three thousand attendees. The next held in Los Angeles in April 1973 had over ten thousand. The sale of *Star-Trek* books and other memorabilia was big business by the mid-seventies. However, it is a sign of how the 'Trekkies' were perceived by the magazine-publishing medium that the only regular magazine devoted to the series was the comic book *Star Trek* which had been published by Western Publishing – the same firm that published Elwood's *Starstream* comic – on an occasional basis since October 1967, becoming quarterly in February 1971 and bi-monthly in July 1973. It ran for 61 issues to March 1979.

Paramount held a tight control over the *Star-Trek* franchise and professional outlets for related fiction were limited. As a consequence there was a huge market for fan fiction and, although there were occasional attempts by Paramount to stop these fanzines, Gene Roddenberry was happy to let them remain, provided they were not for profit. The earliest fanzine, *Spockanalia*, had grown out of New York fandom, edited by fellow Lunarians Devra Langsam and Sherna Comerford. It had first appeared in September 1967 and besides the articles had included a story by Ruth Berman, 'Star Drek'. Berman subsequently rewrote that as a non-Trek story and it became her first professional sale, 'Ptolemaic Hijack' (*Worlds of Fantasy* #4, Spring 1971). The second issue of *Spockanalia*, in April 1968, contained a humorous story by Lois McMaster, 'The Free Enterprise', in the days before she became a major science-fiction author. *Spockanalia* reached a circulation of about five hundred.

Further fanzines appeared. *ST-Phile* from Kay Anderson and Juanita Coulson in January 1968, *Warp Nine* in February 1969, and *T-Negative* from Ruth Berman in June 1969. These were small-circulation, mimeographed magazines looking just like any other science-fiction fanzine except for the preponderance of *Star-Trek* articles, discussion and stories. *T-Negative* was one of the more highly regarded fanzines and is perhaps most notable for publishing the first of Jacqueline Lichtenberg's Kraith stories, 'Spock's Affirmation', in issue #8 (August 1970). The character of Spock fascinated the fans and the Kraith series explored Spock's early life. Lichtenberg had been an *If*-first, with her story 'Operation High Time' (January 1969), which started her Sime-Gen future where humanity has split into two vastly different but symbiotic life forms.

Star-Trek fanzines proliferated in the 1970s, far too many to cover here.[59] Leading ones were *Eridani Triad* edited by Gail Barton and Doris Beetem, which appeared in June 1970; *Masiform D*, Devra Langsam's successor to *Spockanalia*, which started in January 1971; *Grup* from Carrie Peak and M. L. 'Steve' Barnes, which started in September 1972 and was the first Trek fanzine to treat adult themes; and *Warped Space* produced by Lori Chapek for the Michigan State University *Star Trek* club, starting in October 1974. Eleanor Arnason appeared in several of these fanzines before she made her first professional sale to *New Worlds* in 1973. Her stories included 'The Face on the Barroom Floor' (*T-Negative*, October 1972), a collaboration with Ruth Berman which Sondra Marshak and Myrna Culbreath later included in their anthology *Star Trek: The New Voyages* (Bantam, 1976). This selected eight stories from various Trek-zines, amongst them Berman's own 'Visit to a Weird Planet Revisited' (*Spockanalia* #5, June 1970), a pastiche where the *Star-Trek* actors find themselves beamed up to the real *Starship Enterprise*. This had originally been written as a response to 'Visit to a Weird Planet' (*Spockanalia* #3, September 1968) by Jean Lorrah and Willard Hunt, where the real Kirk, Spock and McCoy are transported to the *Star-Trek* TV set. Jean Lorrah, like Jacqueline Lichtenberg, would go on to write not only professional *Star-Trek* novels but also other works of science fiction and fantasy. The *Star-Trek* fanzines, like the general sf fanzines, were a route to the professional scene.

One of the most notable appearances in a *Star-Trek* fanzine was by James Tiptree, Jr., whose 'Meet Me at Infinity', which was a script she had drafted for the series, appeared in *Eridani Triad* #3 (September 1972).

A noticeable aspect of these fanzines and stories is that the majority of them were produced by women. What is clear about many of the *Star-Trek* fan stories is that they are about relationships, either between individuals, most notably Kirk and Spock, or between cultures, or indeed within the *Enterprise* 'family'. Women writers, some of whom may have not felt comfortable submitting to the traditional sf magazines, still seen erroneously as a male preserve, may have felt more at home within the ready-made *Trek* universe, and the fact that so many women were producing the fanzines encouraged even more women to write. The fact

59 For a detailed study of *Star Trek* fanzines and fan fiction, I recommend Joan Marie Verba, *Boldly Writing* (Minnetonka, MN: FTL Publications, 1996, revised 2003).

that Arnason, Bujold, Berman, Lichtenberg, Lorrah, even Tiptree, all made their way into the professional sf scene via their fascination for *Star Trek* is evidence enough that the space-opera field continued to attract new writers in the same way that, in past decades, it had appealed to Leigh Brackett, C. L. Moore and Marion Zimmer Bradley. It signalled a start to the concept of shared-world magazines and anthologies. One could argue this had already begun many years before with the growth of interest in H. P. Lovecraft's Cthulhu Mythos, but that was chiefly a male preserve. The current fascination with shared worlds was triggered by the interest by female fans in *Star Trek* and soon moved on to other fictional worlds and characters, starting with Marion Zimmer Bradley's Darkover series. Bradley began her own amateur magazine, *Starstone*, in January 1978, as a forum for stories and articles about Darkover. It ran for five occasional issues until 1982 and included material by Jacqueline Lichtenberg, Diana Paxson and Bradley herself.

With the further development of modern science fiction in the current sf magazines and anthologies, a gap became apparent between the two fan bases. In 1976, *A Piece of the Action*, a newsletter produced by the *Star Trek* 'Welcommittee',[60] reported the results of a survey taken amongst fans concerning the projected *Star-Trek* movie. Amongst the responses, the majority of *Star-Trek* fans stated that they were not primarily science-fiction fans.

Star-Trek fans soon embraced *Star Wars*. The July 1977 issue of *Warped Space* sported a *Star-Wars* cover and the August issue featured three stories based on the *Star-Wars* universe. It was not long before *Star Wars* also had its own fandom and the explosion in science-fiction films and TV resulted in the growth of multi-media fanzines covering *Dr Who*, *Battlestar Galactica*, *Blake's 7* and many more. SF media fandom continues to this day and has effectively splintered from science-fiction fandom and the sf magazines into a separate subgenre, though the two worlds would occasionally collide.

During the seventies, though, the overlap between the fields remained and some of the fiction inspired by *Star Trek* and *Star Wars* appeared in general sf amateur magazines. We have already seen how *Star-Trek* stories appeared in the Canadian *Stardust*, and how the final issues of *Galaxy* ran a 'Star Warriors' serial by Steve Perry. The students of Ohio State University produced their own sf and fantasy amateur magazine *Rune*,[61] and its

60 The 'Welcommittee' had been created by Jacqueline Lichtenberg in 1972 as the first port of call for *Star Trek* fans who wanted to know more about fandom.

61 This is not to be confused with the long running fanzine *Rune* which had been the newsletter of the Minnesota SF Society since 1967 but which later flowered into a remarkable fanzine in its own right.

first issue, dated Fall 1974, tried to appeal to a cross-section of fandoms. There was a Lovecraftian story, a pastiche of the Tom Swift dime novels, a Tolkienesque fantasy, an interview with Isaac Asimov, even a stab at Tarzan's 'ape dictionary', and alongside all this were not one but two *Trek* items. One was a story set on Vulcan, 'Premonition' by Carol Shuttleworth. The other was a clever parody of *Star Trek* written like a Gilbert and Sullivan light opera, 'HMS Trekastar' by Karen Anderson, which had first been performed in 1967 and again at other conventions in 1968 and 1969. *Rune* then vanished for a year and reappeared as *Starwind*, in new editorial hands. It was thereafter a straightforward sf amateur magazine, reflecting the world of science fiction and fantasy and divorced from *Star Trek*.

Whereas science-fiction writers and fans had generally been supportive of *Star Trek* when it had appeared in 1966,[62] *Star Wars* provoked a mixed response. Leading the anti-campaign was Ben Bova, who complained to *Time Magazine* that an article they had run on *Star Wars* in their issue of 30 May 1977 had misquoted him, implying that he had liked the film. Bova was quoted as saying '*Star Wars* is the costume epic of the future. It's a galactic *Gone With the Wind*.' Bova's response appeared in the 20 June *Time* where he made it clear that he did not like the film. 'Those of us who work in the science fiction field professionally look for something more than Saturday afternoon shoot-'em-ups', he wrote. A reader of *Analog* read Bova's comments and reprimanded him about them: 'your opinion as editor should reflect the interest of the science fiction readers, not writers. Space Opera (of which *Space Wars* [sic] is a cinematic example) is a valid and very enjoyable form of science fiction.'[63] Bova's immediate response was that *Star Wars*'s 'only relation to science fiction is to degrade our genre in the eyes of the public'. He saved his more detailed comments for an editorial in *Analog* in June 1978, by which time he had also seen *Close Encounters of the Third Kind*. Setting aside all the marvels of the special effects, which he likened to seeing our first decorated Christmas tree, Bova argued that the stories tried to please the public by delivering a diet of wish-fulfilment summed up by the phrase 'Trust the Force'. In neither case was there an adequate scientific premise to the actions and, more importantly, to the climax or solution. Bova's conclusion caused quite a stir in his use of words: 'neither film can be regarded seriously as science fiction. In fact, they bear the same relationship to science fiction as the Nazi treatment of Poland bore to the Ten Commandments.'[64] Many readers criticized him for his choice of words even when they supported

62 See discussion in the previous volume, *Transformations*, pp. 272–73.
63 Letter from Lowell G. Johnson in *Analog* 98:2 (February 1978), p. 170.
64 Ben Bova, 'Trust the Force', *Analog* 98:6 (June 1978), p. 10.

his argument. Arlan Keith Andrews, who would later become a regular contributor to *Analog*, accused Bova of having a 'narrow technological view of the Universe' and said that the 'sense of wonder engendered by *Star Wars* and *Close Encounters* deserves better treatment by SF editors than to be compared (unfavourably) to Hitler's invasion of Poland'.[65] Bova repeated his basic argument that Hollywood's approach to sf was anti-intellectual and thereby cheapened science fiction. But on the whole most readers seemed to be in favour of *Star Wars* rather than against it. That also seemed to be the case amongst many of Bova's fellow writers. Baird Searles, writing in *F&SF*, was heartily in favour of it, saying of the director George Lucas, 'Here at last is a filmmaker who *knows* (and respects) science fiction.'[66] Charles Brown, writing in *Isaac Asimov's SF Magazine*, called it 'a glorious and exciting experience' and said that Lucas had taken 'all the clichés from 1940s *Planet Stories*, treated them with love and warmth, and ha[d] given them new life'.[67] *Galaxy* ran a 'pro and con' feature, with Jay Kay Klein for and Jeff Rovin against.[68] Klein, who rated the film 'the best science-fiction picture made so far', also believed that the film set standards for what the public wanted to see. Rovin, however, saw this as a backward step away from the steady improvement in recent films to the 'by-gone froth' of the pulps. Joanna Russ was also vehemently against the film, calling it 'sexist, racist and morally idiotic'.[69]

The debate raged through the professional and amateur magazines for many months. At the heart of the problem was how the film depicted science fiction. Long-time sf fans, aware of the evolution of science fiction, would know that the film was a throwback to pulp space opera of the thirties and forties, and could enjoy it for that alone, wallowing in the sense of wonder and marvelling at the special effects. But sf fans were also aware that the film did not reflect the state of science fiction as it stood in 1977 and their concern was that the public would believe that the film was representative. All the good that had happened in dragging sf out of the gutter could be lost overnight. There was hope amongst the detractors that future films would become more sophisticated in content, but when *Superman* premiered in December 1978, it was obvious that the new wonders of special effects were allowing film-makers to recreate the marvels of the comic-book heroes with no pretence to characterization or story. Although *Close Encounters* and *Alien* were more adult in treatment,

65 Arlan Keith Andrews, letter in *Analog* 99:1 (January 1979), p. 177

66 Baird Searles, 'Films', *F&SF* 53:4 (October 1977), p. 149.

67 Charles Brown, 'On Books … & a Movie', *Isaac Asimov's Science Fiction Magazine*, 1:4 (Winter 1977), p. 120.

68 *Galaxy* 38:8 (October 1977), pp. 63–72.

69 Joanna Russ in *Future* #4 (August 1978), p. 33.

they were still little more than hackneyed sf plots decked out, as Bova observed, in new Christmas tree lights.

Lucas did not deny what he was trying to achieve. He was well aware of the depth in science fiction and had in 1971 created a well-received Orwellian film of an oppressive future society, *THX 1138*, for which, ironically, Bova wrote the novelization. When reviewing the book, Darrell Schweitzer commented rather presciently that you would read the book for a certain level of entertainment, like you would an 'Edgar Rice Burroughs novel'.[70] For it was indeed to Burroughs that Lucas turned for inspiration for *Star Wars*. In the press-release material for the film he is quoted as saying, 'I wanted to give young people some sort of faraway, exotic environment for their imagination to run free.' He was very aware in this context that he was dumbing down science fiction. In a later interview he said:

> Buck Rogers is just as valid as Arthur C. Clarke in his own way. They are both sides of the same thing. Kubrick did the strongest thing in film in terms of the rational side of things, and I've tried to do the most in the irrational side of things because I think we need it.[71]

Lucas went purely for entertainment. The film was a fairy-tale dressed in the trappings of science fiction. The test was whether the new fans created by *Star Wars* would eventually gravitate towards the mature science-fiction magazines or seek their thrills elsewhere. It is true that in the immediate aftermath of *Star Wars* the subscription levels of the sf magazines rose, though news-stand sales dropped. The latter was partly a problem of distribution, but there was also a vicious circle of demand and availability. The traditional science-fiction digest rapidly looked dull and old-fashioned alongside the magazines that responded to the film fan base.

Movie and media magazines had been around as long as the cinema, and those concentrating on science-fiction films – or more specifically monster films – had existed since Forrest Ackerman created *Famous Monsters of Filmland* in 1958. That had led to a rush of monster magazines aimed at juvenile readers. The first magazine to provide a more serious, adult survey and analysis of science-fiction and horror films was *Cinefantastique*, started by Frederick S. Clarke in Fall 1970. He had dabbled with an earlier fanzine version while at college, and even the first issue of the relaunched magazine was in a semi-professional form, with a circulation of only 1,000. But the magazine soon attracted a loyal readership and sales reached around 30,000. Clarke refused to run much advertising,

---

70 See *Luna Monthly* #40, September 1972, p. 25.
71 George Lucas interviewed in *Rolling Stone*, 25 August 1977.

to allow himself critical freedom, so the magazine was always expensive to produce and ran on the borderline of profitability. This did not stop Clarke running critical analyses of films and previews and exposés that often infuriated the major film-makers. Nevertheless, *Cinefantastique* set the standard and was the head of the field in its coverage of *Star Wars*, *Star Trek* and the wealth of successors.

In its wake came other sf media magazines: *Starlog* (from August 1976), the British *Starburst* (January 1978), *Fangoria* (August 1979) and *Cinefex* (March 1980) to name but a few. The leading title was *Starlog*, published by Kerry O'Quinn and Norman Jacobs and edited by Howard Zimmerman. It owed its initial success to its coverage of *Star Trek* but it broadened its scope to covering not just new but also classic sf films and looking at the books and authors behind them. It also looked further to science fiction in all its forms and included features and interviews with writers and artists. Issue #6 (June 1977), for instance, had an article about Robert A. Heinlein and the making of *Destination Moon*. Issue #8 (September 1977) ran an interview with Harlan Ellison; issue #10 (December 1977) had a piece by Isaac Asimov on faster-than-light travel; issue #14 (June 1978) ran a feature on Virgil Finlay, while issue #17 (October 1978) featured an interview with Joe Haldeman. There were interviews with artists Don Dixon and Dave Mattingley and with writers Alan Dean Foster, Ray Bradbury and even David A. Kyle.

Although these media magazines carried no fiction, they were still called 'sci-fi magazines', superseding in the public's mind the real fiction magazines. Like the serious semi-professional 'fan' magazines – *Algol*, *Thrust, Science Fiction Review* – these magazines also explored the world of science fiction, but with the emphasis on movies rather than books. There never really was a safe middle ground, though there would be movement on both sides.

One attempt to blend the two was *Questar*. This was started by William G. Wilson of Jefferson Borough, Pennsylvania in 1978, initially as a one-man operation produced in his basement. It was typical of many semi-prozines of the period, produced with more hope than money, but it was able to use a *Star-Wars* cover, which doubtless attracted attention. He soon teamed with Robert Michelucci, who had recently compiled *The Collectors Guide to Monster Magazines* (1977), to form MW Communications in Pittsburgh. The third issue introduced internal colour illustrations for features on the leading films. It was rapidly becoming a quality production, running to 64 pages printed on coated stock, though the content remained variable. Wilson's original interest had been chiefly in the cinema and comic books, and the magazine ran detailed coverage of new movies plus several black-and-white comic strips, with art by Steve Ditko, Fred Hembeck and others. It was an odd mixture of the new and the old, both clearly aimed at a juvenile readership. With the fourth issue it began a new strip, 'Just Imagine: Jeanie', illustrated by Ron Frenz and with a script by Forrest Ackerman. The added feature of *Questar* was that it ran fiction, a story or two in each issue, though nothing too remarkable. It ran the first stories by C. J. Henderson, who became a regular contributor to small-press magazines. Although the fourth issue carried no fiction, it featured an interview with Larry Niven which telegraphed a shift to a great coverage of written sf.

Issues appeared as finances allowed but with the June 1980 issue the publisher secured national distribution and tried to sustain a bi-monthly schedule with extra pages and full-colour photography throughout. James Warhola was a regular contributor, his cover for issue #10 being voted one of the 12 best magazine covers of 1980 by *Marketing Bestsellers Magazine*. The coverage of written sf increased, with interviews with A. E. van Vogt, Robert Bloch, John Norman, George Zebrowski and others, and a shift to articles on popular science, perhaps influenced by the success of *Omni*. Circulation rose from around 5,000 to 40,000. Based on the published letters, most of the readers were chiefly film buffs. *Questar* nevertheless continued to run short fiction, mostly very short and minor. From the twelfth issue (June 1981), now subtly renamed *Quest/Star*, they brought in Horace Gold as fiction editor. Gold planned to use both new and reprint material as, in his view, the readership was different to that of the regular sf magazine and thus unaware of most science fiction. Gold's 1954 story 'Man of Parts' was reprinted in the June issue while the October issue reprinted both 'Now+N, Now–N' by Silverberg from *Nova 2*, and 'Born of Man and Woman', Richard Matheson's timelessly powerful story from *F&SF* in 1950. However, Gold had little opportunity to acquire new material. The only new story he published, beautifully illustrated by James Warhola, was 'Exit the Master' by David Curtis, which explores the fate of the earth as witnessed by explorers returning five million years hence.

Quest/Star had a full facelift, and shifted to nine issues a year. With the change the editor proclaimed: 'We are not a 'science fiction' magazine, but a magazine about science fiction. This approach, to cover the entire world of SF rather than concentrate on just one aspect of it, will be what separates us from the rest of the pack.'[72] The October 1981 issue sold around 90,000 copies, including 25,000 subscribers. However, the magazine was underfinanced to cope with such sudden growth. This was exactly the same problem encountered by *Galileo*, and it is not the last we

---

72 William G. Wilson, Jr. quoted in *Science Fiction Chronicle* 2:9 (June 1981), p. 5.

shall see of it. MW Communications had no such finances and so *Quest/ Star* became a victim of its own success.

Quest/Star was an attractive magazine that was starting to do interesting things. Wilson's belief that a magazine covering all aspects of sf had a market may well have been right, judging by the sales, though it may have been hanging on the coat-tails of *Omni*. The blending of movies and fiction, though, was certainly a trend that would feature time and again during the eighties and nineties and was a formula that worked, for a while at least, for a new magazine that appeared in April 1981, *Rod Serling's 'The Twilight Zone' Magazine*, which I shall discuss in the next volume.

Super Science

The leading media magazines soon established a significant level of readership, certainly in excess of a hundred thousand. *Starlog* even promoted itself in its own advertisements as 'the most popular science-fiction magazine in publishing history'. Though not entirely true – it was still not technically a science-fiction magazine and it did not reach the sales of either *Amazing Stories* or *Astounding* at their peak – it nevertheless shows how it perceived itself and gives some idea of the scale of its market.

The publisher, Kerry O'Quinn, was keen to develop this market, especially the interest in science and the interface with science fiction. This led him to produce a companion title to *Starlog* called *Future*, subtitled 'The Magazine of Science Adventure', which went on sale at the end of February 1978 (first issue dated April). This magazine embraced the future and sought to explore it through art and speculative articles as well as interviews and features on science-fiction writers. In many ways it presaged *Omni*, though, as we shall see, whereas *Omni* explored all aspects of scientific development, *Future* concentrated on what science was forecasting. Although *Future* ran no fiction, it still called itself a science-fiction magazine. Editor Howard Zimmerman summed up *Future's* purpose as follows:

> In *Future* you will find what may be considered a strange mixture of elements for a 'science fiction magazine'. In actuality, they are all different aspects of the same search. What we have done in this issue, and will continue to do, is to examine a single question, 'What is the shape of tomorrow?' from as many perspectives as we can free ourselves to see.[73]

73 Howard Zimmerman, 'Perspectives', *Future* #1 (April 1978), p. 78.

The first issue was still too close to *Starlog* to feel much different as it ran several film features, but it also featured a number of items of science news, an item on space artist Chesley Bonestell at 90, an article by Isaac Asimov on 'Society in the Future' and an interview with Frederik Pohl conducted by Ed Naha. Naha commented: 'Pohl realizes that, in 1978, it's possible for an SF fan never to actually *read* science fiction. For a lot of present day buffs, television and movie science fiction is the *only* kind of science fiction.'[74] Although Pohl believed that 'printed SF ... will be around forever', he was nevertheless identifying a clear divide within science-fiction fandom that would continue to fragment.

Future issues of *Future* continued to run interviews with leading science-fiction writers and artists plus speculative articles on what tomorrow might bring, many also by sf writers. Norman Spinrad, in issue #2 (May 1978), was not too far from the mark when he imagined that the 'average' twenty-first-century American would own a 'media net console' that was 'a marriage of a world-wide, but also highly localized complex of television networks with miniaturized computer technology'.[75] He went on to describe something very close to the existing World Wide Web.

Future became *Future Life* from its ninth issue in March 1979 at the same time as an editorial change, with Ed Naha and Robin Snelson as the new co-editors. There was a price rise to cover the cost of going fully slick, but otherwise there was little change in content. *Future Life* was a place where science-fiction writers could talk about anything they wanted and not just about the future. In issue #6 (November 1978), David Gerrold took great exception to proposals by a California senator to prohibit the employment of homosexuals as teachers and quite possibly as college lecturers, which would also lead to their books being removed from libraries. This would affect not only gay writers but also writers on gay subjects, and Gerrold listed dozens of science-fiction books which dealt positively with homosexuality. Gerrold's comments were generally supported by the magazine's readers, including Jose Alcarez, associate publisher of the first gay sf and fantasy magazine, *Aura*. Alcarez reprinted Gerrold's article in the first (and, alas, only) issue of *Aura*, published by Torch Publications in New York in 1979.

Harlan Ellison began his own column, 'An Edge in My Voice', from issue #20 (August 1980), where he spoke on any matters that annoyed him. Lou Stathis provided a music column which covered mostly rock and experimental music.

Although *Future Life* reported sales of around a hundred thousand copies,

---

74 Ed Naha, 'The View from a Distant Star', *Future* #1 (April 1978), p. 30.
75 Norman Spinrad, 'Total Media', *Future* #2 (May 1978), p. 76.

the magazine was clearly having financial problems. In an announcement in issue #23 (December 1980), O'Quinn complained about the treatment that small publishers had from news-stand retailers where feedback on sales and the financial returns can take many months. Part of the problem was that *Future Life* was being distributed with the media magazines rather than the science magazines, a divide that readers can cross more easily than distributors and vendors.[76] With issue #24 (February 1981), *Future Life* ceased to have news-stand distribution, relying solely on subscriptions and sales through specialist dealers and major bookstores. Evidently this was not enough, for the magazine was forced to close down with its issue #31, dated December 1981. It was one of many magazines from comparatively small publishers that would fall foul at this time of news-stand distribution problems.

Future Life had given science-fiction writers a status, recognizing their views as observers and commentators on trends within both science and society. It was all part of the growing acceptance of science fiction in the marketplace, even if it was still shunned by the literary and scientific establishment. *Future Life* was the kind of magazine that Hugo Gernsback would have found delightful, and it was as key a part of continuing his grand design for the popularization of science as any science-fiction magazine. If anything, the traditional sf magazine was in danger of being supplanted by the sf media magazines. What *Future Life* lacked was sufficient funding to deliver a magazine of diverse scientific news and one that could cope with the financial exigencies of news-stand distribution. The level of advances that some publishers were now paying for the leading writers, as highlighted above, showed that science fiction had a market that was worthy of considerable investment. If magazines had the same level of investment, who knew what might happen.

The answer to that came when Bob Guccione, the publisher of *Penthouse*, announced plans in early 1978 to publish a magazine focusing on science, parapsychology, science fiction and fantasy. A budget of $5 million was allocated, which included $3 million for promotion. This caused Charles Brown to comment, 'For that price, they might as well buy all the other magazines and eliminate any competition.'[77]

The real passion behind the project came from Guccione's wife, Kathy Keeton, a former ballet dancer who had retained a childhood passion for science fiction and escapist literature. It was she who wanted a magazine that explored all realms of science and the paranormal, that delved into all corners of the unknown and projected some of those discoveries into

76 See news story in *Science Fiction Chronicle* 3:3 (December 1981), p. 1.
77 Charles Brown, '*Nova* Coming', *Locus* #208 (January/February 1978), p. 1.

fiction. It was Guccione, though, who developed this concept into a vision and laid the groundwork for the magazine. At the outset the magazine was called *Nova*, a name it retained till almost the last moment.

The project plan was written by Dick Teresi, who was then phasing himself out from editorial work at *Good Housekeeping*:

> I was commissioned to write the first proposal of the magazine, on which the dummy was based. I worked during the launch as a consulting editor. When I wrote the first plan for *Omni* (when it was called *Nova*), I included science fiction in the blend because I noted that all great magazines had had fiction, and also I knew many scientists who grew up on science fiction. It was a natural.[78]

The projected start date was September 1978. Guccione brought an editorial team together, though the catalyst was Frank Kendig. He was a freelance writer and the former editor of *Science Digest* and the *Saturday Review of Science*. He and Guccione had had some preliminary discussions but it was not until some three months later that Kendig discovered that he was the magazine's executive editor. He arrived at Guccione's apartment only to discover that he was chairing the first editorial meeting:

> I was led into a room with a large oval table and maybe 12 people sitting around it. I was introduced as the new executive editor of *Nova*. I was told that the assembled folks were the staff of the new magazine. Among them were Ed Rosenfeld (the original articles editor), Trudy Bell (senior editor, then working at *Scientific American*), Frank DeVino (art director) and Judith McQuown (fiction editor). I think Barbara Seaman was there too, as a contributing editor. Bob then announced that this was *Nova*'s first editorial meeting and turned it over to me to run which I did. Nobody there had actually been offered a job. Nobody had discussed money or any other terms. It was a very unusual meeting. When it was over, Bob abruptly left the room leaving the rest of us there bewildered.[79]

Guccione had called in Judith H. McQuown as the fiction editor. She ran her own consultancy business for publishers and financial industries. She had been involved in science-fiction fandom in the late fifties under her maiden name of Judith Hershkowitz when she had been married briefly to Lin Carter. She retained her interest in science fiction but Kendig was unsure of her experience and, after letting her go, he contacted Ben Bova.

---

78 Personal e-mail, Teresi/Ashley, 26 August 2006.
79 Personal e-mail, Kendig/Ashley, 19 August 2006.

Bova had already been approached by Guccione and Keeton while still at *Analog* but at that time Bova was not ready to leave:[80]

> I declined as politely as I could, because I still had a few odds and ends I wanted to finish up with *Analog*, and I wanted to be a full-time writer. When they hired Frank Kendig, as executive editor, Frank invited me to lunch and invited me to be the fiction editor. Again I declined, but I recommended Diana King, who had been my associate editor at *Analog*. Diana took the job, then just as the first issue of *Omni* was hitting the presses Diana suddenly quit to get married ... At about the same time I had made the decision to quit *Analog*, so Frank invited me to lunch again. He pointed out that there was a hole in the staff that was partly my responsibility. After thinking about it for a couple of minutes, I agreed to step in as the fiction editor, at least *pro tem*.[81]

Bova was appointed on 15 August, just a month before the first issue was due on the stands.

Trudy E. Bell continued as science editor. She had been an associate editor at *Scientific American* and was a former mission controller for the Pioneer space project. She had recently contributed an article to *Analog* on the definition of planets, 'And Then There Were Nine' (June 1977).

Everything was on schedule for the first issue when the Boston television station WGBH, which produced the science series *NOVA*, brought an injunction against the publisher over the use of the name. Rather than delay the first issue, the magazine's name was changed to *Omni*. A dummy of the first issue had already been prepared with the name *Nova*, and one of the reasons why *Omni* was chosen was because the word fitted in neatly with the original design.

Despite all these problems and changes, *Omni* appeared on the bookstalls on time on 19 September (the first issue dated October 1978). A full-size slick, saddle-stapled, it ran to a magnificent 184 glossy pages, beautifully illustrated throughout, yet selling for just $2. It had a print run of a million copies. No other sf magazine could compete with it. *Omni*, though, was not a science-fiction magazine. Bova preferred to think of it as a magazine 'that deals with the future',[82] although it was even broader than that. It was a magazine of popular science in all its forms and it used photography, art, fiction and speculation to explore the wonders of

---

80 When Bova was interviewed for *Science Fiction Review* on 17 March 1978, he commented that he had already had discussions with Guccione and Keeton and was impressed with what they were planning. When asked whether he would accept the editorship of *Nova* if Guccione phoned him tomorrow, Bova responded, 'Probably not.' See issue #27, September/October 1978, pp. 16–17.

81 Ben Bova interview, *Rigel* #1, Summer 1981, p. 21.

82 Ben Bova interview.

science and pseudo-science in the best possible way. The first issue ran not only fiction – stories by Isaac Asimov, Theodore Sturgeon, Ron Goulart and veteran James B. Hall (all selected by Frank Kendig) – but features on UFOs, ageing, the Turin Shroud, robots, and an interview with Freeman Dyson about the Dyson Sphere.

The first issue sold 850,000 copies and over the next few months the magazine built up a subscription list of 125,000. Although news-stand sales dropped after initial interest, it still sold an average of around 760,000 copies per issue in the first year, and that increased to over 840,000 in the next year. In addition, about a third of its pages were given over to advertising which attracted significant revenue. Within a few issues *Omni* was established as the most successful new publishing venture of the decade.

Bova had always believed that there was a large market for an intelligent but not overly technical magazine about scientific development. *Omni* rode the crest of the latest major wave in public awareness of how technology was going to change people's lives with the advent of personal computers, video games, mobile phones, camcorders, even microwave ovens! Guccione's idea was to show how science was the new religion, but in doing so he also made science and technology look sexy, giving it a gloss and vitality that it had never had in the technical magazines.

In this respect Guccione was not trail-blazing. Hugo Gernsback had done exactly the same 60 years before when he developed *The Electrical Experimenter* into the more glamorous post-war *Science and Invention*. More than any other popular science magazine of its day, *Science and Invention* had brought new technology to the general public and had shown not only how it would change their lives but how they could contribute to it. He encouraged readers to experiment and invent and to look to the future through 'scientific fiction'. It was the popularity of the fiction in *Science and Invention* that prompted Gernsback to launch *Amazing Stories* in 1926. Now, 60 years later, Bob Guccione was doing exactly the same – only better. Unlike Gernsback, Guccione knew how to spend money to good effect; his money on promotion and his top payment rates gave the magazine its widest possible readership and attracted the best possible writers. Payment rates at the start were advertised as between $800 and $1,250 per story, four times the level Bova had been able to pay at *Analog* for stories of equivalent length, but both Kendig and Bova confirmed to me that they actually paid $2,000 per story.

Bova was soon attracting good writers with quality fiction, covering both fantasy and science fiction. Early stories included 'The Chessmen' by William G. Shepherd (November 1978), a curious fable of a chess set with one set of pieces communist and the other set capitalist; 'A Thousand

Deaths' (December 1978), an especially violent story by Orson Scott Card set in a future where the Soviets control the United States; 'Count the Clock That Tells the Time' (December 1978), another of Harlan Ellison's introspective stories, this one written in a transparent tent at the World SF Convention; and 'Whether Pigs Have Wings' (January 1979) by Nancy Kress, about a benign alien whom we have all encountered before. The February 1979 issue shows the diversity of the material that Bova was selecting. 'The Ancient Mind at Work' is one of Suzy McKee Charnas's vampire stories, which became the opening chapter of her novel *The Vampire Tapestry* (Simon & Schuster, 1980). Robert L. Forward, who had already appeared with an article, 'Goodbye Gravity' (January 1979), made his short-story debut with 'The Singing Diamond', a surprisingly lyrical, high-tech story about dense particles of matter that can be trapped in a diamond. 'The Blizzard Machine' is a tall tale by Dean Ing about a snowmobile that breaks the sound barrier. The March 1979 issue contained one of Orson Scott Card's most beautiful and emotional stories, 'Unaccompanied Sonata', which shows that human artistic creativity can never be crushed.

Bova also published work by Robert Sheckley, Gene Wolfe, Robert Silverberg, Philip K. Dick, Norman Spinrad and Alfred Bester, yet the author who scooped the awards in the first year was George R. R. Martin. 'The Way of Cross and Dragon' (June 1979) is a challenging story which questions the very roots of religious faith. 'Sandkings' (August 1979), like 'Nightflyers', shows Martin's ability to create a chilling horror story from a solid science-fiction base, in this case the bizarre fate of a cruel collector of exotic alien creatures. Both stories won the Hugo award in their respective categories, 'Sandkings' also winning the Nebula, and both topped the *Locus* poll. Bova won his sixth Hugo Award for Best Editor in 1979.

It seems highly suitable that it was in *Omni*, the magazine that celebrated scientific advance and revolutionized popular awareness and acceptance of high-tech, that the word 'cyberspace' was coined by William Gibson in his story 'Burning Chrome' (July 1982). This story and Gibson's earlier 'Johnny Mnemonic' (May 1981), both of which preceded *Neuromancer* (1984), are regarded as the texts that began the cyberpunk revolution which typified the fiction of the eighties and which I shall discuss in more detail in the next volume.

The fiction represented only a third of *Omni*'s contents, and in addition to the articles on science, UFOs and the paranormal, there was also a profusion of artwork. Although it ran no graphic stories, *Omni* was as important in the popularization and promotion of science-fiction art as any of the graphic magazines, including *Heavy Metal*. *Omni* helped popularize in the

United States the works of H. R. Giger, De Es Schwertberger and Robert Venosa, and featured some of the most remarkable scientific photographs published up to that time, including the work of celebrated *Life Magazine* photographers Fritz Goro and Roman Vishniac.

Omni conducted a number of surveys of its readership, with some surprising results. Teresi recalled:

> If I remember correctly, we had a weird audience, one that at first scared our ad salespeople. In general, our research showed that we had a lot of males, a lot of single males among them, with discretionary income. And they did *not* read other magazines. They did not watch much popular television. (They did go to movies.) They did *not* read the competing popular science magazines but they *did* read *Scientific American* (about a 20 percent overlap between the two magazines) and they read tons of books, fiction and nonfiction. This is an odd audience and our sales staff at first didn't know what to do with it. Fortunately, the advertisers told them. For example, MasterCard, which has no real interest in science, wanted to be in *Omni* because we had young readers no one else could reach because they don't read other magazines and don't watch much TV.[83]

Although *Omni* caused a storm in the publishing industry it was ignored, at the outset, by the scientific press. One critic remarked, 'Yet, if one judges by the amount of attention paid to *Omni* by the 'establishment' science press, one would think its birth was no more significant than that of some small, esoteric journal.'[84]

The establishment could not turn a blind eye forever. Imitations inevitably appeared. In October 1980, Time, Inc. launched *Discover*, another heavily illustrated magazine on the wonders of science, though with no fiction and less than half the number of pages of *Omni*. It did not gamble on such a wide readership, printing 400,000 copies of the first issue. In fact, Time had missed out on pre-empting *Omni*. In the mid-sixties Time-Life had published the *Life Science Library*, a series of books drawn from the unused resources of *Time* and *Life* magazines. The series was highly successful. Frank Kendig told me:

> Clearly, a market had been identified and Leon Jaroff, then *Time*'s science editor, almost immediately proposed a new magazine, without success. He brought it back unsuccessfully for years and then was suddenly given the okay a short time after *Omni* hit the stands. Leon was the founding editor of *Discover* magazine. Then Nick Charney and John Veronis, who

---

83 Personal e-mail, Teresi/Ashley, 26 August 2006.
84 Eugene Garfield in *Current Comments* #11 (12 March 1979), p. 70.

had founded and later sold *Psychology Today*, bought the aging *Saturday Review*, a weekly, and turned it into four separate monthly magazines, covering The Arts, Business, Education and Science. To everyone's surprise, *The Saturday Review of Science* made money but the other three didn't and all four magazines were folded. I had edited that magazine and a few years later was hired by Hearst to turn *Science Digest* into a full-scale popular science magazine along the lines of *The Saturday Review of Science*. Hearst was aware of the numbers at the time but didn't put up the money until after *Omni* went on sale and proved that the market existed.[85]

Science Digest which, since it had first appeared in January 1937, had been in the standard digest-size format, was reborn in the larger, fully illustrated slick format with its issue for November/December 1980. Sales boomed, reportedly around five hundred and forty thousand, with a shift to younger readers, many college-based. *Science Digest* ran more articles of popular science but it ran no science fiction. However, its Australian edition, initially called *Omega*, which began with its January/February 1981 issue, ran two stories per issue. *Omega* had an Australian circulation of 40,000, the largest that any indigenous sf-related magazine achieved and, as a consequence, sales to that magazine made authors eligible for membership of the Science Fiction Writers of America. *Omega* was important in the re-emergence of Australian sf, which I shall explore in more detail in the next volume.

There was also *Beyond*. This was a 24-page tabloid science magazine which also ran one or two stories per issue. The idea was for three issues a year, one per term, distributed free as part of college newspapers across the United States, funded by advertising procured because of its guaranteed large circulation. It was published by Alan Weston Publishing in Hollywood and edited by Judith Sims. It promised a remarkable payment rate of 25 cents a word. The mixture of articles in the first issue (Fall 1981) was clearly aimed at students, with features on computers (by David Gerrold), cameras, the Rubik Cube, science anomalies and a *Star-Trek* quiz. There was one item of fiction, 'Night of Black Glass', a dark fantasy by Harlan Ellison, which was given the centre spread. Three other issues appeared carrying fiction by Robert Silverberg, Steven Barnes and Horace Gold, amongst others, but then the magazine ceased, with no reason given for it folding. As Weston produced other types of college magazines, presumably the process was profitable, but *Beyond* vanished and remains one of the least known of the science fact/fiction magazines.

Omni, in the meantime, was creating its own offspring. In early 1980,

85 Personal e-mail, Kendig/Ashley, 23 August 2006.

Ben Bova and Don Myrus (one of the staff editors at *Penthouse*) assembled a large-format slick anthology *The Best of Omni Science Fiction*. It sold over three hundred thousand copies in three months,[86] prompting the possibility of an all-sf slick magazine. This first volume was all reprint, including non-fiction and pictorial features as well as stories, but future volumes, of which there were another five, included several new stories.

Omni had been distributed widely in Britain from its first issue[87] so it was strange in November 1981 to see a slimmed-down version of just 32 pages being marketed as a weekly partwork called *Omni, Book of the Future*. This was published by Eaglemoss Publications, who had previously issued such partworks as *The Living Countryside* and *You and Your Camera*, and who had obtained a licence to compile a selection of articles and stories that would build into 'the weekly library of scientific fact and speculation'. The staff at Eaglemoss knew nothing about science fiction so they commissioned David Langford to select stories from *Omni* which were not only suitable for a British readership but which could also be spliced up and serialized over two or more parts. The editor, Jack Schofield, overruled Langford's initial choice, preferring to use Asimov's 'Found!' from the first issue of *Omni* as the first story to be sliced in two. There were hopes that if the partwork succeeded it could run new material in future issues, and Michael Scott Rohan came on board as fiction editor and Peter Nicholls of the Science Fiction Foundation also served as consultant. A set of five weekly issues were prepared as a pilot run, with a print run of 100,000 copies, and released at the end of November and during December 1981. The only other story reprinted was 'The Test' by Stanislaw Lem, from the October 1979 *Omni*, in the last two parts. Sales were poor and the project was, thankfully, dropped.[88] There was a later, more dignified attempt at a British edition of *Omni* in 1984, which I shall discuss in the next volume.

By one of those odd quirks of fate, Britain had a home-grown equivalent of *Omni*, albeit a pale alternative, which appeared at exactly the same time. This was *Ad Astra*, conceived and edited by James Manning out of his home in Clapham, south London. The publisher of record was Rowlot Ltd. Manning explained the thinking behind the magazine:

> The basic philosophy of the magazine is to cover science fact, astronomy and space exploration in simple terms so that people can understand not only what is going on, but its importance. Secondly, to publish

---

86 See letter from Ben Bova to *Locus* #240 (December 1980), p. 11, which stated that news-stand sales were over 70 per cent of the print run of 400,000.

87 The British edition ran until 1982 under the editorship of Bernard Dixon.

88 For David Langford's amusing account of his involvement with *Omni Book of the Future*, see *Cloud Chamber* #10, January 1982 reproduced online at www.ansible.co.uk/cc/cc10.html

science fiction stories from not only known authors ... but also from people who are just starting. Finally, there is a middle ground of future speculation/mysteries which embraces such subjects as UFOs, astrology, alternative energy, etc.[89]

This is identical to the premise behind *Omni*, though, as Manning told me, at the time he was planning the magazine he had no idea that *Omni* was in the offing. By comparison, *Ad Astra*'s budget was minuscule. The first issue, dated October/November 1978, ran to only 28 quarto pages. Although it was on quality, coated stock, allowing for reproductions of photographs, it was all in black and white and the general design was basic. There was some decent interior artwork by David Hardy, alas also in black and white, but it was just not in the same league as *Omni*. Manning printed 10,000 copies of the first issue and managed to secure distribution through W. H. Smith, so that the first issue was sold out. By the fourth issue the print run was up to 22,000 and Manning was growing in confidence. He introduced full-colour covers from issue #4 and switched from bi-monthly to a six-weekly schedule.

Ad Astra can be seen as an *Omni* in miniature, with the same good intentions and with a huge effort and dedication by the editor to make it work. The first issue featured articles on the moons of Mars and Jupiter and the newly discovered 'moon' of Pluto, Charon. It featured an astronomy article by Patrick Moore, who was also a columnist for *Omni*, plus a sky chart for the November stars. Manning had secured a new story by renegade author and rock star Mick Farren, 'The Ants are Going', an amusing slant on the fate of the first planned starship. Unfortunately he also ran a very immature comic strip, 'Frank Fazakerly' by Bryan Talbot, which damaged the tone of the magazine.

The second issue ran 'There Will Always be an England' by actor Edmund Dehn. This had won first prize in a science-fiction contest run by a local commercial radio station, Radio London, for stories set in London in 2001. The story depicts an England destroyed and a lone madman still hopeful that he can restore the land. Dehn wrote no more sf but went on to appear in several sf films and TV series and has done many voice-overs and book narrations, including the leviathan task of reading the entire *Gormenghast* trilogy by Mervyn Peake on audiotape (Isis Books, 1995).

Ad Astra was soon attracting work from the leading British sf writers, although as it rarely ran more than two stories per issue, the scope was limited. Nevertheless, it ran new stories by Ian Watson, Geoff Ryman, Brian Stableford, Tony Richards, David Langford, Robert Holdstock, Garry

<hr/>

89 Personal letter, Manning/Ashley, 26 March 1979.

Kilworth and John Brunner. Their stories fitted in well with the magazine's general atmosphere of delving into the deeper mysteries, such as Ian Watson's subtle reworking of history, 'The False Braille Catalogue' (#4, June 1979) and Geoff Ryman's reinterpretation of how Einstein formulated his theory of relativity in 'Einstein at Berne' (#5, August 1979). In addition to the science articles, which included one from Isaac Asimov on comets and asteroids, there were interviews with writers, including Norman Spinrad (#7, November 1979), the Strugatsky Brothers (#8, January 1980) and Joan Vinge (#16, September 1981), plus articles on Philip K. Dick (#6, September 1979) by Charles Platt, and L. Ron Hubbard (#12, October 1980) by George Hay. The magazine also extended its coverage to the cinema, using film promos on its cover in the hope of boosting sales.

Manning worked hard at developing the magazine but it remained a costly production with limited return. Manning was convinced that there was a market of at least fifty thousand in Britain but he needed the finances to expand. During the autumn of 1981 he believed he had secured a deal with a European publisher and distributor but this dragged on and the unpublished seventeenth issue remained dormant. Unfortunately, the deal fell through and although Manning clung to the hope that he could revive *Ad Astra*, it faded away.

Although it lasted for only sixteen issues, and ran just over thirty new stories, *Ad Astra* was Britain's longest running magazine in the years between *New Worlds* and *Interzone*. *Interzone* appeared seven months after *Ad Astra*'s last issue and would usher in a new Golden Age for British sf, which I will explore in the next volume.

Omni, however, was set to prosper for many years, but not without its changes. After nearly two years' involvement, Frank Kendig resigned as executive editor, the challenge and thrill of establishing a new magazine having now somewhat dissipated. Encouraged by Guccione and Keeton, who did not want further reshuffling of staff, Bova was elevated to the post, placing him in overall charge of the magazine. He appointed Robert Sheckley as fiction editor. The changes happened in October 1979 and took effect from the January 1980 issue. Sheckley found that the office work was too restricting, even at three days a week, and that it was eating too much into his writing time and, though he persevered for nearly two years, he resigned in July 1981. His place was taken by Ellen Datlow, who had served as associate fiction editor during Sheckley's tenure. Datlow would remain with the magazine for the rest of its life. At the same time, Bova was made a vice-president and editorial director, with Dick Teresi, succeeding as executive editor. From this elevated position, Bova no longer had much to do with the magazine beyond writing the 'First Word' editorial, but was involved far more in public relations and as a figure-head. The frequent travelling and TV appearances limited even more the time he needed for writing and it was found that the promotion was not materially affecting sales, so Bova resigned in September 1982, four years after his *Omni* adventure had started.

The success of *Omni* can obscure whether the magazine did anything to further science fiction. It clearly reached an audience interested in popular science, and the sales of the *Best of Omni* anthology, which was marketed specifically as science fiction, showed the scale of the market – one which the traditional sf magazines could only dream of attaining. Sales of *Analog* had peaked at 116,521 in 1973, the most that any digest sf magazine had achieved since the fifties,[90] but this was only a third of the sales of the *Best of Omni* and a seventh those of *Omni* itself. *Omni*, therefore, helped make science fiction big business, paying authors a top rate for quality material. But would that material have sold elsewhere? Or, to take it back one stage further, would that material have been written at all?

Clearly most of the stories would have been written anyway. George Scithers had a vicarious thrill when visiting Ben Bova at the *Omni* offices in being able to tell him, after Bova had handed Scithers the latest issue, that he had already read and rejected all the ficton in that issue.[91] However this is more a statement about the content of *Asimov's* than it is about that of *Omni*.

Orson Scott Card considered the matter and told me:

> By the time *Omni* appeared, I was already writing novels, which were so much more lucrative than magazine sales to the standard magazines that I suspect I would have written far fewer short stories had there not been a market that paid as well as *Omni*, with an editor who knew and liked my work. And because *Omni*, unlike *Analog*, was open to more 'weird' fiction besides strictly hard-sf, I could write stories like 'Deep Breathing Exercises' and 'Quietus', which are clearly not *Analog* stories. 'Unaccompanied Sonata', on the other hand, is a story I had tried to write some time before, but I didn't have a handle on it until *Omni* happened to be the short story market of choice. Still, I wonder if I would have written it when I did, or in the fairy-tale-like voice I used, if I'd been aiming it at *Analog* or *F&SF*.[92]

90 The first issue of *Fantastic* in 1952 reportedly sold over 300,000 copies because of the presence of a Mickey Spillane story.

91 Related to me by George Scithers in a personal e-mail, 13 August 2006. Darrell Schweitzer believed that it was the October 1979 issue which contained the first instalment of an excerpt from Heinlein's *The Number of the Beast*, plus stories by Stanislaw Lem, Jean Shepherd and Walter Tevis.

92 Personal e-mail, Card/Ashley, 25 August 2006.

Omni also lured Robert Silverberg back to short-story writing for very sound reasons:

> I wrote my first story for *Omni* after an absence of six years or so from short story writing because I was offered about six times what I might have received from a conventional magazine, and my rate got higher from there later on.[93]

Bova himself believed that *Omni*'s greatest achievement was in giving a home to the earliest cyberpunk fiction. Almost certainly *Omni*'s presence created a liberal atmosphere in which authors could think creatively about technology's effects on society, without the restrictions or expectations of a genre magazine such as *Analog* or *Asimov's*. In effect, *Omni* was the gateway that filtered the science fiction of the pre-technological revolution of the sixties and seventies into the cybertech eighties.

SF Destiny

Soon after James Baen left *Galaxy* in August 1977 to become a senior editor at Ace Books, he announced that he would be publishing *Destinies*, a science-fiction magazine in pocketbook format. Baen took pains to emphasize that it was a magazine and not an original anthology. Volumes were referred to as 'issues', the cover always labelled it 'the paperback magazine' and 'the science fiction magazine'.

Of course, the general public and book dealers would not have known the difference. To them it was a paperback book of short stories and other features and was displayed in the book section not the magazine racks. At first glance it would seem to readers just like any other original anthology.

The original-anthology market had soon recovered from the Elwood phenomenon, if it had suffered at all. During 1978, bookstall browsers would have found Terry Carr's *Universe 8*, Robert Silverberg's *New Dimensions 8*, Judy-Lynn del Rey's *Stellar #4*, Damon Knight's *Orbit 20* and Roy Torgeson's *Chrysalis 2*, and that was just amongst the regular series. There were further one-off volumes such as the *Analog Yearbook*, *Millenial Women* and *Cassandra Rising*, all previously discussed, plus the start of the horror-fiction series *Shadows*. It was into this seemingly abundant market that *Destinies* appeared in October 1978, the first issue dated November/December.

It was in standard pocketbook format, running to 316 pages and selling

93 Personal e-mail, Silverberg/Ashley, 29 August 2006.

for $1.95, an average price for paperbacks at that time, though more expensive than the regular digests. It was published on thick book paper and the type size used was 12-point so that the volume looked thick, far thicker than it needed to. Nevertheless, despite the large type and the profusion of internal illustrations and adverts, each issue carried around seventy thousand words of fiction and features, more than the average digest magazine, so appearances were not deceptive.

Despite the format, *Destinies* was assembled like any other magazine and certainly more so than those anthology series which were closely related to magazines such as *New Worlds* and *QUARK/*. It was given a volume number as well as an issue number, it ran book reviews and other regular features, including a science column by Jerry Pournelle, stories were grouped on the contents page by length rather than page order, and each story was illustrated with headings just as in a magazine. The finer points of these niceties would probably have escaped most readers, but most would have noticed that *Destinies* was not your average paperback collection. In fact, *Destinies* was trying to do everything that Baen would have liked to achieve at *Galaxy* had he had the budget and control. It was important, though, that he delivered the goods rather than producing what might otherwise have looked like a gimmick.

Baen generally kept himself behind the scenes and let his contributors speak for him, but he revealed some of his purpose in the third issue. Baen was a firm believer that science should be mankind's salvation and that the human race would not survive without expansion into space, but that society at that time lacked the will. 'Generating that will is what *Destinies* is all about', he wrote, calling the magazine 'the fun-filled crusade for the future of our species'.[94]

The emphasis in each issue, therefore, was on how technological advance was our salvation, and this led to a high number of science articles. The message in Jerry Pournelle's column, especially in the second issue, was 'only technology can make us free'. Poul Anderson contributed a series on the nature of science as depicted in science fiction. Harry Stine looked at the 'Third Industrial Revolution', Frederik Pohl wrote about predicting the future and Charles Sheffield considered how we would get about in space. Baen would also secure advance publication of excerpts from Robert A. Heinlein's autobiographical reminiscences, 'Expanded Universe' (Summer–Fall 1980).

Dean Ing wrote several articles on nuclear warfare, including a series, 'Nuclear Survival' (began Summer 1980), about how to survive a nuclear war. Ing also contributed one of the more significant stories to the first

94 James Baen, 'The Plot', *Destinies* #3, April/June 1979, p. 7.

issue, appreciated more in hindsight than at the time. Ing had only recently returned to writing science fiction and was establishing a reputation for his near-future techno-thrillers. 'Very Proper Charlies', the basis for his novel *Soft Targets* (1979), shows how easily open societies such as the United States are vulnerable to terrorists. Ing's solution is to use the media to ridicule them, one that may have its shortcomings, but his depiction of how terrorists use the media to establish their cause was chillingly prescient.

These articles demonstrated not only Baen's crusade but how he saw the market-place, especially following the success of *Omni*, which he regarded as *'Destinies'* only real rival for the hearts and minds of the new generation of science fiction/fact readers.'[95] Baen did not have *Omni*'s budget for either production or acquisition: he paid six cents a word, the same as the other major anthologies and *Analog* and *Asimov's*, and he could not produce a magazine of such beauty as *Omni*, but what he lacked in presence he could make up for in passion. Baen wanted his magazine to inspire readers to embrace the new technology. In that sense *Destinies* had the same driving force as *Omni* and *Future Life*, and all were true sons of Gernsback.

Not all of the fiction had the same gloss and sparkle. The authors had the ability to be more subtle, to get under the skin and to plant seeds to mature over time. Gregory Benford's 'Old Woman by the Road', in the first issue, is really a parable about how things can't stay the same but must change. Along the same lines, though much more way out, in the same issue is Clifford Simak's 'Party Line', which begins with the universe starting to contract and humanity understanding that they have to plan now to survive. Orson Scott Card also wrote a parable urging individuals to explore beyond their immediate world in what otherwise reads like a story of oppressive government, 'But We Try Not to Act Like It' (August/September 1979). David Drake shows the stupidity of humans in 'Cultural Conflict', in the second issue, when they manage to wipe out the dominant intelligence on a planet without realizing it. Depressingly, war, violence and terrorism continue to feature in several of the stories, not all of them showing technology to its advantage. Stephen Leigh's 'Encounter' (April/June 1979) concerns a man made into an invincible weapon, giving rise to the problem of what to do with him. Charles Sheffield's 'Skystalk' (August/September 1979) has man's crowning achievement, the space elevator, as the inevitable object of terrorists. What stands out amongst these stories is Gordon R. Dickson's award-winning 'Lost Dorsai' (February/March 1980), which shows how even amongst these powerful warriors, pacifism can sometimes be a powerful weapon.

95 James Baen, 'Welcome', *Destinies* #2, January/February 1979, p. 1.

There were stories that conveyed a sense of wonder and mystery. James Hogan's 'Silver Shoes for a Princess' (October/December 1979), for instance, tells of a young girl and her robot mentor on a journey to a distant star, with only hints of the purpose,[96] while Joan Vinge's 'Voices from the Dust' (Spring 1980) brings ancient Mars alive in the minds of two scientists. There were also humorous stories, but the prevailing mood of most fiction in *Destinies* was dark and depressing, tending to show what a mess humanity had made of Earth. Larry Niven summed it up in his brief and thankfully light-hearted bar-room story, 'The Green Marauder' (February/March 1980), where human and animal life on Earth is seen as a product of a plague that wiped out a far earlier civilization.

In August 1980, three years after joining Ace, Baen resigned and followed publisher Tom Doherty, who established Tor Books. Susan Allison, who had assisted Baen on the early volumes of *Destinies*, took over as editor at Ace Books, but did not wish to edit *Destinies*. This had been Baen's personal project and he compiled two more volumes on a free-lance basis, using the remaining material on hand. The final volume appeared, undated, in August 1981. There was also a batch of stories that Baen had originally bought for *Destinies* but which, as the series developed, he decided were not sufficiently hard-sf. These were assembled by Richard McEnroe in a '*Destinies* Special' anthology entitled *Proteus: Voices for the 80s*, published in May 1981. Unfortunately these stories are almost all misfits and were best left out of *Destinies*.

As an experiment in producing a paperback magazine, *Destinies* was only a partial success. Though the first issue had been reprinted and purportedly sold over 150,000 copies, subsequent reports placed sales for early volumes closer to 60,000 and dropping to 30,000 for later volumes, not sufficient for Ace to continue it. Baen had also found the pressure of producing a bi-monthly magazine, as originally planned, far too demanding in addition to sustaining Ace's book line. As a consequence *Destinies* slipped from bi-monthly to quarterly and then became irregular.

But schedules and sales aside, *Destinies* was rather a mixed bag. The positive and inspiring non-fiction was not always matched by the fiction, which could be downbeat or, at worst, anti-progress. Few stories were outstanding. Only 'Lost Dorsai' won an award, and only two others were nominated, both low-tech stories which dealt with benign aliens. Richard Wilson's 'The Story Writer' (April/June 1979) portrays an old pulp writer who tells people stories of their lives and realizes that he is recounting the history of very noble aliens. Baen was not getting the high-tech stories he needed. In fact the best stories, those that have passed the test

---

96 Hogan eventually used this as the basis for his novel *Star Child* (1998).

of time in *Destinies*, are those, like Wilson's, that came from the soul and not from the mind. The science-fiction field was changing. A decade on from Campbell's death the high-tech story no longer held the appeal. Traditonal science fiction had become depressing and downbeat, whereas true science was looking exciting and sexy. Readers wanted the flash and excitement of *Star Wars* with the freedom that science would bring and looked to those story-tellers who could weave wonder with emotion and give the reader a glimpse of the beyond.

Baen did not abandon the idea of the pocketbook magazine and would later revive the *Destinies* model as *Far Frontiers*. But at the start of the eighties it was science that captured the mind but wonder that captured the heart.

5

Looking Back:
The Gateways in Perspective

The story of the science-fiction magazines during the seventies has been long and complicated. The decade was one of so much change and uncertainty that at the time it was not clear in what direction it was heading. We have already seen Bruce Sterling's rather dismissive assessment that by the end of the seventies sf had become 'confused, self-involved and stale'.[1] It was certainly confusing, and one reason why this book is so long is in order to unravel that confusion. More recently, Roger Luckhurst reassessed the seventies from two opposing viewpoints: first that it was a period of breakthrough in the aftermath of the New Wave revolution and as a result of the emergence of academic appreciation; and secondly that it was one of shutdown and anarchy. This caused him to reassess the decade as an 'interregnum' between the New Wave of the sixties and the Cyberpunk movement of the eighties.[2]

The problem in assessing the seventies is the large number of different initiatives moving in different directions under the control of different editors and publishers. During previous decades, despite growing rivalry from comic books and paperbacks, the sf magazines had remained firmly on course, directed chiefly by John W. Campbell, along with, from the fifties, Horace Gold and Frederik Pohl. There was a main highway which everyone found easy to navigate, and even if they wandered off down the byways, the highway was always there to return to, solid and reliable.

But a number of factors from the sixties and early seventies, not least the upheaval caused by the *New Worlds* brigade and Harlan Ellison's *Dangerous Visions*, plus the death of John W. Campbell, Jr., had fragmented that highway into many minor roads and it was difficult to know which

---

1 Bruce Sterling, 'Preface' in William Gibson's *Burning Chrome* (London: Gollancz, 1986), p. 9.

2 Roger Luckhurst, *Science Fiction* (London: Polity, 2005), pp. 167–8.

to follow. Many readers lost their way altogether and abandoned the field, while others found a favoured route, stayed with it and did not explore further.

Thus the science-fiction market fractured. We have seen how a separate *Star Trek* fandom grew, originally an offshoot of core sf fandom, but very rapidly taking on a distinct identity and with evidence that many *Star-Trek* fans did not read other forms of sf. *Locus*'s survey of its readers, based on a reliable 800–900 responses, showed that while in 1975 42 per cent of readers also shared an interest in *Star-Trek* books and fandom, by 1980 this had dropped to 27 per cent.[3] This split grew with the success of *Star Wars* and other films so that an entire wave of sf-media fandom evolved, with their own magazines led by *Starlog*, which actually declared itself a 'science fiction magazine', even though it carried no fiction.

Similarly, a separate role-playing-game (RPG) fandom developed around sf and fantasy board-games and the emerging computer games, with its own magazines. These games became a substitute for reading or writing sf.

Young readers who might have been attracted to the core sf magazines instead became absorbed by *Star Trek* or *Dungeons & Dragons* and never crossed the divide. Potential new readers were therefore being lost, as evidenced by the increase in the average age of readers of the magazines. The average age of *Locus*'s readers, for example, rose from 24 in 1971 to 31 in 1981 and continued to rise. The percentage of those under 21 dropped dramatically from 36 per cent in 1971 to 4 per cent in 1981. *Algol* had similar results, with the number of readers aged 15-20 dropping from 12.3 per cent on 1975 to 1 per cent in 1982. *Analog* had two surveys in 1958 and 1981. Unfortunately it used different age bands and the second provided no averages, but in 1958 the percentage of readers aged under 25 was 30.7 per cent, and in 1981 the percentage under 24 was 14.6 per cent. This trend continued. When *F&SF* took a reader survey in 1982, 4.6 per cent of readers were under 18 and by 1995 this had dropped to 2 per cent. There was no doubt that from the seventies onwards the average age of magazine readers was rising. New recruits were not being attracted to the magazines. They were, though, still reading books. A survey by Waldenbooks in 1988 of their five book clubs showed that the Otherworlds SF bookclub had the youngest average age of all the clubs, with 41 per cent under 25.[4]

It was to this younger market that *Isaac Asimov's SF Magazine* successfully appealed in 1977. It is unfortunate that *Asimov's* published no reader

3 See 'Locus Survey Results', *Locus* #247 (August 1981), pp. 12–13.
4 See news item, *Locus* #331 (August 1988), p. 4.

survey at this time so it is not possible to determine the average age of its readers, though the circumstantial evidence from the letter column and the feedback reported by its editors is that readers were generally younger.

Apparently magazines were keeping many of their core readers, who were growing old along with them, but, apart from *Asimov's*, were not attracting younger readers. Since *Asimov's* was able to attract these readers, it's not as if they were not prepared to read magazines. It must be that the other sf magazines no longer appealed to young readers as they once had; the comic-book field, films and now role-playing games held a greater lure.

It cannot be a coincidence that the attraction for younger readers fell away at the same time that the field was maturing, a process which was more evident in the anthologies and magazines during the seventies than it was in books. That does not mean that there weren't mature sf books available during the seventies; there obviously were, with many of them directly evolving from the magazines. But the growth in sf-book publishing was primarily in formulaic adventure books and retro-pulp, a phenomenon cited by Robert Silverberg when he turned his back on writing sf because his publishers failed to keep his more recent, mature work in print.

The revolution that had begun with the explosions in Michael Moorcock's *New Worlds*, Harlan Ellison's *Dangerous Visions* and Damon Knight's *Orbit*, had shaken the dust and debris out of short-story sf, and this continued in further anthology series, notably Silverberg's *New Dimensions* and Terry Carr's *Universe*, and in a reinvigorated *Analog* under Ben Bova and an ever-receptive *F&SF*. Between them they restructured sf out of the debris by a process Damien Broderick has called 'diligent consolidation'.[5] This was happening primarily in the magazines and anthologies, but at the cost of losing the younger and less sophisticated readers, many to the attractions of *Star Trek* or RPGs. We must also remember that at the start of the seventies there was an upsurge in the popularity of fantasy fiction – indeed, it was fantasy more than sf that popularised the RPG – and this was soon followed by the revival of interest in horror fiction following *The Exorcist* and the arrival of Stephen King. These fields had much more to offer the younger reader in terms of escapism and simplistic story-telling, which magazine science fiction had moved away from.

The science-fiction magazine was, to some degree, caught between a

5 Damien Broderick, 'New Wave and Backwash, 1960–1980' in Edward James and Farah Mendelsohn (eds), *The Cambridge Companion to Science Fiction* (Cambridge: Cambridge University Press, 2003), p. 62.

rock and a hard place. In order to mature it needed more sophisticated readers who could appreciate the greater depth of new fiction being produced, but this meant that it was not encouraging the next generation into the field. This dilemma was never more evident than with the success of *Star Wars* in 1977. The argument that ensued, led by Ben Bova, was that *Star Wars* was degrading the sf field by pandering to the lowest common denominator, and Bova believed that this risked science fiction being dragged back into the pit of immaturity from which it was still struggling to escape. Despite the advances made under John Campbell in the forties, and Horace Gold and Anthony Boucher in the fifties, science fiction was still coming of age. The feminists had inveighed against it, Kate Wilhelm specifically calling the field 'immature'. Stanislaw Lem was equally critical, arguing that sf was held back by its devotion to its pulp roots and the desire of its fans for formulaic adventure fiction. According to Lem, 'Americans are children.'[6]

At this same time that it was being challenged from within, science fiction came under intense academic scrutiny in the new-found critical magazines. Indeed, it was not just academic scrutiny. Writers became more critical of themselves, and the pages of *Algol*, *Thrust* and *Science Fiction Review* were as full of criticism and analysis as anything in *Science-Fiction Studies* or *Extrapolation*.

All of these factors showed that if science fiction was genuinely trying to mature, it had to rebrand itself so that its readership understood what was happening. Otherwise it was running the severe risk of confusing and alienating its market, which had fresher fields to move to. Of the traditional magazines, only *F&SF* had been consistent in presenting a mature image via its covers and overall content (including a lack of interior illustrations), and it can be no coincidence that this was the only core magazine significantly to increase its circulation during the seventies.

Ben Bova had soon got to grips with moving away from Campbell's latter-day formula of psi powers, military conquest and political chicanery. It was noticeable during the seventies that Campbell's surviving stable of writers faded not just from *Analog* but from most of the magazines. It was easier (and more profitable) for them to sell novels and collections to the book market, because that market was still lagging behind the innovations of the magazines and anthologies. The majority of books published in the seventies drew upon the popular style of fiction developed by the leading writers in the fifties and sixties. For every daringly original new book by Samuel Delany or Ursula Le Guin, there were plenty of tried and

6 Michael Kandel, 'Remarks 1: Stanislaw Lem', *The New York Review of Science Fiction* #155 (July 2001), p. 7.

tested, familiar and very popular works by Poul Anderson, Harry Harrison or Mack Reynolds.

The old guard was being replaced by a wave of remarkable new writers, all maturing in the magazines before establishing themselves in the book field. The roll call of writers whose first sales were made between 1969 and 1979 is quite breathtaking, easily the equal of the talent that emerged 20 years before. Some of these emerged via the Clarion and other workshops that began around this time. Others were encouraged and helped by the new wave of editors. I listed many of the Clarion alumni in Table 2.2 and won't repeat all that here, but it is important to remind ourselves of at least some of the major names who first appeared during this decade. They include, in the order in which they first appeared in print, Joe Haldeman, Chelsea Quinn Yarbro, Vonda McIntyre, Pamela Sargent, Michael Bishop, Connie Willis, George R. R. Martin, Jerry Pournelle, Octavia Butler, Howard Waldrop, John Shirley, Joan Vinge, John Varley, Garry Kilworth, Kim Stanley Robinson, Geoff Ryman, Bruce Sterling, Paul Di Filippo, Pat Cadigan, Charles Sheffield, Somtow Sucharitkul, William Gibson, Orson Scott Card and Barry Longyear.

What stands out with these writers is the sheer diversity of their work. In *Transformations*, when I catalogued the new writers, I considered them as primarily Campbell or Gold or Boucher authors. That scarcely applies here. Only a few of these authors, Jerry Pournelle and Barry Longyear being the most obvious, are closely identified with their initial editors (Campbell and Scithers). Almost all of these authors could sell to most of the editors of the day, and they were producing work that not only replicated the best of the old, but was generating a new brand of mature and expanding science fiction. These were the writers providing Broderick's 'diligent consolidation'.

The liberation of science fiction meant that the new generation of writers had no restrictions on their creativity. Some of them – Howard Waldrop and Rudy Rucker spring to mind – were perhaps so idiosyncratic that the major markets were uncertain about them, but this was where the semi-prozine came to the rescue. The markets diversified like never before during the seventies. If your work was too unusual for *Analog* or *Galaxy* or *Universe* or *Asimov's*, there was always *Unearth* or *Shayol* or *Galileo* or *Orbit*. In fact, the options were more than generous. It was very different from the sf boom of the fifties where the opportunist magazines that mushroomed in the wake of the success of *Galaxy* or *Astounding* did so in imitation of them. Most tried to be *Galaxy* clones, even in pulp format. If anything, in the seventies the opposite was true. No one tried to imitate anyone. They tried to develop their own individuality and the majority of writers were now sufficiently sophisticated and liberated that they could adapt to almost any market.

This is why critics have looked back on the seventies as being both confused and transitional. Liberated by the revolutions of the sixties and the demands of the seventies, authors made good use of their new-found freedom and rebuilt sf by casting out the old rule book. If anything, it became harder to define science fiction by the end of the seventies. The field encompassed much that would otherwise have been classified as fantasy and horror fiction, but the hard core of sf was also affected. Stories became more human, more emotional, more literary. This was partly due to the increase in women writers, but not entirely. Many of the stories by Barry Malzberg would not be classified as science fiction under older, stricter definitions. The same applies to the works of Harlan Ellison, Robert Silverberg, George Alec Effinger and John Shirley. These authors wrote deeply personal, deeply visionary stories that often defied defini-tion. That was what made sf in the seventies so exciting. Writers were once again able to experiment and push boundaries. It did not always work, but they learned from that and pushed further, opening ever-new gateways. Genuine hard-core sf was still there, of course, but the works of many of the major names, new and old, were more lyrical, more intense in their study of cultural interfaces and human relationships. The work of John Varley, George R. R. Martin, Vonda McIntyre, Pamela Sargent, James Tiptree, Jr., Michael Bishop and that of many like them may have featured the nuts-and-bolts of science fiction, but only to showcase the human dilemmas within.

There were some who believed that science fiction had, as a conse-quence of all of this, become respectable, particularly because of the new-found academic acceptance. But this was too much too soon to expect of a field in the process of change. Science fiction was being challenged by the experimentalists still championing the literary revolution, by the academics who had opened the field to inspection, by the feminists who argued it was stereotyped and immature, by black writers (or at least Charles Saunders), who argued that sf held nothing for them, and by outsiders looking in, such as Stanislaw Lem, who felt that sf was following the wrong rules. It would take a while for writers to respond to this, but the new generation was more prepared for the challenge than most of the old guard. The seventies saw science fiction reforming and striking out in new directions.

There were other forms of respectability. Science fiction had still not been accepted by the literary establishment – miracles take a little longer. But there was the scientific establishment, who increasingly recognized that science fiction had a part to play in exploring and creating the future. Bob Guccione saw technology as sexy, and *Omni* was a major magazine that ran serious science fiction as part of a quality package aimed at the top end of the market, the movers and shakers of the new technological age. *Omni, Future Life* and *Destinies* helped to direct at least one of the subroutes of science fiction into cultivating our new-found love affair with technology and thus helped usher in the cybertech age.

In *Transformations* I stated that the true Golden Age of science fiction was in the early fifties, because that was when the greatest concentration of talent was brought to bear on re-creating a more sophisticated form of science fiction out of the ashes of the pulps. The seventies was not a Golden Age, it was too diverse for that, and too fragmented. But there was an energy stimulating the new science fiction that had not been felt for 20 years, and that made the decade daring and exciting and, yes, as Bruce Sterling believed, 'confused'. More material was produced in the seventies that challenged preconceived conventions than in any previous decade.

Some did not like that. The familiarity and security of traditional science fiction had gone, but not completely. You could still find it but you had to look for it. It was more likely to surface in paperback novels, mostly those from Del Rey Books, than it was in the sf magazines and anthologies. And, of course, it was there in excess in the cinema, in the blockbusters *Star Wars, Superman* and *Close Encounters*.

So the seventies saw a gap growing between the traditional sf reader, nurtured on Campbell and Gold, and the newly liberated magazines. One of the challenges facing the magazines was whether they could.rebrand their image to look more sophisticated, so as to attract the more mature reader, while at the same time not wholly alienating the younger reader. Part of the problem was the magazine's appearance. The digest size, which had been so modern in the fifties, was now unfashionable and out of place on the stalls. The new media magazines and the style and glitz of *Omni* and *Heavy Metal* were far more attractive and beguiling, but also expensive. Had it not fallen foul of the paper shortages, *Vertex* would have shown that a slick magazine could be published. *Shayol* showed it could be done on a relatively modest budget. *Galileo* had found a convenient half-way house. *Cosmos* perhaps did it the best but it was seriously underfinanced, and that was the fundamental problem: to shift to the new, sexy, slick format needed money and that did not come easily.

Another gap was growing. At one extreme was the small-press magazine where the focus was on minimal overheads with sales primarily by subscription, but showing restraint so that you did not overreach yourself, as *Galileo* had. At the other extreme, you could launch a major magazine provided you had substantial financial backing or a profitable existing business. Guccione could do it with *Omni*, but Goldfind couldn't with *Cosmos*. There were variations between these extremes but they tended to favour one or the other. At the big-business end was Joel Davis. When he launched *Asimov's* and took over *Analog*, he did it knowing that he had an existing profitable business, a good distribution network, a sound subscription base and money-making ways to recycle the magazines as anthologies and sell foreign rights. Edward Ferman at *F&SF* knew the business well and knew how to benefit from his subscriber deals, even when news-stand sales were falling, but he was shifting away from the big-business model to a smaller 'cottage industry'. Magazines had to be either big business and entrepreneurial or small and safe. Both sides had different tactics to capture their readers, either the big glitz or the shrewd business operations. There was very little middle ground. *Galaxy's* demise was in part attributable to Abramson's disastrous financial deals and his unwillingness to invest in sound distribution. *Amazing's* decline was caused in large part by Arthur Bernhard's refusal to undertake a subscription drive, even though Elinor Mavor had worked out how this could benefit the magazine. Both found themselves stranded.

For most of the seventies, the leading magazines had held on to their main readership. Overall the figures were relatively stable. *Analog's* average circulation in 1970 had been 110,000 and in 1978 (the last available before the change of publisher) it was just under 105,000. *F&SF's* had been 50,300 in 1970 and 62,000 in 1980. But beneath these figures were worrying changes. *Analog's* news-stand sales, which had been 70,000 in 1970 had fallen to just under 55,000 in 1978. The same applied to *F&SF*, which had fallen from 31,000 to 19,000. Subscriptions had risen to compensate but, as was evident from the fates of *Galileo* and *Questar*, it was expensive to meet that demand if it was cut-price, and it was essential that subscribers renew and keep renewing. At least if the magazine had a good news-stand display it could attract casual readers, but that could not happen with subscribers. Distribution had always been the bane of magazines, not just the sf magazines, but increasingly during the seventies the distributors lost interest in the smaller magazines. Good distribution was costly, while subscription drives had long-term benefits but short-term costs and were at the mercy of a deteriorating and more expensive postal service.

The major magazine chains that had sustained crateloads of fiction titles in the forties and fifties were a thing of the past. The traditional science-fiction magazine was becoming something of a dinosaur. This was perhaps the ultimate irony. At the very time when sf had found its greatest liberation and, at least in books, a huge and profitable market, the news-stand sales of magazines were shrinking. The casual readership was dwindling, lured away by the glitter of the cinema, the excitement of role-playing games, and the safe familiarity of the paperback novel. It was a challenge that the magazines had yet to come to terms with, but was one that was crucial to solve in the eighties.

The economic rollercoaster of the seventies had not helped. This had contributed directly to the deaths of *If*, *Vertex* and *Galaxy*, and each prospect of economic revival had to be viewed with caution. *Cosmos*, *Destinies* and *Asimov's SF Adventure* could not be seen as luxuries. They either paid their way or died. And even though *Destinies* was profitable, that was only because James Baen's personal time and cost was not put into the equation. Producing a magazine is extremely time-intensive, and therefore costly. Joel Davis could overcome this by spreading overheads over several magazines. Edward Ferman managed it by retreating into his own home and cutting overheads. Bob Guccione did it by a huge investment to capture advertising.

Yet maybe there was hope on the horizon. We have seen how both the media and RPG magazines might be part of the solution. *Starlog* had considered buying *Galaxy*, but was put off by the debts. TSR came to the rescue of *Amazing*. And we shall see at the start of the eighties how a merger of sf, weird fiction and media interest would prove a success with *Rod Serling's 'The Twilight Zone' Magazine*. Was the child going to save the parent after all? Or was another salvation or enemy on the horizon?

During the seventies an increasing number of computer networks had been developed and by the early eighties several successful experiments had been conducted to link them. The fully functional internet was still a decade away but, with remarkable prescience, Dick Geis, writing in 1980, foresaw the following:

> I do think we will have one day a small console attached to the TV set. You buy a feed from a local cable company – you are allowed to view the contents page of a new issue of a magazine, or allowed to see the cover of a book, plus a descriptive blurb – and you key in a purchase of that magazine or book … You could also pay for the right to record (copy) all of part of the book or magazine.[7]

Geis's thinking was moving towards the idea of internet trading 15years before Amazon.com became a reality, and had a vision of the online magazines or webzines that would mushroom in the 1990s. Whether

7 Richard E. Geis, 'Alien Thoughts', *Science Fiction Review* #35 (May 1980), p. 4.

these would prove the answer to the magazine distribution problem or yet more nails in the coffin is something I shall explore in the next volume.

As the eighties began, there was a certain degree of hope restored in the sf magazines, but they could never be complacent. There would always be new challenges and surprises. Over the years SF had been able to meet those challenges because the writers proved infinitely adaptable. As a result of the seventies liberation, the writers were even more adaptable. Science fiction in the magazines was more mature, more human, more literate and, thanks to the growing public fascination with technology, more topical. Science fiction had redesigned itself during the seventies and now, refitted and refurbished, it was ready to take on the next wave of challenges.

Appendix 1

Non-English-Language
Science-Fiction Magazines

The phenomenon of the science-fiction magazine is not confined to the United States and Britain. As I explored in *The Time Machines*, there are grounds to argue that the earliest sf and fantasy magazines originated in Sweden and Germany. Nevertheless, the development of the sf magazine is, by and large, a US phenomenon. Most of the science-fiction magazines in non-English countries have either been local editions of *Astounding*, *Galaxy* or *F&SF* or were filled with translations from other US magazines. Franz Rottensteiner believed in 1973 that between 80 and 90 per cent of all science fiction published in Western Europe consisted of translations from English.[1] Little indigenous work was appearing prior to the seventies, with a few obvious exceptions in France, Russia, Japan and Germany, as detailed in *Transformations*. In most countries the preferred and more marketable publication of science fiction was either in paperback or in the digest-form series novel, such as the *Perry Rhodan* series in Germany, which was translated into many European languages. Yet, as Danish author and translator Ellen Pedersen remarked, 'One sign of a healthy, commercial science fiction field is the existence of a magazine.'[2] Arkady Strugatsky was of the same view, believing that it was only through a science-fiction magazine that the field could develop and mature.[3]

The traffic in science fiction was almost all one way. Very little non-English sf was published in the United States or Britain until the seventies and even then it was of limited scope. This volume has already looked at the impact of Stanislaw Lem in the United States and the influences of *Perry Rhodan* and *Métal Hurlant* in the 1970s, though these were geared to specific market niches. There was some attempt to broaden horizons

1 See F. Rottensteiner, *View From Another Shore* (New York: Seabury Press, 1973).
2 Ellen M. Pedersen, 'The Micro-World of Danish SF', *Locus* #288, p. 28.
3 Arkadi Strugatski interview in *Locus* #321, October 1987.

during the decade, starting with the first World SF Convention to be held in a non English-speaking country, in Germany in 1970. The first European SF Convention was held in Trieste in 1972 and the first World SF Writers Conference was held in Dublin in 1976. The latter led to the creation of World SF, an international organization of sf professionals, which came into being in 1978 under the presidency of Harry Harrison.

The 1970s otherwise saw local science-fiction magazines in transition, with only a few countries having a magazine that lasted a sufficient number of issues to develop an identity and encourage local writers. Most of these magazines had small circulations and many were produced by fans. The political climate in many countries made it difficult to publish science fiction with any social or political comment, though it is also true that science fiction was often viewed as juvenile literature and thus of no consequence. The last 30 years has seen a steady maturing of science fiction across the world, but not all countries in the seventies were in a position to have sf magazines of any significance. Some countries, such as Albania, Greece and China, were only just developing their sf magazines at the end of the seventies, and I have saved discussion of those until the next volume. Other countries, such as Brazil, which had a brief emergence of science fiction in the sixties was forced underground again until the eighties.

The following, therefore, is a summary of the magazine scene in the major countries during the 1970s. It is organised by continent and then alphabetically by country.

EUROPE

Belgium[4]

Belgium has never had any consistency when it comes to science-fiction magazines, a problem complicated by the country being divided linguistically, the northern part, Flanders, speaking Flemish (virtually identical to Dutch) and thus linked to Holland, and the southern half speaking French. Invariably their books and magazines tend to be closely associated with the neighbouring countries and, as in those countries, there is a greater interest in Belgium in the adult comic book than in traditional narrative science fiction. One of the most popular of all comic-book series, *The Adventures of Tintin*, was the creation of Belgian writer Georges Remi ('Hergé'), while perhaps the best-known Belgian sf comic-book serial was

4 My thanks to Eddy C. Bertin and Guido Eekhaut for their help with this section.

Le Rayon U created by Hergé's erstwhile collaborator Edgar Pierre Jacobs in 1943.

It is also true that the Flemish writers were generally more influenced by magic realism and the fantastic than their Dutch equivalents. The leading writer in the 1920s and 1930s was Jean Ray, who continued to have an impact on more recent authors such as Thomas Owen, Hubert Lampo and Johan Daisne. It was not until the seventies that the English New Wave began to influence Belgian sf even more than US sf.

Most Belgian magazines have been either small-circulation fanzines or short-lived prozines, consisting primarily of translations. The most recent of these, *Atlanta* (discussed in *Transformations*), had folded in 1967. The next was *Apollo*, a joint venture with the Dutch publishing house De Schorpioen, under the editorial control of folklorist and literary agent Albert van Hageland. Van Hageland had previously edited the pulp-novel series *Utopia*, which ran from June 1961 to May 1963 but was poorly distributed and eventually folded in favour of westerns and crime books. The series had run abridged versions of novels by mostly US and German authors. Ten years later Van Hageland tried again with *Apollo*, another attempt at much the same, though this time it was a large-flat format magazine of 48 pages. It ran from May 1972 to November 1973, a total of 20 monthly issues. It published some original Belgian and Dutch novels alongside the translations, plus a short story (usually supernatural), each issue. Contributors included Paul Van Herck and Eddy C. Bertin, both of whom would become known outside Belgium. It had a companion weird-fiction magazine, *Horror*, which saw 28 issues from January 1973 to May 1974 and relied almost entirely on translations.

Fans found themselves relying more on the publications of the Belgian SF Association, known colloquially as SFan. It had been organized by Julien Raasveld in November 1969 and Raasveld relaunched and retitled his existing fanzine as the club's official magazine *Sfan* from March 1970. Unfortunately, the club went through a few internal upheavals, including a change of top membership in November 1970. Raasveld was voted out as chairman and his magazine was replaced by *Info-Sfan*, edited by Simon Joukes. *Info-Sfan* was renamed *SF Magazine* from issue #32 (January 1974). From issue #57 (July 1977) Guido Eekhaut became editor and it absorbed his fanzine *Rigel* (which he had started in June 1976), taking on its name. The magazine passed through several more editorial hands until it ceased with issue #77 in April 1981. It published the works of several Flemish writers, including Frank Roger, Alex Reufels, J. P. Lewy, Yves Vandezande and Robert Smets. The Fan Club also organized the local sf convention and presented SFan Awards. It did far more than any professional

magazine in Belgium to encourage local writers, who otherwise had few
outlets unless they published in Holland or France. Robert Smets and
Guido Eekhaut commented in 1987, when listing several writers who
came from Flanders, that 'most of these wrote interesting stories but saw
their talents confined to fanzines and semi-professional publications'.[5]
Belgium had yet to establish a major market for its local writers.

Denmark[6]

Although Denmark was the home of one of the world's greatest fantasists,
Hans Christian Andersen, neither sf nor fantasy became a tradition in
Denmark, and it was not until the influx of US sf after the Second World
War that a fragile sf market developed. The emphasis was on books, and
such magazines as were attempted seldom lasted long. *Planet-Magazinet*,
which appeared in pocketbook format in January 1958, edited by Knud
Erik Andersen, and reprinted chiefly from *Astounding*, survived for just
six monthly issues. It was over seventeen years before another attempt
was made.

Månedens Bedst Science Fiction ('The Month's Best SF') was a large-flat-
format magazine of 100 pages, which ran for 16 issues from September
1975 to April 1977. It relied heavily on reprints from US sources and was
initially successful but hit a sales slump during the summer of 1976 from
which it failed to recover. The last four issues were delayed and reduced
in size to a slim, poorly illustrated digest of 68 pages. It was not regarded
as being of high quality. Its editor, Frits Remar, was more experienced in
crime fiction and he brought in Jannick Storm and Niels Søndergaard to
advise on the last few issues, but by then it was too late. Sales needed to
reach 10,000 to break even but they only averaged 5,000. Remar told me,
'My policy was, after a start with the good old names, to bring the New
Wave, Harlan Ellison, etc., to Denmark, and to open up for new Danish
writers, but that failed unfortunately.'[7] Remar had the added problem
that he found it difficult to secure enough good new stories for each issue.
He bought rights to several US anthologies to have better material to hand
but then found the agent from whom he had acquired the rights did not
own them, which added to the publication delays.

When *Månedens Bedst* failed, Niels Søndergaard and other fans joined

---

5 Robert Smets and Guido Eekhaut, 'SF in Flanders', *Foundation* #40, Summer 1987,
p. 53.

6 My thanks to Frits Remark, Carsten Schiøler and Niels Dalgaard, Ph.D. for their help
with this entry.

7 Personal letter, Remar/Ashley, 19 August 1977.

with publisher Bent Irlov, to produce a successor magazine of higher quality. *Science Fiction Magasinet* began in June 1977, aiming for a bi-monthly schedule. Again it mixed mostly US/UK translations with a few original stories. It also had a 10,000-copy print run but the magazine was poorly distributed and folded after seven issues.

Science fiction was served better by smaller fan-operated publications. The Danish fan club Science Fiction Cirklen was founded in 1974 and issued a magazine, *Proxima*, the first issue of which was dated October 1974. It was edited by Carsten Schiøler for the first ten issues, followed by Eric Swiatek and Niels Dalgaard from #11 (March 1977). It was chiefly a magazine of review and comment but ran at least one story per issue, including some original fiction. 500 copies of each of the first three issues were printed and these needed to be reprinted, so the print run rose to 700. *Proxima* did not pay for material but strove to be a quality product and has continued to appear, and is now the longest-surviving Scandinavian magazine.

France[8]

France has long had a major science-fiction tradition. It had two important magazines, *Fiction*, the French edition of *F&SF*, which had started in October 1953 and *Galaxie*, the French edition of *Galaxy*, which had had a short-lived existence in the fifties but which was revived in May 1964. Both magazines were edited by one of France's most important editors, Alain Dorémieux, who had taken over as editor of *Fiction* in December 1958. Michel Demuth became editor of *Galaxie* from January 1970. *Galaxie* was almost entirely reprint, including fiction from *If* and *Worlds of Tomorrow*, but from the November 1974 issue it began to include new French stories. Though *Fiction* reprinted mostly from *F&SF*, it drew from other diverse sources, including *Weird Tales*, and usually featured one or two French stories per issue. Rather significantly it called itself 'La Revue Littéraire', which gave it a literary finesse and allowed it to become a venue for the discussion of science fiction. From 1959 there was also a *Fiction Special* with one or two issues a year, many of which contained all original French material. Similarly there was a *Galaxie Bis* or 'Special' from December 1965, which sometimes appeared four or even six times a year and which ran longer material from *Galaxy* or occasionally other sources.

8 My thanks to Richard D. Nolane, Pascal J. Thomas, Remy Lechevalier and Jean François Ledeist, who provided much of the basic data for this section.

It was through *Fiction* that many of the leading French sf writers had emerged in the fifties and sixties, notably Philippe Curval, Gérard Klein, Stefan Wul, Jacques Bergier, Michel Demuth, Roland Topor and Daniel Walther. French sf writers tend to be more politically sensitive than most of their US or British counterparts, and the student riots of May 1968 led to a new generation of politically aware writers, inspired to some degree by the British and US new wave movements and especially by the works of Philip K. Dick and J. G. Ballard. Premier amongst them was Jean-Pierre Andrevon who, coincidentally, debuted in the May 1968 *Fiction*. Andrevon held strong socialist views and his fiction reflected ecological and military concerns. Alongside Andrevon, Michel Jeury introduced a radical element into his work and other writers followed, most notably Daniel Walther, Jean-Pierre Fontana, Dominique Douay and Jean-Pierre Hubert. At the same time, older-style writers left the magazines for the various paperback series that were rampant in the seventies, such as Ailleurs & Demain ('Elsewhere & Tomorrow') and Anticipation. Philippe Curval, for instance, one of the most popular and original writers of the period, was less in evidence in *Fiction* in the seventies, though the magazine did serialize his *Dune*-like novel 'Les Sables de Falun' (October–December 1970). Just as happened when Moorcock changed *New Worlds*, the new style of writing alienated some readers, and sales of *Fiction*, which had been as high as thirty-five thousand, dropped to around ten thousand at the start of the seventies,[9] doubtless also affected by the growing sales of the paperback series.

The third rung of France's regular magazines was *Horizons du Fantastique*, published and initially edited by Dominique Besse. It ran for 37 issues between January 1968 and Winter 1975.[10] It had a broader policy, running stories and features on horror and the occult, as well as favouring more traditional science fiction, which made it a good market for both established and new writers. It ran fiction by Pierre Barbet, Gérard Torck and Stefan Wul as well as Henri-Luc Planchat, Yves Olivier-Martin and Jean-Claude de Repper, amongst other new writers. Although it featured some stories by other European writers, it carried no US or English translations. It also ran a special film section and from February 1969 it generated a highly popular companion movie magazine, *L'Écran Fantastique*, which continues to this day.

With heightened interest following the 1970 World SF Convention in Heidelberg, the first European SF Convention in 1972 and the first

9 See news story in *Luna Monthly* #17, October 1970, p. 8.
10 Issue #38 (Spring 1976) was printed but not distributed, though copies occasionally surface.

National SF Convention in France in 1974, the seventies were a boom period for French sf. Many small publishers and fans were encouraged to produce their own new wave magazines. *L'Aube enclavée* (*The Enclaved Dawn*) from Lucien and Henri-Luc Planchat, lasted only six issues from 1970 to 1972, rising from fanzine to semi-prozine (up to two thousand copies) with issue #3, but, alongside translated stories from England and Spain, it discovered one of the major names of the French New Wave, Serge Brussolo, who debuted with 'L'Évadé' (1972). Another New-Wave magazine was *Argon*, published in flat-slick format by Alain Detallante and edited by Daniel Lamy. It lasted seven issues, from April to October 1975 but published several writers of the new generation, including Pierre Pelot who had also sold to *Fiction*. *Chroniques Terriennes*, another of the New-Wave magazines, was planned as a quarterly but lasted only one issue in May 1975. Edited by Hervé Desinge and Lionel Hoebeke it ran mostly French material plus a story by John Brunner.

The major new contemporary sf magazine was *Univers*, a quarterly launched by the publishing house J'ai Lu in June 1975, and edited by Yves Frémion under the editorial directorship of Jacques Sadoul. Since this was issued in pocketbook format and ran a J'ai Lu imprint sequence number, it is often referred to as an anthology series, though its content was more akin to a magazine. *Univers* reprinted primarily from such original anthology series as *Orbit* and *New Worlds*, but also ran some original material and gave space to articles, reviews and interviews. Frémion was a known political radical and *Univers* was an opportunity to promote more extreme fiction. But it proved popular, with sales of around thirty thousand copies, though it was eventually stopped after 19 issues, in Fall 1979 and converted into an annual anthology under Sadoul's editorship. The most radical French editor, though, was Bernard Blanc who, like Frémion, promoted political sf and had spearheaded the revolutionary movement in sf at the start of the seventies. With publisher Rolf Kesselring, Blanc edited *Alerte!*, an irregular magazine in more ways than one. It saw only five issues, its first four spread over two years between Autumn 1977 and June 1979, published in pocketbook form. Plans to shift to a standard magazine format with issue #5 in 1979 collapsed when Kesselring's firm went bankrupt. *Alerte!* ran work only by French writers, with the emphasis on proactive, militant and radical sf and essays. Its circulation was never high, and though not representative of most French sf, demonstrated the extremes to which the genre could go. Blanc shifted his allegiance to *SF & Quotidien* (*SF & Daily Life*), a digest edited by Stéphane Gillet, which appeared in November 1980 and continued the emphasis on French New Wave.

There were plenty of other magazines that appeared during these boom years, most of them short-lived. Inevitably the success of *Métal Hurlant* led to a number of imitators such as *Neutron, Ere Comprimée* and *Piranha*, the latter also running short fiction and movie-related material. Editions de France, in Paris, brought out a French edition of the British tabloid *Science Fiction Monthly* called *Science-Fiction Magazine*, edited by Jean-Luis Ferrando. It was in the same tabloid format but used mostly French artwork and augmented the slim contents with traditional French stories, articles and reviews. *Horizon 3000*, edited by Alain Tremblay, ran mediocre adventure fiction and featured articles on UFOs. It saw just one issue in July 1976. *Mouvance* was a series of thematically based original anthologies edited by Raymond Milési and Bernard Stephan, containing material solely by French writers, which appeared on an annual basis from 1977 to 1985 and proved especially popular.

Editions OPTA, which published *Fiction* and *Galaxie*, launched a third magazine, *Marginal*, in November 1973, edited by Michel Demuth. It was packaged like an anthology and featured reprints, mostly from earlier issues of *Galaxy*. They also published a challenging anthology, *Les Soleils Noirs d'Arcadie* (*The Black Suns of Arcadia*) in 1975, edited by Daniel Walther in the style of Harlan Ellison's *Dangerous Visions*. Around this time, Dorémieux stepped down as editor of *Fiction* and planned his own magazine, *Nova*, but the project fell through. Michel Demuth took over *Fiction* from May 1974 and was succeeded by Daniel Riche from May 1977. Unfortunately, OPTA ran into financial difficulties when it was abandoned by its parent company and was declared bankrupt in September 1977, bringing an end to *Marginal* (in May 1977) and *Galaxie* (August 1977). Remarkably, a new corporation was set up within weeks, Les Nouvelles Editions Opta, and *Fiction* continued to appear without a break in its schedule. It was, though, seriously underfinanced and encountered payment problems. Quality suffered and issues were delayed (despite a continuity of cover dates). Riche resigned as editor in August 1979 after having achieved much with little. Dorémieux returned as editor and injected life back into the magazine. During most of the eighties its circulation was a modest 6,000 but it remained the backbone of short fiction in France and was still the primary route into publishing.

While *Fiction* was at a low ebb in 1978, there was hope when a new magazine appeared, *Futurs*. It was edited by a collective of four, Gérard Klein, Philippe Curval, and Gricha and Igor Bogdanoff, and appeared in a large-flat, semi-slick format with good graphics and good-quality translations. The emphasis was as much on commentary and reviews as on fiction. Unfortunately, the cost of production was excessive and although it reportedly sold around thirty thousand copies, it folded after just six issues in December 1978. It left its mark, as it received the European SF Award in 1978 for the best professional magazine. It was revived by another publisher in March 1981 and was edited by Pierre Delmotte, again in flat slick format. The emphasis was on French stories and there was a smattering of English material which was marred by poor translation. Delmotte, who did not know the sf field well, aimed for popular but rather shallow material, trying to capture the *Star-Wars* market, but the magazine was again underfinanced and failed after three issues. Delmotte was assisted by Jacky Goupil who produced his own semi-professional magazine, *Opzone*, starting in March 1979, described as the French equivalent of Andrew Porter's *Algol*. This was a critical magazine and ran no fiction at the outset, but later ran one or two per issue. It had a small circulation of about five hundred, and was generally well received, but folded after nine issues[11] for lack of finance.

As has been evidenced time and again in Britain and the United States, when a country has a number of sf magazines, especially of a radical and varied content, it will encourage new writers, and the seventies was a boom period in France. However, by 1981, when a left-wing government took control, the wind was taken out of the sails of the political sf movement and by then the New Wave had settled. The upsurge in new magazines had ceased and once again *Fiction* and Dorémieux remained the backbone to sustain French sf into the eighties.

Germany

Germany has no tradition in publishing science-fiction magazines, even though the country can lay claim not only to the first magazine of weird and macabre fiction, *Der Orchideengarten* (1919–21) but also to possibly the world's first-ever magazine of popular science and superstition, *Relationes Curiosæ* (1683–91).[12] The pattern, especially after the Second World War, was on pulp-style dime novels, known as *Hefte* (staples), so called because the booklets were bundled and stapled in single signatures, usually of 64 pages. The leading sf series was *Utopia* which started in 1953 and was published by Erich Pabel, and though he experimented with a magazine, *Utopia Sonderband* ('special volume'), which saw 26 issues from 1955

11 *Opzone* began as a fanzine with issue #0. The last issue, #8, was so delayed that a stopgap issue #8 was produced in advance, giving the impression that there were ten issues.

12 See Ahrvid Engholm, 'A Magazine of the Fantastic from 1682', *Foundation* #72 (Spring 1998), pp. 88–93.

to 1959 (see *Transformations*), it made little impact. Their content was almost all US/UK translations. The *Perry Rhodan* series, started in 1961, dominated the German sf publishing scene and encouraged many imitations, and there seemed little purpose to be served by producing another specialist magazine. Such attempts as were made were all short-lived. *Comet*, from Tandem Verlag, saw eight issues from May 1977 to June 1978, However, though it was expensively produced in slick format with many full-colour illustrations, it managed to sell only fifteen thousand copies at best. This fell to under eight thousand after the fourth issue, when the format and size shrunk. It was originally edited by a triumvirate of Hans Joachim Alpers, Ronald Hahn and Werner Fuchs, selecting primarily US translations, but from issue #4 (February 1978) it was taken over by Renate Stroik. One final, special, larger issue was published as *Comet Sonderband* in Autumn 1978, but it still found no market. The same fate befell *Andromeda*, which since 1955 had been the official journal of the Science Fiction Club of Germany. In October 1978, under the editorship of Hans-Jurgen Frederichs, it was revamped as a semi-professional, semi-slick magazine, rather like Porter's *Algol*, retaining the emphasis on non-fiction and news, but with one story per issue. There were plans for the fifth issue (July 1980) to go fully professional but the demand was not there and neither were the finances and thereafter the magazine reverted to being the club journal. At the same time, the publisher of a karate magazine launched *2001*, aimed at a younger readership. It emphasised TV and cinema, the first issue sporting a *Star-Wars* cover and feature article, and later issues covered *Star Trek* and *Superman*. The first issue was entirely on quality coated stock but later issues were mostly newsprint. The fiction in the first two issues consisted of US translations, but later issues included several original German stories. However, it rapidly failed after five issues, from April 1978 to January 1979, the last retitled *Nova 2001*.

More success might have been expected of *Perry Rhodan Sonderheft*, started by Erich Pabel in Spring 1978, edited by Hans Gamber. It sought to combine the success of *Perry Rhodan* with the popularity of *Star Wars* and looked more like a glossy film magazine. Sales were excellent at the outset and it was renamed *Perry Rhodan Magazin* from issue #6, shifting from quarterly to bi-monthly and eventually to monthly in 1980. It ran interviews, features and several stories, mostly US translations, but, by 1981, sales were falling. It went through a succession of editors, ending with Hans-Jurgen Frederichs for its last four issues, and folded in June 1981.

It was clear that the glossy slick sf magazine would not work in

Germany, and the only successful sf magazine of the eighties, *Heyne SF Magazin* which started in November 1981, was in trade-paperback format. Moreover, the German editions of both *F&SF* (which had run since 1963) and *Isaac Asimov's SF Magazine* were issued as trade paperbacks and were really a series of anthologies rather than specific reprint issues. Unlike other countries, none of the German magazines helped launch the careers of any major writers.

Hungary[13]

Hungary has a tradition of science fiction dating back to the early nineteenth century, though the only names known in the English-speaking world are Mór Jókai and Frigyes Karinthy. In the years since the Second World War, Soviet sf dominated Hungary until Péter Kuczka emerged to champion the genre. He started the Kozmosz series of sf books with publisher Móra Ferenc in 1969, helped organize the first sf convention in Hungary in 1971 and was a founding member of the first European SF Convention in Trieste in 1972. In September 1972, through Móra, he launched Hungary's first sf magazine, *Galaktika*, which sold out its initial print run of 39,800 copies. He was assisted on many issues by László Fazekas. *Galaktika* was originally quarterly and issued in large-digest format, running to 128 pages. It was not until 1985 that it expanded into full-flat-magazine format, by which time it was selling over 50,000 copies a month, and was ranked amongst the most respected periodicals in the world. It was a struggle at the outset when Kuczka received much opposition from the sf fan base in Hungary. One viewpoint was expressed by János Kis, vice-secretary of Hungary's Central Science Fiction Club in 1978:

> A small group of professional writers have monopolized the field of SF in Hungary. Thus the fans have neither any rights to intervene in the publishing of books nor any hope to appear, ever. These evil conditions are caused by Mr Peter Kuczka, who hates any co-operation. This leaves its mark on the quality of appearing publications.[14]

While the local fans felt aggrieved, it was evident that Kuczka was trying to do his best for Hungarian sf by producing a magazine of high quality. His attitude was similar to Stanislaw Lem's. Attila Németh comments:

> Peter Kuczka was a noted poet in Hungary, and after the crushed 1956 revolution he was prohibited from publication. As a kind of

13 My thanks to Attila Nemeth for his help with this entry.
14 Personal letter, Kis/Ashley, 28 December 1977.

compensation they gave him the editor's chair at Móra's Kozmosz line. It was natural for him to seek out respected Hungarian authors of prose and verse to produce highly experimental SF, to raise the genre to the level of 'high literature'. He was afraid that associating *Galaktika* with the fan-movement would drag it down again to the dreaded pulp ranks. With this, of course, he made many enemies in the Hungarian SF community.[15]

Each issue was a blend of translated material from a wide variety of sources (despite the title, it was not drawn chiefly from *Galaxy*) plus several Hungarian stories, reviews and articles. Many issues were themed, either by author or subject. The first issue, for instance, ran an article on and several stories by Robert Sheckley. Issue #2 featured Ray Bradbury, #3 French sf, #4 A. E. van Vogt, #5 artificial intelligence, #6 Italian sf, and so on. By publishing material from such diverse sources, *Galaktika* became one of the most cosmopolitan of sf magazines, far more so than any English-language title, and presented such a fund of ideas and approaches to storytelling that it inspired a whole new generation of writers. Those whom Kuczka published and helped develop in *Galaktika* included Béla Kasztovsky, István Nemere, Gyula Fekete, Zoltán Csernai, Péter Szabó, László Lörincz and Mária Szepes, all of whom are now amongst Hungary's leading sf writers. With or without the support of fandom, Kuczka was determined that *Galaktika* would present the best that he could find and he succeeded. The 1974 European SF Award was the first of several awards that he and his magazine would receive.

Italy

The majority of science fiction published in Italy during the fifties and sixties was of non-Italian origin and, as quoted in *Transformations*, the leading publisher, Mondadori, did not recognize the existence of any Italian sf writers. Since 1952, Mondadori has published *Urania*, the name given to a series imprint which published novels, collections and anthologies but which was never a magazine, even though it is sometimes called that. As one Italian commentator, Fabio Calabrese observed, as late as 1985:

> *Urania* is a science fiction series which contains almost one thousand novel titles. With its very wide circulation at a controlled price, it exerts a heavy influence when it comes to building up readers' tastes and

---

15 Personal e-mail, Németh/Ashley, 5 October 2006.

therefore to fixing market potentialities. Yet it has never offered even the smallest possibility to any Italian writer.[16]

Calabrese regarded the years 1968 to 1972 as a 'black hole' in sf publishing but steadily, after 1972, the sf field began to expand. Though the series *Galassia* often squeezed an extra short story in per volume, usually of Italian origin and ran several Italian novels, during the 'black hole' period there had been only one genuine sf magazine, *Nova SF*, from Libra Editrice in Bologna, edited by Ugo Malaguti. It was published in pocketbook form, containing both translated and original stories plus reviews and features. It first appeared in May 1967, planned as a bi-monthly, but it struggled to maintain even a quarterly schedule, almost ceasing in 1969. Thereafter it was rather more consistent and by the time it folded in December 1980 it had published 42 issues. It encouraged several Italian writers, and there was a special issue in July 1976 composed entirely of work by Italians, including Vittorio Catani, Adalberto Cersosimo, Giovanni Mongini and Mauro Antonio Miglieruolo. Otherwise, the magazine consisted almost entirely of translations of US stories from the fifties and sixties. *Nova* was successfully revived in 1985 and continues to this day.

Steadily through the early seventies and then exploding in 1973, the publishing houses introduced many new science-fiction pocketbook series. The major ones were from Editrice Nord in Milan, including Cosmo Oro, Cosmo Argento and Fantacollana, which included many major classics by Frank Herbert, A. E. van Vogt, Philip K. Dick, Philip Jose Farmer and others, but there was also Millemondi from Mondadori, also in Milan, and Futuro Biblioteca from Fanucci in Rome. All of these were pocketbook series, not magazines. They also included translations of the Doc Savage novels, which ran from July 1974 to December 1975, from Mondadori, and the Perry Rhodan series, which began in March 1976, from Solaris in Milan, but passed through several publishers and editors before folding in July 1981. Like its US counterpart, the Italian *Perry Rhodan* also ran a few short stories.

The boom in magazines started in April 1976 with *Robot* from Armenia Editore in Milan, edited by Vittorio Curtoni who had previously co-edited *Galassia*. This was a 128-page digest magazine which was published monthly and which, in addition to running the usual translations of classic American sf, ran more contemporary stories by Michael Bishop, Harlan Ellison, Ursula Le Guin and James Tiptree, Jr., and usually included one or two Italian stories per issue. *Robot* also ran nine special supplements, all translations of anthologies or collections. The first one, a supplement with

16 Fabio Calabrese, 'Italian Science Fiction: Trends and Authors', *Foundation* #34, Autumn 1985, p. 49.

issue #9 (December 1976), was a translation of the first volume of the original *History of the Science Fiction Magazine* series that I edited in 1974. Supplement #4 (with issue 18, September 1977) was an original compilation of time-travel stories. Amongst the Italian writers featured in the magazine were Lino Aldani and Vittorio Catani. *Robot* ran for 40 issues until July 1979 and was resurrected in 2003.

Fantascienza followed in May 1976. This was a flat-format, A4-size, 70-page slick magazine from Ennio Ciscato Editore in Milan, edited by Maurizio Nati. It was attractively illustrated, including film coverage. The emphasis was again on major US writers and any work by Italians was restricted to columns and reviews. It proved expensive to produce and failed after three issues, in October 1976, when the publisher suddenly disappeared.

Next was *Altair*, started in October 1976 by Editrice Il Picchio in Milan and edited by Antonio Bellomi. This was a slim monthly digest of 128 pages that catered chiefly for fans of space opera. It ran a lead novel, including some translations of Murray Leinster, Poul Anderson, Walter Ernsting and even 'Vargo Statten', but also included original work by Luigi Naviglio and Ugo Malaguti under Americanized names (such as Jack Azimov). Short stories, included mostly as padding, were all by Italian writers. After eight issues the magazine relaunched itself as *Spazio 2000* from June 1977, but it delivered much the same. Armanda Dell'Onore took over as editor from June 1978, and the lead novels became even older material. The magazine ceased after another 19 issues in December 1978.

Gemini, edited by Luigi Randa (Antonio Bellomi) from publisher Mameli Gatti (who later operated as Solaris), was much the same as *Altair*, with old, translated space-opera lead novels and Italian padding. It ran for 19 issues from September 1977 to January 1979. However, it had a companion magazine *Verso le Stelle* (*Towards the Stars*), also a digest, which ran mostly short fiction almost all of which was by Italians. But the quality and intent was still the same. It managed ten issues from October 1978 to July 1979.

Curiously, an Italian edition of *Asimov's Science Fiction Magazine*, *La Rivista di Isaac Asimov* from Mondadori fared little better. It ran for just 11 issues from Spring 1978 to November 1980. There was little doubt that, despite the publishing boom in Italy in the mid seventies, the preference was for adventure novels and the desire for the new sf that had been maturing in the United States was not strong. By the early eighties the boom was over, but it would return.

One interesting phenomenon in Italy at this time was the semi-professional magazine *Kadath*, produced by Francesco Cova in Genoa. Cova was a fan of *Weird Tales* and he soon made contact with other devotees in

Britain and the United States. The first issue (October 1979) was in Italian, as was the second (May 1980) except for Adrian Cole's story. From the third issue (November 1980), which was devoted to the work of Brian Lumley, the magazine was almost entirely in English. It was an attractive, slim, A4-size magazine on top-quality coated stock. While it found only minor interest in Italy, it proved popular in England and America, and Cova switched to all-English contents from #4 (July 1981), a special *Weird Tales* issue. However, the magazine was expensive to produce and to mail and Cova's time was limited so only two more issues appeared, in July 1982 and Fall 1984, with new material by Manly Wade Wellman, Ardath Mayhar and Brian Lumley.

The Netherlands[17]

A survey conducted by the fan magazine *Holland-SF* found that only 22 per cent of the magazine's readers read their sf in Dutch, most preferring to read it in English.[18] Moreover, less than 10 per cent of the sf published in Holland each year is by Dutch writers and only 1 per cent of all books published in Holland are science fiction. This all suggests that indigenous Dutch sf is in the minority. A proliferation of paperback series dominated the sf scene in the 1970s, making it almost impossible for an sf magazine to be noticed or to gain any share of the market. The few attempts that were made to produce a professional magazine happened in the seventies. The best was *Morgen* (*Tomorrow*), edited by Manual van Loggem and published in Schiedam. It ran minimal American material, relying primarily on French, Dutch, German and Belgian contributors, including stories and articles by Julien Raasveld, Eddy Bertin, Rein Bleistra, Paul van Herck and Wim Burkunk. It lasted for only six issues, five between October 1971 and November 1972, and a final supplement three years later. Loggem later produced a cross-cultural anthology of Dutch sf, including stories from *Morgen*, that was published in the United States as *New Worlds from the Lowlands* (Merrick, 1982).

Germany's *Perry Rhodan* series had been published in Holland but in 1970 the publisher, Born, stopped the series after Volume 35. Following protests by several Dutch fans, the series was restarted and at the same time, in 1971, a local Perry Rhodan club was formed which published its own magazine *SF Magazine Terra* – later *SF Terra* – in July 1972. In the nineties, *SF Terra* would make a bid to become a prozine, with mixed results.

17 My thanks to Jaap Boekestein and Kees Buis for their help with some of the information for this entry.
18 See report by Annemarie van Ewyck in *Locus* #354 (July 1990), pp. 44, 47.

Two of the fans involved with the club, Kees van Toorn and Robert Zielschot, produced their own Rhodan fanzine, *Atlan*, and in 1977 both attempted to convert it to a professional magazine. It led to two separate magazines, both called *Essef* and both appearing in January 1977. Zielschot continued with the name while van Toorn relaunched his as *Orbit* from Autumn 1977. Zielschot's *Essef* lasted for nine issues from January/March 1977 to 1979, with the emphasis on comic strips, though it also serialized two space-opera novels from the German, 'Octavian III' by K. H. Scheer and 'Ren Dhark' by Kurt Brand. *Orbit* was the more professional and survived the longer, from Autumn 1977 to Summer 1987, winning the European SF Award in 1978. *Orbit* relied more on translations from US and German sources and rarely ran more than one Dutch story per issue. Useful though it was as an additional source of short sf, *Orbit* was not a market for new fiction. Dutch writers had more opportunities contributing to paperback anthologies which were more prominent in the seventies and generally sold better. One of the most popular series was *Ganymedes*, a 'Yearbook' published by Bruna SF and edited by Vincent van der Linden, which ran for 11 volumes from 1976 to 1989, the last volume delayed by three years.

Otherwise, the fan magazine *Holland-SF* which was produced by the Netherlands Contact Centre for SF (NCSF) and which has appeared since 1966, has been almost enough to cater for the core of sf fans in providing news, studies and reviews. It has a circulation of around four hundred. It runs the occasional short story but that is as likely to be American or British as Dutch.

Norway

Although Norway is the home of one of the earliest of all genuine science-fiction novels, *Nicolai Klimii iter subterraneum* (*Nicholas Klim's Underground Journey*) by Ludwig Holberg, published in 1741, there was not much advance in genre sf until the mid-1960s when two active devotees, Jon Bing and Tor Åge Bringsværd, began a programme of translating novels and compiling anthologies and introduced American and British sf into Norway. This was the start of the Lanterne science fiction series which showed publishers the popularity of sf. Amongst their pioneering works was the original anthology, *Malstrøm* (Oslo, 1972), containing works solely by Norwegian writers. In September 1971 Terje Wanberg became both publisher and editor of a Norwegian edition of *F&SF*, called *Science Fiction Magasinet*. The first two issues were drawn entirely from *F&SF* but thereafter

Norwegian material was included as well as a letter column, which helped revive interest in Norwegian fandom. The Norwegian science-fiction club, which had started in 1966 but had been lying dormant, was revived in 1974 by Johannes Berg. He started a club magazine, *Algernon*, which, despite its small circulation, was highly respected. *Science Fiction Magasinet* sold reasonably well but was still underfinanced. It sought to lift its profile by changing its name to *Nova* from February 1973 and relaunching itself as a new magazine. It published works by several of Norway's emerging writers, notably Øyvind Myhre, Dag Ove Johansen, Thore Hansen and Reidar Jensen. Myhre also edited the magazine from 1975 to 77. By now it was publishing more translations and less original material and had broadened its coverage to fantasy. Sales gradually fell away and publication ceased in 1979 under its final editor, Johannes Berg.

Romania

For many years Romania was the only Eastern European country to have a science-fiction magazine. *Colecţia Povestiri ştiinţifico-fantastice* (*Collection of SF Stories*) first appeared in October 1955 as a twice-monthly supplement to the weekly science magazine *Ştiinţă şi tehnică* and arose as a result of a competition for a science-fiction story. Amongst the winners was Adrian Rogoz who became the editor of the magazine and saw it through nearly twenty years and 466 issues. Also amongst the contributors to that competition was Ion Hobana and between them Rogoz and Hobana remained the backbone of Romanian science fiction for over forty years. *Colecţia Povestiri ştiinţifico-fantastice* usually featured a serial episode or long story plus a short story per issue. *Ştiinţă şi tehnică* had been a science magazine aimed at the young to encourage their interest in technology. Rogoz recognized the value of developing young minds. He later wrote, 'The most promising field to spread the seeds of science fiction are the youth.'[19] Rogoz was following the same route as Hugo Gernsback and, like Gernsback, he encouraged the development of fan clubs in Romania, the two major ones, the Timisoara Club and the H. G. Wells SF Club, both being formed in 1969. The Timisoara Club organized the first National SF Convention in Bucharest in April 1972. But, also like Gernsback, Rogoz did not publish fiction that was juvenile, but sought out fiction that explored bold new ideas. He ran translations of Ivan Yefremov's *Andromeda* (1957)

---

19 Adrian Rogoz in *Colecţia Povestiri ştiinţifico-fantastice* #386 (August 1970) quoted at http://hgwellssfclub.tripod.com/id1.html.

and Stanislaw Lem's *Solaris* (1974). It was estimated by the writer Florin Manolescu that there were twice as many stories by Romanian authors as there were translations in the magazine. The list of writers whom Rogoz helped is long and includes Romulus Barbulescu, Vladimir Colin, Sergiu Farcasan, Marcel Luca, Lucian Ionica, Mircea Opriţă, and Mircea Şerbănescu. Following the enactment of a new law in Romania governing the control of the press, the magazine was closed down on 15 April 1974, the official reason being the paper shortage.[20] There may also have been concern over the fan organizations that had grown through Romania and which were fostered by the magazine. It was these clubs that sustained sf in Romania during the next decade. From November 1972 the H. G. Wells Club printed the fanzine, *Paradox*, edited by Marcel Luca and Cornel Secu, while in 1976 the literary review *Student Forum* made space for a regular section on science fiction. Ion Hobana compiled an anthology of sf that was representative of current sf in Romania in *O falie in timp* (1976), and in 1978 he edited a special Jules Verne issue of the Writers' magazine *Secolul* (#207). All this bid fair for the re-emergence of sf in force in Romania in the eighties. Looking back over Rogoz's achievement, Cornel Robu saw the 466 issues of *Colecţia Povestiri ştiinţifico-fantastice* as 'the "soul" of the sf movement'[21] in Romania. That soul could not be stifled and the magazine would be reborn in 1990 as *Anticipatia*.

Spain[22]

The story of science fiction in Spain in the seventies is effectively the story of *Nueva Dimensión*, the country's only sf magazine at the time, published in Barcelona. The magazine ran for 15 years, from January 1968 to December 1983, a total of 148 issues. The Spanish required that a professional journalist be identified as the editor of all periodicals, so the editor of record was José M. Armengou from issue #1 to issue #85 (January 1977) and then Fernando Mir Candela until #111 (April 1979). However, the true initial editor was Sebastián Martínez, assisted by Domingo Santos (who became full editor from issue #111) and Luis Vigil. *Nueva Dimensión* followed the familiar pattern of publishing translated stories and some original material. Many of its issues were composed entirely of stories from Spain and Latin America or elsewhere in Europe, and the choice of

20 See Eugen Stancu, 'Perception of a Literary Genre, Science Fiction Literature in Romania, 1955–1974', *Carnival*, #36, March 2001, p. 46–53.

21 Cornel Robu, 'Milestones of Postwar Romanian Science Fiction', *Foundation* #49, Summer 1990, p. 12.

22 My thanks to Miguel A. Martínez for his help with the information in this section.

material was predominantly contemporary, meaning that most Spanish readers were gaining a better understanding of worldwide sf than anyone in Britain or the United States. The editors favoured more unusual or surreal stories, including New-Wave material, with items by Avram Davidson, Thomas M. Disch, R. A. Lafferty and J. G. Ballard, but also ran many stories by Poul Anderson, Isaac Asimov, Gordon R. Dickson, Robert Sheckley and Robert Silverberg.

They produced several special-author issues, starting with Cordwainer Smith (#22, May 1971), Harlan Ellison[23] (#29, February 1972), Arthur C. Clarke (#31, April 1972), John Wyndham (#35, August 1972), Robert A. Heinlein (#57, July 1974) and Philip K. Dick (#145, May/June 1982). These weren't confined to US writers. Several European and Latin American authors were honoured, including Gérard Klein (#26, October/November 1971), Hugo Correa from Chile (#33, June 1972), Juan G. Atienza (#43, March 1973), and, amongst the special issues, Domingo Santos himself (#2, July 1970).

They published material from Latin America, notably Argentina, where the magazine also circulated and was often the only current sf available. This led to trouble when the March 1970 issue (#14) was seized by the Spanish authorities for publishing 'Gu ta gutarrak' ('We and Our Own') by Argentinian writer Magdalena Mouján Otaño, a story which, in seeming to support the Basque separatists, was treated by the Spanish Secret Police as an offence against the State. Martínez reported on the problem:

> The question is that all the copies of *Nueva Dimensión* 14 will be destroyed and we will have to pay a fine or go to prison. My guess is that it will cost us about US$5,000. We have been always in a bad financial situation and will not have money to pay for this. Most probably this will mean the disappearance of the magazine ... I prefer to go to prison for not having money than to give them the opportunity of seizing the money I owe authors.'[24]

Donald Wollheim requested that British and US writers contact the Spanish Embassy in Washington and the US ambassador in Spain to exercise clemency.[25] The outcome was that there was no trial and Martínez had to remove the story from all issues and replace it with something else, in the end an inoffensive comic strip, and that issue also had to be

23 Santos reported that Ellison had generously sold them the translation rights to his stories for $1 in total.

24 Letter by Martínez to Donald A. Wollheim dated 27 June 1980 and reported in *Luna Monthly* #15, August 1970, p. 3.

25 See Wollheim's article 'Nueva Dimension in Jeopardy' in *Luna Monthly* #15, August 1970, pp. 3, 19 and the follow-up item in *Luna Monthly* #19, December 1970, pp. 3–4.

passed by the censor. By that time issue #15 had been published, but issue #14 eventually went on sale. Needless to say, the few issues that were distributed which included the story are now exceedingly rare. The story was, eventually, published in issue #114 (July 1979), which shows what a difference a decade made in Spain. The incident gave the magazine some attention, which improved sales, and from issue #20 (March 1971) it went from a bi-monthly to a monthly schedule.

Besides being a forum for publishing good-quality fiction, it was also a focus for fandom. It published many articles and reviews plus an active letter column. These features were printed on different coloured paper at the end of every issue and became known as the 'green pages'.

The magazine always looked top-quality. It received a special award from the 1972 Worldcon committee for excellence in magazine production and the same year won the first European SF Award for the best professional magazine. Until issue #109 (February 1979) its format was slightly wider than digest with 128 pages (occasionally 160); thereafter it shrunk to regular digest size but increased to 192 pages.

The magazine suffered various financial setbacks, mostly from a series of unscrupulous distributors. At one point they lost all their distribution in Latin America, which was almost half of the total sales. In 1977 their distributor absconded with the money from news-stand and library sales and they tried to recoup the money from a special sale of back issues. The magazine continued, but the changing economic and political climate in Spain by the end of the seventies left *Nueva Dimensión* increasingly vulnerable and, despite a valiant effort by Santos to keep it going, it ground to a halt in September 1982, with one extra-large farewell issue (#148) released a year later.

Sweden[26]

Swedish science fiction in the seventies was almost entirely the responsibility of Sam J. Lundwall and John-Henri Holmberg, with Lundwall the chief activist for magazines. Sweden had previously had two long-running magazines, *Jules Verne Magasinet* (*JVM*) which ceased in 1947 and *Häpna* which ceased in 1966. Lundwall tried various ways to resurrect both titles. He brought out four single-sheet issues of *Häpna* in 1969 in order to protect the name but plans to revive it fully never materialised. At the same time, Bertil Falk revived *JVM* as a quarterly magazine but

26 My thanks to Sam J. Lundwall and John-Henri Holmberg for their help with this entry.

dropped it after ten issues in 1971. He sold it primarily by subscription and succeeded in raising the print run to 1200 copies by issue #6, but it remained a slim, 32-page quarto magazine. Falk reprinted some stories from the original series of *JVM* along with more recent US translations and just a handful of new stories by Bertil Mårtensson, Sture Lönnerstrand and Dénis Lindbohm.

Also in 1971, Lundwall began translating and editing a science-fiction line for the publisher Askild & Kärnekull and he succeeded in getting them to relaunch *JVM* in 1972. Like Falk's version, it was in quarto format. Lundwall continued the numbering from the original series plus Falk's issues, so began with issue #343. Askild & Kärnekull reached an agreement with Ed Ferman to reprint stories from *F&SF* and this remained the main part of the magazine, although Lundwall added articles and features and included reprints from elsewhere. In 1973 Lundwall set up his own publishing company, Delta, and acquired the rights to *JVM*. He changed the format to large digest and made the magazine available by subscription only, which provided advance funding to help publish it, but limited its availability. The Swedish genre-sf market was small, though it had more than trebled between 1970 and 1975. Even so, Holmberg commented in 1974 that the 'bookstore sales on an average quality SF paperback seldom exceed 500 copies'.[27] The majority of sales were either to libraries or via the Swedish Science Fiction Book Club, which was organized via Lundwall's Delta, and had 8,000 subscribers. It was hoped many of these would also subscribe to *JVM*. About 80 per cent of the sf books published in Sweden were translations, so the market for new writers was slim and not especially profitable. *JVM* was the only real medium for new writers to get published. Holmberg has calculated[28] that during its first ten years under Lundwall (1972 to 1981), *JVM* published roughly 280 stories, of which 10 per cent (29) were original Swedish items by 15 different authors. Chief amongst these were Dénis Lindbohm, with eight, and Sten Andersson with four. Lundwall did seek an international flavour, though, and peppered a diet of US sf with material from elsewhere in Europe, especially Italy. However he published only 20 stories by women writers during that period, and only one by a female Swedish writer. Despite Lundwall's own liking for unusual and experimental fiction, he tended to favour more traditional material for *JVM*.

Amongst other writers whom Lundwall launched or encouraged in the seventies were Ahrvid Engholm, Börje Crona and Bertil Mårtensson.

27 John-Henri Holmberg, 'SF – Report from Scandinavia', *Algol* #23, November 1974, p. 20.
28 Personal e-mail, Holmberg/Ashley, 20 September 2006.

Lundwall has kept *JVM* going, mostly on a bi-monthly schedule, and passed through issue #500 in the year 2000.

Turkey

Turkey may seem a surprise addition to the magazine stakes, yet it produced not one but two sf magazines. The emphasis was on cinema and TV but both *Antares*, which began in March 1974, and *X-Bilinmeyen* (*X-Unknown*), which started in April 1976, ran fiction, mostly by Turkish writers. *Antares* was edited by Sezar Erkin Ergin, and grew out of a newsletter issued by the SFFC, the Turkish SF Club organized in 1972. *Antares* was inspired by the interest in *Star Trek*, the film *2001* and the books of Erich von Daniken, so it had a wider coverage beyond fiction. *X-Bilinmeyen*, which also started as a slim, eight-page newsletter issued by an SF Club, relaunched itself in January 1977 as a 32-page, glossy, large-flat-format magazine. Its main coverage was of TV and films (especially *Star Trek*), scientific developments and strange phenomena, such as the Loch Ness Monster. It was edited by Selma Mine, one of Turkey's leading sf writers, who contributed fiction to most issues, including several advance serials of her books. Although the contributors were primarily Turkish, the magazine did later run a few stories by Isaac Asimov, Ray Bradbury and even Vargo Statten. In January 1980 it changed its name to *Evren* (*Cosmos*) and the emphasis shifted to popular science, with items reprinted from *Science Digest* and *National Geographic*. It sustained a monthly schedule throughout, folding with issue #64 in December 1981.

Yugoslavia[29]

Prior to the Yugoslav Civil War of the early 1990s and the crumbling of the former republic of Yugoslavia, the country had a thriving science-fiction community. When Jack Williamson visited the country in 1979 he saw science fiction spreading like an 'epidemic', and it had been growing throughout the seventies. In March 1969 the entertainment magazine, *Duga* (*Rainbow*), which included a set of 'coloured' supplements, introduced a green science-fiction section, *Kosmoplov*. In fact it was primarily a supplement on space travel and later called itself 'the magazine for astronautics and science fiction', with perhaps a quarter of its contents featuring sf, usually one or two translated stories. The supplement ran

29 My thanks to Krsto Mazuranic and Dr. Zoran Živković for their help with this entry.

for 24 slim issues, ceasing on 15 June 1970. In April 1972 the Belgrade publisher BIGZ started *Galaksija*, sometimes referred to as an sf magazine but which was really a monthly covering popular science. It ran a page or two of science fiction, including artwork, but nothing of significance. However, in 1976 its editor Gavrilo Vučković started an annual 'almanac' called *Andromeda* which ran many features about sf, a few local stories, and much artwork, though all in black and white. It was expensive but sold well enough to appear on an annual basis for three years, with some thought given to it shifting to a more regular magazine format. In the second volume the editor organized a short-story competition which had over three hundred entries. The winner was Miodrag Marinkovic.

By the time *Andromeda* was published, a genuine sf magazine had appeared: *Sirius*. It was published in Zagreb by the Yugoslav daily newspaper *Vjesnik*, and edited by Borivoj Jurković, the first two issues prepared in close association with the newly formed Yugoslav SF organisation SFera. Its first issue was full of translations, including two by Stanislaw Lem, but in the second issue an original Croatian story appeared by Zvonomir Furtinger, one of Yugoslavia's old-guard writers, who became a regular. Soon there were two or three local authors in each issue, sometimes double that, and, on one occasion in 1978, Jurković put together an all-Yugoslav issue called *Yu Sirius*. Alexander Nedelkovich, who stated that the magazine ran 'the best Yugoslav SF',[30] estimated that over five hundred original Yugoslav stories appeared in the magazine's first ten years. Authors who became main contributors included Branko Belan, Goran Pavelić, Branko Pihac, Vladimir Janković, Miroslav Bagaric, Milanče Marković and Slobodan Ćurčić, with perhaps the most popular being Damir Mikulicić, who favoured hard sf but with a lyrical touch. He would go on to win the SFera Life Achievement award for his science fiction in 1999. His collection *O* (Kentaur SF Series, 1982), includes some of his best work from *Sirius*. Their work contrasts with much of the US sf being reprinted which was chiefly from the magazines of the fifties but included some more recent material by Roger Zelazny and Harlan Ellison amongst others. *Sirius* had a workmanlike appearance. It was unillustrated, apart from the covers, with little editorial presence, and just a few brief features, but it evidently delivered what readers wanted as it rapidly hit sales of 30,000. *Sirius* was the backbone for a major developing market in Yugoslavia and would survive for 156[31] issues until 1989.

---

30 See Nedelkovich's chapter on Yugoslav SF in Neil Barron (ed.), *Anatomy of Wonder* (New York: Bowker, 1987).

31 There were seven 'double issues', #121/2, 146/7, 155/6, 157/8, 159/60, 161/2 and the final issue, 163/4.

THE AMERICAS

Argentina[32]

The 1970s was a bleak period in publishing in Argentina because of the succession of oppressive military regimes. The military coup of 24 March 1976 led to many journalists and publishers being imprisoned and killed by the new dictatorship because of their political views. Amongst them was Héctor Oesterheld, regarded as the father of Argentinian sf, who had been the leading native contributor to *Mas Alla* (*Beyond*), which had run from 1953 to 1957. He also edited the final few issues. Oesterheld was arrested and almost certainly executed in June 1977, not for his science fiction but for his biography of revolutionary Che Guevara. With his death, at age 58, went one of the prime movers in Argentinian sf. The new regime also saw the end of the literary little magazine *El Lagrimal Trifurca* which had been edited by Francisco and Elvio Gandolfo since June 1968. Though it focused mostly on poetry and general literature, it ran occasional stories and features on science fiction.

Science fiction books and comics were generally ignored by the military regime because they were regarded as juvenile, but the economic and political climate was too fragile to encourage many publishers to experiment. A few translated books appeared, but the only magazine to appear at this time was *La Revista de ciencia ficción y fantasía*, a local edition of *F&SF* which saw three issues between October 1976 and February 1977. It was edited by the Uruguayan-born Marcial Souto and, though it was primarily reprint, he ran one or two original stories per issue from José Pedro Diaz, Norman Viti and fellow Uruguayan Mario Levrero.

Soon after it folded, another magazine put in a brief appearance, *Umbral Tiempo Futuro*, edited by Fabio Zerpa in Buenos Aires. It ran from November 1977 to the summer of 1979, though the last two issues were delayed. It featured a range of stories, including translations of old items by Jack London, Mark Twain, Wilkie Collins and William Hope Hodgson, running the whole range of weird and scientific fiction and including articles on scientific mysteries and UFOs. Although it ran a high percentage of stories by local writers, little was of much merit.

Souto remained the main driving force in sf publishing in Argen-

32 My thanks to Hector R. Pessina, Sergio Logioco and Christian Vallini Lawson for their help with information over the years. The most detailed survey of Argentinian sf is Claudio Omar Noguerol 'A History of Science Fiction and Fandom in Argentina', *The Mentor* #76-#78 (October 1992–April 1993). Coverage will also be found in the introduction to Adriana Fernández and Edgardo Pígoli (eds), *Historias Futuras: Anthology of Argentine Science Fiction* (Buenos Aires: Emecé Editores SA, 2000).

tina, developing several book series. Amongst these appeared a one-shot, pocketbook-size magazine, *Entropia*, in July 1978, which reprinted several New Wave stories, a movement which had found a core of interest in Argentina. Souto persevered and in September 1979 he and Jaime Poniachek launched *El Pendulo entre la ficcióne y la realidad* (*Pendulum between Fantasy and Reality*), usually known as *El Pendulo*. It began in June 1979 as a supplement to the magazine *Humor*, a satirical magazine that was in tune with public political opinion and then appeared as a separate publication for four issues from September to December 1979. The fiction in this series was all translated from American sources, except for one story by André Caneiro, but it included many features, cartoons and comic strips by local writers. It ceased publication, not for lack of popularity but because production costs as a semi-slick magazine were too high, and it was absorbed back into *Humor*. Then, over the next couple of years, the sales of *Humor* tripled as the crumbling Argentinian junta caused the public to become bolder, and *El Pendulo* reappeared in May 1981, this time in pocketbook format. *El Pendulo* became the focal point for new science fiction in Argentina just as *Mas Alla* had 25 years before. Even though *El Pendulo* had a rocky few years ahead and had folded by 1988, when a survey was taken amongst members of the Argentine SF & Fantasy Circle in 1990 it was voted the most popular magazine. Its popularity and the return of democratic government to Argentina opened a new door on sf, which I shall cover in the next volume.

Canada (French-speaking)

Although English is the first language of 80 per cent of all Canadians, that is true of less than 20 per cent of those living in Quebec. Even so, there had been no tradition of French sf amongst the Québécois, with only isolated books prior to 1974. However, in that year not only did several sf books appear, including a book series, 'Demain Aujourd'hui', but it also saw the first issue of *Requiem*, which would steadily evolve into today's major French-Canadian sf magazine, *Solaris*. *Requiem* began as a fanzine produced by college students under the direction of their French teacher, Norbert Spehner, at the Édward-Montpetit College in Longueuil, Montreal. Spehner had been encouraged by the World SF Convention which had been held in Toronto the previous year. He was not a native Canadian but had been born in France and only settled in Quebec in 1968. Interestingly, his successor on the magazine, Élisabeth Vonarburg, was also born in France and did not move to Quebec until 1973. Both were aware of science fiction being published in France, much of which was also available in Quebec. The French magazines *Fiction* and *Galaxie* had been distributed in Quebec since 1969.[33] Vonarburg believed that it was important to be able to discover sf in your own language and not via translation, and both *Fiction* and *Galaxie* were crucial to her early appreciation of science fiction and fantasy.[34]

The first issue of *Requiem*, dated September 1974, ran to 24 quarto pages and sold for 75 cents. It was printed offset from typed sheets and looked no different from the scores of similar fanzines that proliferated throughout the United States and Canada. It contained the usual mix of fannish articles and illustrations. Contrarily, its one substantial piece of fiction, 'The Army on Mars' by Pierre Lenoir, was printed in English. Spehner commented in his editorial that he had plans to make the magazine like the newszine *Locus* but, although it did carry some news items, it rapidly developed in another way. Fiction took a central role along with critical articles and the first assessment of French-Canadian sf. Its cultural role was recognized by the Canadian Council for the Arts which provided it with a subsidy from 1976. During its first few years *Requiem* discovered several writers who have continued to be major contributors to French-Canadian sf, including Daniel Sernine (#5, July 1975), Michel Bélil (#10, June 1976), Jean-Pierre April (#14, March 1977), René Beaulieu (#20. March 1978) and, significantly for the magazine, Élisabeth Vonarburg with 'Marée haute' ('High Tide') in issue #19 (January 1978). Maxim Jakubowski picked the story for his anthology of French sf, *Twenty Houses of the Zodiac* (NEL, 1979) and Vonarburg's career was launched. That same year (1979) she organized Quebec's first sf convention. She became literary editor from issue #28 (September 1979), which was the first issue with the name change to *Solaris*.

It was also in 1979 that Jean-Marc Gouanvic began his literary magazine *imagine ...*, first issue Fall 1979. This made the year something of a landmark, and Gouanvic later noted that it was only from 1979 that a genuine 'system of "literary communication"' had come into existence which allowed for a formal discussion of science fiction in Quebec.[35] From the start the emphasis in *imagine ...* was on fiction, with Gouanvic determined to demonstrate that French science fiction had a character distinct from that of US sf but every bit as important. The stories, especially those by Jean-Pierre April, were highly political and it was clear that *imagine*

33 See news item in *Luna Monthly* #4, September 1969, p. 4.

34 See Élisabeth Vonarburg, 'US SF and Us', in James Gunn (ed.), *The Road to Science Fiction Volume 6: Around the World* (New york: New American Library White Wolf, 1998).

35 See Jean-Marc Gouanvic, 'Rational Speculations in French Canada, 1839–1974', *Science-Fiction Studies* #44 (March 1988), p. 71.

... had a strong voice for nationalism at the time of the referendum in Quebec on independence, which was held in May 1980.

Whereas *Requiem* had given French-Canadian sf an identity and a voice, *imagine* ... sought to give it a purpose. We shall explore in the next volume what the two magazines achieved.

ASIA

Israel[36]

Israel had flirted briefly with a few science-fiction magazines in the late fifties, though both *Mada Dimioni* (*Imaginary Science*), which saw thirteen issues, and *Cosmos*, which saw four issues, relied totally on reprints from US sources, those in *Mada Dimioni* published anonymously. The first attempt at a fully fledged sf magazine came in December 1978 when, following the success of *Star Wars*, Eli Tene and Aharon Hauptman launched *Fantasia 2000*, with Tene as publisher. A large-flat-format slick magazine, with beautiful artwork, *Fantasia 2000* began as an Israeli edition of *F&SF*, including Isaac Asimov's science column, but from the start it ran some original Israeli stories and features, plus news and author profiles. After 16 issues Tene moved on to the advertising business and Aharon Hauptman took over as full editor, with a new publisher, Hyperion in Tel Aviv. Hauptman became the main driving force in Israeli sf over the next couple of years until a dispute with the publisher led to his resignation in December 1982 after issue #31. Thereafter there was a rapid decline in the magazine's fortunes. As in other countries, the magazine acted as a focus for fans and helped spark the country's first convention in March 1981. Under Hauptman it ran some Israeli fiction of note, such as the work of Shira Tamir, Hillel Damron, David Melamed, Ivsam Azgad and Igal Tzemach (who won the magazine's 'best story' award), but of these only Melamed has had a story collection published and continues to sell to literary magazines. *Fantasia 2000*'s circulation peaked at around five and a half thousand, which was sufficient to sustain the production costs, particularly as, Hauptman told me, 'the editors and translators were not paid'.[37] The magazine ceased in August 1984 after 44 issues.

Fantasia 2000 proved very popular and is still fondly remembered today. Its success encouraged a wider publication of sf both in book form, from

36 My thanks to Aharon Hauptman and Inbal Saggiv for their help with this entry.

37 Personal e-mail, Hauptman/Ashley, 18 September 2006. Hauptman was paid a small fee at the outset but that soon stopped.

the publishing house Am Oved, and in a flurry of other magazines. *Cosmos* was the Israeli edition of *Asimov's SF Magazine*, edited by D. Kol for the publisher Atid in Ramat Hasharon, but it was underfinanced and poorly promoted and died after six issues, all published in 1979. It found room to squeeze in a few Israeli stories. There were also single appearances of *Olam Hamachar* (*World of Tomorrow*) in 1979, with mostly articles on speculative science, and *Mada Bidioni* (*Science Fiction*) in 1982, which ran just one translated novel.

Japan[38]

Japanese science fiction is so closely linked in the Western consciousness with monster movies such as *Godzilla* as well as the *anime* cartoons and *manga* comic books that it is easy to overlook that Japan has had a thriving science-fiction publishing industry for nearly fifty years. During the 1970s Japan was the most important publisher of science fiction outside of the United States, Britain and Russia, and second only to the United States with regard to regular science-fiction magazines. Its premier title, *SF Magazine*, has been published regularly since February 1960 (that issue actually appeared in December 1959), making it today the third-longest continuously surviving sf magazine after *Analog* and *F&SF*. It published its 600th issue in April 2006, the number being that high because it publishes a special extra issue each year. It had started as a Japanese edition of *F&SF*, but soon included original material and has long since moved away from its base, running items from a variety of sources, plus plenty of original stories.

In all that time, *SF Magazine* has been published by Hayakawa-sobo in Tokyo. Its founding editor, Masami Fukushima, remained at the helm throughout the sixties, but the seventies saw a rapid turnover of editors. Masaru Mori was editor from August 1969 to April 1974. Like Fukushima, he was a dedicated fan of science fiction, while his successors were hard-headed businessmen. Ryozo Nagashima was editor for only a year, until May 1975, and Taku Kurahashi for just two years, until August 1977. Then Hiroshi Hayakawa, the president of the company and son of the owner, became the figurehead editor until April 1979, though the managing editor was Kiyoshi Imaoka. *SF Magazine* helped establish and develop most of the leading sf writers in Japan, notably Shinichi Hoshi, Sakyo Komatsu, Yasutaka Tsutsui and Ryo Hanmura. Komatsu became inter-

38 My thanks to Takumi Shibano, Takeshi Abe and Shinji Maki for their help with this entry.

nationally renowned in 1973 when his disaster novel *Nippon Chimbotsu* (*Japan Sinks*), became a world-wide bestseller. His stories and novels won the Seiun ('Nebula') Award for five of the ten years from 1970 (the first year the award was presented) to 1979. Tsutsui's fiction was often satirical and he was as at home in the mainstream as he was in the genre magazines. In fact, Tsutsui was rather critical of the sf magazines when compiling his annual best-of-the-year anthologies, where he selected material mostly from non-genre magazines. He believed in 1975 that the sf genre would soon crumble in Japan,[39] but though it has had its highs and lows it is still as popular as ever.

Other authors who emerged in the early years of *SF Magazine* include Taku Mayumura, Ryu Mitsuse, Aritsune Toyota and Kazumasa Hirai, while in the seventies came Koji Tanaka, Masaki Yamada and Musashi Kambe. Yamada's first story, the novella 'Kami-Gari' ('Godhunting') in *SF Magazine* (July 1974), concerned the discovery of a group of godlike beings who have worked through the centuries to control mankind. It is a good example of the direction that much Japanese sf had taken, seeking to interpret the present through the past rather than explore the future. Another popular contributor, though a late starter, was Yoshio Aramaki, who did not sell his first story until 1970 when he was 37, though he soon won the Seiun Award in 1972 for his novella 'Shirakabe no Moji wa Yuhi ni Haeru' ('The Writing on the White Wall Glows in the Setting Sun') (*SF Magazine*, February 1971). Several of these writers became fascinated with the US and British New Wave, which appealed to the Japanese outlook. One of Tsutsui's best known stories was 'Tatazumu Hito' ('Standing Woman')[40] where the punishment for those who speak out against society is to be transmuted into a plant. Aramaki's 'Yawarakai Tokei' ('Soft Clocks')[41] provides a scientific explanation for Dali's surreal images transplanted to Mars. It was through writers such as Tsutsui and Aramaki that Japanese sf began to redefine itself, shifting from the technological US approach to a more surreal existentialism, more in keeping with Japanese literary tradition.

Whereas *SF Magazine* under Fukushima was loyal to the US core, under Mori it became more open and ran work by women writers. Fukushima had not been supportive of women,[42] whereas Mori rapidly introduced

39 See reference in David Lewis, 'Science Fiction in Japan', *Foundation* #19, June 1980, p. 26.
40 First published in *Shosetsu Gendai* in May 1974 and translated for *Omni*, February 1981.
41 First published in *SF Magazine*, February 1972 and translated for *Interzone* #27, January/February 1989.
42 See Lewis, 'Science Fiction in Japan', p. 28.

work by Le Guin, Emshwiller, Tiptree, Wilhelm and Joanna Russ – 'When it Changed' was run in the October 1974 issue. Mori also worked with Koichi Yamano in introducing more British writers into the magazine. Moorcock's Jerry Cornelius stories began to appear from May 1973, along with work by Langdon Jones, John Brunner, Keith Roberts and others.

Koichi Yamano was the editor most keen to promote the New Wave in Japan. He believed that the British New Wave opened the door for sf in Britain to fulfil its destiny,[43] and could see similar benefits in Japan. He had a theatrical background with an interest in avant-garde and absurdist drama and believed that this was the true direction of literature. In July 1970 he launched *NW-SF*, a semi-professional magazine with some news-stand distribution but sold mostly through subscription. Its circulation was around five thousand. It began as a quarterly but soon slipped to just one or two issues per year, so there were only 18 issues between July 1970 and December 1982. He was assisted in compiling the issues by Kazuko Yamada, one of the few women sf writers in Japan at the time, who also encouraged a feminist approach. Yamano did much to promote British writers in Japan and his work helped redirect the New Wave and prepare Japanese readers for the cyberpunk revolution of the eighties.

No other magazines in Japan did as much as either *SF Magazine* or *NW-SF* to develop the genre, though they certainly contributed to the promotion of the field. January 1974 saw the first issue of *Kiso-Tengai* (*Fantastic*) from Seiko-sha, edited by Tadao Soné. This ran mystery stories as well as SF but did not find a market, folding after ten monthly issues. Soné set up his own company, Kiso-Tengai-sha, and relaunched *Kiso-Tengai* in April 1976, concentrating solely on sf. This time it met with considerable popularity, selling as many as fifty thousand copies a month and sometimes exceeding the sales of *SF Magazine*. At a time when *SF Magazine* had shifted to more modern sf, *Kiso-Tengai* wallowed in traditional American pulp fiction, including work by Edmond Hamilton, Hal K. Wells, Clark Ashton Smith, John Russell Fearn and Henry Kuttner, plus fifties and sixties material by Poul Anderson, Damon Knight, Keith Laumer, William Tenn, James Blish and others. It ran similar material by Japanese writers and attracted new writers through regular story competitions. Amongst its discoveries were Chiaka Kawata, with 'Yume no Kamera' ('The Dream Camera') in 1976, and Motoko Arai, who won their first story competition in 1977 when she was still a teenager and went on to become one of the most popular writers of the eighties.

Kiso-Tengai ran for 67 issues until October 1981, though the name

---

43 See Koichi Yamano, 'English Literature and British Science Fiction', *Foundation* #30 (March 1984), pp. 26–30.

would return briefly in the late 1980s. Its popularity only began to fade with the appearance of *SF Adventure* in May 1979, published by Tokuma-Shoten and edited by Yoshio Sugawara. It began as a quarterly but rapidly became bi-monthly and then monthly from June 1980. It ran similar material to that in *Kiso-Tengai*, but with more Japanese fiction by major names, and established a major award, Nippon SF Taisho (the equivalent of the American Nebula) in 1980, which brought with it a prize of one million yen (then about £2,500 or $4,000). *SF Adventure* was a highly visual magazine with an emphasis on art and it became the most popular magazine of the early eighties.

The only other Japanese magazine to appear in this period was *SF Hoseki* (*SF Jewel*) from Kobun-sha, which also published the popular mystery magazine *Hoseki*. This began in August 1979 as a Japanese edition of *Isaac Asimov's SF Magazine*, with each bi-monthly digest-size issue running up to three hundred pages. It also ran original material and features but its editorial staff, under Hisanori Tanaguchi, knew little about sf, and appealed to readers to see what they wanted. As a consequence it grew popular amongst fans. However, internal disputes within the company led to the magazine folding after only 12 issues in June 1981.

Japanese sf came closest to US and British sf in its transformation in the seventies from the traditional, technological approach to a more contemporary form of expressionism, but whereas Western sf had taken some thirty years to achieve this, Japan crammed it into a decade, making the seventies one of the most exciting periods in Japanese sf. With *SF Magazine* and *SF Adventure* locked in rivalry, Japanese sf looked very healthy and alive as it entered the eighties.

Appendix 2

Summary of Science-Fiction Magazines

The following lists all professional English-language science-fiction magazines and series anthologies covered by this volume together with issue and editorial details. It also covers relevant fantasy and weird fiction associational titles including many small-press and semi-professional magazines. It excludes magazines that concentrate solely on horror or macabre fiction and also those which are totally non-fiction. It also excludes comics, though *Heavy Metal* is listed.

Titles are listed in alphabetical order. Individual issues are listed for each year together with a cumulative total at the end of each column. This total relates to specific physical issues and not the issue number itself, where double issues are often counted as two. The cumulative total continues from those detailed in Volumes 1 and 2. Dates shown are cover dates. The list overlaps slightly with the previous volume and starts in January 1970. The cut-off date for this volume is December 1980, though issues for 1981 or 1982 are shown if discussed in the text.

Months are abbreviated to their first three characters. Seasonal dates are shown as Spr (Spring), Sum (Summer), Aut or Fal (Autumn or Fall), Win (Winter). Seasonal issues and undated issues are shown in the column corresponding to the month of sale. Combined months are shown as Jan/ Feb, etc. Reprint editions are not listed unless their contents vary significantly. All magazines are published in the United States unless otherwise noted.

Ad Astra (UK)
Publisher: Rowlot London.
Editor: James Manning.

1978						Oct/Nov	(1)
1979:	Jan/Feb	#3	#4	#5	#6	#7	(7)

1980:	#8		#9	#10	#11	#12		#13	(13)
1981:		#14		#15				#16	(16)

Amazing (Science Fiction) Stories

First issued in April 1926; see Volumes I and II for details prior to 1970.

Publishers: Ultimate Publishing, Flushing, NY, August 1965–February 1979; Ultimate Publishing, Scottsdale, AZ, May 1979–June 1982.

Editors: Ted White, May 1969–February 1979; Elinor Mavor, May 1979 September 1982.

1970:	Jan		Mar		May		Jul		Sep		Nov		(447)
1971:	Jan		Mar		May		Jul		Sep		Nov		(453)
1972:	Jan		Mar		May		Jul		Sep		Nov		(459)
1973:	Jan		Mar			Jun		Aug		Oct		Dec	(465)
1974:		Feb		Apr		Jun		Aug		Oct		Dec	(471)
1975:			Mar		May		Jul		Sep		Nov		(476)
1976:	Jan		Mar			Jun			Sep			Dec	(481)
1977:			Mar				Jul			Oct			(484)
1978:	Jan				May			Aug			Nov		(488)
1979:		Feb			May			Aug			Nov		(492)
1980:		Feb			May			Aug			Nov		(496)

[continues in Volume IV]

Analog

First issued in January 1930; entitled Astounding Stories *and then* Astounding Science Fiction *until September 1960. See Volumes I and II for details prior to 1970. Website http://www.analogsf.com*

Publishers: Condé Nast Publications, New York, February 1961–August 1980; Davis Publications, New York, September 1980–August 1992.

Editors: John W. Campbell, Jr., December 1937–December 1971; Ben Bova, January 1972–November 1978; Stanley Schmidt, December 1978–current.

1970:	Jan	Feb	Mar	Apr	May	Jun	Jul	Aug	Sep	Oct	Nov	Dec (481)
1971:	Jan	Feb	Mar	Apr	May	Jun	Jul	Aug	Sep	Oct	Nov	Dec (493)
1972:	Jan	Feb	Mar	Apr	May	Jun	Jul	Aug	Sep	Oct	Nov	Dec (505)
1973:	Jan	Feb	Mar	Apr	May	Jun	Jul	Aug	Sep	Oct	Nov	Dec (517)
1974:	Jan	Feb	Mar	Apr	May	Jun	Jul	Aug	Sep	Oct	Nov	Dec (529)
1975:	Jan	Feb	Mar	Apr	May	Jun	Jul	Aug	Sep	Oct	Nov	Dec (541)
1976:	Jan	Feb	Mar	Apr	May	Jun	Jul	Aug	Sep	Oct	Nov	Dec (553)
1977:	Jan	Feb	Mar	Apr	May	Jun	Jul	Aug	Sep	Oct	Nov	Dec (565)
1978:	Jan	Feb	Mar	Apr	May	Jun	Jul	Aug	Sep	Oct	Nov	Dec (577)
1979:	Jan	Feb	Mar	Apr	May	Jun	Jul	Aug	Sep	Oct	Nov	Dec (589)
1980:	Jan	Feb	Mar	Apr	May	Jun	Jul	Aug	Sep	Oct	Nov	Dec (601)

[continues in Volume IV]

Andromeda (UK)

Original anthology series.

Publisher: Orbit Books, London.

Editor: Peter Weston.

1976:			#1			(1)
1977:				#2		(2)
1978:					#3	(3)

Ares

Gaming magazine.
Publisher: Simulations Publications, Inc., New York, March 1980–January 1982.
Editor/Creative Director: Redmond Simonsen, March 1980–January 1982.

		Mar	May	Jul	Sep	Nov	
1980:		Mar	May	Jul	Sep	Nov	(5)
1981:	Jan	Mar	May	Jul	Sep	Nov	(11)
1982:	Jan						(12)

[continues in Volume IV]

Ariel

Publisher: #1, Morningstar Press, Leawood, KS; #2–4, Ballantine Books, New York.
Editor: Thomas Durwood.

1976:					Aut	(1)
1977:					#2	(2)
1978:		#3			#4	(4)

The Arkham Collector

Small-press magazine. See Volume II for details prior to 1970.
Publisher: Arkham House, Sauk City, WWI.
Editor: August Derleth.

1970:			Sum			Win	(8)
1971:		Spr	Sum				(10)

Asimov's Science Fiction Magazine

See *Isaac Asimov's Science Fiction Magazine.*

Asimov's SF Adventure Magazine

Publisher: Davis Publications, New York.
Editor: George H. Scithers.

1978:					Sep	(1)
1979:	Spr	Sum	Fal			(4)

Aura

Semi-professional magazine.
Publisher: Torch Publications, New York.
Editor: Jose Alcarez.

1979:		#1				(1)

Beyond

Publisher: Alan Weston Publishing, Hollywood, CA.
Editor: Judith Sims.

1981:					Fal	(1)
1982:	Win	Spr			Oct	(4)

Beyond the Fields We Know
See *Dragonfields.*

Bizarre Fantasy Tales
Publisher: Health Knowledge, Inc., New York.
Editor: Robert A. W. Lowndes.

1970:		Fal		(1)
1971:	Mar			(2)

Chacal
Semi-professional magazine.
Publisher: Nemedian Chronicles (#1), Daemon Graphics (#2), Shawnee Mission, KS.
Editors: Byron Roark and Arnie Fenner (#1), Arnie Fenner (#2).

1976:		Win	(1)
1977:	Spr		(2)

[continued as Shayol]

Chrysalis
Original anthology series.
Publisher: Zebra Books, New York for paperback edition (all volumes); Doubleday, New York, for hardcover editions from Volume 8.
Editor: Roy Torgeson.

1977:			#1			(1)
1978:			#2		#3	(3)
1979:	#4		#5		#6	(6)
1980:	#7			#8		(8)
1981:				#9		(9)
1983:		#10				(10)

Clarion
Original anthology series.
Publisher: Signet Books, New York, (#1–#3); Berkley Publishing, New York (1977).
Editors: Robin Scott Wilson (#1–#3); Kate Wilhelm (1977)

1971:		#1		(1)
1972:		#2		(2)
1973:			#3	(3)
1977:	(#4)			(4)

Cosmos Science Fiction and Fantasy Magazine
Publisher: Baronet Publishing, New York
Editor: David Hartwell.

1977:		May	Jul	Sep	Nov	(4)

Counter Thrust
Amateur magazine.
Publisher: University of Maryland Student SF Society.
Editor: Steven Goldstein.

1976:	#1				(1)

The Cygnus Chronicler (Australia)
Small-press magazine. The first two issues were a fanzine newsletter.
Publisher: The Eperex Press, Canberra.
Editor: Neville J. Angove.

1977:				Oct		(1)
1978:	Mar					(2)

Relaunched as a semi-professional magazine.

1979:					Dec	(3)
1980:	Mar	Jun	Sep		Dec	(7)

[continues in Volume IV]

Dark Fantasy (Canada)
Small-press magazine; began as a fanzine. Issue #13 (Summer 1977) was lost by the printer and never published. After Day's death a special tribute issue was published in 1984.
Publisher: Shadow Press, Gananoque, Ontario.
Editor: Howard [Gene] E. Day all issues except the final one, which was edited by Gordon Derevanchuk.

1973:						Sum			Fal			(2)
1974:		Mar					Jul			Oct		(5)
1975:	Jan							Sep				(7)
1976:				May				Sep			Dec	(10)
1977:	Jan							Sep				(12)
1978:	Jan				Jun	Jul					Dec	(16)
1979:	Feb	Apr				Jul			Oct			(20)
1980:		Mar								Nov		(22)
1984:							Aug					(23)

Dark Messenger Reader
See *Eldritch Tales*.

Destinies
Paperback magazine akin to original anthology series. Also Proteus, *issued in May 1981, was a Destinies Special.*
Publisher: Ace Books, New York.
Editor: James Baen.

1978:					Nov/Dec	(1)
1979:	Jan/Feb	Apr/Jun		Aug/Sep	Oct/Dec	(5)
1980:	Feb/Mar	Spr	Sum		Fal	(9)
1981:		Spr	3/2			(11)

The Diversifier

Small-press magazine. Saw one further issue retitled Paragon.
Publisher: C.C. Clingan, Oroville, CA, operating as Castle Press from #4.
Editor: C. C. Clingan (jointly with A. B. Clingan to #23, and with Ralph S. Harding from #25) #1–26/7; Ralph S. Harding and Joey Froehlich, #25–28/9.

1974:				Jun	Jul	Aug	Sep	Oct		Dec	(6)
1975:		Feb		Apr		Jun		Aug		Oct		(11)
1976:	Jan		Mar		May		Jul		Sep		Nov	(17)
1977:	Jan		Mar		May		Jul		Sep		Nov	(23)
1978:	Jan		Mar		May/Jul							(26)
1979:		Feb/Mar										(27)

[The] Dragon

Gaming magazine. Had earlier issues as The Strategic Review *newsletter. Website http://paizo.com/dragon.*
Publisher: TSR, Inc., Lake Geneva, WI.
Editors: Tim Kask, June 1976–February 1980; Jake Jaquet, March 1980–November 1982.

1976:				Jun		Aug		Oct			Dec	(4)
1977:		Mar		Apr	Jun	Jul		Sep	Oct			Dec	(11)
1978:	Feb		Apr	May	Jun	Jul	Aug	Sep	Oct	Nov	Dec	(21)
1979:	Feb	Mar	Apr	May	Jun	Jul	Aug	Sep	Oct	Nov	Dec	(32)
1980:	Jan	Feb	Mar	Apr	May	Jun	Jul	Aug	Sep	Oct	Nov	Dec	(44)

[continues in Volume IV]

Dragonbane

See *Dragonfields*

Dragonfields (Canada)

Small press magazine. Began as two separate magazines, Dragonbane *(Spring 1978) and* Beyond the Fields We Know *(Autumn 1978), which merged for last two issues.*
Publisher: Triskell Press, Ottawa, Ontario.
Editors: Charles de Lint and Charles R. Saunders.

1978:		Spr		Aut		(2)
1980:		Sum				(3)
1983:				Win		(4)

Eerie Country

Small-press magazine, companion to Weirdbook.
Publisher: Weirdbook Press, Buffalo, NY.
Editor: W. Paul Ganley..

1976:		#1		(1)
1979:	#2			(2)
1980:		#3	#4	(4)

[continues in Volume IV]

Eldritch Tales

Small-press magazine; first issue called The Dark Messenger Reader. *Issue #2 was lost and eventually published out of sequence.*
Publisher: The Strange Company, Madison, WI, #1; Yith Press, Lawrence, KS, #2–30.
Editor: Crispin Burnham (with E. P. Berglund on #1).

Year	Jan	Feb	Mar	Apr	May	Jun	Jul	Aug	Sep	Oct	Nov	Dec	No.
1975												#1	(1)
1978			Mar							Oct			(3)
1979				Apr								#6	(5)
1980						#7							(6)

[continues in Volume IV]

Enigma (Australia)

College student magazine that turned quasi-semi-professional from October 1975.
Publisher: Sydney University SF Association.
Editors: Leith Morton, #1, 1970; Richard Faulder and R. Whight, #2–#3, 1971; Van Ikin, #4, 1972–Dec 1979; David Wraight, April 1980–1981.

Year	Jan	Feb	Mar	Apr	May	Jun	Jul	Aug	Sep	Oct	Nov	Dec	No.
1970											#1		(1)
1971			2–1					2–2					(3)
1972			3–1					3–2			Nov		(5)
1973		Feb			May			Aug			Nov		(9)
1974		Feb			May			Aug			Nov		(13)
1975			Mar			Jun				Oct		De	(17)
1976			Mar			Jun			Sep			Dec	(21)
1977			Mar				Jul			Oct			(24)
1978			Mar								Nov	Dec	(27)
1979	Jan						Jul					Dec	(30)
1980				Apr			Jul					#33	(33)
1981			#34										(34)

Eternity Science Fiction

Semi-professional magazine.
Publisher and Editor: Stephen Gregg, Sandy Springs, SC. (Clemson, SC for second series).

Year	Jan	Feb	Mar	Apr	May	Jun	Jul	Aug	Sep	Oct	Nov	Dec	No.
1972							Jul						(1)
1973					#2								(2)
1974					#3								(3)
1975		#4											(4)
revived:													
1979							#1						(5)
1980		#2											(6)

Fantastic Stories/Science Fiction

First issued in Summer 1952; see Volume II for details prior to 1970.
Publisher: Ultimate Publishing, New York, August 1965–January 1979; moved to Scottsdale, AZ, April 1979–October 1980.

Editor: Ted White, June 1969–January 1979; Elinor Mavor, April 1979–October 1980.

Year	Jan	Feb	Mar	Apr	May	Jun	Jul	Aug	Sep	Oct	Nov	Dec	No.
1970:		Feb		Apr		Jun		Aug		Oct		Dec	(160)
1971:		Feb		Apr		Jun		Aug		Oct		Dec	(166)
1972:		Feb		Apr		Jun		Aug		Oct		Dec	(172)
1973:		Feb		Apr			Jul		Sep		Nov		(177)
1974:	Jan		Mar		May		Jul		Sep		Nov		(183)
1975:		Feb		Apr		Jun		Aug		Oct		Dec	(189)
1976:		Feb			May			Aug			Nov		(193)
1977:		Feb				Jun			Sep			Dec	(197)
1978:				Apr			Jul			Oct			(200)
1979:	Jan			Apr			Jul			Oct			(204)
1980:	Jan			Apr			Jul			Oct			(208)

combined with Amazing Stories.

Fantasy and Science Fiction
See *Magazine of Fantasy and Science Fiction*.

Fantasy Tales (UK)
Semi-professional magazine.
Publisher: Fantasy Tales, London, Summer 1977–Summer 1987.
Editors: David A. Sutton and Stephen Jones.

Year	Spr	Sum	Win	No.
1977:		Sum	Win	(2)
1978:		Sum		(3)
1979:	Spr		Win	(5)
1980:		Sum		(6)

[continues in Volume IV]

Forgotten Fantasy
Publisher: Nectar Press, Hollywood.
Editor: Douglas Menville

Year	Feb	Apr	Jun	Oct	Dec	No.
1970:				Oct	Dec	(2)
1971:	Feb	Apr	Jun			(5)

Galaxy Magazine
First published in October 1950. See Volume II for details prior to 1970. Variously titled Galaxy, Galaxy Science Fiction *or* Galaxy Magazine.
Publisher: Universal Publishing, New York, July 1969–Sep/Oct 1979; Galaxy Magazine, Inc., Boston, July 1980.
Editor: Ejler Jakobsson, July 1969–May 1974; James Baen, June 1974–October 1977; John J. Pierce, November 1977–March/April 1979; Hank Stine, June/July 1979–Sep/Oct 1979; Floyd Kemske, July 1980.

Year	Jan	Feb	Mar	Apr	May	Jun	Jul	Aug	Sep	Oct	Nov	Dec	No.
1970:		Feb	Mar	Apr	May	Jun	Jul	Aug		Oct		Dec	(181)
1971:	Jan	Feb	Mar	Apr	May/Jun		Jul/Aug		Sep/Oct		Nov/Dec		(189)
1972:	Jan/Feb		Mar/Apr		May/Jun		Jul/Aug		Sep/Oct		Nov/Dec		(195)
1973:	Jan/Feb		Mar/Apr		May/Jun		Jul/Aug		Sep	Oct	Nov	Dec	(203)
1974:	Jan	Feb	Mar	Apr	May	Jun	Jul	Aug	Sep	Oct	Nov	Dec	(215)

Year	Jan	Feb	Mar	Apr	May	Jun	Jul	Aug	Sep	Oct	Nov	Dec	(no.)
1975:	Jan	Feb	Mar	Apr		Jun	Jul	Aug	Sep	Oct			(224)
1976:	Jan	Feb	Mar		May		Jul		Sep	Oct	Nov	Dec	(233)
1977:			Mar	Apr	May	Jun	Jul	Aug	Sep	Oct	Nov	D/J	(243)
1978:		Feb	Mar	Apr	May	Jun			Sep		Nov/Dec		(250)
1979:			Mar/Apr			Jun/Jul			Sep/Oct				(253)
1980:							Jul						(254)

[continues in Volume IV]

Galileo

Semi-professional magazine at outset but turned fully professional from #11/12.
Publisher: Avenue Victor Hugo Publishers, Boston, MA.
Editor: Charles C. Ryan.

Year	Jan	Feb	Mar	Apr	May	Jun	Jul	Aug	Sep	Oct	Nov	Dec	(no.)
1976:									Sep			Dec	(2)
1977:				Apr			Jul			Oct			(5)
1978:	Jan		Mar		May		Jul		Sep				(10)
1979:			#11/12				Jul		Sep		Nov		(14)
1980:	Jan		*										(15)

The March 1980 issue reached proof stage but was never published.

Haunt of Horror

Publisher: Marvel Comics Group, New York.
Editor: Gerard Conway.

Year	Jan	Feb	Mar	Apr	May	Jun	Jul	Aug	Sep	Oct	Nov	Dec	(no.)
1973:						Jun		Aug					(2)

Heavy Metal

Website http://www.metaltv.com/
Publisher: HM Communications, New York.
Editors: Sean Kelly, April 1977–December 1979; Ted White, January–November 1980.

Year	Jan	Feb	Mar	Apr	May	Jun	Jul	Aug	Sep	Oct	Nov	Dec	(no.)
1977:				Apr	May	Jun	Jul	Aug	Sep	Oct	Nov	Dec	(9)
1978:	Jan	Feb	Mar	Apr	May	Jun	Jul	Aug	Sep	Oct	Nov	Dec	(21)
1979:	Jan	Feb	Mar	Apr	May	Jun	Jul	Aug	Sep	Oct	Nov	Dec	(33)
1980:	Jan	Feb	Mar	Apr	May	Jun	Jul	Aug	Sep	Oct	Nov	Dec	(45)

[continues in Volume IV]

If

First issue was March 1952. See Volume II for details prior to 1970. The magazine's official title was If, Worlds of Science Fiction but during the 1960s it became increasingly presented as Worlds of If, which became its formal title from March 1972.
Publisher: Universal Publishing, New York, July 1969–November/December 1974.
Editor: Ejler Jakobsson, July 1969–January/February 1974; James Baen, March/April–November/December 1974.

Year	Jan	Feb	Mar	Apr	May	Jun	Jul	Aug	Sep	Oct	Nov	Dec	(no.)
1970:	Jan	Feb	Mar	Apr	May		Jul/Aug		Sep/Oct		Nov/Dec		(151)
1971:	Jan/Feb		Mar/Apr		May/Jun		Jul/Aug		Sep/Oct		Nov/Dec		(157)
1972:	Jan/Feb		Mar/Apr		May/Jun		Jul/Aug		Sep/Oct		Nov/Dec		(163)
1973:	Jan/Feb		Mar/Apr		May/Jun		Jul/Aug		Sep/Oct		Nov/Dec		(169)

1974:	Jan/Feb	Mar/Apr	May/Jun	Jul/Aug	Sep/Oct	Nov/Dec	(175)

[continues in Volume IV]

Infinity Science Fiction

Original anthology series, derived from earlier magazine – see Volume II for details.
Publisher: Lancer Books, New York.
Editor: Robert Hoskins.

1970:	#1					(1)
1971:	#2					(2)
1972:			#3		#4	(4)
1973:			#5			(5)

Isaac Asimov's Science Fiction Magazine

Website at http://www.asimovs.com/
Publisher: Davis Publications, New York, Spring 1977–September 1992.
Editor: George H. Scithers, Spring 1977–15 February 1982.

1977:	Spr		Sum		Fal		Win						(4)
1978:	Jan/Feb		Mar/Apr		May/Jun		Jul/Aug		Sep/Oct		Nov/Dec		(10)
1979:	Jan	Feb	Mar	Apr	May	Jun	Jul	Aug	Sep	Oct	Nov	Dec	(22)
1980:	Jan	Feb	Mar	Apr	May	Jun	Jul	Aug	Sep	Oct	Nov	Dec	(34)

[continues in Volume IV]

Kadath

Small-press magazine.
Publisher and Editor: Lin Carter, New York.

1974:	#1	(1)

Kadath (Italy)

Small-press magazine.
Publisher: Kadath Press, Genova.
Editor: Francesco Cova.

1979:		Oct	(1)
1980:	May	Nov	(3)

[continues in Volume IV]

Macabre

Small-press little magazine. First issue June 1957. See Volume II for details prior to 1970.
Publisher: Macabre House, New Haven, CT.
Editor: Joseph Payne Brennan.

1970:	#21	(21)
1973:	#22	(22)
1976:	#23	(23)

The Magazine of Fantasy and Science Fiction

First issued in Fall 1949. See Volumes I and II for details prior to 1970. Website www. fsfmag.com
Publisher: Mercury Press, Inc., New York, March 1958–January 2001 (based in Cornwall, CT, from February 1971).

Editor: Edward L. Ferman, November 1964–June 1991.

1970:	Jan	Feb	Mar	Apr	May	Jun	Jul	Aug	Sep	Oct	Nov	Dec (235)
1971:	Jan	Feb	Mar	Apr	May	Jun	Jul	Aug	Sep	Oct	Nov	Dec (247)
1972:	Jan	Feb	Mar	Apr	May	Jun	Jul	Aug	Sep	Oct	Nov	Dec (259)
1973:	Jan	Feb	Mar	Apr	May	Jun	Jul	Aug	Sep	Oct	Nov	Dec (271)
1974:	Jan	Feb	Mar	Apr	May	Jun	Jul	Aug	Sep	Oct	Nov	Dec (283)
1975:	Jan	Feb	Mar	Apr	May	Jun	Jul	Aug	Sep	Oct	Nov	Dec (295)
1976:	Jan	Feb	Mar	Apr	May	Jun	Jul	Aug	Sep	Oct	Nov	Dec (307)
1977:	Jan	Feb	Mar	Apr	May	Jun	Jul	Aug	Sep	Oct	Nov	Dec (319)
1978:	Jan	Feb	Mar	Apr	May	Jun	Jul	Aug	Sep	Oct	Nov	Dec (331)
1979:	Jan	Feb	Mar	Apr	May	Jun	Jul	Aug	Sep	Oct	Nov	Dec (343)
1980:	Jan	Feb	Mar	Apr	May	Jun	Jul	Aug	Sep	Oct	Nov	Dec (355)

[continues in Volume IV]

Magazine of Horror

Publisher: Health Knowledge, Inc., New York.
Editor: Robert A.W. Lowndes.

1970:	Feb		May	Sum	Fal	(34)
1971:	Feb	Apr				(36)

Midnight Sun

Small-press magazine.
Publisher and Editor: Gary Hoppenstand, Columbus, OH.

1974:			#1	(1)
1975:			Sum/Fal	(2)
1976:		Apr	Aug	(4)
1979:		#5		(5)

New Dimensions

Original anthology series.
Publisher: Doubleday, New York (hardcover), Vols 1–2; Avon Books, New York (paperback), Vols 1–2; Science Fiction Book Club, New York (hardcover), Vol. 3; Signet Books, New York (paperback), Vols 3–10; Harper & Row, New York (hardcover), Vols 5–10; Pocket Books, New York (paperback), Vols 11–12.
Editor: Robert Silverberg (jointly with Marta Randall for Vols 11–12).

1971:				#1	(1)
1972:				#2	(2)
1973:				#3	(3)
1974:			#4		(4)
1975:	#5				(5)
1976:	#6				(6)
1977:	#7				(7)
1978:	#8				(8)
1979:	#9				(9)
1980:			#10&#11		(11)
1981:		#12			(12)

New Worlds (UK)

First issued in 1946; see Volumes I and II for details prior to 1970. Had become a semi-professional magazine by 1970 and converted into a paperback anthology format from 1971. Reverted to semi-professional from 1978–79.

Publishers: New Worlds Publishing, October 1968–March 1971; Sphere Books, London, Summer 1971–Spring 1975; Transworld Publishing, London, Summer 1975–Summer 1976; Coma Publications, Manchester, 1978–1979.

Editors: Michael Moorcock, May/June 1964–#6, 1973; Hilary Bailey, #7, 1974–#10, 1976 (#7 jointly with Charles Platt); Michael Moorcock, #212–214, 1978; David Britton, #215, Spring 1979; Charles Platt, #216, September 1979.

1970:	Jan	Feb	Mar #200					(200)
1971:			Mar					(201)

relaunched as a paperback anthology

1971:					#1		#2	(203)
1972:		#3		#4				(205)
1973:	#5				#6			(207)
1974:							#7	(208)
1975:		#8				#9		(210)
1976:				#10				(211)
1978:		Spr		Sum		Win		(214)
1979:		Spr			Sep			(216)

[continues in Volume IV]

New Writings in S.F.

Original anthology series started in 1964. See Volume II for details prior to 1970.

Publisher: Corgi Books, London (paperback) all volumes; Dobson Books, London (hardcover) to #20; Sidgwick & Jackson, London (hardcover) #21–29.

Editor: John Carnell, Vols 1–21; Kenneth Bulmer, Vols 22–30.

1970:	#16	#17				(17)
1971:		#18	#19			(19)
1972:	#20			#21		(21)
1973:		#22			#23	(23)
1974:		#24				(24)
1975:		#25		#26		(26)
1976:	#27		#28		#29	(29)
1978:				#30		(30)

Nickelodeon

Small-press magazine, continuation of Trumpet, *which had seen ten issues from February 1965 to Fall 1969 and an eleventh issue in 1974.*

Publisher: Tom Reamy.

Editors: Tom Reamy and Ken Keller.

1975:	#1	(1)
1976:	#2	(2)

revived as Trumpet *and continues the numbering.*

1981:	#12	(3/14)

Nova

Original anthology series.

Publisher: Hardcover, Delacorte Press, New York, Vol. 1; Walker, New York, Vols. 2–4.

Editor: Harry Harrison.

1970:	#1			(1)
1972:		#2		(2)
1973:		#3		(3)
1974:			#4	(4)

Nyctalops

Amateur/Semi-professional magazine. April 1976 was a combined issue #11/12.

Publisher and Editor: Harry O. Morris (operating as Silver Scarab Press, Albuquerque, from #4)

1970:			May			Oct	(2)
1971:	Feb			Jun		Oct	(5)
1972:	Feb				Aug		(7)
1973:		Apr					(8)
1974:				Jul			(9)
1975:	Jan						(10)
1976:		Apr					(11)
1977:			May				(12)
1978:	Mar						(13)
1980:	Jan						(14)

[continues in Volume IV]

Odyssey

Publisher: Gambi Publications, New York.

Editor: Roger Elwood.

1976:	Spr	Sum	(2)

Omni

Science-based magazine which also ran fiction.

Publisher: Omni Publications, New York.

Fiction Editors: Ben Bova, October 1978–December 1979; Robert Sheckley, January 1980–September 1981.

1978:										Oct	Nov	Dec	(3)
1979:	Jan	Feb	Mar	Apr	May	Jun	Jul	Aug	Sep	Oct	Nov	Dec	(15)
1980:	Jan	Feb	Mar	Apr	May	Jun	Jul	Aug	Sep	Oct	Nov	Dec	(27)

[continues in Volume IV]

Orbit

An original anthology series launched in 1966. See Volume II for details prior to 1970.

Publisher: G.P. Putnam, New York, #1–13; Harper & Row, New York, #14–21

Editor: Damon Knight.

1970:	#6		#7		#8	(8)
1971:				#9		(9)

1972:		#10									#11		(11)
1973:							#12						(12)
1974:			#13	#14							#15		(15)
1975:				#16							#17		(17)
1976:						#18							(18)
1977:							#19						(19)
1978:								#20					(20)
1980:											#21		(21)

Other Times (UK)
Small-press magazine.
Publisher: P. P. Layouts, London.
Editor: Andrew Ellsmore (#1), Leo Bulero (#2).

1975:											Nov/Jan		(1)
1976:		Feb											(2)

Pandora
Small-press magazine.
Publisher: Lois Wickstrom; Denver, Colorado, # 1–2; Sproing, Inc.; Denver, # 3–7.
Editor: Lois Wickstrom.

1978:											#1		(1)
1979:	#2			#3							#4		(4)
1980:			#5				#6						(6)

[continues in Volume IV.]

Paragon
Small-press magazine; a revival of The Diversifier.
Publisher: Castle Press, Oroville, CA.
Editor: C. C. Clingan.

1980:					May								(1)

Perry Rhodan
American publication of a German series, issued in the US as a paperback magazine. It appeared twice monthly between August 1973 and September 1976. From March–August 1977 two volumes were issued as one.
Publisher: Ace Books, New York, May 1969–January 1978; Master Publications, Van Nuys, California, October 1978–July 1979.
Editor: Forrest J. Ackerman, May 1969–July 1979.

1971:								#6	#7	#8	#9	#10	(10)
1972:			#11	#12	#13	#14	#15	#16	#17	#18	#19	#20	(20)
1973:	#21		#22	#23	#24	#25	#26	#27 #28	#29 #30	#31 #32	#33 #34	#35 #36	(36)
1974:	#37 #38	#39 #40	#41 #42	#43 #44	#45 #46	#47 #48	#49 #50	#51 #52	#53 #54	#55 #56	#57 #58	#59 #60	(60)
1975:	#61 #62	#63 #64	#65 #66 #67	#68 #69	#70 #71	#72 #73	#74 #75	#76 #77	#78 #79	#80 #81	#82 #83	#84 #85	(85)

```
1976:  #86   #88   #90  #92  #94  #96  #98 #100 #102
       #87   #89   #91  #93  #95  #97  #99 #101 #103 #104 #105 #106(106)
1977:  #107 #108  #109 #111 #113 #115      #117
             #110 #112 #114 #116           #118                    (118)
1978:                                           #119/124          (119)
1979:  #125/130        #131/136        #137/#5                    (122)
```
                                                    [continues in Volume IV]

QUARK/
Original anthology series.
Publisher: Paperback Library, New York.
Editors: Samuel R. Delany and Marilyn Hacker.

```
1970:                                           #1        (1)
1971:      #2            #3            #4                  (4)
```

Questar
Media and comics magazine with increased fiction content from #10.
Publisher: MW Communications, Pittsburgh, Pennsylvania.
Editor: William G. Wilson, Jr.

```
1978:           #1            Sum                         (2)
1979:           Mar                     Aug          Nov  (5)
1980:  Feb                    Jun       Aug     Oct   Dec (10)
1981:  Feb                    Jun               Oct       (13)
```

REH: Lone Star Fictioneer
Semi-professional magazine.
Publishers and Editors: Byron Roark and Arnie Fenner, Shawnee Mission, KS

```
1975:           Spr          Sum       Fal               (3)
1976            Spr                                       (4)
```
                                                    [continued as Chacal]

Rune see *Starwind*

Science Fantasy (Yearbook)
Reprint magazine, first issue entitled Yearbook.
Publisher: Ultimate Publishing, New York.
Editor: Sol Cohen.

```
1970:                        #1        Fal               (2)
1971:  Win      Spr                                      (4)
```

Science Fiction (Adventure) Classics
Reprint magazine. Began as Science Fiction Classics *in 1967, retitled* Science Fiction Adventure Classics, *Winter 1969–November 1972,* Science Fiction Adventures, *January–May 1973 and September 1974–November 1974. Issues #9–#11 (Winter–Summer 1970) were retitled* Space Adventures (Classics) *which became a separate magazine. See Volume II for data prior to 1970.*
Publisher: Ultimate Publishing, New York.
Editor: Sol Cohen

1970:						Win	(9)
1971:	Spr		Sum		Fal		(12)
1972: Jan	Mar	May	Jul	Sep	Nov		(18)
1973: Jan	Mar	May	Jul	Sep	Nov		(24)
1974: Jan	Mar	May	Jul	Sep	Nov		(30)

Science Fiction Greats

Began in Winter 1965 as Great Science Fiction. *Title changed to* S.F. Greats *from #13 (Winter 1969). See Volume II for details prior to 1970.*
Publisher: Ultimate Publishing, New York.
Editor: Sol Cohen

1970:	Spr	Sum	Fal	Win	(20)
1971:	Spr				(21)

Science Fiction Monthly (UK)

Publisher: New English Library, London.
Editor: Aune Butt, #1–5; thereafter Julie Davis, both under editorial guidance of Pat Hornsey.

1974:	#1–1 #1–2 #1–3 #1–4 #1–5 #1–6 #1–7 #1–8 #1–9 #1–10 #1–11	(11)
1975: #1–12 #2–1 #2–2 #2–3 #2–4 #2–5 #2–6 #2–7 #2–8 #2–9 #2–10 #2–11		(23)
1976: #2–12 #3–1 #3–2 #3–3 #3–4		(28)

S.F. Digest (UK)

Publisher: New English Library, London.
Editor: Julie Davis.

1976:	#1	(1)

Shayol

Small-press magazine.
Publisher: Flight Unlimited, Kansas.
Editor: Pat Cadigan.

1977:			Nov	(1)
1978:	Feb			(2)
1979:		Sum		(3)
1980:			Win	(4)

[continues in Volume IV]

Skyworlds

Publisher: Humorama, Inc., Rockville Center, New York.
Editor: Jeffrey Stevens.

1977:			Nov	(1)
1978:	Feb	May	Aug	(4)

Something Else (UK)

Small-press magazine.
Publisher: Pan Visuals, Manchester.
Editor: Charles Partington.

1980:	Spr			Win	(2)
1984:	Spr				(3)

Sorcerer's Apprentice

Gaming magazine.
Publisher: Flying Buffalo, Inc., Scottsdale, AZ.
Editor: Ken St Andre, Winter 1978–Winter 1979; Liz Danforth, Spring 1980–Spring 1983.

				Win	(1)
1978:				Win	(1)
1979:	Spr	Sum	Fal	Win	(5)
1980:	Spr	Sum	Fal		(8)

[continues in Volume IV]

Space Adventures

Reprint magazine, spin-off of Science Fiction Adventure Classics. *Issues are numbered #9–#14.*
Publisher: Ultimate Publishing, New York.
Editor: Sol Cohen

1970:	Win	Spr	Sum		Win	(4)
1971:		Spr	Sum			(6)

Space and Time

An amateur magazine that later became semi-professional. First appeared in Spring 1966. See Volume II for details prior to 1970. Website http://www.cith.org/space&time.html
Publisher and Editor: Gordon Linzner, New York.

	Jan	Feb	Mar	Apr	May	Jun	Jul	Aug	Sep	Oct	Nov	
1970:		Feb					Jul					(9)
1971:			Mar	Apr		Jun			Sep			(13)
1972:		Feb			May			Aug			Nov	(17)
1973:					May		Jul		Sep		Nov	(21)
1974:	Jan		Mar		May		Jul		Sep		Nov	(27)
1975:	Jan		Mar		May		Jul		Sep		Nov	(33)
1976:	Jan		Mar		May		Jul		Sep		Nov	(39)
1977:	Jan		Mar		May		Jul		Sep		Nov	(45)
1978:	Jan			Apr			Jul			Oct		(49)
1979:	Jan			Apr			Jul			Oct		(53)
1980:	Jan			Apr			Jul			Oct		(57)

[continues in Volume IV]

The Space Gamer

Small-press gaming magazine that turned professional
Publishers: Metagaming Concepts, Austin, Texas until January/February 1980; thereafter Steve Jackson Games, Austin, TX.
Editors: Howard Thompson, March/April 1975–August/September 1976; C. Ben Ostrander, October/November 1976–January/February 1980; Steve Jackson, March/April 1980; Forrest Johnson, May/June 1980–May 1982.

1975:	Mar/Apr	Jun/Jul	Sep/Oct	D/J	(4)
1976:	Mar/May	Jun/Jul	Aug/Sep	Oct/Nov	D/J	(9)

1977:		Feb/Mar	Apr/Jun		Jul/Aug	Sep/Oct	Nov/Dec	(14)
1978:	Jan/Feb	Mar/Apr	May/Jun		Jul/Aug	Sep/Oct	Nov/Dec	(20)
1979:	Jan/Feb	Mar/Apr	May/Jun			Sep/Oct	Nov/Dec	(25)
1980:	Jan/Feb	Mar/Apr	May/Jun		Jul Aug Sep Oct Nov Dec			(34)

[continues in Volume IV]

Stardust (Canada)

Small-press magazine.

Publisher: Charisee Press, Toronto; Stardust Publications from #3.

Editor: Forrest Fusco, Jr.

1975:				#1		(1)
1976:	#2		#3			(3)
1977:		#4				(4)
1978:	2–1		2–2		2–3	(7)
1979:		3–1				(8)
1981:	3–2					(9)

Startling Mystery Stories

Publisher: Health Knowledge, Inc., New York

Editor: Robert A. W. Lowndes

1970:	Spr	Sum	Fal	(17)
1971:	Mar			(18)

Starwind

Small-press magazine. First issue entitled Rune.

Publisher: Rune Press, Columbus, OH; Starwind Press from issue #2.

Editor: Warren DeLio, Autumn 1974–Spring 1976; Elbert Lindsey, Jr., Fall 1976–Autumn 1978.

1974:		Aut	(1)
1976:	Spr	Aut	(3)
1977:		Aut	(4)
1978:		Aut	(5)

Stellar

Original anthology series.

Publisher: Ballantine Books/Del Rey Books, New York.

Editor: Judy-Lynn del Rey.

1974:			#1		(1)
1976:	#2			*	(2)
1977:				#3	(3)
1978:		#4			(4)
1980:		#5			(5)
1981:	#6		#7		(7)

* There was a companion *Stellar Short Novels* in October 1976.

Sword & Sorcery Annual

Publisher: Ultimate Publishing, Scottsdale, AZ.

Editor: Sol Cohen.

1975:	#1	(1)

Thrilling Science Fiction

Formerly titled The Most Thrilling Science Fiction Ever Told *and* Thrilling SF Adventures. *Began publication in 1966. See Volume II for details prior to 1970.*
Publisher: Ultimate Publishing, New York.
Editor: Sol Cohen

1970:		Spr		Sum		Fal		Win	(18)
1971:		Spr		Sum		Fal		Dec	(22)
1972:	Feb	Apr		Jun	Aug	Oct		Dec	(28)
1973:	Feb	Apr		Jun	Aug	Oct		Dec	(34)
1974:	Feb	Apr		Jun	Aug	Oct		Dec	(40)
1975:		Apr		Jul					(42)

Unearth

Small-press magazine.
Publisher: Unearth Press, Boston, MA (last issue from Cambridge).
Editor: John M. Landsberg and Jonathan Ostrowsky-Lantz.

1977:	Win	Spr	Sum	Fal	(4)
1978:	Win	Spr	Sum		(7)
1979:	Win				(8)

Universe

Original anthology series.
Publishers: Ace Books, New York, #1–2; Random House, #3–5; Doubleday, #6–17 and revived #1; Bantam Spectra, revived #2–3.
Editor: Terry Carr.

1971:					#1		(1)
1972:					#2		(2)
1973:						#3	(3)
1974:		#4					#5 (5)
1976:			#6				(6)
1977:	#7						(7)
1978:	#8						(8)
1979:			#9				(9)
1980:				#10			(10)

[continues in Volume IV]

Vertex

Publisher: Mankind Publishing, Los Angeles.
Editor: Donald J. Pfeil.

1973:		Apr	Jun		Aug	Oct	Dec	(5)
1974:	Feb	Apr	Jun		Aug	Oct	Dec	(11)
1975:	Feb	Apr	Jun	Jul	Aug			(16)

Void (Australia)

Small-press magazine; switched to anthology series after #5.
Publisher: Void Publications (later Cory & Collins), St Kilda.
Editor: Paul Collins.

1975:				#1	#2	(2)
1976:	#3	#4				(4)
1977:	#5					(5)
1978:		#6–8*		#9–11**		(7)
1979:		#12–14†				(8)
1981:		#15–17‡				(9)
1983:	#18					(10)

*Called *Envisaged Worlds*; **Other Worlds*; †*Alien Worlds*; ‡*Distant Worlds*.

Vortex (UK)
Publisher: Cerberus Publishing, Thame, Oxfordshire.
Editor: Keith Seddon.

1977:	Jan	Feb	Mar	Apr	May	(5)

Weirdbook
Semi-professional magazine. Began in 1968. See Volume II for data prior to 1970.
Publisher: Weirdbook Press, Buffalo, New York.
Editor: W. Paul Ganley.

1971:	#4					(4)
1972:	#5					(5)
1973:	#6			#7		(7)
1974:					#8	(8)
1975:			#9			(9)
1976:		#10				(10)
1977:	#11			#12		(12)
1978:		#13				(13)
1979:			#14			(14)

[continues in Volume IV]

Weird Heroes
Original anthology series promoted as a 'new American pulp'.
Publisher: Pyramid Books, New York.
Editor: Byron Preiss.

1975:				#1	#2	(2)
1976:			#3	#4		(4)
1977:	#5	#6		#7	#8	(8)

Weird Mystery
Reprint magazine.
Publisher: Ultimate Publishing, New York.
Editor: Sol Cohen.

1970:			Fal	Win	(2)
1971:	Spr	Sum			(4)

Weird Tales
First issued in March 1923. See Volumes I and II for details prior to 1970.
Publisher: Weird Tales, Inc., a division of Renown Publications, Los Angeles,

Editor: Sam Moskowitz, Summer 1973–Summer 1974.

1973:		Sum	Fal		Win	(282)
1974:		Sum				(283)

[continues in Volume IV]

Whispers

Small-press magazine which also had spin-off anthology series. From June 1975 on, most issues were treated as doubles. The anthology series is shown as A1, A2 etc.

Publisher: Whispers Press, Fayetteville (and other sites), NC.

Editor: Stuart Schiff.

1973:			#1		#2	(2)
1974:	#3		#4	#5		(5)
1975:		#6/7			#8	(7)
1976:					#9	(8)
1977:			#10/A1			(9+1)
1978:			#11/12			(10+1)
1979:			A2 #13/14			(11+2)

[continues in Volume IV]

Witchcraft & Sorcery

Small-press magazine. Continued the numbering of Coven 13 *from Volume II.*

Publisher: Fantasy Publishing Co. Inc., Alhambra, CA.

Editor: Gerald W. Page.

1971:	Jan/Feb	May		(2)
1972:	#7	#8		(4)
1973:		#9		(5)
1974:			#10	(6)

Worlds of Fantasy

Trial issue released in 1968. See Volume II for details.

Publisher: Universal Publishing, New York.

Editor: Lester del Rey, #2; thereafter Ejler Jakobsson.

1970:		#2	Win	(3)
1971:	Spr			(4)

Worlds of If

See *If.*

Worlds of Tomorrow

Began in April 1963, and suspended between May 1967 and Summer 1970. See Volume II for details prior to 1970.

Publisher: Universal Publishing, New York, Summer 1970–Spring 1971.

Editor: Ejler Jakobsson, Summer 1970–Spring 1971.

1970:		#24	Win	(25)
1971:	Spr			(26)

Appendix 3

Directory of Magazine Editors and Publishers

The following lists the editors and publishers of the science-fiction magazines covered by this volume, together with the first and last issues they edited and the total number. It includes all credited managing, executive, associate and assistant editors. The cut-off date is December 1980, though where magazines continue beyond that date the last issue of the editor's tenure is given.

Abramson, Arnold E.
Publisher, *Galaxy*, July 1969–September/October 1979 (87 issues); *If*, July 1969–November/December 1974 (32 issues).

Achée, Durand W.
Publisher, *Beyond*, Fall 1981–October 1982 (4 issues).

Ackerman, Forrest J
Managing Editor, *Perry Rhodan*, April 1969–July 1979 (122 issues).

Adomites, Paul
Managing Editor, *Questar*, February 1981 (1 issue).
Editor, *Questar*, June 1981 (1 issue).

Alcarez, José
Associate Publisher/Editor, *Aura*, 1979 (1 issue).

Allison, Susan
Assistant Editor, *Destinies*, November/December 1978–Spring 1981 (10 issues).

Angove, Neville J.
Publisher/Editor, *The Cygnus Chronicler*, October 1977–December 1983 (19 issues).

Ashby, Richard
Associate Editor, *Vertex*, October 1973–April 1975 (10 issues).

Ashmead, John

Assistant Editor, *Isaac Asimov's SF Magazine*, August 1980–15 February 1982 (20 issues).

Baen, James

Managing Editor, *Galaxy*, November 1973–May 1974 (7 issues); *Worlds of If*, January/February 1974 (1 issue).

Editor, *Galaxy*, June 1974–October 1977 (33 issues); *Worlds of If*, March/April–November/ December 1974 (5 issues); *Destinies*, November/December 1978–Fall 1981 (11 issues).

Bailey, Hilary

Editor, *New Worlds* #7–#10, 1974–1976 (4 volumes).

Benjamin, Judy-Lynn

See Del Rey, Judy-Lynn

Berglund, E. Paul

Co-editor, *The Dark Messenger Reader*, Winter 1975 (1 issue).

Bernhard, Allan

Associate Publisher, *Amazing Stories*, May 1979–June 1982 (16 issues); *Fantastic*, April 1979–October 1980 (7 issues).

Bernhard, Arthur

Publisher, *Amazing Stories*, May 1979–June 1982 (16 issues); *Fantastic*, April 1979–October 1980 (7 issues).

Berry, John D.

Assistant Editor, *Amazing Stories*, October 1973–June 1974 (5 issues); *Fantastic*, November 1973–May 1974 (4 issues).

Blocher, J.

Managing Editor, *Starwind*, Autumn 1978 (1 issue).

Bloom, Britton

Assistant Editor, *Amazing Stories*, February 1980–June 1982 (13 issues); *Fantastic*, January–October 1980 (4 issues).

Bolling, Cynthia M.

Assistant (to the) Editor, *Galaxy*, June 1975–December 1976 (14 issues).

Bova, Ben

Editor, *Analog*, January 1972–November 1978 (83 issues); *Analog Annual*, 1976 (1 volume); *Analog Yearbook*, 1978 (1 volume).

Fiction Editor, *Omni*, October 1978–December 1979 (15 issues).

Executive Editor, *Omni*, January 1980–September 1981 (21 issues).

Breeds, D. S.

Assistant Editor, *Isaac Asimov's SF Magazine*, Fall 1977–September 1978 (7 issues).

Brennan, Joseph Payne
Publisher/Editor, *Macabre*, June 1957–1976 (23 issues).

Britton, David W.
Editor, *New Worlds*, Spring 1979 (1 issue).

Bulmer, Kenneth
Editor, *New Writings in SF*, #22–#30, 1973–1978 (9 volumes).

Burke, Anne W.
See Jordan, Anne

Burnham, Crispin
Editor (and Publisher from #2), *The Dark Messenger Reader/Eldritch Tales*, Winter 1975–Spring 1995 (30 issues).

Butt, Aune
Editor, *Science Fiction Monthly*, February–June 1974 (5 issues).

Cadigan, Pat
Associate Editor, *Chacal*, Spring 1977 (1 issue).
Executive Editor, *Shayol*, November 1977–Winter 1985 (7 issues).

Campbell, Jr., John W.
Editor, *Analog* (formerly *Astounding SF*), December 1937–December 1971 (409 issues).

Carnell, Edward John
Editor, *New Writings in SF*, 1964–1972 (21 volumes).

Carr, Terry
Editor, *Universe* 1971–1987 (17 volumes).

Carrington, Grant
Associate Editor, *Amazing Stories*, May 1972–May 1975 (18 issues); *Fantastic*, April 1972–June 1975 (19 issues).

Carter, Lin
Publisher and Editor, *Kadath*, 1974 (1 issue).

Charnock, Graham
Associate Editor, *New Worlds*, August 1969–April 1970 (8 issues).

Clingan, A. B.
Co-Editor, *The Diversifier*, June 1974–November 1977 (23 issues).
Editor, *Paragon*, May 1980 (1 issue).

Clingan, Chet C.
Publisher/Editor, *The Diversifier*, June 1974–May/July 1978 (26 issues).

Clum, Barbara
Assistant Editor, *Cosmos*, May–November 1977 (4 issues).

Cohen, Sol
Publisher: *Amazing Stories*, August 1965–February 1979 (77 issues); *Fantastic*, September 1965–January 1979 (73 issues).
Publisher and Editor, *Great SF/SF Greats*, Winter 1965–Spring 1971 (21 issues); *The Most Thrilling SF Ever Told/Thrilling SF*, Summer 1966–July 1975 (42 issues); *Science Fiction Adventure Classics*, Summer 1967–November 1974 (30 issues); *Space Adventures*, Winter 1970–Summer 1971 (6 issues); *Science Fantasy*, Summer 1970–Spring 1971 (4 issues); *Weird Mystery*, Fall 1970–Summer 1971 (4 issues), *Sword & Sorcery Annual*, 1975 (1 issue).

Collins, Paul
Publisher and Editor, *Void*, August 1975–February 1977 (5 issues).

Conway, Gerard F.
Editor, *The Haunt of Horror*, June–August 1973 (2 issues).

Crawford, William L.
Publisher, *Witchcraft & Sorcery*, January/February 1971–September 1974 (6 issues).

Danforth, Liz
Editor, *Sorcerer's Apprentice*, Spring 1980–Spring 1983 (11 issues).

Davis, Hank
Assistant Editor, *F&SF*, November 1974–August 1975 (10 issues).

Davis, Joel
Publisher, *Isaac Asimov's SF Magazine*, Spring 1977–September 1992 (190 issues); *Asimov's SF Adventure Magazine*, September 1978–Fall 1979 (4 issues).

Davis, Julie
Editor, *Science Fiction Monthly*, July 1974–May 1976 (23 issues); *S.F. Digest*, Summer 1976 (1 issue).

Day, Howard E.
Publisher/Editor, *Dark Fantasy*, Summer 1973–November 1980 (22 issues).

de Lint, Charles
Publisher, *Dragonbane*, Spring 1978 (1 issue).
Publisher/Editor, *Beyond the Fields We Know*, Autumn 1978 (1 issue), *Dragonfields*, Summer 1980–Winter 1983 (2 issues).

DeLio, Warren
Editor, *Rune*, Autumn 1974 (1 issue); *Starwind*, Spring 1976 (1 issue).

del Rey, Judy-Lynn
(Judy-Lynn Benjamin prior to 21 March 1971.)
Managing Editor, *Galaxy*, July 1969–July 1973 (33 issues); *If*, July 1969–June 1973 (28 issues); *Worlds of Tomorrow*, Summer 1970–Spring 1971 (3 issues); *Worlds of Fantasy*, Fall 1970–Spring 1971 (3 issues).
Editor, *Stellar*, 1974–1981 (7 volumes).

del Rey, Lester
Editor, *Worlds of Fantasy*, September 1968–Fall 1970 (2 issues).
Associate Editor, *Worlds of Fantasy*, Winter 1970–Spring 1971 (2 issues).
Managing Editor, *Galaxy*, June 1968–May 1969 (12 issues); *If*, June 1968–May 1969 (12 issues).

Delany, Samuel R.
Co-editor, *QUARK/*, November 1970–August 1971 (4 volumes).

Deraps, Anne W.
See Jordan, Anne.

Derleth, August W.
Publisher and Editor, *The Arkham Collector*, Summer 1967–Summer 1971 (10 issues).

Dickey, Jeff
Associate Publisher, *Beyond*, Fall 1981–October 1982 (4 issues).

Dozois, Gardner
Associate Editor, *Isaac Asimov's SF Magazine*, Spring–Winter 1977 (4 issues).

Drake, David
Assistant Editor, *Whispers*, July 1974–October 1978 (7 issues).

Durwood, Thomas
Editor, *Ariel*, Autumn 1976–October 1978 (4 issues).

Dytch, Albert
Managing Editor, *Galaxy*, September–October 1973 (2 issues); *Worlds of If*, July/August 1973–November/December 1973 (3 issues).

Edelstein, Scott
Assistant Editor, *Eternity SF*, July 1972–February 1975 (4 issues).

Effinger, George Alec
Associate Editor, *The Haunt of Horror*, June 1973.
Assistant Editor, *The Haunt of Horror*, August 1973.

Ellsmore, Andrew
Editor, *Other Times*, November 1975–February 1976 (2 issues).

Elwood, Roger
Editor, *Odyssey*, Spring–Summer 1976 (2 issues).

Faulder, Richard
Co-editor, *Enigma*, Volume 2, 1971 (2 issues).

Feder, Moshe
Assistant Editor, *Amazing Stories*, November 1972–July 1975 (16 issues); *Fantastic*, October 1972–August 1975 (17 issues).

Fenner, Arnie
Publisher/Editor, *REH: Lone Star Fictioneer*, Spring 1975–Spring 1976 (4 issues).
Publisher, *Chacal*, Winter 1976–Spring 1977 (2 issues); *Shayol*, November 1977–Winter 1985 (7 issues).
Assistant Editor, *Chacal*, Winter 1976 (1 issue).
Editor, *Chacal*, Spring 1977 (1 issue).

Ferman, Edward L.
Editorial Assistant: *F&SF*, November 1958–January 1959 (3 issues).
Managing Editor, *F&SF*, April 1962–October 1964 (30 issues).
Editor, *F&SF*, November 1964–June 1991 (320 issues).
Publisher: *F&SF*, November 1970–January 2001 (358 issues).

Fones, Robert K.
Editorial Assistant, *Analog*, December 1976–July 1978 (20 issues).

Froehlich, Joey
Co-Editor, *The Diversifier*, March 1978–February 1979 (3 issues).

Fusco, Jr., Forrest
Editor, *Stardust*, Summer 1975–March 1981 (9 issues).

Gail, Anna
Assistant Editor, *Amazing Stories*, February 1980–June 1982 (13 issues); *Fantastic*, January–October 1980 (4 issues).

Galef, David
Assistant Editor, *Galaxy*, March/April 1979 (1 issue).

Ganley, W. Paul
Publisher/Editor, *Weirdbook*, 1968–Spring 1997 (30 issues).
Publisher/Editor, *Eerie Country*, July 1976–Summer 1982 (9 issues).

Gohagen Omar
See Mavor, Elinor

Gold, Horace L.
Fiction Editor, *Questar* June–October 1981 (2 issues).

Goldfind, Norman
Publisher, *Cosmos*, May–November 1977 (4 issues).

Goldfind, Rosa
Editorial Assistant, *Cosmos*, May–November 1977 (4 issues).

Goldstein, Steven
Editor, *Counter Thrust*, 1976 (1 issue).

Gregg, Stephen
Editor (and Publisher, first series), *Eternity SF*, July 1972–February 1975, July 1979–February 1980 (6 issues).

Harding, Ralph S.
Co-Editor, *The Diversifier*, March 1978–February 1979 (3 issues).

Harrison, Harry
Editor, *Nova*, 1970–1974 (4 volumes).

Hartwell, David
Editor, *Cosmos*, May–November 1977 (4 issues).

Hedberg, Ken
Assistant Editor, *Galaxy*, June/July–September/October 1979 (2 issues).

Holdsworth, Ruth
Assistant Editor, *Analog*, August–December 1974 (5 issues).

Hoppenstand, Gary
Publisher and Editor, *Midnight Sun*, 1974–June 1979 (5 issues).
Associate Editor, *Starwind*, Spring 1976.

Hornsey, Pat
Executive Editor, *Science Fiction Monthly*, February 1974–May 1976 (28 issues).

Hoskins, Robert
Editor, *Infinity SF*, 1970–1975 (5 volumes).

Hughes, Terry
Assistant Editor, *Amazing Stories*, August 1974–February 1979 (21 issues); *Fantastic*, July 1974–January 1979 (21 issues).

Ikin, Van
Editor, *Enigma*, #4, 1972–Dec 1979 (27 issues).

Jackson, Steve
Publisher, *The Space Gamer*, March/April 1980–September/October 1985 (50 issues), and editor for his first issue.

Jakobssen, Ejler
Editor, *Galaxy*, July 1969–May 1974 (42 issues); *If*, July 1969–February 1974 (32 issues); *Worlds of Tomorrow*, Summer 1970–Spring 1971 (3 issues); *Worlds of Fantasy*, Winter 1970–Spring 1971 (2 issues).
Associate Editor, *Worlds of Fantasy*, Fall 1970 (1 issue).

Jaquet, Jake
Editor, *The Dragon*, March 1980–November 1982 (33 issues).

Johnson, Forrest
Editor, *The Space Gamer*, May/June 1980–May 1982 (25 issues).

Jones, Stephen
Publisher, *Fantasy Tales*, Summer 1977–Summer 1987 (17 issues).
Co-editor, *Fantasy Tales*, Summer 1977–Winter 1991 (24 issues).

Jordan, Anne
(Anne W. Deraps to December 1976 and Anne W. Burke to December 1979.)
Assistant Editor, *F&SF*, December 1975–February 1984 (99 issues).

Kaplan, Mark
Editorial Assistant, *Analog*, October 1979–July 1980 (10 issues).
Associate Editor, *Analog*, August–December 1980 (5 issues).

Kaplan, Rose
Managing Editor, *Cosmos*, May–November 1977 (4 issues).

Kask, Tim
Editor, *The Dragon*, June 1976–February 1980 (34 issues).

Katz, Arnie
Associate Editor, *Amazing Stories*, January 1970–March 1972 (14 issues); *Fantastic*, February 1970–February 1972 (13 issues).

Keller, Ken
Associate Editor, *Nickelodeon*, #1–#2, 1975–1976 (2 issues).
Publisher and Editor, *Trumpet* #12, 1981 (1 issue).

Kelly, Sean
Editor, *Heavy Metal*, April 1977–December 1979 (33 issues).

Kemske, Floyd
Assistant Editor, *Galileo*, September 1976–January 1980 (15 issues).
Editor, *Galaxy*, July 1980 (1 issue).

Kendig, Frank
Executive Editor, *Omni*, October 1978–December 1979 (15 issues).

Kindt, Mark
Assistant Editor, *Rune*, Autumn 1974.

King, Diane
Assistant Editor, *Analog*, May 1973–July 1974 (15 issues).
Associate Editor, *Analog*, August 1974–June 1976 (23 issues).
Fiction Editor, *Omni*, October 1978 (though resigned before issue assembled).

Kleinman, Cylvia
Managing Editor, *Weird Tales*, Summer 1973–Summer 1974 (4 issues).

Knight, Damon
Editor, *Orbit*, 1966–1980 (21 volumes).

Kushner, Ellen
Assistant Editor, *Destinies*, November/December 1978–April 1979 (3 issues).

Lambert, Diane
Assistant Editor, *New Worlds* #8–#10, 1974–1976 (3 volumes).

Landsberg, John M.
Co-editor, *Unearth*, Winter 1977–Winter 1979 (8 issues).

Lankin, Alan
Assistant Editor, *Asimov's SF Adventure Magazine*, Summer–Fall 1979 (2 issues); *Isaac Asimov's SF Magazine*, September 1979–23 November 1981 (28 issues).

Laursen, Byron
Associate Editor, *Beyond*, Fall 1981–October 1982 (4 issues).

Lazarus, Henry Leon
Assistant Editor, *Asimov's SF Adventure Magazine*, September 1978–Spring 1979 (2 issues).

Leigland, Bonnie
Managing Editor, *Galaxy,* July–December 1974 (6 issues); *Worlds of If,* July/August–November/ December 1974 (3 issues).

Lindsey, Jr., Elbert
Assistant Editor, *Starwind*, Spring 1976 (1 issue).
Editor, *Starwind*, Autumn 1976–Autumn 1978 (4 issues).

Linzner, Gordon
Publisher and Editor, *Space & Time*, Spring 1966–Present (100 issues by 2007).

Lowndes, Robert A.W.
Editor, *Magazine of Horror,* August 1963–April 1971 (36 issues); *Startling Mystery Stories*, Summer 1966–March 1971 (18 issues); *Bizarre Fantasy Tales*, Fall 1970–March 1971 (2 issues).

McCaffery, Vincent
Publisher, *Galileo*, September 1976–January 1980 (15 issues).

McCarthy, Shawna
Assistant Editor, *Isaac Asimov's SF Magazine*, November/December 1978 (1 issue).
Associate Editor, *Isaac Asimov's SF Magazine*, January 1979–November 1980 (23 issues); *Asimov's SF Adventure Magazine*, Spring–Fall 1979 (3 issues).
Managing Editor, *Isaac Asimov's SF Magazine*, December 1980–June 1982 (20 issues).

Manning, James
Editor, *Ad Astra*, October 1978–September 1981 (16 issues).

Marcus, Charles
Associate Editor, *Vertex*, April–August 1973 (3 issues).

Margulies, Leo
Publisher, *Weird Tales*, Summer 1973–Summer 1974 (4 issues).

Martin, Chuck
Assistant Editor, *Rune*, Autumn 1974.

Mavor, Elinor
Editor, *Amazing Stories*, May 1979–September 1982 (17 issues, first 6 issues under alias Omar Gohagen); *Fantastic*, April 1979–October 1980 (7 issues, as Omar Gohagen).

Menville, Douglas
Editor, *Forgotten Fantasy*, October 1970–June 1971 (5 issues).

Meshkow, Marian
Assistant Editor, *Asimov's SF Adventure Magazine*, September 1978–Spring 1979 (2 issues).

Meshkow, Sanford Zane
Assistant Editor, *Isaac Asimov's SF Magazine*, January/February–September/October 1978 (5 issues).

Michelucci, Robert
Publisher, *Questar*, March 1979–October 1981 (11 issues).

Mohan, Kim
Assistant Editor, *The Dragon*, October 1979–November 1982 (38 issues).

Moorcock, Michael
Publisher: *New Worlds*, October 1968 to March 1971 (18 issues).
Editor, *New Worlds*, March 1971; anthology 1971–1973; Spring–Winter 1978 and September 1979 (11 issues).

Moore, Nick
Managing Editor, *Rune*, Autumn 1974.

Morris, Harry O.
Publisher and Editor, *Nyctalops*, May 1970–April 1991 (18 issues).

Morton, Leith
Editor, *Enigma*, #1, 1970.

Moskowitz, Sam
Editor, *Weird Tales*, Summer 1973–Summer 1974 (4 issues).

Ostrander, C. Ben
Editor, *The Space Gamer*, October/November 1976–January/February 1980 (19 issues).

Ostrowsky-Lantz, Jonathan
Co-editor, *Unearth*, Winter 1977–Winter 1979 (8 issues).

Owen Thomas L.
Assistant Editor, *Galileo*, September 1976–January 1980 (15 issues).

Page, Gerald W.
Editor, *Witchcraft & Sorcery*, January/February 1971–September 1974 (6 issues).

Partington, Charles
Publisher, *New Worlds* Spring 1978–September 1979 (5 issues).
Publisher and Editor, *Something Else*, Spring 1980–Spring 1984 (3 issues).

Pelligrini, Ed
Editorial Assistant, *Analog*, August 1978–March 1979 (8 issues).
Assistant Editor, *Analog*, April–September 1979 (6 issues).

Pfeil, Donald J.
Editor, *Vertex*, April 1973–August 1975 (16 issues).

Phillips, Evan
Assistant Editor, *F&SF*, October 1979–September 1982 (36 issues).

Phillips, Meg
Assistant Editor, *Isaac Asimov's SF Magazine*, Fall 1977–July 1980 (29 issues);
Asimov's SF Adventure Magazine, September 1978–Fall 1979 (4 issues).

Pierce, John J.
Editor, *Galaxy*, November 1977–March/April 1979 (10 issues).

Platt, Charles
Editor, *New Worlds*, August 1969–April 1970 (8 issues); Co-editor, *New Worlds (Quarterly)* #6–#7, 1973–4 (2 volumes); Editor, US edition, #6, 1975 (1 volume); Co-Editor, September 1979 (1 issue).

Porter, Andrew
Assistant Editor, *F&SF*, April 1967–October 1974 (91 issues).

Preiss, Byron
Editor, *Weird Heroes*, 1975–1977 (8 volumes).

Preston, Colleen
(Colleen Vandervort from March 1980 issue.)
Editorial Assistant, *Analog*, April–September 1979 (6 issues).
Associate Editor, *Analog*, October 1979–July 1980 (10 issues).

Randall, Marta
Co-Editor, *New Dimensions*, 1980–1981 (2 volumes).

Reamy, Tom
Publisher and Editor, *Nickeoldeon* #1–#2, 1975–1976 (2 issues).

Reginald, Robert
Associate Editor, *Forgotten Fantasy*, October 1970–June 1971 (5 issues).

Roark, Byron
Editor, *REH: Lone Star Fictioneer*, Spring 1975–Spring 1976 (4 issues).
Editor, *Chacal*, Winter 1976 (1 issue).

Ross, Steve
Associate Editor, *Vertex*, April 1973–April 1975 (13 issues).

Ryan, Charles C.
Editor, *Galileo*, September 1976–January 1980 (15 issues).

St. Andre, Ken
Editor, *Sorcerer's Apprentice*, Winter 1978–Winter 1979 (5 issues).

Saunders, Charles R.
Editor, *Dragonbane*, Spring 1978 (1 issue).
Co-editor, *Dragonfields*, Summer 1980–Winter 1983 (2 issues).

Schiff, Stuart David
Publisher and Editor, *Whispers*, July 1973–October 1987 (16 issues).

Schmidt, Stanley
Editor, *Analog*, December 1978–Current (339 issues at the end of 2006).

Schochet, Victoria
Associate Editor, *Analog*, July 1976–March 1979 (33 issues).

Schweitzer, Darrell
Assistant Editor, *Isaac Asimov's SF Magazine*, January/February 1978–15 February 1982 (45 issues); *Asimov's SF Adventure Magazine*, September 1978–Fall 1979 (4 issues).

Scithers, George H.
Editor, *Isaac Asimov's SF Magazine*, Spring 1977–15 February 1982 (49 issues); *Asimov's SF Adventure Magazine*, September 1978–Fall 1979 (4 issues).

Seddon, Keith
Editor, *Vortex*, January–May 1977 (5 issues).

Shaw, Alan
Assistant/Associate Editor, *Amazing Stories*, July 1970–September 1972 (14 issues); *Fantastic*, August 1970–August 1972 (13 issues).

Sheckley, Robert
Fiction Editor, *Omni*, January 1980–September 1981 (21 issues).

Silverberg, Robert
Editor, *New Dimensions*, 1971–1980 (10 volumes); Co-Editor, 1980–1981 (2 volumes).

Simmons, Alice
Editorial Assistant, *Galaxy*, September/October 1979 (1 issue).

Simmons, Julie
(Julie Simmons-Lynch after May 1981.)
Associate Editor, *Heavy Metal*, April 1977–February 1978 (11 issues); Managing Editor, March 1978–December 1979 (22 issues); Executive Editor, January 1980–January 1993 (109 issues).

Simonsen, Redmond A.
Editor/Creative Director, *Ares*, March 1980–January 1982 (11 issues).

Sims, Judith
Editor-in-Chief, *Beyond*, Fall 1981–October 1982 (4 issues).

Stanton, Elaine
Assistant Editor, *Vertex*, April 1973–April 1975 (13 issues).

Stathis, Lou
Assistant Editor, *Amazing Stories*, September 1975–June 1976 (5 issues); *Fantastic*, August 1975–August 1976 (6 issues).

Stein, Irwin
Publisher *Infinity SF*, 1970–1973 (5 volumes).

Stevens, Jeffrey
Editor, *Skyworlds*, November 1977–August 1978.

Stine, Hank
Editor, *Galaxy*, June/July–September/October 1979 (2 issues).

Suarez, Andrea
Editorial Assistant, *Analog*, July–November 1976 (5 issues).

Sutton, David A.
Co-editor, *Fantasy Tales*, Summer 1977–Winter 1991 (24 issues).

Tarrant, Kay
Assistant Editor, *Astounding* (later *Analog*), March 1938–October 1973 (428 issues).

Tarrants, J. Timothy
Managing Editor, *Counter Thrust*, #1 (1 issue).

Thompson, Howard
Publisher, *The Space Gamer*, March/April 1975–Jan/February 1980 (26 issues).
Editor, *The Space Gamer*, March/April 1975–August/September 1976 (7 issues).

Torgeson, Roy
Editor, *Chrysalis*, 1977–1983 (10 volumes).

Vandervort, Colleen
See Preston, Colleen.

Vogel, Henry
Publisher, *Eternity SF*, July 1979–February 1980 (2 issues).

Wein, Lee
Associate Editor, *The Haunt of Horror*, August 1973.

Weinstein, Lee
Assistant Editor, *Asimov's SF Adventure Magazine*, Summer–Fall 1979 (2 issues); *Isaac Asimov's SF Magazine*, September 1979–23 November 1981 (28 issues).

West, Becky
Assistant Editor, *F&SF*, October 1979–August 1981 (23 issues).

Weston, Peter
Editor, *Andromeda*, 1976–1978 (3 volumes).

Whight, R.
Co-editor, *Enigma*, Volume 2, 1971 (2 issues).

White, Ted
Editor, *Amazing Stories*, May 1969–February 1979 (52 issues); *Fantastic*, June 1969–January 1979 (51 issues); *Heavy Metal*, January–November 1980 (11 issues).

Wickstrom, Lois
Publisher and Editor, *Pandora*, October 1978–#17, 1987 (17 issues, jointly with Jean Lorrah from #10).

Wilhelm, Kate
Editor, *Clarion*, 1977 (1 volume).

Will, Elaine
Assistant Editor, *Galaxy*, March–October 1977 (8 issues).

Wilson, Robin Scott
Editor, *Clarion*, 1971–1973 (3 volumes).

Wilson, Jr., William G.,
Editor, *Questar*, March 1978–February 1981, October 1981 (12 issues).

Wraight, David
Editor, *Enigma*, April 1980–1981 (4 issues).

Appendix 4

Directory of Magazine Cover Artists

The following identifies, so far as is possible, all cover artists from 1971 to 1980 for the magazines listed in Appendix 2. Covers reprinted from earlier magazines are excluded. For anthology series, cover artists are listed only for the paperback edition. Where magazine dates are bi-monthly (e.g. Jun/Jul) the first month only is shown.

Achilléos, Chris
Galaxy
1973: Jul
Heavy Metal
1980: Dec

Acuna, Ed
Vertex
1974: Dec
1975: Feb.

Adams, Neal
Dark Fantasy
1976: Dec.

Adkins, Dan
Amazing Stories
1971: Jul, Sep.
Fantastic
1971: Jun.

Adragna, Robert
Heavy Metal
1980: Sep.

Alexander, Paul C.
Asimov's
1978: Jan.
Asimov's SF Adventure
1978: Sep.
1979: Spr, Sum.

Ames
Galaxy
1975: Aug.
1976: Feb.

Anderson, Brent
Space & Time
1974: Jul.
1975: May.

Anderson, Craig
The Diversifier
1976: Nov.
Paragon
1980: May.

Anderson, Darrel
Eternity
1973: #2.

1975: #4.
1979: #1.
1980: #2.

Anderson, Richard
Analog
1979: Nov.

Anderson, Sue
Vertex
1974: Oct (with Stevan Arnold).

Arnold, Stevan
Vertex
1974: Oct (with Sue Anderson).

Austin, Alicia
Universe
1971: #1.

Bailey, Dennis R.
Counter Thrust
1976: #1.

Bambara, Frank
Weirdbook
1973: #6.

Barber, Tom
Amazing Stories
1976: Mar, Dec.
1978: Nov.
1979: Feb.
Chrysalis
1977: #2.
1979: #6.
1980: #7.
Galileo
1976: Sep, Dec.
1977: Apr, Jul.
1979: #11/12.
Unearth
1977: Fal.

Barkey, Joe
Ares
1980: May.

Barlowe, Wayne Douglas
Asimov's
1980: Nov.
Fantastic
1980: Jul.

Barnes, John
Sorcerer's Apprentice
1980: Fal.
The Dragon
1980: Jan, Jun.

Barr, George
Asimov's
1978: Nov.
1979: Oct.
1980: May.

Barr, Ken
Questar
1978: #1.

Bash, Kent
F&SF
1980: Nov.

Bear, Greg
F&SF
1976: Aug.
Galaxy
1977: Apr.

Beekman, Doug
Amazing Stories
1976: Sep.
Fantastic
1976: Nov.

Bender, Howard
The Diversifier
1975: Feb.

Bergen, David
S.F. Digest
1976: #1.

Berry, D. Bruce
Weirdbook
1978: #13.

Betcher, Mark
Midnight Sun
1979: #5.

Bevans, Tom
F&SF
1979: Oct.

Bhalla, Tony
Ad Astra
1980: Oct.

Bierley, John
Fantastic
1977: Feb.

Bijl, Liz
Heavy Metal
1980: Oct.

Billman, Dave
Space & Time
1976: Jan.

Bird, Sheila Jayne
The Diversifier
1978: May.

Birkhead, Sheryl
The Diversifier
1974: Jul.

Black, Brad
Starwind
1978: Aut.

Black, Craig
Galaxy
Credited with Sep 1979 cover but
not used.

Blackshear, Thomas
Shayol
1979: Sum.

Blamire, Larry
Galaxy
1980: Jul.
Galileo
1978: May, Sep.
1979: Nov.

Blish, Judith
F&SF
1972: Apr.

Boas, Marcus
Fantastic
1975: Oct.
Heavy Metal
1978: Nov.
REH: Lone Star Fictioneer
1976: Spr.

Bodé, Vaughn (with Larry Todd)
Amazing Stories
1972: Mar, Jul.
1974: Aug.
Fantastic
1971: Oct.
F&SF
1971: Jan.

Bolton, John
Heavy Metal
1980: Mar.

Bonestell, Chesley
F&SF
1971: Nov.
1972: Mar.
1974: Aug.
1975: Mar.
1976: Oct.
1977: Oct.
1978: Mar.

Boyle, Brian (Studio)
Galaxy
1972: Sep, Nov.
1973: Jan, Mar, Sep, Oct, Nov,
Dec.
Worlds of If
1972: Sep, Nov.
1973: Mar, May, Nov.

Brautigam, Don
Destinies
1978: Nov.

Bruning, Richard
Space & Time
1976: Jul.

Buckman, Diana
Void
1975: #1.

Buinis, Lonny
Galaxy
1978: Nov.

Burge, Jerry
Witchcraft & Sorcery
1971: Jan.
1972: #8.

Burnham, Lillian
Eldritch Tales
1979: Dec.

Burns, Jim
Heavy Metal
1978: Mar, Sep.
Science Fiction Monthly
1976: Feb.

Burton, Alan
The Dragon
1979: Nov.

Caldwell, Clyde
Chrysalis
1978: #3.
1979: #4.
Heavy Metal
1978: Aug.
1979: Apr.
Questar
1978: Sum.
Space & Time
1972: Nov.
Unearth
1978: Win, Spr.
1979: Win.

Campanile, Dario
F&SF
1975: May.

Canty, Thomas
The Dragon
1978: Apr.

Cat, Roland
New Worlds
1979: #215.

Cazamayou, Philippe
Heavy Metal
1978: Jul.

Chaffee, Douglas
Fantastic
1971: Dec.
1972: Dec.

Chandler, Toss
Pandora
1980: #5.

Charette, John
Dark Fantasy
1978: Jul.
Space & Time
1978: Oct.

Chastain, George
Midnight Sun
1975: Sum.

Chaykin, Howard
Ares
1980: Mar.

Cherry, Jim
Heavy Metal
1979: Sep.
1980: Aug.

Cirocco, Frank
Space & Time
1974: May.

Clifton-Day, E. M.
Science Fiction Monthly
1975: Jun.
1976: Jan.

Cochran, Connor
All work signed Freff.
Galaxy
   1975: Jan, Mar.

Cohen, Richard Ion
Heavy Metal
   1979: Dec (with Jon Townley).

Colman, Gareth
Science Fiction Monthly
   1975: Feb.

Conklin, Bruce
Dark Fantasy
   1978: Dec.
Space & Time
   1980: Oct.

Conway, Bob
Space & Time
   1977: Jan.

Cooper, Susan
Pandora
   1980: #6.

Corben, Richard
Ariel
   1976: Aut.
Heavy Metal
   1979: Jul (with Rick Courtney).
Nickelodeon
   1975: #1.

Cosentini, Cecilia
Galaxy
   1978: Apr.

Couratin, Patrick
Heavy Metal
   1980: Feb.

Courtney, Rick
Heavy Metal
   1979: Jul (with Richard Corben).

Cox, A. B.
The Diversifier
   1976: Jan.

Weirdbook
   1974: #8.
   1975: #9.

Coye, Lee Brown
Whispers
   1974: Mar.
   1978: Oct.

Dalzell, Bonnie
F&SF
   1976: Apr (with Rick Sternbach).
Galaxy
   1977: May, Jul.

Davidson, Kevin
Vertex
   1973: Jun, Dec.

Davis, Don
Amazing Stories
   1972: Sep, Nov.
   1973: Dec.
F&SF
   1973: Apr, Aug.
Vertex
   1974: Feb.

Davis, Pat
Stardust
   1975: #1.

Day, Dan
Dark Fantasy
   1980: Nov.
Space & Time
   1979: Oct.

Day, Gene (Howard E.)
Dark Fantasy
   1973: Sum, Fal.
   1974: Mar, Jul, Oct.
   1975: Jan, Sep.
   1977: Jan, Sep.
   1979: Oct.
The Diversifier
   1975: Oct.

1979: Feb, Jun.
Destinies
1979: Apr, Aug.
Universe
1972: #2.

Elrohir, Elladan
See Rahman, Ken.

Emshwiller, Ed ('Emsh')
F&SF
1972: Nov.
1974: Apr.
1976: Nov.
1979: Feb.

Erichson, Kurt
The Diversifier
1974: Aug.

Fabian, Stephen E.
Amazing Stories
1975: May, Jul.
1976: Jan, Jun.
1977: Jul, Oct.
1978: Jan, May, Aug.
Asimov's
1980: Jan, Aug.
Asimov's SF Adventure
1979: Fal.
Dark Fantasy
1976: Sep.
The Diversifier
1978: Mar.
Eternity
1972: Jul.
1974: #3.
Fantastic
1975: Feb, Apr.
1976: Feb, Aug.
1977: Jun, Sep, Dec.
1978: Apr, Jul, Oct.
1979: Jan.
Fantasy Tales
1978: Sum.
Galaxy
1974: Nov, Dec.

1975: Sep.
1976: Mar, Jul, Oct.
1977: Mar, Jun, Sep, Oct.
1978: May.
Nyctalops
1978: Mar.
REH: Lone Star Fictioneer
1975: Spr, Sum.
Weirdbook
1977: #12.
Whispers
1973: Dec.
1976: Dec.
1979: Oct.
Witchcraft & Sorcery
1973: #9.

Farley, G. M.
Weirdbook
1971: #4.
1972: #5.

Farrington, K.
Weirdbook
1976: #10.

Feibush, Ray
Science Fiction Monthly
1974: Apr.
1975: Apr, May.

FitzGerald, Russell
QUARK/
1970: #1.

Fitzpatrick, Jim
Fantasy Tales
1980: Sum.

Flood, Martha
Unearth
1977: Sum.

Foglio, Phil
The Dragon
1979: May, Dec.
1980: Mar, Dec.

Foss, Chris
Amazing Stories
1980: Aug.
Science Fiction Monthly
1974: Mar.

Frazetta, Frank
Ariel
1977: #2.
Questar
1980: Oct.

Freas, Frank Kelly
Analog
1971: Jan, Feb, Mar, Apr, May,
Jun, Jul, Aug, Dec.
1972: Apr, Jun, Aug, Sep, Dec.
1973: Apr, Jun, Jul, Nov.
1974: Jan, Mar, Jun, Sep.
1975: Feb, Oct.
1976: May, Sep.
1977: Aug.
1980: Feb.
Asimov's
1977: Win.
1978: Jul.
F&SF
1971: Apr.
1977: Jul.
Galaxy
1977: Aug.
Galileo
1979: Sep.
The Haunt of Horror
1973: Aug.
Odyssey
1976: Spr.
Science Fiction Monthly
1976: Mar.

Freeman, Gary
Sorcerer's Apprentice
1979: Win.

Freeman, George
Dark Fantasy
1978: Jun.

Freff
See Connor Cochran.

Fritz, Steve
Witchcraft & Sorcery
1971: May.

Frolich, Dany
Space & Time
1972: May.

Fulkerson, Jude
The Diversifier
1977: Jan.

Gaadt, George
Questar
1980: Aug.

Garcia, John
Ares
1980: Jul.

Garrison, Jim
The Diversifier
1975: Jun.
Space & Time
1974: Mar.
Weirdbook
1973: #7.

Gasbarri, Fabio
Dark Fantasy
1978: Jan.

Gaughan, Jack
Analog
1972: Oct.
1973: May, Sep.
1974: Feb, May, Nov.
1975: Mar, May, Dec.
1976: Jun, Nov.
1978: Dec.
Asimov's
1978: Mar.
1979: Feb, Apr, May.
1980: Mar.
Cosmos
1977: Sep, Nov.

F&SF
>   1971: Feb.
>   1973: Jun.
>   1976: Mar.
>   1980: Feb.

Galaxy
>   1971: Jan, Feb, Mar, Apr, May,
>   Jul, Sep.
>   1972: Jan, Mar, May, Jul.
>   1973: May.
>   1974: Mar, Apr, Oct.
>   1975: Apr.

If
>   1971: Jan, Mar, May, Jul, Nov.
>   1972: Jan, Mar, May, Jul.
>   1974: May.

Odyssey
>   1976: Sum.

Worlds of Fantasy
>   1971: Spr.

Worlds of Tomorrow
>   1971: Spr.

Gelotte, Mark
Space & Time
>   1971: Jun, Sep.
>   1973: May, Nov.
>   1974: Nov.
>   1975: Nov.
>   1976: May.

Giger, H. R.
Heavy Metal
>   1980: Jun.

Gilbert, Mike
Analog
>   1974: Dec.

Gildea, Steven
Unearth
>   1977: Win, Spr.

Giraud, Jean ('Moebius')
Heavy Metal
>   1977: May, Jun, Jul.

Greenier, Al
Space & Time
>   1973: Jul, Sep.

Guertin, Jeannine
F&SF
>   1974: Sep.

Haas, Robert
Shayol
>   1978: Feb.

Hague, Michael
Ariel
>   1978: #4.

Haldeman, Jack C.
Amazing Stories
>   1974: Oct.

Haman, Brad
Galaxy
>   1978: Sep.

Hamilton, Frank
Eerie Country
>   1980: #3.

Hammel, Jim
Pandora
>   1978: #1.

Hammell, Tim
Dark Fantasy
>   1976: May.
>   1979: Feb, Apr.

Hannan, Bill
The Dragon
>   1976: Jun.
>   1977: Jul, Sep.

Hardy, David A.
Ad Astra
>   1979: Nov.

Amazing Stories
>   1974: Jun.

F&SF
>   1971: Jun.
>   1972: May, Oct.

1973: Jan, May, Jul.
1974: Jan.
1975: Feb, Apr, Aug, Nov.
1976: Jan, May, Jun, Sep.
1977: May, Nov.
1978: Jan, Apr, Jun, Oct, Dec.
1979: Apr, May, Aug, Dec.
1980: May, Jun.
Galaxy
1974: Sep.
Science Fiction Monthly
1974: Sep.
Worlds of If
1973: Jan, Jul, Sep.

Harlib, Amy
Galaxy
1978: Feb.

Harper, Steve
Fantastic
1971: Feb.

Harrison, Rick
Space & Time
1979: Jan.

Healy, C. Lee
Sorcerer's Apprentice
1980: Spr.

Herron, Don
The Diversifier
1974: Oct.

Hickman, Steve
Amazing Stories
1977: Mar.
Destinies
1981: Win.
Fantastic
1976: May.
Weird Heroes
1977: #6, #8.

Higgins, David
Ad Astra
1978: Oct.
1979: Jan.

Hildebrandt, The Brothers
Fantastic
1980: Apr.
Stellar
1976: #2.

Hinge, Mike
Amazing Stories
1971: Nov.
1972: May.
1973: Jan, Mar, Aug.
1974: Dec.
1975: Sep.
Analog
1976: Apr.
1977: Feb, Jul.
1978: Oct.
1979: Mar.
Fantastic
1972: Apr, Oct.

Holloway, James
The Dragon
1980: Sep.

Hughes, Bill
Forgotten Fantasy
1971: Feb, Jun.

Hunt, James E.
Space & Time
1978: Jan.

Hunter, Mel
F&SF
1971: Mar, Oct, Dec.

Jackays, Paul
The Dragon
1978: Dec.

Johnson, Jr., Earl
Space & Time
1974: Jan.

Jones, Eddie
F&SF
1974: May.

Vortex
　1977: Apr, May.

Jones, Jeff
Amazing Stories
　1971: Jan, May.
　1973: Oct.
　1974: Feb.
Fantastic
　1972: Aug.
　1974: Sep.
Galileo
　1978: Jul.
Weird Heroes
　1977: #5.
Witchcraft & Sorcery
　1974: #10.

Jones, Pauline
Science Fiction Monthly
　1975: Sep.

Jones, Peter Andrew
Heavy Metal
　1978: Dec.
　1979: May.

Jupp, Mike
Ad Astra
　1979: Jun.

Jusko, Joe
Ares
　1980: Sep.
Heavy Metal
　1978: Jun.
　1979: Nov.

Kaluta, Mike
Fantastic
　1972: Feb.
　1973: Feb.

Kanarek, Michael
Heavy Metal
　1980: May.

Kato, Gary
The Diversifier
　1977: May.
Space & Time
　1974: Sep.
　1977: Nov.
　1979: Apr.

Kelly, Ken
Amazing Stories
　1975: Nov.

Kirby, Josh
Vertex
　1973: Oct.

Kirk, Tim
Forgotten Fantasy
　1971: Apr.
Nyctalops
　1972: Aug.
Whispers
　1973: Jul.
　1974: Jul.

Kirkland, Vance
Pandora
　1979: #4.

Klein, Todd
Eerie Country
　1979: #2.

Knecht, Fred
Galileo
　1980: Jan.

Kochich, Carl
Chrysalis
　1979: #5.

Kofoed, Karl
Asimov's
　1979: Jun, Jul.
　1980: Jul, Dec.

Koszowski, Allen
Space & Time
　1977: Mar.
　1980: Jan.

Krenkel, Roy G.
Weirdbook
1977: #11.

Kupperberg, Alan
Space & Time
1972: Feb.

Kuras, Thomas F.
Eerie Country
1980: #4.

Kurowski, Cliff
The Diversifier
1976: May.

Last, Martin
QUARK/
1971: #4.

Leaning, Sean
Stardust
1978: Sum.

Lehr, Paul
Analog
1978: Mar.
1979: Jan, May, Sep.
1980: Jan, Apr, Jun.

Linton, John
Whispers
1975: Dec.

Lloyd, David
Fantasy Tales
1979: Win.

Loge, Daniel
Eerie Country
1976: #1.

Lundgren, Carl
Galileo
1977: Oct.

McCall, Robert T.
Analog
1978: Nov.
1979: Jul.

MacDonnell, Kevin G.
Void
1975: #2.

McGowan, Rodger
Vertex
1974: Apr.

McKie, Angus
Heavy Metal
1979: Mar, Jun.
Science Fiction Monthly
1975: Nov.

McIntyre, Rob
Destinies
1980: Feb.

McLane, Paula
Fantastic
1971: Aug.

McLean, Wilson
Amazing Stories
1980: Feb.

Mahoney, Ron
Questar
1979: Mar.

Mann, David
Beyond
1982: Spr.

Maroto, Esteban
Fantastic
1973: Apr.
1974: Jan.

Martin, Michael
Eldritch Tales
1976: Win.

Mase, Georgia
Starwind
1976: Aut.
1977: Aut.

Massena, Jay
Space & Time
1975: Mar.

Matthews, Rodney
Vortex
1977: Jan, Feb, Mar.

Mattingly, David
Amazing Stories
1980: May.
F&SF
1980: Jul.
Questar
1980: Feb.
Stellar
1981: #7.

Maurus, Bob
Witchcraft & Sorcery
1972: #7.

Mavor, Elinor
Amazing Stories
1979: Aug, Nov.
Fantastic
1979: Jul, Oct.
1980: Jan.

Mayer, John F.
Midnight Sun
1974: #1.

Mayerik, Val
Heavy Metal
1978: Jan.

Mazey and Schell
F&SF
1974: Nov.
1975: Jan, Jul, Sep, Oct, Dec.

Meltzer, Davis
Destinies
1980: Sum.

Miller, Frank
Space & Time
1975: Jan.

Miller, Ron
Amazing Stories
1974: Apr.

Fantastic
1974: Jul.
Galileo
1978: Jan.

Moebius
See Jean Giraud.

Montxo, Algora
Heavy Metal
1979: Aug.

Moore, Chris
Ad Astra
1979: Sep.
1981: Jun.

Morello, Robert
Heavy Metal
1978: Apr.

Morgan, Jacqui
F&SF
1973: Oct.

Morris, Harry O.
Nyctalops
1970: May, Oct.
1971: Feb, Jun, Oct.

Morrissey, Dean
The Dragon
1978: Jul, Sep.
1979: Aug.
1980: Apr.

Morrow, Gray
Fantastic
1971: Apr.
The Haunt of Horror
1973: Jun.
Perry Rhodan
1972: #14, 15, 16, 17, 18, 19, 20.
1973: #20–#36 inclusive.
1974: #37–#60 inclusive.
1975: #61–#85 inclusive.
1976: #86–#103 inclusive.

Moy, Glenn
Fantastic
　1974: Mar.

Murrow, Phil
Stardust
　1976: #2.

Newkirk, Claude
Galaxy
　1971: Nov.

Newsom, Tom
Vertex
　1973: Augpr.

Nicollet, Jean-Michel
Heavy Metal
　1977: Apr, Oct.

Niño, Alex
Heavy Metal
　1978: Feb.
Weird Heroes
　1976: #3.
　1977: #7.

Oliff, Steve
The Dragon
　1978: May.
　1980: Oct.

Olson, Richard
Galaxy
　1978: Jun.

Osterman, Dan
Space & Time
　1971: Apr.

Palladini, David
F&SF
　1977: Apr.
　1978: Nov.

Pastor, Terry
Ad Astra
　1979: Aug.
　1980: Dec.

Payne, Michael
Science Fiction Monthly
　1975: Aug.

Pearson, Joe
Sorcerer's Apprentice
　1978: Win.

Pederson, Jr., John
Amazing Stories
　1971: Mar.
　1972: Jan.
　1973: Jun.
Fantastic
　1972: Jun.

Pekul, Darlene
The Dragon
　1980: May.

Pelham, David
Science Fiction Monthly
　1974: Oct.

Pelletiere, Chris
Weirdbook
　1979: #14.

Penney, Roger
QUARK/
　1971: #3.

Pennington, Bruce
Science Fiction Monthly
　1974: Feb, May, Jul, Aug, Nov.
　1975: Jan, Jul.

Petillo, Robert
Fantastic
　1980: Oct.

Pini, Richard
See under Wendy Pini.

Pini, Wendy
Galaxy
　1974: Jul, Aug.
　1975: Jan, Jun.
　1977: Nov.

with Richard Pini.
1975: Feb, Oct.
Worlds of If
1974: Sep.

Pitts, Jim
Fantasy Tales
1977: Sum, Win.
1979: Spr.
Nyctalops
1976: Apr.

Pohl, Carol
F&SF
1973: Sep.

Potter, J. K.
Heavy Metal
1979: Oct.
Nyctalops
1980: Jan.

Powers, Richard
Analog
1978: May, Sep.

Poyser, Victoria
Sorcerer's Apprentice
1979: Spr, Fal.

Preston, Fiona
New Worlds
1979: #216.

Proctor, George
Heavy Metal
1977: Nov.

Punchatz, Don Ivan
Heavy Metal
1980: Jan.

Rahman, Ken ('Elladan Elrohir')
The Dragon
1977: Jun, Dec.
1978: Feb.
1979: Apr, Oct.
1980: Feb.

Raney, Ken W.
Dark Fantasy
1980: Mar.
Space & Time
1975: Jul.

Reese, Ralph
Weird Heroes
1976: #4.

Ridge, Glenn
Fantastic
1974: May.

Rigg, Derek
Heavy Metal
1979: Feb.

Riley, Steve
The Diversifier
1975: Aug.

Rivoche, Paul
Stardust
1979: 3-1.
1981: 3-2.

Roberts, Tony
Heavy Metal
1980: Apr.

Rogers, Monte
Vertex
1975: Aug.

Roggeri, Bruce
If
1971: Sep.

Roland, Harry
Fantastic
1973: Jul.
1975: Jun, Aug.

Romero, Ed
Eternity
1973: #2.
1975: #4.
1980: #2.

Space & Time
1972: Aug.

Rush, John
Destinies
1979: Oct.

Sanchez, John
Analog
1979: Apr, Aug.

Saviuk, Alex
Space & Time
1971: Mar.
1977: Jul.

Schaffer, Bob
Galaxy
1979: Mar.

Schell
See under Mazey.

Schelling, George
Analog
1977: Sep.
Cosmos
1977: May.

Schilling, Dan
Fantastic
1973: Nov.

Schoenherr, John
Analog
1971: Sep, Oct, Nov.
1972: Jan, Feb, Mar, Jul, Nov.
1973: Jan, Mar, Aug, Dec.
1974: Apr, Aug.
1975: Jan, Jun, Jul.
1976: Jan, Aug.
1977: Mar, Jun.
1980: Aug, Nov.
Galileo
1978: Mar.

Schomburg, Alex
Analog
1978: Jan.

Asimov's
1979: Mar, Aug, Dec.
1980: Feb, Apr, Sep, Oct.
F&SF
1977: Mar.
1978: Aug.
1979: Jun.
1980: Apr.

Schwartz, Stephen
The Diversifier
1977: Nov.
Space & Time
1980: Apr.

Shapiro, Sheryl
Stardust
1978: 2-1.

Shaw, Barclay
Ares
1980: Nov.
F&SF
1979: Mar, Jul.
1980: Jan, Mar, Sep, Oct.

Shore, Bob
Analog
1980: May.

Sirois, Al
The Diversifier
1976: Sep.
1979: Feb.

Skinner, Cortney
Galileo
1979: Jul.
1980: Mar (not issued).

Smith, Andrew
Midnight Sun
1976: Apr, Aug.
Starwind
1976: Spr.

Smith, Kenneth
Galaxy
1971: Jun.

Sokolov, Andrei
Analog
  1975: Aug.

Solé, Jean
Heavy Metal
  1977: Dec.

Sorayama, Hajime
Heavy Metal
  1980: Nov.

Soulen, Ric
Rune
  1974: Aut.

Spurgin, Randall
Nyctalops
  1975: Jan.
Space & Time
  1977: Sep.

Stathopoulos, Nick
Enigma
  1979: Jan, Jul, Dec.

Staton, Joe
Fantastic
  1973: Sep.
  1974: Nov.

Steacy, Ken
Stardust
  1978: Win.

Steadman, Broeck
Analog
  1980: Jul.

Steranko, Jim
Infinity
  1970: #1.
  1971: #2.
Weird Heroes
  1975: #1, #2.

Sternbach, Rick
Analog
  1973: Oct.
  1974: Oct.

  1975: Apr, Sep.
  1976: Feb, Jul, Dec.
  1977: May, Dec.
  1978: Apr.
  1980: Dec.
F&SF
  1974: Feb.
  1976: Apr (with Bonnie Dalzell), Jul.
  1977: Feb, Jun, Aug.
  1978: May, Sep.
Galaxy
  1974: Jan, Feb, May, Jun.
  1975: Jul.
  1976: Jan, May, Sep, Dec.
Worlds of If
  1974: Jan, Mar, Nov.

Stine, Roger
Asimov's
  1980: Jun.
Shayol
  1977: Nov.
  1980: Win.

Stinson, Paul
Beyond
  1981: Fal.

Streff, Mike
The Diversifier
  1977: Mar.

Sullivan, John
The Dragon
  1977: Oct.

Summers, Leo Ramon
Analog
  1972: May.
  1973: Feb.
  1974: Jul.

Sutherland, David
The Dragon
  1977: Mar.

Sweet, Darrell
Stellar
 1977: #3.
 1980: #5.

Swenston, Steve
The Dragon
 1980: Jul.

Tanner, Bert
F&SF
 1972: Feb.
 1973: Feb.

Theakston, Greg
Worlds of If
 1974: Jul.

Thomas, Jim
Nickelodeon
 1976: #2.

Tiani, Denis
The Diversifier
 1976: Mar.
Nyctalops
 1972: Feb.
 1974: Jul.

Tibbetts, John
Eldritch Tales
 1978: Oct.
 1979: Apr.
 1980: Jun.

Till, Paul
Unearth
 1978: Sum.

Todd, Larry
See under Vaughn Bodé.

Townley, John
Heavy Metal
 1979: Dec (with Richard Ion Cohen).

Trampier, David A.
The Dragon
 1978: Jun.
 1980: Aug.

Trevisani, Fran
Space & Time
 1978: Apr.
 1980: Jul.

Trilling, Jo Ellen
Heavy Metal
 1979: Jan.

Utpatel, Frank
Whispers
 1975: Jun.
 1977: Aug.

Valenza, Anji
Galaxy
 1978: Mar.

Vallejo, Boris
Questar
 1981: Feb.

Van der Steur, Gary
Weird Tales
 1973: Fall.

Van Dongen, H. R.
Analog
 1980: Sep.
Stellar
 1978: #4.

Vess, Charles
Space & Time
 1978: Jul.

Walker, Norm
Vertex
 1974: Jun, Aug.

Walotsky, Ron
F&SF
 1971: May, Jul, Aug.
 1972: Jan, Jun, Jul, Dec.
 1973: Nov, Dec.
 1974: Mar, Jul, Dec.
 1975: Jun.
 1976: Feb, Dec.
 1977: Jan, Dec.

1978: Jul.
1979: Jan, Sep, Dec.
1980: Dec.
Heavy Metal
1978: Oct.

Warhola, James
Questar
1978: Nov.
1980: Dec.

Watt, Denise
Amazing Stories
1975: Mar.

Weidinger, James P.
Aura
1979: #1.

Weinberg, Cynthia Tolker
Pandora
1979: #3.

Weiss, Alan
REH: Lone Star Fictioneer
1975: Fal.

West, Joseph A.
The Diversifier
1974: Dec.

Whelan, Michael
Asimov's
1978: Sep.
Destinies
1979: Jan.

White, Tim
Beyond
1982: Oct.
Science Fiction Monthly
1975: Mar, Oct, Dec.
1976: May.

Wilber, Ron
The Diversifier
1977: Jul.
Space & Time
1976: Nov.

Wilkins, Edward Blair
Ad Astra
1979: Apr.

Wilson, Gahan
F&SF
1980: Aug.

Wilson, George
Perry Rhodan
1976: #104–#106 inclusive.
1977: #107–#118 inclusive.

Wilson, Phil
Questar
1979: Aug.
1980: Jun.

Winder, Ray
Science Fiction Monthly
1974: Dec.

Windsor-Smith, Barry
Ariel
1978: #3.

Wing, Chuck
Space & Time
1977: May.

Winnick, Gary
The Diversifier
1974: Sep.
1975: Apr.
1977: Sep.

Wise, Denis
Stardust
1976: #3.
1977: #4.

Wolff, Inc., Rudi
F&SF
1974: Oct.

Woodroffe, Patrick
Ad Astra
1980: Jan.

Woods, Joan Hanke
Galaxy
1977: Dec.
Sorcerer's Apprentice
1979: Sum.

Wrightson, Berni
Heavy Metal
1977: Aug.

Yamada, Tony
Vertex
1975: Apr.

Yates, Chris
Science Fiction Monthly
1974: Jun.

Zabel, Joe
Space & Time
1976: Mar.

Appendix 5

Schedule of Magazine Circulation Figures

It was not until 1962 that American magazines were obliged, by law, to carry a Statement of Management and Circulation. This applied to all magazines that carried advertising and appeared four or more times a year. Publication of this data was a requirement of the magazine being allowed a second-class mailing permit from the postal authorities, but it also allowed advertisers to know the size of the potential readership, and the magazine could charge rates accordingly. As a consequence, the data appeared regularly, though there are a few occasions, usually with the change of publisher, where data was either not published or where figures are repeated. All of the figures below are taken from the Statements as printed in the individual magazines.

The data take two forms. The magazine was required to publish (1) the average paid circulation per issue over the preceding twelve months and (2) the circulation of the issue published prior to the time of filing. In both cases the data was broken down under several headings: (a) the total number of copies printed, (b) the number sold through news-stands and other dealers, (c) the number sold by subscription and (d) the number lost or wasted. In the chart below I provide the yearly average sales figures, which is the total of (b) plus (c) above and I show next to that the proportion of sales as a percentage of the print run (known as the 'sell through'), and the percentage of total sales sold via news-stands etc. (figure b). A general rule of thumb is that if the sell through is above 40 per cent then the magazine is likely to be in profit, or reasonably healthy.

The report is usually filed on 1 October, but sales figures can take up to three or four months to filter through. Consequently the yearly average is not a straight calendar year but is probably summer to summer. The years are thus shown as combined years.

Because this is the first time that these figures have been available I include below the earliest figures from 1962/63 and take them through to 1980/81.

Year	Analog			F & SF			Amazing		
	Circu-lation	Sell-through	% News-stand	Circu-lation	Sell-through	% News-stand	Circu-lation	Sell-through	% News-stand
1962/63	79,690	55.9%	78.9%	52,076	48.0%	71.6%	43,929	48.2%	96.1%
1963/64	81,408	56.1%	75.2%	53,288	48.1%	68.1%	35,471	43.2%	94.7%
1964/65	85,884	60.0%	71.2%	53,831	46.8%	69.1%	46,319	47.1%	95.3%
1965/66	88,828	61.4%	69.3%	51,134	45.6%	67.5%	47,958	48.3%	95.5%
1966/67	94,786	62.6%	66.5%	51,602	47.1%	63.8%	40,345	41.1%	95.5%
1967/68	100,863	64.6%	66.2%	50,536	47.8%	64.9%	38,551	39.6%	95.8%
1968/69	108,383	66.3%	64.8%	50,299	48.1%	61.9%	34,791	37.2%	96.1%
1969/70	110,330	65.0%	63.5%	50,301	49.0%	62.4%	30,298	36.2%	96.3%
1970/71	109,240	64.1%	61.3%	46,185	46.7%	60.4%	28,500	36.2%	96.1%
1971/72	111,794	65.1%	61.0%	42,194	45.3%	60.6%	27,402	39.5%	95.0%
1972/73	116,521	66.4%	60.7%	43,963	45.6%	55.2%	26,577	39.2%	93.2%
1973/74	114,009	64.1%	57.4%	52,355	51.4%	49.7%	23,631	34.9%	93.9%
1974/75	110,742	63.2%	54.7%	55,908	53.0%	45.0%	22,825	34.4%	93.5%
1975/76	110,458	64.2%	54.7%	51,732	51.3%	44.9%	24,800	36.8%	92.7%
1976/77	105,008	60.2%	52.5%	57,486	54.5%	38.0%	25,702	37.8%	93.3%
1977/78	104,612	59.9%	52.4%	57,900	54.5%	40.1%	22,784	34.5%	93.3%
1978/79	Not reported			57,728	53.8%	36.3%	22,332	33.8%	93.7%
1979/80	Not reported			62,071	56.6%	35.1%	17,339	26.3%	94.8%
1980/81	92,394	54.6%	41.7%	60,233	57.9%	31.7%	17,784	34.0%	95.8%
% change 1970–80	-15.4%	-9.0%	-42.4%	+30.6%	+24.0%	-31.5%	-37.6%	-6.1%	-37.8%

Year	Asimov's			Heavy Metal			Omni		
	Circu-lation	Sell-through	% News-stand	Circu-lation	Sell-through	% News-stand	Circu-lation	Sell-through	% News-stand
1976/77	–	–	–	144,232	51.4%	88.5%	–	–	–
1977/78	108,843	55.5%	61.3%	202,818	54.4%	83.6%	–	–	–
1978/79	94,759	48.1%	51.1%	204,015	59.0%	83.5%	759,848	73.9%	88.3%
1979/80	Not reported			183,886	57.5%	83.1%	843,039	72.8%	79.6%
1980/81	103,069	58.5%	23.2%	172,116	58.4%	84.6%	763,910	64.2%	72.3%
% change Start–1980	-5.3%	+5.4%	-64.2%	+19.3%	+13.6%	+14.1%	+0.5%	-13.1%	-17.7%

Year	Galaxy			If			Fantastic		
	Circu-lation	Sell-through	% News-stand	Circu-lation	Sell-through	% News-stand	Circu-lation	Sell-through	% News-stand
1962/63	77,677	67.0%	91.1%	63,000	57.2%	96.8%	32,555	33.0%	97.2%
1963/64	73,536	65.7%	90.8%	64,500	63.2%	96.7%	27,115	39.6%	96.0%
1964/65	72,610	64.6%	92.4%	64,840	65.6%	96.0%	41,753	41.7%	96.3%
1965/66	73,400	68.0%	91.0%	63,930	62.8%	95.9%	41,017	41.0%	96.4%
1966/67	74,700	69.2%	90.8%	64,100	63.5%	95.5%	40,167	40.8%	96.7%
1967/68	75,300	69.1%	90.7%	67,400	65.8%	94.1%	36,910	38.9%	97.4%
1968/9	51,479	43.6%	81.6%	44,548	39.4%	92.0%	31,129	33.0%	97.6%
1969/70	46,091	45.4%	75.9%	35,230	32.3%	83.7%	28,768	34.3%	97.7%
1970/71	45,498	38.0%	79.0%	37,974	33.4%	88.5%	23,600	30.1%	96.7%
1971/72	51,602	53.6%	78.2%	47,525	53.3%	83.0%	25,124	36.2%	95.6%
1972/73	54,524	52.0%	74.2%	45,994	52.8%	72.7%	25,604	38.3%	94.2%
1973/74	47,789	43.3%	70.8%	50,355	51.2%	70.4%	23,631	34.9%	93.9%
1974/75	56,361	52.8%	45.7%	Merged with Galaxy			22,498	33.3%	93.9%
1975/76	52,831	56.3%	50.5%				19,630	28.8%	92.4%
1976/77	81,035	64.5%	36.6%				21,037	31.1%	93.3%
1977/78	Not published						18,370	28.2%	93.8%
1978/9	Not published						18,370	28.2%	93.8%
1979/80	Not published						Not published		
1980/81	Ceased publication						Ceased publication		
% change 1970-end	+78.1%	+69.7%	-17.5%	+32.6%	+53.3%	+5.5%	-22.2%	-6.3%	-24.5%

Select Bibliography

In addition to all the original individual science-fiction magazines covered in this volume, any individual works cited in specific footnotes, and collected works of short stories by many of the writers active during the period covered by this book, the following are the principal books and other reference material that I have consulted in the compilation of this volume.

Aldiss, Brian W., *Billion Year Spree*, London: Weidenfeld & Nicolson, 1973, and the revised version, *Trillion Year Spree*, London: Victor Gollancz, 1986..

Aldiss, Brian W. and Harrison, Harry, *Hell's Cartographers*, London: Weidenfeld & Nicolson, 1975.

Anthony, Piers, *Bio of an Ogre*, New York: Ace Books, 1988

Asimov, Isaac, *I. Asimov: A Memoir*, New York: Doubleday, 1994.

—— *In Joy Still Felt*, New York: Doubleday, 1980.

—— *In Memory Yet Green*, New York: Doubleday, 1979.

Barron, Neil, *Anatomy of Wonder*, 3rd edition, New York: Bowker, 1987 and 4th edition, New Providence: R. R. Bowker, 1995.

Benton, Mike, *The Illustrated History of Science Fiction Comics*, Dallas: Taylor Publishing, 1992.

Bishop, Michael, *A Reverie for Mister Ray*, Hornsea: PS Publishing, 2005.

Blackford, Russell, Van Ikin and McMullen, Sean, *Strange Constellations, A History of Australian Science Fiction*, Westport, CT: Greenwood Press, 1999.

Chapdelaine, Sr., Perry A., Chapdelaine, Tony and Hay, George, *The John W. Campbell Letters*, Franklin, TN: AC Projects, 2 volumes, 1985, 1993.

Clute, John and Nicholls, Peter (eds), *Encyclopedia of Science Fiction*, London: Orbit, 1993.

Collins, Paul (ed.), *The MUP Encyclopedia of Australian Science Fiction & Fantasy*, Melbourne: Melbourne University Press, 1998.

D'Ammassa, Don, *Encyclopedia of Science Fiction*, New York: Facts on File, 2005.

Davin, Eric Leif, *Partners in Wonder*, Lanham, MD: Lexington Books, 2006.

Day, Bradford M., *The Checklist of Science Fiction and Fantasy Magazines 1892–1992*, privately published, 1993 (revised edition).

Del Rey, Lester, *The World of Science Fiction: 1926–1976*, New York: Del Rey Books, 1979.

Di Fate, Vincent, *Infinite Worlds*, London: Virgin Books, 1997.

Disch, Thomas M., *The Dreams Our Stuff is Made Of*, New York: The Free Press, 1998.

Greenberg, Martin H. (ed.), *Fantastic Lives*, Carbondale, IL: Southern Illinois University Press, 1981.

Gunn, James, *The Road to Science Fiction*, New York: New American Library/White Wolf, 6 volumes, 1977–98.

Hassón, Moisés, *Indice Revistas de Ciencia Ficción, 1947–1989*, Santiago, Chile: private, 3 vols., 1995-6.

Heinlein, Virginia, *Robert A. Heinlein: Grumbles from the Grave*, New York: Del Rey Books, 1989.

James, Edward, *Science Fiction in the 20th Century*, Oxford University Press, 1994.

James, Edward and Mendlesohn, Farah, *The Cambridge Companion to Science Fiction*, Cambridge University Press, 2003.

Le Guin, Ursula K., *The Language of the Night*, New York: Putnam, 1979.

Lester, Colin, *The International Science Fiction Yearbook*, London: Pierrot Publishing, 1978.

Lofficier, Jean-Marc and Lofficier, Randy, *French Science Fiction, Fantasy, Horror and Pulp Fiction*, Jefferson, NC: McFarland, 2000.

Luckhurst, Roger, *Science Fiction*, Cambridge: Polity Press, 2005.

Lundwall, Sam J., *Science Fiction: What It's All About*, New York: Ace Books, 1971.

McAleer, Neil, *Odyssey: The Authorised Biography of Arthur C. Clarke*, London: Victor Gollancz, 1992.

Malzberg, Barry N., *The Engines of the Night*, Garden City: Doubleday, 1982.

Miller, Stephen T. and Contento, William G., *Science Fiction, Fantasy, & Weird Fiction Magazine Index (1890-2005)*, CD-ROM, Oakland, CA: Locus Press, 2006.

Mitchell, D. M., *A Serious Life*, Manchester: Savoy Books, 2004.

Moskowitz, Sam, *Explorers of the Infinite*, Cleveland, OH: World Publishing, 1963.

—— *Seekers of Tomorrow*, Cleveland, OH: World Publishing, 1966.

—— *Strange Horizons*, New York: Charles Scribner's, 1976.

Nicholls, Stan, *Wordsmiths of Wonder*, London: Orbit, 1993.

Nyberg, Amy Kiste, *Seal of Approval: The History of the Comics Code*, Jackson: University Press of Mississippi, 1998.

Paradis, Andrea (ed.), *Out of This World*, Kingston, Ontario: Quarry Press, 1995.

Parnell, Frank and Ashley, Mike, *Monthly Terrors: An Index to the Weird Fantasy Magazines*, Westport, CT: Greenwood Press, 1985.

Phillips, Julie, *James Tiptree, Jr., The Double Life of Alice B. Sheldon*, New York: St. Martin's Press, 2006.

Platt, Charles, *Who Writes Science Fiction?*, Manchester: Savoy Books, 1980.

—— *Dream Makers, Volume II*, New York: Berkley Books, 1983.

Pohl, Frederik, *The Way the Future Was*, New York: Del Rey Books, 1978.

Reginald, R., *Science Fiction and Fantasy Literature: A Checklist, 1700-1974*, Detroit, MI: Gale Research, 1979.

—— *Science Fiction and Fantasy Literature, Volume 2: Contemporary Science Fiction Authors II*, Detroit, MI: Gale Research, 1979.

Rosheim, David L., *Galaxy Magazine, The Dark and the Light Years*, Chicago: Advent, 1986.

Rottensteiner, Franz, *View from Another Shore*, Liverpool: Liverpool University Press, revised edition, 1999.

Sawyer, Andrew and Seed, David (eds), *Speaking Science Fiction*, Liverpool: Liverpool University Press, 2000.

Scoleri, Joe, *The Maverick's Space & Fantasy Gamer's Guide*, Jackson, CA: privately published, 1999.

Seed, David (ed.), *A Companion to Science Fiction*, Oxford: Blackwell, 2005.

Staicar, Tim (ed.), *The Feminine Eye, Science Fiction and the Women Who Write It*, New York: Frederick Ungar, 1982.

Sutin, Lawrence, *Divine Invasions, A Life of Philip K. Dick*, New York: Citadel Press, 1989.

Swanwick, Michael, *Being Gardner Dozois*, Baltimore, MD: Old Earth Books, 2001.

Thompson, Don and Lupoff, Dick, *The Comic-Book Book*, Krause Publications, 1998.

Tuck, Donald H., *The Encyclopedia of Science Fiction and Fantasy*, Chicago: Advent, 3 volumes, 1974, 1978, 1982.

Tymn, Marshall B., and Ashley, Mike, *Science Fiction, Fantasy, and Weird Fiction Magazines*, Westport, CT: Greenwood Press, 1985.

van Belkom, Edo, *Northern Dreamers*, Kingston, Ontario: Quarry Press, 1998.

Warner, Jr., Harry, *All Our Yesterdays*, Chicago: Advent, 1969.

—— *A Wealth of Fable*, Van Nuys: SCIFI Press, 1992.

Watson, Noelle and Schellinger, Paul E. (eds), *Twentieth-Century Science-Fiction Writers*, Chicago: St James Press, 1991.

Weinberg, Robert, *A Biographical Dictionary of Science Fiction and Fantasy Artists*, Westport, CT: Greenwood Press, 1988.

Weston, Peter, *With Stars in My Eyes*, Framingham, MA: NESFA Press, 2004.

In addition the following academic or news magazines (not all of which are still published) have been regularly consulted:

Algol (later retitled *Starship*), editor Andrew Porter, Brooklyn, New York.

Extrapolation, editor Donald M. Hassler, Kent State University, Kent, Ohio.

Fantasy Commentator, editor A. Langley Searles, Bronxville, New York.

Foundation, editor Edward James, The Science Fiction Foundation, Liverpool.

Locus, editor Charles N. Brown, Oakland, CA.

Luna Monthly, editor Anne Dietz, Oradell, NJ.

The New York Review of Science Fiction, editor David G. Hartwell, Pleasantville, New York.

Science Fiction Chronicle, editor Andrew Porter, Brooklyn, New York.

Science Fiction Eye, editor Stephen Brown, Asheville, NC.

Science Fiction Review (also entitled *The Alien Critic*), editor Richard E. Geis, Portland, OR.

Science Fiction Studies, editor Arthur B. Evans, East College, DePauw University, Greencastle, IN.

Thrust, editor Doug Fratz, Gaithersburg, MD.

I have also consulted the following websites:

Cameron, Richard Graeme, *The Canadian Fancyclopedia* at http://members.shaw. ca/rgraeme/home.html

Canada's National Association for Speculative Fiction Professionals, *SF Canada,* at http://www.sfcanada.ca/index.html

Hall, Hal W., *Science Fiction and Fantasy Research Database* at http://lib-edit.tamu. edu/cushing/sffrd//

Kelly, Mark R., *The Locus Index to Science Fiction Awards* at http://www.locusmag. com/SFAwards/index.html

Lovell, Ray, *Bibliography for the Magazine of Fantasy and Science Fiction* at http://www. sfsite.com/fsf/bibliography/bibliography.htm

Index

This index covers all of the main text and Appendix 1, but not Appendices 2–5. An 'n' indicates the reference is in a footnote; *passim* means there are passing references between the pages noted. Names beginning with 'Mc' are indexed alongside 'Mac' and 'St. as spelled 'Saint'.

Printed and bound by CPI Group (UK) Ltd, Croydon, CR0 4YY

13/04/2025

14656573-0008